ghosts

ghosts

69 stories that won't let you sleep

edited by Annabella Smith

SWEETWATER
PRESS

SWEETWATER
PRESS

Ghosts

ISBN-13: 9781581737820

Book design by Miles G. Parsons
Contributors: Karyn Kay Zweifel, Nina Costopoulos, Holly Smith,
Lynne L. Hall, Ian Alan, Brice Camp, Amis O'Bryan

Printed in Italy

Table of Contents

cry baby holler

"Stop it, Bobby!" She laughed as she slapped his hand away. The boy took the laugh as a signal to continue. The girl laughed again and slipped loose, sliding across the seat of the Chevy and pushing down on the door latch.

"Where are you going, Cheryl?"

"Can't catch me!" She threw the taunt over her shoulder as she half-ran, half-walked down the asphalt road. The boy struggled out of the car—the springs in the upholstery had given out years ago—and stood watching her, his arms resting on the rounded curves of his '49 Chevy.

The road was swallowed up by a large rectangle of soft darkness: the mouth of Swann Bridge. Cheryl's footsteps slowed as she approached the black gaping entrance, and she looked behind her for Bobby's comforting presence.

"I wouldn't go in there if I were you, Cheryl!"

She took it as a dare, and her slender form melted into the shadows in a matter of moments. Uneasy, Bobby began to walk down the gentle slope toward the bridge.

The waters of the Warrior River sang softly, unseen below the thick hand-hewn timbers that formed the roadbed of the bridge. Between the crisscrossed slats glowing slightly in the light of the crescent moon, Bobby could see the stark white stone of Scarum Bluffs. He shuddered, remembering the legend of the Indian murdered there whose blood could never be washed away from the rock.

Cheryl was just ahead, standing stock-still in the center of the bridge. Over the sighing and cooing of the water, a new sound rose. He quickly stepped up alongside her, and Cheryl reached out and clasped his hand tightly as they listened.

It started out broken, hesitant at first: the sound of a baby waking in an unfamiliar place. Gradually the sound gained strength and duration, building to the cry of an infant lost and alone, rage battling with fear in every shrieking call.

Tears glistened on Cheryl's cheeks. Bobby, too, was affected, feeling strangely chastened as he led his girlfriend out of the bridge, not speaking a word. His romantic hopes for the evening were abandoned, and they climbed back into the car to head for home.

••••••

Thomas Brown trudged slowly down the center of the road, his boots stirring up a little cloud of dust as he walked. The sack over his shoulder was heavy. The blacksmith in Oneonta had been able to repair the plow blade, sparing Thomas the unexpected expense of a new one, and so he had spent some of his carefully hoarded cash on a small bag of white sugar and five yards of pretty gingham. The seven-mile walk from town was pleasant in the late October sunshine.

A jingle of harnesses coming up from the bridge made Thomas move to the side of the road. Before long, a small wagon appeared, drawn by a mule and carrying Thomas's neighbor from across the road, Cornelius Cole.

"Howdy, Mr. Brown," Cornelius pulled his mule to a stop. "Been to town?"

"Yeah, Cornelius, my plow blade snapped off. But Earl got it fixed, so I reckon I'll get another season or two out of it."

"We'll be puttin' in a bit more cotton this year," Cornelius commented. "Never thought I'd see the day when cotton got to 13¢ a pound."

"Makes me scared to put in more, though, remembering that it only fetched just over 5¢ a pound ten years ago," Thomas said with a grin.

Cornelius returned the smile. "God willin', we'll all prosper this comin' year. Gee-up!" he commanded the mule. "You need anything else from town?" he asked as he moved off.

"No, thank you, Cornelius. Give my best to your family."

"You do the same, Mr. Brown."

Rachel was feeding the chickens when Thomas reached the top of the hill. He slipped an arm around her waist, and they surveyed the gently sloping fields his wife had inherited from her uncle. To the west they could see the white scar of Scarum Bluffs. The massive stone formation was nearly hidden by a line of trees bright with fall foliage, a line that curved gracefully to mark the bed of the Warrior River.

"Nice place, Mrs. Brown," Thomas teased, nuzzling her neck. They had been married a scant six months.

"You made it so, Mr. Brown," Rachel retorted. "I believe that house you built will stand a hundred years or more." The white clapboard house, three rooms one behind the other, stood just below the crest of the hill. Just to the right was a barn, considerably older and currently unoccupied except for Rachel's chickens and a couple of cats.

"Supper's ready," she continued. "I made some cornbread, and went over to Roscoe's for a little butter, too." She felt her husband stiffen. "I traded him a dozen eggs for it, Thomas. His hens have stopped laying for some reason."

"Prob'ly scared by that pack of dogs he keeps," Thomas grumbled. He worked the pump outside the kitchen door, moving the handle furiously up and down until water splashed out into the bucket. He scrubbed his hands and sputtered as he threw water on his face to sluice off the road dust. Rachel watched him with affection.

"You'll be takin' the pump in for repair, next, if you don't stop being so hard on it. Roscoe is a good boy. He misses his father."

"He misses his father's hard work, more like it. I've never seen anyone lazier."

"You should know. You worked with him for years."

Inside the kitchen, warm from the heat of the stove, Rachel and Thomas sat down to their supper of cornbread, green beans, pickled beets, and lima beans seasoned with fatback. Just before they finished, they heard a horse gallop wildly up to the doorstep and stop at a shouted command.

Rachel slid back her chair and went to the door.

"Evenin', Roscoe."

Thomas came to stand behind his wife, his hand on her shoulder. "What brings you out, Roscoe?"

"How's the hired hand tonight?" The young man slid off his horse and slapped Thomas on the shoulder as he entered the kitchen.

Rachel felt Thomas stiffen again and sighed. Her uncle had hired Thomas six years ago, when she was just thirteen and her cousin Roscoe had been twelve. Thomas had proved to be a natural farmer, with a sixth sense when it came to farm animals and growing things. Rachel had fallen in love, and when her uncle died in an accident eighteen months ago, he had left half his farm to her and Thomas and half to his only son, Roscoe.

Roscoe lifted up the lid to the pan on the stove and sniffed deeply.

"Have you had supper?" Rachel asked politely. "Let me fix you a plate."

"Don't mind if I do," Roscoe sat down and grinned at Thomas. "If I'd known you were goin' to town today, Thomas, I'd have loaned you the mule and wagon."

"Didn't want to inconvenience you, Roscoe," Thomas said shortly.

"No inconvenience, Cuz." He attacked the food on his plate with such vigor that Rachel shook her head.

"You need to find a wife to cook for you, Roscoe," she said with a laugh. "You eat like you haven't had a bite in days."

"No one can match your cookin', Rachel."

Thomas scowled and threw his napkin on the table. "Let me get the water for washin' up, Rachel." He took the bucket and went outside, barely restraining himself from slamming the door behind him.

Rachel busied herself at the sink, scraping the dishes. "What brings you out this evening, Roscoe?" she called over her shoulder.

"I came to ask Thomas for some help fixin' the roof. It's gotten so I have a bucket in every room, now."

"Your father loved that house. He'd be glad to see you take care of it."

"He shoulda left me the means to care for it, then."

"He nearly lost everything in '99. We should all be grateful to have a roof over our heads."

"I'm planting more cotton next fall. That filthy mongrel across the road made enough this year to buy a mule, and if he can do it, I can, too."

"You already have a mule, Roscoe," Rachel pointed out impatiently. "And a fine horse, and a big house, and a cow—you're very lucky."

"It's not right that I have to work so hard and he just brings in the cash year after year," he continued stubbornly.

"Cornelius has six children, four nearly grown, and they all work hard from dawn to dusk."

Thomas brought the bucket of water in and sloshed some into the kettle to heat up for dishwater. "If you'd get married and have some children, in a few years you could have more success than him. We've got better land."

"It ain't right."

Rachel turned to Thomas. "Roscoe needs some help with the roof at the house, Thomas. Can you give him a hand tomorrow?"

"Glad to." His tone belied his words, and Rachel hurried to dispel the tension.

"What news from town, husband?"

"I brought a paper. I'll read you some." He drew the newspaper out of the sack and settled himself at the table again. "Any coffee?"

"Here." She set a cup in front of him. "I'm afraid we're out of sugar."

"No, we're not." He rummaged through the bag again and brought out the sack of sugar.

"Oh, goody!" She threw her arms around him and smacked his cheek. "I'll make a cake tomorrow."

Roscoe stood up, barely covering his mouth as he belched.

"'Scuse me," he mumbled. "I'll be headin' out now. Thanks for supper, Rachel. See you tomorrow, Thomas."

After he left, Rachel stood behind her husband and rubbed his neck and shoulders while he commented here and there on the news from Oneonta and the world.

"Four miners died in an explosion in Birmingham," he said. "I'm glad I left the mines."

"I'm glad God sent you down this road, Thomas Brown." She bent over and kissed the crown of his head. "God's sending us something else, too."

It took a moment for her meaning to sink in, then he stood up and gathered her into his arms. "Are you sure?" he whispered.

She smiled and nodded. "He'll be a summer baby. He'll get here about the same time the blackberries do."

With a whoop, Thomas picked her up and swung her around. Then he suddenly set her down. "Can I do that anymore?" he asked anxiously.

"I reckon," she said with a smile. "Until I get so big you can't pick me up."

●●●●●●

The lights bobbed up and down, in and out of the trees, making the darkness seem more oppressive. Dogs raced through the underbrush, stopping occasionally to sniff and raise their heads to howl. Behind them, in camouflage jumpsuits made pointless by orange vests, three hunters followed, shotguns cradled in their arms and lanterns dangling. "They sound like they're on to something," one man grumbled as he disentangled himself from another blackberry vine.

"It's a big 'un, I know it," said the man in the lead. "Buddy sounds more excited than usual."

"We grow 'em big in Blount County." The third hunter was breathing heavily as they reached the crest of the hill above the south bank of the Warrior River. They paused to listen again for the dogs.

"How much did you say that dog cost you?"

"Well, I traded a couple other dogs and then paid him twelve hundred on top of that. His daddy was a champion coon hunter in '92, and I 'spect Buddy'll be next year. Hush."

The dogs' cries escalated to a frenzy, echoing and reechoing across the narrow valley. Then, abruptly, the barking stopped.

"What's wrong?" asked the second hunter.

"I dunno, but I'm gonna go see," came the reply as his friend crashed down the hill to the road that wound its way to Swann Bridge.

All five dogs clustered outside the opening to the covered bridge, whining, their tails between their legs.

"You don't suppose they got a bear trapped in there, do ya?"

The experienced hunter laughed. "We don't have any bears around here."

Buddy, the prize coonhound, ran anxiously between his master and an unseen border three feet from the bridge entrance.

"He acts like they got the coon cornered in there."

The third hunter moved to kick the dog past the threshold of the bridge.

"You idiot, don't kick my dog!"

"Sorry." He retreated sheepishly.

Just then, an eerie wail floated up from the riverbed below.

"What was that?"

The cry came again, long and drawn out, and the dogs whimpered and cowered close to the men.

"Do coons cry?"

"That's no coon," came the whispered reply. The voice sobbed and wailed again, the plaintive moan of a baby abandoned. The men stood in a tight little group, circled by the coon dogs. Again the cry repeated itself, sobbing and whimpering until it trailed off to an exhausted finish.

"What was that? Is somebody hurt? Should we go see?"

"There's nothing down there. You'd just break your neck in the dark, crawling around all the rocks. Let's go."

Fortunately, their pickup truck was on this side of the river. No one wanted to enter the dark mouth of the bridge and cross to the other side.

"Have you heard that before? What was it?"

One man shrugged. The other lit a cigarette and exhaled softly before answering. "It's been going on as long as I remember. It's why this is called Cry Baby Holler."

They climbed into the truck, the dogs leaping into the back, grateful for the human companionship and unconcerned about the interrupted hunt.

"Let's go get a drink."

•••••

Thomas folded the newspaper with a snap. Rachel, sitting placidly across from him with a pile of yarn in her lap, looked up.

"What would you think of us growin' pecans?" he asked. "I keep hearin' more and more about it, and I think it would be a good source of extra income."

"It seems like you already have plenty to do, but I know you'll do what's best, Thomas." Pregnancy had given Rachel an aura of calm well-being, which sometimes enveloped Thomas as well. He laughed and came over to hug her before moving to lay two more logs on the fire.

"We'll be goin' to bed soon, Thomas," Rachel protested mildly. "Should we save the wood?"

"We'll have plenty of firewood. I've decided to sell off the timber on those five acres down by the river. Now that we're gonna have a baby, we'll need a horse to get back and forth to town."

"We can always borrow Roscoe's mule. That's what Uncle intended."

"My wife ride on a mule? Never!"

Rachel giggled as she wound the yarn in a ball. "I'd break the poor thing's back now I've gotten so big."

"Why, you must have gained all of ten pounds, you heifer."

"Oh, stop it, you." She threw her half-wound ball of yarn at Thomas just as a gust of wind blew smoke back down the chimney into the front room.

Down by the river, the tall trees tossed and danced, shaken by the chill February wind. Four men, oblivious to the cold and clad strangely in white, hurried their horses across the bridge and up the rise.

"Old man Staton's farm is up on the ridge to the left," the leader shouted over the noise of the river and the wind. "His son has been talking a lot around town about how the black man has cheated him out of his fair share."

"He's one of us, then."

Roscoe blinked to see four figures draped in white on his doorstep. Their heads were covered by odd masks and they appeared menacing, but when the leader spoke, Roscoe recognized with relief the voice of the storekeeper from Cleveland.

"Hail, brother! You have been selected for the honor of initiation into an organization of the highest caliber."

"Yeah, William? Come on in here and tell me about it." Roscoe held open the door and gestured for the men to come in. "You put your horses in the barn?"

"Do you believe in the natural superiority of the white man?"

Roscoe nodded, his eyes narrowing.

"Do you believe in maintaining that natural superiority at all costs?"

He nodded again, a smile beginning to curve the outside corners of his lips.

"Do you pledge to support and uphold your white brothers in the face of any adversity?"

His face now broken by a wide smile, Roscoe nodded a third time.

"Will you submit to the rules and regulations, agree to abide by the decisions of your leaders, and hold in confidence the identities of your fellow members?"

"Yes! I can't wait to get started! Was it you, Will, that chased that teacher all the way back to Boston where he belonged?"

The man's answering smile was revealed as he removed his mask. The three men with him followed suit.

"I hear Cole's been giving you trouble."

"That Cornelius has been doing something to my fields so my cotton won't grow. My corn had the blight last year, my hens won't lay any more, I just can't hardly make ends meet. What's this world coming to when an honest white man's farm starts failing and a no-count black man's getting rich?"

"We can help, Roscoe. All you gotta do is help us out. That's what we do, we help each other out."

Down the road, Ida Cole had just put the lamp out, over the protests of her oldest daughter.

"Just let me finish this chapter, Mama, please!"

Ida smiled. "You'll wear out your eyes, girl, and then where will you be? Out in the cotton fields all your life?"

"Not me! I'm gonna go to school and be a teacher and wear fine clothes. You'll see!"

"I believe you, Baby. Now let's go to sleep. Your daddy and your brothers should be back from Tuskegee tomorrow, and they'll be full of new ideas to try out."

Hoofbeats rang out on the hard-packed dirt road leading up to the little house, and Ida's mind flew from one thought to another. Horses riding fast at night rarely brought good news. A rifle butt pounded the door, jarring Ida's three youngest awake and causing all four children to huddle near their mother, shivering.

"Hey!" A falsetto voice ripped through the thin wood of the door. "We wanna talk to you!"

Ida held a hand over her son Zeke's mouth. He was so frightened he could barely keep still. Ida was figuring furiously how to protect her family. Another blow to the door, and the wood shuddered, cracking under the force.

Ida made up her mind. Holding six-year-old Zeke in her arms like a baby, she ran to the back door of the cabin. She looked out. To her relief, the night visitors had not thought to post anyone around back. She gestured for the other children to follow, and they ran out into the night just as five men dressed in white burst through the front door.

Ida and her children hid in the barn. "They'll come out here next, Mama!" Mary whispered. "What do they want?"

Ida looked at the sixteen-year-old girl and gestured again for the children to follow her into a stand of river cane next to the barn. Soon enough, the men were in the barn, and Ida could hear their conversation.

"Where did they go?"

"There wasn't enough time to hitch up the mule. They must be out visitin'."

"I know where they went! I read in the paper they were givin' out free seeds over in Tuskegee. They must have left this mornin', 'cause I saw that woman on the road yesterday."

"Let's leave 'em a present."

"You got that kerosene?"

Covering her mouth in horror, Ida realized the light of the fire they intended to set might reveal their hiding place. Quickly, she sent each child out of the cane down toward the riverbank, praying the shadows would hide them well.

Ida stayed, hoping to put out the fire as soon as the men left. But they stayed and left the barn standing, so they could shelter themselves and their horses as the wind whipped the flames into a fiery inferno, sending sparks climbing high into the winter sky. Ida wept as she watched her home burn, and then she turned to find her children and a safe place for the rest of the night.

••••••

Sarah Groves rolled her car window all the way down, letting the cool night breeze wash over her and clear the cobwebs from her head. She'd been driving since dark, after spending the weekend with her sister in Birmingham. If she wasn't in her place at the mill by 7:30 a.m. on Monday, though, she'd lose her job.

"There's a war on, sister," the foreman liked to say. "Production can't stop for anything. Our boys need their uniforms, and that's why you're here!"

The mill made low-grade cotton fabric, and since last December, they had been running two shifts. The work wasn't hard, just boring, and the tremendous noise of the mechanized looms crashing hour after hour had made Sarah a little hard of hearing.

She sighed in relief as she saw the lights of Oneonta up ahead. Only nine more miles until home. The old house surrounded by pecan trees was practically falling down around her ears, but it was hers, free and clear. She'd had romantic fancies about living on a farm when she was a kid in Birmingham, but twelve years married to a small farmer washed that romance right out of her. When Dave died last year, she'd gladly sold all but one acre and the house.

She thought she heard the kids stirring behind her, and she twisted her head to look. No, Mary Ellen, who was eleven, and Petey, five, were sound asleep. Sarah smiled at the little boy's wide-open mouth and soft snores. Petey sounded amazingly like a miniature Dave when he slept.

Swann Bridge was up ahead, and Sarah slowed the car down to a crawl. She hated driving across the bridge, the way her tires whined and thumped across the heavy timbers. It didn't seem logical that the bridge would support itself, much less the weight of the car as she crossed, and she always had vague pictures in her mind of the bridge cracking in two, tossing her into the water below.

At night the bridge was even spookier. It was dark, and you never knew when another car might suddenly come thundering onto the bridge from the other side. Right after she and Dave had gotten married, a snake had fallen out of the rafters onto the top of the car with a thump and she had shrieked so loudly her throat hurt for days. Dave thought it was funny, but he'd grown up going back and forth across the bridge.

Tonight she drew her arm inside the car but kept the window rolled down—the breeze felt so good. She heard a moan and thought it was Petey in his sleep. She glanced back but saw he hadn't stirred. The sound was repeated, this time louder and more prolonged. Panicked, Sarah stopped the car in the middle of the bridge and reached back to shake the kids awake. "Are you okay?"

"What, Mom?"

Another cry filled the bridge, chilling Sarah to the bone. It reminded her of a baby crying—it sounded so lost, so forlorn. The river below made a hushing sound, but the cries would not be stopped. They grew in strength and sorrow, and Sarah couldn't make herself move from the spot. Her eyes filled with tears, and her children sat bewildered in the backseat, waiting for the sad wails from an unseen baby to die away again.

••••••

"That sneaky hen managed to hatch five baby chicks, Thomas!" Rachel held one out to her husband, who was washing up at the pump.

"Isn't this a wonderful spring?"

"Can we have fried chicken every other day?" He laughed as she hurried awkwardly to return the chick to the barn. Her belly was full and round now, and he loved to rest his hands across the smooth, firm skin as she slept. The baby's leg or arm would sometimes thrash out, creating an odd bulge that shivered across her midriff. The whole farm was filled with new life.

It had been a perfect spring, with just enough rain and plenty of prematurely hot weather. The cotton was thriving, and the corn was already two feet high. Thomas was in the fields every day till dusk and awake before dawn, but he loved the rhythm of this life. Now he had a fine horse, and Rachel rode out to the fields every day to bring him dinner and a bucket of cool water.

As they sat down to supper, Rachel told him bits and pieces about her day. "After lunch, I heard Bessie mooing up at Uncle's place. She sounded really distressed, so I went on up there."

Thomas looked at her, his mouth too full to comment, but she knew what he would say.

"That poor cow hadn't been milked in a day or more, Thomas! I couldn't leave her in misery, could I?"

Thomas swallowed. "Where was Roscoe?"

"He came out to the barn—scared me half to death—said he'd overslept."

"I just don't understand that boy. He complains about poor crops, but his cotton's full of weeds and he sleeps all day."

"He said he'd signed a lease on the Cole land, too, and he'll put cotton in. He wants to plant a pecan orchard like ours up by the house, and I said you'd give him some advice."

"You've taken more care of those trees than I have. Without your attention, they'd have probably shriveled up and died by now."

"I think it was a good idea."

"They won't bear enough to make any money till after junior there is in school." Thomas pointed with his fork at her belly.

"That's good—it'll keep him in shoes!" Rachel pushed herself up from her chair with a little grunt to clear the table and start the dishes.

"A colored lady came to the house when I was starting supper tonight. She was looking for Ida Cole—her cousin or something."

"It's a shame they left—though I understand why they did after the house burned. He was a fine farmer. I could've used his mule last month, too—two mules can plow twice as fast as one."

The next morning Rachel was making pies from the last of her dried apples when Roscoe appeared on her doorstep. "Come on in, Roscoe. You want a cup of coffee?"

"No, thanks, Rachel. Too hot." He lounged back at the table, tilting the chair back on two legs.

"What brings you over here on a weekday?"

"Is Thomas here?"

"No, he's at work," Rachel said pointedly.

Roscoe let the chair legs down on the floor, leaning over the table and idly tracing designs in the flour Rachel had scattered to roll out the pie crusts on. "My cotton's not doin' too well," he said, not meeting her eyes.

"You really have to keep it hoed." Rachel tossed the dough down on the table and began to forcefully roll it with a rolling pin smooth and worn with use.

"I need help on my farm." Roscoe began to tap his foot under the table.

"You should start callin' on the Wilson girls. There's five of them—surely one would suit you."

He laughed unpleasantly. "My dogs are prettier and prob'ly cleaner." He started to get up from his chair. "What's that?" He shook his foot and a kitten scurried out from under the table, mewling loudly.

Rachel laughed in relief. "It's just a kitten—Tabby had a litter a month ago, and they keep gettin' in the house. Look—she must have gotten into the flour—her paw prints are all over your boot."

"I'll be goin' now." His chair legs dragged across the floor, making an angry scraping sound.

Rachel stood back from the table, surprised by her cousin's suppressed fury. A strand of dark hair had straggled loose from her bun and draped across her forehead. With the back of one flour-dusted hand, she tried ineffectually to push it out of her eye. Roscoe reached out, and she flinched. He gently tucked the hair behind her ear.

"Shall I—shall I tell Thomas to ride over when he's through?" Rachel stammered.

Roscoe only turned and looked at her as he mounted his horse. With a shake of his head, he rode off and turned right, away from his farm, toward the bridge and town.

This close to summer, daylight lingered on until eight o'clock, so Rachel always planned a light, late supper. Tonight they'd have apple pie, some cold leftover chicken, and fresh string beans from her kitchen garden.

Thomas was tired, and they didn't speak much during the meal. "I'm ready to go to bed," he confessed right after supper. "I've still got two acres near the river to hoe tomorrow, and the corn needs tending to."

"I could help," Rachel offered. As Thomas patted her shoulder and smiled tiredly, they heard horses gallop up to the yard. "Who could that be?" Rachel picked up the lamp and walked to the door.

"I'll get it." Thomas took the lamp from her hand and moved in front of her to the door just as someone began to pound on it.

"Open up," came the falsetto cry.

Thomas opened the door with a jerk. "What d'you want?" he asked. Over his shoulder, Rachel glimpsed the spectacle of the nighttime visitors and gasped. They were dressed in white from their heads to the tips of their boots. Any other time she might have laughed at the sight, for the men looked as if they had pillowcases on their heads, with eye slits slashed crudely through the fabric. But at night, and in a group of five, the robed masked men were strangely menacing.

"Do you, Thomas Brown, believe in the natural superiority of the white man?" The falsetto voice came from the man at the far left—the tallest figure.

"Well, I 'spect I've known some smart white folks. I've known some pretty dumb ones, too, though," Thomas drawled. Rachel could tell by his slower-than-normal speech that he was weighing every word before he let it drop.

"Do you believe in the natural rights of white men?" The speaker in his urgency let the falsetto drop, and Rachel struggled to put a face to the familiar voice.

"I've had a hard day, and I don't have time for this foolishness," Thomas said.

"That, sir, is an unwise thing to say." Another man spoke, making no attempt to disguise his voice.

"State your business with me," Thomas insisted.

Rachel's eyes traveled frantically from man to man as they stood in a semicircle at her doorstep, sweeping from head to foot trying to find any clue to the identity of this menace to her home.

"We are looking for loyal white men," the original speaker said, remembering the falsetto. "Finding none here, we ride." He turned, striding to his horse in the shadow of the barn. The other men followed him, and as they turned, something about the left boot of one of the silent men caught Rachel's eye. Marching across the toe were the distinctive five-toed tracks of a kitten. She gasped and stumbled back into the kitchen, falling into a chair.

"Don't worry, Rachel, they're gone." Thomas stroked her hair and tried to soothe her, but all she could do was clutch her belly and weep.

•••••

The doctor smiled again and shook the new father's hand for the third or fourth time, trying to free himself so he could begin the long drive home. He'd already run the gauntlet of proud relatives in the living room and spoken at length to his patient's anxious mother.

"Really, Doc, I can't tell you how much I appreciate it. I mean, this is just wonderful. It's a miracle! Didja see the little fella's toes? They're just so, so tiny! And all that hair, he looks just like me, don'tcha think?"

The older man extricated himself gently, patting the man on the shoulder and hurrying down the stairs to his buggy and elderly Nell waiting patiently. He'd sent someone out to feed and water her six hours ago, but still, she nickered softly to see her old friend approach.

"That's a good girl, a good old girl," he said, pulling a small apple out of his black bag and offering it to her. "I've brought another one into this world, girl, so now you do your job. Let's go home." He spread the blanket across his knees and picked up the reins, but she needed no encouragement. She moved away from the curb at a brisk walk.

It was nearly midnight, but the doctor still kept an eye out for traffic as they crossed the streets of the small town, heading for his farm above the Warrior River. Old Nell didn't much care for those noisy, sputtering automobiles, and neither did Doc, for that matter.

"You really ought to retire that old horse, Charles," his wife scolded him regularly. "You'd get to and from your patients faster. After all, this is 1922—it's the twentieth century, and you should act like it!"

"Bless your heart, Clara, I'm only acting my age," he'd chuckle. "When Nell's old enough to retire, I will too. My patients need me in one piece, not scattered by the roadside somewhere. I'll take my horse and buggy any day over that smelly, noisy, mechanized monster!"

After they were safely out of town, Doc dozed a bit. Nell knew the way home and needed no urging. His head nodding up and down in time with the soft clip-clop of her hooves, the doctor and his horse wound their way downhill toward the approach to the Swann Bridge.

A baby's cry, shrill and anxious, made the doctor's head snap up. "Peggy, I told you to take care of the child," he muttered. "I've got my hands full with the mother, here!"

He shook his head, disoriented. It was dark, and he was alone, except for old Nell, who stood still in her tracks. Oh, it was the bridge. He'd dreamed he heard a baby cry.

"I'm getting too old for these long deliveries, Nell," he chuckled, and clucked gently to get her started again.

Another wail rang through the bridge. Moonlight slipping through the side slats revealed a shiver running across Nell's back, a strange rippling motion of her silky skin.

The doctor sat quite still, the reins motionless in his hands. The sob broke up, then built again as a plaintive moan. The cry was familiar to this old family doctor—the cry of a baby alone and frightened.

"There, there," he murmured. Whether he was placating himself, the horse, or the unseen baby, he had no idea. Tears welled up in his eyes, and threatened to spill over. "Hush, now," he said softly, over and over, until the pitiful cries died away.

•••••

Rachel was down the road collecting blackberries in an enameled dishpan when the first pains struck. They left her breathless but dispelled for a full fifteen minutes, long enough for her to get back to the house. She had just sat down in the kitchen chair, panting slightly, when a fresh wave broke over her. She sucked in great drafts of air, a little scared, but mostly excited.

When these pains too passed, she pulled the shotgun out of the cabinet and carefully loaded it, just as Thomas had taught her. Walking slowly outside, she aimed the gun straight up into the air and fired.

The roar sent the chickens in the yard running and squawking, and the recoil made her stagger. But the gun's report rolled across the fields and down to the river valley, and she knew Thomas would soon be on his way to her.

He'd been riding the horse to the fields the past week since her time was close, so he could return quickly if she needed him. She didn't allow herself to think of the sinister visitors they'd had a few months ago. She had almost been able to dismiss their presence as a bad dream, faintly remembered, but not quite.

"Are you okay?" Thomas flung himself off the horse before it even came to a full stop and stumbled a bit in his haste to reach her side.

"I'm fine," she laughed. "But that old rooster thinks he's been shot." She pointed to a venerable old Rhode Island Red, who reeled and tottered around the yard, still shaken by the shotgun blast.

"Why'd you call me, then?"

A pain snatched low in Rachel's back, then widened and grew, marching steadily across her belly to writhe there evilly for a few moments. Thomas watched as the pain wrote itself on his wife's face, and he clasped her by the upper arm to keep her from swaying and falling.

"Come on, sweetheart, let's go to bed," he said, gently steering her to the kitchen door. When the pain loosed its grip she panted slightly and smiled.

"It'll be hours yet, that's what Lonie says, and she's birthed dozens," she protested. "Let's sit at the table and have a drink of water."

The next pain seized her fifteen minutes later, so harsh and unforgiving that she vomited up the water Thomas had drawn for her. She cried this time, ashamed of the mess, but Thomas soothed her.

"That's all right, you just come with me. Let's lie down. You'll feel better." He led her to the bedroom, sandwiched between the sitting room and kitchen, which was cool and dark with the curtains closed tightly against the hot summer sun.

She lay there for a while, dozing in and out. The pains were infrequent, coming every fifteen to thirty minutes, and it was not yet time to fetch the midwife. Thomas tried to read an old newspaper and then went out and fed the chickens and then wandered aimlessly around the house. Right before dusk, Rachel struggled out of bed.

"I want to walk around a bit," she said, over Thomas's protests. "I'm too restless to stay in bed. Lonie said walking was good, so long as I felt okay."

When the moon rose over the river, Rachel's pains were coming regularly, every ten minutes, and clutching her tightly for a full sixty seconds.

"I want to lie back down," she said, and they walked back to the bedroom.

He helped her loosen her clothes and got a cool cloth to lay across her forehead.

"I'm going to ride across the bridge to get Lonie now, okay?" Thomas stood in the doorway, lit from behind by the oil lamp flickering brightly on the kitchen table.

Rachel lifted up her arms, begging for a kiss before he left. He came to her, gently smoothing the hair away from her eyes and mouth. She was pale. "I'll try to be brave, Thomas," she whispered. "I love you."

"I love you, too, Rachel," he said fiercely. "Don't worry about a thing. I'll be right back."

Rachel listened to the thunder of the horse's hooves pounding down the road and tried to relax, knowing that another pain would soon overtake her.

Thomas had just reached the bridge when a ghostly figure detached itself from the shadows.

"Who rides?" the man demanded, and Thomas recognized the white robes and crude mask with a rising sense of panic.

"My wife, she's having a baby, I've got to get the midwife," he said. "Let me by!"

"It's Thomas Brown," said another figure, materializing from the trees beside the bridge road.

"No friend of the white man," said the first one.

"A traitor who refused to join our brotherhood," hissed a third form in white.

"You don't understand, she's frightened, she's just a girl," cried Thomas. "Please, you've got to let me get the midwife!"

In the house up on the ridge, Rachel allowed herself first to moan through clenched teeth as the pains swept through her body and then to cry out with a full-throated bellow. A sudden warmth seeped through her clothes. With horror, she realized she had entered the final stage of her labor.

"I understand she's too good for you," growled a white-robed figure whose shape was faintly familiar.

"How do we treat traitors here?" called the leader to the five men assembled. One man now held Thomas's horse, and as unfriendly hands reached to pull him from the saddle, he began to realize how serious his plight was.

Rachel's moans would begin low, almost guttural in the back of her throat. Then, as the pain wrapped itself around her, tightening cruelly, the cry would build to a harsh crescendo of wordless agony. In the scant seconds between pains, her breath came out raggedly.

"Soon, soon," she panted. "Ah, Thomas, soon now."

"Death is for traitors," chanted the men. "Death to traitors!" Thomas struggled savagely now, knowing that these men were beyond all reason. His struggles were in vain. The familiar figure in white approached with a knife in his hand, and whispered cruelly as he drew the blade across Thomas's throat.

"She's mine now, Thomas—you can be a hired hand in hell."

Rachel made a last, herculean attempt, shrieking with the effort, and the baby heaved out and onto the wet, sticky bedclothes beneath her. The baby gasped, and cried, at first tentatively but then with the lusty yowl of a healthy newborn.

When Rachel awoke, she was laying on clean, dry sheets and the baby slept peacefully beside her. Lonie rose from the rocking chair when she saw Rachel's eyes open. "Is he all right?"

Lonie's eyes widened in shock.

"Is the baby all right?"

The midwife's expression relaxed. "Of course he is, dearie, he's just perfect."

"What took you so long?"

"What do you mean, Rachel? I came as soon as I heard."

"After Thomas left, it took so long," Rachel murmured, her eyes fluttering closed.

"You sent Thomas to me?"

"Lonie." Rachel recognized her cousin's voice at the sitting room door, but she was too tired to puzzle out the meaning.

"Don't tell her yet," Roscoe whispered to the midwife. "I don't know where Thomas ran off to, but his horse turned up back at the barn. There's no sense in upsetting her."

Lonie eyed Roscoe with some degree of suspicion. He'd come to her door late last night with a tale of hearing his cousin screaming, but she didn't trust this boy. She shrugged and turned back to the bedroom.

"Lonie, can you stay with her for a day or two? I can pay you."

The midwife shrugged again and nodded as she sat back down in the rocker.

A few hours later, Rachel was moving slowly around the house. When Lonie told her Thomas was missing, she didn't believe it.

"Thomas went to get you," she insisted. "He didn't run off. He wouldn't do that."

Lonie was inclined to agree, but she kept her own counsel.

The day after Lonie left, Roscoe arrived at Rachel's doorstep leading the mule with a long cylindrical shape, wrapped in a sheet, draped over its back. Her heart rose up into her throat.

"Rachel, sit down for a minute," Roscoe said, pushing her down into a chair. "I'm afraid I've got some bad news."

She began to shake her head and then moan softly as Roscoe spoke.

"I think Thomas got scared when your baby was coming, Rachel. He must've run away, and the horse threw him."

The baby began to whimper in the next room as Rachel's cries steadily grew. She threw off Roscoe's restraining hand and ran outside to tear the sheet away from the mule.

Thomas's vacant face stared up at her, with a terrible wound, bloodless but gaping, across the throat. It was an ugly parody of his wide smile that had so often greeted her.

"I'm afraid he drowned, Rachel," Roscoe said, standing next to her. "It must have been a terrible accident."

"It was no accident!" The cry burst from her, a furious, shrieking accusation. "I know about you! I know what you are!" Sobbing wildly, she darted back into the house, slamming the door in his stunned face.

"Rachel, you're upset, I understand that!" Roscoe pounded at the door. As the kitchen door splintered and Roscoe tumbled in, Rachel snatched up the baby and flung herself out the front door.

When she reached the barn she didn't even pause to throw a saddle on Thomas's horse. She knew she had to ride to safety and get away from the man who murdered her husband. Ruthlessly she crashed her heels into the horse's side, gripping the baby with one hand and the horse's mane with the other. They flew down the road, the horse neighing in protest at the return to the bloody scene of its master's death.

At the opening of the bridge, the very spot where Thomas's blood had poured out, the horse balked, stopping dead in its tracks. Forward momentum carried Rachel and the baby she held so tightly up and over the horse's head. As they tumbled toward the unforgiving rocks below, the baby cried out—a long, drawn-out forlorn wail.

grace: the witch
of pungo

All manner of witchcraft is practiced in old Virginia. In fact, even more than Puritan New England, Virginia was rife with practitioners of the black arts. Throughout the nation's early history, some even said that Satan's power visibly reigned in Virginia, more than any other place in the world.

That having been said, the authorities and residents of colonial Virginia had a much more relaxed attitude toward the practitioners of witchcraft than their New England counterparts. By and large, they accepted practitioners of the magical arts as something of an unfortunate inevitability. But they also knew that obliterating witchcraft altogether from the colony would be next to impossible. As in its sister commonwealth, colonial Massachusetts, Virginia, too, had its witch trials.

Almost anyone could be accused of being a witch or warlock. If you were too tall, too short, too attractive, left-handed, or had prominent features different from those of the community around you, you could be charged with being a witch. The records of the time detail the trials of many who were falsely accused of witchcraft. In 1622, Goody Wright of Virginia was accused of casting a spell on a young family. Soon after the couple's first child was born, the young family experienced a run of bad luck and accused Goody of casting a malevolent spell upon them. Now it appears that Goody Wright did indeed have some psychic abilities, such as precognitive sight and the ability to communicate with animals. But the sole ground upon which she was arrested and accused of witchcraft was based on the fact that she was left-handed, an anomaly at the time.

Local folklore abounds with descriptions of witches meeting in small—and sometimes large—covens and dancing in the moonlight. One old-timer said, "Oh, yes, witches dance. I've seen 'em! They dance and can put the hex on you no matter where you are. It's best to stay clear from the witches on the Sabbath."

As in Massachusetts, accusing someone of being a witch became something of a local pastime. If anything bad happened to you, if crops failed, or if a horse or a mule got sick and died and there was no other obvious explanation to account for it, then witchcraft was automatically assumed, and the person upon whom the ill fortune fell began looking for a scapegoat. In many cases, those who had been falsely accused turned around and successfully sued their accusers after their acquittal. Malicious slander, it seems, was a much easier case to prove than was the charge of practicing the black arts.

This was the kind of history that had excited May Phillips her entire life. Ever since she had been a small girl growing up in Virginia Beach, she had been fascinated with the stories of Virginia witches and warlocks. Like most people in Princess Anne County, May was fascinated by the story of Grace Sherwood, perhaps Virginia's most famous witch. Conventional history tells us that Grace Sherwood was accused of blighting a neighbor's field in 1698. Over a period of years, suspicion about Grace Sherwood grew, and eventually county officials and local residents accused her of being a witch. History also tells us that she was quickly convicted because she failed the most reliable test of the time to determine if someone was a servant of Satan. The practice was called "Witch Ducking" and consisted of tying the accused witch's thumbs to her big toes and dropping her in a body of water. If her heart were pure, God would come down and hold her beneath the surface of the water to prove her innocence. If, however, she were a servant of the Dark One, she would bob up to the top of the water, proving conclusively that she was a witch.

On July 10 of 1706, at the stroke of ten, Gracie Sherwood was bound according to tradition and thrown into the western fork of Lynnhaven Bay. To this day, it is known as Witch Duck Point. Sherwood, naturally, floated to the top, satisfying the hundreds of onlookers that she was indeed a witch. She was jailed for a time at the Ferry Plantation House, but was later released. Conventional wisdom holds that she lived out the rest of her days quietly and never practiced witchcraft again. She died in 1740.

At least, that is the accepted history.

May Phillips was not satisfied with common knowledge and conventional wisdom. She had made an in-depth study of the controversies and events of Grace Sherwood's very colorful life. What she unearthed in local records, old newspaper articles, and gleanings from local storytellers convinced her that Sherwood's power was truly great and that she had never given up the practice of witchcraft.

As it turns out, according to May, Grace Sherwood was a woman ahead of her time. She was attractive and intelligent and not content to be a protected wife. She wore men's clothing, worked in the field, rode horses, and spoke her mind often. This seemed not to bother her husband, James, who was more than happy to share the many tasks around their farm that were usually reserved for men folk.

The breeches, riding boots, and ruffled linen shirt that Grace wore showed off her ample figure, much to the horror of other wives living in the area. Such behavior was unseemly and scandalous to her more matronly neighbors. But Grace delighted in making them uncomfortable. She would send anonymous notes to them and would secretly take things from their property only to return them later. Grace was a practical joker and could never understand why her victims all took themselves so seriously. The Witch of Pungo was also a skilled midwife and an expert in herb lore. She could combine roots, herbs, and berries to suck the poison out of a wound in no time. She could prepare poultices and lotions for a variety of ailments, but it was her magical skills that made her infamous.

May discovered reports that Grace Sherwood had been seen literally floating above the treetops near her home. She had even been caught teaching a local girl how to fly on a broom. One night, a pair of woodsmen startled Grace while she was apparently performing the witch's Sabbath. At one glance from the Witch of Pungo, both men were struck blind for a day. It was even rumored that the witch could transport herself across the ocean to England or Ireland, bringing back whatever she needed to make her magic potions.

May Phillips could still remember the very first time she heard an old storyteller spin the yarn about Grace Sherwood and the herb rosemary. Needing the fresh herb for a magical potion, Grace shrunk herself down to the size of a coin and then, so the story goes, transported herself in a hollowed-out egg across the ocean to England. There she secured fresh rosemary and packed it into the egg. She flew back to Virginia in the blink of an eye, grew back to normal size, and proceeded to make her potions. Local legend holds that rosemary grew nowhere in North America until the Witch of Pungo brought it here.

Sherwood had the ability to change herself into a cat, a raven, a dog, a wisp of smoke, and even a spider. With these powers, the old-timers said, she was able to keep an eye on the residents of the little town of Pungo. It was in these various forms that she was able to eavesdrop on them and learn of their malicious slander against her. Time and time again, Grace Sherwood would sue her neighbors for this crime, and more often times than not, the court found in her favor.

James Sherwood died in 1701, and the tide changed for the worse for Grace Sherwood and her three sons. Several years later, Grace sued a local woman who had been spreading the "rumor" that the witch had cast a spell on her. The court was indifferent to the charge and, even though they found in favor of the widow Sherwood, awarded her only twenty shillings in damages.

Charges and countercharges flew. Reports of supernatural activity in the small community increased almost exponentially. Ghosts of the dear departed were seen wandering aimlessly throughout the countryside. Strange lights were seen floating in the trees. Cows stopped giving milk, and prize bulls seemed unable to perform their duties. One of the stories that May Phillips liked most of all was the report that Grace Sherwood had turned a local busybody into a horse. The woman in this case described in detail how Grace Sherwood had floated through the keyhole as a wisp of smoke and transformed herself into a black cat. Then, with a swish of her tail, she transformed the old busybody into a horse, jumped on her back, and rode her through the countryside all night long. When the old woman awoke the next morning feeling uncharacteristically exhausted after a long night's sleep, she miraculously remembered the bewitchment and attributed it to Grace Sherwood.

Shortly thereafter, the busybody found herself the forewoman of a jury whose job it was to declare the guilt or innocence of Grace Sherwood, who had been brought up yet again on formal charges of witchcraft. While women did not normally serve as jurors in colonial Virginia, in the case of witchcraft, local women were frequently asked to sit in judgment of another woman. As far as May Phillips could determine from her research, this entailed a thorough examination of the body of the accused, something a man would never be allowed to do. A tell-tale sign called Satan's Mark would be somewhere on the body of the suspected witch indicating that she had made a pact with the devil. In the case of Grace Sherwood, two moles on her privates condemned her. It was in support of this accusation that the county court ruled that she must further be judged by ducking. Before they threw Grace Sherwood into the bay, she cursed the townspeople, telling them that they, too, were going to get the ducking of their lives.

After Grace floated to the surface of the water, proving once and for all that she was a witch, the townspeople retrieved her and took her to jail. Along the way, the beautiful summer sky rapidly darkened over with thick clouds. Thunder and lightning crashed. Then the heavens opened up, and a flood like none ever witnessed before began to punish the townspeople leading Grace away to jail. They were blinded by the deluge and tripped in the mud of the flooded roads. Even the wind, as the stories go, sounded like angry dogs and demons nipping at Grace's persecutors. Grace Sherwood just laughed throughout the event.

May Phillips chose to regard all of these tales as whimsy. To her, Grace Sherwood was one of our nation's first liberated women and was made to suffer for it. Colonial Virginia had no place for a woman who spoke her mind and made her own way in life. The shortcomings and weaknesses of others, May thought, would always be displaced onto the strong and confident.

Once she was released from prison, Grace Sherwood supposedly led a quiet and uneventful life. But May's research provided her with enough evidence to suspect that the Witch of Pungo continued to work her magic spells on the residents of the small community. But what had she been doing for those years leading up to her death? No records, no stories could May Phillips find.

When Grace Sherwood died, it rained for seven days and seven nights. She had warned her neighbors that this would happen. The local residents feared that the witch's watery curse had returned for good. The earth gave up Grace's coffin on the eighth day of rain, and it floated on the runoff from the torrential downpour. Then the rain stopped. Her sons collected the coffin and buried her again. Once more, it rained for seven days and seven nights. Then, as before, the witch's coffin floated out of the earth.

Local legend has it that an area farmer discovered the coffin the second time. Atop the coffin quietly sat a black cat that just stared at the man. When the farmer approached the coffin, the cat arched her back and hissed, leapt off the coffin, and disappeared into the woods. Soon, the word spread far and wide that Grace Sherwood, the Witch of Pungo, was back. This time, she had transformed herself into a black cat. The residents were terrified. "We've gone too far," one man said. "We should have left her alone," exclaimed another. A handful of Pungo residents were so afraid they simply moved away, never to return.

May Phillips laughed when she thought about people being so afraid of a black cat that they would literally leave their homes and move away. But now as she sat on the ground next to Grace Sherwood's grave, she anticipated what was going to happen next. The moon was full and bright, and, as happens on every night of the full moon, cats from all over the city gathered at the witch's grave.

May came here often over the years. Tonight she even brought her own pet cat Grace (named after the witch) along with her. It wasn't long before the felines all began to howl at the bright moon. May's kitty joined in. A few moments later, a thin wisp of smoke crept up from the ground of Sherwood's grave and took the form of a large black cat with emerald green eyes. The ghost cat stared at May, but neither was startled—or even surprised—for they had met many times before. Soon, the ghost of Grace Sherwood in the form of a cat was singing along with the rest of her feline companions. As they sang, the cats gathered around a young girl who knew well the importance of being a strong woman and making her own way in life.

May Phillips just smiled and enjoyed the music of the night.

the ghost of yankee creek

Enormous forks of lightning splintered the ebony sky. Thunder roared across the fields, shaking the ground with savage power.

The little house, white clapboard with blue shutters, withstood the onslaught of rain and wind, but the windows chattered in their frames at every roll of thunder and gust of wind. Isolated at the end of a winding, unpaved road, its bright lights shone bravely, trying without success to hold back the gloom of the stormy summer night.

"I don't know, Alex," Hal Evans was telling his eleven-year-old son. "Even if the storm stops, the ground's gonna be really wet. It can wait till next weekend, can't it?"

Alex slumped down in despair. "If I don't research six wild animals by July 30, I won't get my merit badge." The pitch of his voice climbed higher. "Dad, I've got to go out!"

"Why not let him go out tomorrow night?" Beth Evans had been eavesdropping on the conversation. "You'll both get what you want."

"What about Sunday School?"

Beth shrugged. "So he misses one day. He'll be all right."

Alex jumped up and ran to the phone, throwing his mom a quick grin on the way.

"Where you goin', Sport?" his dad called.

"Gotta call Les," the boy replied, his hand on the receiver.

"Wait till this storm's over," his father suggested. "I don't think it's a good idea to use the phone during an electrical storm like this."

Alex made a face, but set the phone down anyway.

The next afternoon, Alex was carefully checking his gear: sleeping bag, plastic tarp, flashlight, Fritos, Snickers, sandwiches, canteen, camera, notebook, pencil, and a little plastic baggie with plaster to make casts of any paw prints he might find.

"Got everything?" his father asked, dropping down on his haunches next to the boy's pack.

"Yep, sure do," Alex replied.

"Not gonna build any campfires, are you?"

"No, sir." Practically surrounded on all sides by national forests, Alex had had the danger of forest fires drilled into him from an early age. Smokey the Bear was a more familiar figure than Mickey Mouse.

"Let's go pick up Les, then."

Les was packed, and the sun was still well above the horizon when Hal dropped the boys off in a field a few miles from the house.

"What are you boys looking for tonight?"

"Creatures like skunks, raccoons, bats, mountain lions..."

"Lookin' for any ghosts?"

"Aw, Dad!"

With a beep of the horn and a wave, he drove off. He stopped the car a few hundred yards down the road and backed slowly up to the spot where the boys stood. "If you need to get home, we're just three miles straight across those fields." He pointed south. "I think old man Coldwater's got his bull penned up these days, but be careful if you cut across any open fields, okay?"

"Yeah, Dad. Thanks." The two boys shouldered their packs and headed off the road toward a bank of trees, not waiting for the car to drive off a second time.

The noise of the car had faded before Les asked a question. "I didn't know we were looking for mountain lions," he ventured.

"Naaah. I just said that. There aren't any mountain lions left around here."

Soon they were among the trees, looking for signs of small wildlife.

"I don't smell any skunks," Alex said.

"They don't make that stink until you threaten 'em," Les pointed out. "I hope they don't mistake your camera for a threat."

"We'd better find a place to make camp," Alex said. "Near the water would be good since raccoons hang out by the water."

"Skeeters are worse by the water, too," Les pointed out.

"Any sacrifice for a merit badge," reminded Alex.

"Yeah, right," Les said gloomily. "Lead me to the water."

The two boys found a level spot above the bank of the creek and spread out their sleeping bags. Les had a Coleman lantern, but they decided against using it, since it might scare the animals away.

"Let's eat," Alex said. "I've got baloney sandwiches and Fritos. What've you got?"

"Banana and peanut butter and Cheetos. We'll have to chew softly. How good can raccoons hear?"

"I'm more worried about the skunks and mountain lions, myself," Alex said cheerily.

"Quit it about the mountain lions, okay?"

The sun had set. Both boys took out their notebooks and pencils, ready to make notes on any creatures they saw, and then they ate with a businesslike efficiency the raccoons they were seeking would have admired. The crickets and cicadas had started their evening song, and Alex was the first to spot the bats swooping and diving through the trees.

"Look," he said. "Nocturnal creatures seeking food." The bats were consuming insects as rapidly as they could catch them. Alex scribbled a few notes, and then picked up his bag of Fritos. "Look," he called quietly. "Nocturnal creature seeking food." He stuffed a handful of chips in his mouth and crunched noisily.

"Don't," whispered Les. "I can't hear if any creatures are coming."

The woods started coming alive with little sounds amplified by the deep blackness that surrounded them. Once their eyes adjusted to the loss of light, they could make out the indistinct shapes of each other and the trees. Suddenly, a heavy rumble tore though the peaceful woods.

"Yikes! What is that?" Alex stood up, scattering his notebook and pencil.

"It sounded like an earthquake!"

Both boys looked anxiously at the treetops—but they were still and undisturbed. When a car's headlights suddenly blinded the boys, they both recognized the source of the noise at once.

"It's the bridge," they chorused in relief. They had followed the treeline on the creek far enough down to be within a few hundred feet of Yankee Creek Covered Bridge. The summer vegetation was so thick they hadn't seen the road or the white structure of the bridge through the trees. A car's tires passing over the thick wooden floorboards made the throaty thrumming sound that had frightened them.

"You wanna drink, Alex?" Les held out his canteen.

He drank deeply, then spit it out in disgust. "Yecch! What is that?"

"It's Kool-Aid, I think." Les took a swig and just as quickly expelled the liquid. "She forgot the sugar again."

Alex rolled his eyes. Les's mother was very, well, unorganized was probably the nicest way to put it. Les was a little touchy though, so Alex was glad the darkness hid his gesture.

"I've gotta find my pencil."

"That mountain lion probably ate it."

"Wha...?" Alex was almost caught, but pulled back just in time. He whacked Les across the shoulder. "Gimme a pencil, barf-breath."

They sat in silence for a good twenty minutes, listening intently to the little noises of the forest and the sound of each other's breathing, before they heard a regular pattern of tiny footfalls trotting in their direction. Les froze, gesturing to Alex to stay still.

A rotund figure, as tall as a cat but much bigger around, waddled between the trees and down the bank to the creek. As it passed him, Alex noticed the hairless tail, like a big rat's, and the tiny little eyes that gleamed and reflected what little light there was under the trees.

The boys tiptoed to the edge of the bank and peered down. The animal seemed unconcerned about their approach, even after they began to descend to the creek toward it. Alex pulled a flashlight out of his back pocket and shined the light through his fingers to diffuse the brightness.

"You'll scare it away," protested Les in a whisper, but the creature just turned to stare at these two nocturnal intruders. Its fur was graduated white to gray, and its eyes stared beadily.

"It's a possum," exclaimed Alex.

"It's not afraid of us," Les said, advancing toward it. Just as he closed within a yard of it, it scurried off down the bank, its white-and-gray back bobbing up and down.

"That's two creatures," Alex said as they climbed back up the bank. "If we see any raccoons tonight, we'll be halfway to our badge."

A long moan interrupted him.

"Whatsa matter, Les, those bananas gettin' to you?" Alex jumped when Les grabbed him around the waist.

"I didn't do that," Les gasped.

"C'mon, it's not funny," Alex protested. Just as he was peeling his friend's fingers loose from his waist, the ghastly moan sounded again, louder—more like a shriek this time.

The boys looked at each other, their mouths open comically, as the noise died away. "I don't like the sound of that," Alex said, trying desperately not to sound afraid.

Les shook his head wordlessly.

The moan repeated itself, but it seemed a little more distant this time.

"Mountain lion?" croaked Les, and the two boys dissolved in nervous laughter. They moved their sleeping bags closer together and huddled for a long moment, waiting for the melancholy groan to come again. When it didn't, Alex brought out a pair of Snickers bars and they feasted again, in silence this time, the only sound the quiet crackle of the paper wrapper slipping off the candy.

"You wanna go home?"

Alex thought about arriving at his house just hours after they had left. He thought about his father's reaction. He considered the merit badge he wanted so badly. "Naah," he said, and stripped the wrapper off a third Snickers, throwing half to Les.

The only noises they heard for the rest of the evening were ordinary wind-in-the-tree sounds and the soft humming of insects. At last, reluctantly abandoning hope of seeing any raccoons at work, the two boys crawled into their sleeping bags. When Les checked his watch, he was amazed at the time. "Hey, Alex," he whispered. "It's only ten o'clock."

"Yeah," his friend said sleepily.

"I thought it was like midnight or something."

"Go to sleep, Les."

"G'night."

When the boys woke the next morning, a fine mist had risen from Yankee Creek. It was a little chilly, and they were glad for the cover of their sleeping bags.

"Les."

"Uh-huh?"

"What was that we heard last night?"

"I dunno."

"It wasn't, like, a bird or anything?"

"I never heard a bird cry like that."

"You think it might've been, well, a ghost?"

"It is possible, I guess. This bridge has been around a long time."

Alex threw off his sleeping bag, stood, and stretched.

"Oh, no," he cried.

"What's wrong?" Les sprang up.

The two boys surveyed the wreckage of their packs. Their notebooks were scattered, and the two bags of chips, half-filled last night, were now empty and shredded. Dainty little paw prints circled the area and led down to the creek.

"Raccoon?" suggested Les.

"That was breakfast," moaned Alex.

"How could we sleep through that?"

"I guess we were tired. Or maybe it was a ghost raccoon."

"Aw, quit it."

Alex made a few clumsy casts of the paw prints, the plaster dotted with bits of leaves and debris from the creek water he used to mix it, before hunger drove them out of the woods to the road. A green Chevy station wagon, its battered condition hinting at long and rough use, was approaching as the boys reached the edge of the road.

"Hey, Mr. Coldwater!" Alex shouted and waved his hands. The dust-covered car slid to a halt.

"Boys need a ride?" The farmer was a native of Jackson County, and both boys had known him all their lives. He had always been old, it seemed, but as tough as nails, they agreed. He'd probably helped chase the Indians out of Oregon a hundred years ago.

Alex and Les threw their packs in the back through the rear window that had broken out long ago. Then they climbed into the car, glad for the ride back to civilization and breakfast.

"Whatcha doin' out so early?" Mr. Coldwater carefully steered the car down the narrow road, bumping across the little white bridge.

"We camped out last night, lookin' for animals to study for our merit badge," explained Alex. Les stirred the pile of accumulated junk on the backseat floorboards cautiously with his foot. He could see part of an old chain, the rusted blade of an old axe, a bit of a bridle, a few tin cans, and a few dozen crumpled cigarette packs. The debris reached nearly to the top of the seat.

"Find any?" Mr. Coldwater lit a cigarette and flung the match out the window. Alex followed its course with his eyes, unsure if the match was still lit.

"Yes, sir," Les piped up. "Found a possum and some bats, and a raccoon ate our food while we were asleep."

"They'll do that."

"Mr. Coldwater, do you believe in ghosts?" Alex wasn't sure what made him ask that, but Mr. Coldwater would be the one to know if anybody did, he reasoned.

The old man paused. "Well, now, I do, mebbe, sometimes." He turned off to Alex's house.

Les lost his fascination with the rubble at his feet. "Are there any around here?"

"Mebbe." They were almost up to the little white house, and Mr. Coldwater paused again. "I'll tell you sometime, but not today. I've gotta get on over to the feed store."

Disappointed, the two boys climbed out of the car and grabbed their packs. "Thanks for the ride, Mr. Coldwater," they shouted as he backed up, turned around, and drove away.

"Ah, hello, boys!" Beth Evans greeted them cheerily. "Just in time for bacon and eggs and then Sunday School!"

"Aw, Mom," protested Alex.

"You boys must've gotten up at the crack of dawn." She ignored his groans as she laid out two more plates. "Any luck?"

"Yeah, we found a possum and some bats."

"And a raccoon broke into our packs in the middle of the night!"

"That must've been scary." She spooned a pile of scrambled eggs onto each boy's plate just as Hal came into the kitchen.

He poured a cup of coffee and then sat down. "Hey, where's my breakfast?"

"These boys got here first, Hal. I'll put some more on. Don't get your feathers ruffled."

The following week, Alex begged again to plan an overnight trip to study wildlife. "Time's running out, Mom," he said. "If I don't hurry, I'll never finish! And we know right where that raccoon lives. I'll stay up all night long and catch him in the act."

"Your grandmother's coming this weekend," his mother said crossly. "And if I don't get this house cleaned up first, I don't know what she'll say."

"I'll help you clean house, Mom," the boy negotiated. "She won't get here till Saturday, so me 'n Les can go Friday night, please, please, please?"

"All right, all right," she conceded. "As long as your dad says it's okay."

It was overcast all day Friday. Hal called Beth from work three times to discuss a change in plans, and Alex was nearly beside himself with apprehension. Finally they agreed that the boys could go, and Alex slung his pack in the backseat of the car quickly before anybody changed their mind again. Picking up Les, Beth dropped the boys off at the entrance to the bridge.

"If it starts raining, you can get in here," she called to their retreating backs. "Have fun!"

Before they were halfway down the bank, they heard a car horn beeping. Alex groaned and turned around. "If she's changed her mind again..." Relief bloomed when he recognized Mr. Coldwater's dusty, low-slung station wagon.

"You boys out huntin' again?" the old man bellowed, thrusting his head out the window.

"Yes, sir!"

Mr. Coldwater carefully steered his car to a spot only partly blocking the road. "You boys gonna have a fire? I'll go get some weenies, and we can have a regular feast, if you want."

"Yeah! That sounds great!"

Alex wasn't sure about campfires, but Mr. Coldwater was an adult and ought to know what he was doing.

"I'll be back. You boys gather the wood."

"Won't the fire scare away the raccoons, Les?" They had piled up a small mountain of deadwood, and Alex started to worry again.

"Aw, don't worry about it. Maybe he'll tell us about the ghosts!"

The old man scrambled down from the road to the campsite the boys had used before. After carefully clearing away all the nearby underbrush, he started the fire. He'd brought a bucket with him, which he filled with creek water and set near the fire. "Can't go startin' any forest fires, now can we, boys?" He winked at Alex.

It was nearly dark, and all three were leaning back, stuffed full of hot dogs and chips. The boys' sandwiches intended for supper were scattered along a trail: bait to lead the raccoon back to their camp.

"Mr. Coldwater, you remember, you were gonna tell us about the ghosts?"

"I was?" Seeing the disappointment on their faces, he relented. "Oh, yeah, that's right. But I don't wanna scare you, since you'll be all alone out here in the woods tonight."

"We won't get scared." Alex leaned forward, eager to hear the tale.

"Well, you know back in the twenties there was an awful lot of bootleggin' goin' on around here." The old man stretched out his legs and shook a cigarette out of the pack. After lighting it and sending a wreath of smoke curling around his head, he continued.

"Folks were makin' a pretty penny on that bootleg liquor, too, and you know money makes people awful mean. Well, my cousin Jack was not quite twenty but he did pretty good, bringing cases down into town and sellin' 'em to interested parties. His daddy was the sheriff, you know, but that's the later part of the story.

"Some folks up in Portland heard Jack was doin' a pretty good business, and they heard he was just a little pip-squeak. Now I was real young— 'bout six, I reckon, but I remember my cousin Jack bein' a pretty strong man. He wasn't mean at all—in fact, he would pull candy outta his pocket fer me.

"Those Portland gangsters—that's what they were, plain an' simple—came roarin' into town lookin' for Jack. They couldn't find him anywhere. He was out collecting liquor from his sources, see, and he'd be gone a day or two. But nobody tol' them strangers nothin' at first.

"The men from Portland got tired of waiting and were actually on their way out of town when they saw a car pullin' onto Main Street, ridin' low like a car does when it's loaded down. Sure enough, it was Jack, and they pulled in behind him. People said they stuck their shotguns out the window in broad daylight and started tryin' to put holes in ol' Jack then an' there.

"But Jack was crafty and managed to give 'em the slip. He turned into a side street and cruised out of town. It was his bad fortune that one of the shots had punctured his radiator, and the ol' car overheated and quit right up there on that bridge.

"The gangsters were lookin' all over for him, and somebody—if I knew who it was I'd've cut his throat years ago—told 'em to look out by Yankee Creek. Meanwhile, the sheriff had heard there was some shootin' in the middle of town, and he was worried about his boy.

"The men from Portland pulled up behind Jack's car, and he didn't even have a chance. They pumped him so full a' holes he looked like Swiss cheese. They were jus' loadin' up the bottles—them that weren't broke by all the shootin'—when the sheriff pulled up to the bridge. He took one look at his son, Jack, layin' there dead, and he went crazy. He killed every last one a' those gangsters—shot two and beat the third one to death. There was so much blood they said the creek would never run clear again."

The boys were quiet, awed by the scope of the tragedy. After a minute, Alex spoke. "What about the ghost, Mr. Coldwater?"

"For a long time, cars goin' over the bridge would jus' stop dead, right in the center. And one night, I was crossin' over to home a little late," he winked again, "and my car just quit. I pulled up the hood, fussin' and fumin', and then I heard footsteps on the bridge. I stood up so quick I cracked my head good on the hood of the car, but there wasn't anybody there. And sometimes, people say they hear screamin' round here, but I never did."

The boys looked around nervously at the dark woods surrounding them and over at the bridge, its bulk barely gleaming in the reflected glow of the campfire.

"Well, I've got to go," Mr. Coldwater said finally, standing up and brushing off his pants. "You want me to help you put out this campfire? I don't think coons'll come around with all this light."

Reluctantly Alex and Les helped the older man douse the fire. After he climbed back up to the road, they heard his car start up and pull away. The forest seemed impossibly dark and full of inexplicable noises.

"Reckon that's the raccoon?" Alex whispered after one particularly loud crash, not too far away.

"Probably so," admitted Les. "It must be pretty late."

Alex turned on his flashlight and shielded the glow with his fingers while he looked at his watch.

"It's only ten-thirty," he murmured. "You wanna get some sleep while I stay up?"

"Naah, I'll stay up with you. That coon oughta be along soon."

The moon was hidden behind a thick screen of clouds. Suddenly, the chorus of insects stilled, and even the night birds ceased their song. Something was crashing through the underbrush, headed straight for the boys' camp.

They could hardly sit still, waiting for the creature to approach. Alex's hand clutched the flashlight tighter and tighter, until he was sure the thin metal casing would surely crumple. When it sounded like the creature was nearly in their laps, Alex switched on the flashlight with a barely suppressed cry.

The flashlight's beam exposed the mild, myopic stare of a fat possum, following the trail of sandwich scraps the boys had laid down hours ago. With a sigh of disappointment, Alex switched off the flashlight.

"You s'pose that's the same one we saw last week?"

"If it is, it's gotten fatter," Les said bleakly. "Do possums eat raccoons?"

"Naah. That raccoon comes out really late, I bet. We'll get him. We'll just have to stay awake, that's all."

Something cold and wet touched Alex's cheek, and he jerked upright. He'd dozed off. Les, too, was asleep sitting up. A light rain was falling, sifting through the tree leaves landing quietly on the sleeping boys. In the distance, thunder crackled faintly.

By the wavering light of his flashlight, Alex gathered up his sleeping bag and stuffed it haphazardly into his pack.

"Les," he shook his friend by the shoulder. "Wake up."

"Huh? Is it here? Did I go to sleep?"

"It's raining. C'mon, let's go to the bridge before it starts pouring."

They clambered up to the road, sliding a little in the mud created by the light rain. Preoccupied by the weather and their awkward packs, they didn't hear the noise until they were right at the mouth of the bridge.

An unearthly howl floated out from the white structure, and Alex dropped his pack. Another scream, and the boys hesitated, not knowing in which direction lay safety. The ghastly cry began again, echoing from the rafters of the bridge. Paralyzed by fear, the boys could only stand in the rain. Within an instant, a white shape floated out of the bridge and away, just as the rain began to descend in sheets.

The boys had no choice but to dash into the shelter of the bridge. Shaking, chilled by more than the rain, they stared at each other and then rummaged through their packs to find their flashlights.

The faint yellow beams offered meager comfort. They shone their lights up and down the structure, looking for signs of anything that might explain the eerie noise and the amorphous form that had escaped the bridge as the rain began.

"What's that smell?"

Les looked at his shoes. "I think I wet my pants," he admitted. "I've never been so scared in my life."

Thunder cracked again, closer now, and both boys jumped.

"I could care less about that merit badge right now." Alex's teeth were chattering. "I wanna go home."

"What time is it?"

"Almost three o'clock. Unless my watch stopped." Alex shook his arm and held the timepiece up to his ear.

The blood drained from Les's face, and he clutched his friend's arm. "Omigosh," he whimpered, pointing out the mouth of the bridge. "They're coming, Alex!"

The twin beams of a car's headlights were bearing down on the bridge at full speed, slicing through the raindrops that fell like bullets.

The boys huddled in the corner of the bridge, waiting for the carful of gangsters to arrive. A cold wind blew over them, and they closed their eyes and shuddered, certain of their doom.

"Hey, you guys, you wanna ride home?"

It was Hal Evans, in the family's blue Monte Carlo. The boys were so relieved they didn't know whether to laugh or cry. They were subdued during the short trip home and slept only a few more hours in their sleeping bags on the floor of Alex's room, with all the lights turned on.

On Wednesday, Alex called Les.

"Hi. It's me."

"Hi."

"I been thinkin'."

"Me too."

"We gotta find out what that was."

Les sighed. "I know."

"You game?"

"If you are."

Hal and Beth noticed there was a certain measure of reluctance in their son's preparations for yet another overnight campout, but they attributed it to an eleven-year-old's short attention span.

"He's probably tired of the project," Beth told her husband.

"He's put a lot of effort into it. I'm glad he's sticking with it."

On Friday afternoon, the boys persuaded their folks to let them take their bikes out to Yankee Creek. "That way, at least we have a chance of getting away," Les whispered to Alex.

"I don't know about this," Alex replied, but then Beth began to stuff a couple of apples in his pack.

"Have fun," she said brightly. "At least there's no rain in the forecast."

The boys pedaled off slowly. Halfway there, they passed Mr. Coldwater on his way to the store. He honked and they waved, wishing he would join them again for a cookout.

"Maybe it's not a ghost," Alex said hopefully as they spread out their sleeping bags in the twilight gloom under the trees.

"Maybe it's a creature from outer space," retorted Les. "It moans, it flies, it comes out only at night. What else could it be?"

Darkness fell. Again the woods became animated with the rustlings and creakings of its nocturnal inhabitants, and every sound made the boys jump. They expected the stout possum to reappear, its friendly shape a comfort to their apprehensive minds. But they waited in vain.

It was nearly midnight, and they were still waiting for a sign of the ghost or even the elusive raccoon. Then, floating over the fields from a great distance, they heard a familiar spooky cry. Alex moved closer to his friend.

"We should go up to the bridge." Les spoke in a harsh whisper.

Alex nodded but didn't move.

"C'mon." Les prodded him with his flashlight.

The cry came again, closer this time. Les shuddered. It seemed to circle the bridge, repeating over and over, louder and louder. Alex forced his legs to move, climbing automatically through the sparse undergrowth that covered the approach to the road. Once they reached the road, their steps slowed to an imperceptible pace.

The uncanny screech came again, almost right on top of them. With a whoosh and another shriek, a shapeless blur streaked over their heads and into the bridge, causing the boys to fall flat on the ground in an instinctive attempt at self-preservation.

"We've got to go see," moaned Les.

"No, I can't go in there," protested Alex, but he allowed his friend to clasp his hand. They crawled into the mouth of the bridge.

The cry came again, shrill and terrifying. With trembling fingers, lying on the rough wooden timbers of the bridge floor, Alex nudged the switch on his flashlight.

"It's broken," he breathed in panic.

Les's flashlight came on, flickered, and went out.

"Shake it," he commanded Alex. Suddenly, both beams shone out, clear and pure. The light swept across the walls, finally pinning down a pair of eyes that glowed with an eerie fire. With another bloodcurdling screech, the great horned owl stretched its wings. It rushed over the boys so low they could discern individual feathers and muscles pumping hard underneath them.

They stood, awed by its power, and watched it dwindle into a speck of gray against the deep black sky.

slaughter pen

Dan Brooks, the Stones River groundskeeper, checked his watch and was pleased to see that it was almost five o'clock. He felt like he had been over every square inch of the 600-acre battlefield about a hundred times that day. The intense summer sun of Tennessee had sucked out whatever energy he had left after the physical labor was done with him. He could have retired a few years ago, but every year he found himself saying, "One more year, one more year." One of these days, though…

The heat had kept sightseers and Civil War buffs to a minimum, allowing Dan to putter around with his thoughts. He knew the park like the back of his hand, having tended to it lovingly for years. However, his long tenure had whittled away the mystique and excitement of its historical significance, so his imagination had long since stopped turning to the brutal and bloody events that had transpired at the battlefield.

Dan used to picture the battle that occurred at Stones River all the time. His imagination would conjure up images of General Bragg's Confederate soldiers surprising the Union soldiers commanded by General Rosencrans, leaving only one Union division ready to fight. He would imagine the gory details of the bloody battle, a battle that claimed the lives of roughly a third of both sides of the conflict. He would get especially fired up when he worked around what was known as "The Slaughter Pen," a cedar grove on the battlefield where fighting was especially fierce—hence the colorful but morbid name.

The one alert division, led by General Sheridan, had taken its position in the small grove of trees, trying desperately to hold the Confederates back while the other divisions scrambled to organize. They held out until their ammunition ran out, at which point they resorted to rocks, fists, bayonets, and whatever else they could find to stave off the Confederate onslaught. Needless to say, this area saw a lot of blood, gore, and death, and the groundskeeper used to picture it all in his mind.

After a while, however, Dan began to see the Slaughter Pen as he saw the rest of the park, as a historically significant place that demanded respect, but also demanded physical labor to ensure its upkeep and his paycheck. He had heard all the rumors about ghosts and ghouls supposedly hanging out in the Slaughter Pen, but he chalked the stories up to the enthusiastic imaginings of overzealous Civil War buffs. According to him, they saw all of that paranormal hogwash because they wanted to see it so badly. With a little creativity and imagination, a person could convince himself that he had seen just about anything.

On that hot summer day Dan was feeling especially pragmatic, ready to finish up his work so he could go home and take a cold shower. He thought to himself that he wouldn't have minded being on this battlefield for the actual fighting, because at least on New Year's Eve in 1862 it wouldn't have been this dang hot. Then he reminded himself of the brutal and bloody details of the gory battle and decided he'd rather grapple with the sun.

Dan wandered over to the Slaughter Pen to retrieve some of his equipment he had left in the shade. As he stooped over to pick up his tools he groaned a little. Maybe it was time to throw in the towel and retire; he was getting too old for this job. At least it was relatively cooler in the shade of the cedars.

As he straightened back up he heard the crunch of footsteps behind him. He had been left in quiet solitude so long that the sound made him jump. He was so startled he dropped what he had just gone to all the trouble to pick up in the first place. He turned around quickly but didn't see anything. "Must've been a squirrel," he thought and stooped over to pick up his equipment, groaning a little louder this time.

A cool breeze blew through the trees as he righted himself. All of a sudden he had that strange feeling like he knew he was being watched. He scanned the trees around him, but saw nothing but the same old trees he'd been looking at for years.

Dan was just getting ready to go store his equipment when he heard it again, the crunch of footsteps behind him. This time when he turned around he did see something—a man with a dark moustache walking through the trees. Another one of those reenactors, it looked like.

"Hey there, park's about to close up for the day. Might wanna start heading back to your car."

The mustachioed man said nothing, looking around with an intense look of concentration.

"You looking for something sir? Better hurry up and find it before we close up shop."

Again, the man said nothing, but continued striding toward the groundskeeper purposefully.

"Say, you look kinda familiar. Have we met? I must have seen you at a reenactment or something." Dan's attempts at small talk were obviously falling on deaf ears. The strange man had his jaw set like he was concentrating fiercely, but what he was doing there was a mystery to the groundskeeper. He was, however, naggingly familiar. The groundskeeper knew the face from somewhere, he just couldn't place it.

"Well look, sir, the park's hours are eight to five. If you wanna come back tomorrow, you're more than welcome to," he said a little testily.

Again the man said nothing. "What a weirdo," Dan thought. He was a little irritable from the heat and fatigue, so he was losing patience. "Suit yourself, buddy. If you wanna sleep here, be my guest." He looked over his shoulder a few times at the mysterious park visitor, seeing the dark, intense man heading off into the woods in the opposite direction. With that he carried his equipment back to his truck and drove toward the main building that served as the Visitor's Center for the park. He would drop off his equipment, get a cold drink from the drink machine, tell whoever he could find about the weirdo out in the Slaughter Pen, hop in his truck, and head home to put his feet up. The idea sounded so good to him that he quickened his pace a bit.

Dan stored his equipment and was pleased to find the doors to the Visitor's Center still open. He walked inside and sighed contentedly at the wave of cool air that hit him. He realized he needed to make a little rest stop before he got in his car to go home, so he took off in the direction of the restrooms.

As he was walking he was thinking how nice it must be to work indoors sometimes. The cool, quiet center was quite comfortable to the groundskeeper who was still mopping sweat from his brow. Sometimes he would go all day without setting foot inside.

He had seen everything in the Visitor's Center a hundred times, but he felt compelled to take a look at some of the pictures hanging on the wall. The first photograph his eyes fell on made him stop abruptly. He felt a chill rush through his body as every hair on his body stood at attention. He could hear the blood rushing in his ears.

"Oh my gosh," he said quietly to himself. "It can't be. There's no way."

The picture he looked at was a portrait, much like any other portrait taken during the Civil War era. It was a portrait of General Phil Sheridan, the general who commanded the division that was obliterated in the Slaughter Pen.

Suddenly, Dan realized where he had seen that weirdo in the park earlier. He had seen him in this picture, a picture taken when he was still alive over a hundred years ago.

He shook his head in disbelief. As he gazed into the eyes of the man in the portrait, he knew beyond a shadow of a doubt that he had gazed into those eyes that day in the Slaughter Pen. He felt like the picture itself was looking at him and he was entranced, hypnotized by the face that he hadn't been able to place.

Abruptly he turned and took off for his car. As he started his car and backed out of the parking place, a thought crossed his mind briefly, "Maybe it is time to retire." He chuckled to himself, but he knew deep down that this time, he meant it.

the ghosts of
swan tavern

"Oh, no, sir," said the antique dealer, "I couldn't take anything less than five hundred dollars."

"Come on, now," replied Bertram Nash, "five hundred dollars for an old painting with no verifiable pedigree? I don't think so." The men stood silent for a second or two as Bert studied the painting. The antique dealer kept a close watch on Bert's facial expression as he studied the old oil. Finally, Bert said, "Four hundred dollars."

The dealer scrunched up his face and counter offered. "Four fifty," he said, "and not a penny less."

"Done!" Burt shot back.

"Well, then, Mr. Nash, I'll just go wrap this up," the man said. "Why don't you look around some more and see if there isn't anything else you can't possibly live without." The two men smiled and Bertram Nash continued browsing the wares of the antique shop. The shop was housed in the old Swan Tavern in historic Yorktown. In fact, the painting he'd just purchased for a steal was a snapshot of the tavern and the colonial life that bustled around it. The Swan Tavern was the heart and soul of what had been called the most untamed township of the New World.

This was Bert's first trip to Yorktown, but he knew its history. The city was a busy port town, with everything that implies. Merchants, traders, colonists, and businessmen kept the money flowing through the town, while ruffians, highwaymen, and other less than savory individuals did their best to tap into it. Tobacco merchants, weary travelers, slavers, and criminals rubbed elbows with well-dressed gentlemen. And then there was liquor. Spirits could be cheaply purchased in colonial Yorktown. The Swan Tavern itself had seen more than its share of drunken patrons in its heyday. Many a drunken merchant had stumbled out of the tavern in his cups only to have a band of thieves cut his purse as well as his throat.

"It's hard to imagine those times," Bert said aloud.

"What's that, sir?" the antique dealer asked.

"Oh, just the whole wildness and violence of the place long ago," he answered.

The older man spoke up. "Well, now, Mr. Nash, this was truly an amazing place. It was the eighteenth-century equivalent of a fine hotel, a four-star restaurant, news outlet, theater, and sideshow all rolled into one. A weary traveler could experience more life here in a night than he could anywhere else."

"Then there was the part Yorktown played in the Civil War," he continued. "In fact, this building was used by the Union army to store gunpowder—well, not this actual building. This one's been restored. Someone set off the gunpowder in 1863 and the whole place went up—took most of this part of the town with it, too."

"Wow," said Bert.

"Yes," the dealer replied, "only left a couple of the original buildings standing. The blast and the fire afterwards destroyed this building right down to its foundation." The man smiled and added, "Things look pretty good now, though."

"That they do," replied Bert. It was then that Bertram Nash noticed a silver-tipped walking stick. "Hey, this looks good," he said.

The antique dealer chimed in. "Oh, that's a very interesting piece.

It was actually dug up out of the ground a couple of years ago. I was having some work done out back, and a plumber unearthed it. It's in pretty good shape, considering."

For some reason he couldn't explain, Bert simply had to have it. The two men haggled back and forth for a few minutes and finally arrived at an acceptable price. Twenty minutes later, Bertram Nash was headed back to Richmond with his treasures. He had thoroughly enjoyed his weekend trip to colonial Yorktown and was leaving with two little pieces of its history. "It's been a good day," he mused as he motored down the highway. He didn't know it yet, but Bertram Nash was leaving Yorktown with more history than he could have possibly imagined.

Bert began to notice the strange occurrences in his house the very same week he hung the painting of Swan Tavern over his fireplace; however, he hadn't yet made the connection. At first, the events were just annoying. Small objects such as car keys, pens, and documents would go missing and turn up mysteriously in places that Bert never would have put them. Even his favorite antique briar pipe seemed to have a mind of its own and, one day, he "misplaced it" twice, only to have the briar show up once in the pantry and again, later, in his master bathroom.

"What's going on around here?" he said aloud. Then he answered himself: "I must be working too hard."

Bert replaced the pipe in its rack on the mantle. He glanced around the room to see if everything was in its place. Satisfied that all was as it should be, Bert walked out of the room. As he crossed the threshold, he couldn't shake the feeling that he was being watched. He stopped, turned, and surveyed the den again. His gaze fell upon the painting that hung over the fireplace, the painting of Swan Tavern.

Later that night, Bert was awakened by what sounded like voices coming from downstairs.

"Did I leave the radio on in the den?" he thought.

He put on his robe and slippers and proceeded down the long staircase of his two-story house. The strange sounds were clearer now, more distinct, and they were coming from the den. As Bert entered the room, he found himself confronted by a most perplexing sight. Sitting at the head of a large antique table in the den was a woman dressed in old European-style clothes. She gave the impression of being a gypsy, replete with a colorful bandanna around her head and large dangling earrings. It was clear by the tarot cards in her hands that she was engaged in telling a fortune, but for whom, Bert couldn't see. It was also clear that she was a ghost.

Bertram Nash watched transfixed as the ghostly soothsayer arranged her cards in the shape of a cross. She addressed someone else sitting at the table whom Bert was unable to see. Then the gypsy arranged a vertical line of cards to the right of the cross-like formation. She turned to her unseen companion and spoke. "What's that?" she said in a thick accent. She paused for a moment and continued. "No, no, no—this isn't your fortune. It's his." With the utterance of that last word, the ghost turned her head and looked straight into Bert's eyes. Quickly, he looked down at the tarot spread on the table, but before he could see his reading, the cards and the gypsy simply vanished.

Bert turned on the lights in the den and nervously walked around, looking for anything that might explain what apparently was a dream. "No, no, not a dream," he muttered, "Something more than a dream, a vision, I guess. A warning of some kind. Oh, I don't understand." He stopped and rubbed his eyes, not knowing what really had just transpired.

A full month passed. Bert's memory of the spectral fortuneteller in his den had begun to fade. In point of fact, Bert had deliberately tried not to spend much time at all thinking about it. He had, however, spent a great deal of time staring at the painting of the tavern over his fireplace. He studied it in detail, examining every brushstroke and line and viewing it from every conceivable angle. All the while, Bert couldn't get over the idea that the painting might actually be staring back at him.

During one of his less-than-focused moments, Bert noticed that the painting's frame was in need of repair. It was only a minor repair, and one that Bert could easily perform himself. When he removed the painting from the wall, he heard a low moan come from behind him. Quickly propping the tavern painting on the mantle, Bert turned to see an antique armchair in the far corner of the den begin to rock back and forth. There was a palpable presence in the room. Bert could feel it. The armchair continued to rock on its own for over an hour before Bert decided to hang the painting back on the wall. As soon as he did, the rocking ceased. He turned, looked at the painting, and stepped backwards a few feet. Finally he understood: whatever was going on in his home was somehow connected to the oil painting. He continued to stare at it. Inexplicably, the painting stared back.

The next few nights were sleepless ones for Bertram Nash. Confused images of colonial life ran through his mind, making it impossible for him to get any rest. "It's that damn painting," he growled. Finally, he decided to put it away. "Maybe then I can get some sleep," he said. Bert went downstairs to the den and took the tavern painting off the wall. A few moments later, the painting was securely locked away in his attic, and Bert crawled back into bed.

Scarcely ten minutes passed before pandemonium broke out. All of the doors and windows in Nash's home were opening and closing of their own accord. Doors swung wide and then slammed shut with unearthly force. Windows moved up and down like machines until glass broke and sills cracked. Bertram was terrified. "The painting is angry," he thought. "I've got to put it back on the wall!"

He ran to the attic and retrieved the painting. Rushing downstairs to the den, he lifted it upward. As soon as the hook on the wall engaged the wire in back of the oil, the pandemonium stopped. Bert tried to catch his breath. "What am I going to do?" he said. "Selling it is out of the question. If I got rid of it, the painting would probably tear the house down!"

It was then that Bert noticed something different about the painting. Something had appeared inside the painting, something that hadn't been there before. Peeking from behind the corner of the Swan Tavern was the painted figure of a man dressed in a dark hood and cape—a single gloved hand protruded from the folds of the cape and clutched at the edge of the building. Bertram began to shake: the cloaked figure was looking directly at him.

There were no nocturnal visitations for more than a month. But the passage of time had not eased Bertram Nash's mind. He found himself checking the hooded figure in the painting with an almost obsessed regularity. There it crouched, staring at him so intently that he felt the figure's eyes on him in every room of the house.

The following Saturday brought with it a powerful thunderstorm. Most of his neighbors had already lost electrical power, but Bert's generator kept his refrigerator running and most of his lights working. He was tending a fire in the den when he looked up and noticed that the painting of the tavern had changed yet again. The cloaked figure was no longer peering around the corner of the Swan Tavern. He was now standing in front of it. Bert couldn't believe his eyes. He stepped toward the painting to get a closer look. In the time it took him to take those steps, the figure had moved again, this time toward the bottom edge of the painting. And then Bert noticed something else: the hooded man seemed to be getting closer.

Bertram Nash quickly backed across the room when, in the illumination of a flash of lightning, he saw the cloaked man crouching in the corner of the den. Bert screamed as the hooded figure stood fully upright and slowly moved toward him. Bertram wasn't able to move at all until he saw the large knife in the wraith's gloved right hand. Now he was able to move, and he ran for his life up the stairs to his bedroom.

Bert slammed the bedroom door and locked it. He ran for the phone on his nightstand to call the police. "I'll just report a prowler. That'll bring them here fast enough," he mumbled. But the phone line was dead. An eerie mocking laughter floated up the stairs toward his room and resounded against the locked door. "What am I going to do?" he thought. "How do I fight a ghost?"

He turned on his nightstand light to look around the room for a weapon of some kind. Then he noticed a silver-tipped cane resting on his pillow. It was the same cane he had purchased with the oil painting in Yorktown. "This is important," he thought, "it just has to be." Bert grabbed the cane and, brandishing it like a sword, threw open the door to his bedroom.

He moved to the head of the staircase and peered down through the shadows and partial light. He could see nothing, but continued to hear the cloaked man's sinister laugh. Then slowly the hooded man stepped to the foot of the stairs and looked upward. The pair stood motionless, one living and one dead, both locked in each other's gaze. Bert saw the ghost smile an evil grin and take the first step up the staircase. Two steps, then three steps, and then four. The ghost kept approaching as light flickered off his knife blade. By the time the ghost was halfway up the stairs, Bertram Nash had decided that he'd had enough.

"Get out of my house!" he screamed. And then he charged. Bert took one large swing with the silver-tipped cane as he collided with the oncoming figure. It felt as if he was passing through a wet sheet, but the ghost provided no resistance. Bert turned and looked up the stairs, but the ghost had vanished.

The power company restored electricity to the houses in Bert's neighborhood about an hour later. But even as he studied the painting in his den, Bert knew somehow that the worst was over.

••••••

In 1935, excavators discovered the skeletal remains of a man buried beneath the stables of the Swan Tavern in historic Yorktown. There was no way to determine the identity of the man, though it was assumed he had been a victim of foul play. One thing seemed clear though: an examination of the right leg of the skeleton revealed a badly healed break that almost certainly would have left the man lame, needing a walking stick to get around. No walking stick, however, was found at the time. Many people in Yorktown had seen the cloaked figure. A young Union officer even challenged the hooded man as he saw him skulking behind the Swan Tavern. When the figure refused to answer the soldier's challenge, the officer, with rifle in hand, ran to investigate, but the cloaked figure had vanished.

••••••

"Sometimes an artist can do too good a job," Bert wrote in his journal. "I don't know what to make of the events of the past month, but one thing seems certain: whoever painted the picture of the old Swan Tavern captured the very essence of the place, and, in doing so, bound forever the souls of those who lived and died in its shadow."

the scourge of
talladega county

The young Creek stumbled as he stepped up on the rough wood planking of the primitive bridge. The other members of his band, at his insistence, had already gone ahead. They were on their way to fight the white man in a mighty battle that would, once and for all, establish the superior force of the Creek.

The white men needed to be fought. It had been only three years since Running Wolf had first caught sight of one of those strange, arrogant creatures. A band of them had ridden by, never seeing Running Wolf crouching in the underbrush. Since that time, they had been steadily encroaching on his village, often riding right up and enticing the women and little ones to come close and see their pretty baubles.

But that was not all they brought, Running Wolf thought darkly. They brought the fever, too, which had stormed through his village in the course of a week, making strong men as weak as babies and making mothers go mad with grief for their children who lay consumed by the heat from within. Those who survived were marked for life, their pitted and pocked faces and bodies mute testimony to the terrible gifts the white man had brought.

Running Wolf's own family—his squaw, five-year-old son, and infant daughter—all fell victim to the sickness. Grief gave Running Wolf the power to be a terrifying warrior. It had propelled him headlong into the preparations for war and brought him miles from home in spite of the battle that raged within his body.

But now the fever wracked his frame. His steps faltered as he forced himself across the bridge, and he shook his head to clear his vision. He nearly fell at the far end of the bridge but managed to stumble on down the path a few more feet. Ahead he saw the curious log dwelling the white men built, and he heard the joyful shrieks of children playing in the just-plowed field. His children, too, would have run and shouted through the rows of beans and corn and squash planted outside the stockade of his village. If they had survived the fever.

He could walk no farther. He collapsed in the center of the grassy path, falling with a barely perceptible thud. From a distance, his slight frame resembled a pile of rags. The two little girls who approached him circled cautiously, and then ran screaming back to the cabin. "Papa! Papa! There's an Indian on the path!"

The man was bent over, examining the plow blade. He jerked upright. "How many?"

"Just one, and he looks dead!"

Roughly, the man shoved his daughters inside and snatched up his rifle before running across to the path. He slowed as he neared the prone figure. It did not stir, but he could see by the steady rise and fall of its chest that it was still alive. Using the tip of his boot, he rolled the body over.

The flushed cheeks and glazed eyes gave the settler all the information he needed to know. As he watched, the deep brown eyes flickered shut, and the breathing slowed even more.

Impulsively, he took off his shirt and stepped down to the creek to wet it in the fast-running, cool March waters. He laid it across the fevered man's brow. "There, you poor creature. Not long now, I reckon."

He hunkered down and watched the man's labored breathing. Suddenly, the Indian's eyes flew open, and the startled settler reached for his gun. The Indian's eyes cleared, and a stream of words flowed from his mouth. The settler didn't understand a single word. The Indian's eyes closed again, and life slipped away.

He took the dead Indian's hand in his own and marveled at the similarities. It was shaped exactly like his, except it was a little smaller, slightly more brown, and, of course, marked with the pockmarks, an unmistakable sign of the affliction that had taken his life.

"Well, I hope you didn't touch him," his wife said later. "You know those savages carry all kinds of horrible diseases."

••••••

Years later, music and light streamed out the open doors of the gristmill that stood on the banks of Talladega Creek. A crowd of thirty people, waiting for the last of their winter's supply of corn to get ground, or waiting for lumber from the sawmill, or gathering at the forge to have their horses and mules shod, had all come out for a Saturday night dance. They had come from a distance of forty miles, some of them, just to see their neighbors and conduct a little business on what was still essentially a frontier.

"I declare, Simon, you've just about spun me off my feet," laughed Sally Stewart.

"I'd like to think I swept you off your feet," he replied gallantly. Then he led her just outside the circle of light thrown out by the merrymaking at the mill. "Sally, you have no kin for me to ask, so I'll ask you directly. Will you be my wife?"

"Oh, Simon." Sally clasped his hand in hers and raised her eyes to meet his. "I will, gladly." A widow of six months, Sally had been struggling to make ends meet on the few acres her husband had cleared before he died.

"The preacher's here already. Would tomorrow be too soon for a weddin'?"

Sally laughed again and shook her head. "March 25th sounds like a wonderful day for a wedding, Simon. All I ask is that you take a bath in the creek before we get married."

"I'd do anything for you, Sally," he exulted. "A hundred baths, if that would make you happy."

The next morning dawned clear, and Sally went down to the creek early. Simon was already there, in the shadow of the newly covered bridge, splashing and laughing and vigorously rubbing strong, homemade lye soap over his arms and face and head.

Sally watched for a moment. Suddenly Simon's happy bellows changed to a cry of fear. She could only watch, stunned, as the big man was dragged beneath the surface of the water by an unseen force.

Later she held his cold, lifeless hand as the carpenter at the sawmill measured his body for a coffin. "Must be a whirlpool or somethin' that comes up in the spring," he commented, taking the stick and laying it even with Simon's feet. "Seems like every year in the spring, somebody jes' drowns for no good reason." He notched the upper end of the stick even with the crown of Simon's head. "I'll git that box built by tomorrow noon. Lucky for you the preacher's here. Not everybody gits buried by the preacher." He turned and left before Sally could tell him it was supposed to have been her wedding day.

••••••

In 1853 the little community of Waldo boasted a cotton gin, a blacksmith shop, a sawmill, and a gristmill. Saturday nights were still a time for dancing and courting, but Saturday afternoons were the time for children to take advantage of the company of others. Small bands would roam around, their elders preoccupied with the price of cotton or the cost of corn.

"Don't play in the creek," was the constant admonition, but the lure of the water was irresistible. The older children knew how to carefully shed their clothes before slipping into the creek so wet clothes never betrayed them. The younger children just splashed on into the water anyhow, trusting in the leniency of adults who were on a holiday of sorts, gathered with other families to tend to business.

"I'm gonna tell," singsonged little Jason McBride to his big brother Bradley, who was splashing naked in the creek. The bridge, source of so many paying customers for the busy miller, blacksmith, and sawyer, cast its shadow across the water.

"You wouldn't dare," hollered Bradley. "If you do, you'll be sorry! I'll tell Mama you've been sneakin' into the sorghum jug when she's not lookin'."

Jason sat down and struggled with his shoes. Although it was almost the end of March, his parents had insisted that he wear his shoes this morning since they were in town. Finally they slipped off his feet, and he ran down to the edge of the water.

As he watched, Bradley began to strike the surface of the water with the palms of his hands, making great gouts of water spray up. "Help me, Jason," he roared, and then his head disappeared beneath the water. It took a moment for the small boy to recover enough to run, screaming, up to the mill.

"It doesn't happen very often," the miller assured Jason's parents. "Just sometimes in the spring the waters rise up. It's perfectly safe most of the time."

The couple were too dazed by the loss of their oldest son to even attempt a reply.

••••••

The mill stood silent for much of the four years of the War Between the States, but hooves regularly thundered back and forth across the covered bridge. One March, not quite a year after the war began, three soldiers passed through Waldo.

"I'm gonna get a bath, right here," announced one, dropping his backpack on the bank of the creek. "This water looks too good to pass up."

"You think Caroline will git a little closer if you sweeten up some?" His friend poked him slyly but also began to unbutton his frayed shirt.

"That ain't what we're goin' home fer, Frank," laughed the third. "We're s'posed to spend all our time at home plantin' crops an' head straight back to our regiment."

Before long all three men were submerged in the water, talking idly among themselves.

"You plantin' just corn, Frank, or some cotton, too?"

"Oh, I reckon I'll plant me a little cotton. The war's not gonna last forever, you know."

"Ol' Jeff Davis said it's our duty to the Confederacy to plant corn."

"I'll plant it to make sure I got plenty to eat come winter," agreed the third soldier.

"I don't care what Jeff Davis says," argued Frank. "Cotton is where I'll make the most money, an' that's what I'm plantin'. Jeff wants to come pull 'em up, he kin do that." He splashed over to a rock where his shirt was laid out and balled it up in his fist, wringing the dirt and sweat of a long hard winter out of the homespun fabric.

His friends shrugged and began ducking their heads under water, trying in vain to dislodge the lice that had taken up residence. The youngest soldier looked around after a few minutes.

"Frank, where'd Jimmy go?"

Frank shrugged, busy hanging out his shirt to dry a little in the warm March sun.

"He was right here, in the water with me," insisted the other. "I didn't see 'im git outta the water." He took a deep breath and dove below the surface, straining to catch sight of his friend in the depths of the swimming hole. He splashed out of the water onto the bank and began to walk up and down the side of the creek, calling as he walked, "Jimmy?"

Frank finished hanging out his shirt and walked back down to the creek, certain that Jimmy was playing a trick. When he caught sight of an arm floating among the cattails on the far side of the stream, he called out in relief. "Jimmy, you dog, you scared poor Thomas half to death!" He splashed through the water and pulled up short. The hand was lying in the water palm down. He parted the cattails gingerly, afraid of what he might see.

Jimmy floated face down, bobbing gently in the current.

······

The war had been over for less than a year, and strangers traveling through Waldo were not uncommon. The residents had adapted to the defeat; after all, no one around the little village had owned any slaves, so life continued much as before.

A little boy, no more than six, had slipped away from his chores at home and sat fishing underneath the cool shade of the bridge. The Confederate army, fleeing, had often burned bridges during the past five years. The Federal army, too, had sent their share of bridges crashing into creeks and rivers. But Waldo was far enough out of the way that the bridge survived. In the dim waters below were fish of enormous size. The little boy was prepared to wait a while in order to present a fat fish to his mother for their supper.

A whistling figure made him look up. "Howdy, mister," he said, friendly enough.

The stranger only nodded and proceeded to unbutton his shirt after setting his bag down on the bank.

"Hot, ain't it?"

The stranger nodded again and sat down to remove his dusty shoes.

"I wouldn't get in that water if I was you," the boy continued.

"And why is that?" The stranger paused, one shoe off.

"Folks drown in that creek in the spring."

The stranger studied the placid water and then turned to stare at the boy. "Looks fine to me. How long's it been since anybody drowned?"

"'Bout a year."

"Do you swim here, young man?"

"Yep, sure do. All summer long, till October, usually."

"Just not in the spring." The man sounded skeptical.

"No, sir. Somethin' comes up every spring. My gran'ma says it's in March, but Mama says she thinks it's April, so they won't let me swim at all till May."

"I think you don't want me splashing around, scaring off your fish."

"Oh, no sir, I don't mind that at all," the boy said earnestly. "I'd just hate to see you drown."

"I've swum against the strongest currents in the Atlantic Ocean," the man boasted. "I think I can manage to paddle around in some little no–name creek."

"It don't matter how good you swim," the boy protested. "And it does too have a name. It's Talladega Creek."

The only reply was a splash as the stranger dove into the deepest part of the swimming hole. The boy sighed and pulled in his line, watching the water with great curiosity.

In seconds, the stranger's head reappeared on the surface. "Nice 'n' cool," he crowed. "Beautiful swimming hole, here."

The boy shrugged and kept watching. The stranger's head disappeared again, and although the boy waited patiently, it never reappeared. He painstakingly counted on his fingers.

"March," he said with some satisfaction. "March 25th. Gran'ma was right." He gathered up his fishing gear and started back along the path toward home.

••••••

Sweat ran down into his eyes, making them sting and blurring his vision. He stopped his work long enough to wipe his face, then picked up the hammer again.

From his perch on the roof of the bridge, he could see the dilapidated mill building and the grassy swath of lawn that led up to it. It was easy for him to imagine the political rallies, revivals, dances, and socials that were a central part of life in Waldo from 1843 until 1930, when Alabama 77 bypassed Old Socapatoy Road and the covered bridge.

The bridge and the mill had fallen into disrepair over the next 50 years, until he had come along with a grand scheme to make the grassy area enclosed by the curving Talladega Creek come alive again. The mill would become a restaurant, and the bridge would draw tourists from all over the Southeast, he envisioned.

But for now, all he had was a falling-down old bridge with no approaches to it and a crumbling mill filled with rusted-out machinery. It would be a while before his dreams were realized. He nailed a few more shingles onto the roof and scrambled down. His first priority was to stop the deterioration, and the interior of the bridge needed a little work to keep the rain out.

It was nice and cool inside the bridge. He had to use a ladder to climb the fifteen feet to the inside since the unenclosed bridge approaching it had collapsed. He hammered up a few boards, expecting to scare out a few birds and maybe some lizards while he worked. The bridge would be a tailor-made hideout for mice and squirrels, he thought, since they could easily scamper up the rough stone pilings and enter the bridge from the holes in the floorboards.

He looked around. There was no sign of any animal life. No messy tangles of leaves and debris marked the home of a squirrel or mouse; no droppings betrayed the presence of birds, large or small. That was strange because barn owls in particular liked the shady, quiet confines of these old open structures. He struck a match and held it high, straining to see the rafters. No bats hung from the massive old beams.

In fact, he hadn't even noticed any spiderwebs, even though he was the first person inside the bridge in a year or more. The structure was completely devoid of life. He suppressed a shiver and hurried down the ladder to head back up to the mill. He had a good three months of hard work before he could even consider opening his doors to paying customers.

The people around Waldo eagerly awaited the opening of the Old Mill Restaurant. Someone had tried to make it into a family amusement park some years back, but it had never really gotten going good. But a restaurant with good, hearty food would surely draw folks from miles around.

On the day of the grand opening, the proprietor greeted all his guests at the door. He knew many of them since he'd grown up in the area. In his head, he was calculating how many $6.95 dinners he needed to sell in order to make the mortgage payment on the old place. It had been a struggle over the last four months, and he had done most of the work himself, but maybe it would start paying off.

"Mrs. Pierce," he exclaimed, taking one old lady's hand between his own. "I'm so glad to see you!"

"You've done well, Lloyd, and I'm proud of you." This slightly bent lady had once been the terror of his life. She had taught second grade the old-fashioned way, with a hickory stick. Her family had been among the original settlers in the village of Waldo.

"I have a riddle for you to solve, Mrs. Pierce. You go eat, and I'll come sit with you while you have dessert." The proprietor spent the next thirty minutes running between the kitchen and the door and the dining room, making sure that everything was proceeding according to plan.

At last he sat down next to Mrs. Pierce with a sigh. "This is hard work, Mrs. Pierce!"

"Hard work is good for you, Lloyd." She patted his hand. "Now what did you want to ask me?"

"I know you grew up around here," he began. "I've noticed something odd about the old bridge. There are no birds nesting there, no squirrels, no lizards, not even any spiders."

She opened her mouth to speak, but before the first words came out, he interrupted her. "I checked to see if the beams were treated with creosote because I knew birds don't like that, but they're not."

She shook her head. "You still haven't learned not to interrupt, Lloyd."

He hung his head, amazed at how quickly she could reduce him to feeling like a seven-year-old.

"I never would have told you this story when you were young," she continued. "In fact, I must be getting pretty senile to tell it to anyone at all, because I doubt anyone would believe me."

Lloyd leaned forward, eager to hear more.

"I was the youngest of five girls," she began. "The next oldest was Lucy, and she was about as contrary a girl as you would ever care to meet.

"We were allowed to swim in the creek just about any time— except March and April. There was some old superstition that people getting into the creek in the spring would drown mysteriously. My mother said she didn't believe it, but she wouldn't let us swim in the spring anyway.

"Well, one March—it was late in March, I remember, because my birthday is March 15, and I was wearing a new hair ribbon my daddy gave me for my birthday—Lucy got it into her head to go swimming."

Mrs. Pierce paused to glare at Lloyd. "You're paying attention, aren't you?"

"Yes, ma'am."

"I was seven, and Lucy was nine. She could swim like a little fish, and she was always teasing me because I hated to get my face wet. Still do.

"Lucy stripped down to her knickers and jumped right into that creek. I was mad because she'd called me a scaredycat, and I turned my back on her. She was swimming and splashing and calling out that the water was so cool, I should jump right in.

"I didn't know what to do. Lucy and I were very close, and I knew she'd tease me unmercifully if I didn't get in. At the same time, Mama had a mean hand with a switch, and she absolutely did not want us in that creek in the spring.

"I had just made up my mind to get in anyway and reached up to take out my new hair ribbon when Lucy gave a shout.

"I thought at first she was playing because we all played like that, to scare each other—you know how kids are. But then I ran right down to the edge of the water and I could see she was really struggling. Just like someone was pulling her, forcing her under the water."

Mrs. Pierce paused and took a swallow from her water glass. The chatter of voices and the chink of forks on plates had receded as she spoke, so that she and Lloyd seemed to be all alone in the old mill, with its plaster walls freshly whitewashed and the machinery cleaned of rust.

"I know you'll think I'm just a crazy old lady, but I saw a hand pulling her down. It reached right up through the water and held onto her forearm so tight I could see the knuckles turning white. But it wasn't just any old hand. It was small and brown and covered over with pockmarks like I've never seen before.

"Lucy died, and I couldn't save her," Mrs. Pierce said simply. "I don't know if that has anything to do with that old bridge out there, but it wouldn't surprise me. Not one little bit."

That night, Lloyd took a walk out by the creek after the restaurant closed. He tried to imagine what it would be like to see somebody drown right in front of your eyes, but his imagination failed. He listened to the water instead. The murmuring sound which had seemed so peaceful just yesterday now carried a menacing undertone. Almost like a voice, muttering in a tone just beyond hearing.

Perhaps it is a voice still murmuring, speaking in a language no one understands. No human witness to the death of Running Wolf in March 1814 understood his words, but maybe some of God's creatures were perceptive enough to comprehend his meaning all the same.

Listen. Maybe it's the rocks and the water repeating the message of a long-dead Creek saying endlessly that he shall have his revenge.

life is like a rose

Geena Freeman took delivery of the armoire at half past six on a Friday evening. For some reason, the cartage company had a hard time locating her Atlanta townhouse. They had an even harder time getting it up the two flights of stairs to her bedroom. By the time they had positioned the wardrobe against the wall opposite her bed, the furniture movers were ready to call it quits and get their weekends started.

After she had thanked them, Geena went back upstairs to inspect her new acquisition. It was an unusually large armoire with ornately carved appointments, and even though it was much too large for the room it was in, Geena was glad to have it. The armoire had been in her family for years. The last time Geena had seen the wardrobe, it had been sitting in her great-grandmother's house in Oakdale, Louisiana, where it had been for many years. Geena even remembered playing around it as a young girl.

The wardrobe had been only one of dozens of pieces of antique furniture that were in her great-grandmother's house. Actually, it would have been more appropriate to say "stored" there. Geena's great-grandmother was an avid antiques collector, so much so, in fact, that her house was a clutter of furniture, lamps, and statuary all jammed together so as to make it impossible to display any of it. Geena remembered that a pair of large art deco black panthers sat on either side of the armoire, which itself had been stuffed with all manner of antique linens and clothes.

After her great-grandmother's death, there had been some trouble with one of Geena's great-aunts who tried to snatch up all the antiques for herself. But cooler heads prevailed, and the furniture was divided up amongst existing family members. Big Mama, as her great-grandmother had been known to the family, had always said, "This is Geena's closet." And now here it was.

Geena smiled, remembering her great-grandmother. Big Mama was a courageous woman, filled with vitality and the love of life. She also had a peculiar thirst for knowledge. She could tell you the history of every antique that she had in her house, including who built or manufactured it, where it had come from, and the families who had owned them before her. But in all those years, Geena couldn't remember Big Mama detailing anything of the wardrobe's history.

Still, the piece was beautiful even if she didn't know where it had come from. Geena had never seen a piece of antique furniture with such attention to detail. Carved flowers, birds, and forest scenes worked their way up the sides of the armoire. It had two large doors that opened up to reveal one large drawer on the right side and two smaller drawers on the left. The bulk of the space was suitable for hanging coats and clothes of all kinds, including full length gowns and dresses that were worn by well-to-do women of a bygone era.

Geena couldn't remember why everyone in her family assumed that the armoire had come from New Orleans. Perhaps it was the fact that wardrobes of this kind were so immensely popular in that city. At one time in old New Orleans, property taxes were levied on homes according to how many rooms they had. Even closets and kitchen larders were considered taxable rooms.

The residents of the Crescent City began building homes without closets and used large armoires to store their clothes as a means of avoiding excessively high taxes. Big Mama used to say, "If you want a good armoire, don't go to Paris; go to New Orleans." It would probably be worth a call, Geena thought, to my parents to see if they know anything of the history of this piece of furniture. Somebody in the family had to know where it came from. Geena decided that she would call her parents later on that weekend.

Geena went to the grocery store to get what she needed to make a late-night supper. She also picked up a small bouquet of roses for her bedroom, inspired by those that were ornately carved on the armoire. When she got home, she arranged the roses in a vase and brought them up to her bedroom and placed them on her nightstand.

"There," she thought. "That brightens the room up a bit." Then she headed back down to the kitchen to make herself a late-night sandwich. Geena, moving down the stairs, was unable to notice that the roses had begun to rapidly wilt. By the time she made it to the kitchen, all of her fresh roses had unexpectedly and rapidly withered and dried.

When Geena reentered her bedroom some hours later, she was shocked to see the wilted roses. It was as if the hand of death had reached out and touched them. "Never buy flowers in a grocery store," Geena thought as she removed the vase.

She came back into the bedroom armed with a rag and a bottle of furniture polish and set to work cleaning the armoire. Removing two of the drawers was easy, but one of the smaller ones seemed stuck, as if it were catching on something. Geena wrestled with it for about a minute before the drawer pulled free. Then she saw what had been jamming it. An old journal filled with handwritten notes and newspaper clippings had been stuffed behind the drawer. Geena recognized Big Mama's handwriting immediately.

As she began to leaf through the journal, Geena realized that it contained a detailed account of the history of Woodlands Manor, a large Italian-style villa in northwest Georgia. Woodlands had been the home of Godfrey and Julia Barnsley and their descendants. It was also the home of the Barnsley Curse. "Wow!" Geena thought. "A curse—how wild is that?" It appears that Geena's great-grandmother had made an extensive study of the Savannah couple, as well as the mysterious happenings that became a part of their life and their death.

Julia was the beautiful daughter of a Georgia shipping tycoon and his overbearing wife. Godfrey Barnsley was a handsome young English cotton broker. The two were married in 1828. They were the toast of Savannah high society. Several fortunes were made and lost by Godfrey over the next few years. The pair lived in England for a time before returning to Savannah in 1830. By then, they had one child named Anna, and she would be the first of seven Barnsley children.

In 1838, his wife weakened from childbearing and afflicted by consumption, Godfrey decided to build the home that he and his beautiful bride had always dreamed of. Perhaps here, he thought, Julia could regain her health, and then they could live out their years in happiness. But it was not to be.

Godfrey bought nearly 400 acres of land in northwest Georgia that had once belonged to the Cherokee nation. Legend has it that the spirit of the spider brought the alphabet and language to the Cherokee people, so they could effectively communicate with one another. The spider spirit also showed them how to enter the spirit world by precisely writing certain letters and speaking certain words in the language that he brought to them. With these gifts, the Cherokee explored the depths and far reaches of the shadow worlds.

As Geena read on, she began to feel an odd numbness in her fingertips that slowly crept through her fingers and across the backs of her hands. She paused and looked at her left hand, inspecting it front and back. She could gain no clue to the faint numbness that was now creeping into her forearms. She decided that she was obviously clutching the book too tightly, so she relaxed her hands and her shoulders and continued reading Big Mama's journal entries.

While Godfrey was surveying his new land, he found what he thought was the perfect place for the new manor house. The site was a high bluff with a beautiful view of the property. Of course, he would have to level the bluff off and prepare the land for construction. It was then that an old Cherokee Indian who lived on the land approached Godfrey and told him that he must not build his house on the bluff. "This land is sacred," he said, adding, "Our ancestors are buried there. They will not let this happen."

Godfrey Barnsley didn't want to offend the old Indian, but his plans were not about to be delayed by the superstitions of savages. He politely announced that his decision was final and that was to be the end of the matter. Speaking in his native tongue, the old Cherokee immediately cursed him. Shortly thereafter, the Indian simply vanished and was never heard from again.

The Barnsleys moved into a log cabin on the property, which they named the Woodlands, while their new home was being built. Living in a log cabin was hard on Julia, but the promise of a grand manor in such a beautiful wooded area was enough to make it worthwhile. However, the cold winters took their toll on Godfrey's beautiful wife. She died of consumption in the winter of 1844. The curse was beginning its work.

Geena found herself getting unusually sleepy. Her eyes wouldn't focus on the old journal entries. She decided to put the book away and call it a night. "Great-grandma," she said, "you'll just have to wait until tomorrow morning." With that, she put the old journal back in the wardrobe, securely closed the doors, and prepared for bed. She had no trouble falling asleep.

Geena dreamt wildly that evening. The images and events in her dreams were detailed and confusing, with one dream bleeding over into the next. She had dreams where she was fulfilled and happy, where she was experiencing gratitude to people she had never known before, where she was having surprising and enriching encounters with strangers. Her perceptions seemed to be heightened in her dreams. She could hear things she wouldn't normally hear and see things she wouldn't normally see. Mostly, her dreams were blissful, and she felt her heart overflowing with love, deep affection for everyone and everything in the whole world, and then ... dreams of dread and death.

Geena drifted in and out of the darker dreams, until one felt so horrible and so real that she woke up, calling out to the empty room. She sat up and turned on the light on her bed table so she could collect herself and let the bad dreams pass. As the dim light filled the room, Geena saw that the wardrobe was open, and instead of being empty, it was filled with a miasma of refracting light and light wisps of smoke that resembled clouds. All of a sudden, Geena felt very cold, the kind of cold that doesn't have anything to do with the temperature of the room, but a feeling as if the warmth in her blood and bones was slowly being drained away.

Cautiously, she got out of bed and, wrapping the bedspread over her shoulders against the cold, she approached the open armoire. As she got closer to it, she saw scenes fading in and out in the swirling mist. Geena saw pictures of woodsmen felling trees. She saw carpenters framing a house, while other people dug in the earth and cleared land. It was then that Geena realized she was watching the construction of the Woodlands.

As the scenes and images changed, fading in and out, overlapping one another, she saw Godfrey Barnsley overseeing the construction. She saw him and his wife, Julia, going over plans, making decisions, and designing the gardens and grounds of what was to be their home. She saw exotic plants and flowers and grandiose gardens that wound in curving paths all through the property. She saw boxwoods and exotic trees being planted in unique formation, and, most of all, she saw roses—hundreds and hundreds of rosebushes dotted the estate in and around the Woodlands.

They were beautiful, Geena thought. It looked like a combination of old English and Italian gardens. In the swirling mist that filled the armoire, she saw curving lines and meandering paths everywhere, just the kind of place a couple deeply in love would hold hands and stroll for hours.

Then she began to witness scenes of sadness. She saw the sadness of Julia and the children while Barnsley was away on business. She saw Julia in the throes of her illness, suffering greatly, but still clinging to the dream of the Woodlands. Finally, she saw the death of Godfrey's wife and experienced the tremendous grief felt by the man. Images of the half-completed estate and the construction falling into disrepair floated before Geena's eyes.

She then saw images of Godfrey Barnsley in a different city, possibly Mobile or New Orleans, sitting at a large table during a séance. She saw Godfrey crying and speaking emotionally to some unseen force in the room.

"He must be talking to the spirit of his dead wife, Julia," Geena thought. And then the scene changed again. In some of the clearest images in the vision so far, Geena saw Godfrey Barnsley walking with the ghost of his wife through the finished Woodlands Manor. Godfrey was talking freely with his wife's ghost. In fact, he was consulting her spirit often and regularly on all manner of decisions. Godfrey would speak to the spirit of his wife and then relay messages from her about the house, grounds, construction, and upkeep to another man who was obviously a carpenter and handyman, or caretaker, who would then follow the instructions to the letter.

The scenes continued to change. She saw for a brief period what looked like a British flag flying over the estate, and she saw soldiers of the Union army ransacking and destroying much of the Woodlands. She felt Godfrey's pain and, surprisingly, Julia's as well.

The room got colder. She saw scenes of death and illness, of despair and longing, all of it suffered by members of the Barnsley family. Geena wondered how many years were actually going by, and then she saw Godfrey Barnsley dying in poverty in the ruins of his estate.

All of a sudden, she felt colder, colder than she'd ever felt in her life, and then she was thrust backward toward her bed. The doors of the armoire slammed shut. Geena then saw the image of a young man standing before her, leaning with his back against the armoire. This apparition appeared more real than anything she had witnessed so far. The man she saw was something more real than a dream, more solid than a hallucination. The ghost was motioning with his hands to something or someone that Geena couldn't see. His arms and hands were outstretched as if trying to stop something from happening, and she could hear him say, "No, no, Preston, no—don't shoot!"

Then Geena heard gunfire and saw bullets careening off the armoire, creating little splinters of wood, while other bullets hit the wall behind the armoire. Then she saw one of the bullets find its mark as a blood stain slowly expanded on the shirt of the ghost in front of her. The wounded man slowly collapsed to the floor. A woman appeared and bent down to help the man. She was weeping. The bleeding man died in her arms as other Barnsley ghosts stood around them and witnessed his passing.

The vision was getting thinner now and less distinct. For the first time, Geena noticed that the sun was coming up outside her townhouse. As the last vestiges of the death scene faded away, the woman cradling the dead man in her arms looked up directly at Geena and said, "Life is like a rose."

No images, light, or mist could be seen now, only an open, empty armoire with a journal resting quietly inside remained. Geena realized that she had witnessed those last scenes while she was sitting shivering on the edge of her bed, but now warmth started to fill her body again. She could feel a rebuilding of her life's energy coming up from somewhere deep inside of her. For some time, she was afraid to move, but as her body temperature increased, she let the bedspread slide off her shoulders, and she stood, walked forward, and picked up her great-grandmother's journal.

That morning, she was reading in detailed prose the events she had seen in pictures the night before. She read about the life and death of the seven Barnsley children. She read about the two who had served in the Confederate army. There were detailed accounts of each of the Barnsley descendants, including one named Preston, a prizefighter who fought under the name of Knockout Dugan. He loved the family home and used his prizefighting fortune to keep Woodlands alive and vibrant.

Preston fell into madness toward the later years of his life and had to be committed to an asylum. Later, escaping from the asylum, he made his way back to Woodlands, where, armed with a pistol and consumed by paranoia and his madness, he shot his brother, Harry Barnsley. Harry died in the arms of Godfrey Barnsley's granddaughter named Addie, and if the vision was to be believed, in the company of all the other deceased Barnsleys.

As she continued to read, Geena discovered that the caretaker she had seen in her vision had the last name of Freeman and was indeed one of her ancestors, in fact, her great-great-grandfather. That's why the spirits had been reawakened, she thought. That's why I had the vision.

Geena closed the journal and sat quietly for a moment. Almost instantly, she knew what she had to do. She decided that she would send the armoire back to Woodlands Manor.

Two months later, the museum at the restored Barnsley Manor, located in Adairsville, northwest of Atlanta, received a beautiful armoire with ornately carved flowers and woodland scenes. It had been donated by one Geena Julia Freeman, who had some distant connection to the Barnsley estate. Along with the donation was a detailed synopsis of everything Miss Freeman had learned about the armoire, condensed from the research of her great-grandmother. It appeared that the donor suspected that Harry Barnsley, Preston's brother, had been shot and died against this armoire. She detailed her sources and evidence, and after she signed her name, she wrote below her signature the motto of the Barnsley manor, "Life is like a rose."

Back in her Atlanta townhouse, Geena smiled at what must be going through the minds of the people who ran the Barnsley museum. Of course, she kept Big Mama's journal and all of the clippings. After all, it was part of her history, just like the armoire. She hadn't been able to discover if her ancestor had actually built the armoire for the Barnsleys, but she suspected it. In any event, he had been a friend and caretaker to the Barnsleys, and now she was able to continue the family tradition by returning the cherished piece of furniture to the family it belonged to.

Geena's great-grandmother had given her the gift of the wardrobe, but the most important gift was the journal itself, and not what was in the journal, but what could be read between the lines. Geena had discovered that death and destruction must occur if life could begin anew. She thought about what the Barnsleys had risked, moving to the wild woodlands of northwestern Georgia, and how they had conquered it.

That was advice you could use at any age: you have to risk, you have to conquer, if you ever expect to grow. She also knew that divine power, whether it comes from God or the Cherokee spirit world, sometimes can destroy as well as it can create.

the haunting of ashville

The first settlers of Ashville arrived in the area around 1817. St. Clair County was then established in November 1818, making it older than the state of Alabama. Ashville was first founded as St. Clairsville. The name was later changed to Ashville in honor of John Ash, who played a vital role in establishing the town. Chosen as the county seat because of its location in the center of the county, Ashville was incorporated in 1822. Given its age and history, it is not surprising that Ashville has a haunted past.

The Indian Drums

General Andrew Jackson came down from Tennessee before Alabama became a state. It was around 1813, and there were no white families living in the Coosa River area yet. Only hunters and traders seemed to be brave enough to scope out the land surrounding Indian villages. General Jackson and three thousand men entered the area and made their headquarters at Ten Islands of the Coosa River, also known as Fort Strother.

Jackson sent groups of men out to search for supplies, giving the men orders to destroy any Indian villages they encountered. It was mid-October when Colonel Dyer discovered he was camped within five miles of Chief Cataula's village on Big Canoe Creek. At the same time, Cataula's men found out about the troops. They knew their village would be in danger of being destroyed and themselves most likely killed in the process. They realized they needed the help of another Indian tribe eight miles away. Late that night they pounded on their war drums, calling for help. The loud, resonate ker-boom, ker-boom, ker-boom of the drums pierced the dark silence of the moonless night.

The sound of the drums reached the ears of Colonel Dyer, who immediately knew what was happening. An attack was inevitable, and Dyer thought it best to strike first rather than be ambushed. He and his men made their way to the village.

The Indians held their own but were greatly outnumbered. Dyer burned the village and took twenty-nine Creek prisoners, a herd of cattle, and some other food supplies back to Fort Strother and General Jackson.

The only Creeks killed in the attack were two of Chief Cataula's sons. To this day, on cold, moonless nights, the ker-boom of their drums can be heard echoing in the darkness.

Old Tawassee

General Jackson removed most of the Creek Indians from the area, but a few were still around. They lived in a place near Dean's Spring called Tawassee, which meant "sanctuary" or "safe place."

By 1829, most of these Indians were gone, but one, a thieving villain, had managed to stay behind. The Indians had been causing problems up and down the river valley. They loved to break into houses and barns, stealing whatever food items they could get their hands on. No one's property was safe.

After being caught carrying two slabs of bacon from Mr. Jones's smokehouse, this particular Indian was whipped and released. Only known as Old Tawassee, the pilferer returned a few days later. Mrs. Jones was out back boiling and beating laundry. Seeking revenge for his thrashing, he snuck onto the Jones's farmland. Only days before he had been warned never to return. He grabbed a stick and knocked Mrs. Jones in the head. She slumped to the ground, unconscious.

As in every small town, news traveled fast. The only Indian left in town, Old Tawassee had no place to hide. The sheriff, Colonel John Massey, wouldn't stand for that type of behavior. Tawassee was soon apprehended, and before he could utter a word in his defense, he was standing under a gigantic oak tree in the town square.

A crowd quickly gathered to see the first hanging in the area. Whispering with curiosity, they watched the Indian intently.

His neck itching from the raw rope, Tawassee glanced down at the wagon beneath him. He blinked. The rickety wagon jerked out from under him. He tried to stretch and wriggle out of the death trap but was suddenly motionless. His lifeless body began to sway in the soft April breeze.

The townspeople simply stared at him. Not knowing what to do with the corpse, they left him there, swinging.

He hung there for days, gently swinging in the wind.

Finally, Dr. Brewster said he would dispose of the Indian. He and his apprentice cut down the body. Together they stuffed him in a box and carried it to Canoe Creek. They lowered the makeshift coffin into the river, secured it, and promised to return in a few months.

Meanwhile, the river rapids rushed across the body, removing the rough flesh, leaving only Tawassee's bones.

After the winter, Dr. Brewster and his associate returned to retrieve what remained of Old Tawassee. Upon opening the box, they found exactly what they had hoped for—nothing but the bones.

After tediously wiring the bones together, Dr. Brewster hung the skeleton in a closet in his office, just down from the town square. Many students learned human anatomy from Tawassee's remains that were used as a teaching aid.

The one-year anniversary of the hanging was fast approaching. The first to be hanged from the large oak in the square, Old Tawassee hadn't been forgotten. The tree had quickly become known as the hanging tree.

The morning of that day was eerily calm for an Alabama spring. No winds blew; no clouds were in the sky. The air was the perfect temperature with no humidity. People were milling about on the street, on their way to and from the market that was always set up that time of year. Suddenly, leaves from the hanging tree burst into the air, as the tree began to shake violently. On a closer look, only the limb from which Tawassee was hanged trembled. Frightened, the townspeople scattered. Since most of them lived several miles from town, the people crammed into the few businesses. Every door was locked and every window shut.

The tree stopped shaking, and the leaves landed softly on the ground. As townspeople began moving about, word spread that it had to be Tawassee's ghost. Spreading like wildfire, the news eventually reached Dr. Brewster. "The ghost of Tawassee has returned for his bones," he heard from several different patients. Laughing at the ignorance of his fellow man, Dr. Brewster ignored the accounts.

But that evening, as he and his assistant, Thomas, were cleaning up to leave the small office, strange sounds echoed through the silent space. Thomas began to tremble. He backed into a corner, crouched, and mumbled, "He's come back to get us!" The sounds continued for several minutes. Dr. Brewster decided they were coming from the closet. Slowly opening the creaky door, he was shocked to find the skeleton of Old Tawassee shaking violently in the dark.

The Courthouse Ghost

As one of two county seats in St. Clair County (a branch moved to Pell City in 1902), the courthouse has always played a vital role in Ashville's history. Court week was held regularly in the spring and again in the fall. The "week" would often turn into three or four weeks, and each time, all the boarding houses in Ashville would be filled with judges, lawyers, and court reporters.

The courthouse was built before the Civil War in 1844 by Littleton Yarbrough, who had his slave make the bricks right on the town square. A man by the name of Jefferson Campbell was hired to lay the bricks. Campbell had the help of an Irish man with a funny limp. The Irishman was known as one of the best brick layers in the state, but he would only work on one condition. He had to have his little brown jug with him as he worked.

Each morning the Irishman would fill his jug with moonshine from Mr. Yarbrough's still. He could make one jug last an entire day. When he wasn't drinking from it, he would slide the jug down the wall as he worked.

The Saturday the men were laying the west wall of the building, the Irishman's wife came down to the site, asking to speak with her husband. He obeyed, scurried down the wall, and limped to meet her, leaving his precious jug where he had been working. Campbell wanted to have the wall finished before dark and grew impatient waiting for his helper to return. He continued to work and finished the wall quickly.

The Irishman returned to find the day's work completed and his little brown jug missing. He searched everywhere but couldn't find it. He finally asked Campbell if he had seen it, but he merely shrugged his shoulders. The only answer the Irishman could come up with was that the jug had been bricked into the wall. He panicked and began tapping furiously on the newly bricked wall. He tapped all the way up and down it, listening for any clue that might show the jug's location. The rest of the crew had gone home for long ago, but the little Irishman continued to tap into the night.

He apparently never found his brown jug because on cold windy nights, lone courthouse visitors can still hear his tap-tap-tap on the bricks of the west wall of the building.

The Ashville Museum & Archives

The Ashville Museum & Archives is located within the historic St. Clair County Courthouse. It contains county records, including wills, deeds, births, and deaths, dating back to 1819. The Census of Confederate Soldiers from 1907 and newspapers from as early as 1879 can also be found there.

One woman was instrumental in gathering and organizing all of the genealogical information found in the Archives—Mattie Lou Teague Crow. The author and editor of several books detailing St. Clair County's history, Mrs. Crow grew up in Ashville and spent much of her life researching and tracing her ancestry. A beautiful white-haired woman with a sweet disposition, she expended vast amounts of energy into the archives. It was definitely one of Mrs. Crow's greatest passions. She died at age ninety-six and is buried in the Ashville Cemetery.

Mrs. Crow loved the museum so much that she still visits it on occasion. The information contained in the museum is used by many students conducting research for reports. Jokingly, the current archivist will warn them that they better get their history correct or Mrs. Crow will come after them. One young girl, after concluding her research, told the archivist that she felt something cold brush against her arm while she was searching for information. She said that Mrs. Crow must have been trying to help her find what she needed.

There have been several other reports of visitors seeing a white-haired lady walking around the museum. Ironically, these accounts would have fascinated Mrs. Crow, who grew up hearing ghost stories from her grandmother and in turn shared them with her children, grandchildren, and great-grandchildren.

the children of arlington mansion

Susan Gray Eagle knew the price of freedom all too well. In fact, she had lost family members in World War II, the Korean War, and Vietnam. Now, as she walked among the graves and headstones of Arlington National Cemetery, the full impact of her ancestors' sacrifice hit home.

Susan was part Choctaw and part Cherokee. The Choctaw and the Cherokee, along with the Chickasaw, Seminole, and Creek Indians made up what was called, in the Civil War era, "The Five Civilized Tribes." Collectively, they represented the Cherokee Nation.

Susan's ancestors had been fighting in American wars since that time and continued to serve proudly to this day. Some of them were even buried beneath her feet in Arlington Cemetery. As she walked among the graves, she wondered aloud as she had so many times before. "What was it really all about?" she asked. "What was it all for?"

As a little girl growing up in Mississippi, Susan would listen to her great-grandfather tell stories about the Civil War and the part that

Native Americans played in it. He told the stories exactly the same way every time. She was so familiar with them that she could recite her great-grandfather's words almost verbatim.

"In late October of the year 1861," he began, "the Cherokee Nation took sides in the Great War of Northern Aggression. The Choctaw, Chickasaw, Creek, Seminole, and Cherokee people sided with the Confederacy." It was at this point that Susan's great-grandfather recited paraphrased passages from the document that made the Indians' decision final.

"I quote now from the Indian document titled, 'Declaration by the People of the Cherokee Nation of the Causes Which Have Impelled Them to Unite Their Fortunes With Those of the Confederate States of America.' In this document, it is recorded that the Southerners disclaimed any intention to invade the Northern states. The Confederacy only sought to repel the invaders from their own soil and to permanently secure the right of governing themselves. They claimed only the privileges put forth in the Declaration of Independence, namely the right to govern themselves and the duty to alter their form of government when it becomes intolerable. These rights are the ones that even the Northern states are built upon.

"But the Cherokee people saw the Northern states violate their Constitution. The sight of this caused us great shock and alarm." The old man would then lift his head upward, close his eyes and continue. "The Cherokee saw the Northerners put all civil liberties in peril and the rules of civilized warfare discarded along with the dictates of common human decency."

The old man would continue to paraphrase the Declaration of the Five Tribes, making sure to emphasize the most important points.

"The states that followed the Union found their civilian powers replaced by a military authority and those laws established by the populace put down at the point of a gun. Free and truthful speech was declared to be unlawful. The president even set the military to control the highest court in the land. Soon he began a most hateful war against the Southern states.

"Now in the past, the people of the Cherokee Nation were not always the allies of the Southern states. However, the Great Spirit revealed to us that our destiny and fortune intertwined with their own."

Again, he lifted his head and closed his eyes, saying, "The war that is now waging is one of Northern avarice and fanaticism. It seeks to annihilate the sovereignty of the Southern states and completely change, forever, the soul of government." With the close of his recitation, Susan's great-grandfather would call out in his native language, signaling the start of a larger ceremony. Then, those gathered tribe members would begin to sing. Susan found it strange that the songs were mostly Christian hymns sung in the Choctaw language. But as they danced in a circle as their ancestors had, Susan Gray Eagle wondered, "What was the war really about?"

Susan saw the first child while she was musing about her life. The tribal gatherings, the stories and traditions preserved by her family, life on the reservation, the music they played, and the songs they sung all faded to memory when she saw the little boy.

The child was dressed in out-of-date clothing and was standing with his back to a headstone some forty yards away. Susan might have not noticed him at all except for the fact that the young boy was waving at her. She automatically returned the wave. As she did, the boy dropped his hand to his side, turned, and walked away. Susan knew that kids would wave at just about anyone, so she didn't give it a second thought. That is, until she saw another child.

This child, too, was staring at Susan from about forty yards away. She wore an old-time play-party dress replete with petticoat. Susan was unable to get a better look at the child to see her face clearly, but she could tell that the girl had curly blond hair tied up in bright blue ribbons.

Susan was about to turn around and leave when the girl with the petticoat waved.

"What's going on here?" Susan muttered. "Have I walked into some sort of school field trip or something?" Susan Gray Eagle's words had barely left her lips when the little girl proceeded to walk off into the cemetery. For some unknown reason, Susan decided to follow her. Along the way, she looked at the graves, reading the names of the fallen heroes who were laid to rest there. Susan also noticed something else; the little girl had vanished completely.

Susan looked all around but couldn't find the girl. Then she remembered that she had been about the girl's age when she made her first trip to Arlington. Her grandfather was part of a tribal committee that was meeting with senators to discuss mining rights on the reservation. She remembered her grandfather saying, "If the South had won the Civil War, we'd have our own state by now, an Indian state."

Susan's grandfather had taken her to the Tomb of the Unknown Soldier in the early morning hours. She remembered that the grass was still wet with dew. She also vividly remembered the military Honor Guard marching back and forth at the entrance of the memorial. The guards, in dress uniform, moved with a hypnotic precision that transfixed her. She, quite literally, was unable to take her eyes off the tomb.

Susan and her grandfather had been silently watching the Honor Guard for about ten minutes when Susan had a vision. She'd heard about visions her entire life but had never experienced one—at least not one like this. She saw a spinning whirlpool of light and energy swirling around the Tomb of the Unknown Soldier. It seemed to reach out for her as if it wanted her to come closer. Instead, Susan grabbed her grandfather's pants leg and nervously stood her ground.

Later that night, she told her grandfather about the vision. "You have a gift," he said. "All of the women in our family possess this power." Then he leaned close, gave her a sly wink, and said, "Some of the men, too."

The next day Susan's grandfather took her back to the tomb and asked her to show him where the unearthly energy was strongest. Without hesitation, Susan walked to a small clearing near a stand of evergreens on the southeastern slope of a hill next to the tomb. Her grandfather laughed and said, "Yes, little one. You've got the sight, all right! Yes, indeed, you have the gift."

The truth was that Susan had not experienced another vision since that day. Now as a grown woman looking for a mysterious blond girl with blue ribbons in her hair, she wondered if she ever would again.

Susan walked over a small rise and noticed another small child standing a short distance away. Then she saw another girl she had never seen before. Yet another girl who appeared to be slightly older than the first appeared next to the other two. Almost in unison, the children waved gently at Susan, turned, and scampered away.

Susan quickened her pace in order to catch up with the kids, but as she came over the next hill, all three of the children were gone. For the first time in ages, Susan felt uneasy. She was wondering what to do next when she caught a glimpse of the children running toward a house on the cemetery grounds. She ran to keep up, but the children vanished somewhere near or into the house. Then she realized where she was. Susan was standing in front of Arlington Mansion, the former home of Robert E. Lee.

In all of her trips to Arlington, she'd never taken a tour of the Lee home, but a child's voice in the back of her mind urged her to do so now.

"Of all the beautiful antebellum homes of Virginia, Arlington Mansion is considered the most majestic," began the tour guide. "It was originally built by the adopted grandson of George Washington as a memorial to the first president of these United States. George Washington Parke Curtis had only one child, and in 1831, Mary Parke Curtis married the young and dashing Robert E. Lee. Robert was the son of 'Light Horse' Harry Lee, the famous hero of the Revolutionary War."

The tour guide was detailing the tranquil and idyllic life that Lee and his bride enjoyed at the mansion, but Susan was being distracted by something. Standing in the corner of the room was one of the children she'd seen earlier. The boy was playing quietly with an old toy horse and wagon. Oddly enough, no one else in the room seemed to take notice of him. The boy looked up at Susan and smiled. "Such a cute child," she thought.

"Robert E. Lee seemed destined to not remain here in his beloved home. In 1846 he left to fight in the Mexican War. Six years later he left to become the superintendent of the military academy at West Point. Shortly after that, the specter of Southern secession cast a cloud over the country and this house. After the war began, Federal troops seized the house and grounds to punish the rebellious general. At first, only Union dead were buried on this site, but in ensuing years, it became the final resting place for all of America's honored dead."

Susan wandered away from the group to find a place to sit down and rest her feet. She had little trouble finding an appropriate spot. As soon as she sat down, a purring cat hopped up in her lap. "Well, where did you come from, sweetie?" she asked. The cat closed her eyes for a moment as Susan began petting it. Then the little blond girl with bright blue ribbons walked into the room. Susan looked up for only an instant, but in that instant, the cat vanished. The disappearance seemed to occur in conjunction with a soft popping sound that startled Susan. When she glanced back up, the girl was gone.

Susan resolved to get back to the tour group. However, no matter where she looked, the group was nowhere to be found. She was about to go upstairs and look when a small boy came walking down the staircase. He appeared to be somewhat agitated and brushed past Susan without looking at her or saying a word. In his hands he carried a teddy bear that was, obviously, his prized possession. Susan followed him into a room with a fireplace. The boy walked up to the fireplace and set the teddy bear in a small chair by it. The spectral child and his stuffed companion started to warm themselves at a non-existent fire. It was at this point that Susan Gray Eagle realized that she was looking at a ghost.

The faint sounds of voices caused Susan to turn around, but she could see no one. Then two more children came in to the room and joined the boy by the fireplace. "My God!" whispered Susan. "They're all ghosts."

Another child walked in, followed by four more. Soon more than a dozen ghostly children were in the room. Each quietly amused themselves. None spoke a single word.

Susan's head began to spin. One of the little girls noticed her distress and walked over to Susan and took her hand. Susan couldn't help but notice how radiant these children were. For the life of her, she couldn't imagine why they were all gathered in this house.

"Surely, you're all not relatives of the Lees, are you?" At that very moment, a stately woman with a dower look on her face marched into the room. Susan and the children watched as the woman walked over to the little chair by the fireplace and picked up the stuffed teddy bear. Then, she turned on her heels and marched out of the room, turned the corner, and headed for the stairs.

The ghostly children, with Susan in tow, followed the woman up the stairs to an opulent bedroom. Everyone watched as the woman put the bear on the bed, resting it against the pillows. The glowering woman seemed to take no notice of either the living or the dead as she left the bedroom. The ghostly children waited until she was gone and began a silent giggle. Then they rushed to the bed and snatched the teddy bear. Susan and the children left the bedroom and headed down the stairs.

"Those little rascals," Susan thought, "are taking the teddy bear back downstairs to the fireplace."

Before Susan was completely down the staircase, she felt a sensation that urged her to go back upstairs. The little girl who was still holding her hand released it and smiled. She ran off to join her playmates by the invisible fire.

Susan walked into another bedroom off the main hall. She saw the ghostly figure of a young and beautiful woman lying on the bed. It was obvious that the woman was ill. Suddenly, two more adults entered the room and stood over the supine form. One was a man dressed in the finery of a colonial country gentleman. He was weeping inconsolably, and it was obvious that the woman in bed was his wife. His female companion, however, did not display any emotion whatsoever. She spoke to the crying man.

"I wish I could hear what they are saying," thought Susan. There was a strong physical resemblance between the two women, and Susan thought that they might be sisters. After a few more moments, the pair of ghosts walked past Susan and stood in the doorway of the bedroom. Unexpectedly, they embraced and kissed passionately. All sorrow for the dying woman had apparently vanished.

Just then, a man dressed in a ruffled shirt and long black coat strode confidently into the room. He clutched a ledger under his left arm. The man moved to the bedside of the sick woman and adjusted the blankets that lay over her. Susan was trying to get a better look at the ledger book under his arm when the man in the white shirt looked up at her. At first, Susan was frightened by the stern look the man gave her, but soon his frown melted into an amiable smile.

"Who are you?" she asked.

Much to her surprise, the man answered. "My name," he said, "is Light Horse Harry."

The sound of children playing diverted Susan's attention, and both of the ghosts in the room vanished with a soft popping sound. Just then, the phantom cat she'd met earlier hopped up on the bed. The animal's tail twitched furiously. It mewed a silent mew, and its actions clearly indicated that it was trying to get Susan's attention. The cat jumped to the floor and ran out of the bedroom with Susan close behind.

Susan crossed the threshold of the room to see dozens and dozens of ghostly children crowding every corner of Arlington Mansion. They were all young, healthy, and happy children. Some of them played with invisible toys while others read tattered books. Each one appeared content and peaceful.

"This is my family," a voice said. Susan turned back to the bedroom to see it filled with smiling children. In the center of the crowd stood the ghost of Robert E. Lee's father, "Light Horse" Harry Lee.

"You stand on hallowed ground, Susan Gray Eagle," he said. "Please come to the window and look out."

Susan walked to the second-story window and peered through it. What she saw took her breath away. The grounds around Arlington Mansion were covered by hundreds—maybe thousands—of ghostly children playing in the warm sun. They were everywhere.

The ghost of Harry Lee said, "I keep a record of them in my ledger, just so I can keep track, mind you."

Susan felt compelled to speak. "But why are they here?" she asked.

"Can't you guess?" replied Harry Lee. "Haven't you longed for a return to the simpler carefree days of your childhood? Well, some of my children have done just that. Others have found their way here to spend eternity in a constant state of wonder and playfulness."

He paused for a moment and continued by saying, "Still, others were brought here by their comrades. Those children are among my favorites."

"War is a terrible thing, Susan. It destroys innocence and steals youth. But sometimes it is necessary. When someone meets the challenge and pays the ultimate price, don't you think it's fitting they should get their innocence back as a reward?"

Susan Gray Eagle began to cry. Now she knew the answer to the question she had been asking for most of her life. The sacrifice that her family and so many others like them had made over the generations was for the children. And not just for the children that soldiers leave behind. The brave men who are buried in Arlington National Cemetery gave their lives to protect innocence and preserve the youth of others. They accomplished this by offering their own precious innocence and youth.

Just then, a National Parks employee tapped Susan on the shoulder to tell her that the house was closing for the day.

As Susan Gray Eagle walked out of the front door of Arlington Mansion, she caught sight of a small boy happily playing in the grass. He looked up at her, smiled, and gently waved. "It's all about the children," she thought. "It's all about the innocence."

the kissing bridge

The photographer entered the shade of the old covered bridge with relief. She had been clambering up and down the river bank for hours, now on the south side, now on the north, once even scaling a tree, trying to find the best possible angle for her shot. Hauling twenty pounds of equipment all over creation in the August heat made her wonder why people thought a photographer's job was glamorous.

Once her eyes became accustomed to the dimness, she noticed the profusion of initials and messages carved into the venerable old beams. The graffiti looked old and carefully inscribed. The bold, angry strokes of paint so common in the city she lived in were conspicuously absent. It was peaceful here, with the light filtering greenly through the branches at either end. Smiling faintly, she ran her fingers across a heart carved near the center of the bridge.

A whispering sound behind her made her turn sharply. No one was there. It was probably some tree branches scraping across the roof of the bridge, she thought. Odd how it sounded like voices. Like a whispered endearment. This fanciful notion made her smile again, and she leaned closer to the wood to study the carvings on it.

●●●●●

"That's it!" The foreman shouted loudly as the final beam was guided into place.

"Set the bolts now, Matthew!"

The young man straddled the huge beam, white and still oozing sap from its fresh-cut surface. Before he took his hammer and knocked the bolt into place, he eased his pocketknife from his pocket. There, hundreds of feet above the murmuring waters of the Doe River, he painstakingly carved the initials MT, intertwining them with the letters JS. This job would give him the money he needed to ask for her hand. And their love would last as long as this bridge remained standing across the river, he vowed.

"You gonna stay up there all day, man?"

The foreman's demand startled the young builder, and his hand slipped. The knife nicked his finger before sailing through the air to land with a tiny splash in the shallows.

"After lunch we'll put the roof on it, okay, Matthew?" The foreman's eyes flashed, the vivid blue evident even from Matthew's perch in the air. He wasn't an ill-tempered man—just a busy one. And that was fortunate for Matthew, because the foreman was also destined to become his father-in-law.

●●●●●

Someone lightly tapped a car horn at the mouth of the bridge, and the photographer looked up from her study of the carved initials. She waved, and the car slowed to a halt as it approached her.

"Hey, young lady." The car was a boxy old Rambler, at least fifty years younger than the driver. His hair was a bright white, and his eyes shone blue even in the dusky interior of the old structure.

"You like this bridge?"

"Yes, sir. I hope these photographs will be in a book I'm working on."

"Pictures can't do this bridge justice. You need to hear its history. There's something mighty unusual about this bridge."

"It certainly does make me feel peaceful to be here," Sarah admitted.

104

"You go see Mattie Billings. She'll tell you a thing or two about this bridge. She lives on this road and can see everybody comin' and goin'."

"Mattie Billings," the photographer repeated. "Where can I find her?"

"'Bout this time every day, she's down at the post office. She gets around for an ol' lady, she does. You like old things?"

"Yes, sir."

A pocketknife materialized in the palm of his hand. "Found this knife buried in silt by the river when I was a little tyke." It was rusty and obviously more than a century old. "It's done its share of carving on this old bridge, I can tell you that."

Sarah examined the knife closely and then handed it back. She stepped back as the elderly man continued across the bridge, giving him a little wave.

"Hey," she shouted. "What's your name?" He just smiled and piloted the car gently off the ramp and onto the asphalt road.

Sarah shrugged and dusted off her hands. She needed to buy some stamps anyway, so she might as well stop at the post office.

••••••

She met him at the door, flying into his arms as if she hadn't seen him in a year. Actually, it had been a little more than two months since he'd joined the army, and she hadn't seen him in uniform. After the first hug, she stepped back and pulled him by his arm out onto the porch.

"My, don't you look fine in that uniform," she said, admiring the smartly buttoned tunic and tight leggings. "Let's take a little walk, shall we?"

He held her arm tenderly as they strolled down the hill.

"You look thinner," she commented, just as the silence between them grew awkward.

He shrugged. The silence lengthened again.

"How's your mother?" She already knew the answer since they were practically neighbors.

"All right, I guess."

They were nearly to the bridge. As they entered the shadowy space, her words came out in a rush.

"I wish you weren't going."

"President Wilson says we have to make the world a safe place."

"France is so far away."

It was easier to speak in the bridge, their faces hidden in the dimness. "I love you."

She turned to him. "You know I've always loved you."

"Will you be my wife?"

Her only response was to stretch up on her toes and kiss him swiftly on the cheek.

"We'll get married next spring. I'm sure I'll be home by then."

"I'll be ready."

They clasped hands and held on as if their life depended on it. Absorbed in each other, they didn't hear the creak and jingle of a horse and rider approaching.

"Good afternoon, folks."

The couple guiltily jumped apart.

"Kissin' Bridge earnin' its name today?" The rider laughed and spurred his horse up the hill.

"I've got to go now."

"When does your train leave?" She fought the urge to cling to his arm.

"Seven tomorrow morning."

She clasped his hand again until at last he tenderly worked it free. With a soft kiss on her cheek, he left.

Halfway up the hill he turned to look back. From that distance he couldn't see the tears glistening. She stood framed by the dark opening of the bridge and the graceful tendrils of the weeping willow on the riverbank.

••••••

Sarah drove slowly along the main street until she came upon the post office. Just stepping outside was a petite, white-haired woman.

"Excuse me, ma'am?" The photographer threw her Jeep into park and jumped out. "Can you tell me where to find Mattie Billings?"

"You've found her. Who are you?"

"Sarah Hamilton. I've been photographing the bridge, and I was told you might know some history about it."

The old lady laughed. "Mercy, yes. I could tell you stories all day."

"Can I buy you a cup of coffee?"

The diner was just across the street, and Sarah carefully held Mattie Billing's elbow as she stepped off the curb. Her bones felt as fragile as a bird's, and her skin had the crepelike texture of great age.

When they had settled into a booth, Sarah pulled out a notebook and pen.

"They say if you declare your love on that bridge, it will last forever," Mattie explained. She fumbled in her billfold for a picture. "See here?" It was the picture of a very young man in an old-fashioned uniform, the edges of the photo tattered from years of handling.

"We pledged ourselves to each other on that bridge in 1917. We were married for sixty-eight years."

Something about the young soldier looked familiar to Sarah, but she couldn't quite place it. She examined it closely before handing it back.

"Are there any other love stories connected to the bridge?"

"My land, yes. Just about everybody in Elizabethton has spent some time spoonin' in that old bridge. Why, on a Saturday night, you just about couldn't get a car through there for all the couples!"

Incredibly, the woman winked. Sarah blinked, not sure she'd really seen it. Then Mattie leaned closer over the table.

"Of course, you'd find all those same couples lined up pretty as you please on the pews of all the different churches come Sunday morning!" She laughed at her own joke, and Sarah smiled.

"But they all lived happily ever after?"

"As happily as folks can, I reckon."

"Mattie!" An older lady, tall and imposing, sailed into the cafe and across to their booth. "You didn't tell me you had guests coming!"

"She's just in town for the day. She's come to take pictures of our bridge."

The woman nodded, a smile forming on her lips. She reached to her shoulder and touched a brooch pinned there, as if to assure herself that it was still there.

"That's a beautiful pin. It's Italian, isn't it?" An oval frame held a delicate mosaic, tiny chips of opaque stone forming flowers in a vase.

"Yes, I got it a long time ago."

"Is Hank waiting outside for you, dear?" Mattie pointed out the window to a man who was waving a cane in great sweeping motions, trying to get the attention of the woman inside.

"Oh my, yes. I'd better go. See you Wednesday night, Mattie?"

"Of course. Bye!"

Through the glass, Sarah watched with some amusement as the woman placated her husband. Reconciled, the couple strolled off arm in arm.

••••••

"I can't stay long." The girl was tall and thin, her hair pulled back into a tight knot at the base of her neck.

"Are you cold?" The young man rubbed his hands together and shifted from foot to foot. "Let's at least get out of the wind."

Shivering a little in her thin cotton dress and holding a sweater around her shoulders, she followed him to the shelter of the bridge.

"I've got a job."

She squealed and started to throw her arms around him but he stopped her.

"I've got to go to Nashville."

"No," she whispered. "You promised me we'd get married!"

"We will," he said fiercely. "I swear it. We'll just have to wait a year, maybe a little longer. Things will get better, and I swear I'll come back to get you."

Now her eyes and nose were red from more than the cold December wind. "You'll never come back. I know it."

"Of course I will." He tilted her chin up to look her in the eyes. "I've never broken a promise to you yet, have I?"

She shook her head, sniffling a little.

"I promise 1934 will be our year," he pulled her close with one arm, reaching into his coat pocket with the other. "Here, you can wear this and think of me."

She studied the little oval pin. "It's beautiful," she whispered. "I've never seen anything like it."

He turned it over so she could see the writing on the back. "It's from Italy. Flowers that will never stop blooming."

"Hank, I love you."

"You'll wait for me?"

She answered him with a tight embrace that lasted until a car horn made them break apart. They stood holding hands, watching as the car clattered across the bridge and down the road.

••••••

"If you'd care to come home with me, dear, I have some old photos of the bridge." Mattie had finished her coffee and was sliding out of the booth. Sarah checked her watch. She wanted to get some late-afternoon shots of the Elizabethton bridge, anyway, so she might as well talk to this entertaining old lady.

"You got married in 1918?" Mattie walked deliberately with small steps, planting each foot with great care.

"Yes, in December. Just after the war. You should see the way we decorated that bridge to welcome home our troops."

"There were a lot of men from here who fought?"

"Oh, yes, Elizabethton sent men to all the wars. Grieved over many of them, too. That's my car." She pointed across the street.

"You must've married very young." Sarah hurried to open the door of a big old Cadillac parked outside the post office. Mattie slipped inside, and Sarah got in on the other side.

"You're fishing to learn how old I am." The key made a grinding noise, and then the engine purred into life. Mattie threw the car into reverse with a jerk and began to back out.

"I'm ninety-three years old." She drove like she walked, with a deliberate pace, calm and implacable.

"I'm sorry, I didn't mean to be rude."

The car glided to a halt at a stop sign. Mattie put on her blinker to signal a left-hand turn. A red car roared past them, after pausing only briefly at the stop sign. Mattie sighed.

"Billy French. He always was a reckless boy. Thirty years married and five children would settle some people down, but not him."

She continued down the street, the Cadillac positioned firmly in the center of the road.

"They say my husband's grandfather helped build that bridge. Of course, half the people in town say their kin helped build it. It was built in 1885, or did I tell you that already?"

They pulled into a driveway that led up a gentle slope. At the top, Sarah looked around curiously at the old house and the barn beside it.

"I know he built this house," Mattie continued with pride. "Of course, all I keep in the barn now is junk and old cars."

Sarah helped Mattie up onto the porch and into the house. The woman directed Sarah to a cabinet in the dining room and asked her to pull out an ancient, round hatbox.

"Somewhere I have pictures of Robert and me on the bridge," she said, rummaging around. "It was when we bought our first car."

••••••

"Yeeeeoooooowwwwww!" The young man did a flip off the side of the riverbank, landing into the water below with a sharp smack.

"You're crazy!" protested the young woman standing next to his car.

"That's right, baby," he replied, breathless from running back up to the car right outside the bridge. "I'm crazy about you." He smoothed his hair back carefully and squeezed a few drops of water out of the ducktail at the back.

"You'd say anything," his date said, laughing.

"I mean it," he said, resting the palms of his hands on either side of her, flat against the two-toned red car. "I love you."

Just then a car filled with teenagers roared up into the center of the bridge. Moonlight poured in through the arched windows. Laughing and screaming, the kids piled out of the car and ran around to switch seats, ringing cowbells and shaking noisemakers. The driver took off with a squeal before the doors swung shut, and he tooted the horn as they careened off the ramp past the couple and their parked car.

"Oh, I bet they're on their way to see *The Thing That Couldn't Die*," the young woman said eagerly. "I want to see that. Can we go?"

Without a word, he helped her into the passenger side and shut the door with a solid clunk.

The moon was full when he pulled up to her parent's house. They hadn't been sitting there more than two minutes before the porch light flashed off and then on again.

"I'd better get inside," she sighed. "Mama worries."

He buried his face in her neck and growled. "She oughtta be worried."

His girlfriend giggled and hopped nimbly out of the car. "See you tomorrow?" Without waiting for a reply, she was gone.

He sat for a few minutes, pondering his options. Then, his mind made up, he drove home.

Back at the bridge, it took some time to figure out how to juggle the paint can and the brush while hanging onto the rope, but the moon provided ample light. The letters were nearly three feet tall and marched unevenly across nearly half the length of the bridge. He stood back to admire his handiwork. The first "M" was a little shaky and the exclamation point dripped, but he was pleased. It looked like a serious proposal: "MARRY ME, RUTH WHITFIELD!"

••••••

"We kept that car till 1955," Mattie said, shaking her head as she looked at the photo. "Of course, we only drove it once a week or so. Robert always walked down to work, and I'd walk back and forth to the store and to the post office. It's such a small town, a car was really kind of frivolous." When she turned to Sarah and smiled wistfully, the photographer could see a shadow of the beauty that had been Mattie's before time wore it away.

"When we were young, couples used to take their buggies into one end of the bridge and the young men would see how much they could slow their horses down before the young ladies complained. In the dark they could slip their arms around their girlfriend and maybe even steal a kiss."

"I guess that stopped when cars became common."

"No," Mattie replaced the photo and began to stir through the box in search of another. "I think the young men still drive real slow through the bridge. Robert did, even after we'd been married for years."

"Have you always live in Elizabethton?"

"Of course." She presented another photo with a flourish. "Where else would anyone want to live? This is a picture of the bridge in 1953 when we welcomed the soldiers home from Korea. See how we strung flowers and crepe paper across the opening?"

••••••

It was dark. Not even a sliver of a moon brave enough to face this Tennessee night, the woman thought as she leaned over the rail to stare into the gleaming black water. She'd come back to town to help bury her grandfather, and it was like stepping back in time.

"Why on earth would you chop off all your hair like that?" her mother had hissed when she arrived at the funeral home after a 2,000 mile cross-country trek. "It's so unbecoming."

"I'm glad to see you too, Mama," she had said, gingerly pulling the older woman into an embrace. "It was a hard drive, but I'm glad I came."

After the funeral, they all gathered in her grandfather's house, standing around tables with dozens of pies, cakes, casseroles, salads, and breads. Her grandfather had been well-loved, and the quantity of food pouring in from his friends and neighbors was mute testimony to that fact.

The woman's classmates and former friends had all been there, too, some with children running around, all of them a little thicker around the middle, a little grayer, a little more tired. None of them questioned her about her life in distant California. They talked about her grandfather or the latest scandal in Tennessee politics (news of which hadn't reached the West Coast) or their own lives bounded by the Doe River and the Appalachians.

Grace found it all very unsettling. After a while, she let their voices wash over her, the mosaic of food spread out before her went out of focus, and she only nodded vaguely in response to the kind queries directed her way. She wandered to the porch and then to the streets beyond. These streets, where she had learned to ride a bicycle, played tag, first steered a car, and walked with her first sweetheart.

Michael must be gone now. She hadn't heard anyone mention him, so he must have moved off the edge of the world—out of Elizabethton.

The darkness was healing. Like a bandage over her eyes and ears and mouth, it screened out the flow of sensory input, brought it down to a manageable level. The only two senses fully functional were her sense of smell and touch. She could smell the rich, fertile odor of the damp leaves piled by the sides of the street. Not too far away, she could smell the river's water and the fecund scent of mud at the river's edge. Her toes, poking through the sandals that were a bit unpractical for Tennessee in October, could feel the dew on the grass. Her fingers glided along the handrail and gripped the splintery old wood of the bridge.

"Hi."

The figure materializing out of the shadows of the bridge made her shriek softly. "My gosh, you scared me," she complained. Then recognition dawned.

"Michael?"

"That's me."

She strained to see his face and then laughed.

"I was just thinking you must've escaped. I've been here two days, and no one's said a word about you."

"I'm still here."

Her hand slipped easily into his, just as if the years had never gone by. Without a word, they walked slowly through the mouth of the bridge.

"Let me show you something," Michael said at last. He patted his pockets for a few minutes. "I don't have any matches. Do you?"

She shook her head before she realized it was too dark for him to see the gesture.

"No."

"Here." He took her hand and drew it up to the beam in the center. Blindly, her fingers moved around and over a familiar shape.

"A heart?"

"Now look inside."

Her fingers now smoothed over a pattern of lines and circles.

"I always heard that if you declared your love on this bridge, it would last forever."

The pattern began to take shape under her fingers.

"I was too shy to tell you. But I never forgot you, Grace."

"G.O. and M.K. Michael, how sweet."

The darkness of the bridge made their kisses sweeter. Their embrace lasted until a beam of light pierced the shadows, announcing a car that thundered across the river and over to town. Silent again, the couple wandered off the bridge, hand in hand.

••••••

"Are you all right, Mattie?"

The old lady had been silent for several minutes, staring at the picture in her hands as if she could change it by a force of will.

"Robert, Jr., never came back," she said softly after a moment. "I never can look at this picture without remembering him."

Sarah touched her gently on the arm. "I'm sorry."

"Robert asked me to go back to the bridge with him in 1986." She placed the photo back in the box and sat up straighter. "He had just come home from the hospital after his second heart attack."

Sarah nodded, unsure how to respond.

Mattie laughed. "We must have made a sight. It was in December, and he was in a wheelchair, so I wrapped him up in three blankets and just wheeled him right on down there.

"It wasn't as cold on the bridge, you see, because the walls acted like a windbreak. We walked up and down the bridge three or four times, talking about all the things that happened to us on there bridge, and then we went inside and had hot cocoa."

She lapsed into silence again.

Sarah couldn't tolerate the quiet for long. "I'm sorry if I've brought back old memories."

Mattie shook her head, a smile growing slowly on her face. "Don't be. Memories are all I have, and I cherish them." She grasped the arm of the sofa and pulled herself to her feet. "Out in the barn, I have some copies of a book about the bridge published at its centennial in 1985. If I can find it, you can have a copy."

They walked out to the porch and across the yard to the barn. To Sarah, it seemed as if Mattie's steps had slowed even further.

"I'll never forget the last thing Robert ever said to me," Mattie said over her shoulder as she picked her way carefully across the lawn. "He said, 'Meet me on the bridge, Mattie.'" She stopped and turned to face her guest.

"The nurse said he was wandering and out of his head, but I believe he knew exactly what he was saying." She turned to continue her passage to the barn.

The old structure was filled with shadows and unexpected gleams of pure sunlight, streaming in through random holes in the siding. Dust mites danced in the sun, and spiderwebs glistened in the shadows. The old barn seemed to be alive with magic. Mattie headed straight for a corner littered with old wooden crates and cardboard boxes.

"I'll just look through here," she declared. "They're in one of these boxes."

Sarah looked around. Still hanging on the walls were old, rotten pieces of leather held together by metal—bridles and harnesses, she guessed. A wheel leaned against the far wall, next to an indistinct pile that might have once been a wagon or a buggy. Far back in the barn, hidden by the darkness and partially covered by a piece of old green canvas, Sarah spied the wide round headlights of an old Rambler. Just as she started to move toward it, Mattie let out a triumphant cry.

"Here it is," she said. "I knew I'd find it!"

Sarah walked over to the other woman and thumbed through the book. They walked back to the house, Sarah ready to head back to capture the bridge in the afternoon sunlight.

"I never showed you Robert's picture, did I?" She led Sarah into the dining room to a framed photo resting on the sideboard.

"He's, he's very handsome," Sarah stammered. "Such blue eyes."

"I'll take you back into town now," Mattie announced. "Let me get my keys."

Sarah didn't speak on the short ride back to her Jeep at the post office. She thanked the woman profusely, promising to send her a copy of the book when it was finished.

"Oh, by the way," she mentioned in what she hoped was a casual tone. "Did you two ever have a Rambler?"

Mattie laughed. "Robert drove a Rambler from 1964 until the day he went into the hospital in 1986. He loved that old wreck."

Sarah gave a little wave as Mattie pulled away. She pulled the jeep off the road near the bridge and scrambled down to the river's edge to catch the last of the afternoon sun for the photograph.

The next day, working in her darkroom, Sarah hummed as she moved around, printing the last two rolls of film she needed for her book. She had put the incident in Elizabethton out of her mind, telling herself she must have imagined it, that there were lots of blue-eyed men around, and old cars were common in the country. She had almost convinced herself.

Sarah pulled the last print out of the chemical bath and pinned it up to dry. She cocked her head to take a look, and what she saw made her unpin it and hold it up close in the dim light.

The long, white, angular bridge over Doe River was surrounded by a soft, definite glow. It looked like the sun had created an aura, a halo of light and warmth. But that wasn't possible, Sarah realized. Doe River ran north to south through Elizabethton. There was no rational explanation for the radiance that enveloped the bridge that had sheltered a century of love.

the star-crossed lovers of don cesar

Young Thomas Rowe took his seat in the theater just as the curtain was rising. He had come to the opera tonight expecting only to enjoy the show one of his fellow students was raving about, and nothing more. The moment the stage lights came up, however, he knew his life was forever changed.

There, in the spotlight, stood the woman of his dreams. A tumble of iridescent ebony hair framed her face and breasts, then fell away down her curving back. Her tawny complexion spoke of a foreign descent, Spanish perhaps. She had luscious red lips and soulful dark eyes that he swore were looking right at him. And her voice! When she opened that luscious mouth and sang, his heart threatened to jump right out of his chest. Grabbing up his program, he thumbed it until he found her name—not far in, since she was playing the starring role. Lucinda! Her name was Lucinda. Lovely, luscious Lucinda.

Mesmerized by her beauty, Thomas only peripherally absorbed the opera's plot of star-crossed lovers Maritana, played by lovely Lucinda, and Don CeSar, played by…someone, who find happiness in the end. Although he was just a poor American student studying here in London and she was obviously a rising star, he was determined they would meet. That determination is what propelled the brash young man, hat in hand, to the back door of the theater.

"My lovely Maritana," he said, bowing elaborately, as she stepped into the alleyway. "Don CeSar at your service. May I escort you to your destination, or, perhaps you'd like to stop for a light supper somewhere?"

Startled, Lucinda stepped back. She gave him a coy smile and appraised him with those big, dark eyes that made his heart flutter. "Why, sir, you are quite bold."

"That I am, mistress, and for that I apologize. But from the moment I first laid eyes on you, I knew I must meet you. Please forgive a man made speechless by your beauty and your talent."

She smiled again, a reply on her lips. But before she could speak, they were descended upon by a rather loud woman. A small, dapper man tagged along behind.

"Lucinda! What are you doing loitering back here? You could be assaulted. Or accosted by strange men," the woman said, giving Thomas a nose-turned-up look. "Come, dear. We must get home."

"Yes, Mother. I'm coming." Lucinda quickly turned back to Thomas, and with a secret smile, whispered. "Your boldness, Don CeSar, is somewhat appealing. Meet me tomorrow around 2:00 at the fountain in Trafalgar Square. I shall only have a few minutes, but perhaps then you can tell me your real name." She smiled over her shoulder once more as she disappeared around the corner of the building.

The next afternoon, Thomas, dressed in his best suit, arrived at Trafalgar Square an hour before the appointed time, too anxious to hang around his small apartment any longer. As he strolled around the square, he ruminated on his good fortune. Why, just a couple of years from now, they'd be entering the 1900s. A new century and his future—and the promise of young love—all ahead of him. True, he didn't have much to offer his lovely Lucinda right now, but that wouldn't last long. He knew as soon as his studies were complete and he returned to his beloved Florida, his fortune would be made. Surely Lucinda's snobby mother would see his promise and respond to his complete and utter devotion to her daughter.

He turned back toward the fountain, and stopped as his heart skipped a beat. There she was, her black hair a halo around her bemused face.

"Don CeSar," she held out her hand. He took it in his and bowed elegantly.

"Maritana."

They sat on the edge of the fountain and talked. He told her of his dreams, the plans he had for when he returned to America, and about how he knew there was a fortune to be made in Florida real estate. She spoke of her singing, which she loved, and her belief in true love—how she believed that even in death, true lovers would meet somewhere on a higher plane. She also talked of the strictness of her parents, which she loathed. Her mother was the worst, always keeping tabs on her. Yes, Lucinda knew she had a wonderful career ahead of her, but sometimes she wasn't sure if it was worth giving up the rest of her life.

The couple met at the fountain at the same time every day. And every day they greeted each other with their affectionate nicknames for each other. Each time they had only a few minutes to converse, but each time as he left, Thomas knew he was even deeper in love. He was certain Lucinda felt the same. So, finally, after weeks of clandestine rendezvous, he insisted on calling upon her at home to plead his case to her mother. Big mistake.

Lucinda's mother was a formidable woman, driven by her snobbery and by her devotion to her daughter's career. Nothing, absolutely nothing, was going to get in the way of that, certainly not this lowly American student with no money and no prospects. She banished him from her home and forbade Lucinda to see him.

For weeks, he tried to change the infuriating woman's mind, but she was resolute. Finally, one day, a tearful Lucinda met him at their fountain, where they still rendezvoused daily, exchanging passionate love words and making promises of what their life together would be like. It was impossible, she cried. Her mother would not relent. Defying her would mean turning her back on her family, something she could not do. This, she said, would be their last meeting. He tried to change her mind, but she was as stubborn as her mother. They kissed sweetly, desperately, and parted that day, never again to see each other. At least not in this life.

••••••

Thomas completed his studies in London and returned to America. He set about making his fortune in Florida real estate, just as he had told Lucinda he would. Soon he was a millionaire—someone with money and prospects, someone worthy of his lovely Maritana. For two years, he wrote passionate pleas to Lucinda, telling her of his new situation and begging her to see him. But for two long years, his letters were returned to him unopened.

Then one day in the post, there it was. On creamy white stationery. A letter from the lovely Lucinda, his Maritana. Eagerly he opened it, and elation quickly dissolved to despair.

My beloved CeSar:
Time is infinite. I wait for you by our fountain, to share our timeless love forever.
Our destiny is time.
Your Maritana

Reading the words, he knew in his soul that she was gone, knew that her letter was telling him that they would someday meet on another plane, in a time and a place where their love could finally be free.

Thomas Rowe went on with his life, building his fortune and even taking a wife. But he never forgot the Spanish beauty who had stolen his heart and taken it with her to that higher plane.

Finally, in 1925, Thomas began building his dream hotel, a resort that would stand as a remembrance to his lost love, his Maritana. He first hired famed architect Henry DuPont, but fired him because his design was too plain. Thomas wanted a monument. Something striking. Something people would point to and marvel over.

He hired a new architect and worked closely with him to make his dream come true. Out of the sands of St. Petersburg grew a grand flamingo-pink castle. Mediterranean-style and accented with Moorish bell towers and majestic turrets, the hotel originally was estimated to cost $1.2 million. It ran almost 300 percent over budget.

That mattered not to Rowe, for money should be no object when love is involved. He named his pink castle the Don CeSar. In the center of the courtyard, he built a replica of the London fountain, the rendezvous fountain, where he'd spent so many happy times with the true love of his life. He opened the hotel with an extravagant gala on January 16, 1928. More than fifteen hundred guests enjoyed dining in the fifth-floor restaurant and dancing in the grand ballroom.

"The Don" quickly became the hot spot for the Roaring Twenties in-crowd, with celebrity guests such as Al Capone, Tallulah Bankhead, and Clarence Darrow making it a favorite party place. F. Scott Fitzgerald was so taken with the resort that he wrote about it in many of his books, once referring to it as a "hotel in an island wilderness." It was, it seems, a favorite dry-out place for the often soused Zelda.

Rowe loved the hotel that love had built, and for the next twelve years he rarely left it. With a suite on the fifth floor, he could often be seen sporting a Panama hat as he made his rounds, greeting guests and engaging them in conversation, always ending with an order to just let the staff know if they needed anything at all.

The Don CeSar reigned as a vacation hot spot until 1940, when Rowe suddenly collapsed in the hotel's ornate lobby. Refusing hospitalization, he was carried to his room, where medical care was brought to him. Realizing that his time was close, the childless Rowe insisted that his will be amended to leave the Don CeSar to his staff, the people he believed could best carry on his dream.

Unfortunately, the nurses there refused to sign as witnesses, believing Rowe incapable of making such a monumental decision. The Don went to Rowe's estranged wife, who let it fall to disrepair. After the attack on Pearl Harbor on December 7, 1941, its operations suffered the effects of cancellations, rotating supplies, and loss of employees as people were drafted into the military. In 1942, it was sold to the U.S. Army for just $450,000. It was turned into a convalescent center for battle-fatigued World War II airmen. After the war, the government stripped it and used it as a regional office, but when, in 1967, needed repairs proved too costly, it was abandoned.

The once immaculate hotel languished on the sands of St. Petersburg beach. Efforts to raze it were met with stiff opposition by residents. It soon became a graffiti-covered eyesore, until the early 1970s, when St. Petersburg revitalization discovered the Don CeSar. And it was then that things got strange.

When renovations began, workers began reporting a distinguished silver-haired man, wearing a tailored suit with one of those starched old-timey collars, hanging around the work site. He never interfered, they said. He simply watched their progress as they sweated in the Florida sun. They asked management about the guy, wondering if he had authorization to be there, but no one seemed to know who he was.

It's not certain who finally put two and two together and figured out that the spirit of Thomas Rowe had returned, perhaps to take delight in the fact that his hotel was being restored to its former glory. Once renovations were complete, he began appearing in the lobby, Panama hat perched on his silver hair, suit and tie in immaculate condition, tending, it seems, to his old duties as host. There are even reports that he has interacted with his guests, inquiring about the weather, the enjoyment of their stay, and their satisfaction with the amenities, always urging them to consult the staff if they needed anything at all. By all accounts, he is courtly and kindly, and though his sudden disappearing act surely gives a start, no one ever reports being frightened.

The story doesn't end there. Since the 1980s, there have been numerous reports of a dark-haired beauty who frequents the Don CeSar. Wearing clothes of another era, she has a tumble of ebony hair and a strikingly lovely face that often wears an expression of bemusement. In the first years of her appearance, she was seen sitting at the hotel fountain, sometimes alone, sometimes with the kindly man sitting next to her. He would hold her hand and smile into her eyes, occasionally brushing her lips with a tender kiss. Guests drifting by sometimes mentioned hearing a whispering of "Maritana" or "Don CeSar."

Today, the Don CeSar once again reigns as a pretty pink playground for the rich and famous, with celebrities as diverse as Britney Spears and Bill Clinton coming here to party. Now called the Don CeSar Beach Resort and Spa, Rowe's hotel sports the AAA Four-Diamond Maritana Grille, a second swimming pool with surrounding tropical gardens, and a full-service spa—four thousand square feet of additional space.

Despite all these "improvements," there has been one tragic loss. During recent renovations, the rendezvous fountain was done away with, putting a crimp in the couples' trysting. Ah, but love will overcome.

Today, the couple is sometimes spotted down by the beach, holding hands, engrossed in each other. When guests spot them strolling together, they profess a need to avoid the lovers, not from fear, but rather from respect for a love that has found freedom on a higher plane.

the line

He flinched as a small projectile flew over his head, making an almost inaudible hiss as it continued its course past his left ear and landed on the ground by his foot. His first thought was dismay—he had always pictured his death occurring when he was surrounded by his comrades, nobly defending the company colors or leading a gallant charge that would ultimately prove to be the turning point for the Confederacy.

Instead, here he was, half-naked, rinsing out his drawers in a creek, not even where he was supposed to be. His friends were building defenses up on the hill. They had all agreed to take turns bathing and washing down at the stream since it had been nearly a month since their last opportunity.

The second fatal shell never came, and the private opened his eyes to look at the bullet that had missed him by a whisker. He rolled it over with his toe. It was a big, green pecan, still in its protective outer covering. He looked up to see that the tree towering over him was indeed a pecan tree. The creek was thickly bordered by trees of all types: redbuds with their distinctive heart-shaped leaves, mimosas with lacy fronds barely stirring in the thick heat of late June, crooked little dogwoods, and tall arrow-straight pines.

He picked his way carefully through the water, headed for a rock that sat in the sun. Spreading his pants out to dry, he splashed again to the bank. He watched the water flowing for a few minutes, idly wondering if the stream might eventually join up to the creek that ran by his mother's house in Athens, Georgia. A fierce longing, quickly squashed, rose up in him: to be that stick, floating harmlessly downstream, toward someplace that was always quiet and safe—a place where a falling pecan didn't sound like death coming down.

He lay back, using his arms for a pillow, and thought about writing Delia about being scared by that pecan. She'd laugh, picturing him with his britches in his hands, crouching, trying to get ready to meet his maker. Maybe the sergeant would have some more paper and envelopes this afternoon. The supply train was supposed to have been through here by now, but Private William Beckman knew better than to count on that.

He could count on a few more minutes of peace, right here by this creek, and he intended to enjoy it. The sky was an old, faded, worn-out blue, like it was already tired of summer. But the branches and leaves that crisscrossed his field of vision were bright, defiant green. Wisteria twined and twisted around every available support, a riot of exuberant growth, and late-blooming honeysuckle tinged the air with faint sweetness.

William reached to scratch absently at a chigger bite on his chest. The birds called to one another beneath the sheltering arms of the trees, but their calls didn't seem too urgent. The laziness of late June seemed to affect every living thing along the winding path of the stream. A lizard sunned itself next to William's pants, blinking languidly. A couple of squirrels chased each other and then stopped suddenly to chatter. William listened to the soothing babble of the water over the rocks and let his eyes close. His imagination drifted back to a June day three years ago, when he was fifteen and sitting on another creek bank with Delia.

He felt a shadow fall over him, blocking the shade-dappled light, and sat up with a start.

The man standing over him was about his age, holding a rifle loosely in one hand and a canteen dangling by its strap in the other. His uniform cap was stuffed roughly into the back pocket of his pants, which were precariously secured above his hips by a belt cinched tight. The tunic coat that hung open, unbuttoned in the heat, was blue.

"Howdy," William said cautiously, gently patting the ground behind him for his rifle and cursing himself for not keeping it close at hand.

"Howdy," the soldier replied. "You seen anybody from the Twenty-seventh?"

"Who?"

"Ohio Infantry. The Twenty-seventh. I went out after a wild turkey and got turned around. I know they're right close."

"Naah, haven't seen 'em." William scratched his head and then flicked a few lice from under his fingernail. "I reckon they're upstream a bit."

The tired soldier turned and trudged away. A few yards away, he turned back. "Say, what division're you from?"

William's mind scrambled to latch onto a number that might make sense. "Hunnerd an' twenny-first," he blurted.

The man nodded and waved. "See ya."

William looked at his pants, still drying on the rock in the middle of the stream. His shirt hung on a bush just out of sight. The soldier had mistaken him for one of his own, and that made a second brush with death in the space of an hour, he thought. Delia would really like this letter.

A figure came crashing through the undergrowth, from the high ground where William had left the men of his company earlier. It was John Coffee, who lobbed a pinecone at William's reclining form.

"You gonna take all day, Smelly?"

"You kin call yerself Smelly, now. I've had a bath, and I'm now fit to spend an evening in the finest company." William stood and stretched.

"You'll have to settle fer us old boys, I'm afraid."

"Saw a bluecoat jes' now."

"What? And didn't take 'im prisoner?"

"I was nearly naked. He went thataway if you wanna go after 'im." William pointed upstream.

"I'll jest have myself a bath instead."

"Y'all finish them fortifications?"

"We left you about a mile or so to dig."

"Hope we'll stay in 'em longer than the last ones."

John Coffee stripped down and waded out into the water. "It seems a shame to dig 'em 'n' then leave 'em," he agreed. He looked into the current. "If I jest had my fishin' pole, we'd have ourselves one heck of a dinner," he remarked.

William gathered his clothes and slipped them on. After refilling his canteen, he turned to trudge up the hill.

●●●●●●

"Anybody want any more Cheetos?" The red-haired woman rattled the bag in vain. No one was in earshot. She stuffed the bag into the wicker picnic basket and stood up. She saw a glimpse of something gray through the trees near the creek and strolled in that direction, noting the signs of wildlife all around her. Squirrels ran and chattered through the trees, chipmunks scurried between the rocks on the banks, and birds flitted everywhere beneath the lofty canopy of pines, oaks, and old pecan trees.

"Jim?" she called. Every time she got near, they slipped off again. Really, it was a bit too hot to play hide-and-seek.

"What?" He was right behind her, holding a map. Josh was right behind him, clutching the bag of Cheetos she had just packed away in the picnic basket.

Sherry looked at her husband blankly.

"I thought I saw you over there." She pointed up a little rise.

"No, but let's go up that way. I think that's where the entrenchments were."

She shrugged and followed him, their son falling into line behind her.

"The bridge that was here was burned," Jim said over his shoulder. "That one there," he gestured to the right, "was built a little after the war. Both armies burned a lot of bridges." He grinned. "But if I were an infantryman in the summer of 1864, I wouldn't mind wading through a creek every now and then."

"Can I go wading in the creek, Mom?" At the prospect of getting in the water, Josh showed more enthusiasm than she'd seen from him in the three days they'd spent touring Civil War battle sites.

"It's a private creek, honey. Maybe we'll find a motel with a pool, and you can swim then." The boy dropped back, discouraged.

A booming sound made all three jerk to a stop, startled. Jim said with a laugh. "Tires on the old timbers of that bridge sound like cannon, don't they?"

"I think that's poison ivy, Jim, isn't it?" She pointed to a suspicious-looking plant. "Are these trenches very far away?"

He stopped walking. "They must've been around here somewhere." A horde of gnats rose up around him like a malevolent cloud. He swatted in vain. "The battle of Ruff's Mill was exactly 131 years and one day ago. The Ohio boys just put on their bayonets and swarmed over the top of the trenches. 'Course, the Rebels were fighting pretty hard. Lots of 'em had family near here."

Sherry shuddered. "I'm ready to go," she said firmly. "Take me back to the twentieth century."

As they drove toward the center of Smyrna, Sherry noticed red-and-white signs sprouting in a number of yards, like a crop of exotic mushrooms.

"Save Our Covered Bridge," she read curiously. "I wonder what that's all about?"

Josh never looked up from his comic book. Jim, although he drove the car, was still lost in the battle of Ruff's Mill. "Um," was all he said, and Sherry began to look for a motel with a pool as they entered the more populated area of the Atlanta suburb.

●●●●●

It was dark before the sergeant told the men to quit digging. William gladly threw his shovel aside and sat down, dangling his feet over the edge of the trench.

"Pretty big," he commented. "Room for a lot more than our regiment."

"I reckon we'll have some company." John Coffee had come back from the stream refreshed, but now they were all dog-tired. "I don't think we were diggin' jest fer us."

"Let's go, boys."

William and his fellow soldiers looked up in surprise.

"Where we goin', Sarge?"

"Back to Kennesaw. Them's my orders."

They looked at each other in amazement. "All that work an' we're gonna leave now?" No one rose to their feet.

"Come on." The sergeant was just as tired. "We got to get there by midnight."

One by one, the men straggled up to form an uneven line. Swearing and muttering, they began the eight-mile hike back to Kennesaw Mountain and the trenches they had dug there last week.

"I 'spect we'll see these ditches again," John told William. "I'd like to think so, anyway. It'd be nice to think somebody had a plan that made sense."

John, William, and all the men of their regiment felt at home in the trenches below Kennesaw Mountain. They could work their way half-crouched through the maze of ditches and get almost anywhere up and down the line. The secret was not to stand up straight. Sometimes a new soldier would forget, and his head appearing above the trench would prove too tempting a target for the Union sharpshooters. Then his fate depended on luck, or the skill of the soldier a few hundred yards away.

Bullets whined and moaned across the tops of the trenches all day. Confederate soldiers returned the fire. The constant noise was something every soldier adjusted to. Sometimes one side or the other would yell taunts and insults, provoking an extra flurry of bullets or even a rock or two, hurled by an angry soldier.

William made his way through the trenches clutching a true prize. He'd traded his tobacco ration for two sheets of paper and an envelope. When he reached the section of fortifications he'd been calling home, he raised his hand above his head.

"Look what I got, John," he called, waving the paper triumphantly. A bullet whined overhead, but he ignored it. "Today's my lucky day. As soon as she gets this letter from me, Delia will sit right down and write me back, you wait and see."

John pulled William's hand down roughly. "You idiot," he said. "Ain't you been here long enough to learn anything?"

Neatly piercing the two sheets of stationery was a bullet hole.

William stared at it in surprise. "I guess today really is my lucky day," he said. "Mebbe I've got nine lives, like a cat."

John shoved him lightly. "If that stationery don't make Delia write back, nothin' will." He sat back down on an overturned bucket to gnaw reflectively on a piece of hardtack. William smoothed out the paper and began to write.

"I heard we're goin' South again," John interrupted him.

"Mebbe that's what we dug them ditches for," William muttered, chewing on his pen and carefully considering his words. "My dearest Delia" sounded a little too serious, but she ought to know by now that his feelings for her were pretty strong.

"If we don't hold this next line, some people say the Union army's gonna overrun all of Georgia." John watched William carefully. His family had gone west to his uncle's farm in Alabama, but he knew William's mother and sweetheart were still ensconced in Athens.

"Uh-huh." Should he start off by saying how much he missed her, or jump directly into his adventures over the past few days?

"That creek we was at, it's called Nickajack Creek. It's jest fifteen miles from Atlanta."

William looked up, startled. "We're that close to Atlanta?"

John nodded, switching a soggy chunk of hardtack from one side of his jaw to the other.

"Atlanta's not sixty-five miles from home."

John nodded once more as William bent over the page again. Now he had some real news to write. He didn't expect that Delia's father, who ran Athens' best hotel, would leave town. But maybe he would consider sending Delia and her mother and sisters out of harm's way. He wrote furiously for a few minutes and then slowed down as he began to recount his encounter at Nickajack Creek and explain the hole in the stationery.

He stopped altogether as he debated how to close the letter. Love? Deepest affection? That sounded about right. But it needed something else. The pauses between the bullets singing overhead began to grow longer and longer, and William realized the sun was setting. Maybe he should tell her that he was fighting for her. That was it.

"As I fight to hold that crucial line above Atlanta, I shall hold thoughts of you close to my heart. With deepest affection, I remain your devoted William."

He stretched, careful not to extend his limbs above the top of the entrenchment.

"What's for supper?" he asked John cheerfully. "Can we light a fire tonight or not?"

••••••

"Concord Village was established nearly two hundred years ago." The woman spoke in the deep drawl of a native Georgian. "It's a practically perfect example of the villages typical during the Civil War."

"I can't believe we're so close to Atlanta." The journalist looked around at the thickly wooded landscape and the creek that murmured gently through the trees. "It's almost like being in another century."

Nancy nodded. "We want to preserve that feeling," she said. "The creek was named after a Cherokee Indian chief, Chief Nickajack. There are some Indian burial grounds nearby and some graves from some early white settlers, too."

"Cobb County started trying to put the highway through here in 1985, is that right?" The reporter scribbled in her notebook.

"Yes, and the Army Corps of Engineers has granted them a wetlands permit so they can start construction. But the highway will probably destroy the ruins of the old woolen mill, which is that way," she pointed east. "It will definitely ruin this location as a recreational area, and the bridge probably won't survive the blasting they'll have to do in order to build the freeway."

"I saw some people here earlier, before you got here. I tried to stop them, to interview them about their opinion on the construction, but I guess they didn't hear me call."

Nancy shrugged. Tourists were not uncommon here.

"I think I have all I need. Thanks for your help." They turned and began to walk back to the parking area at Ruff's Gristmill. She consulted her notes. "Your group's called Protect Endangered Areas of Cobb's History, right?"

"That's right. P-E-A-C-H. Will you send me a copy of the article when it comes out?"

"I'd be glad to." They shook hands, and the reporter drove off with a little wave.

••••••

It was the Fourth of July, and William couldn't help but feel a twinge of nostalgia for the celebrations he'd witnessed before the war. Now, he supposed, the Confederacy would celebrate something like it, but he wished sometimes that it had never come down to all this. Here he was again, bent over and hustling up and down the ditches, shooting and getting shot at.

They had abandoned the fortifications at the base of Kennesaw Mountain a day or two ago. The Federal troops had followed close behind. The last few days had been a confusion of marches and shouting and shooting. William wished that he and his friends had dug the trenches a little deeper, but they could improve upon them. It was only a little harder to dig now that there was constant fire overhead.

Suddenly the frequency of the firing increased dramatically. Somewhere, William heard an officer yelling.

"They're coming over the top, men! Hold your ground!"

William looked around to see John crouching next to him, his face pinched and grim. "Gotta hold this line, John," William grunted. "Can't let 'em get by."

They took turns cautiously peering over the embankment and firing, then falling back into the trench to reload. Each time William looked over the brink, a wall of smoke and fury seemed to be edging closer. He couldn't make out any individual soldiers, just indistinct blurs, first one hundred yards off, then fifty, now ten.

"Fix bayonets!" An officer screeched, a clear note of panic.

William and John had abandoned their bayonets months ago. They had large hunting knives, though, and had them loosely tucked into their belts.

Both soldiers had fought before. They and about half of their regiment survived the battle at Missionary Ridge and a number of small skirmishes. For William, the memory was dreamy and disconnected, an incoherent roar of artillery, the sharp smell of gunpowder, masked by a cloud of smoke. He remembered men falling on either side, but the most painful memory was the agonized screams of the horses when they were hit. That seemed the greatest injustice of all. The poor dumb animals, led into this chaos against their wills, without even the comfort of knowing that their death served a higher purpose.

As William stuck his head above the trench, a figure resolved itself out of the smoke. To William, crouched in the trench, the soldier in blue seemed impossibly large and too close to shoot.

With a shout, John leapt up and whacked the Union soldier across the side of the head with his rifle butt. When he fell, John quickly finished him with a neat slice across the neck. William watched, fascinated and sickened, as the blood spurted out of the soldier's throat. The man had shaved that morning and nicked himself on the chin, right next to a deep dimple.

William's hand reached involuntarily to his own chin, hidden by a beard. He'd grown the beard to hide a boyish dimple just like the Union soldier's.

"William!" John kicked him, hard. "Shoot!"

He snapped out of his reverie and loaded his gun. With mechanical precision, they shot and stabbed at the men coming at them for what seemed like hours before they heard a bugle sound.

"That's retreat," John shouted. "Let's go!"

"I can't leave," William said. "I promised Delia I'd stay."

"You're crazy!" John pulled at William's belt, hauling him backwards. "We can hold the line back here. Come on!"

William resisted for just a moment, then felt John go limp. "John?"

He shook his friend.

"John?"

The battle roared around him, the sound now louder and more immediate. Looking around, William saw they were all alone in the trench—except for the dead men. And some vaguely blue shapes that were swirling around in the smoke to his left.

William tossed John over his shoulder and climbed awkwardly out of the trench. He staggered a few hundred yards before he saw an officer directing the retreat.

"John," he gasped. "He's hurt."

"There's a house over there, about a half-mile away. Take him there. The doctors'll see to him." He clapped William on the shoulder. "Good man. Anybody left in the entrenchment?"

William shook his head and shuffled off in the direction he'd been told. John lay still across his back, but William didn't think about what that meant. He wanted to get John somewhere safe and get back to the line. Any other thoughts were meaningless.

Men were piled up on the porch of the big house like firewood. Someone yelled at William to lay John down outside, but William walked right into the frenzy that filled the house. He found a man with bloodstained hands and shook him by the shoulders.

"This is John," he shouted.

"I can hear you, son." The surgeon spoke kindly.

"Take care of him. I've got to get back to the line."

The man held out his arms and William gently passed his friend over. He squeezed John's hand and turned to leave.

••••••

Nancy was tired. She had spent the day in court, fighting with county officials and lawyers about the Concord Historical District. The battle seemed endless, without respite, one petty legal struggle following upon the heels of another.

She turned left onto Spring Road, past the big mall with its satellites of Taco Bell, KFC, and Hardees. Every store was draped with a big, brightly colored plastic banner declaring the virtues of the products inside. The traffic, the signs, the condensed litter of an affluent, late-twentieth century society seemed to scream at her that to resist the future was impossible. She snapped off the radio, cutting off a litany of snarled traffic in midstream. There—one manifestation of progress was eliminated.

A few blocks down Spring Road the buildings were spaced a little farther apart. A little more green surrounded the concrete, although it was still dominated by offices, businesses, and stores. Two miles away from the mall, the office buildings disappeared, replaced by single-story bungalows built at the century's midpoint. Solid, practical houses with aluminum awnings, sensible lawns, and American cars in the driveways. The trees along Spring Road at this point were tall, embracing the sky with wide-spread branches. They were planted fifty years ago or more by the same down-to-earth people who built and bought the bungalows. A wide strip of lawn bordered the road, was briefly interrupted by a sidewalk, and then continued to the doorsteps of the houses.

Nancy could breathe more easily now, and she rolled down her window to take advantage of the breeze that only began to stir about seven o'clock on a midsummer evening in Georgia. It was not a cool breeze by any means, but it managed to convey a promise of relief from the sultry air, a promise that might or might not be kept.

Spring Road became Concord Road at a sharp bend, and the four lanes narrowed into two. Trees crowded even more closely around the road now, and the houses, set farther back, looked like they had been there before the road was paved. At last the road began to slope gently down toward the creek, and Nancy pulled aside to let a stream of cars heading back toward town pass through the one-lane bridge.

She glanced to the left, and her heart skipped. Up on the hill were row after row of ragged trenches, the dirt thrown carelessly to one side. The trees she knew as veritable old giants were mere saplings, overshadowed by other trees she'd never seen. Long rifle barrels protruded from the trenches, each one marked by a puff of smoke as it fired.

Approaching the trenches were rough lines of men in Union blue. As she watched, horrified, they halted to pull long pieces from their pack that glinted evilly in the sunlight: bayonets. They fixed the weapons on the ends of their guns and advanced into the little puffs of smoke. Some fell. More came forward to take their places. They scrambled over the edge of the trenches, and Nancy shuddered, imagining the carnage taking place as the battle moved into hand-to-hand combat. She heard the cannon roar and felt her skin crawl with a chilling premonition of danger. She saw a figure on a horse ride across the battle line, exhorting his troops, heedless of the risk to himself. And as she watched him, clearly encouraging them to hold their position, she felt as if he were talking to her. She felt a sense of protection—of being watched.

The cannon roared again, and the sound of a car horn made her tear her eyes away from the compelling, unnerving battle scene. It wasn't a cannon at all. It was the last car from the opposite direction, its tires thundering across the bridge. As she swung out into the road, she glanced up to the left again. The trees were familiar, the fortifications long overgrown, the men in gray and blue long at peace. Or most of them, anyway.

••••••

William walked slowly down the road to the creekbed. The guns still thundered around him, but they sounded strangely distant. Men were streaming past him heading south, and some men on horseback stopped to talk to him, gesturing widely. He only shook his head and walked, step by step, north to the edge of Nickajack Creek.

There were a few stones piled up, remnants of the bridge that had stood there before someone—Confederate or Federal, William didn't know—had decided the bridge made it too easy for armies to move back and forth across the creek. William sat down on the stones and methodically began to load his gun.

"This is the line, Delia," he whispered. "This is the line I will hold."

In front of him, across the creek, stood a line of soldiers in blue. At a shouted command, they began to cross the creek, holding their guns and ammunition above their waist to avoid the splashing water.

William began to shoot left to right. He'd shoot one, and then carefully reload and shoot the next. He didn't know how many he'd shot before he felt something strike him hard in the chest. As he spun down, off the pile of rocks and toward the ground, he noticed the mimosa tree above him was in bloom. The vivid pink blossoms, looking like absurdly painted miniature feather dusters, spiraled down toward his face. Or maybe he was spiraling up toward them. The sky became bright, then white.

••••••

Calvin Phillips walked slowly down his driveway to fetch the newspaper. It was almost dark, and there might be a hint of a breeze off the creek to cool him off. He breathed deeply, noticing a faint scent from the late-blooming honeysuckle that wound itself around the trees by the road. The smell was nearly overpowered by the smell of exhaust from the cars passing to and from Smyrna. But the traffic was practically nonexistent now, at 8:30 on a July evening. The narrow Concord Road wound its way down to Nickajack Creek and the single-lane covered bridge that crossed it.

Calvin peered through the shadows at the mouth of the bridge. Someone was there, standing motionless at the entrance. Calvin moved a little closer to warn the man that sometimes cars came through the bridge at high speed and that he should move to one side before he was struck.

"Hey!" he shouted.

The figure did not move.

Calvin walked a little closer, then shook his head in disbelief. The forage cap with the black leather brim. The tunic buttoned smartly up the middle. The round canteen on a long leather strap. The long-barreled rifle. It was unmistakably an infantryman from the Confederate Army.

"Hey!"

Still the man did not budge.

"What do you want?" Calvin was now distinctly uneasy, but determined to make a stand here, practically at the foot of his own driveway.

The soldier's lips were moving. Calvin moved a little closer.

"This is the line, Delia." The whisper was so faint it barely carried above the song of water over stones in Nickajack Creek. "This is the line I will hold."

the fisherman of lake bistineau

The air looked yellow and moist; it smelled sweet in the early morning as Joseph Chantalle pulled a rasher of fish from the muddy bottom of Lake Bistineau. The lake looked smoked. The sinking moon was green and looked like it was hanging from a string, like a child's toy.

Joseph was extremely tall and, as his mother always said, he had a good bone structure. But he'd always been thin and out of joint, the sort of boy that other boys liked to poke with a stick, like a dead cat. But Joseph was also the best of little boys. He loved his mother and father very much, he did his chores on time, and he was very protective of his little sister.

So every morning Joseph expected to smell his mother's bacon, or see his father from his bedroom window walking out in the early morning moonlight to milk the cows, or even hear his little sister fussing over her dolls in the room next door. But every morning Joseph was disappointed.

Instead of hearing the warm sounds of family, Joseph would wake before dawn, splash cold water on his face, and stare at his antique and ghostly image in the mirror. He felt as miserable as a cow.

"Who are you," he'd ask the mirror, "cat got your tongue, or what?" He began to think that his face was looking thinner and thinner, and he thought it would be time to get a haircut soon. Even his fingernails were longer than he'd ever remembered, and he worried that his mother wouldn't be able to clip them for him while he sat on the edge of the bed listening to her tell ghost stories.

Joseph loved stories about dark, scary, abandoned places, about old mills where ghosts would scare exploring children. And even though Joseph's mother had led him to believe that Lake Bistineau was haunted, he still loved to fish every day, often alone.

Joseph loved Lake Bistineau and he loved Louisiana. His father had taught him that of all the places in the world, Louisiana was the one place where everyone wanted to be. He'd told him tales about the British, the French, and American armies fighting over the territories. Louisiana was a mysterious place, his father told him, and mysterious places were hard to come by these days.

This made it even harder for Joseph to understand why his entire family had packed up in a moving van and left him behind. He had run after them screaming as loud as he could, but it had been as if the family could no longer see or hear him. And Joseph had sobbed for days, just as any abandoned boy would.

His world was no bigger than the end of the road leading to the house, Lake Bistineau, and the reaches of farm land where his family had kept cows for decades. He had been to Acadia once to see a picture show, but Joseph lived in a small world, unable to imagine where his entire family could have made off to. At night, after he'd come home from fishing, Joseph would bury his head in his dusty pillow and sob until it felt like his ribs would come rattling apart.

As Joseph slopped dead catfish into a plastic sand pail, he heard the soft sputter of a trawling motor. His world was covered in moss and haze, a world of green stuff, and he rarely saw other humans. When he did it was never pleasant. Someone would see him from a distance, wince or shudder, and take off running.

A fisherman and his son pulled up shore side, but before they could cut the engine, they spotted the shred of a boy in rotted and molding coveralls holding up a string of fish carcasses. Joseph looked so entirely dead, but the man and his son never even considered it a prank or a Halloween costume. They opened their mouths to scream, but the screams came out hollow, and they pushed away from the shore, the sacrilege called Joseph waving his terrible wave.

Joseph wanted something, but he didn't know what it was. He wanted his family back, of that he was certain. He wanted to go to school and play with the other children. He wanted to feel like someone loved him. But there was more that he wanted, he just couldn't figure out what it was. Dark matter oozed from his fishy lips each time he tried to speak to a passerby, and sometimes it seemed people stared right through him. He thought he could smell the earth rotting around him. His whole body was coming apart, like the fragile, liquid bones of a catfish.

Joseph shrugged off the encounter and turned back for the long walk through the piney woods to his family's farm. The trail through Shooter's Gap was nearly impassable with kudzu this time of year, but Joseph paid no mind, his sodden boots seeming to glide right through the dark green vines. His father had told him that eventually kudzu would cover the earth, that people would live in houses made entirely of kudzu. But Joseph was always afraid of snakes hiding out in the deep overgrowth of green leaves.

When he stepped out into Wren's Hollow, the sun was high in the sky, making Joseph sweat until he felt slimy, like he hadn't bathed in months. A young doe came bounding out of the woods and stopped to look at Joseph as if she wanted a nuzzle.

"Hey there, little girl," he said, but the doe bounded right past him like nothing terrible had just tried to rub her milky skin.

"I'm nothin' but an empty voice," he thought. "Even the kindest of animals act like I'm not here."

Joseph had no idea what he'd do with the rest of his day; he never did. It was too hot to fish, and he was tired of leafing through his old comics. The stories never changed, and the paper was starting to yellow and crumble. Sometimes he'd ride his bicycle through the house, crashing from room to room because he knew it never mattered, that he'd never get in trouble. And some days he'd just lounge around in the barn, throwing rocks at rats.

Joseph approached the long dirt road that led to his family homestead. He looked straight into the sun and thought, much as he did every day, that the sun looked like a hole in the sky. I could slip right through that hole, he thought. But Joseph didn't know that the boredom of his daily routine was about to change forever.

Approaching the farm house where he was raised, the yard where his daddy had first taught him to play catch, and the front porch where he'd sat with his folks drinking lemonade, Joseph noticed a yellow car had pulled up with what looked like a family. "What's this mess," he thought. Joseph was afraid to approach any closer because he'd become accustomed to negative responses from strangers. But before he had a chance to slip into some bushes, a large black dog came loping down the road, barking in his direction. Joseph began backpedaling and slipped and fell backwards, afraid he was about to be mauled by the beast. But the dog just hovered over him, drooling and looking about aimlessly like Joseph was there but not there.

"Don't worry, he won't bite," Joseph heard from the softest voice ever.

Looking up into the glaring sun, Joseph saw a young girl in a blue dress with white lace and a head full of brown ringlets. He couldn't remember the last time he'd seen anything so pretty, and she reminded him of his little sister.

The little girl leaned over toward Joseph and held her hand out to help him up.

"Don't worry," she said again, "It's OK. Everything will be OK."

Joseph stood up and smiled down at the little girl. He looked as if this was the happiest day of his life. It was the first time anyone had spoken to him in years it seemed.

"Whatcha doing here?" the girl asked. "I'm Penelope." But Joseph couldn't answer back; his mouth just wouldn't work anymore. It seemed to him that he'd never connect again with another person. He'd watched his mother and father pack up their car, driving off with tears on their cheeks while he'd chased them down the red dirt road screaming that he was still there. Everyone he knew and loved had moved on and left him. There were no more cows in the barn, the paint on the house was flecked and chipping, and everything else was brittle and rusting. Joseph opened his mouth again to speak to the girl, but he could only mouth the words. She couldn't hear or understand him. "This is the saddest I've ever been," he thought, collapsing on his rear end, staring up at the girl while tears welled up in his drying sockets.

"We're moving into this house," Penelope said, "you can be my new friend."

Joseph reached up to clasp her outstretched hand as she said, "Come on, let's go exploring."

Joseph pulled himself up in a cloud of dust. Penelope thought he smelled like a cardboard box and his hand felt like mush, but she was too kind to tell him. Since her own little brother had died, Penelope knew about sad and empty children who couldn't find their way back home. She knew about ghosts and how to see them. She wasn't afraid. They were too sad to ignore.

Joseph thought Penelope smelled like clean laundry, and she made him feel warmer than he had in weeks. She reminded him of soup and hot bread. She reminded him of his mamma. Penelope led Joseph slowly back down the long road, away from the house. "Let's get you back home," Penelope said, which puzzled Joseph who thought he already was home. But he allowed himself to be led away by this passive, sweet presence. She was so warm and comforting, Joseph would have let the girl lead him anywhere.

Joseph and Penelope walked for what seemed like hours, past moss covered oak trees, past green fields with the grazing cows Joseph always loved. This was Joseph's story, walking this road. He had a vegetal taste in his mouth and a loud cicada-like buzzing swarmed his ears, but Joseph began thinking about walking down this road holding his mother's hand. He thought of the old days as he clung tightly to Penelope's hand. It felt to him that it was time to go to bed; his body felt like something seeping out of the world. He felt like water, like air.

Penelope led Joseph farther and farther down the country road than he could ever remember walking. But Joseph didn't worry about getting back to the house ever again. He felt too much at home with this girl. Finally, Penelope stopped walking, and Joseph saw off to one side of the road a lovely hill of green grass. Over the entry to the gate leading to the hill was a sign that read: Loving Family Cemetery, Home for the Lost, Home for the Wayfaring Soul.

Penelope opened the gate and gently pushed Joseph through. No sooner had Joseph entered the gates than he could feel something warm cover his entire body.

"Goodbye, little boy," Penelope said.

a ship aflame

"Aye. It's true. She burned as purty as can be." The toothless old salt was drunk again. He came in practically every night and drank himself into a stupor, mumbling to himself and cackling away like he'd lost his mind. Maybe he had, thought Jon, the bartender. After all, he was eighty if he was a day. Maybe he was senile.

"Bartender! Another rum!" The old man shouted.

Jon skirted the bar and walked to the table.

"Old man, you've had enough. Look around. The place is empty. It's time for you to be off to your bed."

"Off to me bed? Nay, son. Me bed is the last place I need to be. Me bed is when they come, hair all aflame, eyes glowing with accusation. They're all there. All, down to the last child. Nay, nay. Not me bed."

Jon could feel the old man's fear. It was a palpable thing that permeated the air around him. Curious, Jon sat. Serving the man night after night, he had caught snippets of his mumblings. There was a story here, he knew. And he wanted to hear that story.

"What are you prattling on about? Who is it you think visits you in your bed? Are you daft or just drunk?"

The old man raised his head and fixed Jon in his gaze. After a second or two, he nodded. "Aye, you want the story, don't ye lad? Well, bring us a rum and settle down. I'll tell you the whole sorry tale."

The rum was poured and Jon settled into the chair across the table. "OK, old man. Tell me your tale."

The old man seemed lost deep in thought for some time, and Jon was beginning to think he'd fallen asleep, when finally he began to speak.

"It happened many years ago. Aye, I was just a young lad of fifteen when I signed on as cabin boy. The captain, he was a cruel man and a greedy one. I had seen him steal from passengers many times. Ahh, but this time...

"It was back in 1710. We sailed from England with a ship load of passengers. German Palatines, they were. Protestants who were coming to New Bern, looking for a new life. Aye, a life of freedom. A life free from the persecution they'd faced for so long.

"I learned this from one of the passengers, a lad a lot like meself. We got on pretty well and became friends during the voyage across the Atlantic. It was his first time at sea, and he was afeered of the tossing of the ship. Thought we were going to overturn at any moment. I was able to help him see that the ship was seaworthy. To ease his mind some."

The old man paused for a sip of rum, his thoughts lost to years gone by.

"There was about forty people—nine families on board. During the voyage, we—the crew, I mean—believed them to be poor people, like ourselves. They dressed poorly. Their possessions didn't seem to be of much worth. Their passage was paid in full, aye, but we thought that must be all they had. They said they were meeting relatives in New Bern who would help them get a start here. We believed them.

"The passage across was uneventful. We had some bad weather, true enough, but nothing to be afeered of. It was the middle of the summer, so for the most part, the waters were calm, while there was enough wind to keep the sails full. I taught young Luka to fish from the bow and, on nights when the moon was full, we sat on deck talking and listening to the sea. Many times sea creatures would come alongside—porpoises, turtles, devil rays. The lad, who had never seen such, was always excited when something like that happened.

"He was close with his family and that was something I remember envying. My own family was naught. Me ma was a woman of loose morals, understand? Never knew who me pa was. I left ma when I was just thirteen years. Bummed around until I signed on me first ship. Luka's family was kind to me during that passage. They made me homesick for something I never had."

The old man looked Jon in the eye. The bartender knew that the point of the story was getting close.

"As I said, everything went fine with the passage. It took us two months to get across the ocean. But finally, we had arrived. We were off the coast of North Carolina, at the mouth of the Neuse River, not far from here. It was closing on late afternoon, but we could've easily made port. The passengers were excited, as you might guess. Months cramped up on the ship and finally, they were about to reach their destination. Their excitement, I guess, was what sealed their fate.

"Anticipating their arrival and in a hurry to get off the ship, the families began bringing all their belongings on deck. We were all shocked to see that, far from being the poor people we thought, they were actually quite rich. We saw gold and silver. There were pouches of jewels. All types of finery. All of it had been below decks all this time, and we never knew.

"I saw the captain eyeing it all, and I was worried. I tried to warn Luka and his family, but it was really too late. The goods had been seen. After an hour or so, the captain gathered the families and told them we weren't going to be able to make port that night. Don't remember now what excuse he gave, but he jollied them all, telling them it was just one more night. One more night aboard ship, and bright and early the next morning they'd be on dry land. They were disappointed, but understanding. They took everything back down below and soon after nightfall they all went to bed.

"Late that night, I was asleep in the crew's quarters when ol' Sam, one of the mates, grabbed me by the arm and hauled me out of me rack. I kept asking what was happening, but he never said. He just kept pushing me ahead. We got into one of the lifeboats. The others were all manned by other crew. Again and again, I asked what was going on. Nobody told me. I didn't know!

"Then I did know. I looked in the bottom of the lifeboat, and there was a pile of booty. It was stuff I'd seen. Stuff the Palatines had on deck earlier. The crew had stolen their stuff. We were rowing away and I tried to call out to tell them to stop and let me off, but no one was listening. They were rowing so hard.

"The next thing, I smell smoke, and when I turn to look at the ship, it's beginning to catch fire. Before long it's ablaze. I started screaming that we had to go back to get the people out. We couldn't just let them burn alive. That's when ol' Sam said, 'They ain't alive, kid.' They'd killed them all, he said. Stabbed them in their beds and stolen their lot. The captain's plan, he said."

The old man's eyes were full of tears and his hands were clenched in fists.

"It was horrible! I couldn't believe that Luka, his family, and all of the Palatines were dead. We'd been such good buddies. I had hoped to visit them once they were settled in New Bern. May have even had a foolish notion of living with them. I don't know. But there before my eyes, the ship was burning. Flames everywhere.

"It kept on burning, too. Long after it should have sunk. The crew began to really get spooked. We all watched as that ship blazed for hours. Not just that, either. It began to move. As if the sails were filled with wind. But there was not even a breath of a breeze that night. Yet the ship was sailing right for us.

"The crews on all the lifeboats rowed furiously to shore, with the blazing ship right behind. We made it. While the ship still sailed back and forth along the shoreline, they divvied up the booty and ran. I never saw any of them again.

"I sat on the shore that night and watched the ship. It burned all night long. At times it would pass out of sight, but then it would return, brighter than before. Back and forth. Up and down. Always coming back to the spot where it had all happened. I remember hoping that Luka and his family somehow knew I had nothing to do with it. I woulda stopped it if I could.

"When dawn broke the next morning, the ship had stopped burning. But it was still there. All of it. Masts, spars, deck. Everything was there, but it was all blackened and charred. And there it sat for the whole day. And when night fell again, the flames once again climbed into the air. I don't know how long that happened. I left that night and made my way into New Bern. I tried to find Luka's relatives to tell them what happened. But no one would talk to a lowly cabin boy. They thought I'd lost my mind, I guess.

"And maybe I have. Maybe I have. Every night when I'm abed, I fall into a deep sleep and am awakened by the smell of smoke. There, standing next to the bed, is Luka and his family and all the families that perished aboard the ship that night. They just stand there, looking at me and burning until I start screaming loud enough to wake the dead. Then they just fade away.

"Every year on the anniversary of the murders, I've returned to the shoreline where I stood that awful night. Every year, I've seen that ship sailing on the waters again. She's sailing and she's burning right purty as can be."

●●●●●

The tale of the ship that burns but never sinks is a well-known story around North Carolina. It's said that on the anniversary of the horrific murders of a shipload of families bound for a new life in New Bern, the ship reappears. It sails up and down the shoreline, burning and burning, but never sinking. According to legend this phenomenon will recur until the deaths of the Palatines have been avenged.

the singing ghosts

"You let me know if I can get you anything, ma'am," the landlord said. "Rent's due on the first and my door's always open to my tenants. Just let me know if you have any problems."

"Thank you very much. I'm sure I'll settle in here quite nicely," Ruth Wilson replied.

The landlord whistled as he walked away. He was really pleased with himself for finding such an ideal tenant. The old lady seemed sweet enough, and she was sure to be a quiet tenant that paid on time and didn't cause him too much trouble. In other words, she was a lot better than a lot of the drunks and ne'er-do-wells that he had had to contend with being a landlord in New Orleans.

Ruth looked around in her apartment. She liked it. Apparently it was built in the 1800s, but it had gone through some transformations since then. The old house used to be all one residence, and then it was occupied by Union troops when they controlled New Orleans. Later it became a factory, and now it was a boarding house. It had been remodeled nicely, with all the little details you expect from an older place, and was just enough space for her, living alone and all.

She put the kettle on her hot plate she had brought with her and settled by the window to sew. She was sewing a christening gown for her third grandchild. She should have been unpacking, but her old bones were already tired from relocating. The boxes could wait for her children or grandchildren to come help her.

She hummed to herself while she sewed and thought, "If these walls could talk..."

If those walls could have talked, they could have told her quite a story. She knew the Union army had occupied this house during the Civil War, but she did not know that it had a particularly strange history.

General Butler was in charge of the Union troops that occupied New Orleans. Looting is a problem in most wars, and this war was no exception. Trying to curtail the violence and infighting that looting can breed, he issued a strict mandate that any soldier caught looting would be shot. Apparently two soldiers either thought he was bluffing or thought they wouldn't get caught. Either way, they were caught red-handed looting an abandoned house in the French Quarter and were hauled off to the grand house, now Ruth's home, for their crime.

What those in power didn't know, however, was that these two were not actually Union soldiers—they were Confederate deserters in disguise. The two never really thought that the General would have two perfectly good "Union" soldiers shot. What a waste that would be! No, he was just trying to scare them a little.

They were in high spirits when they got to the temporary jail, so they bribed a guard to get them a bottle of liquor, which they consumed with a quickness. Soon they were laughing and carousing and caterwauling a popular Northern song called "John Brown's Body," hoping that the Yankee tune would ensure that their true identities would never be known.

They kept this behavior up around the clock, getting drunk and singing the same old song. Then they got the bad news. It seems that the anti-looting decree applied to all soldiers, Union or Confederate, and it had not been issued as a threat. Somehow they managed to find two pistols and on the night before they were to be tried, they shot each other in the chest.

Had Ruth known the macabre tale, she would have been nonplussed. She was a salty old lady who had seen too much of the world to be terrified by a silly old ghost story.

The kettle began to whistle, so Ruth heaved her old bones out of her rocking chair and made a cup of tea. She blew gently on the steaming cup of tea and gazed out the window at her new view. She had been born and raised in New Orleans and loved the city with all her heart. After her husband died she couldn't bear to stay in a house full of so many memories, so she cleaned out the house and moved to Constance Street.

As Ruth was admiring the view, she heard the sounds of rowdy singing on the floor above her. She grimaced when she heard it. The place was so nice, but what good was it if drunkards kept you up all night with their excessive noise. She waited to see if it would stop, and when it didn't, she took her broom and knocked the handle against the ceiling.

"That did the trick," she said happily, and returned to her tea. The sun was going down and the evening's first partygoers were filtering out of the woodwork. She took that as her cue to put herself to bed, turning off the lights and snuggling under the goose down comforter her grandmother had made for her.

About two o'clock in the morning, the old lady was awoken from her slumber by singing. "Oh no, they're at it again," she thought. They were even louder this time, singing in robust but slurring voices. It sounded like the "Battle Hymn of the Republic." Of all the stupid songs to be singing at two in the morning, she thought.

The broom trick didn't work this time, so Ruth called her landlord. When she voiced her complaint, he mumbled knowingly, "Oh yeah, the singing," and then said something sleepily about taking care of it. She thought it was odd that he knew about this problem and failed to mention it to her. "Can't trust anybody these days," she thought to herself.

Whatever the landlord did apparently worked though, and she managed to get a good night's sleep after that.

Ruth awoke the next morning, yawned, stretched, and put the kettle on. While she waited for the water to heat she picked up the sewing she had left by her rocking chair. She carefully threaded the needle, noting that each time it got a little harder to do. She had slowly begun to stitch a hem when the singing started again.

This time it was really loud. She could hear the words and everything: "John Brown's body lies a-mouldering in the grave, John Brown's body lies a-mouldering in the grave, but his soul is marching on." She thought the melody was the "Battle Hymn of the Republic," but the words were very intelligible despite being slurred.

"Why don't you at least learn a new song," Ruth yelled in the direction of the singing, hammering her broom handle into the ceiling, to no avail. She made a call to the landlord, who was conveniently unavailable.

"I reckon I better get used to it," she said with a sigh, and reluctantly picked up her sewing, casting a disapproving and peevish glance toward the raucous singing every few minutes.

As quickly as it had started, the singing stopped.

"Well that's a relief," she thought to herself and took a few contented rocks in her chair. She wondered how long she would have to put up with all that racket. As it turned out she didn't have to wait much longer at all.

Ruth was rocking gently and stitching some lace onto the sleeve of the dress when she noticed the spot of blood on her hand. Ordinarily a careful seamstress, she was surprised. She didn't remember poking herself with the needle.

"Getting senile, are we old girl?" she thought to herself. She wiped off the spot of blood, grateful that it hadn't gotten on the beautiful fabric she was using to make the gown.

This time she felt it, a drip. Then another. She looked up and gasped in horror. Directly above her the ceiling was dripping fresh red blood, a small stain at first but quickly growing bigger. It looked like it was seeping through from the room above her. She jumped to her feet, dropping the tiny white dress into the puddle of blood that was beginning to form at her feet.

As quickly as she could, she was down the stairs and out the door, screaming all the way. She called her landlord and the police in hysterics from a pay phone. She waited for them outside the building but did not dare go back inside. They did a search of the place and came back out.

"I didn't see any blood," the landlord said with a condescending expression that implied she was just some crazy old coot. She didn't appreciate it. She may not have been a spring chicken, but she still had her wits about her.

"But what about the upstairs tenants? I know something horrible must have happened up there," Ruth said in frustration and disbelief.

"Look, lady. I'll level with you. Nobody's lived up there since the war, and by the war I mean the Civil War. Coupla soldiers shot themselves up there and since then people have seen and heard some pretty strange stuff. I didn't wanna scare you off, but that's the truth. Believe it or not."

Oh, she believed it alright. Somehow, she knew he was telling the truth. The singing, the blood, she knew it was not just her imagination.

"I'm breaking my lease and moving out. Charge me what you will. I'm not setting foot back inside that place. There is death living in that house," she said.

Ruth asked her children to move out her boxes because she refused to return to the room. Good thing she hadn't even had a chance to unpack.

Her children didn't believe her, of course. They expressed concern and urged her to have Alzheimer's tests done, convinced that she had dementia at the very least.

But then her son, leaving the apartment with the last load of his mother's things, happened to look up to the third floor from the sidewalk. He never told anyone, but through the window he saw two ragged men in Civil War uniforms, swaying clumsily and singing an unfamiliar tune.

whispering waters

"Listen to this, Papa." The young woman bent over the newspaper, straining to make out the smudged type by the lamplight. "The Iowa Equal Suffrage Society has adopted the motto of the State with the change of a single word, thus: 'Our liberties we prize, our rights we will secure.'"

The man seated in an armchair, dozing next to the fire, only grunted. "Ephesians 5, verses 21 through 24."

His daughter rattled the paper. "What about Ephesians 6, verse 5? Are we to take that to mean slavery is acceptable?"

"Don't try my patience, Jenny. God created Adam first, not Eve. It is not our place to question the wisdom of our creator."

"Yes, Papa." She was silent a few moments longer, then spoke again. "Mrs. Johnson and her daughters went to Des Moines to visit her sister again. I wonder if they are back yet?"

Her father only grunted, and she sprang up out of her chair like a mechanical toy and paced the parameters of the room. "Winterset, Winterset," she singsonged in a tone perilously close to mocking. "Do they call it that because winter sets in early and stays late?"

"You are restless this evening, my dear," her father commented, barely opening his eyes. "Regardless of why they named it, you had best become accustomed to it. I plan to stay here until my retirement and beyond, God willing."

"I miss Ohio," she started to say but bit back her tongue. What's past was past. Ohio and her life there were as lost to her as Iowa was lost to the Indians, she supposed.

"I will feel brighter in the morning, Papa," she said, trying to sound certain. "It is time for me to retire, I think." She kissed the crown of his head and lit a lamp to take upstairs. In Cleveland they had had all the modern conveniences, like gaslights in every room, but it seemed all they had in Winterset was corn. Corn to the east and corn to the west. Corn to the south and corn to the north. And in the winter, even that distraction was gone. The fields lay bleak and barren, waiting for the advent of spring and the farmer's attentions.

The congregation her father had come to lead was fairly large, about thirty families, but all the young ladies Jenny's age were married and mistresses of their own place. Jenny, at age nineteen, was a distinct oddity.

In fact, she was a somewhat more agile and singular version of the Misses Lavender. They lived alone on the edge of town, the spinster daughters of the town's first banker. They subsisted, somewhat precariously one might assume, on some kind of pension. The first time Jenny had come to call they had hovered over her like bees over a fragrant rose.

"Oh, what a lovely bonnet," one exclaimed. "Is this truly the fashion now?"

"However do you get around in that skirt, my dear?"

Jenny rather expected one of them to pull out a magnifying glass and begin to scrutinize the stitchery on her gloves. She almost enjoyed the attention, until she had a sudden vision of herself thirty years from now latching onto a newcomer like a dog snatching at a bone.

"Have you joined our literary society yet, Miss Cooper?" Miss Lavender—the one who looked a little more like a plum than a prune, Jenny thought unkindly—was pouring tea. Jenny would have to stay a little longer.

"We have begun to read *Saint Elmo*," continued the elder Miss Lavender. "Do you enjoy reading?"

"Oh, yes," said Jenny, glad for a familiar topic. "I read that last year. Right now I'm reading *Leaves of Grass*, by Mr. Whitman."

The ladies were shocked into silence. After a moment, the younger ventured a word. "Does your father approve of such reading?"

Jenny wished the ground would open up and swallow her. To put herself in a bad light was one thing. But to make her father appear permissive or to make it appear that his daughter would not bow to his wishes was even worse.

"I'm afraid he has not noticed my little excursion into this book," she stammered. "I've not enjoyed it, and I really think rereading *Saint Elmo* would be a pleasure. When did you say the literary society meets?"

"On Tuesdays, dear." The elder Miss Lavender leaned over and patted her hand. "Do come join us. We usually meet at Mrs. Scott's house. She has such a big parlor in that nice new house of hers."

Jenny had hurried home that day and hidden her copy of Mr. Whitman's book that her best friend had given her when she left Cleveland. She didn't even think to ask Papa for his approval of her reading material—Mama had always allowed Jenny to read anything that interested her. But Mama had always been a little less strict than Papa, Jenny though guiltily.

Tonight she picked up her copy of *Saint Elmo* with a sigh. They would discuss the final chapters tomorrow at Mrs. Scott's house. Then on Wednesday she had the church supper to look forward to, with all the ladies vying to present the most elaborate dishes. Thursday she would write letters, and Friday she could prepare the Sunday school lesson for the little girls of whom she had been given charge. Saturday, well, perhaps Saturday she could find some mending to do.

Jenny nodded off into sleep, then awoke with a jerk. Not even the combination of the book and a catalog of her life's exciting events could keep her awake, she thought wryly.

The next morning she found herself late leaving for the club meeting. "How," she scolded herself silently, "can you possibly get so far behind when you have absolutely nothing to do?" She picked up her skirts a bit and took long, steady strides, not quite running, her book tucked under one arm and her muff under the other. Jenny spun around the corner to Mrs. Scott's house and collided full force with a figure just closing the gate. Her book flew to the left, her muff landed in the street, and her hat was thrown off her head by the power of the impact.

"Oh, I am so sorry," gasped the young man, whose hat had also been knocked off by the blow. "Are you all right?"

Red-faced, Jenny assured him that she was. "It was my fault, completely," she insisted. "If only I had been paying attention."

"Let me get that for you." He retrieved the book for her and read the title with interest before placing it into her hand.

"*Saint Elmo.* You must be a member of the famous literary club."

Jenny blushed further, feeling like her face must surely explode.

"Well, I am," she admitted. "I'd already read it, but when we moved here I had so little to do that I needed the company, and the Misses Lavender invited me first thing."

Then it occurred to her that she was rattling on to a complete stranger, on the streets of a very small town on whose goodwill her father's future depended. "I'm late," she concluded abruptly. "Please, do excuse me." And she swept up the sidewalk to the shelter of Mrs. Scott's front porch. She had barely tucked her hair back under her hat before Lizzie, Mrs. Scott's parlor maid, swung the door open. The assembled ladies greeted her, and the discussion began.

Jenny's mind wandered, returning again and again to the encounter on the street. A warmth stole over her cheeks again, and she impatiently dismissed her foolish wanderings.

"But was Agnes truly repentant when she approached Saint Elmo at the end?" Mrs. Wright could discuss each phrase of the book in excruciating detail. She often did.

Jenny glanced out the windows. The clouds were thick, and might bring snow before the week was out. If it had been icy, she might have landed at the stranger's feet.

"Do you think Agnes was sincere, Jenny?" A voice boomed to the left of Jenny's chair.

She snapped to attention, turning to face Mrs. Allen. "I, ah, I was just looking at the snow."

"What? Did it start snowing already?" Mrs. Allen, a formidable matron, heaved her bulk out of the chair to peer out the window.

"No, I mean, I was thinking it looked like snow," Jenny explained weakly. She seemed to do nothing but embarrass herself and her father lately, she thought with despair. All the ladies were now clustered around the window, looking for a telltale flake.

Mrs. Scott clapped her hands. "Let's have refreshments now, ladies, shall we?" Lizzie scurried into the room with a tray of tea cakes and the teapot.

That night, Jenny and her father had just finished supper when someone knocked at the front door. Jenny, too curious to sit patiently in the parlor, followed her father to the foyer as he opened the door.

"Good evening, sir," said a young man, taking off his hat with a bow. "My name is Joseph Brooks, and I had the pleasure of, ah, meeting your daughter this morning when I accompanied my cousins, the Misses Lavender, to their literary club."

"Yes?"

"She left this behind, and I came to return it."

Jenny's heart jumped when she saw her muff in his hand. Her father accepted it and bowed, ever so slightly, to the visitor.

"Thank you, sir, and good day." Her father closed the door with a soft and final thud.

"Papa," she moaned.

"What?" He turned around to face her, more quickly than you might expect from a man of his bulk.

"You might have invited him in since he was kind enough to return my muff," she protested.

"You didn't tell me you had met a young man," her father rumbled.

"Well, I didn't, really, that is, we weren't introduced."

"Do not forget, young lady, how important it is for me to maintain a certain decorum in my own and my family's life." He stalked into the parlor, leaving her muff lying on the bench in the foyer.

Jenny followed behind him, struggling to maintain her composure. "Shall I read to you, Papa?" She reached for the black, leather-bound Bible which lay in its usual place on the table beside his chair.

"Proverbs 31." He leaned back and closed his eyes.

"Who can find a virtuous woman? For her price is above all rubies," Jenny began. "The heart of her husband doth safely trust in her, so that he shall have no need of spoil. She will do him good and no evil all the days of her life."

As she read, she couldn't help but think of her mother and wondered if her father thought the same. This was one of his favorite passages for her to read aloud. He had always said she looked like her mother.

After less than an hour of reading verses her father selected, Jenny excused herself and drifted upstairs. As she passed through the foyer, she slipped her hands in the folds of her muff, imagining they were still warm from the stranger's hands. She was nearly upstairs before she realized her fingers had closed on a scrap of paper.

She closed the door to her room and sank onto her bed, unfolding the note with uncertain fingers.

"I do not know your name," it read, "but I hope one day I will. Do you read poetry as well as novels? Perhaps you will recognize this:

How say you? Let us, O my dove,
Let us be unashamed of soul,
As earth lies bare to heaven above!
How is it under our control
To love or not to love?

Jenny kept the note and the muff beneath her pillow that night. She heard the nine o'clock train pull out of the station, its lonely cry trailing it west toward Omaha. She heard the late express go through without even slowing down, headed east as fast as coal and steam and modern engineering could take it. That train also howled in protest at the solitary, cold Iowa night, and Jenny felt an answering cry fill her heart.

"Did you sleep well, Papa?" she asked at breakfast.

He threw her a sharp glance. "Of course. I always do." He ate a few more bites of egg and ham before continuing. "What are your plans today, Jenny?"

"I thought I might help Sarah make an apple cake for the church supper tonight," she answered casually. "Then I have some calls to make."

"Not to the Misses Lavender, I'm sure." He did not even bother to look at her. He got up from the table and stretched. "I'm going to my study now. See that I'm not disturbed until dinner."

Jenny kept her eyes on her plate. "Papa, I..."

"If the young man wants to meet you, he can surely come to church," he interrupted her. "If he has any objections to church, then he's certainly not a suitable caller."

Jenny rang the little bell to summon Sarah to clear the table and then snatched up her coat and muff and went outside. She dared not leave the garden, but she strode round and round its perimeter until her cheeks were flushed with the cold. It took her nearly half an hour of walking before she realized it was a hot, flaring anger that drove her. She marched back inside and sat down at the writing table in the parlor.

"Dear Caroline," she wrote. "Sometimes I believe Papa never intends for me to marry. And, sometimes, I believe it is for entirely selfish reasons. As long as I remain in his home, he never has to worry about meals, or clothing, or entertaining the often dreadful women in his congregation. I do it for him! Although I cannot be entirely in agreement with those dreadfully strident suffragists like Mrs. Bloomer, I can certainly see the value of independence every now and then!"

Jenny took a deep breath, laid aside her pen, folded the letter, and thrust it deep into her pocket. She would reread it later and possibly mail it. Her best friend in Cleveland was still unmarried, like her, but had no lack of callers. In Iowa it seemed there were no unmarried men, except perhaps the one man her Papa refused to let her see.

Jenny went to the cellar and fetched a few jars of applesauce. She and Sarah spent the better part of the morning making apple cake, and before she knew it, it was time for her to dress for church.

"You look lovely this evening, my dear," her father said, ceremoniously lending her his arm for the walk next door to the church. "I am sure everyone in Winterset feels blessed to have you in their midst."

Jenny shook her head slightly, feeling the unaccustomed weight of her mother's diamond ear-bobs on her earlobes. "Do you mind that I wear them, Papa?" she asked tentatively.

As he shook his head, she saw the muscles of his jaw tighten momentarily, perhaps to suppress some emotion like sadness. Or, she thought suddenly, anger.

Jenny took her customary place in the front, just to the right of the pulpit, and tried to read her Bible as she waited for the service to begin. Her back seemed curiously exposed, and she fought to keep herself from turning and gawking as the congregation gathered behind her.

The sermon seemed tediously long, although she tried loyally to follow her father's complicated train of logic. Afterward, the congregation assembled in the little frame Sunday school hall, attached to the church with an open dogtrot.

"My, doesn't this look wonderful!" enthused Mrs. Allen. Her diminutive husband followed at her heels. He was the county sheriff and seldom spoke when his wife was around. They both filled their plates and moved on.

Jenny's eyes scanned the crowd, searching for a tall, scarcely remembered figure, or the lean, wrinkled forms of the Misses Lavender. She had just about abandoned hope when a touch on her elbow made her jump.

"Miss Cooper?" It was the younger Miss Lavender, followed closely by the older. "We have been so fortunate to have a guest, you know, our cousin from Chicago,"

"Really he's our second cousin, dear," the other interrupted. "Now, where did he go?"

At last Jenny's eyes latched onto a figure in black moving through the crowd toward them. Her mouth became mysteriously dry, and her heart pounded so loud she wondered if perhaps she was having palpitations. At last he arrived and took her hand in his.

"Miss Cooper," he cried, bending low over her hand. "I have heard so much about your astonishing powers of literary criticism."

She giggled.

He stood and his eyes gleamed, reflecting her amusement. "May we join you for supper, Miss Cooper?"

"I would be delighted, Mr. Brooks, is it?" It all seemed such an intriguing little charade, pretending that their encounter on the sidewalk outside Mrs. Scott's house had never taken place. As they talked, largely ignoring the food on their plates, it was as if they were only reacquainting themselves, old friends after a long absence.

"What do you do in Chicago, Mr. Brooks?"

"Oh boring things, mostly to do with trade and agriculture. I am trying very hard to establish myself."

"I would follow you anywhere," thought Jenny, and then she wondered where that wild thought had sprung from.

"You enjoy poetry, sir?" Her mind had flown just as quickly to the captivating scrap of verse he'd tucked into her muff.

A fugitive and gracious light he seeks,
Shy to illumine; and I seek it too.
This does not come with houses or with gold,
'Tis not in the world's market bought and sold.

His half-smile caught her heart just as a shadow fell over them.

"The best poetry ever written is found right here, young man," her father growled, shaking his Bible at eye level. "And the best stories, too, for that matter. I could have nothing else to read for the rest of my life and be content."

"I couldn't agree more, sir." Joseph Brooks sprang from his chair and began to quote again. To Jenny's delight, he chose a passage from Proverbs.

"She openeth her mouth with wisdom, and in her tongue is the law of kindness. Her children arise up and call her blessed; her husband also, and he praiseth her. Many daughters have done virtuously, but thou excellest them all."

He made a little bow in Jenny's direction, which prompted another scowl from her father. "Where is your family from, Mr. Brooks?" The two men faced each other, standing in the center of the room.

"Mostly from right here, Reverend Cooper, these fine fields and homes. My father, rest his soul, came from Chicago, and I work with his brother now. My mother was cousin to the lovely Misses Lavender."

"Any brothers or sisters?"

"No sir, my mother died along with a baby sister, twenty years ago."

"An orphan, then."

"In a manner of speaking, yes sir, I am."

"Well." Reverend Cooper nodded curtly and turned to speak to some church members who were leaving.

"I'd like to call on your daughter, sir," the young man called after him.

"We'll see," said the minister, without turning around.

Jenny had flushed again when the young man had spoken. He sat down again, next to her, and spoke very softly.

"May I? Call on you? You set more than my hat spinning Tuesday morning, Miss Cooper. I've been so distracted that the Misses Lavender tried to dose me with castor oil."

She stifled a giggle and then saw that he had intended to make her laugh. "I'd be honored, Mr. Brooks, but I really can't say for myself. You'll have to get permission from my father."

"Anything." His eyes locked on hers with such sincerity she felt her heart constrict again.

"You be a good boy and fetch the buggy for us, Joseph." Miss Lavender the elder swooped down, fracturing the moment.

The quarter moon shone so brightly that night Jenny could barely keep her eyes closed. Again she heard the nine o'clock train and then the late express, but this time their songs seemed full of hope as they rushed across the fields.

"That boy's a Catholic," her father roared as soon as she entered the dining room for breakfast. "Penniless, too!"

Jenny recoiled from the force of his words.

"Papa," she began.

"Don't you start," he warned. "If I let him call on you, you'd just get your hopes up. He's not suitable at all, and that's the last word."

Too stunned even to cry, Jenny turned and walked stiffly back up to her room. She threw herself across her bed, heedless of her dress, and buried her head beneath the pillow.

Her mind raced from one thought to another, sometimes alighting on reckless schemes to circumvent her father's will. "I'll run away," she thought, "and live with Caroline in Cleveland!" But she knew she never would. At last she began to sob, with a fury that first surprised her and then drained her of her energy. Near noon she fell asleep, too deeply to hear Sarah's timid knock and call to dinner.

When she awoke, she slipped downstairs for pen and paper. Once she returned to the privacy of her room, she began to struggle over the composition of a letter.

After many false starts, she finally had a draft she felt she could send.

"Dear Mr. Brooks," it read. "Please forgive my boldness in writing you, and I pray that God will forgive me for disobeying the deeply felt wishes of my father, whom I respect and love.

"My father believes the barriers between my upbringing as a Protestant and your own as a Catholic are too great to overcome. He is further concerned about your ability to secure an adequate livelihood to support a family.

"I cannot express how profoundly your presence in Winterset has affected me. These circumstances bring the great poet Coleridge to mind:

For hope grew round me like the twining vine,
And fruits and foliage, not my own, seemed mine.
But now afflictions bow me down to earth;
Nor care I that they rob me of my mirth.

"I cannot ask that you abandon religious habits you have formed from birth. Yet I recall your sincerity when you expressed a desire to call upon me. If there is hope, please acquaint me with it. I fear dejection will not turn me into a poet, but merely a bitter person."

Having finished the letter, Jenny sealed it and carried it to the kitchen, concealing it in her pocket.

"Sarah, are you about to go home?"

"Yes'm."

"I need you to carry these preserves to the Misses Lavender on your way." Jenny hastily put a few jars into a basket and then scribbled a note to tuck in with them. As Sarah turned to put on her hat, Jenny slipped the letter to Mr. Brooks beneath the jars. "Leave the basket there," she called as Sarah left. "I'll collect it when I see them on Tuesday."

At supper that evening, she and her father barely exchanged three words. Just as she was excusing herself, he spoke.

"I trust you will obey me in this matter, Regina," he said gruffly. "I am acting with your best interests at heart."

She nodded, too filled with a stew of conflicting emotions to trust herself to speak.

When she heard the nine o'clock train pause at the station, she rested her forehead against the cold glass and wondered if Joseph Brooks was boarding. She read fragments of poetry until late into the night, only falling into a restless sleep when her lamp flickered and went out, its supply of oil exhausted.

Sarah lightly tapped on her door the next morning.

"I'm coming, Sarah," Jenny called, struggling out of the twisted sheets that had tried in vain to contain her sleep.

"Oh, Miss, breakfast is over. Your father said to let you sleep. But I had something for you," the girl continued.

Jenny yanked open her door and restrained herself from covering Sarah's mouth. If her father heard anything, he would be most suspicious.

"What?" she whispered.

"A gentleman at the Lavender house gave this to me when I left the preserves," Sarah whispered in reply, pulling an envelope from her apron pocket. "Should I not have accepted it?"

A flying kiss on the cheek was the only response from Jenny, who snatched the letter from Sarah's fingers and closed the door in the surprised girl's face.

"My dear Miss Cooper," the letter began. "I have received with a heavy heart the correspondence of your father. I will with joy become a member of his congregation, if that were all he required to pay suit to you. Of my financial situation, I can make no amends, save that to assure you that the future holds much promise. I am afraid that will not satisfy your father.

"I dare not hope that the strength of your affections for me would cause you to receive this letter with happiness. I will accompany my cousins again to the literary club on Tuesday, and if fate is kind I will glimpse your lovely face. To hear your voice again is beyond all hope.

> Far off thou art, but ever nigh;
> I have thee still, and I rejoice;
> I prosper, circled with thy voice;
> I shall not lose thee though I die.

The next three days were interminable. Her father's watchful, brooding presence weighed heavily on Jenny, and as she had so many times over the past five years, she ached for her mother's bright countenance and calm disposition to lighten the gloom.

Tuesday morning the light waking her was so muffled and diffused that she feared the worst. Crossing to the window, she saw that big, fat snowflakes were spiraling down steadily. She dressed and went downstairs.

"Sarah," she called, glad to see the girl already in the kitchen preparing breakfast. "How bad is the snow?"

"Well, not bad at all, Miss," Sarah responded, "if you're a farmer. It's this kind of snow that makes the corn grow come spring."

Exasperated, Jenny left the kitchen to join her father at the table.

Her father intoned the blessing, and then asked, "Do you have plans today?"

"Just my literary club, Papa," she said, spooning some eggs on her plate.

"Snowing pretty hard this morning," he commented.

"It will stop soon, I'm sure. Would you like me to drop by Mrs. Simpson's house on my way home? I hear she's still feeling poorly."

"That would be a kind thing to do, daughter." They finished their meal in silence.

By half past nine, the snowfall had mercifully slowed to a few lazy flakes circling to the ground, and the dark gray clouds were thinning. Jenny wrapped up tightly in her coat and muffler, stopping at the last moment to slip her mother's ear-bobs on her ears.

Sarah dropped a plate in the dining room, and Jenny let out a little shriek. Sarah came running, full of apologies, and held the door for her.

Jenny's nerves were strung to a high pitch, and she nearly flew out of the house to avoid her father. He would surely comment on her ear-bobs, a sign of increased vanity on what was to him an ordinary Tuesday morning club meeting.

Her steps slowed as she turned the corner to Mrs. Scott's house. She didn't know how she would contrive to speak to Mr. Brooks without risking discovery by the whole circle of ladies inside the parlor.

The muffled sound of hooves on the soft blanket of new snow made her jump and whirl around. A brown horse with white stockings was pulling an unfamiliar buggy.

"Miss Cooper?"

"Oh, it's you, Mr. Brooks!" Jenny was relieved to recognize his lively brown eyes between his hat, pulled low, and a muffler that covered his mouth.

"I know it's most unusual, but would you care to take a short ride with me?"

With a surge of courage, Jenny took his outstretched hand and climbed into the buggy.

"That's the Misses Lavender's horse, isn't it?" she asked. "Where did the buggy come from?"

"The livery stable." He turned the buggy left, and within a few moments they were out of town, surrounded by fields on all sides, glowing with their fresh covering of snow. "The ladies decided that since it was snowing, a covered buggy was called for. I was happy to oblige."

Jenny became suddenly shy, and neither spoke until the road began its gentle slope down to Middle River.

"I shouldn't have done this." The words burst out of her.

"I've loved you since I saw you," he said at the same time.

They were quiet again.

The horse slowed to a standstill on the middle of the bridge, glad of the shelter and forgotten by the man who held the reins.

"I have a plan," he said urgently, aware of Jenny's discomfort in the darkness of the bridge. "My uncle knows a man who is selling a new kind of corn—a hybrid that grows faster and doesn't get the rust. If I invest in his idea, we could be married in a year!"

"I don't understand," Jenny stammered. "What can you invest?"

"I'll work for him for free, or something. Please say you'll marry me, Jenny."

He touched her hand, and even through the wool of her gloves she felt the intensity that sparked between the two of them.

"It's dark now," he continued. "But if we go on, just a little further, see how bright it could be!" He pointed to the opening of the bridge, where the snowy fields shimmered with an uncommon light.

Quickly, without speaking, Jenny stripped off the ear-bobs. She took his hand and turned it up, dropping the diamond jewelry in his open palm.

"Take them," she said breathlessly. "Invest them. I'll be in Winterset until you can come back."

"Are you sure?"

She nodded, and he raised the ornaments to his lips and kissed them gently.

"Take me back," she whispered. "I'm late."

Jenny sat through the discussion of *Saint Elmo* in a daze, barely responding even when her fellow club members spoke directly to her. She relived those moments alone in the carriage over and over, until the whole episode began to feel like a dream.

At home, her silence was so pronounced that her father commented on it. "You're not taking ill, are you? We would miss your company at the church supper tomorrow night."

Listlessly, Jenny assured her father she was fine and excused herself to go to bed. She fell right to sleep, but her dreams were tortured, with odd fragments of poetry spinning from the mouths of incongruous people and pierced by shrieking train whistles.

Wednesday morning her bones felt leaden. She missed breakfast and only appeared downstairs a few minutes before dinner. She had only pulled a comb across her hair and barely fumbled with the row of buttons on her dress. Her father frowned as she sat down at the table.

"I hope you will take more care with your appearance this evening," he chided her. "Good grooming is the mark of a good upbringing."

"Yes, Papa," she said dully.

She knew without a doubt that Joseph Brooks would not be at church this evening. Jenny could not even grasp how to make it through the afternoon without sinking into the black despair that threatened. To contemplate a full twelve months of this deadening, thick melancholy was beyond her comprehension.

At last it was half past five, and she and her father were bundling up for the short walk to the church.

"You're not wearing the ear-bobs tonight?"

"No, not tonight, Papa." Her brain moved so sluggishly she could not think of an appropriate response.

"Come along, then." He grasped her elbow, rather too tightly, and they proceeded through the door.

Thursday morning Jenny was struggling to finish a letter to Caroline without mentioning recent events. Sarah appeared at the parlor door and dropped an awkward little curtsy.

"Your father would like to see you in his study, ma'am," she said, avoiding Jenny's eyes. Her father rarely invited her to interrupt his workday. Curious, Jenny tapped at his half-open door.

"Come in," he said, bent over his work. After a moment, he laid down his pen and motioned for Jenny to have a seat in the leather arm chair in front of his desk.

"Sarah tells me she delivered a basket of preserves to the Misses Lavender last week," he said without preamble.

Jenny studied her hands, laid neatly in her lap.

"And she says a young man gave her a letter to carry back to you," he continued. His voice was so calm it terrified her. She made no reply, but a great shudder tore across her torso, and she seemed to shrink.

"She has been dismissed. Bring me the letter."

Jenny rose and turned to go, too numb to feel compassion for poor little Sarah.

"Jenny, what did you do with your mother's ear-bobs?" The whisper blasted her with more force than a hurricane. She could only shake her head and hurry from the room.

His heavy footfall sounded on the stairs moments after she reached her room. She heard a telltale jingle, and then a click as the tumbler fell into the lock.

"When you're ready to speak, you may come out. In the meantime, I shall summon Sheriff Allen to recover my stolen property."

"No," she whimpered, but too quietly for her father to hear.

She held out until nightfall, when she pounded on her door and shouted until she was hoarse. Her father came upstairs to unlock the door.

"The thief is now in jail," he announced with satisfaction. "We shall recover your mother's ear-bobs soon. Will you give me the letter now?"

"No, Papa, I can't," she whispered. "Please, don't make me."

"Then you shall stay in your room. I will not have my child flaunting my authority."

Jenny paced the parameter of her room, frantic. At last, when she heard the nine o'clock train leave the station bound for Omaha, she opened her window. Holding her skirts scandalously high, to free her legs for the climb, she clambered out of the window and dropped, praying wordlessly. Her feet slammed into the roof of the porch and she began to slide, slowly at first but then with growing speed, hurtling toward the edge of the roof and a ten-foot drop to the ground.

Jenny landed with a grunt in the abundant foliage of the holly bush outside the kitchen door. Scratched on her face and hands, she was otherwise uninjured. She picked herself up and began to walk resolutely to the east, the center of town, to the small county jail next to the Winterset train station.

It was a simple, square building, solidly constructed of stone with iron bars across a single, high window in the back. The streets were deserted. After the nine o'clock train, there was no reason for anyone to be out.

She did not know why she had come or what she could do, but she seized the doorknob and rattled it just the same. To her amazement, it opened.

"Mr. Brooks?" she whispered.

"Miss Cooper?" The familiar voice cracked in surprise.

As her eyes adjusted to the gloomy interior, she saw that the space she occupied was a tiny little anteroom to the jail cell itself.

"I'm sorry," she said, ineffectually.

"You didn't do anything," he pointed out, his voice gaining strength.

"I want to help you get out," she said.

"There's the key." He pointed to a nail in the wall to the left of the door. It held an iron ring with a solitary key attached.

She unlocked the door and swung it open.

"Where will you go?"

"West, I suppose." He shrugged. "Why are you doing this?"

"I, ah, I love you, Mr. Brooks."

"Will you come with me?"

She shuddered involuntarily, a great, encompassing motion that shook her as fully as a mother cat shakes her kitten.

"Yes," she whispered.

"Meet me on the bridge, then. I'll get a horse."

Suddenly he was gone, and she looked around in surprise. She had just made a decision to turn her life upside down, yet the world looked oddly the same.

She was half a block down when she heard voices in the jail behind her. "He's gone!" someone shouted.

"He must've broke out and then gone and kidnapped the girl," someone else yelled. She realized it was Sheriff Allen.

"Get your horses! They can't have gone far!"

Five men galloped past her, heading west, as she cowered behind the corner of a house. She turned right and began to run toward the livery stable.

In a matter of minutes, she had grabbed a horse and led it outside. Perched precariously on its side, clutching the mane for support, she urged it west, out of town to Roseman Bridge.

A mile ahead of her, the moon illuminated a black speck against the snow, a solitary figure on horseback. Behind her she heard the shouts and calls of the posse, swollen now to nearly a dozen men.

The wind picked up and snatched a sentence or two from the sheriff's mouth, sending it flying down her way. "He's headed down the bridge road! You and Frank go round and ford the river. We'll get him on the bridge."

The gait of the horse threw her up and down, jarring her roughly with every step. Still she rode, trying to catch up with Joseph before he fell into their trap.

At the crest of the hill, she turned off the road, onto the river path, in a desperate attempt to make it to the bridge before Joseph. Her horse, confused, shimmied back. She slid off and hit the ground.

Dazed, she heard the horses from the sheriff's posse thunder past. Moments later, gunshots split the night.

Jenny staggered to her feet in time to see a riderless horse dance out from the mouth of the bridge.

●●●●●

The men greeted each other with few words as they settled into their accustomed spots on the banks of the Middle River.

"You hear Reverend Cooper's daughter died?"

"Yep." They cast their lines and sat in silence again for a while.

"How old was she? Fifty?"

"'Bout that."

"She never was the same after that Brooks boy."

"I dunno why they never caught him."

"He disappeared into thin air, my daddy said. Right there off that bridge." He pointed to the bridge wreathed in mist a few yards down stream.

"I dunno," said the other man doubtfully.

"Reckon she went crazy?"

"Who?"

"Miss Cooper."

"Dunno." The fisherman reeled in his line and slipped another worm deftly onto the hook. After casting once more, he spoke again.

"I heard her mama was crazy. Locked up somewhere back east."

"Huh."

The weight of the mist-shrouded morning again took its toll. It was a good five minutes before either man spoke.

"What's that, Stephen?"

An odd little susurrant sound seemed to mock the gurgle of the water flowing unseen in the fog below the bank.

"Dunno," the other man said softly. "Sounds like somebody whisperin'."

"You 'spect it's Michael, come along to play a trick?"

Something cold and wet pushed its way into the first man's side and he yelped.

"Dog snuck right up on me, didntja, boy?" He rubbed the dog's ears as the creature whimpered.

The whispering sound continued, a little louder now.

"It's comin' from the bridge, Stephen. Let's go see if ol' Michael's playin' a trick on us."

They heaved themselves to their feet and walked slowly through the swirling vapor to the mouth of the bridge.

The dog whined again and pushed its belly flat against the ground.

"Whatsa matter, Sport?"

The dog just cried again, its fur standing up.

"Go on in and look for Michael, Stephen," the other man urged.

"I dunno," his friend said doubtfully. "Listen. It almost sounds like poems. Michael don't know any poems, does he?"

The two men walked slowly into the bridge, side by side, leaving the dog whining softly outside.

"Boy, it's cold this mornin', ain't it?"

"It's June, you idiot." He playfully shoved the other one, inadvertently placing his feet in the center of the bridge.

"It is cold here." They looked at each other, their features indistinct in the gray light of dawn.

The whispering grew louder, so that words were almost distinguishable. It sounded like a man and a woman, murmuring their pledges, safe within the sheltering darkness of the bridge.

The whispers died away. But when raucous laughter rang out from unseen lips, its reluctant audience hurried out of Roseman Bridge, glad to return to the light of day.

tales of a
haunted city

Nowhere in America will you find a city richer in history than Charleston, South Carolina. First called Charles Towne in honor of England's King Charles II, Charleston was the first permanent settlement in South Carolina. It was established in 1670 by a group of two hundred colonists from Barbados.

The early days were, no doubt, wild and woolly, with the town often subject to attack from Spain and France, who still laid claim to the land, as well as from Native American pirates. Despite this, Charleston's lucrative seafaring trade and its religious tolerance made it a popular site for settlers. By 1742, it was the fourth largest city in America, with a hugely diverse population that blended English, French, Scottish, German, and Iberian cultures.

Charleston played a pivotal role throughout American history. Two signers of the Declaration of Independence were born here, and three were jailed for treason in Charleston's Provost Dungeon. Its rich Carolina soil, perfect for the cultivation of rice and indigo, spawned a rise in gentlemen planters and, combined with its shipping industry and unfortunately, its slave trade, the city soon became the cultural and economic center of the South. In addition, the first shot of the Civil War occurred here, when Confederate soldiers fired on Fort Sumter.

Thanks to the fact that General William Sherman was once posted here and seemed to have a soft spot in his heart for the city, Charleston was spared the razing experienced by most Southern cities. And where Sherman left off in preserving the city, Charleston's good citizens picked up. Acutely aware of their place in American history, they have diligently worked for decades to preserve and restore Charleston's numerous historic homes and buildings. Centered in Charleston's historic district, these buildings number more than one thousand four hundred and include the three hundred-year-old homes of rice lords and shipping magnates, antebellum homes, historic civic buildings, churches, and even cemeteries.

You know what this means don't you? I bet you do. I bet you know that all these historic buildings, filled with so much history, mean a plethora of ghost stories. From patriots to pirates, from gentried gentleman to ladies of the evening, from frightened slaves to headless torsos, Charleston has certainly earned its reputation as "America's Most Haunted City."

The Old Exchange Building and Provost Dungeon

Because of its extensive shipping trade, its rice and indigo exports, and its unfortunate slave trade, Charles Towne developed into the fourth largest city and was one of the wealthiest towns in colonial America. This phenomenal growth in trade necessitated the construction of a building to accommodate the heavy import-export market and to provide a place to conduct both public and private business.

Charles Towne's first effort in urban planning, the Exchange and Custom House was designed to reflect the self-image of the town's elite. The town fathers chose the foot of Broad Street as the site for their new building. The center of the waterfront, it was an area where inland streams converged with major maritime traffic thoroughfares, and had long been the symbolic center of the city.

Several important civic buildings had once occupied the site, including the Half-Moon Battery, an original fortification of Charles Towne. In the name of urban planning, adjacent street markets were moved to another block because they were unsightly.

The Exchange Building was erected in 1771. Shiploads of cut, dressed, and beveled Portland stone were imported for the building's façade. It was one of the most important buildings in Charles Towne—indeed in the whole of colonial America. The last building built by the British government in the American colonies, it served as the office for the king's customs collector and was used as a space for public gatherings and lavish entertainment.

It was elegantly constructed in the popular Palladian architecture style, but its design and the construction materials were unique for the time. Only two other colonial buildings—Philadelphia's Town Hall and Boston's Faneuil Hall—came close in stature, but even those venerable buildings could not match the architectural distinction of Charles Towne's new Exchange and Custom House.

Perhaps the town fathers didn't exactly have that urban planning thing down pat, though, for they decided to use the nether regions of their fine and elegant Exchange Building as a dungeon. Called the Provost Dungeon, it was a damp, unwholesome cellar located deep beneath the Exchange Building. Men and women prisoners, transported in irons, were crowded together in squalor.

Despite the fact that the Exchange and Custom House was built and, for a time, was controlled by the British, it played an important role in American history. In 1773, Charles Towne citizens met in the building's Great Hall to protest the Tea Act. While the citizens of Boston dumped their tea into the harbor, in Charles Towne tea was seized and stored in the Exchange Building and was later sold to fund the patriot cause.

In 1774, South Carolina's delegates to the Continental Congress, the group that drafted the Declaration of Independence, were elected in the Great Hall. Then, in 1776, South Carolina declared independence on the steps of the Exchange Building and Custom House. Charles Towne was the birthplace of two signers of the Declaration of Independence, Arthur Middleton and Edward Rutledge. After they penned their names to that venerable document, they, along with St. Luke's Parish native Thomas Heywood Jr., found themselves charged with treason by the British and tossed for a while into the filthy dungeon.

They weren't the only patriots jailed. In 1780, after a lengthy siege, the British marched into Charles Towne and took over. They jailed leading citizens in the dungeon, requiring that they sign an oath to the King to secure their release.

Isaac Hayne was a South Carolina patriot who took the oath of allegiance to avoid imprisonment. His entire family was ill with smallpox in Charles Towne, and being incarcerated was not an option at that time. He was assured by the British that he would not be required to take up arms against his country. The British, however, broke their promise and drafted him into the Royal army.

They broke theirs, so he could break his, Hayne reasoned. He rejoined the American Army and fought against the British, who unfortunately captured him. He was thrown into the Provost Dungeon and was charged with treason. Without a jury trial, he was convicted and hanged within forty-eight hours. His execution was controversial and caused the two British officers who sentenced him and carried out the execution many problems for years to come.

As Hayne was being paraded through Charles Towne on the way to the gallows, his sister reportedly called out to him, "Come back, Isaac! Come back!" To which her brother replied, "I will if I can."

Many believe that Isaac Hayne has kept his promise. It's his ghost, they say, that haunts the Provost Dungeon and the Old Exchange Building, which now operates as a museum. Ghost tours also are conducted here, and reportedly on several occasions, there have been strange occurrences—unexplained shadows on the walls, chains swinging or rattling, strange noises—that were so frightening, entire tour groups broke and ran from the dungeon.

••••••

In addition to the ghost of Isaac Hayne, many believe the ghosts of Charleston's many pirates haunt the Old Exchange Building. In the late 1700s, Charles Towne was a favorite port for some of the Atlantic's most notorious pirates. The infamous Blackbeard, as a matter of fact, held the entire city for ransom, capturing vessels sailing into the harbor and taking hostages at will. He refused to release the hostages unless the town gave him much needed medical supplies.

Although many think the Old Exchange Building could be haunted by ol' Blackbeard himself, it makes more sense that the ghost is another famous pirate. See, Blackbeard met his fate elsewhere, but Stede Bonnet, known as the "Gentleman Pirate," was captured, along with his crew, in December 1718. Bonnet and twenty-two of his crew were hanged on December 10, 1718, at White Point. It seems likely that it's these old buccaneers who may be responsible for much of the building's poltergeist activity, which includes unexplained images and the balls of light known as "orbs" seen in many photographs taken here. Orbs and other flashes of light often captured on film are thought to be ghostly presences that are either too shy or too weak to make an appearance.

Dock Street Theater

The original Dock Street Theater was the first theater to be built in America. It opened on February 12, 1736, with a bawdy Restoration farce by George Farhquar entitled The Recruiting Officer. The theater was located on the corner of Dock and Church Streets, facing Dock Street, which was later renamed Queen Street.

For the next several years, the theater featured plays and operas and was a popular Charleston attraction. Its true fate is unknown, but it's presumed that it was burned in 1740, when a huge fire devoured the city's historic French section.

In 1809, a hotel was built on the site by Alexander Calder and his wife. The couple renovated several buildings on the Church Street side, adding a grand stairway and a drawing room. The Planter's Hotel offered superior lodging, excellent food, and innovative drinks—it's the home of the Planter's Punch, a tasty and fruity little rum concoction. It became popular with planters from middle South Carolina, who came to town for some fun and relaxation during the horseracing season.

In 1835, the hotel was remodeled, with the addition of a wrought iron balcony, whose silhouette against the spire of St. Philip's Episcopal

Church has become one of the most photographed images in the city. For fifty years, the hotel was the principal hotel in Charleston, popular with plantation owners and seafaring merchants alike.

During these heyday years, the Planter's Hotel became the home of Nettie Dickerson. Nettie moved to Charleston in 1838 and took a job at St. Philip's church, located across the street from the hotel. Nettie was a comely miss, but at age twenty-five, she was considered past her marrying prime.

What's a girl to do? Initially, Nettie decided if she couldn't get a man of her own, she'd take someone else's. Her job at the church gave her the opportunity to meet many church members looking for a little action on the side, and she became mistress to a succession of men, none of whom was willing to leave his family for her.

Eventually, she began to resent their hypocrisy in sitting piously on the front pew at church every Sunday, after spending Saturday night drinking and carousing with her. On one stormy evening, as she was about to enter the church, a lightning bolt crackled overhead. It jagged its way across the sky and struck the cross on the church spire. Hmm, thought Nettie, must be a sign from God.

I'm thinking she misinterpreted that sign, however. The next day, she quit her job at the church, vowing that she'd have more out of life. She then moved into the Planter's Hotel and began a new career—in the world's oldest profession. Nettie was good at her job and she soon became a wealthy woman, though she was, of course, snubbed by the "polite" society of Charleston.

Through her years at the Planter's Hotel, Nettie gained a reputation for her outrageous behavior. During violent rainstorms, she would don a bright red ball gown, and, having developed an affinity for lightning since her "epiphany," she would stand out on the hotel balcony watching the lightning crackle across the Charleston sky. On one such meteorologically active evening, God must've decided it was time to set her straight about her interpretation of his previous "sign." A lightning bolt streaked across the sky and struck the balcony railing where Nettie had rested her hands. She was immediately electrocuted.

One of the hotel's most famous guests during the time Nettie lived there was an actor named Junius Booth. An imposing entertainer with a full, rich, baritone, Booth stayed at the hotel when performing in Charleston. Booth was the father of three sons, two of whom also became actors. His most famous son did not earn his fame on stage, however. No, John Wilkes Booth's infamy came from the shot he made from a theater balcony—a shot that struck and killed President Abraham Lincoln.

After the Civil War, the Planter's Hotel went out of business and fell to disrepair. It was certain to simply disintegrate there on its foundation, but in 1930, the building became a Works Progress Administration project. It was restored, renovated, and reopened. It was taken over by the city of Charleston and was once again named the Dock Street Theater, even though Dock Street had long since been named Queen Street. Today the Dock Street Theater is home to the Charleston Stage Company, a community performing group. It also houses Charleston's Cultural Affairs office and The City Gallery, an exhibition venue for local artists.

It also, of course, is home to a couple of haunting spirits. Nettie Dickerson is one. She appears, most often wearing a gaudy red ball gown, on the theater's second floor. She floats around the theater, apparently unaware of anything going on around her. She never interacts with the living and may be totally oblivious to the fact that she's dead. Those who have seen her say one of the most frightening aspects about Nettie is that she seems to be walking—or floating, as the case may be—cut off at the knees. Seems when the theater was last restored, the second floor floorboards were raised twelve inches, which brings them to about Nettie's knees.

The other ghost that treads the floorboards of the Dock Street Theater is Junius Booth. No one is sure why he's chosen this particular theater, considering that he was a famous and well-traveled actor, but he has been seen enough times to earn his spot in the local ghost tours.

The Old City Jail

Night had fallen and rain had been pelting down on him for more than two hours, when ol' Jack the fur trader came upon the Six Mile House. The lights glowing from the inn's windows looked warm and inviting. "Finally," he thought, "a dry place to sleep."

"Come in, good sir! Come in." The inn's proprietess met him at the door. "Take off that wet cloak and sit by the fire. Ooooh, you are a big, strong fella, aren't you!" She cooed as he shed his wet outer garments.

Jack looked askance at the lady, a comely lass. Her flirty words, he thought, seemed inappropriate. "Thank ye, ma'am. It is a mite cold and wet out there. I'd appreciate a place to sleep tonight."

"Of course, of course. My name is Lavinia. And, what, handsome sir, is your name?"

"Jack," he replied. He was surprised as the lady took his arm and led him over to a chair in front of the fire. Her manner was much too friendly for his taste. Jack had no illusions about his appeal to women. He basically had none. He was a big fella, true enough. But he was nothing to look at, with a pock-marked face and a nose that covered half his face. The straggly beard didn't help anything either. So he couldn't help but wonder why this beautiful woman was showing such an interest.

He'd heard about places where unsuspecting men would rent a bed for the night and never be seen again, murdered for their meager savings and belongings. He had no intention of letting it happen to him. He turned down the lady's offer of dinner, despite the fact that his stomach was rumbling at the savory aromas coming from the kitchen. He had strong suspicions that there might just be something a little extra in the food—like rat poison.

Miss Lavinia seemed disappointed at his refusal of her food. She pouted a bit, but eventually showed Jack to his room. Still suspicious, he made himself a pallet of his furs in one corner of the room, and placed other furs underneath the covers on the bed to make it look like he was slumbering peacefully beneath them. Then he crawled into his makeshift bed and eventually drifted off to sleep.

Late into the night, Jack was awakened by a sound. His heart pounded as he strained his ears, listening for the sound that had awakened him. Suddenly, there was a loud crash and when he looked across the room, there was an empty hole where the bed had been. It had dropped into the basement through a trap door. He crept over and looked down into the hole. There he saw John Fisher, Lavinia's husband, butcher knife in hand, furiously stabbing into the furs on the bed.

Scrambling, Jack grabbed his hat and cloak and dashed out into the rain. He didn't stop until he'd found the sheriff's office and reported his story of near murder. He even followed the sheriff's deputies back out to the inn, where a search of the basement beneath the trap door turned up a graveyard of skeletons.

Seems John and Lavinia Fisher had been at their murder game for quite some time. They would lull their guests into a warm, cozy sleep. Then, in the middle of the night, the guests' beds would drop into the basement and they would be stabbed to death. All their valuables would be added to the Fishers' assets.

John and Lavinia were tried, found guilty of murder, and tossed into the Charleston City Jail to await execution. They were executed on the same day in 1820. John was first. "Please don't kill me," he pleaded. "It wasn't me. It was my wife. She made me do it!"

The rowdy crowd was unsympathetic. "Be a man!" They screamed.

After John was hanged, Lavinia was brought out. Dressed in her white wedding dress, she ascended the gallows stairs with an evil smile on her face. After stealing a quick kiss from her dead husband's lips, she turned to the crowd and in an unwavering voice screamed, "Do any of you have a message for the devil? I'll be glad to tell him!"

The crowd was silenced by her maniacal laughter as the rope was placed over her head. The snapping of her neck was the only sound heard when the lever was pulled and the floor dropped from under her. Lavinia Fisher was the first woman to be executed in the United States.

I guess the devil's still waiting for those messages from Lavinia, for, according to legend, she has yet to leave this earth. Seems her spirit is still hanging (sorry 'bout that) around the Old City Jail. And she may not be the only one.

Charleston's Old City Jail was constructed in 1802 and served as the city's jail until 1939. When first built, it consisted of four stories topped by a two-story octagonal tower. It was remodeled by Charleston architects Barbot and Seyle in 1855, at which time they added a rear octagonal wing, expansions to the main building, and Romanesque revival architectural details. The octagonal tower and the top story of the building were substantially damaged in the great earthquake of 1886, and those two elements were removed.

In addition to John and Lavina Fisher, Charleston's City Jail housed a variety of prisoners. The last of the nineteenth-century pirates were jailed here in 1822, as were the participants of the Denmark Vesey slave revolt. Denmark Vesey was a slave who, after winning a $1,500 lottery, purchased his freedom. He became prosperous and won respect from slaves and owners alike. His hatred of slavery drove him to organize a revolt to free all slaves. But he was betrayed, and he and other participants were held in the Old City Jail before their executions. In addition, during the Civil War, both Confederate and Union prisoners where held here.

The evil face of Lavinia Fisher is often glimpsed from a top story window, where she was held in a meager cell. By all accounts, she's a hostile ghost, especially to female visitors. She's also pretty strong, with the ability to fling objects across a room. She's been seen wandering the hallways of the jail—still wearing her white wedding dress. Reportedly, numerous psychics have tried to banish her spirit, but she refuses to leave.

Other spirits still haunting the jail include several members of the Denmark Vesey slave revolt and a Confederate soldier.

The Old Slave Market

In the eighteenth century, Charleston was the major point of entry for slaves being imported into the country. During this time, three out of four imported slaves were brought into Charleston and traded here. By 1790, city blacks outnumbered whites in Charleston, and curfew laws for slaves were enacted. At 10:00 p.m., bells would toll, and any slaves caught in the streets without written permission from their owners were jailed and severely beaten.

In 1808, foreign slave trade was abolished, but the country's plantation economy depended heavily on slave labor. This led to the creation of a domestic slave trading system, and Charleston again became the major center for slave collecting and selling.

Plantation owners traveled from all over the country to buy and sell their slaves in Charleston, helping to make the city into the cultural and commercial hub of early America. During the antebellum period, Charleston also was the center of commercial activity for the South's plantation economy.

For many years, the slave trade was carried out in the street on the right side of the Exchange and Custom House. But in 1856, a city ordinance was passed that prohibited trading in the streets. No problem. The slave traders simply built a series of buildings with sales rooms on Chalmers, Queen, and State streets.

The largest of these slave markets was owned by Thomas Ryan, a sheriff and Charleston city alderman. Occupying the land between Chalmers and Queen streets, Ryan's Mart—now the Old Slave Mart—contained a shed with an arched entranceway, where slaves were traded; a four-story brick building, with offices and a jail, where slaves were held before trade; a kitchen; and a morgue.

When slaves were traded in the shed, they were displayed on auction tables, three feet high and ten feet long. According to legend, fiddlers were employed at the slave markets, a carryover from the foreign import days. In those days, the fiddlers played music for the slaves to dance to but not for the entertainment of the slaves or the customers. The dancing was intended to loosen the muscles of the slaves, which might have become atrophied during their long voyage from Africa—to make them more marketable.

The last slave auction was held in Ryan's Slave Market in 1863. Around 1878, the Slave Mart was renovated and used as a two-story tenement. It changed hands many times in the next few years, and was even used for a time as an auto repair shop. In 1938, it was bought by Charleston resident Miriam Wilson, who turned it into a museum featuring African and African-American arts and crafts. It was placed on the National Register of Historic Places in 1973. The museum was closed in 1987, but, recognizing the historical significance of the Old Slave Mart, the city of Charleston purchased the property in 1988.

Today, the Old Slave Mart, located on one of Charleston's only remaining cobblestone streets, is once again being operated as a museum. It's the only remaining building once used for slave trading in South Carolina. The museum, with its story of African-American history and the city's slave trade, is just one effort Charleston is making to face its ignoble history in the trade of human flesh.

As for the haunted history of the Old Slave Mart, there have been numerous reports of the echoing sounds of dancing feet as well as sightings of slaves in chains.

Charleston City Hall

In 1801, Charleston's city fathers constructed an elegant building to serve as a branch of the First Bank of the United States. One of eight branches, Charleston's branch served as the Office of Discount and Deposit.

The building's design is attributed to Charleston gentleman architect Gabriel Manigault. The building is constructed in the Adamesque architecture style, also known as Federal. This style, popular in Europe during the 1800s, interprets the Neoclassical style and uses decorative motifs of Roman art, such as sphinxes, scrolls, medallions, and urns.

The building's semi-circular projection on the north side and its round basement windows are characteristic of a Manigault design. The original red brick, trimmed in striking white Italian marble, was covered in stucco in 1882. Inside, a bulge was placed in the iron railing of the second floor balcony to accommodate the ladies' wide hoop skirts.

Congress revoked the bank's charter in 1811, and the building was turned over to the city of Charleston. It became the City Hall in 1818, and city council meetings have been held there ever since, making it the second oldest council chamber in the country. When the mayor and council meet here twice a month, they sit at the original Charleston-made 1818 black walnut desks.

Throughout the years, the city has acquired many paintings and objets d'art, each with a special connection to Charleston, which are displayed within City Hall. Among the paintings are two portraits of General Pierre G.T. Beauregard, the Confederate general in charge of the first battle of the Civil War.

Beauregard was an officer in the United States Army when the Civil War began. He immediately offered his services to the Confederacy and was placed in command of the defenses of Charleston. When Union Major Robert Anderson refused to evacuate Fort Sumter, it was Beauregard who led the attack on the fort. The April 12, 1861, shelling of Fort Sumter with canon fire is considered the first battle of the Civil War.

When Anderson finally evacuated—with no lives lost on either side—Beauregard emerged a hero.

In his next engagement, he and General Joseph Johnston led Confederate troops to victory in the first Battle of Bull Run. He moved on to Tennessee, where he took over command of the Battle of Shiloh when General A.S. Johnston was killed. He almost won it, too, but he called off the attack prematurely on the second day. When General Ulysses Grant's forces were reinforced, Beauregard found it necessary to retreat.

Beauregard was sent back to defend Charleston from September 1862 until April 1864, a chore he masterfully carried out. As a cultural and commercial hub, Charleston was considered an important target for the Union. During his time in the city, Beauregard successfully defended against formidable siege operations commanded by Union General Gillmore and Admirals Dupont and Dahlgren.

In May 1864, Beauregard re-enforced General Robert E. Lee in the defense of Richmond, Virginia, defeating General Benjamin Butler in the Bermuda Hundred Campaign near Drewry's Bluff in his most brilliant battle to date. Following this resounding success against Bulter, Beauregard began believing his own press. Developing delusions of grandeur, he proposed to Lee and Confederate President Jefferson Davis that he lead a grand invasion of the North. He'd defeat Butler first, see. Next he'd hit Grant and his forces. With his superior military skills, it'd be no problem to take 'em out in short order. And, voilà! The North would be his…uh…theirs!

Lee and Davis weren't convinced. To get Beauregard out of their hair, Davis sent him to command the forces in the west. Since all of his forces were engaged elsewhere, Beauregard was unable to stop General William Sherman's forces in their March to the Sea. He surrendered, along with his old buddy J.E. Johnston, in April 1865.

After the war, Beauregard returned to Louisiana, where he wrote several books on the Civil War and engaged in a war of words with Davis. The two published bitter attacks on each other, each blaming the other for the defeat of the Confederacy.

He also served in the government and became involved with the railroads. He served as president of New Orleans, Jackson, & Mississippi

Railroad and president of the New Orleans & Carrollton Street Railway, for which he invented a system of cable-powered street railway cars.

Beauregard is remembered fondly for his service in Charleston. Two portraits of the distinguished general hang in places of honor in the Charleston City Hall. The first was commissioned in New Orleans just as the Civil War was breaking out. Internationally-known artist George Healy began the portrait in New Orleans and, along with his brother Thomas, also an artist, followed Beauregard to Charleston to finish it. When Beauregard attacked Fort Sumter, the brothers left Charleston.

George, being a Northern man with Northern sympathies, returned to his home state of Massachusetts. Thomas, however, considered himself a Southern man, and returned to New Orleans. Because of his victory at Fort Sumter, another, smaller, portrait of Beauregard was commissioned—this time with Thomas doing the honors. He faithfully copied his brother's painting, but added two soldiers and a cannon in the lower left corner.

Perhaps it's the presence of these two portraits that have prompted Beauregard's return to Charleston. Maybe, an egoist even in death, he wants to live out eternity in a place where he was much admired. Whatever the reason, reports are that the spirit of Pierre Gustave Toutant Beauregard still wanders the halls of City Hall.

the phantom rider of mystic

John Cuthrie had known old May Allen his entire life. She had been a friend of John's mother when he was young. After his mother died, May didn't come around as much, which pleased John. Young boys generally don't like being around old women, and John was no exception. Also, May Allen reminded him of his mother, and he preferred not to relive the painful memories of her death.

John's mother and May Allen went to the same church, and sometimes he would attend Sunday services with them. The two women were shape-note singers at the small southern church outside Mystic, Georgia.

Shape-note singing was a simplified approach to singing church hymns. Even though it was praise music, John thought that the shape-note hymns had an eerie quality to them. Everyone sat on elevated pews arranged in a large square and engaged in call and response with the hymn leader. Frequently, that leader was May Allen.

May's late husband had given her an expensive diamond necklace with a matching set of earrings that she wore to church every Sunday. John thought that the jewels were much too fine for May, and, as a small boy, resented her for flaunting them. After all, his mother could never have fine things and neither could most of the people in their small rural church. John felt that May Allen had no right being so high-hat.

May Allen's other prized possession was an old hill pony named Red. The two were inseparable. No matter where old May was, Red was never very far behind. Even after May was too old to ride, she would drive down the road in her old car at a snail's pace with Red trailing close behind. Whether it was Sunday services, the market, or their small town post office, you'd see Red tied to a hitching post wherever May was doing business.

John and Red liked each other at first, but horses have a sense about people. As John grew into a discontented and angry teenager, the old pony began to keep his distance. When John would approach him, Red would snort loudly, turn sideways, and paw at the ground with his front hooves. John got the message and stayed away. Soon, he disliked Red as much as he disliked May.

As John grew up, he had numerous run-ins with the local law. These were small offenses at first and nothing of any consequence. Later, though, his offenses turned into real crimes, and soon everyone in and around the community of Mystic considered him a menace. "Bad seed" they called him.

Before too long, John had had enough of the town of Mystic, and he decided it was time to leave forever. The last person who saw him before he left was old May Allen, who chastised him vigorously for ruining his life. She said, "Your mother would be brokenhearted to see the mess you've made of things. Straighten up and act like you've got some sense!" In response, John said some very unkind things and then he left.

To a young man, forever isn't quite as long as he thinks it's going to be. So it was fifteen years after he'd "gone for good" that John found himself back in Mystic. Life in the big city hadn't been what John expected, and things had gone from bad to worse for him. He'd even spent some time on a county prison farm. Unfortunately, John's experiences hadn't taught him anything about the straight and narrow. Instead, he was a bitter man who came back home because, frankly, he didn't know where else to go.

Old friends and neighbors knew nothing about John's life of crime after he'd left Mystic. They were hoping only that the years away from home had mellowed him and tempered his anger. Little did they know that John was already contributing to the increase in petty crime within their community.

Old May Allen had died two years after John left town. Red, her constant companion, refused to eat after her death and died a short time later. Some say he died from grief. Red just could not stand to be separated from his beloved mistress. The part of the story that was most interesting—to John at least—was that May Allen had been buried in her expensive jewels. John visited May's grave, not so much to pay respects to his mother's best friend, but to get the lay of the land. John, you see, had decided to rob the grave and steal the diamond necklace and earrings.

John picked the night of the next full moon to commit his crime. If the weather cooperated, he'd be in and out of the cemetery and halfway to Atlanta to sell the jewels before anyone noticed.

Now grave robbing is a nasty business at any time, but on this hot summer's night, John found it particularly difficult. It was very hot and humid, and he was covered in sweat before he dug his first shovelful of earth. An approaching thunderstorm threatened to make it much worse, so John wasted no time.

The earth was reasonably moist from a wet and rainy spring, and it made the work go quickly. Soon John was engaged in a continuous rhythm of digging. He paused once to keep his eye on a slithering snake. The light of his lantern illuminated the snake as it moved along the edge of the grave. From time to time, he would catch glimpses of a predator's eyes in the night underbrush.

Occasional flashes of lightning in the distance silhouetted the headstones and memorials. He was most disquieted by the sounds of thunder that seemed to resonate through the ground itself. The claps of thunder sounded much closer to John than they should've been. He looked up to see just how far away the approaching storm really was and then continued to dig.

Periodic blasts of hot breeze on his face and neck reminded John of the hot summer days of his youth. Those memories were not pleasant ones. He pushed them aside and kept digging. Amid the sounds of shoveling earth and the approaching storm, John thought he heard something moving among the tombstones. Though he could see nothing, John couldn't shake the feeling that he wasn't alone.

Suddenly, John felt his shovel hit something solid, and he experienced a rush of adrenaline. He continued to dig until the coffin was uncovered. Soon thereafter, he used a crowbar to force the simple wooden coffin open. There before him was the rotting corpse of May Allen with her jewels glittering by lantern light. Moments earlier, it began to lightly rain, but John hadn't noticed. The thrill of discovering the diamond necklace and earrings pushed everything else from his mind. John, beginning to be covered in mud, set to work removing the jewels. He began by removing earrings from lifeless flesh. John was surprised that the sight of his mother's dead friend hadn't bothered him very much. Earrings in hand, he turned his attention to the diamond necklace. "Give it up, Worm Food," he said aloud as the necklace came free.

It was raining harder as John pulled himself out of the open grave. For several minutes, he inspected his prizes by the light of his lantern. He marveled at how the jewels glistened in the light. Then he felt the ground shake as a clap of thunder rumble all around him. A blast of hot breeze pushed through the rain and broke John's reverie. Quickly, John put the jewels in his pants pocket and, glancing one last time at the corpse of May Allen, he headed toward his car to make his getaway.

It was a good twenty-minute walk to where he had hidden his car, and as he made his way through the rain and the woods, for the very first time, John felt afraid.

Petty theft, assault, arson, vandalism—John could now add grave robbing to his list of dubious accomplishments. He put his hand in his pocket and fingered the diamonds to make sure they were still there. Satisfied that they were secure, he quickened his pace and began to run through the woods. Then, abruptly, John stopped and surveyed the woods behind him. "Is someone following me?" John thought. But no matter how hard he looked, he could see no one. It was raining harder now, and the ground shook with thunder. It was as if the storm was following him trying to thwart his escape.

Ten minutes later, it occurred to John that he must have taken a wrong turn on his way back from the cemetery. Five minutes after that, he realized that he was probably lost. John stood still in a small clearing. Holding his lantern high, he looked around trying to decide where he was. Suddenly, from somewhere behind him, he heard a loud noise that sent shock waves through his spine. The sound was the scream of a wild animal and was something between a panther's howl and horse's neigh. Whatever it was, it was large, and it was getting closer.

John Cuthrie's feet were virtually stuck to the ground. No matter how hard he tried, he couldn't force his legs to move. Rustling in the woods and brush behind him signaled the approach of something—something fearful, something large. Then a large shape leapt out of the woods and knocked John to the ground as if he were nothing more than a dead branch.

John looked up to see the ghostly shape of a horse standing before him. The animal lifted its head, screamed again, and reared up on its hindquarters before stomping the earth. With each stomp of its hooves, the ground shook. The ghostly animal snorted a blast of hot sweet breath, and John realized that the unseen presence he had previously felt was now standing before him. The thunder had been its hooves, and the hot breeze had been its breath, the breath of death! The sight of the spectral beast illuminated by flashes of lightning frightened John, but there was something familiar in its movements. Then fright turned to terror as he recognized the sideways twist, snorting, and pawing of the horse. It was the ghost of May Allen's horse, Red.

The phantom horse snorted and reared upward again before charging John, who scrambled to his feet and ran for his life. "He knows what I did to May's grave. He knows I have the jewels," he thought. Red was almost upon him, so John dodged in and out of thickets in a vain attempt to evade the vengeful horse.

Red's ghost charged through the trees and underbrush. The horse struck at John with his forequarters but John kept running. No matter where he ran, though, Red stuck to him like glue and was never far behind. John could feel the sickly sweet aroma of its hot breath on his neck. With each blast of breath, fear tore at John's soul.

The next few minutes seemed like hours as their game of cat and mouse continued. Finally, John hid behind a large tree and listened for sounds of his pursuer. All John could hear were the sounds of the woods and rain. He remained still and didn't move. For the first time in years, John Cuthrie prayed.

After a few minutes had passed without any sight or sound of his adversary, John thought it safe enough to step out from behind the tree. When he did, he found himself standing face to face with Red's ghost! The horse gave a quick jerking turn of his head and, with an unearthly snort, knocked John flat on his back. John looked up in abject terror to see a rider upon the horse. He wiped the mud and sweat from his eyes. John was staring at the rotting corpse of May Allen sitting astride her beloved pony.

May's corpse got down off Red and slowly walked toward John. "My God!" he thought. "She looks just like she did when I left her in the grave." Covering his face with his hands, he screamed in desperation. Red stepped closer and pawed thunderously at the earth several times.

"What do you want from me?" John asked.

A reply hissed out of May's black and yellow teeth. "My jewels," she said, "give me back my jewels."

John frantically searched his pocket for the diamond necklace and earrings. For a brief moment he feared that he might have dropped them during the pursuit. Finally, he felt the jewels. He tossed them to the ground between May's corpse and where he lay, as if they might form a barrier to her approach. Rotting flesh and bone picked up the jewels and put them back where they once had been.

May stood up straight as if she were admiring the jewels in a mirror. Earrings hanging on dried flesh and a necklace surrounding exposed bone presented a morbid and surreal picture. Then the corpse looked at John with vacant sockets and hissed, "Your mother would be brokenhearted to see the mess you've made with your life. What are we to do with you, John Cuthrie?"

It was then that John heard himself begging for his own life. He promised to mend his ways and be a better person. He would make it up to the people of Mystic any way that he could. "Please," John cried, weeping uncontrollably, "please don't kill me!"

The ghostly pair stood over him, silent and near motionless. Then May Allen hissed, "See that you do, young man." She turned and mounted Red. Dead horse and rider disappeared into the woods. As they did, the sound of thunder faded away and the breeze cooled.

The next morning, John staggered out of the wet and rainy woods, exhausted and in shock. In the days that followed, the town buzzed with stories about poor May Allen's grave being desecrated. It was collectively accepted that a transient had been the culprit and was long gone by now. The townspeople were relieved that May's diamond necklace and earrings were still on her body and had been untouched by the grave robber. Two days later, May and her jewels were re-buried in a brand new coffin. John didn't go to the service, but he was certain that May did, indeed, have her jewels again. He also knew that no one but May would ever have the necklace and matching earrings. She and Red would see to that.

Though he was never able to fully tell anyone in Mystic what had happened to him that night, no one really cared. You see, John is a different man now. He's happy and contented for the first time in his life. He spends his time farming and raising horses. Oh, he also sings in the church that his mother attended when he was a child. It seems that John Cuthrie has become quite an accomplished shape-note singer.

the villages

It was a dark and stormy night—well, it should have been. It was actually a balmy Alabama evening. A diaphanous haze thick with the acridly sweet scent of mimosas blanketed the darkness where three teenagers drove aimlessly.

Like most teenagers, these three were looking for something that at least slightly resembled entertainment. Sheffield was a very small town to them, and in their words "there wasn't anything to do." Unlike many of their contemporaries, these three weren't "into" drinking or drugs or "other things." They were fairly well behaved—for teenagers, anyway.

The leader of the little group was the oldest. Arti was a handsome, tall, dark-headed guy with bright blue-green eyes that tended to have a mischievous twinkle. At sixteen, not only was Arti the instigator of most of the friends' excursions and adventures, he was also the driver.

Robert, at fifteen and a half, was the next eldest. He was smaller in stature than Arti. He had soft brown hair and deep brown eyes that were very expressive against his pale skin. Robert had begun to date Maggie, who was just a little younger at only fifteen. Both boys gave her a great deal of grief about being the baby of the bunch. Maggie had shoulder length red hair, green eyes, and alabaster skin with a smattering of freckles across her nose and cheeks.

Robert had met Maggie at the mall—it being "the only place to go" in town. Dating then and dating now are very different things. Dating then meant meeting somewhere and hanging out with your friends, and then maybe stealing a kiss when you dropped your date off at her door. Your date had to be accepted by your friends back then. Arti was Robert's best friend and had been since the first grade. It was very important that Arti like Maggie, and he did, to Robert's relief.

On this particular night, Arti was at the wheel and up for adventure. They had already gone by their ordinary haunts and had become bored with them.

"Where can we go tonight? There's nothing going on!" Robert whined from the passenger seat.

The three bounced ideas around for several minutes before Arti excitedly said, "I know! I know! Let's go to the old abandoned house in the Villages!"

"Cool!" was the response from the other two.

The old abandoned house was built before World War II in a small quaint neighborhood of stuccoed houses with tiled roofs known as the Villages. The Villages had originally been built on the other side of the Tennessee River in Florence for the workers constructing Wilson Dam, which began in 1918. These homes were moved to Sheffield sometime shortly before the dam was completed, between 1924 and 1927. The original use of the building was thought by the teenagers to be an army barrack, a school, and lastly an apartment building. Whatever it was to begin with, it was abandoned at the moment and was a perfect candidate for exploration and adventure.

Arti turned into the slumbering neighborhood and headed for the darkened target. The house dominated the street. Unlike the other petite bungalows of the Villages, this structure was four stories tall. It loomed an inky silhouette against the azure evening sky. All three friends felt a little foreboding feeling as they passed the expansive façade and cruised around to the back of the hulking abandoned shell of a building.

Arti had done some exploring there earlier in the day and

discovered a way in. He had placed a nail against the doorframe, so he could tell if anyone else had gone into his newest conquest. All the other doors had been secured, as well as the multiple sets of windows throughout the home. Arti was first to the door; nope, the nail was still in place! "Looks like we have it all to ourselves!" he said happily.

Robert and Maggie tumbled out of Arti's car and looked up, awestruck. It was truly a massive place. Arti opened the door, and the three ventured into a great room that spanned about twenty-five feet wide by forty feet in length. Along one side of the "great hall," as they called it, were six sets of French doors. It was a beautiful space. There were fireplaces at both ends of the room, and again, two sets of French doors to the stairwells on either end.

Arti had found an old telephone line spool to use as a table and several wooden crates for seats, which was where he chose to put the boom box and flashlights and Cokes and candles and chips and any other thing he thought to bring that might increase their sense of creature comforts. They took their time exploring the vast ballroom-like space. They lit candles on the fireplaces and on the spool, where they also put a large flashlight pointed at the ceiling to bounce light all around, dissipating much of the darkness and giving the great hall almost a cozy feel.

"Let's see the rest of the place," said Robert. And they were off. The three bounded noisily up the stairs and through the many empty and dilapidated rooms. The stairwells were wide with large beautiful arched windows at every landing. Many of the walls between the rooms had been torn out, most likely in preparation for renovation. For the teenagers, it meant they could see from one side of the house to the other on every floor.

The three friends scampered about, playing hide-and-seek and wild games of tag until they decided perhaps they were getting much too loud, and Arti pointed out, "You know, breaking and entering is like a crime, okay."

Maggie suggested going back down to the great room. It was her favorite, and it was also closest to the car if they needed to get out quickly. No one wanted the police, or more importantly, their parents involved. They sat down at the spool table and gleefully snacked, gossiped about high school dramas, and listened to the Cure, Billy Idol, and Boy George.

Arti was in the midst of laughing about what exactly Boy George was when Maggie grabbed his arm and said, "Did you hear that?"

"Hear what?" both boys replied.

"I don't know. It sounded like footsteps over there in the stairwell."

Before Arti could turn off the boom box, the battery-powered flashlight on the table flickered and went out. The music also stopped suddenly, as if all the batteries had drained in a matter of seconds.

"Um, that's kinda creepy," Robert whispered, as he snuggled closer to Maggie, who was listening intently to whatever it was she heard.

"Did it just get colder in here?" Arti was now also whispering.

"Yea, I'm freezing. Maybe we should leave now?" Maggie murmured to Arti.

He was beginning to feel really uneasy and started to gather up everything he had so carefully laid out for the evening's entertainment. Little did he know the real entertainment was about to arrive.

At that moment, the French doors to the far stairwell flew open, and a cold breeze rushed in past the friends, blowing out the candles. Robert grabbed his lighter and relit his candle instantly. "Ol' quick draw!"

"Sshh! Listen!" Maggie was standing up with the boom box in her hands and starting to edge toward the exit. Arti and Robert followed her lead and slowly made the motions of evacuation. Then they froze. In the deafening silence, they heard footsteps.

The sound was growing louder, almost as loud as the sound of the heartbeats of the three intruders. Whoever or whatever it was, was coming downstairs, coming to the great hall, coming to the three terrified teenagers.

The footsteps simply got louder and faster, until they were booming, and seemed not only to originate from the stairwell, but from the entire building. The three stood frozen, peering into the shadows, desperately trying to see who or what their pursuer was.

The booming was so loud now that the windows were rattling. The group headed for the door. Their feelings of panic were overwhelming, and as they reached the door frame, the booming steps reached the bottom of the stairwell in an incredible thud. Arti turned and yelled out, "Hello, who's there?" into the darkness of the great hall. Nothing could have prepared him for his answer. A bone-chilling bloodcurdling demonic scream of a man in anguish, ending in the snarl of some rabid beast, split the air around the three teenagers.

"Get out! Get out! Get out!" Arti screamed. He pushed his pals out the door toward the car, and as he moved to shut the door, he was flung with tremendous force onto the ground outside. He wasted no time in figuring out what had happened. He just ran for the car, slid into the driver's seat, rammed the keys into the ignition, and spun the tires—getting the gang "the heck outta here!"

At a safe distance, which incidentally was through two cities and across the Tennessee River bridge in another county, they came to a stop. All of them were pale, panting, and on the verge of hyperventilating. Arti interrupted the heavy breathing and pounding heartbeats. "Is everyone okay?"

"Arti, what's that on your cheek? There's something red on your face. Turn on the overhead light. Let me take a look at you," said Maggie.

On the right side of Arti's face, a hand print was clearly visible against his once olive, now ghostly white, complexion. They all took turns placing their hands in the reddened impression, only to discover that it was abnormally large.

"Creepy!" Robert shuttered.

"Oh, Arti! It hit you!" Maggie was concerned understandably.

"What was that thing?" stammered Robert. "What in the world was that thing!? What was it!?" he sat in shock still panting.

"I don't know, but I don't think I'm going back there. I've had enough of playing patty cake with demons. How about y'all?" Arti was getting his sense of humor back. The teenagers giggled and boasted about what they would have done if they had gotten the chance. "I'd open up a can of whoop exorcism on his butt if he tried that patty cake stuff with me!" growled Robert as he beat his chest Tarzan style.

"Then I'd give him an offer he couldn't refuse! See you later buddy!" this time in his best Alabama gangster impersonation. They laughed. Maggie said, "I don't know about you guys, but I think that was the most exciting thing that ever happened to me! Talk about entertainment! Arti, you sure do know how to pick 'em!"

"Yea, umm, I think maybe abandoned buildings are gonna be taken off my list of things to do! What do y'all think?"

They all agreed.

A few years later, the abandoned building was renovated and became lovely condos. The three teenagers grew up and went to college and still get together on occasion and ride around remembering the adventures of their youth. One evening, they decided to drive by the Villages just to see what, if anything, had changed. As the three slowly glided past the gleaming renovation, they noticed the structure was dark. "I wonder what else is living there with all those people," Arti considered aloud. As they crept on into the night, a bright light flickered inside.

bookin' it

Does the spirit of writer Jack Kerouac haunt his favorite bookstore? Many people believe so.

Haslam's Book Store in St. Petersburg first opened its doors in 1933. It was the middle of the Great Depression, and to increase business, owners Mary and Charles Haslam sold handicrafts, roses, doilies, and used magazines in addition to books. The store survived and grew, and by the 1960s, it was a thriving business.

Jack Kerouac came to St. Petersburg under duress in 1966. He and his wife were living with his mother, and when she left their Lowell, Massachusetts, home to avoid the cold winters, they went with her. The voice of the Beat generation didn't give St. Petersburg a ringing endorsement, often calling it "Salt Petersburg, the town of the newly wed and the living dead."

Kerouac was only in his mid-forties by the time he reached St. Petersburg, but an addiction to Johnnie Walker Red and Benzedrine had taken its toll on his body, his mind, and his spirit. He'd used up his youth hard and fast in a revved-up, wild, and desperate road trip in search of enlightenment. He was the first to howl "Sex, Drugs, and Rock 'n' Roll," the battle cry of disenfranchised youth everywhere. Except, of course, his cry was made before rock 'n' roll came about, so he'd cried for bebop instead.

Bebop jazz had, in fact, been the inspiration for his stream-of-consciousness writing style, a style Kerouac called spontaneous prose. He would start with a thought, a sentence, or an idea, and play it for all its essence. Then he'd move on to the next, feeling a rhythm build and working off it like riffs on a guitar, ignoring the sanity of punctuation and drawing in his reader with the cadence of his beat.

He was a prolific writer, and a fast one, having written *On The Road* in just three, coffee- and Benzedrine-soaked weeks. In addition to his unorthodox punctuation, he wrote the entire manuscript in one long, continuous roll. Perhaps that's why it took seven years to sell it!

Published in 1957, this mostly autobiographical, but embellished, story of his travels with friends became the defining work of the Beat generation and made Kerouac the king of that generation, a title he despised. The fame it brought him may ultimately have been his downfall.

By the time he arrived in St. Petersburg, his publishing days were behind him. The road trip was in the rearview mirror, and enlightenment had eluded him. He was here, settled in a strange town, angry and disillusioned. He drank heavily, saturating an already diseased liver, and spent days locked away in his 10th Avenue home, eyes glued to the boob tube.

But it wasn't all bad. He'd found a couple of friends who dropped by to talk, and he'd found succor in the local bookstore, where he could browse the shelves and immerse himself in words.

Charles Haslam didn't recognize the disheveled man as a famous writer when he first entered the store. It wasn't until later, after the man had spent quite some time browsing through the shelves and left, that Charles noticed the books of Jack Kerouac had been pulled from the bottom shelf and placed right at eye level. As he was replacing them, he happened to glance at the photograph on the back panel of *On The Road*.

Aha. Now he understood. Sad, he thought, that a man such as him should be in such a condition. He had heard, of course, that Kerouac had moved here, and, too, had heard of the unflattering comments he'd made about St. Petersburg. If he didn't want to be here, thought Haslam, then he should just leave. Didn't need him around messing up the shelves if that's the way he felt.

Kerouac wasn't going anywhere, and he seemed to enjoy the bookstore, for he visited often, spending hours browsing through the ever-growing inventory of books. An ongoing argument arose between him and Haslam about the store's alphabetical arrangement of books. Seems Kerouac's books always ended up on the bottom shelves, a problem he would remedy each time he came, moving them to a shelf at eye level and facing them forward. And each time, Haslam would move them back.

The put-out store owner spoke to the writer about the problem several times, asking him to leave the books where they were, and many times a lively discussion about book placement ensued. Neither would yield his position.

Of course, the point was rendered moot (or was it?), on October 21, 1969, when Kerouac suffered a fatal abdominal hemorrhage.

Many people suspect, the owners of Haslam's included, that Kerouac is still overseeing the placement of his books here. Since his death, Haslam's has greatly expanded. With more than three hundred thousand books, it is now the state's largest independent bookstore. So if Kerouac is here, at least he's got plenty to do.

It was after the store's expansion into the building next door in the 1970s that weird things started happening, things that led employees and owners to believe that a spirit had moved in. Customers and employees began reporting incidences where they felt the presence of someone when there was no one there. At times, someone would feel the tap of an invisible hand on his shoulder. There were sudden cold spots, and most tellingly, books would mysteriously fly off the shelves. On several occasions, it was Kerouac's books that fell.

It happened to Ray Hinst, third-generation owner of Haslam's. A few years back, Hinst says, he was restocking the fiction shelves, when he heard the distinctive sound of a book hitting the floor behind him. When he turned around to look, a copy of Kerouac's *On The Road* lay at his feet. It was just past midnight and he was there alone. Or so he thought.

The haunting of Haslam's has piqued the interest of local paranormal research groups, who've visited with their equipment and "sensitives," people who are able to feel and see otherworldly entities. They say, indeed, the place has ghosts, and yes, they believe Jack Kerouac is one of them.

The research team has determined that the benevolent spirit of a middle-aged man with salt and pepper hair looks remarkably like the photograph of Kerouac on the back cover of *On the Road*. The spirit is elusive, however, choosing not to speak. He follows the group around and watches the activity with a bemused expression on his face. The team says he likes the books and really enjoys being there. It's a place where he found comfort in life and seems to still find it in death.

In addition to Kerouac, the team says they've encountered a little boy spirit, who likes to take the books off the shelves, and a little girl, who wanders around the store confused. They believe she's the spirit of a little girl who was killed in a car wreck in front of the store. They also report seeing a man and woman who sit close together reading.

Hinst says he doesn't object to the presence of these spirits, as long as they're not scaring off the customers. He can "live and let live," he says, although "live" might not be exactly the right word. He does note that perhaps there's a good reason Kerouac seems to be leaving the books on their shelves. What with all that expansion and the addition of thousands books, his works now have better placement—right about eye level.

fool's gold

California still haunts me. In fact, there is no part of my day, waking or sleeping, that is not populated with shades of those long dead, and memories of my life when it was full of hope and the promise of love.

I have been evicted from yet another boardinghouse for waking the occupants in the dead of night, screaming and wrestling with one of my many ghosts. Although it is barely October, there is frost every evening, and soon I must find a place to stay or risk death by exposure.

Exposure. Perhaps that would not be an undesirable end. After all, it is the hiding of events and facts that has brought me across the continent to this cold, forsaken state of dour, pale people. October in California is a time of bright sunshine and even brighter company; the people there are not forced to abandon their outdoor pursuits until the rains come in late November. Even then, the rains are welcome, for their random action often uncovers new and profitable sources of great wealth.

But the wealth I speak of is a false one. I would happily trade every pinch of gold dust ever found in California for a return to my former state of relative poverty and happiness. Even though I have nearly five pounds of the treacherous substance, secreted in various hidden pockets and seams of my coat and pack, I cannot find a place to stay or even buy a home, for these demons pursue me night and day.

I know there is a reckoning to come, and I fear it even more than the specters who appear before me at every turn. Perhaps I should make my way down South for the winter, plying my trade and trying to settle some part of my soul. No matter where I travel, though, I must cross water, and every one of those streams and creeks and rivers are spanned by the damnable bridges, identical to the one that became the instrument of my downfall.

I was not, you see, born to become the itinerant peddler I am today. My parents sent me to college in the year 1843, at a great personal sacrifice. I then became a teacher, married my sweetheart, and produced two offspring in short order. One daughter and one son, a tidy little balance to match my tidy little life.

Then in 1849, I was struck by an illness so profound that it left my life—and most probably my afterlife—in ruins. That many others succumbed to this fever gives me no comfort. Those other victims do not give me any companionship, or ease my fears of what is to come, or soothe me when my terror strikes.

My wife had been petitioning me to purchase a carriage. It was not seemly, she said, for her to ride in a rude wagon when her husband was such a person of importance in our little town. But I saw no means of financing such an extravagance. Her nagging irked me. The cries of my two young children made my skin crawl. The local children, whom I was supposed to enlighten, seemed a dull and loutish bunch. Their parents, whose support I must maintain in order to keep my position, seemed equally as tedious, if not more so. So the fellow who appeared at the tavern one evening, slim and well-muscled and bursting with vitality, had found in me a most receptive audience.

"There's gold just lying on the riverbanks, waiting to be picked up," he explained. "You take a flat pan, swirl the water and stones around, and pick out the gold." He pulled out a little pouch. "It looks like this." The pieces scattered on the polished bar top, some smaller than the head of a pin but others nearly the size of a pea, gleamed and glittered wickedly.

"When I left, my daughters were panning $15 to $25 a day in gold dust. It's easy work."

I shouldered my way up through the crowd to study this man more closely. Like me, he appeared to be a gentleman. He spoke well, and I listened with growing excitement as he described the principal routes to the gold fields.

"You can go by ship, but I hear there's so many people waiting for a ship in Panama that it takes longer than the overland route. And people are dropping left and right from scurvy on the ships, too."

"How long does it take to get there by land?" My neighbor, a bank clerk by trade, was as captivated as I.

"It depends. You can get to the mountains in eight weeks or so, even with a loaded wagon. Then you can go through the Sierras by Peter Lassen's trail, which might take six weeks, or take the Truckee River crossing, which could take four or five weeks."

"Isn't that the route the Donner party took?"

The stranger nodded somberly, and the crowd surrounding him recalled the grisly tale of cannibalism and death by the group caught in an early snow.

My dreams that night were filled with visions of great riches, towering, snowcapped mountains, grand mansions, and elegantly clad women, none of whom, I am ashamed to report, bore the slightest resemblance to my wife. The next morning I hurried to the tavern to speak in private to the man from California.

"How much will it take to get me there?" I was already determined to go at any cost. It seemed the perfect solution.

"You going alone, without your family?" His brown eyes swept over me, assessing, I thought, my physical stamina and courage.

I nodded eagerly.

"You'll need at least $100 once you're there to buy your equipment and such. It'll take another $50 to get there, but only if you're starting out with a good horse."

I asked a bit timidly, if he was returning to California soon himself.

"Matter of fact, I was thinking of leaving next week," he drawled.

"I'm taking Pete Lassen's trail 'cause it'll take me around some of the highest mountains instead of through them. May's late to get started, and I don't want to get caught by the snow."

"I could pay you to be my guide, if you would permit me, sir."

"There are a few other adventurers here who are interested in a guide," he said. "If you're ready to go by next Thursday, I'll have you in the gold fields by September 10. You can pay me $15 just like everybody else."

Fifteen dollars was half a month's salary for me. But, I calculated, if his daughters found $15 a day in gold and I could work twice as hard, his fee was negligible.

I returned home and informed my wife of my decision. She was stunned but could see that argument would be fruitless. Those ridiculous women at Seneca Falls notwithstanding, my wife knew her place. She began to pack hurriedly for a temporary return to her parents' house. She would live there with the children until I came home, within fifteen months, I assured her, leading a horse laden with my newfound wealth.

I arranged in a few short days for the sale of our meager furnishings, with the bulk of the proceeds going into my pocket for a grubstake, as the stranger from California so quaintly phrased it. All but one of my fellow townsmen dropped out of the expedition, so we were a group of three leaving Illinois one late May day.

We were only two weeks into our journey when my neighbor, the bank clerk, decided to turn around. The journey was tedious and long, but my guide convinced me that we were making good time, being on horseback and unencumbered by families, wagons, or livestock. As we labored through the Rockies, we saw many household items by the side of the trail, abandoned by travelers who had overburdened their wagons. Barrels of china, chairs, tables, even a piano were all left to rot in the sun and be buried by snow from September to April or longer.

My first sight of the Sierras gave me such a shock that my guide laughed. It had taken several days' riding to come close enough to comprehend their size, but when I finally did, I nearly lost all courage. I felt so puny on my horse that I thought we would be forever lost among those massive peaks. We pushed on, though, and I was glad for the route that enabled us to avoid the most difficult climbs.

We left the mountains on September 1, and my excitement began to mount steadily. Here at last was the promised land. The site of my future prosperity, the night we crossed Deer Creek and camped, the gold fields an easy day's ride south, I proposed we celebrate with a bottle of brandy I had carefully hoarded during the long journey.

I fell into a drunken stupor before midnight and woke before dawn, queasy, cold, and stiff. I soon realized my bedroll was gone. Panicked, I stood to look for my horse and pack. All gone. My guide had stolen everything but the clothes on my back, even going so far as to remove the wallet from my pocket while I slept.

I leaned over and vomited violently. Even now, I will not touch brandy for the bitter memories it invokes. But in September of 1849, I still had the courage to continue my quest, and struck out on foot for the gold fields.

I didn't get far. Before dark I found myself on the banks of a large river blocking my access to the future, with only one apparent crossing. The bridge looked dilapidated, although the tollkeeper assured me it had been built at great expense only two years before.

"I get ten to fifteen people an hour crossin' sometimes," he cackled. "Comin' and goin', but mostly goin'. You lookin' to git rich too, young man?"

I allowed that I was, but that I'd suffered a temporary setback in my financial affairs.

This made him hoot with laughter. "Welcome to California, boy! Don't you trust nobody, 'cause nobody's gonna trust you!"

I found it difficult, at that point, to ask for the privilege of crossing on credit, but I did my best.

He shook his head emphatically.

"No, sir, no credit, no free passage." He cackled again. "Unless you're a man of the law, why, then I'd have to let you pass!"

Discouraged, I retreated a few hundred yards back along the trail and prepared to spend a cold, hungry night considering my options. A family party of about six set up camp next to me right at dusk, and I hurried over to their campfire to introduce myself.

They were kind enough to tell me that passage over all bridges in California was free on Sundays, to allow the faithful to attend church. I was surprised to hear of such civility in such a wild country, but it seemed like Providence was smiling on me. Tomorrow, my fellow travelers told me, was Sunday. I had lost track of the days during my passage through the terrible Sierras.

I was hungry, cold, and discouraged when I arrived at Marysville. The little town was a stew of mud, men, and mules. I had to provision myself, so I asked for work at several establishments.

"A schoolteacher?" The storekeeper thought this was quite a joke. "Look, Samuel, here's a schoolteacher from..." He turned back to me. "Where'd ya say you was from?"

"Illinois." I didn't appreciate being the source of his amusement, but I hadn't had a meal in three days.

"Illinois! He wants to work!" A man half as large as a house came lumbering over. Samuel, I suppose.

"Illinois, you'd better git yourself some gear and git out to them fields," he told me. "You won't find any work in town 'cause nobody's gonna hire you for fear you'll run off after that gold as soon as you can."

I had to admit he had a certain logic. I begged him for a job anyway.

"Look, in Illinois, I gits $1 a pound fer flour, $2 fer a pound of bacon or dried beef, $30 fer a shirt, and $100 fer one a them serapes over there," he gestured toward a bright garment tightly woven out of wool. "Now, am I gonna trust a complete stranger with all these things that are pretty near worth their weight in gold?"

They did give me a few slices of bread in exchange for sweeping the floor. I headed east, out of town, since I could not go either south or west without crossing a toll bridge. Already the covered, barnlike structures were becoming a symbol of my desperate state of mind. Through their shadowy depths, I was sure, lay my salvation. I could not have been more wrong.

I walked until nearly dark, parallel to the Yuba River, a wild and ferocious torrent that roared out of the Sierras, which brooded over the landscape some fifty miles east. I saw little activity on either side of the river until I reached yet another covered bridge.

A little knot of men had gathered at the mouth of the bridge, shouting and gesturing. On the other side, I could see tents pitched all across a field and men hunkered down by the side of the river, washing dirt or building elaborate contraptions to wash greater quantities of dirt. Again, as at Marysville, there was a confusion of men, mud, and mules, but there was no air of carnival here as there had been in the town. This was deadly serious work.

"You can't get away with that, Jim Cooper!" A burly man with crossed forearms seemed to be the center of the storm. He stood squarely in the center of the bridge opening, while another smaller man hovered around him.

"You took at least $5 worth of gold dust, and now you're saying I owe you for crossing back? That's robbery, and you know it!"

"I weighed that dust, and it was less than a quarter of an ounce. You left with a loaded mule, you're comin' back with a loaded mule, it's a dollar each way. See there?" The big man pointed to a sign nailed to the side of the bridge.

To my dismay, tolls here were higher than any I'd seen yet. It cost twenty-five cents to cross on foot, fifty cents with a mule, and a dollar if your mule had a pack. I had no desire to argue with the formidable man guarding the mouth of the bridge, but the first sign of any gold mining I had yet seen was on the other side of the river, so I had no alternative.

Just as I approached the man, I sensed some movement underneath the bridge out of the corner of my eye. I looked, and there was a young man, swinging by his arms from one crisscrossed support to the next, across the river, going to desperate measures to avoid the toll.

I walked up to the tollkeeper with as much dignity as I could muster.

"Sir," I said, "is there a penalty for cheating the tollkeeper out of his toll?"

"Sure is," he roared. "Who are you?"

"Should you collect such a penalty, would you be obliged to reward the person who led you to catch such a scoundrel?"

"No!" He scowled at me so fiercely that I began to think I should follow the young man under the bridge, instead of reporting him.

"Well," said another man, "we would certainly be most grateful. You wouldn't believe the lengths some people go to avoid our toll, which is, I think, quite reasonable." It was the smaller man who had been hovering around earlier.

"Then, sir, cross the bridge with me and I shall show you your culprit!" I decided I was not agile or foolhardy enough to swing across the underside of the bridge.

The three of us crossed, but not before the burly man picked up a shotgun from the inside corner of the structure. When I saw the gun, I was well satisfied with my decision not to cheat them of their toll.

"You there," he shouted at the figure, who had just dropped off the last support and was clambering down the stone pier to reach the riverbank. "The toll is a quarter, whether you cross over or under, and now you'll pay triple!"

When the agile young shirker appeared before us, I saw he was little more than a boy.

"Aw, Mr. Cooper," he said. "I've been at Marysville, and I lost all my money. I've got a little dust in my pack, back at camp, and I'll pay you, really I will!"

"But you didn't intend to, is that right, Jack?" The other man, Mr. Cooper's partner, could also put forth an intimidating stare.

"Of course he wasn't going to pay us!" Mr. Cooper—the burly man—grabbed the young man's arm and twisted up until the boy's face went white.

"I'll pay you now, really—come with me, we'll go get it!"

Half carrying the boy by his upper arm, Mr. Cooper marched off in the direction of a little cluster of tents. I tried to melt into the crowd that had gathered, but Mr. Cooper's partner grabbed my arm.

"Didn't fergit about the toll, didja?" He grinned, and the awful stench of his breath wafted over me.

"Ah, of course not!" I cast about in my mind for an explanation, but found none. "I was, actually, wanting to know if you would have some employment for me since I was the unfortunate victim of a swindle just three days ago."

He laughed. "The swindle started the day you left fer California, man, haven't you figgered that out yet?" We walked back across the bridge, which creaked and moaned with the rising evening wind. "All those men over there, they'll not make more than they need to buy more supplies, and then that deposit'll run out and they'll need to build a stamp mill to git the gold out or have to move on to another deposit." He leaned over to me, confidentially, and I had to force myself not to withdraw from his offensive odor.

"You wanna get rich, you build yerself a bridge. That's the way to make a livin' and not break yer back in the process!"

It seemed as if he were right. When we emerged, there were three more men waiting to pay their toll, and a farmer with a wagon drawn by two oxen. Nearly two days' wages for me in Illinois, and all in the space of a few minutes.

After collecting the money, my companion turned to me again. "You've got long legs," he said. "Ain't afraid to climb, are ya?"

In fact, I am afraid of heights, but I saw no other reply was wanted, so I said no. He handed me a hammer and a canvas sack of shingles, and told me to attend to the roof where some shingles had blown off during a recent storm.

With some difficulty I ascended to the roof. A few rough boards had been nailed to the side of the structure to aid in my climb. Apparently these repairs were frequently needed. Once on top, the river was so far below me and rushing at such a speed that I felt near fainting with fear. I could not stand up but lay on the roof, clutching the shingles and praying that the shingles I held would not come unstuck from the bridge and send me tumbling to my death in the torrents below.

After a time, my senses steadied. I studiously avoided looking down at the water and crawled on my hands and knees across the structure, looking for places where shingles were missing. I nailed six or seven new ones into place before I heard a shout from below.

"Hey, you! You gonna spend the night up there?"

I crawled to the edge and awkwardly climbed down. Mr. Cooper and his partner were standing there to greet me, both smiling broadly.

"Fun, huh?"

"I did not come to California for fun, sir," I replied stiffly. "May I ask what wages I will receive for my labors?"

"When you're finished, we'll pay you, oh, I dunno, what do you think, Joseph?"

"Two bits?" suggested the smaller man.

"Since that is the price of passage over your bridge, I would expect a slightly higher renumeration."

"My, he do talk fancy, don't he?"

Mr. Cooper laughed and slapped me on the back. "Hungry?" he asked. "I think we owe you a plate of beans for catching young Jack at his tricks again."

I was, of course, famished, and ate not one but two plates of beans for supper. They suggested I bed down in the bridge for the evening, in a corner. I was glad for the shelter.

The next morning I forced myself to climb back up to the rooftop. It took me all morning to finish, and then I crawled over the roof twice to make sure every missing shingle had been replaced. When I looked south, toward the gold field, I saw hundreds of tents dotting the landscape, some on the edge of little streams, others dwarfed by huge mounds of dirt, stripped of their value by the industrious miner. Everywhere was squalor, men toiling with a single-minded purpose that boggled my mind. I had no idea how to apply for a claim, how to work one if I got it, and for the first time I began to seriously question my ability to succeed.

I clambered down and presented the hammer and depleted sack of shingles to Joseph Kyle with a flourish.

"I hope I have proved my worth to you, sir," I said. "I believe my labor is worth a dollar at least."

To my surprise, he agreed at once. I followed him inside to the safe, which he carefully unlocked before handing me a coin.

"You gonna go try yer luck?"

"I do not yet have the means to equip myself, sir."

"I've got to go to Marysville tomorrow. Stay here and watch the bridge with Jim. We'll pay you two bits."

I hesitated, but felt I had no alternative. After agreeing, I stepped back outside in the bright sunshine. Jim Cooper was arguing fiercely with a bent old man, heading south across the bridge. His mule was loaded with gear. This, I came to see, was Mr. Cooper's primary sport—abusing travelers who had no other choice but to cross at his bridge.

"I'm no storekeeper! I'm no miner! Your gear is worth less than nothing to me! I'll have cold, hard cash or you'll not cross, old man!"

Seeing an opportunity, I stepped up to the miner.

"I'll purchase your spare pick for two bits, sir, and solve your dilemma."

He grumbled a bit, claiming that he'd paid $3 for it in Yuba City, but he needed the toll and gave in.

After the miner had crossed, Mr. Cooper clapped me heartily on the back. I winced. The man had hands like hams.

"You've caught the right spirit, now," he shouted. "Pin 'em down and squeeze 'em till they scream for mercy!" He called to his partner. "Hey, Joe, this one's got the makin's of a real California businessman!"

I didn't want to spend what little money I had to cross the bridge, so I positioned myself beneath a massive pine tree to watch the travelers come and go. Toward the end of the day, another miner appeared who had been drinking rather too zealously in Marysville. He had no mule and no money left, but tied to his pack were three flat miner's pans. I again offered to help him cross the bridge by purchasing one of the pans, and we struck a deal.

"Didn't I see you up there, repairing the roof yesterday?"

I admitted that I had been.

"I hope that old skinflint paid you well," he grumbled. "The last man who took that job fell and died for these greedy bastards."

I was shocked to hear that my feelings of danger had been so well justified and resolved to make as much profit as I could from this infamous team of tolltakers.

The next day I watched over the south end of the bridge, while Mr. Cooper assaulted travelers making their way back to the gold fields. My job was relatively easy because most miners leaving had at least a little gold dust, being on their way to buy supplies or find amusement at Marysville, Yuba City, or even on their way to San Francisco or home to their families. On the north end of the bridge, travelers were either newcomers to the fields or miners coming back, usually penniless.

Once Mr. Cooper suspected me of holding back a toll, having miscounted the number of miners who crossed. He lifted me up by both forearms and shook me until my teeth rattled. The thought had crossed my mind, since fifteen men, six with mules, one buggy, and three wagons made their way across heading north, just in one morning.

I assured Mr. Cooper I had given over every pinch of gold dust and every coin, and I turned my pockets inside out as proof. Somewhat mollified, he took me across and showed me where he scratched a tally in the dirt with a long stick.

"I don't trust nobody," he growled. "You'd be wise to do the same." Between us that day, we caught three people trying to steal across without paying. From one I extracted a serviceable tent, after escorting him to campsite to retrieve the toll. Mr. Cooper agreed to let me have the tent in exchange for my day's wages—a true bargain, he told me, as I was well aware.

That night I pitched my tent near the river, almost underneath the south end of the bridge. In secret, I began to chop gingerly at the rocky, sandy soil of the river's edge. For weeks, I worked only after I was certain that Kyle and Cooper were asleep.

Almost immediately I began to find small particles of gold, which I sewed into the seams of my tent. By day, I worked with either Kyle or Cooper, ensuring that every person paid their toll, and squeezing triple tolls from those reckless enough to try to sneak by our vigilant gaze.

One morning, several hours before dawn, I was wakened by the sound of hoofbeats on the bridge above. I scrambled up the bank and stood at the mouth of the bridge, blocking the horse and its three riders.

"Is that you, Cooper?" The man squinted through the darkness at me.

"No," I said gruffly. "But the toll's a dollar just the same."

"My baby's sick," came a woman's voice from behind the man. "She's got a fever, and I've got to get her to Yuba City."

"Toll's a dollar." I was stubborn. The baby set up a thin wailing cry.

"Please, please let us by," the man begged. "I can bring you a dollar in the morning."

I was obstinate. I turned them away. I suppose they tended the brat themselves or forded the river three miles down, although it was a dangerous crossing. No one deserved mercy from me, least of all a man wealthy enough to own a horse.

Kyle and Cooper were scouring the area for other likely bridge locations, and one or the other was absent almost every day. It took two men to guard the bridge, and I had apparently proven my loyalty. Soon my wages were increased to seventy-five cents a day, and I had collected all the gear I needed from desperate travelers at greatly reduced prices.

I felt not a single twinge of compassion. These travelers were no more deserving of pity than myself, and I had certainly not received any kindhearted treatment from tollkeepers or merchants, fellow travelers or miners since I had left my home months ago.

Every night I covertly scratched in the dirt at the river's edge. The piles of dirt in my tent were so high there was barely enough room to turn around, much less stretch out and sleep. But I barely slept, so feverish was my desire to wring wealth from the unwelcoming California soil. At last I felt like I had removed every possible scrap of gold without calling attention to my labors. I spread the dirt back around, packed it down tightly over the course of a week, and moved my tent downstream a few yards.

"Movin', Teacher?"

The nickname they had attached to me rankled somewhat in view of their illiterate scorn for learning, but I accepted it. I had no choice, really.

"I thought the mosquitoes might be better if I moved."

"As long as you can still hear footsteps on the bridge at night, you can pitch that tent anywhere you like." Kyle grinned at me, exposing his mouth full of rotten, stinking stumps, and I forced a smile in return.

One day, a family approached the north end of the bridge while Cooper was eating his lunch or, more likely, toting up the week's earnings. Their oxen were bone-thin, the wagon nearly empty except for a half-empty barrel of flour, and the children's faces were pinched and wretched. The man wouldn't speak, and his wife approached me about the toll.

"We've only just made it here," she began in a low voice. "We were snowed in for a week in the mountains, and the tollkeeper at the Feather River Bridge took our last dollar. I've got two picks left, and a miner's pan, and some flour. You can have it all, if you'll just let us through."

"Now what'll you do over there with no pick?" I pretended kindness as I walked her to the river's bank and gestured toward the fields. "You think one of those miner's gonna lend you a pick?"

The last glimmer of hope in her eyes died.

It was Saturday. Near sundown. All the woman had to do was make camp for the night and tomorrow morning we'd have to pass her through, free. It was a law Cooper and Kyle didn't dare break, for their bridge charter would be revoked immediately as penalty. Newcomers to the state were seldom aware of the law.

"Nice ring," I commented. She was twisting a ring savagely around and around on her finger. It was quite loose. Her fingers were long and elegant, and I could see that she had once been an attractive woman. Of course, out here, any woman was attractive. I had not seen a woman since that early morning rider a month or more ago.

"Here," she said bitterly, thrusting the ring in my hand. "Take it. I hope you rot in hell."

The next day I noticed my tent was sagging in the center. I took some extra poles and shored it up. I had sewn so much gold into the seams the weight was pulling it down. I decided to begin hiding my gold in the seams of my clothes.

I was working that night, systematically digging up the dirt and sand that made up the floor of my tent and taking it to the river to wash away the silt, when I heard a floorboard on the bridge above me creak. Living under the bridge and working on it day after day, I had come to know all the different kinds of noises it would make. This was definitely the sound of someone, probably small, trying to creep across unnoticed. I set my pan under my cot and stole up the bank to the opening of the bridge.

There was a full moon that had helped me as I worked, but its light now threatened to expose me to the prowler on the bridge. I slipped through the shadows as best I could and hugged the walls as I followed the intruder. Two-thirds of the way across he froze, sensing a presence near him. I threw my arms around his neck and pinned him roughly to the ground.

He was thirteen at most. He lay there and tried not to cry as I glowered at him. "Where do you think you're going, you rogue?"

"I was just headed back to camp, sir."

"Toll's twenty-five cents." I held out my hand, knowing full well he didn't have a penny.

"I don't have it, sir." A tear slipped down his face, and he lay there, immobile, too frightened to wipe it away.

"Get off the bridge, then." I kicked him and then waited till he struggled to his feet and trotted back out the south end of the bridge.

I went back to my tent and retrieved my pan from under my cot. I was quietly washing a pan full of silt and pebbles when I noticed movement on the river. It was that damn boy, attempting to get across. He'd dragged a log to the water's edge, found a tent pole, and was trying to perch on the log and pole his way across the current. I watched him, curious. He would move forward a few feet, then the current would catch him and pull him sideways, downstream. Sometimes the current would turn the log completely around, and he would get a dunking.

The whole scene was washed with a silvery, mystic light, and the boy never made a sound. Only the endless rushing clamor of the water accompanied his struggle. At last, when he had about thirty feet left to go, the log rolled over and the boy didn't come back up. I studied the surface of the water for a long minute, waiting to see his head break through, but it never appeared.

A big hand clapped on my shoulder. I jumped, and nearly screamed. It was Mr. Cooper.

"Any luck tonight, Teacher?"

"I, I don't know what you mean," I stammered.

He sighed. "You're not as smart as I thought. I told you, never trust anybody. But you thought I trusted you."

A second figure appeared on the river's edge, it was Mr. Kyle. "What have you got? About $2,000 in dust? Your tent nearly collapsed with the weight."

"You think we're stupid?" sneered Mr. Cooper. "We thought we'd see how much you could dig up before we stopped you. Tomorrow, you'll go to jail. It's illegal to jump somebody's claim, you know."

"They hanged that miner down on the American River, didn't they, Jim?" Mr. Kyle was idly fingering the collar of his shirt.

"You can have it all," I stuttered. "I meant to give you your share, really, I was going to."

"I'll tell you what, Teacher," Mr. Cooper said softly. "You just take it all out of your little hiding place and bring it up to the tollhouse. We'll talk about it then."

They both turned and walked back up to the tollhouse in silence.

I ripped out all the seams as quickly as I could. In my pack (I got it with a cup and plate for a quarter), I put the gold and about a dozen smooth river stones. I grabbed my pick and slipped up to the bridge.

I hid in the rafters on the south end of the bridge and threw the rocks with great force onto the wooden planking. As I expected, Cooper came running to the bridge with his gun, shouting over his shoulder.

"I'll shoot the little bastard, Joseph, with great pleasure!" He stopped at the opening of the bridge, expecting to see me silhouetted against the moonlight pouring in the other side.

With a banshee scream, I jumped from the rafters down onto his neck. When he lay still and quiet, I headed inside for Joseph Kyle.

The sun came in a pleasant little pattern on my face, through the stitches I had hastily sewn last night to repair my tattered tent. I lay on my cot, contemplating the soothing sounds of a Sunday morning. It must have been nine o'clock before the first miner crossed the bridge.

"Oh, my gosh! Murder! Help!" He ran back toward the camp, and I waited until several witnesses returned with him before emerging from my tent, stretching and yawning.

"What's happened?" I asked.

James Cooper lay face down in a pool of blood. His body was mangled, face and torso cruelly torn with vicious stabbing blows from a pick. His sightless eyes glared up at the rafters when the miners rolled him over.

"He was a ruthless jerk, but he didn't deserve this," one miner commented. "Didja hear anything last night, Teacher?"

I shook my head. "I'm afraid I drank too much last night," I said. "I passed out around ten."

When the lawmen came, they found Joseph Kyle in front of the open, empty safe in the tollhouse. They questioned me at great length until I remembered some of the events of the previous night.

"I was really drunk," I broke down and began to sob, the strain telling on me. "I heard two horses crossing, going north. If I'd only gone up to see, I might've..."

A lawman patted me roughly on the shoulder. "The thieves would've probably murdered you, too," he said. His foot struck a bottle that had rolled under my cot. "What's this?"

"Brandy," I said with a rueful little smile. "I drank it all."

They let me stay on at the bridge. I moved into the tollhouse. But livestock were spooked by the bloodstains on the floorboards at the mouth of the bridge, no matter how many times I scoured them clean. Some horses would only pass through the bridge if they were led blindfolded around the irregular splotch that marked the end of James Cooper.

Soon, to keep from losing all my trade, I was out there scrubbing every day. I even tore the boards up and replaced them, but the stains came back. No matter how I washed and rubbed, the blackish-red blot reappeared, about two feet across, with trails and spatters in every direction. I put a box outside, for people to drop the toll in, so I wouldn't be distracted from my chore. It didn't matter how many times I cleaned the floorboards, the stains returned.

The wind began to moan around the bridge all the time, too, and the hushing of the water's current sounded like the laughter of a young boy. I finally left Yuba River Bridge and wandered south.

I had plenty of money. But one day when my landlady put on the face of the woman whose wedding ring I took in lieu of the toll, I began to scream. I left San Francisco after that and wandered east. I bought a peddler's pack, because peddlers are supposed to wander, but

I'm not a very successful peddler because I do not chat for long before the customer begins to look like my wife. Or a thirteen-year-old boy in the moonlight. Or a desperate woman clutching a baby.

Today I am in Kentucky. It is warm here, but a different kind of warmth than California. On the road out of town there is a bridge with wooden shingles on top, just like a bridge I used to know. I plan to climb on the bridge.

My seams are heavy with gold. If I change my mind once I am in the water, my treasure shall carry me down. It is the best use of that treacherous metal I can devise. How far down it shall carry me, I cannot say. How far down I deserve to go, I do not know. I can only hope that somewhere I will find the mercy I lost so long ago.

ghost soldiers of the french quarter

It isn't a stretch to say that every house in New Orleans is haunted. And most New Orleanians would be offended if you told them their house wasn't haunted. In a city so layered in death and trapped below sea level between a lake and a river, it's very difficult for ghosts to find their way out of the city.

There are many reasons for visiting New Orleans, but ghost hunting is one of the most common. The Louisiana Society for Spectral Studies lists the Beauregard-Keyes House in the French Quarter, once called the Vieux Carre by its French settlers, as one of the most haunted houses in all of New Orleans. As a National Landmark, the Beauregard-Keyes House welcomes a lot of tourists every year, and it is rare for the New Orleans visitor to come away without a tale of some spectral strangeness.

Though legends of ghosts in the Beauregard-Keyes House abound throughout its history, Dr. Byrum Emory discovered the first haunting here; he was the first to document the hauntings on film. A researcher in paranormal activities, Dr. Emory uncovered hundreds of files on the history of the Beauregard-Keyes House while researching his first book on special hauntings in the Southern United States. Dr. Emory had earned a grant to study at the New Orleans Historical Society, and he had been reading reports of hauntings in the French Quarter when he stumbled across the story of General Beauregard, an officer in the Confederate Army. A native of Louisiana, General Beauregard had retired from the military to the mansion on Chartres Street. He had been an important figure in several key periods of the Civil War. He'd been at the Battle of Shiloh and Fort Sumter, and he'd earned a stunning victory at Bull Run.

It was in 1967 that Dr. Emory first began research on the Beauregard-Keyes House. Looking through General Beauregard's diaries, Dr. Emory noticed a strange notation in the middle dated October 20, 1891, just a couple of years before Beauregard's death:

Allowed to May how maybe I'd make a trip to Missippi by train come December for Christmas holidays if feeling less homely. Heard noise in parlor adjacent to bedroom while sleeping last night. Woke to find parlor door strangely opn, but no one but me and May home for the night, servants having gone for wkend. Slipped down the hallway in stocking feet after hearing grinding noise like something from the blacksmith's. Told May to get my gun and May was scared witless. Got own gun myself out from under mattress and walked stealth like down hall to more rough noise, light comin from out of room. Suddenly spectral shape appears in hallway and I back into corner near stairs, scared beyond holy God. Prayed to God for deliverance from rude presence such as the devil only portents hisself. God only knows I says I ain't nothing but a old man done my time in Tennessee Missippi Virginia by God I earned not to be treatd so roughly. Spectral nightshade come full over me my heart come near to fallin from my chest. I fired my colt clean through the shady beast. Bullet destroys clockface on the wall passing clean through spectral haunting. Spectral haunting turns down stairway, floats off into street. I allowed how I was frighted to death never having seen such a mess and scared to near death for May to come to senses.

This kind of notation was right up Dr. Emory's alley, feeling as he did both an insatiable curiosity and a kind of empathy for the famous Civil War general who had received such an unwarranted scare so late in life. He wondered what the ghost wanted. Why had it chosen to show itself after the General and his wife had already lived for so long in the house? Had something, perhaps, happened to someone in the house that Beauregard didn't know about? For a certified connoisseur of ghosts and hauntings, this diary notation satisfied two needs for Dr. Emory: a mystery to solve and the opportunity to see some actual ghosts.

Dr. Emory made an appointment with the curator of the Beauregard-Keyes House for a private viewing. It's very difficult for a spectral researcher to get clear readings with a lot of noisy tourists in the room, and Dr. Emory was certain that if alone, he'd actually see a ghost or two. But what Dr. Byrum Emory couldn't have imagined was the house being home to so many ghosts.

Dr. Emory arrived at the house early in the morning and he first noticed that it had a kind of rarified air about it. It certainly suggested to Dr. Emory that it had been the scene of carnage, of unhappy deaths. But the strongest sense he had was that most of the ghosts in the house were located in the upper rooms where General Beauregard had first recorded the appearance of a ghost. Dr. Emory began perusing the rooms with all the detachment of an anthropologist at work, which is what he actually was, an anthropologist of the souls of the departed. Dr. Emory liked to think that he studied the secrets of human behavior, behavior that was held in check until a person could die. Ghosts seemed to have no sense of consequence. They were already the universe's great homeless, souls without the comfort, or the rules, of society.

The curator of the museum, Dr. Miles Jeffries, had insisted he accompany Dr. Emory through the house, first to make sure Dr. Emory respected the condition of the house's many antiques, but also because he wanted to see for himself if the house was the site of any famous hauntings. At the top of the grand staircase, Dr. Jeffries opened the first of three doors on the left, and the two scholarly men walked into a musty room that felt as if it had been closed up for a while.

"Do you sense anything Dr. Emory?" Jeffries asked as he watched Dr. Emory sniff each of the walls, gently caressing the plaster as if searching for a sign of life within.

"Not just yet. I have to wait, and we have to be as quiet as possible. Ghosts have to find the world inviting before they show themselves, and they have to have a need to tell something. Ghost behavior is no accident."

Dr. Emory continued to move quietly throughout the room just as any detective would search a crime scene. Dr. Jeffries stood motionless in the doorway, ready to flee at any moment.

"I can't seem to pick up anything in here," Emory said. "I'm sensing a deep electrical current in the air, something working on the atmosphere, but it's simply too nonspecific to locate."

But just as Emory was ready to walk out of the room, a strange blood stain began to appear on the floor at their feet. The four-poster bed began lurching about the room in agony. A high-pitched scream, so loud the two men winced in pain as they covered their ears, filled the room, and later they learned it could be heard throughout the French Quarter.

It was certainly clear that a horrible death had happened here, that a ghost had been waiting for someone as sensitive as Dr. Emory to come along so it could tell its tale.

"Let's leave it in peace," he said. "We'll learn more about it as we get a sense of the entire house." As the two men began backing out of the room, the stain began to recede, and the screaming died down. Drs. Emory and Jeffries proceeded to the next two rooms on the hall, and in each, the very same ghostly circumstance made itself clear.

"Each of the three rooms has its own ghost," he explained to Dr. Jeffries. "This is clearly the site of a mass murder of some sort."

"Well, uh, what are we to do about it? I've heard legends that a massacre took place here, but I've no evidence to suggest it actually happened."

Dr. Emory rolled his eyes and sighed. "The evidence, sir, is right before you. The evidence is in the haunting, and I can assure that we'll find more evidence throughout the house. I can't imagine that these three ghosts would limit themselves to just these rooms."

As Emory and Jeffries walked back down the hallway toward the grand staircase, they began to hear the shouting of men and a metallic clanking as of men loading muskets. From the top of the staircase Dr. Emory witnessed a sight he'd never imagined. Hundreds of the ghostly forms of Confederate soldiers filled the foyer as if they'd just come from battle. Some were still loading their weapons and firing through the window dusty flashes of gunpowder.

"God save us," Dr. Jeffries screamed. But Dr. Emory was too busy taking notations of the ghastly scene in front of him. It was as if the house needed to actually be taken seriously for the ghosts to manifest themselves.

"But what does this have to do with the strange behavior we witnessed in the bedrooms?" Dr. Jeffries asked.

"We may never know, but we do know that the Beauregard-Keyes House is a magnificent site of spectral specimens. And you do realize," Dr. Emory said with a wry grin on his face, "we have to walk through that crowd of ghost soldiers in order to get out. That is, unless they decide to settle down."

The mystical battle waged on. The two men could even hear the sounds of musket and cannon fire coming from outside the house. But the ghosts never seemed to mind the living being witnesses to their hellish battle. It seemed precisely as Dr. Emory suggested, that the dead needed a willing believer in the true power of ghosts before they'd perform the mystery of apparitions.

Dr. Emory knew as well that it would take years of research to discover why this band of soldiers were holed up in the house and what had caused the bloody deaths in the upstairs room. He knew that spectral research was the work of a driven scholar, a vocation not for the weak of heart.

But Dr. Jeffries was weak of heart, so Dr. Emory knew he'd have to lead him by the hand to part the ghostly sea of battle-hardened soldiers. As they moved toward the entryway the ghosts indeed stepped aside to let them through. Then, as they reached the doorway, the ghosts disappeared back through the walls of the house. I'll have much more work to do here, thought Dr. Emory, a fact confirmed when he turned around to look back up the grand staircase. At the top of the stairs stood an apparition of what could only have been the noble form of General Beauregard.

"What happened here old man?" Dr. Emory asked the ghost. "What do you have to tell me?"

ghostly rescuers

Captain John M. Harper stared out the wheelhouse windshield. Sleety rain was pelting down, and he was fighting the wheel against a roaring wind. As his boat chugged down the Cape Fear River, it was being tossed about like a canoe. The winter storm had blown up without warning, not that it was a problem. His steamer, a product of the best technology the late 1800s had to offer, could handle whatever the river could throw at it.

"Aye, Captain," said the man beside him, the boat's sole passenger. "It was right there in Brunswick Town. The Brits took them prisoner—all three of them Highlanders. The Revolution had been going for just a few months when they were captured. They were transported to Brunswick Town by barge. Shackled like slaves, they were."

The man's Scottish brogue was as thick as the red hair sprouting every which way from his head. He'd invited himself into the wheelhouse two hours ago and had been talking nonstop about an ancestor and two other Scots captured during the American

Revolution. The captain listened peripherally as he piloted his steamer through the rough waters.

"They were all sentenced to die, but my great-grandfather escaped. Thae's why I'm here with yae today."

"Umm," was about all Harper could manage. It occurred to him that he wasn't quite as grateful for that happenstance as his passenger seemed to think he should be. Two hours and the man had barely taken a breath. It was already a difficult situation. Fighting the storm and the river currents demanded his full attention. Having the Scot prattling away in his ear was distracting.

Suddenly, there was a loud scraping sound. The boat gave a lurch as it came to a quick halt, pitching the passenger onto his rear and almost throwing Harper out of the captain's chair.

"What was that?"

Harper didn't answer at first. He swung the wheel around and tried to power the boat around. "We've hit a sandbar," he explained tersely. He swung the wheel again and tried to power on through. No go. His first mate rushed in.

"We're hard aground, Cap'n," he said. "Ain't goin' nowhere 'til the tide rises."

Harper nodded. "Aye, nothing for it. Have the red lights run up, so we'll be seen. Well, sir," he turned to the passenger. "What say we wait this out below? It'll be warmer down there, and I'll put on a pot of coffee."

It was just past midnight and the cabin was quiet. Finally, even the Scot had stopped talking. He was hunched on the bench seat in the boat's galley, his head lolling back. Harper himself was drowsing, faintly aware of the soft creaking of the boat.

Suddenly, the cabin door flew open, and a deckhand rushed in. He slammed the door behind him and leaned back against it, rain draining from his mackinaw and puddling in the floor. Harper could see how white his face was against the yellow of his rain hat and coat.

"What is it, Johnson?"

"Cap'n!" The man was trembling. "I..I...I…"

Harper sat up. "Is it the boat? Have we come loose?"

The man shook his head. "Nay, Cap'n. We're still hard aground."

"Then what?"

"On the deck…Just now. I saw a…gh-h-ost!"

"What are you talking about, man?"

Johnson took a deep breath and started again. "I was standing on deck, Cap'n. And I looked beside me, and there was a man standing there. He wasn't wearing a mack, just a shirt and pants, and he was soaking wet. His skin was dead white. It gave me such a fright. While I was standing there, he turned and gave me this look, Cap'n. It was terrible. His eyes had this glassy dead look to 'em. Then he turned and looked out over the river and pointed out. He was pointing due west. I…I asked him what he wanted. He looked at me again and turned and started pointing again. Then…Cap'n…He just disappeared! Right there in front of me. Just faded into thin air!"

"Johnson, have you been drinking?" Harper looked the man in the face and leaned closer. He was pale and he was shivering, but he didn't seem to be drunk. He couldn't smell liquor on him.

"Nay! Captain, you know me. You know I never touch the spirits! I saw it, I tell you. I saw it….disappeared right into thin air. What do you suppose it means?"

"Nothing, Johnson. It doesn't mean anything," Harper went to the stove and poured a cup of coffee. "Sit down here and warm up. You just got too cold, is all. You just thought you saw what you saw."

Johnson kept shaking his head, but he sat down and began to drink his coffee, mumbling to himself.

Captain Harper donned his mack and hat and stepped back out into the rain. He took a turn around the deck, checking every nook and cranny, but found nothing. Looking overboard, he could see that they were, indeed, still aground, but the tide was rising. In another two hours, they'd be free.

Two hours time proved Harper right. The tide rose high enough to float the boat off the sandbar. Harper put his first mate at the wheel, and he was standing on the deck staring into a cold misty dawn as the boat picked up its course from the night before. His deckhand, Johnson, had left the cabin and was standing next to him.

"Listen, Cap'n! Do you hear that? It sounds like someone calling for help."

Harper cocked his head and listened. Indeed, he did hear a cry.

"It's coming from that direction," he pointed to the west and signaled the first mate to slow their speed. "There! Steer to port!"

As the boat turned to the left, the two men were joined by three other crew members as well as the Scottish passenger. All were lined along the rail, staring ahead.

Harper squinted. Surely the mist was obscuring his view. He couldn't be seeing what he thought he was seeing. There, adrift in front of them, was an old wooden rowing barge. It was carrying two men. They were dressed in mere rags and their hands and feet were shackled.

"Help us, sir. Please help us," one of them called out.

"Johnson! Get a rope! Toss it out to them. Hurry before we pass them!"

Johnson already had a rope in hand. He tossed it out, but it landed in the water, not because he had missed the mark, but because the barge was no longer there.

Harper blinked to be sure. But no, it was gone. He knew he'd seen it. It had been there. He had heard the cries. And he wasn't the only one. His entire crew had seen the same thing.

Johnson stood for a stunned moment, then turned to his captain. "I told you, sir. I told you. I saw a ghost last night. You thought me daft. But now you know. I saw what I saw."

The captain shook his head. He didn't know what to say. The rest of the crew stood in stunned silence, which was broken by a cry from the Scot.

"Captain! Look ahead there. It's a capsized boat, is it nae?"

Harper strained his eyes, afraid of what he'd see. But, yes, ahead he did see the belly of a boat bobbing up and down in the waves. He looked harder and saw two men clinging desperately to the hull.

"Johnson! Drop the life boat. You and Mays go. Get those men aboard, quickly."

Johnson jumped into action, loosening the ropes that held the lifeboat against the boat's railing. He jumped in after Mays and began rowing, half believing that the boat and the two men would disappear by the time he got there.

Not this time. As they pulled alongside, he reached out and grabbed onto an arm, an arm of flesh and blood. It was cold as the dickens, but flesh and blood for sure. He and Mays pulled both men into the lifeboat and quickly rowed back to the boat.

Both men were still alive, and the crew rushed them into the warm cabin, giving them some soup and dry clothes. As the two began to warm and were able to talk, they related an eerie story.

They were the only survivors, they said, of a crew of seven. Their boat had overturned in the storm right around midnight that night. The captain and first mate had been lost when the boat overturned, and three more had drowned before they could grab onto the hull. Somehow, these two made it to the overturned boat and had found the strength to hold on through the long, cold night.

"It was an odd thing," croaked one as he looked to his fellow survivor for confirmation. "Every time I thought to give up and let go, I felt a tug, as if someone had grabbed my arms and was pulling me back up."

His buddy nodded. "Aye, I felt the same. As if someone were holding us up."

Johnson studied their faces. "Midnight, you say?" When the men nodded, Johnson gave his captain a knowing look.

"It was around midnight, wasn't it, sir?"

Harper nodded.

"What? What was around midnight?" one of the survivors asked.

"A man. He was on our deck, standing right next to me. He was wearing a blue shirt and black pants and he had long hair pulled back into a que. He was pointing off to the west and seemed to be trying to urge me into action."

"Long hair? In a que? But that's our captain! He made it? Where is he?"

"Nay, nay, mate. I'm sorry, but he didn't make it."

"But..."

A look passed between the captain and his deckhand. "And, Captain, think about it. That barge we saw, the one that wasn't there? If it hadn't been for that, we would have never found these two. We would have sailed right on by them."

Harper nodded. "Yes, Johnson. I know. It was a rescue," he said. "It had to be that—a ghostly rescue."

Captain John Harper was a well-respected and well-known Cape Fear riverboat captain. He was a down-to-earth guy, not given to flights of fancy. So, when he told his fantastic tale of the rescuers from the deep, they listened.

They knew him to be honest to a fault. And they knew how seriously he took his responsibilities to his men. So, when he looked them straight in the eye and asked his question, it gave them pause. Do you think it could be true? he would ask. Is it possible that a drowned captain had come back to save his men?

They'd study his face and nod. Yes, maybe, they'd say. Maybe it was possible. For they knew what he was thinking; what he was wondering. It was his hope, they knew, should the occasion ever arise, that he, too, could become a ghostly rescuer.

the trapped ghost of hopewell

"Great, another old house," Rob thought to himself dully as he climbed the steps of the old antebellum home. For the life of him he couldn't figure out why his girlfriend was so into all this old stuff.

"Wow. What a cool place! I wonder how many people have walked up and down these stairs since it was built," Lydia thought to herself excitedly, a typical thought for her and exactly why she was so into all this old stuff.

She liked antique homes, antique stores, antique just-about-anything. She was a dreamy and imaginative girl who always believed she had been born in the wrong century. Something about the past had always intrigued her, and her imagination allowed her to enjoy everything it had to offer in the way of tours, classes, artifacts, graveyards, or just about any other relic you could think of.

Her boyfriend did not share this obsession with history. While she preferred the old gabled antiquity of an antebellum home, he preferred new, shiny, modern things, technology, the present, the future. It seemed that no matter where they went on a trip or off the beaten path, there was some old house or historic site that Lydia just had to see.

Sure enough, this road trip proved to be no different. At Lydia's insistence and persuasion, they had already had to pull off on the side of the road for every historical marker they passed. They stopped for lunch at a diner in Virginia, and lo-and-behold, there was a travel brochure for local historical attractions. Rob groaned inwardly, but he was not really surprised—even he knew that Virginia was chock full of history, particularly Civil War history, due to the state's proximity to enemy Union territory.

Lydia found a blurb about an antebellum house in nearby Hopewell and didn't have to try too hard to convince Rob to make the short trip. He made a half-hearted protest, but it was more teasing than serious. He decided to try to be a good sport about it as he drove toward the house, using a crude map scribbled on a diner napkin.

They found the house easily enough, parked, and walked up the stairs. A tour was beginning momentarily, and Lydia's eyes shone too excitedly for her boyfriend to refuse her.

"These tours are all alike," he sighed to himself as he leaned against the railing of the sprawling front porch. This was exactly the kind of thing Lydia liked about these old houses—sprawling front porches littered with rocking chairs, porch swings, and any other surface one could sit on and escape the sweltering summer heat.

At last the tour began and they filed into the old home. Their noses were immediately greeted by a smell that Lydia loved and Rob hated— the unmistakable smell of old stuff. Lydia hung on every word, but Rob lagged at the back, his hands in his pockets, his mind wandering. While Lydia oohed and ahhed at the antique furniture and décor, the warped floor boards and the faded fabrics, wishing that she could live in just such a house, Rob checked his watch, wishing that this tour would wrap up soon so they could get back in the road. He wanted to make it to Philadelphia in time to crash with some of his friends.

As the tour group turned down a hallway, Rob broke away from the group. Lydia gave him a puzzled look, and he mouthed the word "bathroom." She nodded and he drifted away from the crowd of eager history buffs.

In reality he wasn't looking for a bathroom. From his experiences of being dragged along on these little historical jaunts, the best way for him to deal with it was to break away from the group and give himself a tour, stopping only when he saw something that interested him in particular.

He soon found himself descending some low, narrow steps into what he guessed to be the basement. Maybe I'll find something creepy or interesting down there, he thought.

The air was stale and close and the basement dimly lit, so dimly lit in fact that the corners were pitch black. He gave the room a sweeping look, trying to see if there was anything worth noticing.

He was just about to give up when, all of a sudden, he heard a noise behind his back, causing him to jump. He was alone in the basement and the sounds of the tour above him had grown faint and distant, rendering the sound behind him all the more startling.

He looked quizzically at the wall behind him. Scratch, scratch, scratch, he heard coming from behind the wall. Is it a rat, he wondered, leaning a little closer. Yes, it was definitely a clawing sound coming from behind the wall. As quickly as it had started, it stopped.

Having decided that the scratching was being done by a rat or a squirrel or some other vermin, Rob began to turn to head back up the stairs. Then, again: scratch, scratch, scratch, louder this time. He turned back toward the noisy wall. He leaned in closer to it, examining it closely, running his fingers along the boards to see if he could find some sort of opening. That must be some rat, he thought to himself, as the scratching became more loud and frantic.

His gaze followed the sound of the scratching as it slid down to the wall and became silent. He tentatively put an ear to the wall near the baseboard, when all of a sudden, something began to thump slowly behind the wall, causing him to bolt upright. The thumping was weak, and was then accompanied by a sort of high-pitched whine.

"These old places must have all kinds of pest problems," he said to himself bravely, comfortingly. "That's why I prefer the modern stuff. Yes sirree, clean and efficient, that's the way I like it," he thought. Although the sound coming from behind the wall seemed much too loud and strong for a rat, it was the only logical explanation.

Then, as the thumping slowly turned back into the scratching, this time more halfhearted, his "logical explanation" flew out the window as he heard a low voice moaning behind the wall.

With that he turned and hurried up the stairs. As he ascended the stairs, he tried to tell himself that his quickened pace had nothing to do with whatever was clawing behind the wall.

He mounted the stairs and gave a quick, cursory look around. When he didn't see the tour group, he decided, somewhat relieved, to wait for Lydia on the porch. His run-in with the giant mutant rat or whatever it was had caused his breath to become shallow, and besides, he needed some fresh air after the heavy, stale air of the basement.

Finally, Lydia drifted out of the front door with the other tourists. Rob smiled a little despite himself; he knew that enraptured look on her face. It would be hours before she snapped out of the romantic reverie.

"Oh, there you are. I guess we lost you," she said, "Did you find the bathroom?"

"What? Oh, yeah, the bathroom," he stammered, "I found it." Then he said in a tone that was more a statement than a question, "Ready to go?"

They strolled hand in hand toward the car.

"So what was your favorite part?" he prompted, knowing that such a response could easily kill thirty minutes of boredom on the road.

"Oh, I loved it all—surprise, surprise," she said, giving him a sidelong smile. "But I especially liked the basement."

"Wow, how cool, the basement," he said in a mildly sarcastic way, playing his assigned part in one of the comfortable routines of their relationship; but, he noticed that his hands tensed up a little on the steering wheel when she mentioned the basement.

She smacked him lightly on the arm. "No really, it was neat. I guess you missed that part of the tour."

"Well," she continued, "as you heard in the tour, the house has had its share of visitors over the years, especially because of the Civil War."

He nodded, blushing a little as he realized that he hadn't been paying attention to anything the tour guide had said.

"Well, there was this nurse who worked in the house who was a Union sympathizer, but of course she didn't tell anybody that. She heard the news that some Confederates were coming to the house to inspect it, so she hid this Union soldier behind a secret wall in the basement."

He felt the blood slowly drain from his face and the hairs on his arms began to rise.

"The Confederates showed up and found all kinds of Yankee paraphernalia in her storage space, so they accused her of being a traitor and hauled her off to prison somewhere."

He could already see where this was going.

"Well, nobody but the nurse knew about the Union soldier hidden behind the wall. He clawed and pulled at the wall, but to no avail. You could only open the wall up from the outside. So he died of dehydration, or malnourishment, or whatever it is you die of when you're stuck in a closed space. Can you imagine how awful that would be? It kinda reminds me of that Edgar Allan Poe short story."

He could hear the blood rushing in his ears as his girlfriend chattered on about the Union soldier trapped behind the wall.

"Then," she said in a way where he could tell she was about to get to the juicy part, the finale, "they were remodeling the basement in the fifties and they found his bones rotting away behind the walls. Isn't that wild? See, isn't history fascinating?" she asked rhetorically, contentedly.

He cleared his throat and tried to ask casually, "So, um, did you hear anything weird in the basement?"

"Weird? No," she said, "although the tour guide said something about how sometimes they supposedly hear the ghost of the Union soldier trying to claw his way out," she said theatrically, waving her hands in Rob's face.

"Oooh! How terrifying," he said in a silly way, trying to be playful. She didn't notice how forced it sounded.

I'm a reasonable guy, he thought to himself. What I heard in that basement was clearly just some kind of animal. Maybe, um, the house settling. Sure, that must have been it.

Rob tried to shake the maddening sensation of knowing he had experienced something but not wanting to admit it to himself. He relaxed his grip on the steering wheel as he saw that his knuckles were turning white and tried to think calmly.

He couldn't. His gut instinct had been right all along. That was no rat; he now knew it for sure. He also knew for sure, as he steered the car northward, that the next time Lydia wanted to go on one of her little historical trips, she could definitely count him out.

business is good

The rain struck the bottom of the pail with a rhythmic ping, ping, ping. Across the dark room, an iron kettle was full, each fat drop threatening to send a cascade of water flowing over the edge. Another bucket and a battered saucepan had also been pressed into service.

Three tousled heads—one fair, two dark—were just visible, nearly hidden by a thick layer of quilts piled high on a bedstead set askew in the center of the room to avoid the rapidly falling drops of rain. A pallet near the foot of the bed held two more figures, mouths open, long limbs tangled in sleep.

A small woman stepped over and between the sleeping children. Her hair was pulling loose from a hastily-pinned knot. Bone-weary, she hauled the brimming containers one by one to the window, tugged open the reluctant sash, poured out the rainwater, and repositioned the container.

The drumming of the rain on the roof and the soft musical counterpoint provided by the raindrops in their receptacles made a soothing sound as she settled into her chair by the fire in the next room. Pulling the mending basket close to her feet, she drew out a shirt that needed patching on the elbow—it was Benjamin's. As if to compensate for being the youngest, he always had to climb higher in the tree, jump farther out into the brook, or run the fastest down the road to meet his father. His clothes showed it.

Above the noise of the deluge she heard the steady thrumming of hooves on the road. No doubt to escape the downpour, although, she thought with a small smile, it could be he was riding hard to catch up with that good fortune that always seemed to elude him.

Seth Allen burst into the door, spreading a hail of drops as he opened his arms wide to encompass his little house and not-so-little family.

"Mary," he boomed, "all my hard work has now come to fruition. I have been awarded the contract to maintain every bridge in the county."

"Sshhh," she said, nodding her head toward the next room. "They've only just gone to sleep."

"I will begin tomorrow by mending the roof of Scott Bridge west of town," he continued in a slightly lower voice.

Mary burst out with a long and delighted peal of laughter. The cat that had been dozing peacefully on the hearth woke, stretched, and stalked out of the room in high dudgeon. Seth only stared at his wife, bewildered.

"Well," he conceded, "it isn't really a contract for all the bridges. It could be, though, in time!"

Mary, shaking her head, laid the shirt back in the basket and stood. Taking her husband by the arm, she led him to the door of the little room where the children slept.

"What do you hear, Seth Allen?"

"They haven't got the croup again, have they?" he whispered anxiously.

"No. Try again."

He tilted his head, straining to hear something unusual in the darkened room. Finally he shook his head, admitting defeat.

"The rain, husband, the rain," she hissed. "This roof's needed mending for six months now, and you've not found the time!" The drops clattered and spit as they landed in their various receptacles. Her voice climbed in intensity. The oldest child, asleep on the pallet, stirred uneasily.

He pulled her back from the door and swept her tiny form into his arms. "Now, now, my Mary," he crooned. "I've always taken care of you before, haven't I?"

Stiff in his embrace, her humor turned sour with the memory of broken promises. "The fence for the chicken run," she began to list. "The extra room for the older boys. The floorboards on the porch. The door to the barn. And now the roof. All promised. And nothing, nothing finished!"

She stepped hard on the side of his foot. Wincing, he released her arm and sat in his chair to rub his foot thoughtfully. "You have a point, Mary," he acknowledged at last. "And you have my solemn pledge that I will be up on the roof at first light, making those repairs."

Only slightly mollified, she reached back into the basket for the shirt. "Mrs. Harrison sent her son over today." She squinted as she tried to thread the needle by the wavering light of the fire. "He said his pa wanted that barn painted by Friday or there wouldn't be another penny in it for you."

Seth threw up his hands. "For what that skinflint is paying me, they should be a little less particular about when I can get to it."

"I could use a penny or two, Seth," Mary said gently. She held the shirt up. "More patches than shirt. And we're down to the bottom of the barrel on the cornmeal."

"It won't take me but a few hours to finish that barn. I'll take Jacob and Joshua with me."

"I hope the rain stops."

"Mary, Mary, Mary," her husband sang as he swooped across the room. "You would make the sun shine his very self, you would, with that bright smile."

She shook her head, but a smile was growing on her lips. She did not protest this time as he drew her into his arms, crushing the half-mended shirt between them.

"Ouch," he exclaimed, jumping back. The needle, neatly threaded, had pierced his forearm. Mary stood on her tiptoes to give him a peck on the cheek before sitting down again to resume her mending.

"There's some supper on the back of the stove," she said.

"Oh, I ate at the tavern." He slumped back into his chair. "I should finish the barn about noon, and then I'll get started on the roof." His voice softened. "I know I've made you many promises before, Mary, but this one I'll keep. I swear it."

"I believe you will, Seth. I know you intend to." She bent over her task again, firmly stitching the patch in place. Finished, she folded the shirt neatly and tucked the needle into the side of the basket so it wouldn't get lost.

"You'd best get on to bed, so you can get up early in the morning."

The two made an incongruous picture, one tall and the other one short, as they walked to the little room tacked on behind the fireplace. But the tenderness was unmistakable as Mary slipped her hand in the crook of her husband's elbow on the way.

"Mamaaaa!" The next morning a little girl flew into the shelter of her mother's skirts just as two of her brothers reached out to grab the white-blond braids that trailed down her back. They skipped up and over the bench by the table, tumbling it to the floor.

Mary slapped at the arms and legs within reach. "Stop that," she said crossly. "Stop tormenting your sister and sit down and do your lessons!"

The older boy, Joseph, obediently turned the bench right side up and sat down. Benjamin sidled up to his mother.

"When we're done can we go help Pa, please, Mama?" He mustered up all the charm in his five-year-old body.

"I reckon," she relented, smoothing his thick, dark hair. "If he goes to work at all today, which I don't know." The rain still came down, the drops singing in the next room as they danced into the buckets and pans.

"I feel sunshine coming," declared Seth from his post in the chair by the fire. "When I went to go check on Josh and Jacob, I think I saw a patch of clear sky over to the west."

"I want to help Josh and Jacob, Pa!" Joseph jumped up, overturning the bench again.

"Only have two axes, son, and besides, making shingles is a man's job," Seth said. Mary added a little more water to the corn mush and decided not to comment.

"At least it's not cold," she sighed as she cleared the table for their meager dinner. "Can't patch an icy roof."

"Ah, Mary, what'd I tell you?" Seth crowed as his oldest sons came in from their work in the barn. A golden rectangle of sun spilled into the room from the open door. The storm had finally passed.

Mary had just seen her husband and four sons off down the hill when a rider approached their house, coming from town.

"Good afternoon, Miz Allen," he said as he dismounted. "Mr. Allen here?"

"No, you just missed him, Mr. Watson." She shooed the chickens back toward the barn. "Care to leave a message?"

"Well, I think it's time we added that room," he said. "Seth told me last summer he could put a room on behind the kitchen."

"I'm sure he'll do a fine job, Mr. Watson, and I'll have him come right over," Mary said. "He's got a barn to finish painting and a couple roofs to mend, but maybe he'll get you fixed up before snow comes."

"Tell him to come as soon as he can," Mr. Watson said as he remounted the horse.

"Tell Mrs. Watson I said hello," called Mary. The man waved and trotted down the hill.

It was well past dark when Seth and the four boys returned, paint-smeared and hungry.

"Remind me, Mary," Seth said wearily as he sat down to warmed-over corn mush and milk, "not to ever offer to paint a barn again. It's too much work and not enough money."

"Mr. Watson came by," Mary said, spooning out supper. "He wants you to get started on that spare room you talked with him about last summer."

Seth bowed his head and the rest of the family followed. "For this food and for thy many blessings, we are most grateful, Almighty Father. Amen."

He put a spoonful of food in his mouth and swallowed before he continued.

"I saw Mr. Lamson today on the way to the Harrison's. You know, he built the West Dummerston Bridge? He wants some help repairing some other bridges, and he says he needs somebody with experience like me."

"That's welcome news, Seth." Mary watched as Josh and Jacob finished their portions in four or five bites. They knew better than to ask for more. She pushed back her chair to go to the stove. All eyes watched as she bent to pull a pan from the oven.

"Baked apples for dessert. We didn't have any sugar left, but I put plenty of honey in." She placed one small, wizened apple on each plate, smiling at their surprise.

"Mary, you're a wonder." Seth set his fork down for just a moment and smiled back at his wife. "Can you and Anna spare the time to go to the store tomorrow? Mr. Harrison paid me today."

"I think we can manage."

"Can I come, Ma?" Benjamin decided to take advantage of his status as the youngest child.

"If your Pa can spare you."

Seth winked at Mary.

"Let's clear up, now. It's getting late." While Mary and Anna started on the dishes, Seth and the two older boys stepped outside. In just a few minutes, an enormous clattering noise filtered down into the main room of the house.

"What on earth?" Mary, drying her hands hastily on her apron, ran outside to peer up at the roof of the house. Silhouetted clearly against the starry night sky was her oldest son.

"Joshua Allen, what on earth are you doing up there?"

"We're mending the roof, Mary Allen." The voice of her unseen husband floated over the peak of the roof.

"That is the most ridiculous thing I have ever heard!" With her hands on her hips, she looked no more intimidating than her daughter Anna. But her husband knew better. With a few short words, he directed Joshua and Jacob down the ladder and back into the house.

"I promised you I'd start mending the roof today, Mary." He took her hands up in his own and squeezed them gently. "I wanted to keep my promise."

He looked so woebegone Mary had to laugh. "You are a big silly goose sometimes, Seth Allen."

"The moon will be rising soon, won't it?"

"I don't know. You should check the *Farmer's Almanac*." She caught herself. "No, don't check it because the children won't get to sleep with you up there pounding and walking around."

"You're right, Mary. But I will get that roof mended. You wait and see."

"I know you will, Seth Allen. You're a man of your word—most of the time."

As Mary bustled about getting one child's face washed, settling squabbles here and there, telling stories, and tucking in, Seth wandered restlessly through the rooms. At last, when Mary sat down in her chair by the fire and pulled the mending basket close, Seth snatched his hat off the hook by the door.

"I'm going to the tavern, love," he announced.

Mary looked up in surprise, but only told him goodbye as he pulled the door shut behind him.

He came in so late she barely stirred as he threw his arms around her. He struggled out of bed at cockcrow the next morning, joining her and the children for a small breakfast of bread and honey. He and the older boys climbed cheerfully to the roof to begin the mending job in earnest.

Joseph, Benjamin, and Anna set to work on their lessons, their recitations and songs punctuated by the irregular tapping and pounding of three hammers. Seth often bellowed a verse or two of song as he worked, until Mary stuck her head out the door and called up to him.

"Seth, your music makes my heart glad, but we can't hear our lessons when you sing so loudly."

"Yes, Mary Sunshine," he called back down. "I'll hold my tunes until you go to the store this afternoon."

The sky was the shade of blue common to autumn, achingly pure, and there was a crisp breeze that hinted at the weather to come. Mary checked the garden as she and her two youngest headed to town.

"The pumpkins will soon be ripe," she commented. "Anna, tie your bonnet on."

They walked down the hill, Mary allowing Anna to skip and run with Benjamin until they reached the bridge on the edge of town.

"Anna, walk with me," she commanded. "You're almost a young lady now."

"I'd rather not be," the little girl grumbled under her breath, so her mother couldn't distinguish the words.

"Benjamin!" Mary called through the bridge opening. "Don't go down to the river, now!"

They were halfway through the bridge when a buggy clattered through. "Hello, Mrs. Chamberlain," Mary said politely after she had discerned the familiar face in the gloom.

"Mary and Anna Allen!" exclaimed the buggy's sole occupant. "How are you?"

"Very well, thank you. We're on our way to the..."

Her sentence was interrupted by a wild banshee shriek as a small figure leaped through the air and landed with a thump on the wooden floor.

Mrs. Chamberlain's horse screamed in fright, followed at once by cries from the two ladies and the little girl. With some difficulty, the woman managed to restrain the terrified horse, whose hooves danced and clattered loudly in the dim space.

"I'm sorry, Mama." The figure picked itself up, dusted off, and proceeded to place a small hand in Mary's. "I was climbing, and I fell."

"Mercy, you gave me such a scare I thought I would just die right here on the spot!" Mrs. Chamberlain held a hand to her chest, breathing rapidly. Mary glared at her son, too angry to find words.

"I'm sorry, Mama," the boy repeated.

"Don't you ever do that again, you hear me, Benjamin Allen?" She shook him by the shoulders.

"Yes, Mama."

"Well, I'll tell you why that gave me such a terrible fright." Mrs. Chamberlain adjusted her hat. "Our hired man, Henry? He was bringing in the cows last night, and he looked down the hill and saw a light, moving around the bridge!"

"Must've been someone coming home late. Sometimes Seth carries a lantern if he's out late, especially if the boys are with him."

254

Mrs. Chamberlain shook her head. "No, the light didn't pass through the bridge and up the road. It hovered all around the bridge, he said."

"Isn't that odd?" Mary was distracted by a movement she caught out of the corner of her eye.

"Then he came down here and looked all around!" She paused and waited for Mary to respond. Mary was straining to see deep in the shadows of the bridge. She thought she had glimpsed a flash of white. "Uh-huh," she said vaguely.

"There was no one here!" Mrs. Chamberlain said triumphantly.

"Oh, my!"

Mary had made out the mystifying shape at the far end of the bridge. It was Anna, and the flash of her white petticoats as she clambered up the latticework of the bridge, trying valiantly to reach the rafters.

Pleased with the astonished reaction of her audience, Mrs. Chamberlain nodded in satisfaction. "I'll be going then. Give Mr. Allen my regards."

Mary recovered enough to answer. "Oh, yes, and you do the same. I'm awfully sorry about Benjamin falling out from the rafters!"

The woman raised her hand in response as she urged the horse forward and off the bridge.

"Anna Allen, you get down from there! Right now!" Mary advanced across the bridge to gather her children and continue their trip to the store.

That night after supper, Seth left the house. It wasn't Mary's place to protest or even comment, but she did feel a twinge of resentment as she began to let out the hem to Anna's dress again. In a month, at least, she'd need a strip of cloth to sew across the bottom to hide Anna's growing legs. Instead of spending money at the tavern, Seth should be spending money for clothes for his children, she thought irritably.

Again, Seth arrived home so late that she barely woke up. They all awoke at the usual time, and Seth and the big boys climbed up to the roof. Mary heard pounding and stomping and shouted commands, but Seth wasn't singing today. Clouds were gathering to the west as she and Anna and Benjamin picked butter beans in the garden. Dinner at noon was a bountiful meal compared to the meals of the past weeks: cornbread, butter beans, and boiled potatoes.

"We'll be finished with the roof in another hour or two," Seth said after accepting a second helping of butter beans. "Then I thought I'd go over to see Mr. Watson."

"When will you start on the roof of the bridge?"

"Oh, I'll get to it, never fear." He smiled broadly at her.

"Will the boys work on the shingles for it this afternoon?"

"That would be a fine idea."

"I know how particular the county is about getting jobs done quickly."

"Yes, yes, Mary, no need to worry." He was getting a bit testy now.

"We're fortunate you have so much work to do. When will you start on the other bridge repairs?"

"I told, you, Mary, I can mind my own affairs!"

Mary averted her eyes. "Yes, Seth."

Mary was relieved to hear him whistling in a pleasant mood as he came up the hill that evening, returning from the Watsons' house. She hoped he would stay home after supper, but he grabbed his hat again and slipped out the door, kissing her and telling her he might be late again.

"Be careful," she called, but he had already closed the door.

The next afternoon she and Anna had just finished the washing when her neighbor came to call.

"Good afternoon, Mary, Anna. I had some fresh pumpkin, and I thought you might like to make a pie tomorrow." Elizabeth Saulter's children were grown, and she often looked for company at the Allen house. Anna, relieved by her mother's preoccupation with the visitor, slipped off to the barn with Benjamin.

"That's most kind of you, Elizabeth. Our pumpkins aren't quite ripe yet, but when they are, I'll bring you some."

The older woman waved the offer aside. "We have more than we need, Mary, and goodness knows you have plenty of mouths to feed."

They sat on the porch in companionable silence for a while before Elizabeth spoke. "Didn't you tell me Mr. Allen was working on the bridge?"

Mary sighed. "Yes, well, he's going to start on it soon, I hope."

"There've been some strange goings-on over there lately, I hear."

"Mrs. Chamberlain told me all about it." Mary smiled. "Their hired man saw some lights or something. Did I tell you what Benjamin did?"

"No."

Mary related the incident, and Elizabeth shook her head with a rueful laugh. "Henry's not the only one to have something strange happen at the bridge." Elizabeth leaned conspiratorially toward her friend. "Leslie Lowe swears he heard the devil on the bridge last night."

"Oh?"

"He was riding along through the bridge, oh, it must've been about ten last night. It was just as quiet as it could be, when all of a sudden, he heard such a banging and a clattering that his old horse, Jerry, took off running as fast as he could. It was all Mr. Lowe could do to hang on!"

Mary nodded at her friend, her eyes wide.

"Mr. Lowe says it was the devil, knocking on the roof of the bridge or maybe a witch, since there was a full moon last night."

Mary closed her eyes for just a moment, thinking. She opened them and asked, "Did you say Scott Bridge?"

Elizabeth nodded again.

Mary's laughter rang out across the yard, bringing the children running. When she caught her breath, she spoke.

"Elizabeth, that wasn't the devil! That was plain old Seth Allen, trying his best to keep his word!"

the lighthouses of south carolina

For centuries, lighthouses were beacons that saved many a ship from certain doom on the shoals of South Carolina's coast. The people who manned the lighthouses were dedicated. They knew that to keep the lighthouse lamp lit was to save lives.

With today's sophisticated navigational equipment, the lighthouses are now a beautiful part of history. But according to legend, a couple of South Carolina's lighthouses are still manned by spirits from the past, who haven't gotten the word that their efforts are no longer needed.

The Blue Lady of Hilton Head

It was August 30, 1898, and word was a vicious hurricane was bearing down on Hilton Head Island. Already the wind was whipping sand into painful swirls that pelted lighthouse master Adam Fripp as he made his way around the lighthouse, securing the grounds.

Fripp had been the keeper of Hilton Head's lighthouse since it was put into operation in 1884. It was actually the second lighthouse built on the spot. The first had been set atop the keeper's house and rose to a height of only thirty-five feet. This height was impossibly short, considering that the island's passage channel was ever shifting.

To alleviate the problem, a ninety-five-foot range-light lighthouse had been erected behind the original. This new, taller lighthouse was constructed of steel in a skeletal style around a solid cylinder. It was mobile, which meant it could be moved around as the channel moved. Now that there were two lighthouses, a range-light system was being used. A large Fresnel light, which could be seen fifteen miles out to sea, was placed on the mobile light house, and a smaller light was placed in the short lighthouse. By aligning the two lights, sailors could safely navigate the hazards around the island.

Despite its spindly appearance, the skeletal lighthouse tower was built to withstand gales and hurricanes. Fripp felt safe enough riding out the storm here, and he knew it was essential that the beacon stay lit, beaming its warning out to the hapless sailors caught in the storm. Keeping the light going could well save lives and that was his job. So there was no question that he was staying.

"Father! Father! Where are you?"

At the sound of his daughter's voice, Fripp rounded the corner of the keeper's house.

"Caroline! What are you doing here? The storm is coming ashore now! You should be in town."

"I wasn't about to leave you out here by yourself. You might need help keeping the light going with the wind so high."

Caroline was his youngest daughter and he doted on her. She'd always been a daddy's girl, dogging his every footstep as a toddler and wrapping him around her teenage finger. Now at twenty-one, she was a beautiful young woman who still enjoyed spending time with her old father. He should've known she'd be worried and come out here.

The wind was coming in harder now. Trees were beginning to bend over and objects were flying through the air.

"Get inside!" Fripp screamed to Caroline. He followed her into the lighthouse, both struggling with the door to shut it against the howling wind.

"Get out the checkers and make us some coffee," he said. "I'm going up to check the lantern."

About halfway up the tight spiral staircase, Fripp was breathing hard. He began feeling a tightness in his chest. At the top, he paused for a moment to catch his breath. It was just fatigue, he told himself. He hadn't slept well last night, worrying about the coming storm. That's all it was.

Striding into the lantern room, he made his checks quickly. Everything was shipshape. He had turned to go, when suddenly there was a loud crashing sound and glass began splintering down. Something had crashed into the lantern! It was shattered and the wind howled into the tiny room, extinguishing the kerosene lamp that was so vital to the sailors.

As he turned back toward the room, an excruciating pain squeezed his chest and radiated down his left arm. Struggling for breath, he tried to make it over to the lamp. He had to re-light it! The pain in his chest worsened. It was squeezing the breath out of him. He collapsed onto the floor, clutching at his chest and gasping for air.

Suddenly, Caroline was by his side. "Father! What's wrong? Are you hurt?"

"No," he gasped out. "My chest is hurting. Caroline, you've got to re-light the lantern! It's imperative. You've got to light it and keep it lit."

"But, Father, What about you? I've got to go for help!"

"No!" He grabbed her wrist. "You can't leave. I'll be all right. Just get the lamp lit. Go." He pushed her hands away. "Go!"

Caroline reluctantly stood and headed toward the lamp. She had spent most of her childhood here, helping her father with his duties. She knew how to light the lamp. The problem was going to be keeping it lit with the wind blowing through.

"Caroline," her father called her back momentarily. "Promise me, Daughter. Promise me that no matter what happens, you'll keep the lamp lit. There are sailors out there in this storm. Without the light to show them the dangers, they'll run aground. They could drown. If the light's lit, they at least have a chance to steer clear. Now, promise me you'll keep it lit!"

Tears streamed down her face. "I promise, Daddy. I promise I will."

Caroline returned to the lamp and, with great difficulty, got it lit.

"It's lit, Father!" There was no answer. "Father!" As soon as she turned away, the wind blew the lamp out again. Caroline was torn. She wanted desperately to go to her father; to go get help for him. But she had promised. She knew how dedicated her father was to his responsibilities. She had promised she would keep the lamp lit, and she knew she had to keep that promise.

All through the long, dark, and windy night, Caroline kept her vigil, sheltering the lamp so that it could beam its warning beacon out to sea. She would call out to her father, but there was never a response. Still, she stayed at the lamp, faithfully keeping her promise to her father.

Finally, morning broke. Heavy clouds still blanketed the sky, but the wind was finally still. Exhausted, Caroline left her post at the lamp and rushed to her father's side, but one look told her it was too late. Her father had died during the night.

Caroline was devastated. She was hailed as a hero for her efforts in keeping the lighthouse lamp lit. Because of her, several ships had been saved. But she believed that had she left and gotten help, her father would still be alive. Her grief would not let her rest. Every night afterward, she would have nightmares about that long night, with her father lying dead on the floor. It was more than she could take, and within weeks, she, too, had died. She was buried in a beautiful blue gown.

The short front lighthouse was decommissioned in 1932 and was later destroyed. The tall skeletal construction lighthouse was deactivated in 1930s, but remains in good condition today. It sits at the Palmetto Dunes Resort on Hilton Head Island, along with the oil house and a cistern.

According to legend, Caroline, dressed in her blue gown, faithfully keeps her promise to her father to this day. She's been seen wandering the grounds around the lighthouse, and there have been numerous reports of the sound of a woman crying coming from inside the lighthouse, especially on stormy nights.

Little Annie of Winyah Bay

Georgetown, named in honor of King George I, was founded in 1729 and became an official port of entry in 1732. Within a few years it had become a major commerce center. Prior to that, all foreign imports and exports had to pass through Charleston. By the time of the American Revolution, hundreds of acres of cypress swamp land had been cleared and more than 780 miles had been dug, making the area the world's second largest rice cultivation center. Georgetown also was a center for the cultivation of Indigo, which is used to make blue dye.

Ships trading in these two commodities had to sail between North and South Islands to enter Winyah Bay, then sail up the river into Georgetown, a sometimes treacherous route because of the rocky shoals. Although the land for placement of a lighthouse on North Island was donated by Revolutionary War patriot Paul Trapier in 1789, it was more than a decade before the lighthouse was finally built. The seventy-two-foot cypress wood tower was erected in 1801, during the last days of John Adams's presidency. In addition to the tower, there was a two-story keeper's house and a large tank for holding the whale oil that was used to light the lighthouse lamp. The lighthouse had been erected only five years when a massive storm toppled it.

It was 1811 before the lighthouse was replaced, this time with a seventy-two-foot sturdy brick building that would not so easily succumb to storms. There is a stone stairway that spirals inside the lighthouse and in 1857, a Fresnel lens was added.

During the Civil War, the lighthouse was used as a lookout point for Confederates, but then it was captured by Union troops. The war played havoc with its exterior, and as part of the post-war repair, it was lengthened to eighty-seven feet.

The lighthouse was manned until 1986, when the Coast Guard installed an automated light. A solar-powered system was installed in 1999. The lighthouse was used for a short time as a juvenile detention center, but then was placed on the National Registry of Historic Places, a move that may see it restored to its original condition.

In addition to the solar-powered beacon beaming from the lighthouse to warn them away from the shoals, the sailors of Georgetown also have a hurricane warning system. Her name is Annie.

Back in the early 1800s, weather forecasting was pretty much your-best-guess-is-as-good-as-mine. In those days, sudden and violent storms would slam into the island with no warning. It was at this time that pretty, fair-haired Annie lived at the lighthouse with its keeper, her father.

Since there was nothing on the island but the lighthouse, Annie and her father would row across Winyah Bay into Georgetown for supplies. Annie's father would always plan their trips by the tides, and they would always return before evening in order to light the lighthouse's whale-oil beacon.

On one glorious morning, Annie's father had awakened and decided it would be a good day for a trip across the bay for supplies. The sun had been shining brightly, and there wasn't a cloud to be seen. They had rowed over to Georgetown early that morning, and had spent a pleasant day shopping and visiting with friends. Annie's father had been enjoying himself so much he hadn't noticed that the wind had freshened and that a bank of clouds was moving over the bay. And they had left later than planned.

Now, as he was rowing strenuously against a swift current, rain began pelting down and the wind suddenly began gusting, kicking up waves that splashed into their small boat. He glanced at the bow of the boat. Annie was clinging to her seat, a look of fear on her sweet little face. The wind grew stronger, and the waves became taller and more threatening. The boat tossed side to side, at the mercy of the raging water. Annie and her father were in a desperate situation, but it was too late to turn back. They were closer to the island than to Georgetown.

Suddenly, a huge gust of wind drove a wave over the boat, swamping it. Annie screamed and her father grabbed her as they both ended up in the choppy water. Taking one of the boat lines, he quickly lashed her onto his back and began swimming toward shore. Reaching it, he crawled out of the surf and collapsed.

When he awoke many hours later, he had no recollection of the terror they had encountered. He did not remember strapping the child to his back, or crawling to shore. He was brought abruptly into reality, however, when he found Annie still lashed to his back. Sadly, she had not made it. She had drowned before they reached shore.

Since that time—even until today—sailors have reported seeing the spirit of a beautiful blonde child. According to legend, she appears on boats plying the water of the bay. She usually appears on a bright, sunny day, pointing back to shore and pleading for the sailors to go back. The sailors ignore her warning at their own peril. The legend says those who keep sailing soon find themselves in a furious storm and may well end up in a watery grave.

the phantom flagman

For most of Simon Everett's young life, people had told him that he was the best youth minister they had ever met. He could talk to just about anyone, and even the most troubled teens found it easier to communicate with him than they did with their parents. More importantly, he was able to provide real world advice and solutions to their real world problems. When somebody would occasionally praise him for his insight and wisdom, he would humbly say, "Thank you. This is what I do."

Unfortunately, being a young man, Simon had much to learn about dealing with people. Frequently, his criticism of their behavior was too harsh, and it was difficult for him to understand that it didn't do anyone any good to be too forceful. He found himself being harsh with people more oftentimes than not, and it became clear to Simon that he was having a problem.

Perhaps he was having a crisis of faith, or perhaps he just hadn't lived enough life yet to know how to really communicate with people. Whatever the reason, he decided that he needed to go on some sort of spiritual vacation to help sharpen his sense of reality. He was an energetic young man, generally imperturbable, with intense staying power as long as you stayed out of his way. But he couldn't take people disturbing him, breaking his stride, or in any way interfering with his personal rhythm. So he decided to spend time alone with his thoughts by going on a journey of discovery.

He made the decision to begin hiking the state of Georgia, leaving his hometown of Columbus. He would let the open road quicken his perceptions, and he would come to rely fully on his own strengths and his own abilities to solve problems and fend for himself. Simon Everett trusted in his ability to master any situation and to size up any person, so he knew he wouldn't have any problem as he hiked through the state.

As he set out along the way of his journey, he immediately learned to patiently trust in the natural cycles of the life he was currently living. He would dedicate himself to covering a certain amount of distance every day, and along the way, he would volunteer at area churches. Occasionally, he would preach, or maybe even stay a day or two in a town, doing work around area churches in exchange for food and board. It was clear to everyone who met him that he was a special young man who was willing to assume responsibility for his own growth and development.

As the weeks turned into months, Simon started to gain some insight into the way he'd been conducting himself as a youth minister. He was beginning to see things that, he believed, probably ought to change. He began to have a sense that he needed to make a clean sweep of things and just, well, start over. Simon recognized that he would often get carried away in his capacity as a minister, and he began to see where his harsh criticism and forceful truthfulness came from; he was, simply, trying too hard.

Going out on the road brings the refuge of solitude where a man can think for himself, and Simon was taking full advantage of it. He was finding his sense of reality reinforced, and he found that some of the issues in his life that he thought of as problems weren't really problems at all; it was just a question of growing up. In any event, as he made his way down the road, he could tell that his journey of discovery was bringing order to his life.

One day after a particularly long hike down a lonely stretch of road, he found himself at a campsite near the town of Blackshear off Georgia Highway 38. It was a lovely little campsite, made even better by the fact that Simon was completely alone. That night, he wrote in his journal, had a meal fit for a king of the road, and experienced all the sounds and images of a spring night in Georgia. He was keenly aware of the all-or-nothing beauties of the great outdoors. He was also experiencing a sense of peace and euphoria that he had never experienced in his life. Yet at the same time, Simon almost couldn't sit still. He was on fire with possibilities for new ministries, new projects, and new ways to help people in his home church, and he furiously wrote in his journal until he just couldn't write any more.

Then he unrolled his sleeping bag, tended to the campfire, and laid down for a well-deserved night's rest. As he lay there about to go to sleep, he found his mind playing with all sorts of disconnected thoughts, and he found himself curiously questioning everything. He was playing intellectual games, doing multiplication tables and word games. He quietly complimented himself on his intellectual slyness in solving some of these self-imposed puzzles that ran through his mind there at the campsite.

But amid the feelings of euphoria and suspense in a mind alight with the possibilities of life to come, there was also a feeling that something strange was about to happen. Simon experienced a feeling of lightness or tingling on his scalp. He paid no attention to it and drifted off to sleep.

As he began to fade off into sleep, he imagined that he was tumbling and falling, as if he'd rolled out of bed. He wasn't sure, but he felt that he might be a little bit afraid, as if he was falling toward some sort of dangerous situation. But he wasn't sure. Then, all of a sudden, it felt like someone grabbed him by the hair on top of his head and pulled him right out of the sleeping bag.

When Simon opened his eyes, he wasn't yet aware that he was dreaming, but he looked down to see himself lying comfortably and peacefully in his sleeping bag at his campsite. Standing next to him was the man who had pulled him out of the sleeping bag by the top of his hair. It was a railroad flagman who smiled pleasantly and tipped his hat.

In one hand, he held a flagman's lantern that was fully lit and shone light all over the campsite. He reached out and took Simon by the hand, and then the two started to walk away from where Simon's physical form lay sleeping.

Now, in Simon's ministry, he had told people not to believe in ghosts, but here he found himself in a dream—or something more real than a dream—apparently walking through a campsite with one. And then the most amazing thing happened: Simon and the ghostly flagman began to float up into the air. Higher and higher and higher they went, slowly gaining height and distance over the countryside. Soon, the campsite was in the distance. The flagman held out his lantern to illuminate the area in front of them, and Simon found himself floating with his ghostly companion over the tops of trees and houses. When they crossed roads, he saw cars and trucks pass beneath him.

Occasionally, the flagman would circle low and pay a visit to an area house. Most of the time, the people inside the house weren't aware that anything was going on, but Simon and his ghostly friend floated in and out of the attics and ceilings, visiting one- and two-story houses. Simon was astounded to see that he could actually focus on things that were on top of shelves and china cabinets. He could read letters on desks and book titles on top shelves, and even listen to the conversations as he drifted from one room to another, one house to another.

Along the way, the flagman took Simon in through the roof of an area church where they were getting ready for some sort of festivity. The choir was singing and people were making punch and generally getting ready for a celebration.

Simon and the flagman sat up in the rafters of the huge country church and just watched the scenes below. The flagman had not once said a word to Simon the entire time, and for some reason, Simon couldn't speak, either. But as he looked around the rafters of the rural church, he noticed a message carved neatly into one of the top rafters. The message read, "Dedicated to the people of Screven," and there was a date Simon couldn't make out. He was about to lean forward to get a closer look at the carved inscription when the flagman grasped him by the hand, and they both floated out the ceiling of the church and off into the night.

Simon was starting to become very uncomfortable with the whole situation. Was this a dream? If it was, how come he couldn't wake himself up? If it was something more than a dream, then it was something more than Simon had ever experienced in his young life, and it frightened him. Where was this grinning ghost taking him next?

It was almost as if the flagman realized that Simon was getting scared because he smiled, held his lantern toward the ground, and the pair floated to the earth. As they were a few feet above the ground, Simon saw old railroad tracks illuminated by the flagman's lantern. A moment later, Simon and his ghostly companion were standing on the crossties.

The flagman held his lantern high, and as Simon looked around, he couldn't make out what it was that he was supposed to see—if anything. He looked over at the flagman, who just smiled and nodded his head and continued to hold his lantern high to illuminate the surrounding area. Then, off in the distance, Simon heard the sounds of an approaching train. His natural reaction was to step off the track, but for some reason, he couldn't get his feet to move. He looked at the flagman, who just smiled and nodded his head and held his lantern aloft, while Simon desperately tried to communicate with him that they needed to get off the railroad tracks.

But still Simon couldn't speak. He looked off in the distance, and he could see the headlamp of the oncoming train. The flagman smiled quietly at Simon and then began to walk forward in the direction of the train. Simon reached out with his hands, trying to pull him back, but couldn't reach the ghost.

The train was getting closer and closer now, and the flagman began swinging his lantern from one side to the other, as if to slow the train. But the train wasn't slowing. The oncoming train got closer and closer. Finally, Simon was able to muster enough strength to shout for the flagman to get off the tracks. The flagman stopped, turned around, looked at Simon, smiled, and nodded his head, and then began walking toward the oncoming train. Simon felt the pulling at the top of his head again, as his feet lifted off of the crossties. He began to float in the air above the railroad tracks.

The fast-moving train was moments from the flagman, who continued to walk on the crossties, swinging his lantern back and forth. There wasn't anything Simon could do except look at him in horror as the train ran headlong into the flagman.

The flagman's lantern skittered to the ground, but even more horrifying was the sight of the flagman's head being knocked off his body and rolling into the brush alongside the railroad track. By then, the fast-moving train passed under Simon in a flash. Moments later, the train was gone.

The flagman's body lay off to one side of the railroad tracks near his lantern, but his head was nowhere to be found. Simon wanted to go down and tend to his new friend, but the pulling sensation at the crown of his head became more intense. Before he could prepare himself, Simon's floating body was snapped backwards like a rubber band.

In a flash, Simon found himself back in his sleeping bag at the campsite. He was covered in a cold sweat and breathing heavily. He sat up and threw off the sleeping bag. For what seemed like hours, he sat with his knees in his chest, trying to compose himself. He had a sip of water from his canteen and tried to relax.

He recorded his dream in his journal, having decided that it was, indeed, just a nightmare. The details were so vivid and the sounds and the smells were all so real. Writing the dream down in his notebook seemed to ease Simon's mind quite a bit. Soon he drifted back off to sleep and woke up the next morning to a bright and shiny opportunity for a brand new day.

He made his breakfast, broke camp, and headed off down the road. Even though the sun was shining, and Simon was feeling generally very good about himself, the events of the previous evening had left him very disturbed and uneasy. Generally, nothing could shock this young man, but today he was feeling weak and unsure of himself.

As he walked along Highway 38, an occasional train would pass by, sending chills through Simon's spine. Soon, he realized if he didn't spend some time around some friendly people, he felt he might go a little bit nuts.

A short time later, Simon found himself at Milligan's railroad crossing on what was called Bennett Road in this part of Georgia, really an extension of Highway 38. It was almost dusk, and Simon couldn't help but think about his dream the night before. Had it been real? Had it been a dream? Was that a ghost or was it just his imagination?

While Simon was trying to figure out just exactly what had happened the previous night and why he was filled with such dread, he noticed something coming down the railroad tracks by Milligan's Crossing. It was a round light floating four or five feet above the railroad tracks, bouncing slowly from one side of the railroad tracks to the other. Simon couldn't see where the light was coming from, but he chalked that up to the tricks that dusk light can play on you.

But as the light got closer, he saw that it was free-floating—no one was holding this unearthly light. The pulsating orb of light, about the size of a basketball, got closer and closer and closer to Simon. And then, in panic, Simon began to run from it. But the light chased Simon down the track, swinging from side to side, bouncing from one track to the other.

It was darker now, and the orb of light was getting closer. As Simon cleared some trees, he saw a small church and made for the front door. There were people inside getting ready for a wedding. He was grateful to see a room full of living people. Simon walked in the church, briefly turning around to see the light floating off into the wilderness that framed the railroad tracks.

Someone greeted him at the door, and Simon introduced himself. Over the next few minutes, Simon in his characteristic fashion had made friends with most everyone there. The warmth and fellowship of these people even chased away his fear. He even agreed to stay for a few days and help them with their wedding celebration and possibly exchange some room and board for some work around the small church. It was then that Simon realized that the church he was standing in looked like the church he had seen in his dream. In fact, this was the very church that he and his ghostly friend had been in the night before.

Simon asked someone, "Is this Screven?"

And they said, "Why, yes it is. This is the oldest church in the area."

As Simon was hanging wedding decorations, he maneuvered his

ladder to catch a glimpse of one rafter in particular. There, just as he had seen it in his dream, was the inscription, "Dedicated to the people of Screven."

Simon stayed for the wedding and even accepted an invitation to be the guest preacher on the following Sunday. His sermon revolved around the theme of quietly holding the illuminating lamp of your faith and love for all to see.

It wasn't until two days later that Simon told the parishioners of Screven Church about the ghostly light that chased him down the railroad tracks and the dream he had had the night before. As it turns out, the ghostly lights were a regular feature of this community, and many people had seen them. There are a great many stories as to where the lights came from, but the most common one concerned a railroad flagman who, sometime near the turn of the century, tried to slow down an oncoming train and had unfortunately died in the attempt. Nobody knows why the flagman was trying to slow down the oncoming train. Perhaps there was livestock on the track or a small child was playing too close to it. But one thing everyone agrees on, when they recovered the flagman and his lantern, they couldn't find his head. And during the evenings, particularly evenings after it rains, some say you can see the flagman waving his lantern back and forth, trying to find his head.

The locals say that no one else has ever been killed on the tracks at Screven. In point of fact, because of the unearthly lights that play in the area, no one ever goes near them.

the river speaks

January 14, 1863

My Christmas package arrived, mostly intact and containing this diary. God's grace alone must have guided the package, for Julia, not knowing where I was, simply addressed it to me by name and regiment number. She is well and the farm all right in spite of the lack of help.

I have not told her much about my injuries. I can hardly bear to think of them myself. But when I remember Sharpsburg, I guess I should be grateful to have escaped with my life. I still dream of it.

My comrades that had been laughing and sharing cornbread with me that morning, I left lying two and three deep in the road, mutilated and torn almost beyond recognition. Some of the wounds were so large I could have passed my fist through them and touched the soldier beneath.

My caretakers here say that I am fortunate to have survived the first few weeks after my surgery. Many, many men died as a result of fevers or complications to their wounds. I do not feel lucky. I feel most times abandoned by God. I have been to hell.

January 18

The man who buries the dead here must be simpleminded. He wanders through the rows of beds calling "Anybody dead here? Anybody dying?" I have talked to him once or twice. He asked if I were well enough to help him with the burials, and I asked him if he really thought I could manage a shovel.

I received another letter from Julia today. She hears of movement in Tennessee by the Yankees and is concerned. I wrote back and told her to hide the seed corn and set the pigs loose to forage in the woods. She'll be fine as long as she doesn't make anybody mad, Confederate or Yankee.

After a week of smelling worse and worse, the man on the bed next to me has finally died. I suppose his wound became infected. Many nights I lay awake worrying that it was my body rotting away. The orderly assured me it was not so, but only until I began to use the crutches and hobble outside, away from the other patients, would I believe him. I am mastering the use of the crutches.

The weather is oddly springlike. I am nearly five hundred miles north and east of home, so it should be colder here. I am glad of the warmth, though, because our makeshift hospital, formerly a barn, has gaps of three inches or more between the strips of siding. I feel sorry for the poor animals who will call this structure home in colder weather.

January 23

They have told me I must go home. My regiment has been dissolved. Most of us died at Sharpsburg and I would be better off if I had, too. I told them I did not want to return home. They said they had no further use for me. I approached an officer who had come to check on some of his men and begged him to let me serve the Confederacy again. After some delay, he agreed. I am to go to Jackson, Mississippi, with a small company in the morning.

The weather has turned cold and wet. The rain runs in little rivulets between the cots so that everything is wet and muddy. There is still a shortage of chamber pots. I will be glad to be quit of this stinking hellhole. I saw a surgeon today for the first time since I was brought here. He was enjoying a smoke on the porch of the farmhouse. I began to approach him but the tips of my crutches sank so deeply in the mud I abandoned the idea. Instead, I spit as loudly and voluminously as I could in his direction.

January 30

I marched as best I could before developing festering sores under my arms from the damned crutches. My new company commander, Cap. N—, had me tossed on top of the supply wagon and so I made my way here to Jackson, Mississippi. I am not the only cripple in the company. In fact, between us all (there are forty), we probably total about twenty whole men.

It is downright cold in Jackson and the rain blows today in almost horizontal sheets. I am not sorry to be here. We passed within fifty miles of my home on our march here, but I did not request leave to see Julia. I doubt she would want to see me in the state I am in now.

We are housed in tents on the banks of a river. The Pearl River, they call it. There is a ruined bridge upstream of our camp a few hundred yards. The people of Jackson are very anxious about Grant's armies. I suppose our presence, piecemeal as we are, is small comfort.

I have been sick for four days with diarrhea. I believe the saltback we were issued in Richmond was wormy, but the company cook insists on putting it in the beans anyway. We are all sick to one degree or another. The Cap's servant who used to cook ran away on January 2 after telling the Cap that Mr. Lincoln had made him free.

January 31

Our Cap is either very intelligent or crazy. He has ordered us to secure the bridge and turn it into a prison for Yankee officers. The approach on the south bank had completely fallen away, so we took some miscellaneous boards and covered over the end of the bridge. After boarding up the north end, except for a narrow opening, the prison was ready for its inmates. We will have a patrol on each bank and one on the river itself in case one of the officers is desperate or foolish enough to try the river as an escape route.

Since I have had a great deal of experience in small boats, having been raised on a river, I am eager to take on the river patrol. It will be easy for me to row and watch since I will not have to stand up for a long time. Tomorrow the prisoners arrive from Vicksburg. The news from Vicksburg is all bad. The siege is taking a terrible toll. I have heard the civilians there are forced to turn to their horses and even to their dogs for food.

The rain stopped but mud is everywhere. We have taken a few leftover boards to make wooden floors for our tents, so they are more habitable than many other quarters I have found in the past two years. The bridge is quite dilapidated. Working on it today I could swear it was swaying on its foundations. There are large gaps between the boards on the side, wider than those at the hospital barn in Richmond. But at least the prisoners will have a roof overhead.

February 1

Twenty captured Yankee officers marched in today. They looked thin but not any worse off than any of the rest of us, I reckon. One man, near the end of the line with his arm in a sling, looked so much like my cousin Sam Watterson that I went up to him to see his face closer.

"Sam?" I asked. He turned to look at me. I still couldn't tell if he was my cousin. It's been at least fifteen years since I saw him.

"You related to the Wattersons of Tennessee?"

He shook his head, and I could tell his arm or shoulder was paining him pretty bad.

"Where are you from?" I was walking alongside them as they filed into the bridge.

"Illinois," he croaked. "Can I have a drink of water?"

Without thinking, I handed over my canteen. He looked at it blankly then spoke again.

"I can't use my hand to unscrew it." I helped him take a drink, then it was his turn to enter the dark bridge.

My comrades gave me a hard time about giving that old Yankee boy a drink. When I told them he looked like my cousin, though, they let up some.

I spent the rest of my shift in a boat on the river. I could hear the floor of that old bridge creak and crack with their weight, but I figured it was strong enough to hold them. Pretty soon one of them called out.

"We want food! We ain't et since we left Vicksburg on Sunday!" They'd been on the road a few days, but it wasn't my job to see that they got fed. I guess that's the sergeant's job. They were still fussing and hollering when I went off to my tent. That idiot Fritch is still cooking for us, and he forgot to soak the hardtack this morning. But I guess a plate of beans is better than nothing at all.

The rain is colder now, but the local folks say it rarely snows around here. That's good, because I lost my blanket back at Sharpsburg, and I don't think I'll be seeing another one for a while. I have a cough, but it's not too bad. The diarrhea is still awful, and I hope Fritch will stop putting that rancid fatback in the beans. I talked to an old man who lives nearby who says his old lady's got a cure for the runs. I hope it works. I promised him a dollar if he'd bring it back to me tomorrow.

February 3

I spent all day yesterday with such terrible cramps I thought I'd die. I couldn't even make it to the latrine so I spent all day lying in piles of my own filth. One good thing about the rain is that I can just hang my drawers from the tent pole outside and they get washed. Sort of. The old man came back right before dark, and I brewed the bark to make a tea. It tasted nasty, but it must have worked. I feel all right today, just weak.

February 4

Got a letter from Julia today. Darn those Yankees. They came and made off with both cows and the mule. She had hid the seed corn, so at least she'll be able to start a crop this spring. And the pigs have been out in the woods foraging for a month now, so they are all right as long as nobody else found them. Julia's all right, too. Thank God. But she's mad enough that I sure wouldn't cross her.

Those Yankees on the bridge were still hollering for food today. I hollered back that their friends in Alabama were drinking milk from my cows and that would have to satisfy these jerks in Mississippi, too. I could see them sticking their hands out between the boards, I guess trying to catch a little rain. I wonder what the sergeant has done for provisions for them. We ain't eating much either, but at least we've got more than the folks at Vicksburg.

The sergeant told us to expect some more prisoners soon. Maybe even tomorrow. If it gets much colder, those Yankees are going to need some blankets or something. I know the wind's blowing right through the sides of the bridge. It rained today, all day, letting up to a light drizzle this evening.

Some of the other men told me the Captain left today to go to Vicksburg. I guess that leaves our sergeant in command.

February 5

The old man brought some potatoes to sell and some eggs. Me and some of the boys split a dozen eggs—they cost $3 but they were worth every penny. I'll roast me a potato tonight. The sergeant let one of the prisoners out to cook for the rest of them—can't build a fire on the bridge, so me and one other soldier watched while he boiled some beans. Didn't look like much, but he said they would be glad for anything. I helped him carry the pot back to the bridge and saw the Yankee that looked like my cousin Sam lying on the floor.

"You sick?"

He just groaned.

"Got the Mississippi runs," said the man next to him. "He's been sick for a couple days."

I still had some of that bark left in my pocket. I pulled some out and stuffed it into the soldier's hand. I don't know why. I guess I was still thinking about Sam.

"Give 'em these," I said. "Brew them in some water. Don't tell anybody I gave 'em to you."

It was dark on that bridge, since we'd closed up one end and blocked off all but a little of the other end. It smelled bad, too. I guess they'd made a hole in the floor in the corner to use as a latrine. I asked them what they were doing for water and they said they were catching a little rainwater here and there. I don't think I'd even treat a dog like that. But then again, they're Yankees.

Still raining and mighty cold. The fog off the river in the mornings makes it hard to see sometimes, but if anybody jumped off the bridge into the water, I'd hear it. They wouldn't get far.

February 6

I went and talked to the sergeant this morning and told him that I'd help forage provisions for the regiment and the prisoners. He showed me a fifty-pound bag of cornmeal just come in and another barrel of salted meat. I agreed that it looked like plenty for a while, and he told me to keep up the good work. He's been watching me, he said.

Then I got outside and saw a whole stream of new prisoners come marching in. They were more stumbling than marching. It seemed like there was no end to the line of soldiers, and I asked the boys bringing them in how many there was.

"Two hunnerd and fifty," he told me.

Now I am no genius. But I don't know how you fit nearly 300 men in a space that's eighteen feet wide and ninety or a hundred feet long. I guess you can; I saw them go in and certainly none of them came out, but I am glad I have my little tent even if it does leak sometimes.

Their cook came out, and I had guard detail again while he cooked some corn mush. It started raining so hard it was putting out the cooking fire, so we rigged up a tarp to keep him a little dry. It's a small kettle and he's feeding a lot of people, so he had to be outside a while.

Jimmy, the other guard, went to the latrine and while he was gone I asked about the Yankee that looked like Sam.

"He's feelin' better," their cook allowed. "But we all need more water. And there's more of us sick than him."

"Just about all of us have the runs, too," I told him. "I wish I knew what kind of bark that old man gave me, and I could make a fortune out of the Confederate Army." We both had a good laugh and he told me that before he'd gotten captured his regiment had a lot of diarrhea, too. And fevers and coughs and measles and smallpox.

Jimmy came back and we quit chatting so friendly. Before I left, we'd carried that kettle back and forth about five times and the bag of cornmeal was more than half-empty. I can get along good on one crutch now. Jimmy asked me on our way back to the camp if I worried about going in the bridge without my rifle. It never occurred to me that the Yankees would try to hurt me. Now don't that sound stupid?

I wish it was spring; I'd go find some greens to cook. I've got such a craving for them I could spit. It's raining like it'll never quit. I guess that's what winter's like in Mississippi. I would almost wish for snow, if I had some decent shoes, just to be rid of this rain.

I hear some fuss going on over at the bridge but I'm dry and I'll wait and see what's going on in the morning. If they need me they can come and get me.

February 7

Well, I couldn't believe it when they told me. The noise last night was some boys bringing in another 130 prisoners. Nobody knows where they come from but my guess is Vicksburg. They are still surrounded and things don't look too good. I suppose they want to be sure the prisoners don't turn on them.

But I don't know how they'll fit all those men in that bridge. I have been all around its foundations patrolling in the water and it is an old bridge. With that many men they won't even be able to lie down. I suppose our sergeant knows what he's doing or maybe even he has orders to do this. But it seems a very hard thing to treat their soldiers like this. I hope they are treating our boys better.

I was under the bridge in the rowboat today and I looked up. I thought I saw the floorboards sagging and I reported it to the sergeant when my watch was up. He said he thought it would be all right.

Their cook was under the tarp we had rigged for him, cooking some beans. I stopped for a smoke and he started coughing very bad. I looked at him and he had bright cheeks, like he'd been out in the wind too long, but he said he had a fever. Some of the new soldiers were pretty sick and nobody could sleep because there wasn't any way to lie down. Some men were sitting and others were taking turns lying down but it was pretty awful in there, he told me. I believe him.

This tent feels like a palace. The mail has not come through for a few days and the men are starting to grumble. It is mail from home that keeps us from going crazy. Or maybe we are crazy. Sometimes I wake up at night and both my legs hurt ached like fire.

February 9

Those Yankees that got here day before yesterday must have been pretty sick. Five of them died last night, and we had some other prisoners drag them out and put them on the riverbank. Sergeant says he'll get up a burial detail tomorrow, but we're shorthanded ourselves today because everyone, including me, has terrific stomach cramps. I tried to tell him the salt pork wasn't fit to eat, but he won't listen. I guess he didn't give the prisoners any or else I'd have heard them moan when I passed under the bridge on my watch. I threw up four times but the river took it all away.

Haskell had the river detail last night and wasn't paying attention. He stopped the rowboat under the bridge to get out of the rain for a smoke, only he was right under their latrine. Ha ha.

The rain has cleared for the first time in a week and if I weren't so weak I'd jump up and say "Hallelujah!"

February 10

I guess the river air is deadly for Yankees. Four more died. The prisoners are shouting for a doctor. I should tell them how much doctoring I got after being wounded. They would shut up right quick. The doctor couldn't do anything for them anyway, because there isn't any medicine left in all of Jackson, the old man told me. The trains aren't getting through.

There wasn't but a few cups of cornmeal left, but their cook made a thin gruel with it anyway. When I helped him carry the pot to the bridge, I was almost afraid to look in. I have fought in some of the bloodiest battles ever, but there is something even worse about treating men like they were lower than an animal. They were moaning and groaning, packed in there so close that when one man turned, his neighbor had to move too or else get stepped on. That started a chain reaction so they were constantly in motion, taking tiny steps first in one direction and then the other.

It was so dark I couldn't see anything but the first few lines of men near the door. But I could hear their feet moving and feel the heat of their bodies. With so many packed in there, they didn't even need any blankets. Except, I guess, the poor guys next to the walls.

The sun was shining again today, but it has turned bitter cold. The old man from town sold me some newspapers to stuff in my shoe, but I would really like to have my blanket back. I suppose some Yankee at Sharpsburg is wrapped up all warm and snug. I am consoled by remembering the lice I surely left in that blanket. I hope those little rascals keep that Yankee up all night, crawling through his hair.

February 13

Every morning they carry out two or three more men. I can't help with the burial detail because I can't manage a shovel. The sergeant doesn't seem to care. The Yankees are just lying there on the riverbank rotting. I guess there are too many of us sick. There seem to be fewer of us, but I haven't been really keeping track. We don't know each other anyway. We formed up as a company less than a month ago, and we're from all over, so nobody really cares about anybody else. I wish I'd get a letter from Julia. It's still cold and our ration of beans is gone. The prisoners don't have anything left to eat either. If the old man would come by, I'd buy everything he had to eat. I'd even eat that maggoty old saltback if Fritch put it in front of me.

Jimmy says it's the air from the river killing the Yankees, but I don't understand why it don't kill us, too. Sometimes they get to coughing on the bridge and the whole thing seems to shake. It makes my chest hurt to hear that cough. Maybe all the sick ones that came in last have all died by now. There are about twenty bodies waiting to get buried.

February 14

No one died on the bridge last night. I must've been right. The weak ones died and now everything will be all right.

I figured out why it seems like there are fewer of us now. Men have been slipping off, going home I guess to get some food. It's dismal here and I don't think it'll get any better anytime soon. If I thought Julia could stand the sight of me, I'd go back home, too. But I wouldn't be any use to her the way I am. I should write and tell her to forget about me, but I'm a coward.

I went up to the bridge and poked my head in after I did my watch on the river. It's truly awful and I know it's not right. I wish there was someone I could talk to, but the sergeant doesn't care, and I guess they'd call it treason for me to complain on account of the prisoners anyway. I don't know why I care. They're only Yankees and they'd kill me if they had the chance. But God knows I'd rather be dead than packed onto that bridge. Sometimes when the wind blows hard I wonder if it will stand up.

I heard from the old man that Vicksburg is still defying Grant. Good for them. It was cold but clear today.

February 15

What would it be like, I wonder, to be standing elbow to elbow with a man and listen to him cough his life out? To feel his last breath hot on your neck, feel his body turn limp and start to slide to the ground, only to get caught by the arms and elbows and knees of people packed in around him?

Three men died in the bridge last night. I guess it's the same fever because their cook told me the men who cough don't die. It's the ones who start heating up from the inside out who eventually die after getting chills and fever and losing their senses. Sometimes I can hear them from my post down in the rowboat, crying out for their mama or their sweetheart. It gives me a chill and then I start worrying that I've got the fever.

We got another bag of cornmeal today, and I helped the cook carry gruel to the bridge. I told the sergeant I'd give every soldier his ration and then give the leftovers to the prisoners, but I split it up evenly in half. There's only thirty of us left, maybe twenty-five, and nearly 400 of them. Less the ones who've died, of course. It didn't seem right to keep so much for ourselves when at least we can go out and forage. I found a woman today who sold me half a ham and I ate it till I got sick. Then I gave the rest to Jimmy.

Still no mail. If the Union Army wanted to make us give up, they should start by keeping the mail from getting through. I suppose that's exactly what they're doing.

February 16

Jimmy came to my tent last night and told me he was leaving. They tried to discharge him in November after he was injured, but he wouldn't go. He lost his left eye. Now he says he's scared. He's seen the elephant, faced hundreds of men with rifles whose sole aim was to shoot him down, but this fever has got him scared.

I'm scared, too, but I don't know where I'd go if I left. Four more men died on the bridge last night. If they keep dying like this there won't be any left by spring.

Jimmy gave me his blanket. He says he's going south anyway and he'll get all the blankets he needs. His family is in Louisiana and will be glad to see him. I wished him luck.

February 18

It started raining again today, and I was sliding in the mud down to the rowboat past the row of corpses and one of them moved. I liked to have died right there. But it must have been a rat or something because I looked very closely and they were all dead. There are more than forty bodies piled up and the sergeant stays in his tent all day. I think he's drunk. If he's got whiskey rations for us, I wish he'd let us have them. I could use it. On the river it gets foggy and I hear the men call and cry out. I get so scared. They sound like they're right there in the boat with me. Their feet shifting and turning to accommodate every soldier's move, whispering on the planks of the bridge; it sounds like they're saying my name.

I sound like a lunatic and maybe I am. That body moving nearly did me in. Why won't the sergeant bury them?

February 19

The old man brought a bushel of apples. I almost cried they smelled so good. He wanted $10 for them and I asked some of the boys for some money and the cook from the prisoners gave me $3. I have six shiny apples lined up by the head of my cot, and I will have one a day until they are gone.

How would you divide a half-bushel of apples between 350 men? I don't even want to think about the scrambling and pushing that must have occurred when their cook went in with those apples. Or maybe they are all too weak to fight over food now.

I don't know why I stay. If I were not such a coward, I would leave. If those men were let out of the bridge, though, they would head straight north to get their guns and come back here to kill us. Is it worse to take a gun and shoot a man or put him in the dark and starve him to death? Maybe there will be no forgiveness for me no matter what I do.

I saw the Yankee that looks like Sam lying among the dead today. The sergeant is openly drunk when he bothers to appear from his tent, which is infrequent. Rain has come in from the west and so it blows and rains intermittently. No mail.

February 20

Four letters from Julia. Troops from Huntsville are foraging around the farm regularly. There are no men left in the area so she says the women just let the soldiers take what little is left. Julia has been nibbling away at the seed corn, she says, but there is still plenty to plant. She will try to start planting in another six weeks.

She has been writing me regularly, but the mail isn't getting through. I have heard no good news about the war. Four men died on the bridge last night. The fever is taking them quicker now their cook tells me. We have gotten a fifty-pound sack of beans but many of the prisoners are too weak to eat.

Julia asks if I will have any leave at springtime to help her with the planting. I must write to her and tell her that I can no longer do the work I once could. I try to imagine what will happen to me once the war is over, but I cannot.

I can't even imagine this war being over. It seems like I have been moving up and down the Pearl River in that little rowboat with my rifle in my lap for all my life. Has it really only been twenty days?

The rain cleared at midday. It seems a little warmer, but I doubt winter is over yet.

February 21

I talked to the cook today while he was fixing their rations. I asked him where he was from and he told me Missouri. I have never talked to somebody from there before.

"Are you a farmer?" I asked him.

"Yes, sir," he said, all proud. "I raise some of the fattest, finest hogs west of the Mississippi!"

I told him I was a farmer, too, or used to be, before the war.

"How many slaves do you have?" he asked me.

When I told him I didn't have any, he didn't believe me at first. I told him me and Julia had about seventy-five acres near Huntsville, Alabama, on the Flint River and grew cotton before the war, but then switched to corn to help feed the army.

He scratched his head. "If you ain't got any slaves, why are you fightin'?"

Well, I am not sure I really know the answer to that anymore, but I tried to answer him truthfully. "Because I didn't want anyone telling me what to do," I told him. "You Yankees were always poking your noses in my business."

He just shrugged and said that's why he moved out West, but he didn't see it as a reason for killing anybody.

"Why are you in the army, then?"

He shrugged again, then looked up and grinned.

"Bounty was good," he said. "I stayed drunk for four days before they found me and shipped me off."

He seems like a nice enough fellow and Missouri sounds like it has some good farmland.

Clear today and still on the warm side. The sergeant came out of his tent and stood in front of all those bodies. They stink pretty bad and it will get worse if he doesn't get somebody to bury them.

February 22

I was helping the Yankee cook carry those beans to the bridge today when my crutch broke—snapped right in two. I spilled the beans and lay there on the ground, helpless as a baby. Couldn't even stand up and the other guards were inside playing cards or something.

That Yankee quickly disappeared and I lay there wondering what it'd be like to get court-martialed. I could see my rifle propped up against the side of the guardhouse.

He came back with a stout stick to use as a crutch. I lay there with my mouth open until he hauled me back up to my leg and stuck that stick under my arm. I didn't ask him why he didn't run away. I think I know why. It's because he's a better man than me.

I asked him if there were any able-bodied men on the bridge who could bury the dead. He said he could find four or five. Three more Yankees died of the fever last night, and one of our men has come down with a fever, too. The sergeant packed him off to the hospital, but all the rest of the boys are pretty worried.

February 23

The sergeant just looked at me with his beady little mean eyes when I asked him if some of the prisoners could bury the dead. Then he asked if I had abandoned my post to come bother him with my stupid questions.

"We hang traitors!" he hollered after me as I left. I guess he's still got our whiskey ration hiding somewhere. I wish I could get my hands on it.

The cook didn't come out today—there is nothing for him to cook. It hasn't rained in three days and those prisoners don't have any water. I can't carry a barrel, but I ordered one of the younger boys—I think he's from Georgia—to take them a barrel of water from the river.

February 24

I am so hungry I could boil my shoe and eat it. I don't feel like writing much. No rain, but the weather has turned colder.

February 25

A train must have made it through because we now have two barrels of salted meat and four bags of cornmeal. The prisoners sent a different cook out. While I watched him I asked him where was the man from Missouri.

"Sick," he said, all mad and sullen.

"Fever?"

He just nodded. "You might as well kill us all now," he burst out, after we'd carried a couple buckets of gruel to the bridge and passed them in. "We're all gonna die here, so why not just shoot us here?"

A gunshot came from behind me and I turned around. There was that crazy sergeant, drunk as a lord, barely able to stand up. I turned around and that poor boy that had been cooking was laying there bleeding to death.

"Didja see that Yankee wretch tryin' to 'scape?" the sergeant grinned at me and it was horrible.

I hobbled off as quickly as I could. I couldn't say anything to the sergeant or he'd have shot me, too. The boy was right, anyway. I'd rather be shot dead myself than have that fever. Sometimes they foam at the mouth or flail around like they lost their wits. It's awful.

March 22

Well, I might as well have been shot dead. I don't remember having any convulsions or foaming at the mouth, but the old man tells me I was really sick. I don't know why he took me in, but he came to our camp and everybody was gone but me and I was lying on the ground shivering, so he threw me over his shoulder and carried me home.

I've been out of my head for almost a month and now it's nearly planting time. The sergeant meant for me to die; I know he must've, because he took my tent, my cot, and my rifle and left me on the ground. He put some papers in my bag that said I've been discharged from the Confederate Army because I'm crippled.

I'm tired and the old man says I should sleep.

March 24

I sat on the porch today and watched these two plant their garden. They will have watermelons, corn, green beans, beets, and squash. I want to help them but the old man says just to watch for now. I am awful tired. The sun feels good. If I am out on the porch I can hear the river but I can't see it.

March 30

I walked all the way back to the bridge today. Two months ago I could go for miles, but I am still as weak as a kitten. The old man says it was his wife's herbals that saved my life and I guess I am grateful.

There was no one at the bridge. The door was open and the only sign that the prisoners had ever been there was the barrel they had water in. The bodies were gone, too, but I don't think they were buried there. I didn't see any signs of digging.

The river sounds like the voices I heard when I was patrolling. Men crying for their mamas, wanting a little comfort when they're sick. Even if I do go home, I don't think I can stand to hear the river anymore. It used to sound so sweet but now it just sounds like men being killed for no good reason.

April 15

Jackson is full of rumors. The old man gets around and hears them all. People are saying that Grant has given up, Vicksburg has fallen, Grant's gone west, or that Grant's on his way to Jackson. Most folks are scared and some are leaving town. Me and the old man and the old lady are just staying put, though. There's not much that can scare me now.

April 20

I went down to the river today for a wash and heard that Yankee from Missouri talking to me. I swear it. It was foggy and I couldn't see, but I swear I heard him ask me how the farming was in Jackson. He didn't sound mad or anything. I turned around and expected to see him walking to me out of the fog but he never came.

Maybe I did imagine it. If I can imagine that my left leg has taken a bullet again, then I guess I can imagine anything.

The old man's crops are doing just fine. I took a hoe to that garden and did just fine. Balancing is tricky, but I can manage.

May 12

There was a great commotion in town as a brigade of men came through. They were fighting the Yankees at Raymond and were outnumbered, so they retreated. Raymond is only ten miles from town. Grant is said to be headed here and many folks are leaving in a panic.

May 14

Rain coming down in sheets. Jackson fell today to Sherman and Grant.

May 16

As I am obviously no threat to anyone, I can move freely about the area. I went this morning to the bridge to see if there was any activity. I ran into a Union soldier, alone on the banks of the river.

"Howdy," he said, nodding. "You live around here?"

I told him I did. He asked me where I'd been hurt and I told him Sharpsburg.

"Did you know they kept prisoners here?"

I said I did and he told me his brother had died here in February. I said I was sorry and that the fever had killed a lot of good men.

"They had 400 men packed onto that bridge," he said bitterly. "I'd shoot every last scoundrel that did that to my brother."

I was quiet. What could I say?

"I hope it haunts them till their dying day," he continued. "I hope they never lie down without remembering what they did."

"They probably will." He looked at me hard and then went away. I sat there and listened to the water a little longer. It's funny how you can hear voices if you listen hard enough.

Then I gathered up as many fallen branches as I could find. I stacked them up against the side of the bridge and lit them. I watched that bridge burn and burn and burn until at last it fell into the water and washed away. The river takes away so much. I wish it could take away my guilt.

the old man at the lake

John and his dad, Mark, were finally on their way to the lake. They had to drive all the way across the state to get there, but the important thing was they were going. They had been planning this trip for months. A whole weekend of camping, fishing, waking up early to catch breakfast, and sitting by the fire all night roasting marshmallows. John was too excited to sit still. He needed this break from work and school. He needed the break from his girlfriend, too. She had been especially annoying that week. Mark was also looking forward to this trip. He hardly saw his son anymore since he started college.

"So how's school, son?" Mark asked.

"Oh, you know," John's usual reply.

"Well, then how's work?"

"The same."

"Aren't we talkative this morning." Mark sighed heavily.

His dad just didn't get that he was tired of talking. Talk, talk, talk. That's all Carmen ever wanted to do—talk. "Hey, Dad, do you think we can just chill this weekend? I really just want to clear my head a little. I'll talk when I'm ready."

"Whatever you say, son."

They continued on in silence.

"So where exactly are we going?"

"Lake Tohlocco."

"Which is where again?"

"Near Ozark."

"Right."

More silence.

"You know your grandfather used to take me here once a year when I was a kid."

Ah, great. Another nostalgia trip, John thought. Just what I needed, a weekend of reminiscing about the old days. He sighed.

John's dad grew up in Ozark. His parents had moved there a few months after Mark was born. The family had a small house just outside of town. Mark's dad made a point to have an annual father-son fishing trip. They took the trip every year until Mark left for college in Tennessee.

Mark had always wanted to do the same with John, but there never seemed to be time. Mark's dad died suddenly from a heart attack the year before. It was only now that Mark had the strength and courage to return to Lake Tohlocco. He knew it would not be the same as when he was a child, but he hoped he and John could reconnect on the trip. John was always so distant, keeping everyone at arm's length.

"Really? Did you guys catch a lot of fish?"

Uncontrollable laughter erupted from his left. "Of course not, your grandfather always forgot his fishing pole."

"How do you go fishing and forget your pole?"

"That's exactly what I used to ask. Turns out he never went for the fishing; he just wanted to spend some quality time with me away from home."

"Oh."

"Don't worry. Our poles are in the back."

"They better be," John mumbled.

"What was that?"

"Oh, okay good."

"Some of the best moments in my life were spent at this lake." Mark continued to talk about his childhood. He told his son about the first fish he caught, the first time he kissed a girl, the first time he watched fireworks over the lake on the Fourth of July. He rambled on about sleeping under the stars and staying up late to watch meteor showers.

John listened as Mark droned on for hours. It wasn't that he didn't like listening to his dad's stories; he just didn't want to hear them for eight hours while stuck in a cramped car. John was ecstatic about finally reaching the lake because it meant an escape from life in the fifties. It also meant an entire weekend in the great outdoors.

The two men quickly unpacked in their rustic cabin. John's room had a window overlooking the lake. As he gazed out onto the still, lifeless water, he couldn't help but think, This must be what heaven's like. He looked to the left and saw his dad setting up the fire pit. "Guess I could go help him," John said to himself.

"How 'bout hot dogs for dinner?"

"Sounds perfect."

As they munched on their supper, John began to open up to his dad. He talked about school, work, and even got some advice about his relationship with Carmen. After dinner, they did a little night fishing. After several hours of not catching anything, Mark decided to call it quits for the evening, and the guys leaned their poles against the side of the cabin. John stayed up late that night to talk to Carmen. While waiting for the fire to die down, he noticed a man walking around the lake. Glancing at his watch, he saw it was about two o'clock. Just thinking he was seeing things, he turned in.

The next morning John's fishing pole was missing. Unsure of where it could be, he mentioned it to his dad. Both men found it strange that a just a few hours before, both poles were leaning against the cabin and now only one was there.

"Who would steal a fishing pole? And why would you just steal one? If you were going to go to the trouble to take one, why wouldn't you just take both?"

"There are other things to do at a lake than fish, John. Don't get discouraged."

"Oh really, what do you have in mind? Wake boarding?"

"That sounds fun. What is it?"

John laughed hysterically at his father's innocence. "Why don't we just rent jet skis?"

"Your wish is my command."

The father and son spent the rest of the day on Lake Tohlocco trying to throw the other off his jet ski. Exhausted, they headed back to their camp in time for dinner. Opting to once again stay up late talking to his girlfriend, John sat out beneath the stars. He heard the rustle of leaves coming from the lake. Turning towards the calm water, he could barely make out a figure. He strained to see more clearly, only to find the man from the night before—this time with *his* fishing pole. John jogged over to talk to him, but when he was close enough to speak to him, the man disappeared. Okay, now I know I'm seeing things, John thought as he headed back to the cabin.

The next morning, his pole was sitting exactly where he had left it two days earlier. John mentioned the incidents to his dad, but his reply was that John wasn't getting enough sleep. "All this fresh air must be getting to you."

Since John had his pole back, they took off for the bait shop. Making small talk with the owner, Mark casually brought up the incidents with the strange man and the pole. The shop owner described the man perfectly.

"No one really knows who it is, but he is seen quite often. Every six or seven years, someone will lose a fishing pole, only to find it the next day."

"Have these incidents ever been investigated?"

"Oh, no, I don't think so. You boys have a nice day. Come back to see us."

John and Mark left the store, slightly more confused than when they entered. As they paused to hold the door open for another customer, the owner called out, "But you be careful, son. Someone always comes up missing within a few days of seeing the man." The men chuckled as they continued to walk away.

Out on the lake, John and Mark had the perfect fishing day. The weather was just right—not too hot and not too cold. The sun was shining; the sky was clear. Even the fish were behaving. John caught six bass, and Mark caught eight. They celebrated that evening with a fish fry. After dinner they packed up what gear they could in order to leave first thing in the morning. Now his nightly ritual, John stayed up with the fire and Carmen. Hearing something in the bushes, he whipped around to find nothing. "I have lost my mind," he said as he turned back towards the fire. Suddenly everything went black as a rope tightened around his throat.

••••••

John sat straight up in bed, his heart pounding and pulse racing. He was sweating profusely. The sun was just beginning to peek through his window when he looked out to see the strange old man walking beside the lake. He continued to stare and watched the gauzy figure slowly fade away into nothingness.

ashley's restaurant

When Ethel Allen stepped into Jack's Tavern that morning, several folks took notice. The teenager was certainly a looker, with that head of long blonde hair and a face dominated by big blue eyes. Those eyes, fringed by long, dark lashes, held the look of a girl on the cusp of womanhood. As she bounced across the floor to the bar, many there wondered at her father's insistence that she work here. She was, after all, only fifteen years old—old enough to cause trouble, too young to handle it.

Jack's Tavern had opened just the year before—New Year's Eve 1933—in celebration of the end of Prohibition. Since that time, it had been a continuous party. There was drinking, socializing, and dancing. Jack's even had one of them newfangled jukeboxes, the first ever in Brevard County!

Owner Jack Allen did his best to keep things in line, but after years of drinking in dark back rooms, the exuberance at no longer having to hide often got out of hand. There were frequent brawls and many domestic incidents—where a spouse would get angry or jealous and cause trouble. So far, no one had been seriously hurt, but it was just a matter of time.

Allen knew people often questioned his sanity at putting young Ethel to work here. He understood their concern, but in his mind, he was keeping her close, where he could keep his eye on her. She had been a beautiful child, and she was growing into an even more beautiful woman. He'd raised her as best he could after her mother had left, keeping close tabs on her comings and goings, and not allowing her to get silly ideas of going out with boys or wearing face paint. He wasn't a hard man, but he'd lost his wife to another man and he had no intention of losing his only daughter as well.

"Hey, Daddy," Ethel said as she tied an apron around her small waist. She went on tiptoe to give him a quick kiss on the cheek.

"Hi, sweetie. I have you assigned to tables 3, 4, and 5. You'll be taking over from Lana. It's been really busy, so hurry up and get ready." He saw her eyes scan the crowd as if looking for someone, and felt a niggle of worry in the pit of his stomach.

Distracted, Ethel nodded, picked up her tray, and glided out to the main floor. Her eyes still scanned the faces of the tavern's considerable crowd because she was, in fact, searching for someone. She was hopefully looking for the gentleman who had been in two nights ago. He'd said he planned to come by tonight. And he'd said he would request her station.

She smiled to herself. The guy was a dreamboat. He was older—at least twenty-five. And he had curly, black hair, with dreamy blue eyes and dimples when he smiled. He'd flashed a money clip filled with cash and talked about living in Hollywood, where there were movie stars everywhere. He'd said she was beautiful enough to be a star, too.

Jeepers! That was her dream—to see herself on the big silver screen. She had seen every movie ever made! Posters of all her favorite stars covered the walls of her room. She especially liked that new type of movie they called the "slasher movie." They were so deliciously scary!

And that's the type of movie this guy said he made. And he'd said he was looking for girls to star in them. She'd been so excited that she thought she'd never make it through the next two days. But here it was Friday, finally. She hoped he showed up soon, or else she might pee on herself out of excitement.

She jumped in and began working her tables, deftly avoiding the pinches and touches inflicted by some of the men who'd had a few too many. She weaved in and out, back and forth, tray held high, working up a sheen of sweat.

She was so busy, she almost forgot why she had such an edge of excitement in her belly, but then, suddenly, there he was. He was sitting at table 3 and smiling up at her. Her heart skipped. Finally! She flashed him her biggest smile and approached the table.

"Hello. How are you?"

"I'm very well, Ethel. It looks like you're really busy."

"Yes, we are, Mr..."

"Ah, now, remember I told you to call me Jim."

She beamed even brighter at him. "Jim," she said tentatively.

"That's better. Well, now, I was wondering if you'd had time to think about what we discussed before?"

She bobbed her blonde head. "Oh, yes...uh, Jim! It's just all I could think about for the whole two days!"

"Good, good. And what do you think? Are you going to do it? Are you going to let me make you the star of my next slasher movie?"

Ethel took a furtive look around to ensure that no one had heard what he'd said. Everyone was bustling about. No one was paying any attention to her and the good looking man. Good thing Johnny wasn't here. He'd be all over her, demanding to know just who the guy was and what he wanted. And her father! Thank goodness for all the business. He was too busy drawing up beers and slinging drinks to notice what she was up to.

"Yes! Yes, I am! I can't leave just yet, though. I have to finish out the shift. But I'm all packed. I'll change clothes in the restroom, and then I can slip away while Daddy is closing up. I'll call him once we get to Hollywood to let him know I'm OK."

The guy nodded. "That sounds good. And have you told anyone else? Anyone at all?"

Shaking her head vehemently, she said, "No one. I promise! I haven't told anyone."

"That's good." He smiled benignly at her. "Now, bring me a Jack and Coke, and we'll plan to meet at the spot we discussed at, say, around midnight?"

"Yes, sir. Midnight sounds good. I'll be there, I promise!"

As he watched her bounce away, he began planning out the opening scenes of his next slasher movie, the one starring Miss Ethel Allen, the young Florida ingénue. Bloodcurdling screams! Unspeakable horrors! Oh, yes, it was going to be a killer, all right, he chuckled. A real killer.

Ethel Allen walked out of Jack's Tavern that night and was never seen alive again. Her poor, mutilated body was found days later on the banks of the Indian River, miles away, near the town of Eau Gallie. It was, said the old *Cocoa Tribune*, "the most mystifying and brutal murder case ever to occur within the confines of Brevard County." And, indeed, it was mystifying, for the murder of Ethel Allen was never solved.

••••••

Fast forward to modern times. Jack's Tavern is now Ashley's Restaurant, an establishment better known for its ghosts than for its food. It is, in fact, one of the most haunted places in Florida.

Many people believe the spirit haunting Ashley's is that of Ethel Allen, who was murdered in 1934. Though her body was found, the homicide remains unsolved. Many people believe she may still be at Ashley's. Customers and employees alike have reported a wide range of happenings here, from the mild to the down right aggressive.

The women's bathroom is a particularly haunted area. There have been numerous reports of an ethereal young woman who emerges from one of the stalls, then just disappears. She flicks lights on and off in the bar, often breaks things in the kitchen, and projects an overpowering presence to employees.

Oh, and that's not all. Some women report feeling as if they're being choked when walking down the hallway to the restroom. There also have been reports of shoulder tapping and, every now and again, a push from an unseen hand. One particularly terrified lady reported that when she looked into the restroom mirror to refresh her lipstick, instead of her own familiar face, she saw a stranger's face—that of a younger woman! As she stared, the face slowly disappeared. Well aware that she was in a haunted establishment, she dropped her lipstick and ran.

●●●●●

So, what do you think? Has Ethel Allen come back to haunt Ashley's Restaurant, the place where in life she felt safe? And was that her face in the mirror? Checking her makeup, perhaps? Making sure she's ready for her closeup?

cold feet

June 1898

"Come on, come on, come on!" She was shooing them into the wagon with no more patience than she showed the chickens in the yard at dusk.

"Mary Ellen, hold Patrick. Toby, take this basket. Lizzie Mae, don't you dare get back out."

Balling a handful of her skirt in her fist, she climbed up to the bench in front and spoke to the mule.

"Gee-up, Patsy!" Obediently the mule began to move.

The sun was hovering just above the horizon as they turned out of the Jackson farm road onto White Oak Creek road. The woman urged the mule to its fastest pace—a walking half-trot—until she saw the dark shape of Alvaton Bridge huddling over the creek ahead.

"Momma!"

"What, Lizzie?"

"Where's David?"

"I thought he was under the blanket. Lift it up. Ain't he there?"

"No, he must've stayed behind at the Jackson place."

"Lizzie Mae, I told you to look out for them."

Lizzie, the oldest child, hung her head, feeling vaguely wronged but knowing all the same that she'd failed her Momma.

With a sigh, the woman coaxed the mule into turning around and heading back the way they'd come. Her mouth set into a tight line, she measured with her eyes the distance of the sun from the horizon. Sunset in about ten minutes.

Anne Jackson was walking down the road, holding David's hand as he struggled not to cry. "Momma!" He ran to the wagon and threw himself into her arms. "I thought you'd forgotten me!"

"I told you to git in the wagon," she scolded him gently. "Thanks, Anne!" She waved to her neighbor and turned the mule around again.

Now the sun had set, and the shadows of the trees on either side of the road were melting into one another, creating a seamless ribbon of blackness that marched without hesitation to the inky rectangle that was the open mouth of Alvaton Bridge. The woman tried to avert her eyes as she steered the mule and her family toward it, but there was a certain macabre fascination intertwined with her fear.

"I want you to sing with me," she commanded as the wagon came within a few hundred feet of the bridge. "Sing!"

She opened her mouth and began to thunder her favorite hymn.

"Just as I am, without one plea..."

Her voice wavered just a bit as the mule's shoes made a hollow drumming sound on the wooden planking of the bridge. "And that thou bids't me come to thee, O Lamb of God..."

The girls added their thin voices to their mother's strong alto.

"I come, I come."

Without hesitating, the woman swung right into the second verse, singing as if her very life depended upon it. The song rose to the rafters of the bridge, hidden by the darkness. The wood of the old bridge seemed to muffle the sound of the hymn, soaking up the notes greedily instead of echoing them back to the singers' ears.

At last they were through the bridge, and the woman's shoulders slumped in relief. Their farm was just ahead, up a little rise. It took barely fifteen minutes for her to get all five children tucked into their blankets.

She held the lamp up high, showering as much light as she could on their still squirming bodies, wrestling to find a comfortable spot on the big bed they all shared.

"Go to sleep, now. I don't want to hear a peep out of you," she admonished them sternly. "Don't fergit your prayers."

She pulled the door nearly to the frame, allowing just a sliver of light to enter the bedroom from the main room of the house where she would sit for an hour or two longer with her sewing or her Bible.

"Lizzie," whispered Toby. "Don't go to sleep yet."

"What?"

"Why is Momma so scared of the bridge, Lizzie?"

"She didn't even git scared when Henderson's old bull got loose and ran right at her," chimed in Mary Ellen. "How come she hates that bridge so?"

"I don't know fer sure," Lizzie Mae said slowly, pulling together the loose strands of a story that were floating about in her mind. "But mebbe, it could be..."

She was interrupted by a wide band of light that burst from the doorway. "I told you to go to sleep!" Their momma stood with her hands on her hips in the open doorway. "You want a switchin'?"

"No'm," they murmured. They lay still as death until she turned and left the room, again pulling the door nearly closed.

Lizzie rolled over and put her mouth near her brother's ear. "Lula tol' me once, somebody was hanged to death on that bridge."

She was gratified by the sharp intake of his breath. "Wrapped a rope around his neck and strung 'im up, until his eyes bugged out like this," she made a face, "and his tongue popped out, all purple and swole up!"

Toby shuddered and Lizzie lay back down, satisfied. Mary Ellen poked and prodded at her.

"Tell me," she whined. "I wanna hear it, too,"

"You're too young," Lizzie retorted in a sharp whisper. "It'd give you night mirrors."

"Tell me," Mary Ellen whined again.

"Hush now, or Momma'll come take a switch to all of us," Lizzie answered and turned her back to all of them. She listened to the soft, even rhythm of baby Patrick's breathing until it lulled her to sleep.

December 1915

Gene McClure cursed again and kicked the side of the truck hard enough to make the whole body shudder. A bale of hay tumbled off the precariously balanced stack that reached a good seven feet above the guardrail, and he cursed again.

His wife leaned around to grin at him. "I know that used to make Nellie go," she said, "But I didn't know kickin' and cussin' made Fords go, too."

His only response was another kick, and she turned around again.

"Least it had the courtesy to break down on the bridge," she pointed out, climbing out of the truck. "We're not gonna get rained on while you get it fixed."

"No, but it'll sure git stuck in the mud on the way home," he muttered sullenly, pacing up and down beside the truck. "I was a fool to ever buy this contraption."

She shrugged her shoulders and climbed back to wait while he figured out a solution. Eventually he threw open the hood of the truck and stood staring morosely down at the engine.

She wished she'd brought her knitting. She hated to sit still and do nothing. It felt unnatural. "Idle hands do the devil's work." The proverb raced through her mind, and she shifted uneasily in the seat.

"Gene," she said at last. "We're not but a mile from home. I'm gonna head back." He looked up from his tinkering and glared at her. "It's almost dark," she said reasonably. "Might as well go milk the cows."

"Fix me some supper," he called out to her retreating back. "I'll take this hay to town tomorrow."

She waved without looking back, and he returned to his study of the engine. The red clay of the road was fast losing its color, turning a murky gray in the failing daylight.

Gene lay down on his back and inched under the body of the truck. Maybe it was something underneath that wasn't working properly. He looked and ran his hands over all the cables he could see, checking to make sure everything was connected to something. He didn't have any idea of how to fix this truck, and his helplessness quickly transformed into anger.

When he heard a footstep on the wooden planking of the bridge, he tried to sit up before scooting out from under the truck.

He finally extricated himself from the undercarriage of the truck and sat up. He'd cut his head. It was now full dark, and the bridge was filled with shadows.

"Who's there?" He strained his eyes to see if anyone stood at the mouth of the bridge. All the stories he'd heard as a child came flooding back to him, and he fought back a little whimper as he felt blood ooze from his scalp and between his fingers.

A slight fluttering noise was the only answer. Bats. That's all it was. He stood up and tried to crank the truck again. No luck. He caught a movement out of the corner of his eye and whirled around. Nothing again. He laughed a little nervously. His fingers ran up to his scalp again, but the cut seemed to have stopped bleeding. What a day.

He kicked the truck again and decided to leave it till one of his neighbors could loan him a mule team to haul it into town. It was blocking the bridge, but there were only four or five families who used the structure anyway. If they needed him, they could come get him. He was going home.

As he walked from the mouth of the bridge, he saw a patch of shadows in the corner detach itself from the surrounding darkness, shifting and swaying in the breeze. Only there was no breeze.

He ran, his heavy work boots making a sucking sound each time they pulled free from the sticky, thick red Georgia mud.

May 1922

"Yeehaa!" The boy leaped high in the air and came down like a bullet, clutching one knee with both arms to maximize his impact. The water flew up and around him in a wide circle, splashing the two other swimmers and provoking screams of protest.

"This is a great swimming hole," the boy said after swimming back to the shallows to join his friends. "How come we never been here before?"

A second boy, taller and stockier than the first, shrugged his shoulders. After a moment, he pointed wordlessly at the dark shape squatting across the creek a hundred yards upstream.

"Folks say all kindsa things 'bout that bridge," he said barely above a whisper.

"Just another bridge, ain't it?" Steve's mother had only come back to Alvaton last month to live with her parents on their farm. Steve's dad had died of pneumonia last winter.

"Aaarrrgghh!" Will's head disappeared beneath the water as his hands flailed uselessly on the surface.

Steve watched, horrified, until Will's head reappeared on the surface a few feet away. Wade popped up shortly after, screaming with amusement.

"Gotcha!" he yelled. "Betcha thought some big snake'd snatched ya, dincha?" He howled with laughter until Will forced his head under.

Wade came up sputtering, and the three boys splashed and played for another hour until a long, low rumble caused them to look up.

"Was that thunder?" Wade asked uneasily.

"Naah, just a big truck goin' across th' bridge."

"It mighta been thunder," Steve argued. "Lookit them clouds." The sky above them had turned a deep purplish-black, the clouds hanging low and pendulous.

"We better head home."

A long, crooked finger of lightning darted from the clouds and reached to the ground, as if to punctuate Wade's nervous statement. The wind blew up with a startling suddenness. The tall oaks, sweetgum trees, and pines that bordered the creek swayed and danced in the unexpected onslaught of wind.

"Let's make a run for it," Steve shouted and dashed for the barnlike structure spanning the water.

Hesitating for a long moment, Will and Wade followed him.

Steve darted into the bridge and flattened himself against the inside wall just before his friends approached. Fat drops of rain were slamming down, their impact creating tiny puffs of smoke to rise from the red dirt, miniature explosions. The day had turned almost completely dark, and the interior of the bridge was crowded with shadows. The frequent flashes of lightning were more blinding than illuminating, creating illusions of motion within and without.

"Boo!" Steve jumped out at Wade and Will. Their terror was so pronounced that they froze in their tracks, their faces almost comical caricatures of fear. Wade's face instantly drained of color, and from Will's mouth tumbled a piercing shriek.

"Omigosh," gasped Wade. "That's not funny."

Steve wasn't laughing. He was taken aback by the intensity of the reaction he had provoked. Both his friends stood outside, pounded by the rain.

"Git outta the rain, you idiots," he finally said.

Their teeth chattering, Wade and Will exchanged a long look before moving into the shelter of the bridge. The thunder sounded like God himself just across the field, and the rapid flashes of lightning gave each boy's face a ghastly glow.

"Really blew up a big one, didn't it?" Steve tried to resume a normal conversation. The other two boys stared over his shoulder, to the deep gloom of the inner bridge.

"Whatsa matter, y'all? You act like you seen a ghost." Steve turned to look behind him. He saw nothing.

Just as suddenly as it had come up, the storm was gone again. "Let's go."

All three boys took off across the field as fast as their legs could take them. They got to Steve's grandma's farm in record time, and scrounged some apples before ascending to the hayloft. The sun, strong again, streaked through all the chinks and cracks in the old siding, making a crisscrossed pattern of golden-silver, with dust motes floating lazily, turning and sparkling like fairy fireworks.

"What's wrong with that old bridge?" Steve lay flat on his back, watching the sunlight.

"Should we tell, Wade?"

The other boy slowly chewed a chunk of apple. "Gotta swear never to tell, Steve," he said at last. He swallowed. "Somethin' bad's bound to happen if you do."

Steve sat up.

"Aaron Johnson tol' his mama, an' the very next day he fell out of a tree and busted his arm up."

Steve nodded and leaned forward. "Tell me," he insisted in a hoarse whisper.

"A man hung himself to death on that bridge," Wade hissed. "He'd been betrayed by his best friend."

"Or maybe it was his girlfriend," Will put in darkly. "Nobody knows for sure."

"He thought about it and thought about it, till he got so caught up in it he wrapped that rope 'round his neck and threw it over a rafter."

"It started stranglin' him but it was real slow."

"His eyes bugged out 'n' he couldn't hardly see anymore," Will interrupted eagerly.

"He stuck his tongue out." Wade clutched his throat and made strangling noises.

"It got all swole up an' turned purple."

"Then he died, swingin' back an' forth on the middle of the bridge!" Wade finished with a flourish.

"Oooh." Steve was properly appreciative. They sat silent for a moment, chewing their apples reflectively.

"You ever seen that ghost?"

"My mama won't ride through that bridge after dark," Wade said flatly. "My gran'pa, neither."

"My uncle saw it once, an' said he's never been so scared in all his life. He thought it was the devil come after him."

"Today when we was waitin' out that storm, I swear I saw that body swingin' in the shadows."

"It don't feel right on that bridge."

"Mebbe we should go back after dark, make sure it wasn't our imagination." Steve tucked the apple core absently into his pocket.

"Naaah. Can't." Wade was fidgeting with his apple core, picking each seed out and flicking it down to the floor below.

"Me, neither." Will's tone was decisive.

Steve said nothing, just looked from one friend to the other. Soon the other boys found excuses to leave and went on their way, leaving an unusually quiet Steve to eat supper with his grandparents and his mother.

"Kin I be excused, please?" he mumbled after wolfing down a second helping of everything. Released, he raced up to his room to wait until dark.

Slipping out of the house after bedtime was easy. His grandparents went to sleep right after sunset, and his mother closeted herself in her room. Steve crept slowly and carefully down the stairs, skipping the third step down because of its loud and telltale creak, and cautiously pulled open the kitchen door.

He was nearly across the yard and to the road when a shapeless form materialized beside him. His heart nearly stopped and then he recognized the furry creature.

"Hey, Prince," he said softly. "Good boy. Attaboy." He patted the collie roughly on its side, and the dog followed slavishly at his heels.

Afraid of holes and other pitfalls in the field after dark, Steve took the long route on the road to the bridge. As he approached the dark, forbidding structure skulking low over the banks of the creek, his footsteps slowed unconsciously. Prince whined and stuck his cold nose into the palm of Steve's hand.

Steve fumbled in his pocket for the candle stub and the matches he'd snitched from the kitchen before supper. As he entered the mouth of the bridge, he paused to scratch a match on the rough wood of the portal. It flared briefly, then sputtered out.

He tried again, and this time the flame caught and held long enough for him to touch it to the candle's wick. Armed with this meager light, Steve stepped resolutely forward into the bridge. By the candlelight—flickering wildly in the draft created by his movement—he could faintly see the great crossed beams that had kept the structure standing firm through decades of high winds and roaring floods. Above, the rafters were black with age. He shuddered, thinking about a rough sisal rope tossed over the rafter with deadly intent.

He moved forward, examining every square foot of the bridge as his circle of light revealed it. At last he was at the far end of the bridge and his light had uncovered nothing more threatening than a big beetle ambling along through the shadows.

Just then, at the far end of the bridge, he heard a faint rustling noise. Steve froze, the candle held high to illuminate as much as possible.

The rustling sound turned into a shuffling noise that seemed to reverberate though the passageway, and Steve's bones turned to water. The shambling footsteps steadily approached the terrified boy, closer and closer to his wavering circle of light. Though Steve strained his eyes until they felt as if they'd pop out with the effort, he could make out nothing beyond a shifting, obscure mass of shadows, only slightly more black than the gloom surrounding it.

At last, unable to withstand the suspense, Steve flung down his candle stub with a shriek of utter terror and fled out into the safety of the open road with Prince at his heels.

September 1938

"Ella, you can't do this," the young man moaned in misery. "I can't stand this anymore!"

The young woman on the wagon seat beside him crossed her arms resolutely.

"I ain't changin' my mind this time," she said. "I cain't marry you 'n' that's final."

"But I love you," he protested. "Don't you care about that?"

"It ain't right. Preacher tol' me so 'n' he's a man of God. He oughta know."

Just then, lightning cracked close enough to make the hairs on the back of her arm stand up. "See there?" she said matter-of-factly. "God sez so."

"Yer mama was only cousin to my daddy," he protested again. "It ain't like we was cousins."

"Too close to marry, an' that's that."

The clouds opened up, and the rains descended. Great sheets flew across the road, battering the wagon, the mule, and the occupants with its fury.

"Let's git outta this rain," the man said wretchedly. "Git up, Bess." The mule headed for the covered bridge down the road, eager to see shelter ahead.

"Don't take me in there, Jonathan O'Kelly," she warned. "I ain't sittin' in that bridge."

He shrugged. "You don't believe in ghosts 'n' things, now, do you? I thought the Bible said that was a sin."

"I've been in that bridge in daylight, but it's too dark in there now." She shrank against him.

It was true. The storm had leached most of the daylight out of the sky and the mouth of the bridge yawned black and empty. "I don't care," he said. "Bess is goin' anyway, whether we want to or not."

The mule trotted into the shelter of the bridge and stopped as soon as it was under cover. "Here, you dumb mule." Jonathan flicked the reins. "Pull the wagon in, too." The mule moved forward a few paces, and the woman moved closer to the man.

He slipped an arm around her. "I wouldn't worry if I were you."

She moaned, a strangely feral sound.

"I've never seen nothin' strange on this bridge, 'n' I've been crossin' it all my life," he said, trying to comfort her.

She crouched even lower on the seat next to him, and he flicked the reins softly to urge the mule farther into the shadows.

"Don't, please, Jonathan," she pleaded.

The man's strong arm circled her protectively.

"Nothin's here, Ella," he repeated.

Her eyes swept from side to side and stopped, riveted by a movement from the far left corner of the bridge.

Intent on the mule and the wagon's progress, Jonathan never saw a thing. Never saw the mass of shadows detaching itself from the darkness. Never saw the swaying, swinging form. But Ella did. She began to babble incoherently, her voice rising to a shriek as she lifted both her arms to ward off the clotted drift of darkness that dangled, suspended from the rafter dead ahead.

The mule and the wagon were expelled from the mouth of the bridge with unnatural force. Jonathan anxiously patted the woman's face and arms.

"Ella?" He queried. "Ella, wake up. Stop this foolishness. Ella?"

His voice trailed off, drowned by the fierce growl of thunder from the west.

January 1946

"Helen, do you suppose it needs more gas?"

The car sputtered and coughed and then jerked along for another hundred feet.

"We're only half a mile from the farm. Jack can get it fixed if we can just..."

The engine sputtered again and Helen stomped hard on the gas pedal. The sudden motion made her hat slide down over her eyes, and she shoved it back, crushing the expensive trim that had seemed so important just two hours ago.

"Oh, come on, you old thing!" She spoke from between clenched teeth and pressed again on the gas pedal, as if by force of will she could make the engine turn over and carry them the half-mile to her cousin's farm.

The car resisted and stubbornly rolled to a stop just inside an old covered bridge. "Well, isn't it just like a picture postcard?" Betty got out and ran her hand along the massive old beams that supported the structure.

Helen stayed behind the wheel, twisting the key and pressing the gas pedal in a vain attempt to keep moving forward. "This is exactly why Howard says ladies shouldn't travel alone," she muttered. "He'll say 'I told you so.'" She struck the wheel with one gloved hand in frustration.

The passenger door opened with a click. "What a lovely old bridge," Betty said brightly, slipping into the seat. "I'll bet it's been here forever."

"My cousins always said it was haunted," Helen retorted tartly. "I'd just as soon be up at Jack's farm by sunset."

"It is getting dark, isn't it?" Betty looked around at the shadows spreading like pools of oil from the corners of the bridge.

"It's downright spooky. Jack told me somebody hanged himself out here a long time ago."

Betty looked around again.

"Where?" she asked in a tiny voice.

"In a corner somewhere. See, over there, where the shadows are deepest?" Helen was still wrapped up in the frustration of this, her first visit to the home place in five long years. As she gestured, she noticed a smudge on the tip of her glove and exclaimed in annoyance.

The gold and red splendor of the Georgia sunset was perfectly framed by the mouth of the bridge. To the right, the shadows shifted and stirred. Betty shivered.

"I wish this car would start," Helen repeated, twisting the key again.

"Maybe we should just walk up to your cousin's house."

Helen's only reply was a small, unladylike grunt as she pressed hard on the gas pedal. She didn't want to traipse up the dirt road, arriving at Jack's door like a bedraggled stray kitten.

As soon as the sun slipped away, the shadows crept across the floor, tendrils splaying longer and wider from each side of the bridge until finally they met in the center, leaving the occupants of the car in a dusky half-light.

Betty twined and untwined her fingers, looking from side to side anxiously as Helen, grim faced, thumbed through the owner's manual.

"Maybe it's the choke," she muttered as she opened the door to stand near the hood of the car. Betty hurried to stand beside her.

"It's getting so dark," Beth insisted. "Please, let's just go on and your cousin can come back and fix it later."

"Sshhh," hissed Helen. "What was that?"

"I didn't hear anything." Betty fixed her hand tightly on Helen's forearm. "Let's go."

Something stirred and rustled in the far corner of the bridge. Helen fixed her eyes on the spot, straining to make out the details, but no definite shape resolved itself.

"Get your purse." Helen opened the car door long enough to snatch up her new pocketbook and then took long, striding steps away from the source of the noise, through the darkest part of the bridge.

"Wait," Betty squealed, slamming the passenger door shut and tottering forward on the spiky little heels of her best shoes. The two women trotted as quickly as they could out of the barnlike structure, only slowing when they were a good hundred yards out of the mouth.

"Who," Betty gasped, "who was it that died in there?"

Helen threw a glance over her shoulder and kept up a brisk pace, heedless of the red dust stirred up by her fashionable shoes.

"It's been a long time," she finally said. "No one knows. But they say he'd been jilted by his lover and that she found his body, twisting and turning, dangling from the rafters just minutes after he died."

Betty's mouth opened into a little red "o."

"She went crazy after that. But anybody'd go crazy stuck out here for long," she concluded. "It was probably just some old raccoon we heard. Look at my shoes." The brightly lit farmhouse lay just ahead.

October 1958

Two teenagers danced around the wagon that had stopped right outside the Alvaton Bridge. The sun was nearly gone, obscured by a bank of clouds on the horizon.

"Hurry, Billy, hurry," urged one. "Someone'll be along in a minute, and we gotta hide the wagon."

In the bed of the wagon lay a supine form, one motionless arm protruding from the rough weave of an old horse blanket. A third teenager stooped over the figure, working feverishly.

"I'm hurryin' as fast as I can, Cecil," he complained, brandishing a hand unattached to the body. "If you'da been more careful throwin' this thing in the wagon, it might not have broke into a million pieces."

The third boy was busy fashioning a noose from a long strand of rough hemp rope.

"Ready when you are, Billy," he sang out.

Cecil and Billy carefully lifted the mannequin out of the wagon bed and carried it to the mouth of the bridge.

"Where should we hang it?"

"Over there, in those shadows," Cecil commanded. "Easy, now." The mannequin's eyes stared straight ahead as they slipped the noose around the cool, slender neck.

"Maybe we oughta dress it? It kinda gleams there in the shadows."

"I think it looks perfect. First person to drive through here's gonna pee in his pants."

They stepped back. The light flesh tones of the mannequin caught and reflected the remaining illumination on the bridge. The head was hidden by the shadows up on the rafters, and the legs were suspended, motionless, just to the left of the mouth of the bridge.

Billy grasped the foot and slowly set the body spinning. They raced out of the bridge, and Cecil drove the wagon a half-mile down the road, hiding it in a little grove of trees before sprinting back to crouch in the cover of some bushes with his friends. As they waited for their first victim, they passed a pocket flask back and forth.

"Sshhh, somebody's comin'!" They could hear the slow clop-clop of a single mule coming to the bridge. No gleam of moonlight or glitter of stars broke the velvet blackness of the country night.

They could hear the old black man mutter to himself or his mule as he entered the bridge.

"Dontcha worry 'bout spirits or haints, now. Jest git along home now and git to supper."

The shriek of terror was so bloodcurdling it made the hairs rise on the necks of the boys hiding in the brush. After a moment, they looked at each other and grinned. The mule and wagon came clattering out of the mouth of the bridge at a nearly impossible speed. The old man rocked back and forth on the bench seat, moaning, before he disappeared from view down the road.

Suddenly, Cecil clutched his midsection and groaned.

"What's in that flask, Billy?"

Cramps bent him over double, and he hobbled into the woods, wracked by great waves of nausea.

He lay curled up on the ground beneath the trees, his head gradually clearing. Whatever had made him sick was now on the ground a foot away. He felt better.

Cecil staggered to his feet and made his way down to the stream to rinse his mouth and duck his head underwater. Refreshed, he returned to the mouth of the bridge.

"Billy?" he called.

He cautiously advanced into the bridge, looking for his friends.

The shadows were so thick that even the bright gleam of the mannequin was masked, its location only given away by a faint shifting and stirring of the shadows in the far left corner of the bridge.

"Billy?" He whispered now, vaguely uneasy by the impenetrable gloom enveloping him. He could hear some movement over by the mannequin, and he suspected some trick. He crept slowly toward the corner, straining his eyes to see through the shadows.

The mannequin didn't look quite right, but that didn't register in his mind until hours later. For when he touched its foot to make it spin a bit on the old, frayed rope, his hand met not with cold, lifeless plastic, but with flesh still warm from the blood that had coursed through its veins only minutes before.

the mailman of the ninth ward

On a warm night in 2005, Tom Emory had yet to realize that New Orleans was gone. The city had been strangled by Katrina, one of the largest hurricanes to ever hit the United States. The vast New Orleans levee system had broken, and flood waters had turned the city into a lewd and grizzly version of Venice, a city built on water and made for love.

But New Orleans was a besotted version of its old self, a mockery of racial politics and class division. The politicians lined up to be heroes, but New Orleans seemed beyond rescue. Hurricane Katrina was a sort of genocide. Entire generations of New Orleanians were wiped out when tons of raw sewage came rushing back into the neighborhoods where it had come from. The water that filled the streets, homes, businesses, schools, movie theaters, and churches was itself awash in human and animal disease, toxic waste, natural gas, and other Gothic horrors.

Paris is the City of Lights, New York is the City That Never

Sleeps, and New Orleans is the City of Ghosts, never more so than now as it succumbed to its fate.

Everyone in the nation had seen the bloated corpses floating down highway exit ramps. Everyone knew the New Orleans Superdome had become a haunted way station for the living dead. And everyone knew of numerous other horrors: the escaped convicts, the zoo animals loose in the city, the people trapped in attics, the rapes and murders, the lost power, the stifling heat, the lack of food or clean water, the clotted and inefficient evacuation routes, the missing jazz musician, the water moccasins, the shooting at helicopters, the nursing home patients left to drown, the children tied to light posts, and the general failed experiment in human civilization.

Everyone knew what had happened to New Orleans except, it seems, for Tom Emory, who was a mail carrier in the Ninth Ward of New Orleans, one of the poorest areas of the country and one of the hardest hit by the flood waters. The postal worker takes an oath, so Tom knew he'd have to find a way to resume his mail route once the waters receded. He set about figuring out a way to get back to his job in the Ninth Ward. Tom had been evacuated to Alabama, where he had distant family in Mentone, the only family he had left. None of them suggested otherwise as he planned his return to New Orleans.

Tom was in his late sixties now, and had been delivering mail on the same route for nearly forty years. He knew everyone in the neighborhood by name, and he was one of the city's unpaid crime deterrents. Knowing everyone by name meant that everyone knew Tom, that everyone knew he was keeping watch over their homes.

Hurricane Katrina had been particularly cruel to Tom, who loved making his deliveries, and who loved everyone on his route—people he'd likely never see again—and a route likely never to resume, at least in his lifetime. He just didn't know it yet.

When Tom returned to New Orleans, he came wearing his starched and pressed postal worker's uniform, his mail bag slung across his shoulder, the image of American pride, patriotism, and good citizenship, precisely what New Orleans would need to survive these horrors. But there was nothing in his mail bag and no one, it seemed, in the houses along his route.

The front porches of the homes along his route were filled with whatever had floated to the surface. The Ninth Ward looked like the city dump. "It looked," Tom thought, "like a holocaust had happened."

The first house on his route was Ms. Mattingly's. Tom walked up her front steps, shoving aside a muddy baby stroller at the top of the steps. "I don't even want to think about how that got here," Tom thought.

Ms. Mattingly had been a retired school teacher and longtime sufferer of neighborhood vandalism and petty violence. She had nurtured a delicate rose garden throughout the years and her front lawn had been pristine. The lawn was now unrecognizable as anything resembling the well-manicured American lawn. It looked like something gluttonous had gorged itself on mud and human waste and then vomited on the homes of the poor.

Tom shook his head in sadness and then knocked on her door, not in hope that she would answer but out of defiance for what had happened to his precious sense of neighborhood. He knocked again as if decorum required it, and when there was no answer again, he stepped back and looked at the orange day-glo number "1" spray-painted next to the door. The rescue workers had created some coding system where they spray-painted the number of bodies recovered from each house. He didn't know if that meant a body had been recovered or if a body was missing. Numbering the dead seemed puzzling to him, and he was bothered by the further desecration of Ms. Mattingly's home.

He reached down to turn the knob, hoping it wouldn't give, but the door opened easily. Tom walked into a room flooded with natural light. What he hadn't realized was that a large section of the back of Ms. Mattingly's house was gone, ripped from the foundation, probably at rest in someone else's backyard, or floating out to sea, or on a warm, clean beach somewhere after a haunted sail through the warm Gulf waters. Otherwise, much of the house looked the way it had before. Most of the furniture was strangely still intact, though stained and warped by the floodwaters. Most of Ms. Mattingly's books looked like they'd been blown from the shelves, and Tom could imagine them floating through the room like an aquarium of human life. "So this is what they mean by a house of cards," he thought.

Tom turned to walk into the kitchen and he remembered that the swinging door had once been a bright yellow. He remembered that when Ms. Mattingly would invite him in for a piece of sponge cake, he was always cheered by the bright colors of the house, by her dutiful needlework hanging on the wall, and by her pet parakeet, Mr. Peepers.

So Tom pushed through the mudded door as if he'd always belonged there, and began speaking to the apparition of Ms. Mattingly sitting at the kitchen table before he realized what he was seeing.

She was staring straight ahead and she looked like a ghostly version of everything else in the house, water-logged and rotting. Her hair was hanging over her forehead as if she hadn't cared for it in days, and Tom suddenly remembered what pride she took in her hair, how he'd always tease her about having the hair of a young girl. But she still had on her gingham house dress and her apron covered in daisies.

"How are you, Ms. Mattingly?" Tom asked. "I've been so looking forward to seeing you again after all these months."

But Tom was stunned that he'd even spoken, so convinced was he that she was actually alive. He was on auto-pilot, completely stunned by the entire experience. But Ms. Mattingly didn't speak back. She turned her head toward Tom, and reached out to him as if begging for help or mercy.

Tom, again reacting as if the apparition in front of him was still the woman he'd come to love over the years, reached out in Ms. Mattingly's direction and gently grabbed hold of her hand. But as he clasped her fingers her ghostly body turned into clean, pure water and flowed down through the cracks in the pinewood kitchen floor. Tom thought the water looked and smelled like baptismal water, and he felt purified by the experience.

In the subsequent months, Tom went house to house trying to recover some sense of what had been lost, some sense of his meaningful life. Each house had its ghosts and each ghost had been a friend to Tom Emory. So he continued making his route, rescuing his friends and neighbors from their river-soaked deaths, blessing and purifying them with his faith in the neighborhood he knew so well and loved so much.

And slowly, slowly the ghosts were laid to rest as step by difficult step Tom walked the Ninth Ward...and life began to return.

emily's bridge

"Would you please turn off that noise?" Without waiting for a reply, the woman driving reached over and twisted the knob, cutting off the radio with a click. The teenaged girl beside her slumped lower in the seat, scowling.

"I can hardly hear myself think," the woman complained. "And if we're going to meet your grandmother before midnight, we don't have any time to waste."

The narrow road through the center of Vermont twisted and turned, headlights only revealing a few hundred feet at a time. A pounding rain obscured the driver's vision even more than the darkness, and the wipers squeaked and whined as they struggled to keep up with the deluge.

"I wish they'd mark these country roads better," the woman complained again. "Who knows if we're still on Route 100?"

The sullen teenager still did not speak, only examined her fingernails in the dim light of the dashboard instruments.

"Honestly, I don't know why I bother." The woman slapped the steering wheel in frustration. "You used to enjoy traveling with me.

What happened?" Before the girl could reply, a blurred shape bounded into the center of the road. A scream tore from the driver's throat. Brakes shrieked. The car spun wildly in a full circle.

Only an instant later, it was all over. The car stood slightly askew in the center of the road, and the two occupants were inside, breathing hard. "Are you okay, Beverly?" The woman reached for her daughter.

"What was that, Mama?" The girl's voice quavered.

"A deer, I guess. I don't know. Thank God we didn't go off the road."

She restarted the engine, and they continued down the road, a little more cautiously now. The road twisted again, and the woman braked, slowing down for the blind curve just in case.

A few minutes later she spoke again. "I haven't seen any road signs for miles. Have you?"

The girl shook her head, mute again.

The rain poured down. Ahead, a structure loomed, its mouth wide and black in the tenuous gleam of the headlights. The driver braked, puzzled by the presence of a barn straddling a major highway.

As she approached, she saw her headlights illuminating more rain on the other side, and she laughed. "Now I know we're lost, Beverly. There aren't any covered bridges on Route 100." She pulled slowly into the structure, her tires making a deep rumbling noise on the old wooden planking.

"But we can get out for a minute and stretch our legs without getting wet, and I want to take a look at that map."

She threw the car into park and opened her door. The rain clattered loudly on the tin roof of the bridge. As she exited the car, stretching, she heard Beverly opening the passenger door. The driver stared with curiosity at the massive wooden beams, black with age and hewn from trees that must have towered a hundred feet off the forest floor. The gleam of the headlights did more to illuminate the road ahead than the interior of the bridge, so shadows hovered close.

Running footsteps interrupted the woman's study of the bridge. She heard the car door slam, and then the car horn blared urgently, the sound bouncing all around until it filled the structure. She ran back to the car and jerked open the door, furious.

"What has come over you, Beverly?" She pushed the girl's hand off the car horn and slid into the car.

Her daughter's ashen face startled her. The girl was trembling, her teeth chattering so loudly she could barely force out her words. "Let's go, Mama," she sobbed. "Get me out of here, okay?"

Stunned, the woman complied, starting the car and pulling out of the bridge into the rainy night. A few miles down the road, she began to query her daughter. "What happened, Bev? I've never seen you so scared in your whole life."

"Didn't you hear it?"

The woman was genuinely puzzled. "Hear what?"

"There was a woman screaming for help. Her voice echoed all through the bridge."

The driver shook her head and said nothing. They drove on, lost in the turbulent darkness of the night.

••••••

"Old maid, old maid, yada-yada-yada." The three little children hooted and called after Emily, but she just picked her skirt up out of the dust and continued, her market basket lightly swinging on her arm.

"Some people should learn to teach their children manners," she muttered, watching the road carefully for sharp stones. Last week she had tripped on a stone while she was walking away from this very group of nasty children, and they had shrieked with laughter. She had begged her father not to make her go to market today, but he had insisted.

"I'll not have you becoming a recluse, girl," he boomed. "God knows why you haven't found a husband yet, but you'll not find one hiding away in your room—that's for certain!"

Emily had peered around his bulk in a mute appeal to her mother, but she had not raised her eyes from her sewing. Emily's shyness was interpreted by most of the ladies of Stowe as arrogance, and she had been additionally cursed with three vivacious, pretty sisters, all younger than herself. She knew what all the matrons of the town whispered about her. "Poor Emily," they tittered behind their hands, "So tall and awkward, it's no wonder she hasn't got a beau! But her sisters are sure to be married in no time."

And of course, they were, one to a dairy farmer who lived north of Stowe and another to a poor but eminently respectable preacher who served a congregation in Morristown. Her third sister, the youngest of all, had snared a lawyer who had whisked her away to live in splendor, Emily supposed, in Burlington.

So Emily suffered in silence for the most part, not even really hoping that someone might come galloping into Stowe to carry her away. It would have to be a stranger, because there were very few unattached men in Stowe, and those invariably cast their eyes toward younger, more pliable women.

Emily had thought that perhaps her father's repeated comments about her matrimonial state might end when she turned thirty—but they did not. In fact, if anything, their frequency had increased over the past six years. Her mother had become more withdrawn, so Emily bore the brunt of her father's disappointment.

"I'll not always have the means to support you, girl," he would grumble as she served his supper. "I'm getting old, and it's time you found someone to take on your care."

She didn't eat much, Emily pondered as she walked down the road toward home. She got one new dress a year, and it had been three years since she'd asked for a new pair of shoes. In fact, the soles of these were so thin, the rocks cut her feet, but she didn't dare ask for new ones. Surely she wasn't that expensive to maintain. She was so caught up by her thoughts that she did not hear the jingle of a horse's bridle approaching or the soft plopping sound of hooves in the dust.

"Oh, Emily," trilled a familiar voice.

Emily looked up to see Jenny Mueller, her eyes alight with mischief, riding in a handsome buggy beside one of the most attractive men in Stowe, Donald Manning.

"Good afternoon, Jenny, Donald," Emily said stiffly, moving to the side of the road. "Pleasant day for a drive."

They rode on after exchanging a few words. Emily tucked a stray strand of hair behind her ear and squinted her eyes against the dust as she walked the remaining quarter-mile to her father's house.

"Jenny's hat was crooked," she thought scornfully. "And her hair was all mussed. I don't doubt that she and Donald have been driving through the kissing bridge."

After she had unloaded the market basket and kissed her mother hello, Emily went to the old upright piano and began to work out a new piece. Her sister in Burlington had sent her the sheet music, and Emily poured her whole heart into the plaintive notes as she played.

••••••

"Isn't this a perfect campsite?" The man stretched out his legs and rubbed his hands in anticipation of the potatoes baking in the hot coals of the fire.

"I still think we should've asked permission," his companion said doubtfully. "Surely somebody owns this land." Above them, to the left, loomed the gentle folds of Mt. Mansfield. The leaves were brushed with the faintest tinge of yellow or red, and the evening breeze held a promise of winter's chill. A few hundred feet in front of them was a line of trees marking the banks of Gold Brook.

"It wasn't fenced," his friend pointed out. "And I sure wasn't gonna pay $15 for some dumb patch of dirt at that KOA. Didja see all those kids running around, screamin' and yellin'?"

The other man just shook his head and poked at the fire with a long stick. "Dinner'll be ready about dark," he said. "I hope you're hungry."

They ate in silence and then rose to take their plates to the stream to rinse them off. A few late fireflies flickered in the trees ahead, but the road and the woods were otherwise devoid of light.

"I'm always surprised at how dark it is in the country," one camper remarked. "It's like walking around in a black velvet curtain."

"I wish I'd brought a flashlight."

A sudden noise, like thunder, startled both of them. "There wasn't any rain in the forecast, was there?"

A light broke through the trees and the two men realized what the noise had been. "It's that old bridge," the first man said in relief. "A car was going across it and made that noise."

"I didn't know we were that close to the road."

"Let's go up to the bridge and check it out."

Inside the old structure, their voices reverberated strangely. They could hear the murmuring, babbling sound of the stream below as it coursed over rocks and pebbles. Suddenly, through the mouth of the bridge, a dazzling stream of light poured in, blinding them.

"What the...?"

The light flashed again and again. Then, just as abruptly, it was gone. The sound of the crickets resumed.

"It wasn't a car, was it?"

"I didn't hear one, did you?"

"No, but maybe it was car lights reflecting off something."

"I dunno. It sure didn't look like a car light to me."

"Whaddya think, it was a ghost or somethin'?" His friend punched him playfully on the shoulder.

He shivered. "Let's get back to the campsite. You bring any brandy?"

••••••

Emily was walking home from the market again, humming a little from the new piano sonata her sister had sent last week. She heard a buggy approaching and she moved to the side of the road.

"Emily." The buggy stopped a few feet in front of her. It was Donald, alone this time, his face shadowed by the overhanging canopy.

"Donald," Emily nodded. "Out for a drive?" Her eyes, shaded by the brim of her hat, ran across his shoulders and down his arms. Even at rest, loosely holding the reins, their strength was apparent. A sudden, unbidden thought of those arms around her in an embrace made the color rise to her cheeks.

"A bit warm, isn't it?" His eyes, too, had been scanning her face and form.

"I imagine it's cooler out by the creek," Emily ventured, and then bit her tongue in confusion. She didn't want him to think that she was hinting for a romantic ride down shady, cool Gold Brook Road.

Donald leaned forward, and Emily noticed what a nice smile he had. Then she noticed his eye and covered her mouth in dismay. "Oh, my," she gasped. "What happened to your eye?"

His grin grew wider. "Aww," he said, "I walked right into a tree branch the other night after I put Amelia here in the barn. Smacked me right in the eye. I felt pretty silly about it."

"Did you try a cold compress?" As soon as the words came out, Emily scolded herself silently for being such a busybody.

"Yeah, nothing seemed to help, really." He fidgeted with the reins and Emily realized he was trying to figure out how to say something. He's shy like me, she thought, and the thought warmed her.

"I've heard that you really like to play the piano," he said. "I'd like to hear you sometime. I wish I had a musical talent like you do."

"But what about Jenny Mueller?"

His face changed. "Her father said my prospects weren't good enough to suit him."

"Oh, I'm so sorry," Emily stammered. "That is, I..."

"I'm not sorry," he said bluntly. "Truth is, Jenny was a little..." He groped for the right word. "A little flighty for me," he finished. "I guess she's pretty young, really."

Emily did not know what to say. She turned a deeper shade of red.

"I guess I should talk to your father about calling on you?"

She nodded, relieved that Donald had at last found the words.

He reached out and lightly touched the top of her hat. "You have such pretty eyes," he commented. "But I can't see them when you hide your face like that."

"Thank you," Emily stammered.

"See you later," Donald called, and the horse and buggy ambled down the road toward town.

Emily stood on the side of the road, her heart pounding. She would not fly into a tizzy, she admonished herself firmly. This probably meant nothing at all.

But still, her footsteps were unusually light as she walked the rest of the way home. Almost like walking on air. And that night as she brushed out her hair before bed, she felt uncommonly pretty.

······

"Stand right here."

The girl obliged, shifting a bit to the left.

"No, no, that's not right. Too much shadow on your face. Turn to the right."

Patiently the girl moved again. She shivered a little in spite of the heavy parka enveloping her.

"Let me try this." The photographer knelt down, angling the camera up.

"For heaven's sake, Bob, it's just a snapshot. Hurry up, would you? The poor kid's freezing." The woman lounging against the side of the car held a steaming cup of coffee. The bright December sun warmed her, although there was more than a foot of snow on the ground.

"This is such a beautiful bridge, I want to show it off in the picture." The man fiddled some more with the lens and then decided to change it.

"Don't move, honey," he warned his subject. "With the blue sky from the opposite end of the bridge and the sparkling snow on the roof, it looks great."

"But I'm cold, Daddy," the girl complained. "Just take a picture of the bridge, okay?" Without waiting for a reply, she wandered farther back into the shadows.

"Hey, Mom?" The girl's voice echoed oddly coming out of the bridge.

The woman leaning against the car straightened up and drained the last of her coffee. "What, baby?"

"C'mere. This is really strange."

As the woman peered into the structure, she gasped. "Catherine, get your parka back on! It's thirty degrees out here!"

"It's not cold right here, Mom." The girl stretched out her arms and whirled around. "Come see. It's warm right here!"

Dubious, the woman advanced to near the center of the bridge. As soon as she got within two feet of the girl, she, too, felt the inexplicable warmth. Her face broke out into a light sweat. Her skin prickled.

"This is weird, Catherine," she protested. "Something's not right. Let's get out of here."

"Aww, Mom, you're no fun." The girl skipped toward the mouth of the bridge, stopping short a few feet away to put her parka back on.

"Brrr. You're right, Mom, it's too cold to be out here without a coat. Beat you to the car!" In an instant, she was away, her long legs flashing in the uncertain light of the bridge.

••••••

Emily's face beaded with sweat, and the stays of her corset were digging painfully into her skin. The market basket was heavy because she had bought the sugar and coffee they needed. She trudged down the road, thankful for having successfully bypassed the Kendalls' house with its horde of rude children.

Donald had not called on her during the past week or communicated with her father, apparently. The only news was from her sister in Burlington. She informed them that she was expecting a baby early next spring. This news had, of course, prompted a barrage of sarcasm directed at Emily from her father. "Some women in this family, at least, are fulfilling their God-given potential. I suppose now we'll have grandchildren to care for us in our old age, and I thank God for that. Eh, Margaret?" He poked his wife, but she just took another stitch and pretended not to hear.

Emily snorted and shifted the market basket to her other arm. She was tempted to leave the basket by the gate when she passed it on her way to Gold Brook to cool off. A few steps farther down the road, she decided to do just that. She hurried a little, eager to reach the shaded, quiet stream, its drowsy murmuring a perfect counterpoint to her melancholy thoughts.

She heard a buggy coming up behind her, so she moved to the side of the road, almost automatically. She had jumped so often this past week at the sound of a buggy and been disappointed so often, that she forced herself not to look around again.

"Emily?"

The buggy had stopped right in front of her, and Donald's familiar face peered around at her. "I'm so glad to see you!" He jumped down and hurried toward her, taking the basket off her arm. "I've had to go out of town, that's why I hadn't called, but I was on my way now to speak to your father."

Against Emily's will, a little bit of relief blossomed at his words. Her conscious mind rejected his facile words, but some part of her responded.

"You're not mad at me, are you?" He took her chin in his hand and tipped her face up toward his.

Caught unaware and defenseless, she could only smile and shake her head.

"Will you please honor me with your company?" With a little bow he indicated to his horse, Amelia, standing patiently in the traces. "I could give you a ride home and then speak to your father."

"I was actually going to leave my basket at the gate and go down to the brook and cool off," Emily replied, amazed at her own boldness.

"I would be most glad to accompany you, then," Donald said, his smile growing larger. "I couldn't think of anyone I'd rather go driving with."

Knowing she was crossing the bounds of propriety, Emily gathered her skirt in one hand to step up to the buggy's seat. The thought of Donald wanting her company brought such a delicious chill running across her skin that the hot July sun was almost forgotten. She didn't care, she thought defiantly, if she was endangering her reputation. What did an old maid like her have to lose anyway?

Donald climbed up to the seat next to her and rested his free arm casually across the back of the bench. With a small smile, Emily leaned into the curve of his arm, reveling in the feeling of being desired.

••••••

"You can't catch me!" The long, lanky form of the thirteen-year-old was scantily clad in a two-piece swimsuit. Her wet, bare feet slapping noisily against the planking of the bridge, she ran through the mouth and down the bank to the water again.

"I'll get you!" Her little sister screamed ineffectively—the older girl's head was underwater and she couldn't hear the threat. From the top of the bank, the younger girl could see the remains of their picnic lunch on the other side of the brook and her parents dozing in the shade.

"Mary Ellen threw mud at me, Mama." She hollered mightily, but neither of her parents stirred. "They don't care," she thought unhappily. "Nobody cares." It was hot up here, out of the water and the shade, so the little girl turned and walked back to the bridge.

"I guess they'd care if I was gone," she grumbled, and that gave her an idea. She ran to the center of the bridge and began to scramble up the big beams, preparing to hide while the rest of the family searched frantically. She'd done it before, with pretty fair results.

Halfway up the beam, she stopped. It was cold here. Not just cool, like a shady spot, but downright cold. Like a refrigerator.

"Patty?" Her sister appeared, silhouetted at the opening of the bridge like a picture. "I'm sorry I threw that mud at you."

"Come here." The little girl beckoned to her sister.

Mary Ellen advanced cautiously. "What?"

"Do you feel that?"

Goosebumps popped up all over the girl.

"How'd you do that?"

Patty shrugged. "I didn't. It was just here."

"Let's go, girls." Their dad stood at the far end of the bridge with a newspaper in his hands. "Your mom's ready to get back to civilization."

"Daddy, come here."

He walked toward them. "Did you find a bird's nest?" When he reached the area where they stood, he recoiled.

"Whoa! That's really cold."

"What makes it do that, Daddy?"

He shrugged. "I don't know. Maybe something with the water in the stream. Let's scoot before your mama starts hollerin' for us."

With their arms wrapped around themselves for warmth, the two girls scurried out of the dim structure and into the bright summer heat beyond.

••••••

Emily wadded up another piece of paper and threw it angrily in the stove, watching it shrivel and turn gray and take flight in one of the currents of heat that whirled inside the cast-iron structure.

She couldn't come up with the right words, no matter how she tried. It had been two months since she had climbed in the buggy and gone to Gold Brook in search of a stray breeze, and now she was chilled inside and out. Donald had never called on her father. Never, in fact, ridden down the road in front of her house again. And she had gone far, far beyond the limits of proper conduct with him. The implications of her impulsive actions that hot July day made her shiver all over.

Even if she did manage to compose a letter to Donald, she had no idea how to get it to him. She could hardly appear on the doorstep of his parents' house, note in hand. Perhaps, she thought with a grim little smile, one of the Kendall ruffians would deliver it for her.

More likely, she thought, they'd tear it open and read it aloud for all the world to hear. And she couldn't bear the shame of that, she thought. Bad enough to be an old maid. But to be revealed as the most foolish of women, one taken in by the most timeworn stories of all, tricked blind by her own vanity. Her thoughts chased round and round, like little mice in an empty room scrambling to find even a crumb of hope.

"Writing to your sister, Emily?" Her father entered the kitchen, shattering the silence. "I expect you'll be starting dinner soon, won't you? Your mother's too tired to cook today."

"Yes, Father," Emily mumbled obediently, rising to her feet and sweeping the paper into her apron pocket.

"You are getting stout, my girl," he commented as he left the room. "Watch your figure or you'll be an old maid forever!"

••••••

It was a picture-perfect autumn day. The trees had put on their most brilliant foliage, the sky was an impossibly deep, rich shade of blue, and not a breath of wind threatened to dislodge a single leaf or move a cloud in to blemish the sky.

"Days like this only happen once or twice in a lifetime," declared the woman, pulling the brim of her hat down to shade her eyes. "I've never seen colors this bright before."

Her friend just grunted softly, preoccupied with trying to thread the film into her camera.

"Look up, Marilyn, look around you," she commanded with a laugh. "You'll be so busy trying to put film in that thing you'll miss it all."

"There." Marilyn snapped the camera closed with a satisfying click. "Let me take your picture so we'll remember this perfect day forever."

"Oh, no, you don't," her friend replied. "Take a picture of the bridge, but leave me out of it. My behind is as broad as that mountain, and I want no record of it."

"Suit yourself." Marilyn busily shot pictures of the trees in their splendor, the brown wood of the bridge in pleasant contrast to the brilliant red foliage, the blue sky, the mountain, and the water in the brook.

"You'll shoot anything that stands still, won't you?" Her friend stood in the mouth of the bridge. "Put your camera down and come see this marvelous old bridge."

They stood admiring the massive old beams, and Marilyn sighed. "It reminds me of that old bridge east of town, you remember?"

"How could I forget?" Her friend hooted. "I got into so much trouble in that bridge, I had to get married!"

Marilyn look startled. "You did not."

"Well, almost," her friend conceded. "My, how Kenny loved to spoon in that old bridge."

"That's what I was thinking. Ed asked me to marry him in that bridge."

"You still miss him, don't you?" The woman slipped her arm through Marilyn's.

"Don't you still miss Kenny?"

"Of course I do. Every day." Just then, a gust of wind snatched off her hat, sending it sailing into the shadows deep in the bridge. Her silver-gray hair, carefully combed that morning, stood up nearly straight, blown by the wind. She retrieved her hat.

"That's odd," Marilyn said. "I was watching those trees outside the bridge, and I didn't see them move."

"The wind certainly isn't blowing now," agreed her friend. "Maybe it was Kenny, saying hello. He always did love to play tricks."

"Oh, I wish you wouldn't say that," Marilyn looked up nervously. "You know I don't believe in that stuff." She shivered, and the two women returned to their car, the perfection of the day somehow marred.

••••••

Emily's mother was bent over, her needle flashing in and out of the fabric she held. Emily noted vaguely that she had never seen her mother sew so fast. Her father's voice thundered somewhere above her, but Emily had stopped trying to make sense of his words several minutes before. "Disgrace," "shame," "sin," "humiliation," "tarnish." Words like these figured prominently in her father's tirade.

Emily laced her fingers over her swollen belly and sat as still as she could, next to the warmth of the fire. It was cold all the time now, and the trees were stripped bare. Emily imagined that they, too, might feel a little humiliated, with their clothing all fallen away, and their bare bones exposed for all to see.

"If you'll not tell me who is responsible for this outrage, then I'll send you to your room until you come to your senses!" He pulled her up roughly by her arm, causing her to gasp with the sharp, unexpected pain. Her mother did not look up from her stitching. Half-dragging her, Emily's father stormed up the stairs to her room, thrust her inside, and slammed the door. Minutes later, Emily heard the rattle of the key in the lock and the tumblers sliding into place.

Emily did not talk for five days. Once a day, her mother brought in a pitcher of water and carried out the chamber pot, with her father glowering in the doorway, his arms crossed. Neither parent spoke to her.

On the fifth day, she gave in. "I don't want to hurt the baby," she said. "If I tell you who the father is, will you let me eat?"

Her father nodded grudgingly, and Emily saw a faint glistening trail its way down the pinched and furrowed face of her mother. A single tear.

"It was Donald Manning. But I don't think he'll have me."

"Oh, he'll have you all right," her father said grimly. "Margaret, fix the girl something to eat."

Emily sat at the kitchen table and did not comment as her father left with his old musket in hand. A few minutes later, she called her mother.

"Mama," she said softly. Margaret turned to her with questioning in her eyes.

"Come here," Emily said. She took her mother's hand and laid it gently across her stomach.

"You can feel it," she explained. "It moves around a lot, especially when I'm trying to sleep. Feel that?"

Margaret snatched her hand away and turned back to the stove. The room was filled with the quiet sound of her weeping and the occasional log settling in the stove.

After a meager meal of bread, cheese, and a wizened old apple, Emily climbed heavily back up the stairs to her room. It was dark before she heard the door slam downstairs, and she could hear the rumble of her father's voice through the floorboards.

He spoke for a good five minutes, barely hesitating in his tirade. Emily's mother spoke so seldom now anyway that the pauses were more for him to catch his breath rather than for his wife to respond. Soon Emily heard his footsteps ascending the stairs. She sat in her chair, unbraiding her hair to prepare for sleep. He threw open the door and spoke without preamble.

"Donald and the preacher will be here at nine tomorrow morning," he said shortly. "I'll expect you to redeem yourself by behaving properly."

She nodded.

"I hope you appreciate all I've done for you," her father said bitterly, skewering her with his eyes. "I've told Donald he can have my best saddle-horse as a dowry."

She nodded again, her eyes in her lap, her fingers frozen in the soft tangle of the single, thick braid. As soon as he left, Emily picked up her hairbrush and began to run it through her hair in long, rhythmic strokes. The baby within turned and rolled lazily, and she savored the sensation. Her hair fell in thick clouds all around her face, and she dreamily brushed it until her eyes felt heavy with sleep.

••••••

"Mama, I had a dream last night," the little girl announced as she carefully poured milk over the garishly colored cereal. "It was about a sad lady."

"Mmmm. Pass the milk, would you, dear?" Her mother held a guidebook open on the table next to her. The waitress had refilled her coffee cup and she stirred milk into it while reading aloud.

"Historic Stowe Hollow Bridge. Two miles north of town on Gold Brook Road." She looked up at her daughter. "You want to go see a neat old bridge today, honey?"

The girl pouted. "I wanna tell you about my dream," she insisted. "You weren't listening to me."

"You're right, I wasn't. I'm sorry." She closed the guidebook, but held her finger inside it as a place marker. "Tell me your dream."

"Oh, it wasn't much," the girl said happily. "Just a sad lady in a white dress with flowers. She had pretty long hair."

"Did she look like me?"

The girl studied her mother carefully, then shook her head.

"Not at all," she said decisively. "This lady had brown hair, and she was fatter and older."

"Thanks, honey." The woman laughed and opened the guidebook, while the little girl cheerfully spooned multicolored mush into her mouth.

It was midmorning before the woman pulled the rental car off onto the shoulder of the road. "Here we are, honey," she said. "We drove straight to it. I'll have to tell your daddy what a good map reader you are."

The girl climbed out of the car, her braids swinging with her movements.

"This is it, Mama," she said excitedly.

"I know, it's the bridge I read about at breakfast."

"No, Mama, I mean this is where the lady in my dream was."

The woman looked closely at her daughter, then knelt down to her face-to-face.

"You dreamed about this bridge last night?"

The girl nodded confidently.

A shiver passed over the woman, but she quickly shook it off. "Let's go over there." She pointed to a field not far from the stream. "I bet we can see the mountain real good from over there."

"I wanna look at the bridge, Mama."

The woman shrugged, and moved closer to the structure, clutching her daughter's hand tightly.

••••••

When her mother gathered up Emily's hair to braid it as always, Emily protested. "It's my wedding day, Mama." She pushed Margaret's hands away.

Margaret inclined her head and moved to get Emily's dress. She helped her daughter pull it over her head and smooth down the white folds delicately embroidered with flowers. The bodice was snug, and the unfashionably high waistline helped to mask Emily's ungainly belly.

"I don't know if Father will want me to wear this," Emily warned.

"It was my wedding dress, and I saved it for you. You'll wear it." Emily caught a fleeting glimpse of the woman who had once ruled this household. She wondered if time had worn her down, or if her father's force of will had changed her mother into this meek, silent specter.

Emily wondered what marriage held in store for her, but time did not allow for long speculation. She had just long enough to run a brush through her hair before her father called her down to the parlor.

Emily smiled wanly at the preacher, who was politely sipping a cup of tea as they waited for the bridegroom. She felt vaguely shamed and wondered if the preacher knew that this whole exercise was a farce, a sham with a foundation in deceit and threats.

"Donald will be here soon," her father assured the preacher. Emily lifted the corner of the curtains to peer out the window. On the frozen, rutted road, the sound of horse's hooves rang with an incongruously joyous air. Donald was bringing the buggy.

Emily's father went outside to the porch to greet his prospective son-in-law. "Donald."

"Morning, Mr. Smith." Donald jumped down from the buggy. "I'd like to see that mare again, if I may."

Emily stood in the doorway of the house. Donald's peremptory demand made her feel even more ashamed. He wanted to examine his payment more closely, she thought bitterly, before he makes the final commitment.

Donald came out, leading the mare with her saddle on. Emily had wandered out to the buggy and touched the fringe on the top with wondering fingers. The buggy that had looked so elegant just six months ago now looked a bit shabby. Amelia, the horse, stood a little swaybacked.

With an effort, Emily hoisted herself up to the buggy seat, trying to recapture the feeling she'd had when Donald had first told her how much he loved her. It had been in the dim recesses of the covered bridge over Gold Brook, and the water rushing beneath the bridge had seemed to echo his words.

Donald swung himself up on the mare's back. With a wild cry, he dug his heels into her side and wheeled out of the yard and onto the road.

Emily's father roared in protest, and Donald laughed mockingly as he rode, "You'll never catch me!"

Emily sat in the buggy, stunned, as her father ran into the house for the old musket. He flew back out to the buggy and mercilessly urged Amelia to follow Donald down to Gold Brook Road. In his anger, he barely noticed Emily's presence. They galloped down the road, the buggy bouncing and flying from rut to rut. Ahead lay the bridge, filled with shadows. One of them was Donald, bent over the straps that secured the horse's saddle. It had loosened abruptly, and he was forced to dismount to cinch it tight.

"You maggot," roared Emily's father. "I'll kill you for this!" He ran, pell-mell, into the bridge while Emily struggled to dismount from the buggy. Her hair blew in clouds around her face, and her white dress caught and reflected the brittle January light.

Donald threw a glance over his shoulder and abandoned his efforts to fix the saddle. He stood and ran to the portal of the bridge.

"I'll never marry her!" His defiant cry cut right to Emily's heart. He swung up to the giant beams of the roof, out of range of her father's musket. Her father roared again in impotent rage, and backed off to get a clear shot. Donald stood on the roof of the bridge. Suddenly, his arms flew up in the air and he cartwheeled violently. He'd lost his balance. As Emily watched, horrified, he slipped and tumbled to the rocks below.

She ran, heedless of the sharp stones and steep bank, down to his crumpled body. Blood pooled around his head, and his eyes stared sightless up at the gray, cold sky.

Emily's keening cries rose through the branches and up to the sky beyond. She would mourn this loss forever.

the girl on the bridge

Robert rolled his window down and sucked in a lungful of North Carolina spring air. It was past midnight and he had been driving for four hours straight. Every muscle ached, and his eyelids were beginning to feel heavy. He knew he needed a break, but he was due back at work tomorrow. He had to keep pressing on.

This particular area of Route 70, just east of Jamestown, was almost deserted. He'd passed only one car since he'd been on it. It was 1975, but there were still areas of this state that were totally rural. Well, he'd be coming up on High Point soon. Maybe there'd be an all-night diner, where he could take a quick break and get some coffee.

Staring ahead into the headlight-illuminated highway for several more miles, he was mesmerized by the flick, flick, flick, of the white lines whizzing by. He glanced down for a second to flip on the radio. When he looked back up, he was shocked to see something in the road just ahead. Slamming on the brakes, he swerved into the other lane, staring as he passed. It was a woman! She was standing in the middle of the lane, just before the road went over a bridge, and she was waving her arms over her head in an effort to get him to stop.

Stopping the car, he glanced around, looking for the woman's automobile. There was nothing. As he sat there, she approached his window and leaned in. She was much younger than he had at first thought, probably around sixteen. She was wearing a fancy white dress that seemed a little old-fashioned, with its long, full skirt and full-coverage bodice. The girl's hair was pulled up into one of those things they called a French twist.

"Oh, thank you, sir! Thank you for stopping. I've just got to get home. My mom is going to be so worried."

Robert looked around again. How did she get out here? Even though she was just a young girl, he was a little nervous about picking her up. It just didn't make sense that she was out here all alone. But what could he do? He couldn't leave her. At least with him, he knew she'd be safe. No telling who else might come by and pick her up. He'd never forgive himself if something happened to her.

"Get in," he said.

"Oh, thank you!" She ran around the front of his car and got in the passenger seat. As he started off he glanced across at her. She was a beautiful young woman.

"What's your name?" he asked.

"Lydia."

"Well, Lydia, where do you live?"

"In High Point. I can tell you how to get there."

"What were you doing out there by yourself?"

Twisting her hands in her lap, she looked agitated. Her voice wavered as she talked. "I'm not sure. My boyfriend took me a to dance in Raleigh. We had such a good time! The band was really swinging. But we stayed too late. We were going to miss my curfew. And my mom just worries so much. My dad died two years ago and she just can't stand to have me out late. I've got to hurry and get home before she gets upset."

They had arrived in High Point.

"Go to the next street and turn left," she said.

He followed her direction. "But where was your boyfriend?"

"Turn right at the next street."

He turned.

"Go through the next stop sign and then turn left."

Robert glanced around the neighborhood they were driving through. The houses were older, probably built back in the 1920s or so. Some had been renovated, but most were in their original condition.

"It's the house on the left, there on the corner. The white one with the green shutters. You can just pull up to the curb and let me out."

Pulling across the opposite lane and over to the curb, Robert looked up at the house situated on a small rise. The porch light was on, and he could see a light burning in the front window.

"Looks like your mom…," his words drifted off, for when he turned back to speak to her, she wasn't there. He hadn't heard the door open or close. The interior light hadn't come on, he was sure. But she was gone. He looked back toward the house, expecting to see her walking up to the porch. But she wasn't there. She wasn't anywhere to be seen.

He sat there in the dark car. What had just happened here? How had she gotten into the house without his seeing her? He had to find out what was going on.

Approaching the door, he tried to get a peek into the front window, but curtains obscured the view. The front room light was on, and he didn't know how she'd done it. But Lydia had to be in there, so he rang the bell. It took only a few seconds before he heard footsteps and the door opened. Expecting to see the teenager's mother, he was surprised instead to find an elderly woman at the door.

"Come on in," said the woman. "I've been expecting you."

"What do you mean? You couldn't have been expecting me. Even I had no idea I was coming here."

"Come on in. I've got some coffee made. I'll explain everything."

"But…"

"Come on."

Confused, he followed her into the house, down a short hallway, and into the living room, where there was a silver coffee service set out on the coffee table. She sat down on the couch.

"Have a seat," she indicated a threadbare chair across from her and began pouring a cup of coffee.

"But, I don't understand," he said, taking the cup and looking around. The house was neat, but worn, decorated in another style, another time.

"Well, let me guess…You brought my daughter, Lydia, home, right?" She pointed to a picture of the young girl he had, indeed, brought home.

Robert nodded. "Your daughter? But…" Lydia had been a teenager, he was sure. This lady was seventy if she was a day.

"Yes, Lydia was my daughter."

"Was?"

The woman nodded her gray head. There was sadness in her faded blue eyes.

"Yes, was. You see, Lydia was killed in a car wreck on this date in 1923. I had let her go to a dance in Raleigh—her very first date—with her boyfriend. I didn't really want to let her go. She was my baby, you know, and I had lost her father just two years before. But she begged me, and I just couldn't deny her. I knew I had to let her grow up.

"So, I let her go. Johnny later told me what happened. He wasn't even scratched in the wreck. My baby was the only one hurt. He said they had been having such a good time that they let time get away from them. They knew they were going to miss their curfew—I had told them they had better be back here at midnight. He said Lydia was panicked, not because she was afraid of any punishment I might give, but because she knew how worried I would be. She was rushing him, telling him to hurry up.

"You see, I lost my husband in a car accident. I had a hard time getting over that terrible night of waiting. Waiting for him to come home. Listening for his car in the driveway. I had practically driven myself crazy with worry. And, then, of course, when the police came to tell me, well, I became hysterical.

"That's why Lydia was in such a hurry to get home. She knew I'd be very upset when she wasn't home on time. So, she was frantic, and she got Johnny all upset as well. As they were going across the bridge on Route 70, Johnny said he was trying to calm her down. He only looked away from the road for a split second, he said. But the car drifted into the other lane. There was a car coming from the other direction and when he swerved back into his lane, he lost control and hit the rail on Lydia's side of the car. She was killed instantly. In just that one split second, my baby was gone."

"But, how…?"

"I don't know how. All I can tell you is that every year on the anniversary of her death, someone shows up on my doorstep, saying they picked my baby up out on Route 70 and gave her a ride home. Each time they say she is in a hurry to get home because she's worried about me. When they get here, she disappears. Until the next year."

What a fantastic story, Robert thought. He'd never believed in ghosts before, but he wasn't sure what to think now. He was sure of what he'd seen. He had seen Lydia and had talked to her. He had been sure of her worry over upsetting her mother.

If the story were true, he thought, then it was ironic that, in being so worried about upsetting her mother over a missed curfew, Lydia had consumed her mother's life with her death. Knowing her daughter's spirit was out there, still trying to get home after fifty years, no doubt kept the loss fresh. It had robbed her of the opportunity to grieve her daughter's death and put it behind her. Dazed, Robert finally stood.

"Well, it's getting late, ma'am, and I have to be at work tomorrow. Thank you for the coffee. I'm very sorry for your loss."

She walked him to the door and thanked him. "It's comforting to know," she said just before closing the door, "that even after fifty years, there're still people like you who are willing to help a young girl in trouble."

Back in his car, Robert couldn't help but glance across at the passenger seat every now and then, half expecting to see the lovely apparition sitting here. But she was gone. A few minutes later, as he was nearing the spot where he had first seen her, he slowed down, his eyes straining ahead. But he passed the area and traveled over the bridge without incident. Looking back into the rear view mirror, he thought,

"Goodbye, Lydia. Rest in peace. At least for another year."

crossings

The girl banged the spoon against the side of the metal bucket. "Soo-ey! Soo-ey!" Her eyes scanned the underbrush, searching for a sign of life. Next to her, two little ones danced and yelped in imitation. "Soo-ey! Soo-ey!"

With relief, the older girl heard the pig crashing through the underbrush. It foraged most days, but Becca said it was better to bring it in before dark. The pig, Patsy knew, was of paramount importance to their family life, and Becca had put her in charge of its care.

The little children squealed and scattered as the big old sow lumbered toward their sister and the feed bucket. The pig and the children turned and headed back for home in the clearing above Sandy Creek.

Edward and Ella were fighting when Patsy and the two youngest came back into the house.

"That's my cat-eye! You traded it to me last Sunday!"

"Did not! You stole it, and I'm gonna tell Mama!"

"Stop it, you two." Becca scooped up baby Frank and plopped him on her hip. "You'll be fast asleep when Mama gets back. If you go fetch me some blackberries, I think I could scrape together a cobbler for dessert. Git on."

Distracted by the prospect of a sweet dessert, the two scampered out the door.

"Don't..." The screen door fell back into place with a loud slam and tottered a bit where the hinge was missing a couple of screws. "...slam it," finished Becca.

"Honestly, when will those two grow up and quit squabblin'?" Patsy picked up a bowl of peas and started shelling them into a cast-iron pot.

"They're too close in age, Mama says. When they get to the ripe old age of twelve, I'll bet they'll turn into little angels."

Patsy shot her sister an exasperated look. "You're not that grown up yourself, smarty-pants."

"Pretty soon I'll be old enough to get married and get out of here," Becca retorted. "Take Frank, I'm gonna light the stove." She handed the toddler to her sister. "Rosa, stand back, now."

The five-year-old watched the ritual lighting of the stove with wide eyes. First Becca pumped the handle to get the kerosene into the burner chamber. Then she quickly struck a match and tossed it at the burner, stepping back to avoid the low whomp of gas igniting. It took two tries tonight.

"I hate that thing," she said, tucking a few straggling strands of hair behind her ears. "I'll get me a modern gas stove, just you wait and see." She and Patsy shelled peas in silence for a few moments, letting Rosa play with the baby.

Edward and Ella burst though the door with a cupful of berries in their bucket.

"Looks like more found their way into your bellies than in the bucket," commented Patsy as Becca took the bucket and rinsed the berries.

"Wash up, now," commanded Becca. "Supper's almost ready." She mixed a little flour, a little sugar, and some water and spooned it over the berries before sliding the pan into the oven.

"Why are you so bossy, Becca?" Ella grumbled. "Do this, do that, morning till night."

"She's bossy Becca, that's why," chortled Edward. "Bossy Becca, bossy Becca!" Soon all the children but Patsy and baby Frank were circling in a ring, chanting noisily. Baby Frank cooed and clapped his hands with delight.

"Hush, now," Becca said. "Let's eat."

"Beans again," Patsy said sadly. "I hate beans."

"Cobbler for dessert," reminded Becca. "It's in the oven."

"Did you light it?"

"Oh, drat!" Becca went back to the oven and bent over to light it. After three tries, she had to concede defeat. "It must be nearly out of kerosene," she said as she sat down again. "The peas barely got cooked."

"Yuck!" Edward spat out a mouthful. "They're hard!"

"They're good for you, Edward. Don't waste food."

"We could eat the cobbler the way it is," suggested Rosa.

"Yuck!"

But after trying it, the children scraped the pan clean and declared the unbaked cobbler a success.

"Can we go swimming, Becca?" Edward was the first to clear his plate.

"Please, please!" begged Rosa and Ella.

"Pwease?" said baby Frank, tugging at Becca's skirt.

"You silly goose, you don't know how to swim!" The oldest girl patted her baby brother's soft, downy head and turned to her other brother. "Have you fed the chickens?"

"Yes, I mean, I'll go do it now!" he darted out the door, slamming it again as Becca winced.

"Ella, Rosa, Patsy, let's do the dishes right quick so Mama won't have to."

Their chores completed, the six children traipsed down the hill to the old ferry road. To the right was the covered bridge that provided the main thoroughfare to and from Goldman. There were usually one or two travelers every hour or so, and Becca liked to sit on a little rise overlooking the bridge, keeping an eye on the passersby as well as her brothers and sisters playing on the sandy beach that lay beneath the red-painted bridge.

She heard a distinctive sputtering noise just east of the bridge and her heart rose. It sounded like the old DeSoto her father drove, and she stood and shielded her eyes from the sun to watch the car approach.

She waved, disappointed, as the LeMays crossed the bridge and headed downhill toward Goldman and their hardware store. Behind her, just as she began to sit down again, she heard a piercing whistle.

"Rebecca Johnston, what are you doing playing around at the kissin' bridge?"

"Johnny Oates, you scalawag, I'm not playin', I'm watching my brothers and sisters."

The lanky boy, dressed in overalls but no shirt, hunkered down in the grass next to her.

"Were the blackberries good?" he inquired solemnly.

Becca's hand flew to her mouth, to wipe away any telltale stain that might have lingered after supper. "How'd you know?" she gasped.

"I ran across those little devils fighting over blackberries on my way to the store," he laughed. "I was hopin' some made it back home."

Becca laughed in response. "They're always fightin'. It comes as natural to them as breathin', I guess."

"How d'you like your summer vacation so far?" The boy picked a long blade of grass and began to fiddle with it, watching the five youngsters splashing around in the creek below them.

"Well, I wouldn't call it vacation, exactly. You look like you've been puttin' in some time in the fields yourself."

"It don't hardly make sense to grow anything anymore, with the prices we been gettin'. My pa says he'd as soon set back and collect a government check, but that makes my ma fly into a fury."

"My father quit tryin' to make a livin' on these hills years ago. He says all he ever harvested was rocks and grief anyway."

The two teenagers sat in silence for a moment before Johnny jumped up. "I better get back to the house," he apologized. "My pa wanted this pack of Camels after supper, and ma was cookin' when I left."

"Bye." Becca watched his long legs stride across the grass and scramble over the rocks to reach the road. Johnny made her feel happy sometimes, with all his jokes and cutting up, but the thought of becoming a farmer's wife dismayed her.

On the other hand, it seemed coldhearted and calculating to ignore Johnny's attentions just because he had the misfortune to be born and raised on a farm. That was about the extent of her choices around here, she had to admit, unless she wanted to make friends with Hank Webber, the minister's son. Heaven only knows, though, where he'll end up, she thought as she stood and brushed off her skirt. Smiling a little at the inadvertent pun, she walked down to the creekbed to collect her family.

They were splashing and shouting so loudly they hardly heard her. Baby Frank was in the middle of it all, on Patsy's shoulders, crowing and clapping his hands every time his brother or sisters shouted.

"Let's go home, now," Becca repeated. "It'll be dark soon, and the skeeters are out. They'll eat you up."

The children protested, but Becca was firm. "Out. Now. Or we can't come back tomorrow."

When they finally straggled out of the water, Becca poked Edward. "Race you up the hill!" With a whoop, she gathered her skirt high above her knees and ran furiously, her long legs pumping, up the path to the house on the hill. She only just beat Edward, who complained that she'd had a head start.

Minutes later Patsy came trudging up the hill holding Rosa's hand and carrying the baby on her hip.

"No fair, Becca, I've been watching Frank all day. He's gettin' too heavy for me." A whining note crept into her voice, and Becca threw her a look of disgust.

"Don't carry him then, Patsy. He can walk."

Tired and cross, all six children cleaned their teeth before kneeling down by the side of the big double bed where Edward, Ella, Rosa, and the baby slept.

"Now I lay me down to sleep," they chanted in unison. "I pray the Lord my soul to keep. If I die before I wake, I pray the Lord my soul to take. Amen." Patsy tucked them in while Becca straightened out the quilts that made a pallet for the older girls.

"Patsy, what's 'die' mean?" asked Rosa sleepily.

"Never mind, Rose Red," Patsy said, stroking her hair.

"It's what that fat ol' pig's gonna do this fall," giggled Edward.

"Hush, now."

"He kicked me," whined Ella. "I want Mama."

"Mama will be back soon. Go to sleep."

The warm glow of the kerosene lamp woke Becca hours later.

"Mama?" she whispered.

"Yes, honey?" Even by the soft, forgiving light of the lamp, she looked worn. Almost old, Becca thought.

"What was it?"

"A girl. A big one, and it went hard on Sally."

"She's all right?"

"Yeah, just wore out. Like me. That baby fought for thirteen hours. I guess it didn't see much out here worth bein' born for."

"Aw, Mama." Becca crept out from the covers and wrapped her arms around her mother. After a moment, the older woman reciprocated.

"I'm sorry, Becca. I'm just tired, I guess." Sarah smiled at her oldest child and suddenly looked more familiar. As she stroked the girl's hair, Becca snuggled up closer, warmed by the luxury of undivided attention.

"Let's go to sleep, honey."

Wordlessly, the girl clambered down to the pallet on the floor and nestled spoon-style next to her sister. As her eyes closed, she heard the familiar murmuring sound of her mother's heavy braid of coal-black hair being loosened and brushed, stroke after stroke, until the girl fell asleep.

The next morning her mother had a skillet full of scrambled eggs nearly ready when Becca wandered into the kitchen.

"I think the tank needs filling up, Mama," she mumbled. "I couldn't get the oven to light last night."

"We had blackberry cobbler for dessert and it wasn't even cooked, Mama!" Edward, although not exactly clinging, was hovering close enough to wrap his arms around his mother's legs if he felt the urge. Ella and Rosa, too, were right underfoot and baby Frank rested effortlessly on his mama's hip. The woman moved around through this small cluster of humanity with an easy grace, seeming to know without looking where to place her feet in order to avoid her children's bodies.

A car rattled to a stop outside, the sound of its labored ascent to the house masked by the noise of breakfast being prepared. "It's Daddy!" shrieked Patsy, and the children tumbled like an avalanche into the yard, even Becca forgetting in her haste the precarious state of the screen door hinge.

Sarah turned off the skillet and walked to the door, wiping her hands on her apron. The sight of her husband, overgrown with joyous children like an old barn covered with honeysuckle, brought a small smile to her lips.

"Yes, yes, of course, I brought you all something, I always do, don't I?" He looked toward the house. When he picked out the shadowy figure of Sarah, he waved gaily. "Even got something for your mother this time, couldn't forget my own true love now could I?"

He disentangled himself from the children, and his lurching gait as he walked toward the house again filled Sarah with a hurtful surprise. He'd come back from France with the injury more than sixteen years ago, but the sight still had the capacity to make her heart ache with a dull echo of the pain she'd felt when she first saw his mangled leg.

"How'd it go?" She closed her eyes for an instant. She had meant to greet him first, ask how he felt, instead of demanding an accounting. She saw the welcome fade from his eyes.

"Great, just great. Cotton's down lower than it's ever been, fifteen million men are out of work, the banks are foreclosing on every other farm in the county, and men are lining up by the dozens to buy cigars."

"I'm sorry, Ed. I shouldn't have asked that way. I didn't mean it, I've just had a hard week and..."

"You want to talk about a hard week? I've driven no less than a hundred miles every day, stopped at every two-bit crummy little store and practically begged men who don't care to please, please buy my cigars!" By the time he finished, he was nearly yelling. But the effort seemed to exhaust him, and he dropped into the chair nearest the stove.

"Mama always says a cup of coffee perks you right up." Rosa's solemn little voice as she tugged on her father's sleeve sent the tension in the room underground for the moment. Ed laughed and pulled the little girl up on his lap. Ella scrambled up to his other knee, and

Edward leaned against his father's shoulder. The two older girls sat down at the table, eager to hear about their father's adventures while he was away.

"Sally had her baby last night, Ed. Another girl."

"She pay you this time?"

"Her mother gave us three dozen eggs."

"Our hens stop laying?"

Sarah briefly closed her eyes again, but her back was to her husband. "That's all she had, Ed."

"I'm hungry, Mama," Ella whined.

"And I could use that cuppa coffee, Sarah," Ed said, tugging gently on one of Ella's braids.

"Here, Becca." Sarah handed Frank to his sister and reached for the matches. She pumped the stove vigorously, and with a practiced flip of her wrist, tossed a lighted match toward the burner pan. It failed to catch, and she tried twice more with no success.

"The tank's empty, Mama," Becca reminded her.

"I'll fill it," Ed volunteered. He spilled the girls off his lap and went to the shed outside for the five-gallon can.

"Nearly empty," he said cheerfully, swinging the can so they could hear a little liquid slosh. "I'll send you down to town this afternoon to get a refill."

After he poured the last few drops into the small cylindrical tank attached to the stove, he set the empty can by the back door. Becca sliced bread and Sarah turned the burner on beneath the eggs and the blue speckled coffee percolator.

"Put the can in the shed, please, Edward," she said without turning around.

"It's empty, Sarah. It can sit there during breakfast."

She didn't answer, just shrugged her shoulders.

After breakfast, Ed brought out the gifts he'd collected during the two weeks he'd been away. "Hair ribbons for my beautiful girls." He presented them with a flourish to Becca and Patsy. "New shooters for my marble players." Ella and Edward held up the oversized marbles and turned them round and round, catching and fracturing the light streaming into the kitchen from the window over the sink. "And for

Rosa, my pretty little flower," he reached into his worn leather valise and carefully lifted out a tiny, mewling ball of fluff. "Her very own mouser!"

"Ooooh, Daddy!" the children chorused. Edward had long refused to get a cat, saying that another mouth to feed was a wasteful expense.

"Kitty?" said Frank, toddling forward to touch the curious bundle.

"Edward?" queried Sarah.

His first reply was an eloquent shrug. "It was free," he explained lamely. "I took to it."

Edward and Ella played marbles in the kitchen, while Becca, Patsy, and Rosa amused themselves with the kitten. Before lunch, Sarah announced that she had plans for the children.

"I'll fix you a picnic lunch," she declared, "to take to the creek, and then you can all go to the hardware store and get the kerosene can refilled."

"Oh goody!" shouted Edward.

"What's for the picnic?" asked Ella.

Sarah thought fast. "Deviled eggs," she said. Ed, still sitting at the table, grinned.

"Here's a quarter for the kerosene, Becca." Ed bent close to his oldest child and whispered as he pressed an extra coin in her hand. "Take them to the store and give them each a nickel to spend on candy, too. Tell them to share with baby Frank."

With a flurry of activity and a few false starts, the caravan of six children set out down the hill to the creek for lunch and a swim, and then across to town.

"Be careful!" Ed and Sarah stood watching in the doorway. Patsy carried baby Frank, Edward toiled under the burden of the kerosene can, Becca hauled the picnic basket, and Ella carried a blanket. Only Rosa was not pressed into service, and she flitted forward and backward between the group and the house at first, reluctantly leaving her precious kitty after many attempts to persuade her.

"Let's swim first!" yelled Ella, dropping the blanket halfway as she scrambled down to the creekbed.

"I'll beat you into the water!" shrieked Edward. "Last one in's a monkey's uncle!" With a loud hoot, he tossed the kerosene can aside. Rosa raced past him, her little legs pumping wildly to keep up.

Patsy set baby Frank down and held his hand as they scrambled to the shallows, where Frank liked to watch the shadowy little fish dart back and forth.

Becca was hot, but she felt like she should maintain her dignity and not splash and play in the water like the children—just in case someone special came across the bridge. Or even, she thought, if Johnny Oates happened by. So she lay on her back above the creek, cushioning her head on her crossed arms, staring upward at the billowing, shape-shifting clouds sailing slowly and majestically across the blue.

"Help, help, I'm drownin'! Help!"

Her brother's cry galvanized Becca, and she half rolled, half ran down the bank to the water's edge. Heedless of her dress, she splashed into the creek up to her knees, her eyes frantically scanning the water's surface for a sign of her brother.

There, under the bridge, in the shadows, she thought she saw a hand rise up out of the water. Just as she took a deep breath, preparing to dive into the deepest area of the creek, a giggle behind her brought her up short.

She whirled around to see Patsy, with baby Frank on her shoulders, and little Rosa, covering their mouths to unsuccessfully stifle their snickers. Becca turned around again in time to see Edward swing down from the cross-bracing on the underside of the bridge, and hang there, hooting like a monkey and grinning at Becca's panic.

"Fooled ya, didn' I?" he taunted. Ella also appeared from behind the stone piers, grinning sheepishly.

Becca sloshed furiously out of the water. As she walked past Patsy, she threw a slap across her cheek so hard the girl rocked with its force.

"Don't you ever, ever play a trick like that on me again, you hear, Patsy Ann Johnston?"

Patsy's eyes filled with tears and Frank began to whimper. "I didn't do anything, Becca, I didn't even know where he was till you jumped in the water, I swear."

Becca didn't reply, only stalked back up the bank to sit and sulk. When the shadow of the bridge was directly beneath the structure, she called to her brothers and sisters.

"Let's eat, you rotten little beggars. Or maybe I should let you all go hungry."

They were all subdued as they ate. Little Rosa slipped her hand into Becca's and squeezed it softly, a mute apology for the trick.

Becca felt bad, seeing the imprint of her hand still on Patsy's cheek. Edward and Ella were wary of Becca's anger and ate at a distance, only speaking to request more food.

"Look, Edward, she's right. That was a really nasty trick. She's the one who's supposed to be lookin' out for us, and she'd catch it if anything happened." Patsy broke the tension as the last deviled egg was divided between Edward and Ella.

"She wasn't watching us, anyway," the boy pointed out. "She was bein' her usual stuck-up self, off moonin' at the clouds."

Ella poked her brother. "Say you're sorry, Edward."

"Sorry, Becca," he mumbled, unable to withstand pressure from all sides. "But you did look funny, all soppin' wet an' mad!" With another holler, he took off across the bridge down toward town.

"Oh, forget him," Becca said, standing up to brush crumbs off her skirt. "Ella, you take the kerosene can. I'll stick the basket and the blanket under the bridge, and we'll collect 'em on the way home."

She held out her arms for baby Frank and touched Patsy's cheek gently by way of apology as she passed her younger sister.

"Becca, it's got a dent in it," Ella cried, picking up the can from where Edward had flung it down in his haste to go swimming.

Becca sighed and ran her hand along the side. "It doesn't feel like it's got a hole in it, anyway," she said. "Let's go."

They trooped across the bridge, still cool inside despite the heat of the summer day. It was dark, with only small pools of light filtering in from the narrow windows below the eaves.

"Spooky old bridge," Patsy commented.

"They call it a kissin' bridge," Becca said. "I guess 'cause it's so dark."

Ella and Rosa ran ahead. It was only a little over a mile to Goldman, and they knew Edward was somewhere close by.

"Have you ever been kissed, Becca?"

The older girl thought for a moment before replying. "Who have I ever met that I wanted to kiss?" she asked.

"I dunno."

Their feet scuffed up a cloud of dirt as they walked. Baby Frank's head nodded as he succumbed to the lethargic pleasures of a full stomach and the rocking gait of his sister.

"He's gettin' heavy, isn't he?" Patsy gave a nod toward the baby.

"Yeah. He'll start walking all the time soon, I 'spect."

"You think Mama'll have another one?"

"I dunno, Patsy." The two walked in a companionable silence the rest of the way to town. Ahead they heard the little girls squeal as Edward jumped out of the bushes at them.

"Gotcha!" he hollered. "I'm the Lone Ranger!"

"The Lone Ranger's a good guy, Edward," Patsy called out. "And if you're not good, you can bet Papa'll want to know!"

Mr. LeMay at the hardware store gave the children a hard stare as they came in the door with the kerosene can.

"No credit," he barked. "And I don't need any more eggs," he added nastily.

"No sir, we've got cash today," Becca said stiffly, holding up the quarter for him to see. Grudgingly he took the can from her and led them out back to the kerosene pump. He pocketed the quarter without a word when the can was filled.

"May we leave it out back here while we go to the store?" Becca asked politely, but inside she was seething with anger.

"I can't watch over it, but if you want to, it's fine by me," he said gruffly. "I've got a business to run."

Becca turned and led the little troupe of children through the alley and out onto the main street.

"Daddy gave me a quarter to share with you," she said as they approached the grocery store. "We each have to buy a little piece of candy for baby Frank, though, since he's too little to get his own nickel."

Ground rules established, they swarmed into the store. Mrs. Byers gave them a warm welcome. "It's Mrs. Johnston's children," she cried, slipping off her stool to come meet them. "How is your mama? You'll have to tell her my girl Eva and the baby are doing so well, we never could've managed without her."

"Thank you, ma'am," Becca mumbled.

Mrs. Byers' stream of words continued as she helped the children choose some candy. "It was a hard birth, you know, but oh, he's been such an easy baby. I think it goes like that, don't you? I know women whose babies came out smooth as silk, just like that," she snapped her fingers, nearly dropping a jar of peppermint sticks.

"But then, my, weren't them babies colicky? I never did see a fussier baby than that LeMay boy. He's fourteen now and still a handful." She toted up the assorted peppermint sticks, licorice strings, and brightly colored jawbreakers on a scrap of brown paper. "Let's see, that's twenty-six cents. Don't give that precious baby those jawbreakers, he's liable to choke on those, why I saw a little girl, she was two years old I think, and she just turned blue."

Becca was having a fierce, wordless struggle with Edward and Patsy, trying to get each of them to surrender a licorice string in order to reduce the bill by a penny.

"Her daddy, though, turned her upside down quick as a wink and pounded her on the back and that jawbreaker popped out, pretty as you please," Mrs. Byers chuckled. "They didn't give that girl any jawbreakers for a while, you may be sure." She stared at the two bedraggled licorice strings the victorious Becca held out.

"Please, ma'am, we don't need these," Becca said. She neatly dodged the kick Edward directed at her shins and held out the quarter.

"Take them, take them," the storekeeper said cheerily. "You each want a little paper to wrap your candy in? Here, take this cracker for the baby, he'll like that much better anyway."

Frank, awake again, reached out his fat, grubby fingers for the saltine the lady held out. "Oh, he's a sweet one, he is," she cooed. "Let me wrap that candy up so it doesn't spoil your supper. Your daddy's home today, isn't he? I thought I heard him come through town this morning,"

"Goodbye!" yelled Ella, and the three younger ones dashed out the door.

"Well," said Mrs. Byers, caught up short. "Well, you be sure to tell your mama I said hello." She stopped to take a breath, and Patsy swooped down to retrieve Frank. "Goodbye, Mrs. Byers," Patsy and Becca chorused, then "Thank you," as they made their escape.

Laughing, they ran all the way to the rear of the hardware store where the kerosene can waited. Edward and Ella were designated to hold baby Frank's hands as he toiled down the road, taking three steps on short, fat legs for every one his big brother took. Patsy and Becca took turns carrying the kerosene can.

"Oh, this stuff stinks to high heaven," Patsy cried as they reached the bridge. "I'm 'bout to choke on it."

"I'll carry it now," Becca offered. "Get the basket and the blanket—they're under the bridge in those bushes."

"I wanna swim some more," whined Edward. "I'm hot, an' I wanna get a drink."

"Go get a drink then, Edward, but don't you dare get back in the creek," Becca ordered. The boy tumbled down the bank, Ella and Rosa close behind. Becca and Patsy continued up the hill toward home, shepherding baby Frank ahead of them. He was tired, but struggled valiantly to climb the hill.

As they reached the side yard, angry voices spilled out through the tattered screen door. "Your children haven't had a new pair of shoes in two years! How dare you put a four dollar pair of shoes on your feet when we can't afford meat for the table?"

"I can't make a living going around looking like a bum!"

"You can't make a living! Go on, get out of here!"

Patsy and Becca looked at the ground, oddly ashamed to be overhearing this exchange. Frank sat down suddenly, hard on his bottom, and began to howl. Just then, the sharp sound of a hand striking flesh rang out across the yard.

Seconds later, Ed stumbled out the door, his bad leg dragging. He held his hand up to his face, where a red welt was rapidly rising across his cheek.

Without seeing the children in the yard, he cranked the car and drove down the hill, honking his horn in farewell to Edward, Ella, and Rosa, straggling up to the house.

When Becca timidly pushed open the screen door to enter the kitchen, her mother sat staring straight ahead. Fresh marks of tears tracked her cheeks, and her nose and eyes were red and swollen, but her voice was stony.

"Your daddy's gone back to work. I've got a sick headache, so keep the kids quiet, all right?" She pushed away from the table and rose to enter the bedroom. "Put the kerosene in the shed." The bedroom door closed with a little click.

Becca set the kerosene can down and rounded up the children.

"Let's go swimming," she suggested grimly. "Mama don't feel good."

"Is it a baby?" squealed Rosa.

"No, dummy, her tummy never got big." Ella shoved Rosa, but not too hard. Becca grabbed *Wood's Natural History*, a book her teacher gave her last year when she graduated, and followed her brothers and sisters back down to the creek. Halfway down, Frank sat down again and began to wail.

"He's tired," Becca complained. "I guess I'll have to carry him."

While the children splashed and played, and baby Frank napped on the blanket next to her, Becca lost herself in details of odd animals in far-off places. Time passed easily, and soon, it seemed, her stomach was growling and the others were clamoring for food.

Frank woke up howling. "His diaper's wet," announced Patsy. "Come on, let's go!"

All six children climbed the hill again, hearing the agitated squawks of the chickens before their yard came into sight.

"Everybody's hungry," said Becca. "You go feed the chickens and I'll start supper, okay?"

The bedroom door was still closed so Becca made as little noise as possible, setting out plates, bread, and butter and one of the last jars of applesauce from the cellar. Pumping the stove, she lit a burner under a pot of water and began to slice potatoes into the water.

A horse's hooves came pounding up the road, and Becca heard the chickens and the children scatter. She went to the door to see who rode up in such a hurry, and heard the bedroom door open behind her.

"Who is it, Becca?" her mother murmured.

The gangly young man trotted up to the door and practically wrenched it out of Becca's hand.

"My wife," he panted. "Mrs. Johnston, she's bleeding and you've got to help her."

"May, that's your wife's name, isn't it?" Sarah's voice became brisk, businesslike, and Becca felt a twinge of anger at this sudden recovery. "She's not due for another seven weeks. What happened?"

"I dunno," the man wailed, and Becca realized he was not too much older than Johnny. "She started feelin' poorly, and then she started bleedin'. Please, please come now, Mrs. Johnston!"

"I'll head that way. But you'll have to ride to Doc Sullivan's house. I can't do much if she's bleedin'."

"We can't afford the doctor!"

Sarah pulled sharply at his arm. "You love your wife, don't you?"

He nodded dumbly.

"Get the doctor. He gives credit, same as me." Sarah crossed her arms and watched sternly as the man mounted his horse and rode away to fetch the doctor. Then she disappeared into the bedroom for a moment for her bag.

She gave each child a quick kiss on the crown of the head, and a firm reminder to them all. "Mind Becca, now. I may be late."

Becca had just finished slicing potatoes into the water when she gasped. "Patsy, I left my book down at the creek!"

Patsy looked doubtful. "It's gettin' dark."

"I know, but I can't leave it out, it'll get ruined!"

"Run and get it, then. I'll watch them."

Becca flew out the door, only to return a moment later. "Don't touch the stove, now."

"We won't, worrywart." Rosa was playing patty cake with baby Frank, and Ella and Edward were huddled in the corner. Patsy fiddled with the wick on the lamp, then laid forks around the table.

"Frankie made a stinky one, Patsy," Rosa announced. "Pee-yew!"

"I got the last one, too," muttered Patsy. She held Frank at arm's length as she carried him into the bedroom where the clean diapers were kept.

"That one's mine, Edward. I got two red ones and one black string."

"No, you ate all your red strings. It's mine!"

The shadows were long, and the breeze nearly cool down by the bridge. Becca lingered a moment after she picked up the little gray book with cardboard covers.

"Rebecca, is that you?" Johnny's lean form materialized out of the darkness of the bridge opening.

"What're you doin', Johnny?" Becca felt a warm sort of pleasure steal over her at the sound of his voice.

Edward shoved Ella, hard. "Give me back my licorice," he shouted. A stray breeze, the first of the evening, stole through the screen door and made the flame under the burner dance. Rosa watched, popping her thumb in her mouth, fascinated by the movement of the bright blue flame.

"C'mere," Johnny urged, pulling Becca's hand. "The sun's just right to make these wonderful shadows on the bridge."

"Aw, Johnny," Becca protested, but she let herself be led along.

"See," he whispered, moving close and pointing over her shoulder. As she turned her head to look, his lips grazed her cheek and she turned back, startled.

The flame was out. But Rosa knew what to do because she'd seen her big sister do it countless times before. She climbed up on the kitchen chair and took down the box of big kitchen matches. She scratched one slowly along the side of the box.

"No, Johnny," Becca said softly, just as his lips met hers.

He dropped his hands and the two flew apart as a massive roar broke the silence, shaking the wooden floor of the bridge.

The sound seemed to tear an answering scream from Becca as she ran out of the bridge toward home. Johnny followed close behind, but the heat was too intense, the flames too bright. Both children crumpled in the grass on the crest of the hill as the house burned and then collapsed in a shower of sparks like a vision of hell itself.

••••••

"I'm sure there's a bathroom, it's a state park, isn't it?" The man was a little testy, four hours in the little blue Toyota beginning to wear on his nerves. "Here we are. Look, bathrooms." He pointed to a small building in the center of a grove of trees. His wife and daughter piled out of the car and sprinted to the structure.

"Looks more like an outhouse to me, Dad," his son commented. "When did you say the bridge was built?"

"Oh, 1860 or something like that. Let's take a look." They wandered slowly over to the weathered old structure, the boy reading with curiosity the graffiti scrawled on the concrete piers.

"Let's see what's on the other side," the man suggested when his wife and daughter joined them. Across the bridge, to the left, was a faintly marked path.

"I'll bet there's a clearing up there, where we can get a good view of the bridge." The woman had her camera. "Let's take a look."

The boy and the girl raced ahead. Their parents, hand in hand, climbed the hill more slowly.

"This is really cool, Dad," the boy announced. "There's these foundations, all overgrown with honeysuckle, and they're all charred and black."

"Must've been a big fire," the man mused.

"How sad," said the woman. "We can't see the bridge from up here. I was wrong. Let's head back down, and maybe I can get a good shot from the creekbed."

"Where'd the kids go?"

"I hear somebody splashing in the creek."

"Sounds like a good idea to me."

"I don't want them to get their clothes wet. We've got another three hours before we'll stop for the night."

Just then, the children appeared before them, flushed and panting. "We hear some kids playing in the creek," said the boy. "Can we go, please?"

"You can wade in, but don't get your clothes wet," their mother said.

"And watch out for glass," warned their dad, as they raced down the hill.

When the couple arrived at the bridge, the two children were standing in the middle of the road, their shoes in their hands, puzzled.

"Not getting in?" called their mother.

"We can't find those other kids," said her daughter. "They were here—we heard them. But when we got down here, they had disappeared."

The woman shivered and wrapped herself in her arms. "It's a little chilly here in the shadow of that old bridge," she commented.

"It sounded like a lot of kids," her husband said doubtfully. "Where could they have gone?"

The boy looked up as if to reassure himself that the sun was in its rightful place. "I'm cold, too," he said uneasily. "Can we go home now?"

The family resumed their road trip in a troubled silence that only began to lift when they returned to the sleek new expressway. Behind them, they left a creek whose quiet, sandy shores sometimes echoes with the joyous laughter of unseen children.

the ghost of the boy hero

"Shhh! We're gonna get caught," John whispered to his buddies, trying to suppress an excited giggle. They weren't exactly breaking the law, for Mount Holly Cemetery was open to the public until dusk, but preteens hanging around anywhere after dark were generally considered suspicious and frowned upon. Sooner or later a police officer would probably show up to ruin their fun.

The boys weren't even sure what they were hoping to find that night in the cemetery. Like all the kids in Little Rock, they had heard the urban legends and ghost lore surrounding the cemetery, of which there was plenty. A lot of Confederate soldiers and officers were buried there because after Vicksburg had fallen to the Union forces, Little Rock was not far behind.

"I heard you can see the ghosts of dead people floating around the graveyard," one of the boys whispered to his friends.

"Oh yeah, right," his friend said sarcastically. "Don't tell me you believe all that stuff about ghouls and ghosts. That's kid's stuff."

For all the detractor's bravado, however, he had to admit guiltily to himself that he did feel a twinge of nervousness. He also tried to forget that they weren't that much older than kids. They couldn't even drive yet; they had dropped their bikes at the rear of the cemetery and crept in on foot.

As they knelt behind an obelisk, they sent Matt, the bravest (or maybe the dumbest) of the bunch, on a scouting mission. He crouched over and scuttled from tombstone to tombstone, peeking out from around the stones that glowed in the moonlight. He thought maybe they were being a little overly precautious, but being sent on a mission lent an air of danger to their outing that he liked.

Deciding he would mess with his friends a little, he ducked behind a mausoleum and waited. When he didn't come back immediately, he knew they would come looking for him.

Sure enough, after some minutes had passed (it seemed like an eternity to both Matt and his increasingly anxious friends), the group decided that they should go and have a look.

They set out as a pack, not wanting to admit to each other that they wanted to stick as close together as possible.

"Matt?" they called out questioningly, raising their voices just enough to carry but not so much as to arouse suspicion.

Matt didn't answer, biting his lip to hold back the laughter.

"Matt!" they called out a little louder this time, startling themselves with the volume of their voices in the deathly quiet graveyard.

Still Matt waited, covering his mouth with his hand as he heard their footsteps move closer, rustling the grass beneath their sneakers.

Just as they began to draw up beside the prankster's hiding place, Matt leapt out from behind the tombstone and screamed bloody murder.

A collective yelp escaped from all of the boys who instinctively jumped closer together. They stood wide eyed and shaking, gasping for breath. Matt collapsed on the ground in peals of laughter, holding his stomach and kicking his legs.

"You should have seen the looks on your faces," he gasped between fits of laughter.

The boys were glad that the furious red flushing their cheeks was not visible in the light of the moon. Their hearts pounded so loudly they were sure each one could hear the other.

"Shhhh," T.J. hissed angrily, "we'll get caught for sure with you making all that racket."

"Oh, don't be mad just because I got you," Matt said, his laughter subsiding to sporadic chuckles. "I was just having a little fun."

"You didn't scare me," Adam sniffed, trying to regain some of his wounded and still shaky pride.

"Oh, come off it," Matt replied. "You screamed like a little girl." With that he did an imitation of Adam's shrill shriek that sent him back onto the ground in a fit of giggles and his friends into a fit of shushing.

After Matt's laughter faded and his friends' composure was regained, they decided to play hide-and-go-seek. What better way to reassert their manhood than splitting up in a graveyard at night. One of them suggested playing in teams, a suggestion so transparently cowardly he regretted having said it the minute it crossed his lips. After another delay-of-game for the taunting the suggestion elicited, they finally got the game underway.

It was decided that a round of Rock-Paper-Scissors would be the most judicious way to determine who was "it," and in the end, Adam's rock beat T.J.'s scissors, leaving him to be the seeker.

"Ready, set, go," T.J. called, crossing his arms across the side of a memorial stone and resting his forehead between them. He began to count slowly, peeking underneath his arm to get a general idea of the direction they were going. It was only fair—the cemetery was way too big to not have a little advantage.

He finally reached one hundred and yelled as loudly as he dared, "Ready or not, here I come!"

With that he took off in the direction he had seen Matt go. He quickly looked from left to right behind the rows of stones as he ran as quietly as he could through the grass. He thought he saw some movement behind a tree.

"I've got you right where I want you," he said to himself smugly as he slowed to a tiptoe. He crept up to the tree, ready to pounce.

"Ha!" he called as he jumped around to the other side of the tree, only to find it unoccupied.

Not yet discouraged, he immediately turned around and took off on the search again. The moonlight should offer an advantage, he thought, as he scanned his surroundings with the keen eye of an experienced hide-and-go-seeker. He analyzed the trees and monuments around him, trying to determine where he might hide if he were on the other side.

Just southeast of him he spied a perfect place. It was a big white marble spire with a marble curb laid out in front of it to mark the plot. From his vantage point he couldn't see behind the curb, thus making it an ideal hiding spot. He chuckled to himself. He could imagine one of his poor unwitting buddies pressed to the ground on his stomach, head down, trying to breathe quietly, unaware of the fact that his hunter was about to close in for the kill.

T.J. skirted around to the right and kept low, ducking behind tombstones. If he snuck up well enough and off to the side of the grave, he could maybe avoid even having to chase his prey. He drew close.

Although he was training his eyes to the plot within the marble curb, he caught a flash of movement just behind the spire.

A grin passed over his face as he thought, "What a moron! How obvious can you get?"

He tiptoed over to the side of the spire, took a deep breath, and swung around the corner, crying "Gotcha!"

The look of expectant smugness was soon replaced with a furrowed brow of confusion.

"Oh, hey kid. Who are you?" he asked suspiciously.

The boy standing before him was small, brown-headed like him. He didn't look too much older than T.J. His skin was really pale and he had on funny clothes. What really startled T.J., though, was the blindfold he was wearing over his eyes.

"What's with the blindfold, man?" T.J. asked nervously, taking a few steps backward. There was no telling what kind of wackos hung out in cemeteries after dark.

The boy did not answer.

"Um, well, I'm T.J. I'm playing a game with my friends if you want to help," he said. "What's your name?"

The boy slowly reached behind his head and untied the blindfold. He slowly lifted it from his eyes and blinked. He squinted his eyes and blinked as if he had just stepped into brilliant sunshine. He looked perplexed as he gazed at his surroundings.

He tried to speak but first had to clear his throat.

"I'm David," he finally managed to croak hoarsely. "Have you seen my mother?"

T.J. regarded him guardedly.

"Nope, sorry pal," T.J. said, edging away from the strange boy. This "David" seemed kind of out of it and T.J. didn't feel like dealing with this character alone. As the boy turned his head, T.J. caught a glimpse of his neck in the moonlight. It was red and raw, like it had been chafed by something.

"Hey, are you alright?" T.J. asked nervously, never looking away from the angry red welts ringing the boy's small throat.

The boy nodded absently and turned away from T.J. Taking that as a cue to make his own exit, T.J. mumbled a "later," did an about-face, and began to jog off. He looked over his shoulder and saw the boy looking around on the ground around him confusedly, seeming to search for something in a slow and disoriented manner.

The strange encounter had taken the wind out of T.J.'s sails. Not caring about the game anymore, he looked around half-heartedly as he headed back to the starting point of the game. There he found most of his friends waiting for him impatiently.

"Where the heck have you been?" they called out to him as he trudged over to join his gang.

"We waited forever and you never showed," Adam said. "I thought maybe it was a trick, but then I got bored and came back and found these guys," he explained.

"More like you got scared," John said teasingly, punching Adam in the arm.

"I did find somebody," T.J. said quietly. He then related to them what had happened, how he had met this weird kid in a blindfold. He felt goose bumps pop up all over his body as he tried to describe the interaction with the kid. It didn't come off sounding as creepy as it had actually been, but the boys' interest was definitely piqued. They hadn't seen anything cool in the graveyard yet. Maybe if they found this weirdo the night wouldn't be a total loss.

T.J. led the pack back toward the monument where he had bumped into the kid named David. As they drew closer he could see the moonlight reflecting the white marble of the pillar.

"There it is," he said, and quickened his pace. Since he wasn't looking for anyone who was necessarily hiding from him, he approached the grave straight on.

As he drew up to the grave he stopped so abruptly that his friends bumped into him from behind.

He looked at the spire with a mixture of nausea and horror. Engraved on the front of it were the words, "Here lie the remains of David O. Dodd. Born in Lavaca County, Texas, Nov. 10, 1846, died Jan. 8, 1864." On the curb surrounding the plot where he thought his friends lay in wait was another inscription: "Boy Martyr of the Confederacy."

"Oh yeah, David O. Dodd," John said knowingly. His dad was a big Civil War buff and therefore he kind of was too. "My dad told me about him. When the Yankees were here during the Civil War they arrested this kid for being a spy for the Confederacy."

"Whoa, cool," his friends said. Espionage was exactly the kind of thing they were into.

Encouraged by their enthusiastic response, John continued.

"He was only, like, seventeen-years-old," he said. The boys looked at the dates and the graves, did some quick mental arithmetic and determined this to be true.

"They held him prisoner over at the Ten Mile House until he was found guilty. They hung him on a cold winter's day, after they blindfolded him with his own handkerchief. But they had messed up the gallows or something. Either the rope was too long or the platform too short, because it took him five minutes to die."

The boys paused and let this sink in. None of them noticed T.J., who looked white as a ghost and trembled with fear. He nearly passed out.

"He was finally strangled and they buried him here," John concluded, pleased for having remembered the story.

"Gosh, he wasn't much older than us," Adam remarked, awestruck by the story.

"Hey, T.J., where'd you say you saw that weird guy?" John asked him. "T.J.?"

T.J. said nothing but stood frozen on the spot. He stared so intently at the spire before him that his friends waved their hands in front of his eyes.

"Earth to T.J.," they said teasingly. They finally had to punch him on the arm to snap him out of whatever little spell he was in.

"Ow, cut it out," he said suddenly, rubbing the sore spot where they had pounded him on the arm. "Let's get out of here already. I'm ready to leave," he said and headed back toward the bike.

The other boys shrugged and straggled along behind him. As they trotted along they laughed and horsed around, but T.J. remained silent. He stared resolutely ahead of him as he led the boisterous boys back toward their bicycles. He knew that he had met the ghost of David O. Dodd. He trembled a little at the thought. The neck wounds, the blindfold, the funny clothes, it all added up. But if he tried to tell his friends he would never hear the end of it. There was no way they would believe him.

Over the next few years the boys matured, the desire for girls and parties and cars eventually replacing the desire to play hide-and-go-seek in a graveyard.

What his friends didn't know, however, was that T.J. became a regular visitor to Mount Holly Cemetery. He only had one destination in mind on his visits. He followed the same path he had followed that fateful night with his friends.

He went back because he had to know if what he had seen was real or just a hallucination. Although he never saw him again, he had to keep trying. He had to know if somewhere in Mount Holly Cemetery the strangled ghost of David O. Dodd, the Boy Hero of the Confederacy, still stumbled about moaning, "I'm David—have you seen my mother?"

alice of the hermitage

A hush fell over the ballroom when Miss Alice Flagg appeared at the head of the stairs. Even to the women in the room, her beauty was mesmerizing. She had huge, luminous dark eyes, and her burnished auburn hair fell loosely to her waist. Adorned only by a small diamond necklace, she positively glowed in the soft white gown she was wearing. The hush continued until she had descended the stairs and was met by Dr. Allard Flagg, her older brother. As Allard took her hand and led her into the ballroom, the crowd again erupted into party sounds.

Allard presented his sister to a tall, blonde woman.

"Penelope, may I present to you my sister, Alice. Alice, this is Penelope Ward, my fiancée."

"It's very nice to meet you, Alice. Allard has told me so much about you. Have you and your mother settled in?"

"Yes, we're very happy here, thank you. It was so nice of Allard to invite us to live here. The Hermitage is such a beautiful home, don't you think?"

Allard, who was owner of the family's Wachesaw Plantation, had built the home on Murrell's Inlet just last year—1849. It was to serve as his summer home and the home of Alice and their mother. Alice loved the home, so close to the ocean, and she was happy to be living here.

She was excited by her brother's life here, as well. In the week since they'd arrived, this was the second party he had hosted in their honor. Neither gathering showed any hint of the austerity that the war would bring in a few short years. Elegantly attired young men bowed gallantly before lavishly dressed young women as soft music played in the background.

At age sixteen, Alice welcomed any reason to get dressed up in a fancy ball gown and to dance the night away. She loved the attention, though she was often taken aback by the reaction of other people to her. She had been an awkward, scrawny child and had only blossomed in the last couple of years. She still saw herself as that child and was surprised by the attention her beauty brought.

The reason for this second party had been to introduce her and her mother to Penelope, who had been away when they first arrived. Allard had talked about her incessantly, and Alice had been eager to make her acquaintance.

After their first meeting Alice had circulated a bit, but returned to Penelope, in hopes of getting to know her better. The two had been engaged in small talk for quite some time, and Alice was uncharitably wondering just what Allard was thinking. The woman, though attractive in a horsy sort of way, was thoroughly condescending, spending the entire time pointing out the financial and social foibles of the other guests. Alice was doing her best to be polite, but, frankly, she was bored.

Of course, she did know what Allard was thinking. She knew that the Wards of Brookwood Plantation were the most powerful planters in the Low Country. They cultivated millions of pounds of rice and oats, and thousands of bushels of vegetables every year. They even had a salt making system on the seashore that yielded up to forty bushels of salt daily.

As parishoners of All Saints Episcopal Church at Pawleys Island, the Wards were regarded as examples for others to follow. The rector considered them to be among the most loyal and devoted of his flock. Certainly they were the most accomplished and highly regarded.

They were the elite of South Carolina, wealthy and powerful. And as much as she loved her brother, she knew it was that wealth and power that appealed to him. It was the reason he planned to marry Penelope, despite the fact that she was a boring snob. He valued her social station over love.

That was something Alice could never understand. She valued love over everything. Despite her privileged upbringing, she had never been a snob, had never considered one's social standing as a reason to love or reject. Take, for instance, the man she had met just that very morning while shopping. He was gorgeous. Tall, with dark hair and blue eyes fringed by the longest lashes. So what if he wasn't rich? Or powerful? She didn't care. He was handsome, and sweet, and he seemed to be really interested in her.

She knew neither her brother nor her mother would approve, but she didn't care. She had to follow her heart. She had told him she would meet him in town that next day, and she planned to keep the date. Little did she know just how much her family would disapprove and to what lengths they would go to stop her budding romance.

●●●●●●

The weeks slipped by, with Alice making excuses to go into town as often as possible. There, she would meet with her handsome beau and they would stroll down to the beach, talking and laughing. By the middle of the summer, they had fallen deeply in love, and Alice was in a quandary. She knew she had to introduce him to her family, but she dreaded it. She knew they, in their snobbery, would look down their noses at him, a lowly turpentine merchant. Finally, though, she could put it off no longer. She told him to call on her at the Hermitage the next day.

Alice was up at first light the next morning. She spent more time than usual dressing for breakfast, carefully curling her hair and choosing just the right frock. Her mother and brother were already seated at the table when she appeared. Deciding to broach the subject right away, she nervously took a cup of coffee and sat.

"Umm…Allard, I just wanted to let you know that I will be having some company today. A young man has asked to call on me, and I've invited him over for tea this afternoon."

Allard gave her a wary look. "Well, of course, you may have callers, Alice, but who is this young man and why haven't you spoken of him?"

"He's a prosperous shop owner, Allard, a very nice man. I like him and I hope that you will, too."

"A merchant? You've invited a mere shop owner to call on you here? At the Hermitage? I won't hear of it!"

Angry, Alice rose. "You won't hear of it? Honestly, Allard. Listen to yourself! How can you be such a snob?"

"Alice, you are a Flagg. You must see that a merchant is below your station. Do you want to spend the rest of your life in squalor?"

"There is nothing wrong with loving a man who actually works for a living. Can't you see it's what's inside that matters, not how much money you have or your 'social station'?"

"I'll hear no more. My word is final. Mother, you'll take Alice with you to Georgetown this morning. I'll handle her caller."

"Of course, dear. Alice, go get ready. We'll be leaving in an hour."

Despite Alice's pleading and crying, Allard refused to change his mind. He sent her off with her mother, and, meeting the young man at the front gate, quickly dispatched him back to town. If he thought that was the end of the situation, however, he was mistaken.

Defiant of her family's wishes, Alice continued to see her young man secretly. Each time she was with him, she fell more deeply in love, and she knew he felt the same. She knew if her family would just get to know him they, too, would love him. After several more weeks, she once again invited him to call on her at the Hermitage. They would take a buggy ride, she said. Surely, once Allard saw her determination, he would relent.

This time she did not mention the young man's impending visit. Instead, she carefully dressed and sat in the window of her bedroom until she saw his buggy, pulled by a pair of sleek bays, coming up the lane. She hurried down the stairs and out to the veranda, a smile lighting her face as she watched the buggy pull up. Her young man helped her into the buggy, and they were about to pull away, when Allard rushed down the veranda.

"Wait!"

Alice urged her beau to go on, but, not wanting to make matters worse, he stopped the buggy.

Allard imperiously pulled the young man from the buggy.

"I have ordered my horse brought around. I'll ride in the buggy with Alice and you may ride my horse."

The young man acquiesced and mounted the horse. Allard rode next to Alice, but there was hardly a word passed between them. Alice was seething, but there was not much she could do. When they finally returned to the mansion, Allard stood on the veranda while she and the man said their goodbyes. He did, however, miss the young man silently handing Alice a small diamond ring. Her beautiful smile was the only answer he needed to his unasked question.

Despite her anger at Allard's tackiness, Alice was ecstatic. She was engaged to be married to the man she loved! Somehow, she'd convince her family. When they finally got to know him, they'd love him too. She just knew it.

She was so happy, that it didn't occur to her that she should hide the ring. That evening at dinner, her mother noticed the sparkle on her finger. Grabbing her daughter's hand, she looked aghast.

"What is that on your finger, Alice? My word, it looks like an engagement ring. The diamond is so small, though!"

Allard glanced at the ring.

"What are you thinking? There is no way you are going to marry that man!" he roared. "Give me that ring, so I can return it to him."

"No!"

"Yes! You will return it to him. Now take it off."

Seeing she would get nowhere, Alice removed the ring and put it in her pocket.

"Now, you will return the ring to him, do you hear me? And I don't want to hear any more about this man. Mother and I have discussed it, and we've decided that you will return to Charleston to finish your schooling. I've booked your passage. You'll be leaving in two days."

Tears of anger and frustration rolled down her cheeks. "You can't do this, Allard. I love him. We're going to be married."

"No, you're not. You will do as I say. I know you think me harsh, but truly it is for the best."

Days later, Alice found herself amid the hustle and bustle of Charleston. Alone, depressed, and still angry, she kept to herself, ignoring overtures of friendship from her new classmates. Some elements of Charleston did not suit her: the city was loud and busy, and sometimes less than refined. When not in class, she stayed in her small room, barely eating and grieving over her lost love. Her hand kept straying to the ribbon around her neck, a pink satin ribbon that held the diamond engagement ring, which she had not returned. She always wore it there, close to her heart.

Days passed into weeks, and weeks into months, and still Alice pined. She lost weight, and though she'd become even more beautiful, she looked pale and fragile, like some ethereal being not of this world.

It was in this frail state that she suddenly became ill. Chills and fever wracked her thin body, and by the time Allard, notified by the school's doctor, reached her side, she was delirious from malarial fever. She hardly had the ability to even acknowledge his presence. He quickly had her belongings packed and they began their trek back to the Hermitage.

The journey was long and arduous, with seven rivers to cross by ferry. It had rained the whole way, and the roadways on Murrell's Inlet were sandy and slippery. Several times, Allard had to get out of the carriage and help push it back onto the roadway. All the while, Alice fretted in the back of the carriage, semi-conscious from a burning fever. By the time they reached the Hermitage, she was much worse.

As Allard was lifting her from the carriage, the pink ribbon became uncovered and he saw the ring dangling there. Furious, he grabbed it from around her neck and threw it into the sea, raising a weak cry from Alice.

"My ring! Give me back my ring." But it was gone, disappeared beneath the gray water.

That night, Alice's body, wracked by pain and illness, and her spirit, diminished by her lost love, gave up the fight. Several days later, she was buried, wearing her favorite white ball gown, in the family plot at All Saints Cemetery near Pawleys Island. A plain marble slab was

placed at the head of her grave—a marker with just one word—
ALICE. Modern day visitors to her grave have worn a path around it,
many believing that by circling it backwards thirteen times, they can
summon her. When she is sighted, she always seems to be searching for
something, one hand clutched protectively to her chest.

According to legend, she's spending eternity searching for her lost
ring and, it's said, she doesn't mind taking whatever is close. One
young lady visiting Alice's gravesite reported that the ring on her
finger suddenly flew off. It was a ring that, because of a weight gain,
she'd been unable to remove for more than a year.

The spirit of Alice Flagg still wanders the halls of the Hermitage,
which is a private residence. She's been seen entering the front door
and silently ascending the staircase to her old bedroom on the second
floor. Usually, she's seen in the evening or late night.

the noisiest mill

As the dark clouds flitted anxiously across the the blank face of the moon, the shadowy bulk of the mill towered over the little girl, all four floors devoid of light and unnaturally quiet. She reached for the comforting warmth of her father's fingers, and he squeezed her hand in response.

"Quiet, isn't it?" He threw open the door to the main floor of the grist mill. "I'll get a lamp lit in just a wink."

A matched flared and flickered and then caught on the wide wick of the kerosene lantern that hung on a nail by the door. The meager light made the hulking machinery of the mill seem oversized and threatening, and Ruth stayed close to her father. Even though she had spent most of her waking hours at the mill since she was born, this big echoing room lost all familiarity by lamplight.

The miller took the lantern and crossed the room, stepping up onto the broad staging platform for the giant millstone, which had been shipped all the way from France. As he carefully began to sharpen it, she watched his fingers fly.

His hands were big, with long stocky fingers, a palm almost as big as his daughter's face, and knuckles that were knotted and gnarled as if in protest at the endless round of lifting, loading, tinkering, adjusting, scraping, and hammering. He maintained all the equipment in the mill, from the giant turbines downstairs that turned the great millstone to the grain-cleaning apparatus that stretched up to the third floor and back down again.

Every time something broke down, he would fix it again, sometimes making small modifications to make the mill run more smoothly. The top joint of his third finger on his left hand was missing entirely, a sacrifice to the mill's machinery and, as he often said, a constant reminder to be alert around the great forces at work in the Kymulga Grist Mill.

He had the utmost respect for the raw power of the creek rushing by right outside their windows. The dam allowed him to control its turbulence somewhat, but that was a tenuous control at best. Coupled with the mighty turbines, the water had the power to make almost anything happen, and he held a reverence for that capacity that approached a sense of awe at times. Other forces that lay beyond his sight but were nevertheless undeniable also commanded his respect. He was a big man, but arrogance was not one of his failings.

"Tell me a story, Papa," Ruth begged. This was the great privilege of coming back to the mill with him at night, once the millstone had cooled from its labors, to watch him sharpen the stone. During the day the noise from the equipment and customers' demands on the miller's attention made storytelling impossible. Ruth and her brothers and sisters cherished whatever time they had alone with their father. Ruth had been granted the honor of accompanying him by herself this evening.

"Well," he began, watching his hands very carefully while he sorted through the stories tumbling around his mind. "A scary one?" He glanced up at his youngest child.

She nodded eagerly and then crossed her arms across her chest, hugging herself and rocking gently in anticipation.

"Not too long ago, there was a fine lady who lived across the creek. She had to have the best of everything, no matter what the cost. But some things are just too dear.

"She went visiting some friends one day, and their son had just brought home a splendid black stallion. His coat gleamed, and his mane was long and silky, his gait was proud, and his neck arched so gracefully that she made up her mind she had to have that horse.

"Her horse and buggy were in the stable. Her horse was a perfectly good bay gelding, nice and gentle and well-accustomed to the lady's ways. But the lady had decided that she couldn't live without that stallion. The young man didn't want to sell and argued that she couldn't handle the horse, but the lady was so stubborn, he finally gave in.

"He warned her that the horse wasn't tolerant of loud noises, and he could easily take fright and run away with her and the buggy, but the lady didn't pay him a bit of attention. She just had the stable boy hitch up that lively black stallion, and she went on her way.

"Well that horse gave her no end of trouble. It kind of got to be a joke around here about the lady and the horse she couldn't control. But she was proud as the devil and twice as stubborn.

"One night she took it in her head to go visit some friends and show off a fancy new dress. Her husband told her not to go, but she ordered that black stallion hitched up to her buggy anyway."

The miller's hands, which had been flying on the millstone sharpening it in preparation for the workday tomorrow, now stilled. He leaned closer to his daughter.

"It was a clear night, and the stars were all out, shining down on the earth like a million angel eyes, watching out for little girls and boys. But they weren't watching out for stubborn proud ladies. No, sir.

"That horse pranced and danced down the road, and clip-clopped through that very bridge out there." He gestured to the left with his free hand.

"He was just at the mouth of the bridge when a sound as big as thunder came roaring by, and he screamed and jerked and reared up. Just as the lady was thrown from the buggy, the engineer of the nine o'clock train to Montgomery gave a friendly little toot on his whistle, and the horse, more scared than ever, turned and trampled that lady to death."

Ruth had crept into his arms as he narrated this part of the story. He held her tight.

"Now sometimes when the stars are watching bright-eyed from heaven and the nine o'clock train is due any minute, you can hear the clip-clop of hooves dancing through the bridge. Sometimes when the train is rushing by, you can hear the scream of a horse or maybe it's the cry of a stubborn lady who wanted her way at any price."

Ruth shivered and then reached up with both little hands to pat her father's cheeks. "Papa, are all your stories true?"

He thought for a moment. "I don't know, Ruth. Sometimes they sound true, don't they?"

"Tell me another," she pleaded.

"Not tonight, Ruth. It's time to go home."

When they reached the door he blew out the lantern and hung it back on the nail. As he closed the door behind them, he held Ruth's hand tightly. "Don't be afraid if we see her," he whispered.

"See who, Papa?"

"The lady. She wanders around some at night in that fancy new dress of hers. But she won't hurt you."

"Carry me, Papa." Ruth held up her arms and her father complied, holding her close as they walked through the night.

••••••

"Marcia, this is crazy." The young man carried a blanket and followed the woman as she led the way down the railroad tracks.

"They quit running trains along here in 1967 or something. Believe me—we lived right next to the tracks, so I oughta know, right?" said Marcia.

"What makes you think they didn't tear down the old covered bridge right after you left?" He grumbled but still followed her.

"I read about it in the paper. It's really cool. You'll like it."

"It's dark, and the skeeters are eating me alive."

"It's because you're so sweet."

They walked along the tracks in silence for a few more minutes, the faint beam of her flashlight feebly illuminating a few feet in front of her.

"Aha! I told you so!"

A few hundred yards to the right was a dark shape that looked like a barn, with stairs leading up to it. Only the rushing sound of water indicated that the barnlike structure was a covered bridge.

"Here's a road. Look, we could've driven right up."

"I forgot," she said sheepishly. "Besides, it's blocked. The park's closed at night."

"Great. So we're not supposed to be here at all, right?"

"Get romantic," she commanded him. "This is supposed to be romantic. Look at all those stars."

They stood hand in hand and stared up at the brilliant night sky, punctuated with millions of gleaming points. When she tugged the blanket out of his arms to lay it out on the grass, he did not protest.

They had just settled down when a hollow knocking sound resounded from the bridge. "What is that?"

"It's a horse. It sounds just like a horse on the bridge."

"That's ridiculous. There's no way for a horse to get on that bridge. It'd have to climb up all those stairs."

The steady clip-clop of the hooves continued, drawing closer and closer. All at once, a thundering roar filled the air.

"Holy cow, it's a freakin' train!" Marcia jumped up, yelling to be heard over the noise. The hoofbeats accelerated, and over the high, mournful whistle of the train they heard a scream—horse or human, they couldn't tell.

Suddenly it was quiet again. The cicadas resumed their noisy song, and the bass harrumph of the bullfrogs started up again.

Marcia touched her boyfriend's arm. Her hand trembled. "Randy," she whispered. "That wasn't a real train."

He looked at her with questioning in his eyes.

"We'd have seen or smelled it," she explained. "Touch the tracks."

They did. The unused steel was cold enough to send chills through their fingertips.

• • • • • •

Ruth and her two middle brothers walked with their father back to the mill just before bedtime. The weather had turned cold, almost overnight, so all four walked quickly to get out of the chilly night air. The mill was dark and cold, but at least the wind wasn't blowing inside. Outside the closed wooden shutters, the creek babbled and moaned like a living creature.

"Ralph, help me swing the stone over," commanded the miller. "Ruth, stay clear, now." With very little effort the great stone was levered up and swung over to a spot where the miller could easily bend over it and prepare it for another workday. The system of balances and counterbalances was perfectly designed so that a single man could manipulate it with ease. The miller was teaching his sons the trade.

Once they had all settled in a semicircle around the miller as he worked, Andy asked for a story. "Papa, tell us that story about the fight on the bridge," he asked eagerly.

"That's a great story, Papa. Please?" Ralph chimed in.

The miller looked doubtfully at his youngest daughter. "I don't know," he said slowly. "I don't want to scare Ruth, and that's a mighty bloody story."

"I won't get scared, Papa." Ruth sat up straighter so she'd look older. "Do tell it," she urged.

Again the miller kept his eyes on the task in front of him as he organized the story in his head. "Well," he began, "this old bridge used to be the only way across Talladega Creek for miles and miles, so anybody with business in town or who had to get to the county courthouse had to come right down here. And if you waited long enough, you'd see most everybody in the area either here at the mill or crossing the bridge.

"Not too far from here lived a farmer—Simon was his name, I think. He had two strapping boys, big and strong and both of 'em just as smart as a whip. They grew up, and like all brothers, they had fights ·every now and then. Sometimes they'd even slug it out, but it never was anything serious because deep down they really loved each other.

"The older they got, the more they started to look alike. They were both six feet tall in their stocking feet and could lift up the back end of a loaded wagon with one single hand without turning a hair.

"Trouble came in the shape of a young woman—Louisa. She was beautiful, but you know what your mama says about beauty."

He paused in his work for just a moment to touch Ruth gently on the cheek. "Beauty is as beauty does," Ruth quoted dutifully. "Go on, Papa."

"Louisa may have had fair skin and golden hair, but her heart must've been black as night. She set out to win both men's love, and when she did, she set them against each other.

"'Oh, Peter is so strong,' she'd say to Paul. 'I believe he could break that big old tree over there in half like a toothpick.' Then Peter would call on her, and she'd say something like, 'Your brother is so smart. He told me the other day that he's figured out a way to get twice as much cotton from your farm as you did just last year.'

"Well, the jealousy between the two brothers grew and grew until it was a monstrous thing. Their father tried to reason with them, to tell them what Louisa was doing, because to anyone else, it was as plain as the nose on your face. But the brothers were blind.

"At last, when she had worked them up to a fevered pitch, she told them that she couldn't decide who to marry. She laughed and said she would never be able to choose unless one of them was gone.

"Maybe she didn't know what she was doing. But Paul was so overwrought that he decided to kill his brother. So he lay in wait, right inside that bridge over there." He pointed to the window on his left, tightly shuttered against the rising autumn wind.

"So Peter was on his way home that night, walking easy with hands in his pockets, whistling a little tune. He figured that this thing with Louisa would end up all right because most things in his life did. He wasn't two steps inside the dark, shadowy bridge before a figure flew at him in a fury.

"Peter fought back as hard as he could, but being surprised put him at a disadvantage. First his attacker had him by the throat, but Peter managed to get his hands round the other man's neck and choked him just long enough to get him to let go. Then the other fellow started kicking and kicked so hard that one of the side slats of the bridge was kicked out, and it floated down the stream.

"Peter let loose with a roundhouse punch that would have flattened any other man, and the two of them rolled and tumbled and fought up one side of the bridge and down the other. Peter still had no idea who his assailant was.

"They bloodied each other's noses, and they could feel their fists were wet with blood, but neither one of them would admit defeat. It's hard to believe, but they kept up this fight all night long, till dawn was peeping in the eastern end of the bridge. Sometimes they'd get tired and crawl off to separate corners for just a minute or two, but then they'd catch their breath and one or the other would fly back into the fray. It was a monumental fight.

"When the first little bit of light started creeping into the bridge, both of Peter's eyes were blackened and one had swollen completely shut. His ribs hurt so badly he could barely breathe, and his throat was sore from being throttled. The other man was just as bad off, but neither one was going to give up.

"Peter's assailant cried out for the first time, and Peter saw the glint of steel as his opponent pulled out a knife.

"The knife was coming straight at Peter's heart, and he twisted it back and plunged it into the chest of his brother just as Paul cried out 'Louisa!' Too late, Peter realized it was his brother, deranged by jealousy.

"Paul died in Peter's arms. Peter left the state that same day. Louisa died a bitter old maid years later. They say the boys' father died of a broken heart. Some nights you can hear whistling coming toward the bridge. If you dare stay, you'll hear the noise of a fight like none you've ever heard before, and the anguished scream of a brother killing the one person who loved him best."

The millstone was turning and turning and Ruth cried out in horror. "Papa, look! Your hands!"

As the stone turned and the miller's hands flashed, drops of blood were flying off, spinning into the air to land on the floor in a gory pattern. The miller laughed and stopped the stone. "It's all right, Ruth. It's just my knuckles got so dry the skin cracked." He held out his hands for her inspection, but she flew into his arms, sobbing.

"There, there, girl," he soothed. "It's all right. It's just a story, that's all. Just a story."

"What on earth does this old thing do?" The machine was rectangular, on four legs, with a spout on one side and evil-looking teeth on the inside of the main housing.

"It shucks corn. How many people have we had today?" The woman's knitting needles made a muffled clicking noise as she set her knitting bag on a stool in the old corn room. A Coca-Cola cooler hummed in the corner, and an idle late summer breeze made the wind chimes on display next to the window sigh.

"Five, I think." The other woman straightened out the little stack of maps next to the cash register and then moved on to organize the wooden toys for sale on a card table next to the door.

"Maybe we'll get a school group or two when school starts up again. Or has it started back already?"

"I don't know. I no longer keep track. I'll be going now, if you'll be all right?"

"Sure. Thanks for taking my morning shift. Did you enjoy it?"

The other woman shrugged. "I wasn't much help to the people coming through, but the diagram explains the mill pretty well. I'm glad I could help you out. I'll do it again, if you want me to sometime."

Edna stood in the doorway to watch her friend walk out to her car and wave goodbye before turning back to her knitting. If she spent an hour a day for the next three months on it, she could have a sweater done for each of her grandchildren by Christmas. Afternoons as a volunteer for the Historical Society here at the old Kymulga Grist Mill were dependably boring—perfect for knitting.

She was just turning to the critical part at the top of the sleeve when she heard whistling. Glad for the distraction, she lay down her knitting and stretched, heading for the door to greet the visitors. She hadn't heard their car, but not everyone followed the sign and parked outside the corn room that the Historical Society had turned into a store. She was at the door when she heard a terrific pounding on the bridge a few hundred yards away. Without thinking, Edna went toward the bridge at a jog.

"Is it a dog fight?" she asked herself as she trotted toward the structure. But she didn't hear any whining or barking sounds that dogs usually make. As she watched, something inside struck the side of the bridge with such force that the siding quivered under the blow. She slowed her steps, not sure if she should approach. She wished she'd grabbed her knitting needles as at least some form of self-defense, but she had left them stabbing the ball of yarn in the old corn room.

Edna stood there, undecided, until she heard the sickening, mushy sound of a closed fist making solid contact with flesh. She shuddered and turned toward the corn room and the telephone. This was a police matter.

More thuds and soft grunts of pain or surprise followed her as she hurried back to the store. Then a car horn and a friendly voice dispelled the noise.

"What's up, Edna?" It was Barclay Smith, another Historical Society member.

"Oh, I'm so glad you're here," she stammered. "We've got to stop them before someone gets killed."

He jerked the car to a stop, raising a cloud of dust in the gravel parking lot. "What are you talking about?"

"On the bridge," she gasped. "It's a terrible fight."

To her surprise Barclay smiled. He climbed out of the car and took her elbow firmly. "Steady now, Edna," he advised. "Let's go see."

The bridge was empty. Although she paced over every inch of the floorboards, there was no sign of any kind of struggle. Barclay leaned against the portal of the bridge and watched her search.

"You act like you expected this," she accused him, as she settled down on a bench in the sunshine.

"I've heard it too," he admitted. "It always happens when I'm here by myself. And it always starts with the sound of a man whistling, walking up the road."

"Let's go back to the mill." Edna stood up, dusting off her slacks. "I feel safer there."

••••••

One night, the miller's house was packed full with strangers and anxiety. Granny Holcomb was there, but Ruth knew she never came unless someone was sick. Ruth's mother wasn't exactly ill, but something was awry. The bulge of her belly had just begun to reach noticeable proportions beneath her full skirt and apron. Under the cover of the unfamiliar activity, Ruth and her two middle brothers crept out of the house to join their father at the mill.

When they opened the door expecting to see the miller at his customary spot on the platform, darkness was all that greeted them. Andy tumbled back out of the shadowy space so quickly that he stepped on Ruth and Ralph. "It's dark in there," he said by way of apology.

"You're not scared of ghosts, are you?" Big brothers are good at goading.

Andy bristled. "Course not."

Ruth stepped back to look at the windows.

"Must be fixing the cleaning system," she whispered, seeing a flickering light in the upper story. "He's got his lantern up there."

Ralph looked up and squinted.

"Maybe if we go up there he'll tell us a story while he's working." He poked at his brother. "If you're not too scared to go up in the dark."

In answer, Andy led the way into the echoing, shadow-filled main room, with its hulking machinery and long, spiderlike extensions that groped blindly up to the ceiling and beyond. Ralph and Ruth followed, the little girl reaching for the warmth of her brother's hand, as much for reassurance as for guidance.

Single file, they crossed the room in darkness, shuffling a bit to avoid tripping over any unexpected obstacles. Although the moon was bright outside, the shutters on the ground floor were all tightly closed and latched. The blackness inside was absolute.

At the back of the big room where the noise of the creek was loudest, they reached the stairs. They climbed up, placing one hand on the wall to guide their progress and staying as far as possible from the open side of the stairs. Andy expected to see the welcome gleam of the miller's lantern as his head emerged at floor level of the second story, but only the cold light of the moon showed. The shutters here were left open, except in the coldest weather, to vent the heat and noise and dust that rose like smoke when the massive machinery was running.

"He must be on the third floor," Andy whispered as Ruth and Ralph joined him at the top of the stairs. "Let's go."

Some instinct made the children move as quietly as they could. No one had told them to go to bed; indeed, in the general flurry of anxious women and preparations, they seemed to have been forgotten. Someone sent the older boys, Robert and Charles, to chop wood for the stove. The two oldest girls were in the middle of all the fuss with such a distracted and grown-up air that Ruth was reluctant to approach them.

The stairs to the third floor were narrower and steeper. Andy led the way, creeping quietly, pausing after every step to listen for a sound that would indicate his father's presence. His heart fell as he peered over the edge of the stairs—the third floor was also empty. The tubelike contraptions reaching up from the floor below, the long boxes that agitated the grain to make the chaff fly up and away, all lay still and noiseless before his disappointed eyes.

But above him, accessible only by stairs so sharply inclined and narrow that they were more of a ladder than stairs, he could see a glimmer of light. Andy gestured to the other two to wait while he tiptoed to the foot of the stairs that led to the fourth and highest floor. No equipment was housed up there. It held mostly odds and ends, bits of obsolete equipment, unused lumber, and so many huge rat traps that the children had always been forbidden to climb these final stairs.

Above him, Andy could hear an unearthly, tuneless sound, a cross between humming and moaning, and the scratching, scrabbling noises of hands at work. Goosebumps prickled along his spine until he recognized the sound as his father's peculiar brand of singing. Tone-deaf and acutely aware of it, the miller was in the habit of muttering or moaning his hymns under his breath, barely above the threshold for hearing.

Andy crossed back to his big brother and Ruth. "I don't know what he's doing, but we're not supposed to go up there," he whispered uneasily. "Let's go home."

"They'll just tell us we're in the way," Ralph pointed out, truthfully enough.

"I want my daddy." Even at a whisper, Ruth's voice threatened to break, and the scant light from the opened shutters showed her lower lip protruding stubbornly. The two boys looked at each other, knowing from prior experience what that lower lip signified.

Shrugging a little, disclaiming any responsibility, Andy started for the steep little stairs. Ruth pushed ahead and began climbing. Andy was so close behind, she was almost supported in his arms as she rose.

Their two heads appeared at floor level at almost the same time. Their father sat in a chair near the window, the red lantern at his feet. A shower of wood shavings had made a little mountain by his side, and he carefully, methodically, ran his plane across the two-foot-long rectangular box he gripped between his knees.

The smell of new wood cut cleanly through the familiar odors of the mill, and Ruth watched her father, fascinated as always by the sureness of his motions and the grace of his hands. His back was half-turned to the stairs, and his plaintive humming had masked the sound of the children's footsteps.

At last Ruth became aware of a frantic tugging on her skirt. Andy was below, gesturing wildly for her to descend. Reluctantly she complied. Something told her that her father was not to be disturbed. Just as her view of him disappeared, she realized what had made the picture of her father so incongruous: the tears sparkling on his cheeks were something she had never witnessed before.

••••••

The rain pounded down so fiercely that its sound cloaked even the rushing noise of the swollen creek outside the corn house. Edna yawned and set down her magazine. Early spring was always slow here at the mill, and the rain made it even less likely that visitors would take the detour from the main road to see the old mill, no matter how historic. They might get five people through here in a week.

"Maybe I should just bring a cot," she mused aloud. Her voice was oddly loud, even competing with the steady sound of the rain. She cleared the frogs from her throat.

"Is talking to yourself a sign of senility?" She laughed and stood to stretch her legs. She picked up a feather duster and idly ran it over the shelves of little knickknacks Historical Society members made to sell here at the mill. Her own handiwork was among them: little needlepoint magnets to hang on your dishwasher to tell if the dishes were clean or dirty.

"As if you couldn't see it with your own two eyes," she chuckled to herself. "The things people buy."

A noise from the main room of the mill made her set the duster down with a little click on top of the glass display case.

"Hello?" Edna moved to the Dutch door that separated the corn room from the main mill. She peeked around the door frame just in time to hear the stairs at the back of the mill creak and groan in protest at the weight they bore.

"That's strange," she thought, crossing the mill floor. "I didn't hear a car." The crunching of wheels on the gravel parking lot usually made enough racket to bring her out of the most exciting of daydreams. She stood at the bottom of the stairs and looked up.

"Hello, there?" she called. "You'll need to come pay the admission price at the store, all right?"

When she received no reply, she got irritated. "Some people," she huffed as she climbed the stairs. "No manners at all, I declare."

Once on the second floor, she looked all around. No one was there. But the stairs behind her creaked distinctly, and she turned sharply.

"Look here," she began, but no one was on the stairs. She walked to the foot of the stairs that rose to the next floor. Above her, unseen in the shadows, she heard footsteps again. She shuddered involuntarily.

"Who's there," she croaked and then cleared her throat to call more forcefully. Just then an unearthly sound came floating down from the highest floor in the mill, the fourth floor, which housed only meaningless scrap and bits of rusted machinery. The noise was a cross between humming and moaning—its very tunelessness made it all the more plaintive. Accompanying the sound, in bizarre counterpoint, was the the scraping, scratching sound of a plane moving patiently back and forth against wood.

404

The miller had five children arrayed in front of his chair this night as his hands flashed and blurred white at their work. "Tell us a story, Papa," they chorused, and he was silent for a few moments, chewing the inside of his cheek thoughtfully.

"Well," he began. "This one is absolutely true. It happened a few years ago, when I first came here. And there's really no proper ending, so don't go complaining about that now."

"We won't, Papa," Ruth assured him, her hand touching his knee. He favored her with a sweet smile before continuing.

"I was looking out the window at the creek one day, you know, like I always do." The dam that stretched across Talladega Creek was of critical importance to the mill. It alone gave the power that enabled the giant turbines below the mill floor to turn. Maintaining the dam required constant vigilance—a stray log could puncture the structure and cause the whole dam to crumble and fall away downstream.

The children nodded, eager to hear the rest of the story.

"I saw something out there, just kind of bobbing up and down. It looked to be nearly six feet long, so I decided I needed to get a closer look.

"I went outside and scrambled down the bank of the creek, right next to the dam. I looked, and saw it was a body. I didn't know what to do. We hadn't lived here that long, and I didn't want to make trouble.

"I stood and watched it for a minute. It was all bloated up and awful looking. Then I got to thinking about whether the man had had a family, you know, and I decided I needed to fetch it out and at least give it a decent burial.

"I went to get a pole so I could get it out of the water, and when I came back, it had floated up over the dam and was riding the current. It was gone out of sight in just a few minutes."

"Who was it, Papa?"

"I don't know."

"Was it a colored man?"

"I couldn't tell, Andy."

"What happened next?"

"I don't know. I suppose it fetched up in the Coosa River somewhere. Or maybe it floated all the way to the sea."

The children were silent for a while, contemplating the rigors of such a journey. "Who was it, Papa?" Ruth asked.

"I told you, I don't know. This story doesn't really have an ending." The miller shuddered. "Poor devil. I hope when I'm gone someone'll lay me in a nice peaceful grave."

"Don't say that, Papa." Ruth put her arms around his neck and hugged him tightly, careful not to get near the grindstone. "You'll live forever. Promise me."

The older ones smiled at the child's naive demand.

••••••

The tires on the car crunched and ground to a stop on the gravel surface outside the corn room. Edna had just slipped the padlock over the hasp and turned in annoyance. The sign at the gate clearly stated that park hours ended at six. When she saw the Iowa tags on the car she relented somewhat. A tall young man unfolded himself from the driver's seat and called over to her. "I know it's almost six, but could we look around a minute? I don't know when we'll be back in Alabama."

Edna shrugged and turned to unlock the door. "Just for a moment," she warned. "There's no time for the full tour."

"Thank you so much," the man said warmly. "Come on, Ellen!" He gestured to the woman still in the car.

"Where are you from?" Edna switched on the light and headed for the cash register.

"Des Moines, Iowa. We came to Childersburg just to see the mill."

"It's $2 each, please." She made change for a five and handed him a map and a diagram of the mill. "The money helps the Historical Society keep up the maintenance, you know." She led them into the main room of the mill.

"We still grind corn here every Wednesday. You can buy a bag if you like. I'll rest outside while you look around, if you don't mind. We've had a lot of visitors today. Mind the stairs and don't go past the third floor."

"Thanks again for letting me in. My great-grandfather was the miller here a long time ago."

"Is that so?" Edna pinned him with a sharp gaze. "You'll have to sign our guest book. What did you say your name was?"

"Watkins. Robert Watkins. This is my wife, Ellen." The woman by his side nodded and smiled.

"Well, I'll be. There was a miller here by that name once. A long time ago." Edna was intrigued. "Let me tell you a little about how the mill works." Forgetting her fatigue, Edna gave the visitors from Iowa a full tour, only skipping the climb up to the third floor. She explained the function of each piece of equipment in complete detail while Robert listened attentively.

Dusk was falling when Edna climbed into her car and drove away, raising a cloud of dust as she pulled out of the gravel parking lot. The cloud hung still and lifeless next to the old mill; not a breath of wind stirred the sullen August air.

"Let's go look at the old covered bridge, Robert." Ellen tugged at her husband's arm and he good-naturedly followed her.

"Isn't this just beautiful?" The last light of the day streamed into the mouth of the bridge, filtered by the leaves of the redbuds that crowded close to the creek and the lattice structure.

As they stood there listening to the hush and murmur of the creek below, a new noise broke into their consciousness. A strange groaning, like giant gears shifting and turning.

"It's the mill," Robert whispered, hurrying outside to look at the massive old building.

The moaning of the turbines steadily grew, and turned into a whining sound as they approached full speed. Then a deep-throated rumbling began, rhythmic and insistent. A clanging, clamoring sound of equipment, rattling and banging, rolled out from the mill and across to the bridge where they stood.

"There's no one there," whispered Ellen. "This can't be happening."

They stood in silence, clutching each other's hand tightly, as the noised swelled and crested over them. In a few minutes the sounds died away, leaving an August night that was lacking even the prosaic cicada's song.

"When did your great-grandfather die, Robert?" They were walking slowly back to their car, ready to head for the lights and noise of Birmingham.

"I'm not sure he did, Ellen. I'm not sure he ever did."

voodoo spirit and the ghost dog

"Voodoo, or Voudon," the tour guide said, "came to the Big Easy some time in the late nineteenth-century, from Haiti, which is an island in the Caribbean."

"When the French came to New Orleans they brought voodoo practicing slaves with 'em. That's how come you have a lot of Catholics and a lot of voodoo. And here in St. Louis Cemetery #1, you have the queen of all voodoo practitioners, Marie Laveau."

The tour guide pointed to a large, two-tiered crypt grown over with moss and water stained. Cemetery #1 smelled like a gas refinery, like the by-product of something useful. But it was really just a way station, a gothic no-man's land too full for more corpses, one of New Orleans tourism's stations-of-the-cross. Many of the crypts had been damaged by vandals, and some of the covers had even been pried off so you could see the caskets within. A New Orleans cemetery is like a small city, what is called a necropolis, a maze of little buildings containing the dead. It isn't too difficult for the average tourist to imagine ghosts coming out at night. You had to visit the cemetery, at least once, though it was in a neighborhood you wouldn't dare enter save for the romance and gothic imaginings, or for a drunken adventure. And even then you'd never go at night, but not out of fear of ghosts or even voodoo. Cemetery #1 was known for its brutal muggings.

But New Orleans cemeteries have a deeper history than modern crime. Where, after all, do you bury your dead in a water-soaked city, and where do you bury your dead when there's a lot to bury?

The early colonials of New Orleans began a long and painful relationship with Mother Nature when the burgeoning colony was flattened by a hurricane. It wasn't unusual in a city below sea level for bodies to wash up out of the sodden ground and float through the streets of the French Quarter. New Orleans was a living ghost town, full of gamblers and whores, as well as floating skeletons and ghosts of the dead. But that never seemed to matter to a young country with citizens looking for the Promised Land. A tropical climate and a climate of lawlessness were too inviting, and New Orleans came to be a jewel on the Western frontier.

Jim had been conducting weekly Friday night tours of "Haunted New Orleans" for years now, and he had the routine down perfectly. Give the college kids a little history, toss in some New Orleans folklore, and make up the rest on the spot. He was used to smart-aleck college kids already stoked up on Pat O'Brien's Hurricanes, but as long as they paid for the tour, he didn't care how much they mocked his stories. He'd have done the same. And there was always the tourist couple down from Skokie or Newark, cities Jim had only heard of, who seemed to know more about New Orleans ghosts than he did. Seems everyone's an expert these days.

"Marie Laveau came to New Orleans a free black woman and almost immediately began to embrace the dark arts. By trade, Marie was a hairdresser, so she would fix up ladies' hair, all the while spreading the forbidden seductions of voodoo. Now if you'll look around the cemetery, you'll see coins on some of the tombs or even feathers and strange markings. These are voodoo offerings and you can leave your own if you'd like. So take a look around, but be careful. You never know what's lying in wait around some of these tombs."

Tonight's tour had its share of ghost aficionados, but none more so than Mark Brown and Charles Leake. They were college buddies from Mississippi whose friendship had formed around their love of ghosts and other legends. Mark had introduced Charles to the lore of New Orleans after taking a college course on Caribbean literature, where he'd written a paper on voodoo rituals. So Mark already knew about Marie Laveau and the transport of Haitian voodoo into Louisiana. He already knew a lot about voodoo zombies, and he and Charles considered themselves experts in voodoo movies.

Mark pulled Charles aside behind a crypt topped with what looked like an avenging angel. It was sinister, meant to look like a dire omen to anyone who might consider desecrating the dead.

"Look at that," Mark said. "You see the gargoyle face on that angel? Well, that's meant to ward off evil spirits."

"Sure, this is cool," Charles said, "but don't you think we need to stay close to the rest of the group?"

"I've got an idea. Why don't we stay behind and spend the night here. We can always walk back to the French Quarter."

"No, no, no. You know this place is dangerous. You heard what the guide said about muggings."

"Nah, they have to say that. It's for liability. Besides, why would anyone mug us? We don't have anything to mug."

"Nevertheless," Charles said, "I'd really rather go back. It's a long night ahead, and what are we going to do in here anyway?"

"We'll be able to say we spent the night in St. Louis Cemetery. How cool would that be? Besides, I brought my voodoo doll, and I bought those spells back at the voodoo shop. What better place to cast a spell?"

"Look, I'm interested and all, but this stuff makes me nervous. Maybe we shouldn't be messing around with the dead."

"Oh, come on. It's just for fun."

Charles had already turned to walk back toward the tour group, and there was no way that Mark was going to stay in a cemetery all night by himself. But by the time they got back to Marie Laveau's tomb, the tour group was gone. Mark and Charles couldn't even hear the chatter of Jim, the tour guide. It was as if they had vanished into thin air, and this even began to make Mark nervous as he suddenly remembered he didn't know the way.

"What are we going to do?" Charles asked. "This is your fault. If we get mugged, you're paying me back."

"Take it easy. Let's just calm down for a minute. If we just sit still for a while, another tour group will come along."

But that never happened. Charles and Mark sat down with their backs against the side of Marie Laveau's tomb, and as deeply as Mark was immersed in the lore of New Orleans ghosts, he absent-mindedly forgot about the legend that said the ghost of Marie Laveau would leave her tomb each night to marshal the forces of the undead to spread the voodoo religion. Laveau's ghost was said to walk the French Quarter, and whisper in the ears of tourists the secrets of voodoo practice, inspiring them to dabble in the black arts.

"Do you think Marie Laveau's actually buried here?" Charles asked.

"Yeah, why not?"

"I don't know. Don't you sometimes wonder if all this witchcraft and ghost business isn't just invented to bring tourists in? I mean without all the ghosts, New Orleans would just be a good place to drink, and you can drink anywhere. They need these ghosts to survive, just like Savannah."

"You're a cynic, man. Of course it's real," Mark said, launching into one of his sermons on the absolute realism of hauntings, how like alien abductions, there were too many eyewitness reports for all of them to be false.

"Look," Mark said, "sure some hauntings are false. My priest was actually asked by a man to perform an exorcism of his apartment because he said beer cans kept moving around, and food was disappearing from his refrigerator. But Father Gerald performed it anyway, even though he thought the man just a drunk. And he probably was just drunk and hallucinating. But you've got to take this stuff seriously. If a priest takes it seriously, man, well...."

While Mark was pontificating on the authority of the Church in recognizing and expelling the dark arts, neither he nor Charles noticed that the door to Marie Laveau's tomb was slightly ajar. The cemetery was full of creaking noises, howling cats, and a strong gusting wind, so neither of the young men heard the sound of scrapping concrete as the door opened. If they'd turned and looked around the corner of the tomb, they could have seen Marie Laveau's yellow eyes and smelled her deathly breathe.

But the ghost of Marie Laveau was entirely aware of the two young men casually at rest against the side of her palace. The ghost of Marie Laveau acted as mayor of St. Louis Cemetery, and she was highly protective of her necropolis and its denizens of the black arts. What Marie's ghost knew that no one else did was that every soul in St. Louis refused to enter the afterlife because the cemetery was such an inviting home, because she was like a mother of them all. Laveau and her minions refused heaven, refused hell, refused even purgatory. They were happy in their walled city of the dead.

But ghosts also cannot abide doubters, so before Charles could even fully engage in argument with Mark, a bejeweled but decomposing arm reached out of the tomb and grabbed Charles by the neck, pulling him toward the tomb's gaping maw. "Oh, God," he screamed, "don't let it get me!"

But the ghost of Marie Laveau was too powerful; it held tightly to Charles's legs, and Mark became overwhelmed by a torrent of roaches and maggots that came pouring out of the tomb's door. Charles was pulled into the tomb of one of the most notorious ghosts in the world, and Mark watched helplessly as the tomb's door slammed shut. He began pounding on the tomb, but his knowledge of voodoo culture had taught him that he might never see Charles again.

Mark fell to his knees and began crying. How would he ever explain this to Charles's parents? How would he explain this to their friends? Would he ever get out of this situation alive? But the cemetery then became more hellish than he'd ever imagined. All of the tombs began to open, and Mark saw all manner of ghosts leave their tombs and begin collecting the gifts left behind by the living. Some picked up flowers and teddy bears, while other ghosts began to manicure the tiny spaces of grass around their graves as if tending their lawns. Mark knew that ghosts wanted to go on as if they were still living.

Mark remained pinned to the wall of Marie Laveau's grave when suddenly a ghost dog, distracted by the form of a living presence in the cemetery, trotted over and began to lick Mark's hand, to do what dogs love to do, comfort human beings. As Mark began to relax, he sat back down and as the ghost dog curled up at his feet, he began to drift off from exhaustion and fear.

When he awoke the next morning, the sun was already high in the sky, and Charles was shaking his shoulders.

"Wake up, man, wake up."

When Mark came to, he was suddenly unsure if the night's events had happened, if he wasn't, perhaps, still in a dream.

"Did all that really happen?" he said. "Were you really in Marie Laveau's tomb all night?"

"I don't know what you're talking about, man. We spent the night in the cemetery, like you wanted."

"But there was a ghost dog and you were pulled into her tomb. I thought you'd gone to live with the voodoo spirits," Mark said.

"I have no idea what you're talking about, dude, but I'm ready for a po' boy or something. Let's get out of here."

"But it all seemed so real."

"It is all real," Charles said. "Isn't that what you've been saying since I met you, that ghosts and haunting were real, that we can access the dead and all that stuff?"

"Yeah, but...."

"Yeah, but nothing. If you think it happened then it must have happened. I don't remember anything but your hairbrained idea to sleep in the cemetery and now I'm ready to eat some lunch and knock back a few beers. And you, my man, you need a shower!"

There was little for Mark to do except wonder if he'd ever know the truth. But as he sat across from Charles over that afternoon's lunch it looked to him as if Charles's eyes were slightly darker, as if something wasn't quite the same.

the headless dog of tug fork

The peddler whistled to his dog and picked up his pace. It had been a long and dusty day, and the thin column of smoke he saw rising from the woods up ahead was a welcome sight. It meant trade, a long cool drink of water, a good hot meal, maybe, and most of all, human company.

"Come on, Rex!" he called, urging on his own tired feet as much as the dog's. The creature was coal black and leggy, with an oversize head and floppy ears, and often the peddler's only source of companionship for days on end. Rex was fine company, except for the fleas, but he wasn't much on conversation. And it was conversation that the peddler craved, like some men craved whiskey or women.

It was a mean little cabin—more like a hut, with big gaps between the logs that the settler hadn't bothered to chink with mud or moss. The yard in front was churned-up mud, dried now and difficult for the peddler to traverse with his heavy, awkward pack. The peddler's nose wrinkled as he picked his way across the ridges and hillocks of dried mud; he didn't smell anything cooking. There was no sign of a garden or any crop being cultivated, so this must be a trapper's cabin, he surmised. Just as he thumped on the door, two underfed, rangy yellow dogs shot out from behind the cabin.

They set upon Rex, and the peddler watched, amused. He'd not seen the dog yet that could take old Rex down. Sure enough, in short order, Rex had sent one cur yelping back to its hiding place, while the second cringed down on the ground and whined in abject submission.

"Git yer dog off my land." The door had opened just a crack, and the peddler jumped to hear a human voice growling from the darkness within.

"Howdy," he said, friendly enough. "I reckon they're just figuring who'll be boss, that's all. No harm done."

"I said git off my land."

"I've got all kinds of sundries for sale today, good sir," the peddler continued. "You might be in need..."

The black barrel of a shotgun appeared from the darkness.

"And a good day to you, too, sir," the peddler said, hastily backing off. "As I said, no harm done!" He backed away from the door nearly fifty feet before the gun was withdrawn and the door slammed shut.

An especially deep rut in the yard caused the peddler to stumble and almost fall to the ground, and he cursed under his breath before turning to head back to the trail. Rex followed, his tail drooping as he sensed his master's mood. It was now near dark with no prospect of shelter, hot food, or conversation in sight.

••••••

The rider let the horse walk at its own pace, and the reins dangled loosely from his hands. The dusty road wound out before him, twisting this way and that. Here and there, a light gleamed between the trees, signs of a growing community. At the top of the hill, silhouetted against the rising moon, was a skinny, straight-pointing finger of brick—the chimney and foundation were all that remained of the old schoolhouse, which had been dismantled last year and carried to town a mile east.

The rider's thoughts ambled as carelessly as his horse, and he mused about the growth of the little town that made a bigger schoolhouse necessary. The building's abandoned skeleton sat up on a little rise, and he could see, clearly in the moonlight, a creature scrambling down the bank toward him and his horse.

He felt a little chill of fear. His hands tightened on the reins, and he clucked softly to the horse, which pretended not to hear.

The creature was drawing near. The rider and his horse were now a scant twenty yards from the old schoolhouse, and the shape cantered forward on four lanky, tightly muscled legs. Its chest was deep and broad, and its tail was a jaunty flag in the moonlight.

The rider's brain registered, faintly, that the creature cast no shadow—and had no head.

He called out loudly, heedlessly now, "Run!" He slapped the reins hard against the horse's flank and dug his heels into its sides, but the horse was tired and took two, three running strides, and then fell back into an ambling walk.

Heart thumping painfully against his ribs and sweat rolling down, stinging his eyes, the rider twisted to look behind him. The horrible creature was loping just behind his horse's rear feet, now crouching, gathering its powerful muscles to spring up on the horse's back.

The rider gave a low moan. The headless monster leapt and landed just behind the saddle. Its weight did not seem to affect the horse in the least—oblivious, it plodded on down the road.

The rider could not tear his eyes away from the bloody spectacle inches away from his eyes. The torso was black, with short, silky fur— clearly, it was an animal in its prime. But where its head ought to be was nothing more than a gaping wound. Peering close, the rider could see bloody tendons, torn flesh, and a hint of gleaming white bone or cartilage.

The rider could bear it no longer. He clenched his eyes shut and turned forward to face the road ahead, the hairs on the back of his neck prickling up in fear of the creature at his back. He wrapped his hands around the saddle horn and prayed wordlessly that he would somehow hang on and live through this terror.

The horse's hooves thudded on a little plank bridge. One, two, three, four, five—at the fifth thump on the wood, the rider dared to open his eyes and twist around backward in the saddle. Behind him was only air, but he could see a shadow on the ground, merging with other shadows before the moon was chased behind a cloud.

"Why, Edward, what's the matter?" His wife met him at the door after he'd stabled the horse. "You're as pale as a ghost!"

He wordlessly removed his hat, and she screamed. When he reached for her, she backed away, whimpering. "What happened to your hair, Edward?"

When he stooped to peer into the looking glass, he saw that his thatch of unruly black hair had changed to pure, glistening white.

••••••

The peddler climbed the twisting, turning trail, and Rex plodded alongside. The man didn't see or smell any wood smoke, and that meant he'd have to find a clearing to make camp. But he wanted to be sure he was off the hostile trapper's land first.

With his head down, watching his feet, the peddler didn't notice the building until he was nearly upon it. It was a simple, square structure, built of sawn wood with two glass windows. The chimney climbed straight and true, and the peddler's heart rose.

"Here we go, boy," he said happily to Rex. The dog's tail levitated. The peddler toiled up the little rise until he reached the building's door. It smelled wonderful—a fresh, new pine smell, and the man breathed in deeply.

"Looks like a brand-new schoolhouse, Rex," he announced, noting the squat little belfry above the door in the rapidly fading light. "Bet they wouldn't mind a guest or two, as long as we're tidy."

Rex gave a short, sharp little bark. He recognized a conversational pause when he heard it.

In the dark, the peddler made his way to a stream nearby and filled the water pail that swung from the bottom of his pack. He gathered some sticks for kindling, and Rex dragged back a respectable-size branch from the edge of the woods.

The peddler began to whistle softly, the prospect of a night within shelter raising his spirits considerably. When a little fire burned merrily in the new brick fireplace, he set on a pot of water to boil. He made himself a potful of corn mush, spooning out half onto a tin plate for Rex. After they finished eating, they curled up together by the fire in a nest of blankets.

••••••

The boys were rowdy. It may have been because they'd had a few nips of old man Jenkins' cider at the party—or maybe it was just high spirits. They strolled up the road in the moonlight. Sometimes at a bend in the road, one would dash ahead to hide behind a tree and spring out at the rest, laughing wildly at their fright. One carried a cane, swinging it out jauntily or tapping it none too gently on the calves of the boys lagging behind. There were five boys, but they made enough noise and expended so much energy running up and down the road that they seemed more like ten.

When the road twisted to the left and began a gentle ascent, one by one, the boys began to lose their exuberance and walk a little closer together. There was no outward sign of anything amiss—the moon still shone brightly and the warmth of the cider, or just good spirits, still sang sweetly in their veins.

But on a bank above them, silhouetted starkly against the gentle black sky, rose a single gnarled finger—an abandoned chimney. The boys had been raised on tales of a headless hound that haunted this stretch of road, but they were too old now for such foolishness. They didn't believe in ghosts.

Still, they walked closer together, their voices hushed. Not until they were past the heap of bricks did their mood rise.

"Whoooooooo!" shouted one, waving his cane high above his head.

"Ooooooooh," groaned another, and he twirled around, spinning in the center of the road. What he saw behind him made him draw in his breath with a soft cry.

"Ahh," he said, and a shudder enveloped his bony frame.

Another boy turned to look, and he, too, could make nothing but a soft aspirating sound of pure terror.

Trotting behind them, with an intentional air, was a large black dog. His tail was not waving, but it was up—a sign of no-nonsense attention to business. His chest was broad and deep, and his fur gleamed with blue highlights in the moon's light.

The dog had no head.

Where his head should have been was a gaping wound oozing a thick, viscous, glistening black fluid; in sunlight, it would have been an unforgiving scarlet. The brave boy who dared to stare, feet moving automatically to maintain his distance from this silent horror, might have caught an occasional glimpse of something white shifting and moving through the gore: bone, perhaps, or cartilage.

Not one of the boys spoke. But at least one of them noticed that the grim apparition cast no shadow, even though the moon shone just as brightly now as before. The boys picked up their pace until they were moving with that stiff-legged gait that is closer to a run than a walk. Some of them moved backward, too afraid to turn their backs on such a terrifying creature. The others simply could not watch the unnerving spectacle of the headless dog calmly loping along the road.

The dog's legs moved faster until it caught up with the little cluster of boys. They spread apart, reluctantly, to accommodate the hound in their midst. Now his tail whipped back and forth, playfully, and he dropped his forelegs down to the ground, leaving his rump up in the air, challenging a boy near the back of the little group. The boy's face turned chalk white and then a ghastly shade of green. He stumbled but managed to sidestep the dog.

Next, the creature ran in wide, teasing circles around the biggest boy in the crowd. He bounded in and out, between and beside the boys, his tail carving loops in the air. Still, the boys walked on in silence.

When the fleetest boy's boots hit the little plank bridge that crossed Tug Fork, they made a thudding sound. The sudden noise elicited a grunt of fear from the last boy in the cluster.

"Uhh," he said, involuntarily.

The dog suddenly lay down in front of his feet, rolled onto his back, and raised his paws into the air, a frisky gesture. The boy stopped so quickly that he lost his balance and would have fallen, except that the boy with the cane snatched his forearm and held him upright.

"Take that," he yelled, and thrust the cane through the creature's rib cage. The other boys, as if released from some evil spell, all took flight like the devil himself was on their heels. The cane stuck fast in the dirt of the road. First with a jerk and then a tug, the boy tried to pull it up—it would not come loose. Seeing his companions disappear down the road, the last boy, too, turned tail and ran like the wind.

••••••

Rex was growling. It was so low that it was more a vibration deep in his broad chest than a true vocalization, but either the sound or the movement woke the peddler. He left his eyes closed for a scant moment and then slit them open just wide enough to survey the room as best he could without turning his head.

The dying firelight gave the schoolroom a faintly hellish glow. Just barely, out of the corner of his eye, the peddler could make out a shape stooped over his pack, which he'd dropped carelessly in the corner by the door. It was the faint clinking sound of metal against metal, hands pawing through the utensils in the pack, that had roused Rex.

The peddler dared to turn his head a fraction. The thief had brought a shotgun, and it lay on the floor beside the peddler's pack. If the peddler had been alone, he would have feigned sleep until the thief was gone—he had no stomach for a fight, and his money was all neatly sewn into a belt around his ample waist, anyway.

But he had no way to communicate his wishes to Rex. The dog's growl grew deeper, and the peddler could see firelight gleaming on his long, sharp teeth as his lips drew back in anger. The big dog's muscles tensed, drawing up to leap at the intruder, and the peddler shifted slightly—they might as well both jump at the same time.

With a roar and a yell, the peddler and his dog launched themselves at the intruder. Rex went for the neck, and the peddler went for the shotgun. Reflexively, the thief's hands went up to protect himself, and his cry of pain as the dog's teeth ripped through flesh sounded vaguely familiar to the peddler—it was the unfriendly trapper from a few miles back down the trail.

Rex released the man's hands and thrust his snout back into the man's belly, seeking a good hold. The man rolled up into a ball and kicked out at Rex, who yipped sharply as the man's feet made contact with his head. The momentum of the kick sent the thief tumbling out the open door, and Rex flew down the stairs in pursuit. The peddler followed, shotgun held loosely in one hand.

The peddler figured it was a fairly even fight until he saw the gleam of metal in the trapper's fist. Again the thief kicked out at Rex, gaining enough time to rise to a crouch, knife at the ready. Before Rex could run back into the fray, impaling himself on the held out blade, the peddler raised the shotgun like a club over the trapper's head.

The trapper grabbed the barrel and flipped the peddler onto his back, where he lay helpless, gasping. Rex dove in, but it was too late. The trapper's knife was sinking deep into the peddler's chest, and blood spurted up, black in the uncertain light of the moon.

As the trapper struggled to withdraw the blade from the peddler's body, Rex sank his teeth deep into the trapper's forearm. With a wild cry of agony, the man swung around, looking desperately for a weapon. The shotgun lay inert upon the ground, its barrel glinting evilly in the moonlight. He laid his hand on it, almost sobbing now in fear. Rex gathered himself for a last lunge at the trapper's throat, and the man found the trigger at the same time.

Bits of gristle, flesh, and fur rained down on the trapper's face. Gobbets of blood ran into his eyes. The shotgun had discharged just as Rex made his leap, and the barrel had been mere inches from his head. Momentum propelled the headless creature forward, and his carcass landed heavily on the trapper's chest, incapable of any further physical attack.

••••••

"Slow down, Danny!" The young man beat against the pickup's back window with the flat of his hand. The truck was careening wildly over the twisting, climbing road. Bits of asphalt were clattering around the tires and sometimes got propelled up into the truck bed, stinging the faces of the occupants.

The brake lights flashed red, and the truck skidded to a stop instants later, tires shrieking madly. A dangerous smell of overheated metal hovered over the vehicle like a pall.

The young man who'd shouted at the driver jumped out with a fluid, easy grace. He jerked open the driver's door.

He sprang to one side just in time—a thick stream of vomit burst forth. Danny had slumped over, his head just over the road, retching fiercely. The shoulder belt was all that kept him from falling out.

When he stopped retching, two of his friends gingerly unstrapped him and laid him out flat in the back of his pickup— maybe the chilly wind would revive him. The event distinctly dampened the spirits of the little party.

They proceeded but had not gone more than a mile before the truck coughed and shuddered. The three people jammed in the cab groaned and looked at each other—they were still eight miles out of town. The two conscious passengers in the pickup's bed barely heard the noise.

The engine quickly recovered, but a hundred yards up the road it coughed again and died. They were halfway up a little hill, and it was dark—even the headlights of the truck seemed pale against the sullen thick shadows. They all piled out, except the drunk, who stirred slightly and moaned. They stood in a semicircle around the engine, the opened hood gaping like a toothless mouth around their heads. Above them the jagged lines of an abandoned chimney reached to the sky like a pointing finger.

"Carburetor," said one shortly.

"Fuel pump," another argued.

After twitching this wire and rearranging that one, the man with the keys jumped back in. The engine turned and held, sputtering just a little at the start. The other two got back into the cab, while the two rear passengers walked around to jump back into the truck bed, close to the shelter of the cab.

"Aww, man," one moaned. "Dave, do you see that?"

Dave could not speak. Next to Danny's limp body, stretched out in the truck bed, was the long, bloody carcass of a black dog. As

Dave watched, horrified, the creature shifted, its big paws skittering to find a purchase on the slick painted surface. As the creature stood up, the reluctant moon sprang out from behind a cloud, flooding the scene with light. Dave screamed.

The dog had no head.

At the end of its neck, where its collar should be, was a ragged open wound. Tattered flesh shivered in the slight breeze, and black blood winked evilly from the dog's once silky fur. The unconscious man didn't stir.

The car horn blared irritably. "What's wrong with you?" the driver thrust his head out the window and shouted at the two young men standing transfixed in the road. They shook their heads, and a shudder coursed through them with such violence that it was nearly comical. Cautiously, without taking their eyes off the horrible apparition, they climbed into the rear corners of the truck bed.

"Get up here!" The driver was motioning them to move up close to the cab, but they just shook their heads, still mesmerized by the bloody sight before them.

When the truck started with a jerk, the dog swayed and started sliding toward the rear of the truck. The young man sitting on that side whimpered and pulled his knees closer to his chest.

The dog caught himself and stood, tail up and legs braced, while the wind of their passage ruffled his fur. If he had a head, he'd be smiling, Dave thought stupidly. His next thought was to swear off tequila for good because this was just too, too weird.

The moon slid behind a cloud and the truck bed was suddenly filled with shadows. The tires thudded onto a different surface, concrete instead of asphalt. The wheels whispered softly, water murmured below them, and somehow, the passengers in the truck bed could breathe a little easier.

When their eyes adjusted to the renewed gloom, the dog was gone, and Danny lay where they had placed him, hands crossed across his chest in an oddly formal way. The look they exchanged grew into an unspoken agreement not to share this experience with anybody—no one would believe it, anyway. Five minutes later, the truck pulled up in front of a house.

"Should we wake up his folks?" The young man who spoke was out of breath because he and the others had just hoisted down Danny's unconscious bulk from the truck bed.

Dave shook his head and found his voice. "Ahh, I hate to," he said doubtfully. "They'll be pretty mad." They propped their friend up between them and half-dragged, half-carried him up the stairs.

When the porch light snapped on, pinning them in its glare, they knew their decision had been made for them.

A woman clutching her robe tightly shut around her thin frame peered out the screen. "Ooooh, Danny," she wailed, her face contorted by sorrow and fear. "Whatever happened to your hair?"

forever faithful

"My God," she said when she had recovered. "Don't sneak up on me like that! How can you move so quietly?"

Claire shrugged, her free arm cradling several stout limbs of respectable size. "I wasn't that quiet," she protested. "Why did you scream?"

"Because you *scared* me."

"No, not now, before."

Her friend looked at her like she'd lost her mind. "I didn't scream."

"Somebody hollered," Claire said stubbornly. "I heard it. You didn't hear anything?"

Her friend shivered again. "No," she said shortly. "Let's get that fire built, shall we?" With a grand, sweeping gesture, she invited Claire to precede her up the bank to their campsite.

"This isn't enough wood," Claire said.

"There's a tree limb down over there that was too heavy for me. Come on. We can handle it together."

By the time they'd gathered enough wood to suit themselves, the forest was enveloped completely in thick, black shadows. Claire giggled as she rummaged through her pack for a flashlight or box of matches.

"It's so dark that I literally can't see my hand in front of my face," she said. "But I can hear that box of matches—it's down near the bottom of my pack."

"Of course," said Natalie. "Anything you really need is at the bottom of the pack—it's Murphy's Law."

They cooked a simple meal of beans and rice, sopping up the juices with thick hunks of French bread. When they finished eating and were sipping coffee to ward off the chill, they built up the fire into a roaring conflagration that seemed to nearly touch the treetops.

"Look at the sparks fly," Claire said dreamily, lying on her back with her bedroll under her head.

Just then a low growl on the trail below made both women sit up. Blood pounded through their veins, and their senses were instantly acute. They listened, but heard nothing more—not even the softest sound of padded footsteps on the forest floor.

"An acoustic trick?" Natalie guessed. "Sound travels better up here?"

Claire shrugged. She sat cross-legged, hunched over her sleeping roll, which was now compressed into a tight little ball in her lap.

"Anything to worry about, Claire?" Natalie's voice quivered a bit.

Claire shrugged again, still listening. Then she forced herself to sound confident. "No big deal, Nat. Maybe some hunter left his dog up here."

Natalie regarded her doubtfully. "They don't allow hunting up here, do they? I'd hate to think we're stuck up here on a mountain miles from anywhere with some whacked-out gun-waving hunter."

"You're right. It was probably some weird acoustic trick, the sound carrying to us from miles away." Claire sat up and dragged the food pack closer to the fire. "Didn't we bring a bottle of brandy?"

They had barely splashed a little brandy into their plastic coffee mugs before there was an explosion of sound on the trail below. They sat, frozen, as a chorus of growls, barks, sharp yips of pain, and occasionally the sickening sound of ripping flesh gave evidence of a mortal battle. The cacophony of pain and anger sounded as if it were no more than ten feet away, just below them on the main path that led down the mountain to their car—and safety.

Finally, the noise died away. Natalie was the first to find her voice. "Claire," she whimpered. She crawled over to her friend, and they just silently held each other, mute with terror.

They shook and rocked, shook and rocked for what seemed to be an eternity. The fire threw out a meager circle of light, illuminating their tent and an area a few feet beyond. Past the firelight was a darkness so black that not even the shadows moved. It was more than an absence of light—the darkness was a palpable, living entity, with a texture like fur and a smell like fear. The two women were utterly, totally isolated.

"Howdy." The figure broke loose from the blackness, pulling free from the shadows and slowly, hesitantly edging toward the warmth and light of the fire.

The sudden deadweight of Claire in her arms somehow translated into a coherent thought in Natalie's mind: "She's fainted—now we're both going to die." She clenched her eyes shut as tightly as she could and thought again, "Dear God, why can't I think of anything to say to You?" The words "we who are about to die salute you" ran through her mind, but she dismissed them impatiently—that was something Roman gladiators said to the emperor. "Is there nothing to say? Am I going to die with all these stupid thoughts running through my head?" she thought.

Nothing happened. No earth-shattering revelations, but no bright, blinding flash of pain either. Natalie slit open one eye to see if she had only hallucinated the presence of a strange old man thirty miles from the nearest town and ten miles up from any passable road.

He was hunkered down by the fire, examining the lightweight plastic bottle they'd carried the brandy in. As she watched, he snapped off the top and sniffed.

"Mind if I try some?" He gestured with the bottle in Natalie's direction, and she squeezed her eyes shut again. Her mind's eye flashed on a possum she'd seen once, its stiff, anxious posture such a ridiculous commentary on its hopeless, uncontrollable desire to live that she had snorted in laughter. She saw herself as that possum now, and although she could not laugh, she could at least force her eyes to open and face whatever lay ahead.

"Sure," she croaked. Claire stirred beneath her and then raised her head, cracking it resoundingly on Natalie's elbow. They both howled in pain, tears coming up quick and hot, while the man surveyed them over the neck of the bottle.

"That smarts," he commented when the two women had calmed down enough to hear him.

"Who are you?" Claire's tone was menacing enough, but her body posture gave her away. She was trying to unobtrusively scoot backward on her rear end.

"Ed." He grinned, and they could see neat little squares of lightlessness, just like the night beyond the campfire, irregularly spaced within his mouth. "Ed Welch. This stuff tastes like lighter fluid." He gestured with the bottle, and the women saw that two-thirds of its contents were gone.

Natalie was beyond being afraid. "Where did you come from?" she demanded.

"Over next ridge a ways. Didn't mean to scare you."

His gaze fell over Natalie to the tent behind her. She turned to see Claire, still sitting and scooting, duck out from the flaps with the flashlight in her hand.

"You'd just better sit still, mister." Claire's tone was still threatening, and now she had a weapon of sorts to back it up.

He threw up his hands, and Natalie noticed suddenly how thin he was. "I don't mean you any harm, really I don't."

"But where did you *come* from?" Natalie repeated stupidly.

"Over yonder." He pointed again, patiently.

"Why did you come this way? Where are you going?"

"Ssshh." The man was instantly alert, cocking his head to listen. From the trail below came a short series of yips, whines, and yelps. Two dogs, by the sound of it, confused or hurt or both.

The women tensed, and Claire let the flashlight hang down by her side, forgotten and useless against this unseen threat.

The noise died away. The man relaxed, his long bony hands dangling over his knees.

"What was that?" Natalie whispered.

"Them's Bill Sawyers' dogs," he replied matter-of-factly. "They'll be at it all night, most likely."

"What's wrong with them?" Claire was intrigued in spite of herself. The man shrugged. "Can't rest, I reckon."

"What do you mean?"

"It was a terrible thing." He shook his head and then raised the bottle again. "Can I?"

The two women nodded, nearly spellbound by this apparition in the wilderness.

"Bill got up about sunrise one morning and decided to go check on some calves up in the pastures. You know he kept cattle for Jess Siler?"

The women nodded again, since this seemed to be the anticipated response. Natalie wondered for the first time if this man was all right in the head.

"There was bear up here then and wolves and wildcats that'd take a calf or about anything they thought they could get away with. So Bill kissed Callie goodbye, whistled up his dogs, and told the children to mind their ma. Let's see, there was..." He whispered to himself and counted on his fingers before continuing. "There were nine of them—nine children in all.

"Bill had lots of dogs, too, for hunting, herding cattle, guarding the cabin, you know. But his two favorite dogs were Lead and Larry. Lead was a big blue-spotted hound, sort of, but really mostly mutt. Larry was just an old black-and-tan dog, floppy ears, and long legs. They loved that man, and he all but let them sleep in the bed with him and Callie—Callie drew the line at that. She was a Welch, come right down to it, and that meant she could be pretty doggone stubborn."

Again the man grinned. Natalie's eyes were drawn to the intricate network of wrinkles that crisscrossed his face, radiating from the edges of his mouth and the corners of his eyes.

"Bill told her he'd be back by dinnertime, or maybe supper if the calves had strayed any. Callie watched him walk out onto that trail that twisted and turned up to the high meadows where sweet grass grows, and then she turned to her own work. There was nothing at all unusual about his leaving.

"When supper came and there was no Bill to say the blessing, Callie was just a bit uneasy. But the children were quick to pick up her scare, so she put it behind her for their sakes. She probably told them stories before they went to sleep—she was good at telling stories.

"Sometimes storytelling reaches back and bites you, though, because she told me that she couldn't sleep a wink that night. She kept thinking up reasons why Bill hadn't come home, and every story made her more worried. She would jump at the least little sound thinking it was him on the path, but it never was. Poor Callie—it was the longest night.

"When the sun first started coming up, Callie jumped right out of bed and stirred up the fire—October mornings get pretty chilly. While she was putting breakfast on, she heard a scratching at the door. So worried about Bill that she could hardly think straight, Callie ran right over and opened it up. On the doorstep was old Lead, the blue-spotted dog. She was glad to see him and called out his name, thinking Bill would be right along in a minute.

"But Lead was acting real funny. He whined and ran up the path a ways and came back whining. When he ran up the path and barked, it was clear as day that he wanted her to follow him. Well, Callie grabbed her wrap and a piece of pone bread and ran out the door—she was so eager to go find Bill. She tossed Lead the bread as a reward, but he didn't gobble it down. He carried it real careful in his mouth and trotted up the path and around a bend.

"Callie followed along behind Lead, and the farther they went, the heavier her heart got. She just started knowing, somehow, that things were not right. The trail twisted and turned, and once, near the top of the ridge, she lost sight of Lead. Then she heard the boisterous barking of Larry, and she started running to the turn in the trail.

"Bill was there. His body was cold, and his face was all screwed up like he'd had an awful lot of pain. But his footsteps and the dogs' paw prints were the only marks on the trail, and there wasn't a mark on Bill, so Callie figured he'd died of the cramps. They call it appenda-something now, I think. Hurts like the devil but can't kill you if you see a doctor quick."

The old man's audience sat, truly spellbound now, having edged their way to the fire's side. They could only nod and murmur, caught up in his story.

"Out of the corner of her eye, Callie saw Lead drop something and Larry turn it over with his nose. It was the hunk of bread she'd given Lead back at the cabin, and she watched, amazed, as Larry carefully bit the piece of food in half, leaving Lead a share.

"I imagine she cried a little to see these two good dogs that had stayed by their master all through the night. And you know how animals are—they understand how you feel. Larry came over to her as she sat with Bill's head in her lap and lay down, pressing close against her while she cried. Lead stood over her shoulder and leaned on her while he cried a little, too. They were mostly confused, though, like they just didn't know why Bill didn't get up and go on.

"Pretty soon Callie dried her tears and started thinking what could she do. Bill was a big man, and she couldn't carry him down the mountain—she had to get some help from another adult. Her sons, her oldest ones that is, were just thirteen and eleven. Her brother Bert lived twelve miles away, and he could help her do what needed to be done to get Bill taken care of.

"Looking up at the sun, she decided she had just enough time before dark to get her children to Bert's cabin. She kissed Bill and laid his hat across his face, but she hated to leave him there alone. She told those dogs very firmly to stay, and although she could tell they wanted to come with her, they did, finally, sit down next to Bill's body. That was a sight she would remember the rest of her life: her tall, lanky husband lying in the middle of the path, flanked by those two loyal creatures sitting proud and tall."

A growl came from the trail below, sounding as close as the edge of the circle of light thrown by the fire. Natalie jumped and shrieked softly, her fingers digging into the soft flesh of Claire's arm. Claire, too, paled, and the storyteller smiled, exposing again those coal black gaping holes between his teeth.

"Callie was a strong woman, and she did not panic or make the children afraid. She took the older ones aside and told them that their pa had died and they had to get to Uncle Bert's before dark. The older ones helped the younger ones, and Callie wrapped up the baby in her shawl. They left the cabin pretty quick and struck out through the mountains. They had to walk fast to get there safely before dark, and it's a long, hard hike even for folks with long legs. Sometimes the little ones would cry, and the bigger ones would have to try to carry them. Callie, of course, was carrying the baby and the rifle and sometimes even one of the little toddlers. With nine children and only two of them over ten, it was not an easy trip.

"At last they were on the ridge across from the cabin. The sun had just gone beyond the mountain, and the shadows were growing fast. Callie hollered and the boys hollered, and pretty soon, Bert hollered back. Him and his wife came to help her get the kids inside, and the children were able to rest. Their aunt fed them a warm meal while Callie told Bert what had happened.

"Bert left at first light the next morning to go to his neighbor's house and get a couple more men. Then they'd all go to get Bill and carry him down to his cabin. Bert's son tagged along, working hard to keep up, trying to match his pa's long stride up and down the mountainside.

"They stopped at Bill and Callie's cabin, like Callie had told them to, so they could get a quilt to wrap Bill in and some bread to feed Larry and Lead—Callie knew those dogs wouldn't have left Bill to look for food.

"We found Bill pretty much as Callie'd described him—lying in the middle of the trail with his hat over his face, a few leaves blown over him. But the trail around him was all churned up, with paw prints crossing and crisscrossing in the dirt. A panther, its throat savagely ripped open, lay underneath the big hemlock tree not five feet from Bill's body. And Larry and Lead, still sitting on either side of their master, were horribly torn up. Long, raking claw marks still dripped blood from their sides, Larry had an ear that was nearly torn off, and Lead had an eye that was nearly swollen shut.

"We threw the bread to them, and they limped up to get it, sharing it just like when Callie had given them a piece, and then they turned and went back to their posts by Bill's side. We went a little farther up the trail and found the bodies of two wildcats, both bearing the unmistakable marks of good old Larry and Lead.

"Of course the wildcats and the panther had smelled Bill's body, and it smelled like supper to them. But Larry and Lead fought like wild things themselves and saved Bill from getting all torn up.

"We started to go up to Bill's body to wrap him in the quilt and carry him home, but Larry and Lead sprang at us as quick as you please. They were going to rip our throats out, too, most likely—they'd fought like crazy all night long to protect their master, and we were just another threat in their eyes. They didn't know we didn't mean him any harm.

"We tried sweet-talking them and ordering them and tricking them away from the body, but they weren't going to budge. Finally, Bert said we'd just have to shoot them so we could get the body home. It was getting dark, and there were plenty of other wildcats around.

"Nobody wanted to shoot Larry and Lead. Not even Bert could bring himself to do it because he knew those poor dogs were only doing what they thought was right. We were all relieved to hear another dog barking down the trail. Larry and Lead seemed to recognize the bark, and they stood up and began to wag their tails and sort of yip in return. I ran down the trail and found a man who'd helped Bill with the cattle before. His dog knew Larry and Lead, and he knew Bill's dogs too.

"Cade, that's his name, he gentled those dogs, talking to them real soft and telling them how sorry he was about Bill. He went up and stroked Bill's face and cried a little, and the dogs moaned, too. Soon enough, he'd convinced those dogs that he meant Bill no harm, and they let him gather Bill up in his arms and walk on down the trail. Those dogs walked right alongside him, proud and sad all at the same time.

"They had a right to lead that funeral procession if anybody did. Bloody, battered, and weak from hunger and lack of water, they finally saw to it that Bill got home."

A low growl erupted from the shadows. Then a bloodcurdling shriek filled the air, followed by more howls, low, murderous growls, and the sharp, ripping sounds of teeth making contact with flesh. The old man sat by the fire, a faraway smile on his face. Claire crept off to the tent and grabbed the two sleeping bags; the women wrapped themselves against the evening chill, and the three kept vigil until the sun came up, listening to the intermittent, savage battle being relived on the trail below.

The old man disappeared shortly after sunrise, and the women broke down their camp and continued on their way. Claire was inclined to believe that the old man was a figment of their imagination, but Natalie argued fiercely that he was real.

"Nobody but a real, live human being could have b.o. like that," she said firmly. "And I don't think a ghost drank all our brandy, either."

They were subdued for the next two days. When they hiked out of the woods and back to their car, they had only three things on their minds: a hot meal, a hot bath, and a warm, soft bed. They drove to the little diner in the nearest town.

"You girls been on the trail long?" asked the waitress, filling their coffee cups for the fourth time and surveying their disheveled appearance with some amusement.

"Three days," Claire confirmed, between heaping forkfuls of boiled cabbage and corned beef.

Natalie had taken the edge off her hunger already. "You go up there much?" she asked the waitress as she waved her fork vaguely toward the mountains and the trail they'd followed.

The woman laughed. "God love you, I was raised up there, and I like it right where I am now, thank you."

"Anybody still live up there?" continued Natalie. Claire saw the gleam in her eye that meant she was engaged in more than idle conversation.

The woman shook her head, backing away from the table. "That's a national park or some such, now. You know that."

"But does anybody live up there?"

The woman started to turn and leave, muttering something about customers, although Natalie and Claire were the only people in the little cafe. "Wait," Natalie urged. "I'm not trying to be nosy or get anybody in trouble. It's just that something really weird happened to us up there." The woman turned back and pinned Natalie with a look that was almost unfriendly.

"An old man came up to us and started telling us stories," Claire interrupted. "But he couldn't have been real, could he?"

The woman's face softened. "Old Ed Welch is real, all right," she said. "Real ornery, but they say that's what it takes to live as long as he has."

"How old is he?" Natalie couldn't resist a triumphant poke to Claire's ribs.

"Probably just a hair shy of a hundred or maybe more than a hundred." The waitress shrugged. "Nobody really knows. But he's crazy as a loon. I wouldn't believe a word he told you if I were you."

Claire poked Natalie, triumphant in her turn. "He told us some stupid story about a man and his dogs."

The waitress sat the coffeepot down on the table behind them and reached into her apron for their check.

"Well, now, I reckon that's the only true story Ed Welch knows," she admitted. "Bill Sawyers and his family were good people."

"It really happened?"

"Yes, ma'am, it did." The waitress placed the check on the table with a note of finality. "Hope you enjoyed your dinner. Come back again, anytime."

The story of Bill and Callie Sawyers was first told by Margaret Redding Siler in her book Cherokee Indian Lore and Smoky Mountain Stories *and is retold here with permission.*

north carolina's haunted mansions

Many of North Carolina's historic homes, some nearly two hundred years old, have been restored to their original beauty. Tour them, and you'll take a stroll down wisteria-scented lanes into North Carolina's history, to a time of antebellum homes, big dresses and corsets, and men on powerful steeds. Generations of families have lived, loved, and died within their walls.

If you accept the possibility of ghosts, then you have to believe that North Carolina's historic homes are haunted places.

The Biltmore Estate

Back in 1888, George Vanderbilt II, the youngest grandson of business tycoon Commodore Cornelius Vanderbilt, had a vision of a grand winter estate on a scale that would rival the summer homes his older brothers and sisters built. It was a family tradition, this penchant for building lavish homes. It was begun by Grandpa Vanderbilt, who, as a self-made man, needed some way to thumb his nose at the snooty Northeastern society.

As an international traveler, intellectual, and extremely rich kid, Vanderbilt could have built his little country retreat anywhere in the world, but in all his travels, he had not found a place more beautiful or more desirable than Asheville, North Carolina. He had made regular visits here with his mother for many years and had fallen in love with the breathtaking scenery and the mild climate.

Vanderbilt's vision was to replicate the working estates of England, a concern that would sustain itself and become a benefit to the community. He planned to name the home the Biltmore—"Bilt," the name of the Dutch town of his ancestors, and "more," the old English word for open, rolling land. Purchasing 125,000 acres, some of which the Pisgah National Forest now occupies, he then hired popular society architect Richard Hunt to design the plans. Hunt had designed homes for other Vanderbilt family members and knew the sumptuous style they preferred.

George's Biltmore House was designed as an imitation of the Chateau de Blois, an early sixteenth–century French chateau of the Loire Valley. It was an ornate design, requiring an immense amount of materials and much manpower, both from local laborers and world-known craftsmen. A man of the future, George insisted on his home having all the most modern high-tech marvels, including electricity, central heating, running hot and cold water to upstairs baths, mechanical refrigeration, an elevator, an electric communication system to call servants, and even a swimming pool with underwater lighting.

During construction of the Biltmore House, Vanderbilt and Hunt trekked across Europe and the Orient, purchasing collectible art, porcelain, furniture, bronzes, and carpets. They filled the home with a collection of more than seventy thousand pieces that reflected Vanderbilt's style and interests. Artwork to adorn the walls included Renoir, Whistler, Sargent, and Pellegrini. There were Sheraton and Chippendale furniture and collectibles, such as a chess set and gaming table that Napoleon Bonaparte owned during his exile at St. Helena, and Chinese vases from the Ming Dynasty. Flemish tapestries, and more than fifty Oriental and Persian rugs were to cover the marble and oak floors. The majority of these items grace the home today.

As part of his plan to make the estate profitable, Vanderbilt commissioned Fredrick Olmstead, the landscape architect who had designed New York's Central Park and the U.S. Capitol grounds, to develop the estate's lands. A pioneer in conservation, Olmstead suggested constructing a combination of a 250-acre pleasure park surrounded by a commercial timber forest. Gifford Pinchot, who later established the U.S. Forest Service, renovated the forest.

The surrounding gardens and park contained transplanted seedlings from all over North Carolina as well as exotic plants, such as bamboo groves. The drive to the mansion was designed to mix deciduous trees, pines, and shrubs to offer an interesting drive all year around.

Biltmore Estate was formally opened on Christmas Eve 1895 with a grand party for friends and relatives featuring a forty-foot tree, a tradition that survives today. At 175,000 square feet, Biltmore was—and still is—the largest private home in the United States. There are 250 rooms, with thirty-four master bedrooms, forty-three bathrooms, sixty-five fireplaces, three kitchens, a bowling alley, a gym, and, of course, that indoor swimming pool.

In 1898, Vanderbilt, an avid world traveler, decided it was time to settle down a bit. While visiting India, he traveled to Paris to propose to Edith Stuyvesant Dresser, whom he had been dating for some time. The couple was married in Paris and honeymooned in Italy. George then brought his young bride to her new home, where he had already completed a private suite for her.

George and Edith loved entertaining family and friends in their opulent mountain retreat. Despite the almost overwhelming size of the house, they strove to make it welcoming and comfortable. It was their family home where their only child, Cornelia, was born and reared. Their guests often included U.S. presidents, European royalty, and the day's most renowned writers, artists, and entertainers.

The estate was constantly alive with music and laughter, but when he desired some quiet time, George would retire to the Oak Sitting Room. This was his favorite room in the mansion, where he enjoyed sitting and reading, especially on rainy nights.

As members of the "idle rich," George and Edith might as well have spent their lives traveling the world, entertaining lavishly, and spending their considerable fortune. The couple, however, felt a responsibility to the community they had adopted as home and its people. In addition to the eighty-person staff of the Biltmore house, the estate employed hundreds of locals on its working farms and a commercial timber operation with its own mill. The Vanderbilts gained a reputation as excellent employers.

George's intense interest in forestry and farming led him to introduce new farming techniques and to found the Biltmore Forest School, the nation's first institute for scientific forestry. The couple started Biltmore Industries to teach traditional handcrafts, such as woodworking and weaving, and Edith started the School for Domestic Science to train young women in housekeeping skills. These training opportunities allowed local people to earn higher wages.

It was, no doubt, an exciting and rewarding life for one of the country's most celebrated couples. But it wasn't to last. Tragedy struck in 1914, when George, away on a trip to Washington, suffered a bout of appendicitis. Despite all the privileges his fortune afforded, modern medicine failed him. He died unexpectedly from complications from the surgery.

Edith was devastated. Not long afterward, she took to sitting in the library, in front of the fireplace, where she and George spent many long evenings, and held quiet conversations with herself. Or so the servants at first thought. They soon realized that she was instead speaking with George. Night after night she returned to the library and talked with her husband just as if he had never left. The servants, of course, could not see him and thought she might be losing her mind, but Edith did see him and she continued to visit with him throughout her life.

The Biltmore Estate Ghosts

There are reports that George and Edith are sharing conversations in the library even today. Late at night, people have reported hearing the sound of her voice speaking softly, just as she did in life. There are also reports of the strong feeling of George's presence in the billiard room and in his favorite reading room, the Oak Sitting Room.

Other apparitions and unexplained phenomena roam the huge estate. Workmen report feelings of being watched, of seeing the apparition of a woman in a black dress, and unexplained noises.

The poolroom seems to be a favorite haunting spot. Visitors and staff have reported the sounds of laughter, music, and water splashing here. One of the most disturbing noises is the sound of insane laughter that seems to emanate from the pool's drain.

Perhaps the estate's weirdest apparition is that of a cat. Numerous visitors and staff have seen it. A headless orange cat strolls the area around the gardens and the bass pond. No word on what it lost its head over.

It's not surprising that the Biltmore Estate is haunted by George and Edith Vanderbilt. They lived an exciting and fulfilling life there. It was a home filled with laughter and love. Besides, if you lived somewhere so magnificent, you'd want to stay an eternity, too.

The Mordecai House

The Mordecai House is the oldest residence in Raleigh. Built in 1785 by Joel Lane, known as the Father of Raleigh, it was originally part of a five thousand-acre tract of land that eventually became the heart of Raleigh, the state capital. Lane built the house for his son, Henry.

It was named for Moses Mordecai, a fellow who was a big fan of the Lane family. Seems he married not one, but two, of the Lane girls. He was first married to Henry's daughter Margaret, with whom he had three children—Henry, Jacob, and Ellen. After Margaret's death, Moses married into the Lane family again, taking Margaret's sister, Ann, as his new bride. The couple had a daughter, whom they named Margaret.

In 1824, Mordecai hired state architect William Nichols to do a little work. Nichols transformed the house into a Greek Revival mansion, adding four rooms and remodeling the original section. The house is considered a significant work by Nichols, who had previously overseen the remodeling of the State House.

The Mordecai family members became prominent citizens and were active in state politics. Moses was a lawyer and a member of the

1805 Court of Conference. Henry later took over Mordecai House, becoming a prosperous planter there, and he served in the state legislature.

The Mordecai family occupied the house until 1967, at which time it was bought by the city of Raleigh and turned over to a preservation group to maintain the home and turn it into an historic park. Today, the home has been completely renovated and many original items, such as art work and furnishings have been returned. It's now designated as a Raleigh Historic Landmark.

Mordecai House Ghost Stories

After Henry died, his daughter, Mary Mordecai Turk, took over the home and lived there for quite some time. There are reports that she still haunts the place. She has been seen numerous times, dressed in Victorian fashion, descending the stairs and entering one of the downstairs front rooms. Unkind remarks about her photograph often result in the photograph being turned over and slammed down.

In October of 2003, a North Carolina paranormal research group, accompanied by Mordecai House staff members and a local television news crew, conducted an investigation at the Mordecai House. They were hoping for a little supernatural action and according to their report, that's just what they got.

The evening kicked off with a taped interview of a new Mordecai House staff member who had experienced several recent incidents. Upon reviewing their tapes, the television crew reported capturing a number of orbs, unexplained balls of light that many believe are evidence of spirits, floating around the staff member throughout the interview. More orbs were seen in the east bedroom.

Later into the evening, a member of the research group was sitting quietly in a chair in the west bedroom—Mary's bedroom—when the chair began to shake, a phenomenon that lasted for several seconds.

In an evaluation of 35 mm photographs taken during the investigation, a photo from the outside into a window of the building showed the appearance of a woman dressed in Victorian fashion. Taken with high speed film, the image appeared complete, like someone was standing at the window.

Observations in a follow-up visit to Mordecai House brought the possibility that the image might be a trick of light rather than an actual spirit. But, then, again, maybe not. Perhaps, Mary Willis Mordecai Turk was there, peeking out the window at her visitors with their cameras. She's probably hoping they'll get a good picture of her—to replace that bad one in the front room!

The Hammock House

Filled to the rafters with history and shrouded in mystery, the Hammock House is Beaufort's oldest, and most haunted, house. It was built in 1709, four years before establishment of the Beaufort Township. Some say the house was built for a local wealthy plantation owner, a boring, but respectable beginning, I guess. But there are other, much more intriguing theories surrounding its origins and history.

Speculation over the location of the house plays a significant role in the theories about its origins. So named because it's built on a hammock—a small wooded hillock—the house sits on a high point near the mouth of the Beaufort Inlet. Because of its location near the water, some contend the house may have served as an inn or tavern for sailors, a plausible idea.

As a shipping town, Beaufort conducted considerable trade with merchant ships, privateers, and even pirates, all of whom used the nearby beach as a landing spot. Sailors could anchor their ships in the bay and row to the house from the inlet, making it an ideal location for an inn or tavern.

An even more interesting theory is the pirate theory. According to this legend, pirates actually built the house to use as a landmark to steer safely into the inlet. That's why it was built on the hammock—to make it more visible. If pirates did, indeed, build it for that reason, they performed a service for other sailors, as well. In researching the legend, a former owner found that all maps and charts of the area from 1733 to 1793 used Hammock House as a landmark for mariners navigating the harbor.

The former owner also examined the idea that the house was built as a fortification, with an escape tunnel from the house to the water. Tunnels were commonly used in houses by water, said the owner, and, he said, the house has a trap door cut in the parlor floor that may have accessed a tunnel to the water.

Whatever its origins, Hammock House has survived both a colorful and a dark history. Of course, you'd expect a house that's almost three hundred years old to have a story or three to tell, but Hammock House seems to have more than its share of tales involving mystery and violent death.

The appearance of the house, however, doesn't hint of the darkness of its past. After years of neglect and abuse, it has been beautifully restored to a close approximation of its original state. The sunny West Indies-style architecture, with its white frame construction, double front porches, and dormer windows, brings to mind tropical breezes and sun-drenched days, not death and mayhem, punctuated by terrifying screams in the night. Appearances can be deceiving.

Hammock House Ghost Stories

Just from the sheer number of deaths known to have occurred here, you have to know there's a ghost or two lurking around Hammock House. Some of them are quite noisy, too.

••••••

Whether or not pirates actually built the house, it's fairly certain that at some point it was used as a pirate headquarters, most notably by Blackbeard the Pirate, who plundered the North Carolina waters in 1718. According to legend, when Blackbeard stayed at Hammock House, he had with him one of his fourteen wives. She was just a girl, really, an eighteen-year-old French beauty he had captured on one of his many raids. Ol' Blackbeard fancied himself a ladies man and considered himself quite irresistible to the opposite sex.

The girl didn't agree. She thought, in fact, that Blackbeard was remarkably resistible. He was her father's age, after all.

She willfully—and quite vocally—rejected his every advance, screaming and crying so that everyone could hear. Her refusals enraged Blackbeard, who was notorious for his temper. When it came time to head back out to sea, he decided to divorce her—pirate style. Just before leaving, he had her hanged from one of the live oak trees in front of the house and buried her beneath it. It's said that on nights with a full moon, you can hear the poor girl screaming.

••••••

The pirate's lady isn't the only spirit hanging around Hammock House. Another spirit is said to be that of Richard Russell Jr., who owned the house in the late 1740s. In 1747, Russell returned to Beaufort from a sea voyage. Maybe he was a little tired and cranky from the trip. Or maybe he was just a slightly more civilized version of Blackbeard. Regardless, he lost his temper with one of his slaves and decided to take him to the attic to punish him. As he was pushing the slave up the stairs, the slave decided to push back. The resulting tumble down the stairs broke Russell's neck, killing him instantly. There are reports of a blood stain on the second floor landing that won't go away, despite cleaning. The landing has been sanded and repainted numerous times throughout the years, but according to reports the bloodstain keeps reappearing.

That blood, however, may not be Richard Russell's, for he's not the only one to die on that second floor landing. It seems that another owner, a beautiful Beaufort woman, was engaged to marry a seagoing man. The fiancé had been on a voyage for several weeks and wasn't due back for another week. The winds had been kind, however, and he made it back to Beaufort several days early. Thinking to surprise his love, he went straight away to Hammock House.

She was surprised, all right. Seems the lady had gotten a bit lonely while her fiancé was away. She was doing a bit of "entertaining" when her fellow arrived, pink-cheeked and looking for love. When he found her in the arms of another, a fight ensued and she was thrown down the stairs. She died in a pool of blood on the second floor landing. According to a psychic who visited the house, the spirit of a young woman haunts the house.

••••••

Then there's the story of the sea captain with a truly terrible temper who once owned Hammock House. He had fallen in love with a woman from Baltimore and the couple was to be married at Hammock House. His fiancée with her entourage of bridesmaids and chaperones traveled from Baltimore to Beaufort by coach, while the erstwhile captain traveled by sea.

Bad weather delayed the captain's arrival by a day and when he arrived, he saw his house ablaze with lights. There was music and laughter and guests mingling on the front lawn. Anxious to see his bride, he quickly dropped anchor and rowed to shore. Without stopping to greet his guests, he hurried into the house. What he saw there turned his good cheer to black anger.

There she was, his beautiful bride-to-be in the arms of another man, a Navy lieutenant by the looks of the uniform. The blackguard! Without a word, the captain drew his sword and ran the man through. Unfortunately, it turned out that the lieutenant was his brother-in-law-to-be. According to legend, the lieutenant's spirit makes an occasional appearance at Hammock House.

••••••

The last bit of death and mayhem at Hammock House concerns a story about three missing Union soldiers. It happened on March 23, 1862. On that morning, the citizens of Beaufort awoke to find that Union forces had taken control of their town. As the day wore on, there came the story of three of the soldiers who were missing. Seems their officers had noticed Hammock House on their way into town. It was abandoned by this time, and the officers thought it would make a good outpost. So they dispatched three soldiers to check it out. They were never seen again.

No one knew what happened to the soldiers until 1915, when the house was being renovated. Workmen digging near the back porch discovered the remains of the soldiers and their uniforms. Of course, no one knows how they came to be buried there or who stuck them in their shared grave.

From pirate's lair to Civil War grave to private home, Hammock House is truly a spirited house.

The Battle House

Long before the white man came to the New World, Native Americans considered the area now known as Asheville as a healing place. The mild climate, coupled with the healing mineral waters of the hot spring nearby, prompted them to designate the area as a neutral ground for their sick.

It didn't take the new settlers long to discover Asheville. As far back as 1795, records show that the area was regarded as a place to come to heal. By the late nineteenth and early twentieth centuries, tuberculosis was one of the deadliest diseases, resulting in thousands of fatalities annually. Climate was considered a factor in the recuperation of this disease, with the heat and humidity of the Deep South being a detriment.

Physicians searching for a place to send their tuberculosis patients soon discovered the Asheville area. The climate here was favorable, they thought. So they came to check it out. It began with just one or two. First came Dr. H.P. Gatchell, a pioneer in tuberculosis treatment. In 1870, Gatchell published a pamphlet promoting the advantages of the Asheville climate and opened a sanitarium, the first tuberculosis sanitarium in the country.

Next came Dr. Joseph Gleitsmann, who opened another sanitarium. He was a man of science who had systematically studied the climate of the United States. In his opinion, Asheville had the optimum combination of barometric pressure, temperature, humidity, and sunlight for the recuperation of tuberculosis. Gleitsmann's work helped to establish Asheville as the country's center for tuberculosis treatment.

As Asheville's reputation grew, large numbers of physicians came— some to convalesce themselves—and ended up staying. They built practices and promoted Asheville as a health retreat. From the late 1880s until the 1930s, Asheville rose in prominence. Boarding houses and sanitariums became abundant.

One of the most prominent physicians to come to Asheville was Dr. Samuel Westray Battle. Arriving in 1885, Battle became Asheville's most influential physician. Through his national reputation as a physician and his many connections, he promoted Asheville as a retreat. He was successful in bringing many wealthy and influential people to the town. Among them was George Vanderbilt, who accompanied his sick mother. Vanderbilt liked the area so well that he stayed and built the grand Biltmore Estate. Another of Battle's patients was Edwin Grove, who stayed on to build Grove Park Inn and the Grove Arcade. Battle was involved in civic activities as well, establishing North Carolina's first chapter of the American Red Cross.

Battle died in Asheville in 1927. That same year, his widow, Jane, built a fine home on Macon Street. Designed by prominent New York architect Warrington Lawrence, the house was built in a Tudor Revival style, unlike any other home in Asheville. It was—and is—the only example of Lawrence's work in Asheville. In 1954, WLOS-TV, Asheville's first television station, bought the house. They operated there for the next fifty years.

Battle House Ghosts

Not long after the station moved in, employees began having unusual experiences. Many sighted the apparition of a young woman wearing a long, old-fashioned dress. She was often seen wandering up and down the hallways and was known to fiddle with the station's electronic equipment. One employee also reported that as he descended the stairway one morning, someone grabbed him. There was, of course, no one there.

In researching the history of the house, they learned that a young servant girl named Alice had died here—the result of a fall down those very stairs. The apparition is thought to be her spirit.

There's another spirit haunting the place, as well. A security guard making his rounds reported seeing a dapper man dressed in a top hat and formal clothing. He later saw a photograph of Dr. Samuel Westray Battle and swore that was whom he had seen. Of course, Dr. Battle died before the house was built, but perhaps his spirit returned to be with his wife, who lived there until she died in 1954.

The Horace Williams House

For more than fifty years, Henry Horace Williams was an esteemed and favored professor of philosophy at the University of North Carolina. He was part of the Hegelian movement, which was a powerful force in American thinking in the late nineteenth century.

The Hegelian movement, based on the writings of philosopher Georg Wilhelm Hegel, was influential in breaking the hold of religious fundamentalism on the country's universities, thereby introducing a climate where a truly scientific philosophy could evolve.

This was the time when the right to teach Darwin's theory of evolution was being divisively debated, in both the state courts and the court of public opinion. Williams's teachings helped to open the minds of his students to ideas other than their sometimes provincial upbringings, often based solely on religious fundamentalism. His influence prevented the passage of a state anti-evolution law, and he was a major factor in the cultural and intellectual awakening that took place in North Carolina in the early 1900s.

Eccentric, slight of build, and bespectacled, Williams was well-liked by students and faculty alike. He was a frugal man who balked at spending money on unnecessary things—indoor plumbing, heat, or telephones. When he first came to the University of North Carolina in 1897, he bought an old farmhouse owned by UNC chemistry professor Benjamin Hedrick.

Built in the 1840s, the house had passed through several owners and had undergone a renovation or two. Despite the renovations, by the time Williams bought it, the place was not aging gracefully. Its survival through several architectural periods had turned it into an eclectic, rambling abode, with interesting features such as the uniquely-shaped Octagon Room added by Hedrick, and a parlor and entrance hall with parquet ceilings added in 1888.

Those unusual features were added, but the conveniences that were becoming necessities by then had somehow been neglected. There were no toilets, no steam heating, no telephones, not even a bathtub. Throughout the fifty years he lived here, Williams refused to have these conveniences added. He professed to be exercising his inalienable right to be individualistic and live his life his own way.

His long-time housekeeper had a different take on it. It was his stinginess that kept him from spending money on these things. It also was his stinginess, she said, that kept him from making basic repairs—such as fixing the crumbling plaster falling from the walls that she had to sweep up every morning. Not even his wife, Bertha, who was an artist, could persuade him to spend money on renovation of their home.

Despite his admitted frugality and eccentricity, Williams was an immensely popular professor. Preferring the Socratic method of teaching, he treasured debate and discourse with his students. He often invited them to his home at night, where they met in the parlor and pondered profound profundities.

One of those students who often met with Williams was writer Thomas Wolfe, who attended the University of North Carolina in the 1920s. In his book *You Can't Go Home Again,* Wolfe said of his esteemed professor: "He was a great teacher, and what he did, and for others before us for fifty years, was not to give us his 'philosophy'...but to communicate to us his alertness, his originality, his power to think."

When he died in 1922 at age eighty-two, Williams bequeathed his home to the University of North Carolina, who turned it over to the Preservation Society of Chapel Hill. The house was beautifully renovated in 1972 and now serves as a cultural resource and exhibition space, and is open to the public.

The Ghost of the Horace Williams House

Horace Williams is reportedly still sharing his philosophy, perhaps with a group of former students who enjoyed his discourses so much that they've returned to debate through eternity. Maybe Thomas Wolfe is among them.

Williams's thin, bespectacled apparition has been seen in his house—and reportedly has been seen wandering the halls of the ninety-year-old Caldwell Hall, the building that once housed the college's philosophy department. By all accounts, he's a mischievous spirit, often mysteriously moving objects from one room to another.

Catherine Berryhill Williams and her sister, Jane Berryhill Neblet, experienced these events firsthand. The girls, daughters of Walter

Reece Berryhill, dean of UNC's school of medicine in the 1940s, lived at the house during their teenage years. Both became acquainted with Williams's spirit soon after moving in.

Catherine remembers many strange incidents. The house still did not have central heating and was instead heated with fireplaces. She remembers that her mother would bank the fires at night and leave the fire utensils on one side of the fireplace. The next morning, the utensils would be moved to the other side. Her bedroom was the parlor, which was Williams's office—and, of course, the place he held his nightly meetings. There was always the feeling of a presence in the room. No one ever felt threatened, she said, but when she had a sleepover, her guests would always insist on extra nightlights.

Jane's room was a small room next to the kitchen. One day, she vividly remembers, she was home sick from school and was lying in bed. Suddenly a figure appeared at the foot of her bed. She denies any delirium and at first thought she was having a nightmare, but then realized that she was awake. The figure, she said, was dressed in black with a white collar. Even though she was frightened, she didn't feel as if the apparition meant any harm. She sat up and asked what he wanted and the spirit swayed back and forth, emitting some sort of moan. Then it faded away.

The next morning, she told her mother about her experience, and her mother asked if she'd ever seen a picture of Horace Williams. She had not, but when her mother showed her a picture, she recognized him right away. He was the spirit that had been moaning at the foot of her bed.

In addition to his mischievousness, Williams would seem to be a fastidious ghost. A caretaker reports that, on occasion, the toilets have flushed by themselves. I'm thinking that's not Horace, however. Bet it's Bertha, who, deprived of the convenience of indoor plumbing in life, is determined to make the most of it in the afterlife!

conjure knob

When we were young, they would roll and tumble across the dusty yard, limbs tangled, teeth bared in mock-ferocious battles. At some signal far beyond the ken of ordinary creatures, they'd separate and rest for a split second, panting slightly, out of breath. Their sleek heads, an identical golden brown, were never found with more than a scant twelve inches separating them, and their smooth brown limbs seemed to move with one aim, synchronized to a song only they could hear.

"I swear those two must think the same thoughts," I heard our mother confide to a neighbor one day. "They'll be playing along, nice and quiet, and then look at each other and poof!" She snapped a damp pillowcase in emphasis before clipping it to the line with its mate. "Without a word, they'll be up and running, off to heaven-knows-where to do heaven-knows-what!"

She laughed, and I could hear the note of pride in her voice. In their hidey-hole underneath the back porch, the boys nudged each other and grinned, teeth gleaming in the dimness.

"Well, I'd worry if I were you," pronounced our elderly neighbor.

"Running loose like that—there's no telling what kind of trouble they'll find. These mountains can be dangerous."

Mama shrugged and wrestled with the tattered chenille bedspread from her big soft bed. "They're good boys," she said. "They watch out for each other. I'm a lucky woman, to have such good boys."

The old crow from down the road just shook her head and predicted gloom. And you know what? If you predict bad things long enough, they will surely come to pass.

They tried to separate the boys when they went down to town for school. They said the boys couldn't both be in the same class, and one of them would have to ride the bus into the next county and go to school there. When Mama heard that, she turned white, and then the color came up high into her cheeks. Shane poked me with his elbow—we were both thinking, "Somebody's really in for it this time!"

Well, they got put into the same class. Old Mrs. Tippin didn't know quite what to do with them, but, looking back, school seems like such a small part of our lives. I couldn't go anyway—Mama would never have allowed it. "Trouble comes in threes, girl," she said more than once. So I stayed quiet as a mouse in my safe corner.

But one thing school did give us, all three of us, thanks to that old grouchy Mrs. Tippin, was the ability to open our minds to the world beyond our mountains. We were hemmed in on all sides by the ranges of the Smoky Mountains—mountains so high that I never really saw a sunset until I went away. But that's not part of the story yet.

What I mean is, Mrs. Tippin taught the boys to read. And even though it was devilishly hard at first, one day something clicked into place, and suddenly I could comprehend, too. My eyes sped over the type, devouring the meaning, the taste of the words, and I couldn't resist a yelp of triumph. Shane, too, was exulting, and I knew his brain had clicked all the elements in place at the same time. I will never, never forget that feeling. And to share it—well, it was beyond explaining.

Now, of course, I can see it a little more clearly. Everything we did, we did together. We took our first steps clinging onto each other, mother tells us. Our first words were not "Mama" but each other's names. We climbed trees at the same time, learned to blow spit bubbles at the same time, learned to whistle and to catch a ball as it hurtled through the air. Learning to read was an accomplishment that might have divided us. When it did not, when it affirmed our oneness, it was pure magic.

Once we began reading, we ripped through all the books in the school library in no time flat. All three of us would read at the same time, my head resting on Shane's shoulder as he held the book, or his head resting on mine. We'd all finish a page, and Shawn would turn to the next one.

The books took us so far away that it scared Mama sometimes. She could call and call and even stand right next to us and holler, and we would not hear her. Her voice was merely the tumult of the sea as we fought our way to new and undiscovered shores.

What really frightened her, though, was the possibility that the boys might go exploring in one of the old abandoned mine shafts that dotted the mountains like cavities—black, crumbling pockets smelling of decay and death. Although they told her over and over that they would not go, she never quite believed them.

I believe she had nightmares about us falling out of her reach. She would wake us up sometimes, moaning louder than the wind outside, and we would creep to the door of her bedroom and peer anxiously at her twisting, flailing form all bound up in the sheet and bedspread. We never knew quite what to do. We were afraid to wake her up, for this moaning, thrashing woman bore very little resemblance to the private, contained mother we knew by daylight. But at the same time, we could tell she was in great distress, crying our names, groaning about rocks falling, and the hard, cold earth.

We had nightmares every now and then, too. Just confused pieces come back to me now. It seems like there was always somebody chasing us, and sometimes, when we got caught, the monster or whatever it was would suffocate us.

What I do remember, vividly, is how this creature in the dark caught us. He would come closer and closer, making a lot of racket, and we were making a lot of racket, too, yelling and trying to run in that thick-footed nightmare way.

Then, just as we thought we were safe, a net would surround us. It was no ordinary net—it was woven out of heavy-gauge chain, like the chain you put around a fence to keep it closed. Looking out from that net gave us a view of the world that was all fractured, cut up into tiny little segments. And of course, it was so heavy that we were pressed to the ground.

It didn't really surprise us when we figured out that all three of us had the same nightmare. We were a little disappointed, though, when we didn't have the same everyday dreams—that is, at first we didn't.

Mama was terrified of the mines. She must have had a brother or father who had died in the mines—just about everybody around there did. And of course, there was our father—but she remained close-mouthed on the subject. We learned quickly not to press her with any kind of questions. She never lashed out, never hit, never even spoke an unkind word. She would be crueler than that, even though I don't think it was intentional.

Mama had a remarkable ability to draw up within herself, and it seemed, at first, to be without warning. Her eyes would turn a murky brown, and her features would set themselves still and hard. While her hands would still perform her tasks, their movements were mechanical, unthinking. She once mistook a cup of salt for sugar because she was so preoccupied, and she often made little mistakes like that when she got this way. She was as cold and unknowable as the mountain above us, shrouded in a chilling fog.

If something happened when we were younger and we would run to her for solace, we could wrap our arms around her, and it would take one or two heartbeats before her arms would reach back around us. It's like she just wasn't there. Her body was present, but vacant. Without a word, she might take up her coat and stride off into the woods, heedless of our cries, sometimes disappearing for an entire night.

We discovered that asking questions was one precursor to this strange behavior—so we learned not to ask questions. But we were never truly certain about what might trigger her absence, so we were more cautious than you might expect wild little children to be. That's why she trusted us about everything except the mines.

It may sound like we had a perfect childhood. And, in a way, we did. The boys were free to do a lot of things most other kids weren't because they didn't have very many chores. Mama didn't keep chickens, and she hauled the water herself. When they were old enough to handle an ax, Mama let the boys chop the wood, but that was about all they had to do.

It never really dawned on us how poor we were. We ate a lot of beans and potatoes and greens that Mama gathered herself from around the woods and streams. Sometimes we were hungry, but there wasn't a single child we knew who wasn't hungry every now and then. Some of the neighbor ladies would chide her for not keeping a kitchen garden or even a few hens, but Mama got along all right.

Mama set traps, which was one reason she roamed the woods at all hours—to check her traps. She had an uncanny way of finding just the right spot where the squirrels would congregate, and I've seen her call squirrels so they'd run down a tree and toward her voice. I got to hate squirrel stew.

She was respected, and girls and women would come and consult with her sometimes, and they would whisper in the kitchen until Mama asked us quietly to go outside and play. These visitors would sometimes leave little gifts—a few eggs, a little fatback, some canned berries. Once, even, a little puppy.

"Can we keep him, Mama," we begged. "Please, can we?" His fat little belly was so distended that we shouted with laughter at his rolling gait. She smiled too, but it was a distant smile.

For some reason, she let us keep that dog out in the yard. He grew and grew, and the boys were forever sneaking him table scraps. One day, I heard a terrible commotion out in the yard. The dog, nearly full grown, had grabbed one of Mama's kittens by the scruff of its neck and shaken it, playfully, I think. Its neck broke, just snapped like a twig. Mama walked up while he held the lifeless thing in his mouth and started roaring and kicking and beating that dog like I've never seen before. It's the only time I ever saw Mama lift a finger in anger.

When the boys got home, she told them the dog had to go. They walked down to town, the dog on a rope, limping and whining. She sold that dog to Mr. Sloan at the store, or traded him for it more likely. When they got home they had a new big sack of flour, and Mama wasn't talking. She didn't speak to us for two whole days, and we started to get a little scared. I think she crept out one night while we slept, but I wasn't sure.

That kitten dying must have affected me more than I knew, though. For weeks, I could hear that kitten crying, mostly at night, but it didn't seem to bother anybody else. And once, I thought I saw a kitten creeping along in the shadows at the edge of the woods, its head twisted at an unnatural angle, but surely I was mistaken.

I remember one time, we must've been about ten, the boys came home with a big old box. We only hesitated a minute, calling out for Mama, before the devil got into us, and we started pulling things out of that box. First, a long pair of black trousers, ripped out at the knee. Then, five or six white shirts so long worn that the elbows were see-through and under the arms were acid yellow stains from somebody else's sweat. Then a whole bunch of women's clothes that we carefully set aside, mindful that Mama could stitch a miracle from a whole lot of nothing.

We had about decided that the box was a waste of time when we got close to the bottom and heard the distinctive rustle of old paper. Tucked away at the bottom, packed so carelessly that some of the covers lay open and bent, were nearly twenty paperback books. They were an odd assortment of romances, Westerns, and an outlandish type of stories we'd never encountered: science fiction. When Mama came back, it was dark and the stove was cold, but we were curled up together on the boys' bed, devouring the first of those books. Mama didn't have much to say. She just took up the clothes and began to see about altering them for us and for her, before she started scratching up a little supper for the three of us. I get the feeling, now, that those boxes of charity from the city churches really got her down.

It was about this time that the boys' everyday dreams started to match up. They were very ordinary, and I don't remember much. There were the people from our daily lives and strange or puzzling juxtapositions of words and place. It gave them a jolt to find out that they shared dreams as well as occasional nightmares.

"There were these rocket ships," Shawn was saying, excited. "And then, what happened next?"

"Well, the wheelbarrow was full of cabbages from old lady Henley's garden, so we stuffed them into the fuel tank. And then there was something about us flying, doing flips and stuff."

Shane was nearly bouncing up and down, he was so thrilled. "Yes, yes, that's it, exactly!" he yelped.

"You boys making up a story?" Mama set bowls of oatmeal in front of us and sat down to watch us eat.

"No, Mama," Shane answered, his spoon suspended in midair. "It's our dreams!" I nudged him, to shut him up. For some reason I didn't think Mama should know about it. But it was too late.

"Me 'n' Shawn are having the same dreams!"

Mama shuddered, and a look of distaste skittered across her face. I saw it—I know I did. She studied her hands for a minute before she got up, not looking us in the eye. Maybe I noticed this because I'm older—only eight minutes older, but older, anyway.

With the shared dreams, Shane and Shawn got even closer. They would wake up in the morning in identical positions, maybe with their legs extended like they were in mid-jump, or once, in a vaguely disturbing dream about water, curled up into a little ball. Mama never mentioned dreams again, and the boys were careful not to talk about the dreams in front of her.

Of course, they didn't really *need* to talk about the dreams— they'd both been there the night before. Talking about the dreams was kind of like remembering an extension of the waking day. "Wasn't that car something else?" Shane might whisper.

Two or three years later, the boys started scheming about how to get their hands on a real car—any car. Mama hated hearing them talk about cars, so they kept it pretty quiet. We knew, of course, that the primary factor was money—we didn't have any, we didn't know anybody who had any, and the only way anybody we knew made money was by working in the mines. But that source of income never seriously crossed our minds. It would kill Mama if they went to the mines, and we knew that like we knew the curve of each other's smile.

The summer we were fourteen, though, the local handyman killed himself. I don't think he meant to. He just started drinking one afternoon, and then decided to drive himself up to the top of Conjure Knob and enjoy the sunset.

Conjure Knob was just an old, bare, ugly ledge at the top of the ridge. We lived halfway up; the town, with the school, Sloan's store, and a couple of mean, scraggly houses rumored to supply all kinds of illicit pleasures, was in a little holler below us. I don't know why it was called Conjure Knob—most folks believed in haunts and spirits, but I don't know anybody who did any conjuring. But people would whisper about strange goings-on there when the moon was full, and they'd shut up quick as a wink whenever the boys came up. I expect they didn't want to scare them since we lived so close.

Nights when the moon wasn't full, kids liked to go up there and drink and act crazy, or carry their girlfriends up there and fool around. At fourteen, we had a hazy understanding of this, but it was too far distant from the real obsession: a car.

Anyway, Tom Stone climbed or maybe oozed into the cab of his dirty misbegotten pickup that afternoon and set out for Conjure Knob. I imagine some people had to have seen him careening down the road, slinging the truck from side to side on the curves with those exaggerated movements drunks make sometimes, but nobody stopped him. The road gets pretty narrow after our place, and the switchbacks are wicked, sharp curves that sneak up on you suddenly.

He must've slung the wheel a little too hard just above our house—you could tell by the skid marks that he fishtailed and then just dropped off the edge of the road. Old Tom might've been all right except the door came open, and he flew out on the way down and just cracked his head wide open on the rocks—like a melon.

When the boys got home from school, his body was gone, but all the gore was still there, spilling down the face of the rocks like some giant, obscene bird droppings. Being kids, we were pretty curious about this, and we studied the scene for a minute before we noticed something else that was pretty extraordinary—Tom's truck.

It reclined, laying on its side like a fat old sow, the rusted-out tailpipe and other parts poking out like gigantic, ugly teats—square on top of our outhouse. It had squashed it as flat as a June bug.

We laughed at that until our bellies hurt, howling and shrieking like we were the devil's own children. Then it occurred to us to look for Mama.

Exchanging a horrified look, we ran as one, screaming wildly for her. The house was empty, although a pan of beans sat soaking on the cold stove. We tore back outside and over to the truck, which now seemed to squat evilly, a two-ton marker of unspeakable grief.

I believe terror gives people unnatural strength. We three spindly teenagers somehow managed to rock that truck back onto its wheels, so we could scrabble through the wreckage below. There was an amazing amount of splintered, broken lumber, but that was all we found. We stood, panting slightly, staring at each other before the boys turned, sprinting into the woods to find Mama. We needed to see her, to touch her, to verify once again that nothing had happened to her.

Mama wandered far and wide, and we were never encouraged to seek her out. In fact, we could rarely find her when we looked when we were little, even though it seems she might have been just under our noses. So we gave up looking for the most part and waited in peace for her to come home.

The boys found her quickly this time. Running fleet-footed through the woods softly padded with pine needles, they burst upon her in a little clearing, bent over her task. They were so relieved to find her, and she hurried to them so quickly, that it was days before they realized that she had been stooped over a bloody carcass of some sort. It was a scene oddly reminiscent of the gore spattered across the rocks above our house, but beyond these shadowy recollections, there was nothing firm to grasp. If she was unhappy at being interrupted, she didn't show it. Perhaps she slipped out later that night to finish her work.

Tom didn't have any family left alive—I suppose they had all killed themselves just like he did. So Mama argued successfully that we should have his truck since it had smashed our outhouse. The boys endured a spate of jokes about using that truck for an outhouse, but truth was that Tom's truck was nothing much to claim. It was a mottled gray, like a November sky, leaden and threatening. Here and there were scaly patches of rust, like mange on a dog's hide. Inside, the passenger-side seat had a spring poking up, and there were, inexplicably, great volumes of blood spattered about the cab, even though Tom had been thrown out the door before he got a scratch on him. The truck had landed on the passenger side, so that side was crushed in, and the door wouldn't open, but the boys didn't mind—they'd pile in through the driver's side. They loved to sit in the cab of that truck and talk, hour after hour, gesturing widely and spinning dreams.

It was about this same time that a strange dog appeared from the woods above the house. He was a leggy old cur, and his skull was caved in on one side, like he'd taken a tremendous bashing. The boys snuck out parts of their dinner to feed him, but he'd growl at odd moments and could never be trusted not to turn and snap at you, suddenly vicious.

He disappeared as abruptly as he had come. For nearly a week after, though, we could hear him howling in the woods like he was in some pain. Mama said one afternoon that he might have gotten caught in a trap, and she left for the rest of the afternoon to find him—or so she said. She didn't come back all night. We never heard the dog again, but we didn't ask Mama what happened to him.

When the boys were fifteen, Mama gave them the keys to the truck. Now their range was expanded dramatically, and their comings and goings became as erratic as Mama's. One gray early morning after they'd come in late, I heard them scuffling on their bed.

"What's wrong?" Shane hissed.

"Nothing, it's nothing," Shawn insisted. "It's just a nightmare. Go back to sleep."

"I don't remember a nightmare," Shane said, confused. We lay uneasy in our beds until the sun came up.

It was only two weeks after school let out that I heard the boys in the yard. Mama had been gone all day, and I first thought the noise was her, arguing with a neighbor or a caller. But it was the boys—fighting! In all their years, they had never been anything less than in perfect agreement. Why, they didn't usually even have to speak to each other. One made a decision, and it was just as much the other's—they were one mind. A shudder coursed up my backbone, and I crept to the door to listen.

"I'm not leaving Mama." His voice was low, but the tone was intense.

"It'll kill her if you go to the mines."

"It'd kill her if you left."

"I can't go to the mines."

"You don't have any choice."

"We can get out of here."

"I won't leave Mama."

Their words were stone hard and bullet quick. It seemed inevitable that their talk would lead to blows. I cowered next to the door, opened just a crack for eavesdropping.

I heard the truck door slam. The engine groaned, turned over, and caught, and the black exhaust reached like a finger to stir my hair through the crack in the door. Something bad, something evil came in, too, like a breath, and I shuddered again before venturing out into the darkening yard.

I could hear the truck's engine whine as one of them—Shawn or Shane, we never knew—pushed it hard, racing up the mountain. I heard the tires squeal and a shout of alarm before I saw the truck floating, dreamlike, in midair above me. I saw it smack against rocks as it tumbled, striking sparks that glowed with a festive air before vanishing, leaving only a ghostly, lingering after-impression. I imagined I saw a white face pressed hard against the glass of the passenger-side window before I hid my face in my arms, whining softly in pure animal terror. I never saw the explosion, but I felt the heat of the flames licking at me like a too-familiar, too-large hound.

I don't remember anything for a while. Mama must have delayed the funeral, because the first thing I remember is their bodies laid out in the front room. Their faces were horribly disfigured from the fire, although the undertaker had tried his best to reconstruct their fine, even features. There was just the faintest trace of decay in the cold, still air.

The night of the wake, I had strange dreams, and I went walking in my sleep. In my dream, I saw Mama stooped over one boy and then the other, muttering, burning something, waving a smoldering piece of paper in the air above their bodies. I crouched in the corner and watched. Her actions became more and more frenzied, her voice louder and louder, until I realized the dawn was seeping in through the cracks in the window shade. I almost thought I saw Shane's leg quiver, just once, and I thought I saw Shawn's finger twitch when Mama's voice broke. Then I must have woken up because Mama was just huddled over them, crying. She'd blown out the candles, and a lazy curl of white smoke rose to the ceiling, the smell of hot wax and charred wick masking all the other odors in the room.

We buried those boys on a hillside, and folks from around here collected enough money to put up a real nice marker. I went with Mama to see the marker one winter afternoon not long after they put it up.

The wind was blowing, but softly. There hadn't been any real snow yet, so the graves still looked raw and new. Just as we crested the little rise, we heard a funny little yipping noise, and Mama gasped.

There, rolling and tumbling on the fresh broken earth, were two golden-white puppies. They growled and shook each other by the scruff of the neck with their sharp little puppy teeth, and they frolicked like they were perfectly at ease on this lonely hillside.

When Mama saw them, all the color drained from her face. She swayed and came close to toppling over except I caught her arm. Those puppies just about made Mama come undone, and I don't have the slightest idea why.

I'm doing just fine. They brought me down to a nice place, and no one asks me questions anymore. I saw my first sunset, and it was so pretty that it brought tears to my eyes. Now I always make sure I'm near the window in the late afternoon so I don't miss a minute of the colors. If I was as picky as some, I might complain about this ugly black mesh screen, but if I press my face real close, it's almost like it's not there at all.

I hear the nurses whispering behind me but I don't turn around. "Triplets," I hear one whisper to the new one. "Two boys and her. Never let her out of the house. She won't speak. Totally..." I see in the window a reflection of the woman as she draws a circle in the air next to her temple and makes a face.

I ignore her. Now birds are wheeling and swooping across the sky, graceful black lines against the fiery glow of the sun. The windows on the building opposite are catching sparks of sunlight like the sparks of the truck rolling down the ravine.

It's time for my medicine. The puppies follow, nipping at my heels, as I line up with everyone else for my little white cup.

happily ever after

"Blasted static." She stabbed at her ear with a long forefinger, inky gray from the newspaper on the table in front of her. The crackling noise did not subside, and she shook her head fretfully before giving in. She popped the flesh-colored plastic lump out of her ear and glared at the device as it lay cradled in the palm of her hand.

"Miracle!" she snorted. "No miracles here! Never worked worth a toot." She slapped her hand down, intending to set the hearing aid on the table, but the force of her hand sent the plastic device skittering off the edge of the table like a live thing.

As she watched it wobble into the shadows between the refrigerator and the wall, she heard the staticky noise again. But it was really more like a scratching noise, so slight that she almost missed it without the amplification of her hearing aid.

The dark rectangle of the window beside the kitchen door was imperfectly masked by cheery yellow curtains. Slivers of the darkness outside seemed to be creeping in, reaching for her as she peered around for the source of the noise.

"A branch," she announced, her voice unnaturally loud. "Scraping on the window screen. And to think I paid that crook thirty dollars to prune the tree branches away from the house." She shifted her chair again, so she wouldn't have to stare at that window, and she squinted down at the crossword puzzle.

"Battle site of 1898—three words." She groped for her pen and heard the sound again. It was not at the window—it was at the door, low, a scrabbling sound just a few inches above the floor. She ignored it this time, humming a little to herself. If she didn't hear it, she wouldn't get scared. And if she didn't get scared, she wouldn't have to call Carolyn or, worse, that sneaky great-nephew Kevin who was always fondling the silver tea set when he thought she wasn't looking.

She glanced up at the clock. Eleven forty-five. Carolyn would be really mad if she called and woke her up, and then Carolyn wouldn't get the bathwater warm enough the next afternoon.

The noise—it would slack off for a moment or two and then start up again. She started to imagine just what it might be but stopped that train of thought before it worked up a full head of steam. Picturing rabid, ten-pound rats or drugged-out junkies crawling up to her back door was the quickest route to a full-blown case of the heebie-jeebies.

She pushed back from the table and hooked her foot on the walker that stood like a mute aluminum sentinel next to the table. Dragging it over to her chair, she checked twice to make sure all four feet were on stable ground and pulled herself up. As each joint moved during the hesitant ascent, it sent a sweet, savage thrill of pain shooting upward and away—proof that she was still alive, she thought grimly.

Next to the sink was a metal extension handle that was meant to reach things in high places. She tested it, feeling its heft, and then set it back down. Leaning heavily on the walker, she shuffled slowly into the room that used to be the dining room but now served as her bedroom since she couldn't climb the stairs. Almost forgotten in the corner, by the fireplace, was a heavy iron poker—just what she needed. Nodding in satisfaction, she worked her way back to the brightness of the kitchen.

She stood in the doorway and listened intently. The scratching noise seemed to have stopped. With slow, deliberate steps, she returned to the table and her crossword puzzle. She sat down, keeping the poker across her lap.

A hand touched her shoulder, and she jerked awake with a yelp of surprise. "Miss Emily, you done it again," scolded Carolyn. "You got to get to your bed before you go to sleep. You'll be sore all day."

Emily just grunted, noting with surprise that the crooked band of darkness that had outlined the yellow curtains last night was now dissolved, supplanted by the creamy yellow of the diffused early sunlight.

"Did I..." she cleared her throat, "I didn't call you, did I?"

"What?" Carolyn asked over her shoulder. "You want some coffee?" She turned on the tap before Emily could reply, holding the pot with one hand and whacking the grounds out of the filter basket with the other. After the coffee started dripping, Carolyn pulled the trash bag out of the can and twisted it closed.

"You want to take a little nap in your own bed, Miss Emily?" She twisted the key in the deadbolt and yanked the knob—the old house was settling, and the doors all stuck. When the door swung open, a small ragged pile of fur tumbled onto Carolyn's feet.

She shrieked, and the ball became animated, unrolling into a discernible shape with a lean torso, stubby legs, and paws so bony they were an anatomy lesson all in themselves. Her fright was so pronounced and the creature provoking it so comical that Emily couldn't contain a snort of delighted laughter.

"Get away from me!" Carolyn kicked out, her foot barely missing the ribcage of the little mutt, who retreated into the corner near the refrigerator. Its paws made light, irregular clicking sounds, and Emily recognized the sound from her vigil the night before.

The dog's tousled black-and-gray coat blended in so well with the shadows that Emily could barely make out the shape cowering in the narrow niche. Its eyes shone brightly, though, and as Emily watched, a tiny crescent of pink tongue appeared, framed by two long teeth.

"It's smiling at me," Emily whispered and collapsed back into her chair.

Carolyn didn't hear—she was rummaging through the broom closet and muttering furiously. "Rabid dogs, God knows what else— just trying to earn a living like everybody else. God knows what might happen next—probably get mugged out on the sidewalk." She produced a broom and brandished it triumphantly. "I'll get that blasted mutt out of here, you'll see!"

The dog whined and shifted uneasily. Emily twisted around to face Carolyn. "I don't think," she started, but it was too late. Carolyn thrust the broom handle into the corner, and the dog burst forth, squealing and yelping. At the same time, something small and flesh-colored skittered out toward Carolyn, who reflexively, decisively, crushed it with one sneaker-clad foot.

The dog headed for the door, but the screen blocked its passage. So it turned and raced in the other direction, toward the living room. Carolyn ran, yelling, in pursuit, while Emily covered her mouth with her hand.

"Don't worry, Miss Emily!" Carolyn screeched like a banshee, and the clicking sounds of the dog's progress grew louder as Carolyn and her prey circled back into the kitchen.

The dog catapulted high into the air just as Carolyn's broom came crashing down, and all three moaned in surprise to see where the creature had landed to avoid the blow. Emily slowly raised her arms, a broad smile melting away—the little dog stood, quivering, square in Emily's lap. Carolyn lowered the broom and whispered hoarsely.

"Don't move, Miss Emily. It might go for your throat."

The dog turned to stare at Carolyn and bared its teeth before swinging its head around to face Emily. Their noses were inches apart, and Emily hardly dared to breathe while the dog inspected her. Then, again, a tiny portion of its tongue protruded, and it seemed to smile before delicately situating its haunches in the old woman's lap.

"I ... uh," Emily paused, "I think it smiled at me, Carolyn. I imagine it's hungry. Do we have something it can eat?"

"You don't want to feed that old nasty dog now, Miss Emily," Carolyn protested. "If you feed it, it'll hang around here forever. Let's just get it off you real careful-like, and call the dog pound." .

Miss Emily shook her head, stubbornly. The dog showed her teeth to Carolyn again, a silent growl. Carolyn sighed and propped the broom against the wall before pulling open the refrigerator door.

"We got some leftover corned beef hash," she announced, inspecting the contents of an old cottage cheese carton. "Dogs'll eat most anything."

"Put it in a bowl," Emily commanded. "Please," she added, softening.

Carolyn's foot sent something sliding across the floor, and she stooped to collect it. "What on earth is this?"

"It's my hearing aid," Emily confessed. "It, ah, it fell out, and you stepped on it."

The younger woman moved to the cabinet and took out an aluminum pie pan, grumbling quietly. "Dogs, busted hearing aids—I suppose we'll have to go get you a new one now. Who knows what'll happen next—the furnace'll go out I suppose, and that nephew always looking at me like it's my fault I don't take care of you right. I swear I don't know why I even bother."

She bent over, grunting softly, to set the pie plate on the floor. "That dog going to eat at the table or on the floor, like a proper dog?"

"Shoo," Emily said, tentatively waving her hands at the creature, which paused just a moment before leaping gracefully to the linoleum floor. It stood a good three feet from the food, gazing at it hopefully, before Emily realized what the problem was.

"Move back, Carolyn," she ordered. "It's afraid of you."

Reluctantly, Carolyn backed away from the dish near the door. When she was all the way to the sink, her back pressed against the countertop, the dog moved forward and inhaled the food in three large gulps. Then it turned to Emily and wagged its tail, very slightly. A small belch escaped it, and Emily laughed at the creature's comical expression.

"I believe it's a little lady," Emily declared. "Look and see, Carolyn. Isn't it a girl?"

Carolyn threw her hands up in the air. "You can't pay me enough to get close to that nasty little thing. It's probably got fleas, scabies, rabies—all kinds of terrible diseases."

The dog trotted over to Emily's chair and, without hesitating, jumped back up into the woman's lap.

"Don't let it do that, Miss Emily," Carolyn was horrified. "You'll get sick."

Emily's hand hovered over the dog, now curled in her lap and gazing up at her. "I think she'll do just fine, Carolyn," she said finally, her hand resting lightly on the creature's back. The fur was unexpectedly stiff and bristly, but not unpleasantly so. And the warmth of the dog lying placidly in her lap was a sensation unlike any she'd had before—a sensation that was most definitely pleasant.

To Carolyn's dismay, they sat like that for most of the morning—the wiry-haired mutt curled up, contented, in Emily's lap. The dog lay motionless while Emily ate breakfast and then worked her crossword puzzle. Once she jumped down and scratched at the door, and Carolyn quickly obliged, opening the door to let the dog trot out onto the porch and into the yard. It was no more than five minutes later that Emily heard the now-familiar scratching sound at the door—it was a noise that seemed anything but threatening in the clear light of day.

"Let the little lady in now, Carolyn," she ordered imperiously. Carolyn made no effort to hide her displeasure. Tightlipped, she muttered to herself as she tugged at the recalcitrant door.

"Lady, huh! A walking germ factory—that's what that thing is. I just don't understand why anybody could invite something like that into the house and feed it good food."

Emily ignored her comments. Without her hearing aid, it was just a mush of syllables anyway. But the scratching, clicking sound of the dog's paws was crystal clear.

"I'll call her Lady, anyway," Emily declared. "Some folks have manners around here." Carolyn harrumphed again but held her tongue.

Lady and Emily quickly adjusted to each other, even if Carolyn did not. The dog gave Carolyn a very wide berth when she was around, and Emily soon fell into the habit of talking to Lady when Carolyn was gone.

"Well, she was in a fine humor today, wasn't she?" she commented to Lady one afternoon when the door banged shut after Carolyn. "She must be having a—what do you call it?—a bad hair day, that's it!" She chuckled to herself. Lady turned and smiled at Emily before settling back down into her lap. Emily hummed and idly stroked the dog with one hand, her other hand holding the pencil to complete her crossword puzzle.

When the front doorbell rang, it startled both of them. Emily had been dozing a little in spite of the television's busy chatter, and Lady was undeniably snoring, although they were, appropriately, dainty snores.

By the time Emily hoisted herself up onto the walker and stumped her way to the foyer, the doorbell had sounded twice more.

"Who is it?" Emily snapped. Lady's two short, sharp barks seemed to echo the question.

"IT'S ME, AUNTIE," a voice bellowed back. "IT'S SAFE. YOU CAN OPEN UP THE DOOR!"

Emily sighed and shook her head. "What a nuisance," she whispered to Lady. "Last person in the world I want to see."

Lady whined in response.

"ARE YOU ALL RIGHT, AUNTIE?"

Emily managed to get two separate keys twisted and felt the bolts slide back. "Of course I'm all right, Kevin, I just don't move as fast as I used to," she said crossly. "What do you want?"

"I JUST STOPPED BY TO SAY HELLO," he bellowed.

For an instant, she thought about saying hello back and slamming the door in his face, but that might be unwise. He could, after all, probably convince some judge that she was senile, and then she could kiss her independence goodbye.

"I'm not so deaf you have to yell all the time. Come on in, I don't have enough money to heat the whole neighborhood." She opened the door wider and maneuvered the walker out of the way.

"WHAT'S THIS, AUNTIE?" He paused just inside the door, staring with distaste at Lady.

"IT'S A DOG, IDIOT!" She shook her head. "Stop yelling at me, Kevin. You'll give me a headache."

"I DIDN'T...," he stopped. "I didn't know you'd gotten a dog," he said in a more reasonable tone of voice.

"She just showed up one day, and I took a fancy to her. She doesn't bark much at all. She has lovely manners." Emily was thumping gracelessly down the hall on her walker while Lady trotted behind her.

"I guess it doesn't have fleas or rabies or anything, does it?" He sat down in a kitchen chair and frowned when Lady took up her post in Emily's lap. Lady bared her teeth in a silent snarl at him before putting her head down.

"Of course not. She's very clean, and like I said, she has exquisite manners." Kevin jumped up again, and Lady lifted her head.

"You never could sit still, Kevin. What do you want?"

"It's a little warm in here. I thought I'd check the thermostat." He disappeared into the dining room and then into the living room beyond. Lady nimbly hopped off Emily's lap and trotted after him, her claws clicking lightly on the hardwood floors.

"The thermostat's in the hall, Kevin," Emily called. "As if you didn't know," she mumbled.

"What's wrong with this dog?"

Emily sighed and pulled herself up to a standing position. "What are you doing, Kevin?"

As she entered the living room, she could see him attempting to reach into the bookcase where she kept her late husband's rock collection. "Have you ever had these appraised?" he asked casually, returning his hands to his pockets. "I don't know much about minerals and rocks, but they look valuable."

Lady stood between Kevin and the bookcase, her gums stretched tight and lifted up over her teeth. She made no sound, but her stance and expression were more threatening than anything Emily had ever seen from the little dog before.

"Of course they're valuable, Kevin," she said crossly. "That's precisely why Edwin collected them. You can have them appraised after I'm gone."

"Oh, don't talk that way, Auntie," he said, shaking his head. "Why, you're just a, just a spring chicken—that's what you are!"

They both looked down at the same instant to see Lady straddling one of Kevin's expensive leather shoes. A tiny puddle the size of a quarter marred the shiny surface, and a few drops dribbled onto the floor. Lady backed off into the corner and grinned at Emily.

"What the...?"

Emily covered her mouth and gasped for breath. She had to turn her head for a moment before she could face her great-nephew with anything resembling a straight face.

"I'm sorry, Kevin," she said, not sounding particularly contrite. "Even ladies have accidents every now and then. Let's go back to the kitchen, and I'll find you a paper towel to clean off your shoe." Lady led them to the kitchen, head held high, toenails clicking merrily on the floorboards.

Emily woke with a start that night, feeling an unfamiliar weight on the blankets covering her. When her eyes had adjusted to the dim light in the room, she recognized Lady's smiling face next to her hips. "All right, Lady," she whispered. "I suppose you've earned a place up here. No accidents, mind!" Lady circled around and lay down, a compact little ball of salt-and-pepper fur, warming more than the bed with her quiet companionship.

More than a week later, Emily missed the weight of Lady's body before she realized what had woken her up. A shrill stream of yaps, angry and loud, flooded the foyer. Emily groped for her walker and then for the telephone, astonished at the quantity of noise her quiet little Lady was producing.

The sound of footsteps, heavy and hurried, distracted her from her frantic efforts. They retreated from the porch and then were gone.

"Lady?" Emily called. "Lady?" Her hands shook as she replaced the telephone receiver.

Click, click, click, clickety-click. The dog's weight compressed the blankets and the mattress momentarily, and then the dog's face appeared, two feet from Emily's face.

"What was that, Lady?" The dog whined in response.

"I've never heard you make such a racket before, Lady. Did you scare them off?" Lady whined again and seemed to smile before nestling down close to Emily's left hip. Humming a bit and stroking the little dog at her side, Emily drifted off to sleep.

"This is the nastiest-smelling stuff I ever saw, Miss Emily," Carolyn complained the next day as she spooned dog food into the aluminum pie pan. "You'd think that dog could at least eat food that doesn't smell so awful."

Emily stroked Lady's bristly fur. "Consider yourself lucky I don't have you cook liver for her," she warned. "This little lady is the best thing that's happened to me since Edwin died."

Carolyn sniffed. "Well, I don't know about that."

Emily's bath was a bit on the chilly side that afternoon, but when she complained, Carolyn was short.

"It's as warm as it always is, Miss Emily," she retorted. "I'm leaving in thirty minutes. You want a bath today or not?"

That night Emily noticed, with a flare of annoyance, that the bulb in the hall light was burned out.

"Can't see, black as tar in here," she grunted to Lady, who cocked her head in silent agreement. "Likely to trip and fall down, and then where'd we be?"

Lady whined. In the kitchen, Emily pulled out a chair and sat down to begin her nightly struggle with the day's crossword puzzle. If she went to bed too early, she woke hours before dawn and that threw her off schedule all the next day. The crossword puzzle was usually good for two hours if she tossed in a little TV for good measure.

"In the nursing home, that's where we'd be. And they don't allow you to stay up past ten, and they sure don't let you bring in your Lady friends!" She cackled at her pun and set to work, Lady warming her lap. Sometimes she would stop and just stroke Lady's fur, enjoying the sensation of the stiff bristly hair against her fingers.

Kevin stopped by for his weekly visit the next afternoon.

"HOW ARE YOU FEELING, AUNTIE?"

"Stop bellowing, Kevin. I told you—it makes my head hurt."

"Sorry, Auntie."

He didn't look sorry, standing there with his hip cocked to one side and leaning against the wall. His foot betrayed his impatience, tapping softly on the old carpet in the dark hall. Lady watched him closely from a post in the corner by the front door.

"Your dog housebroken yet?"

"She's always been a lady to those who deserve it," Emily retorted. "I don't feel much like visiting, Kevin."

"Well, I'll be on my way, then. Do you have everything you need?"

"Yes, yes." She was literally shooing him out the door when she remembered. "Oh, I suppose there is something you could do for me. The light's burned out here in the hall. Could you change the bulb for me?"

Emily moved to the kitchen to collect a stepstool and a light bulb while Kevin watched, his restlessness barely held in check. Emily was acutely aware of his intolerance of her deliberate, crablike pace. At last, with a sigh of indulgence, he snatched the light bulb in its little cardboard container out of her hand.

"I've got an appointment, Auntie," he said as he folded out the stepstool and climbed up on it. "You sure a forty-watt bulb is strong enough?"

"It'll do, Kevin," she muttered on her way to her chair in the kitchen. "Good enough for an old fogy like me, I reckon."

He pretended not to hear her as he stretched to reach the light socket. "These high ceilings," he panted, "most impractical things I've ever seen." Giving the bulb one final twist, he stepped down and folded the stepstool with one hand, returning it to the kitchen and throwing away the burned-out bulb.

"See you, Auntie," he said, patting her on the shoulder on his way out. "Lock up behind me, okay?" He was down the hall and gone before she had a chance to reply.

Unexpectedly tears welled up in Emily's eyes. Lady whined and launched herself up into the woman's lap, anxiously looking up into her face.

"Oh, I'm just a silly old woman, Lady," Emily sniffed, stroking her fur. "Don't mind me." She sat quietly for a few minutes, until her tears dried up, and then she reached for her walker.

This was Lady's cue to jump down, and she did, standing a few paces away as Emily propelled herself to a standing position. Together they moved to the hall, and Emily reached for the switch.

With a pop and a sizzle, the new bulb expired. Emily stumped her way through the dark hall of the house she'd known for sixty-eight years, ever since her husband had carried her over the threshold as a blithe and agile eighteen-year-old. Suddenly, Lady stopped dead in front of her and began barking furiously.

"What's wrong with you, Lady?" For a moment, Emily was struck with terror, remembering the would-be intruders who had provoked Lady's barks before. But then, she realized, it had been dark, and now it was early afternoon. There was absolutely nothing to be afraid of here in this house she'd known for so long.

She moved ahead, in spite of the torrent of sound coming from Lady's squat little form. Too late she saw the gleam of white underneath the foot of her walker. Too late, she realized Lady's warning. Emily tumbled down, hip meeting floor with a jarring finality. The woman lay as inanimate as the flattened cardboard light bulb box in the dark hall, while Lady raised an unearthly howl of pure anguish.

The halls were bright with a cold, cheerless light reflected by the uniforms and walls of the nursing home. During daylight hours, the barren whiteness was fractured by the figures moving through. A man in a wheelchair, both legs amputated at the knee, wheeled aimlessly up and down the corridor. His bright red-checked shirt was slightly damp around the collar, and spittle gleamed like secret jewels in the crevices around his mouth.

"'M goin' home tomorrow," he would announce periodically. "Yessir, home's where m' heart is."

A bone-thin woman roamed, a purple sweater draped over her shoulders, restlessly rubbing her hands together over and over as if to warm them. She would never speak, but others might occasionally burst out with shouted oaths or uncontrollable sobs. It was a noisy place, for when the residents were quiet, the TV blared its imperious messages.

"How's the new one?" The evening shift was just coming on duty, and the night nurse in charge liked to keep up with her patients.

"No change, really." The outgoing nurse pulled up a chart and flipped through it. "She's still feeding herself, though, and she's quiet. She'll adjust pretty soon."

The object of their discussion sat placidly in a wheelchair placed in front of the TV set, her left hand moving deliberately through the air a scant six inches above her lap. As the hand reached the edge of her thigh, she would raise it and move it through the air again. Her right arm lay curved in her lap, cradling a small pocket of empty space.

"Is she talking yet?"

"No, but we noticed she was humming a bit this morning after breakfast." "No visitors?"

The other woman shook her head.

"Have a good afternoon."

"You too, Ella. Watch out for Mrs. Lee. She's been on a rampage today." After dinner, the nursing home slowly subsided into its nighttime rhythms.

By nine, the residents were all in their beds and the TVs were off. The stark white corridors were as empty of sound as they were of color.

Click, click, clickety-click. The nurse looked up—nothing there. She returned her attention to the novel she was holding, dog-eared with a tattered paper cover.

Click, click, clickety-click. She looked up again with a sigh of annoyance—nothing there. She stood and walked down the hall to the supply room where the nurse's aide was putting away some towels.

"Did you drop something, Jean?"

The woman turned, startled. "No."

"Did you get your radio fixed?"

"It's still broken. Why?"

"I thought I heard static."

Ella shrugged and returned to her station. Near the end of her shift, she took her little penlight and walked from room to room, checking each patient. Mrs. Sommers was standing in the bathroom in the dark, having forgotten why she got up. In the third room, Ella gently tucked the covers around Mr. Ellis who'd lost his legs last month. And in the next-to-the-last room on the corridor, she stood with her penlight trained for a long minute on the chest of the newest resident. It neither rose nor fell. She snapped on the overhead light, exhaling loudly.

She plopped down on the edge of the bed to take the woman's hand and look for a pulse, even though she knew she wouldn't find one. The woman's hand was like ice, and the joints were gnarled and knotted. As Ella laid the hand gently back down on the bed, her hand grazed a spot on the bed, near the patient's left hip, that was unquestionably warm. And sticking up from the open weave of the institutional blanket were four or five salt-and-pepper hairs, short and wiry.

on river road

Now my Grandpa was always a great one for telling stories. Matter of fact, he had a story to fit almost any occasion. At the drop of a hat, he would start to spin his tale. It got to be a joke among us young ones that Granpa would turn his head and spit and then clear his throat and pronounce, "That reminds me of a story I heard once..."

But there was one story he didn't ever tell us youngsters. He saved it for me until I was a grown-up man with a family of my own. I was in my twenties, I suppose, and I'd found me a wife a few years back, and we'd got right down to business and had two children, wham-bang, just like that.

Now having children is a hard thing for a woman—I don't deny that. But I don't suppose anybody ever thinks about how hard it can be on a young man, too. First, your wife swells up like a balloon and won't let you near her for love or money. My wife, Lissy, got real peculiar both times she was pregnant, and I don't just mean her eating habits. She'd complain that her clothes were rubbing her skin raw, or she'd start boo-hooing about how her ankles had disappeared. I tried to be patient, Heaven knows I did, and I don't think Lissy ever knew how crazy she was making me.

Then came the baby. Oh, boy, if I thought things were weird before the baby came, I was stunned at the changes once he got here. That little squalling, smelly bundle turned my whole life upside down. Our heads would barely hit the pillows before that child would start screaming. I could count on supper being interrupted at least twice. And if I ever, ever thought about getting close to Lissy, well, I believe that baby had some sort of radar or something—I could just think about giving Lissy a little hug, and that baby would wake up and holler with a vengeance.

Then she went and got pregnant again.

So there I was, with a wife doubly preoccupied. I wasn't getting any sleep, I wasn't getting any good food, and Lissy didn't have time to do the wash or clean the house—much less keep me company. Worst of all, I wasn't getting what a man needs most from his wife—affection.

Now I know what I did was wrong. Believe me, I know it with my heart and soul—and I'd never do it again, even if I had the opportunity and I was a million miles from home. But I took to visiting a little roadhouse on River Road after work, just for a little bit to enjoy a brew or two and some like-minded company. Me and the boys might shoot some pool, and we would certainly shoot the breeze. Most of us were married with young children at home, so there wasn't, in our minds anyway, much hurry to get home.

Well, there were a few women who liked to hang around that roadhouse, too. One of them took a fancy to me, and I was partial to her, too. We took up with each other, I'm sorry to say. Now Riverbend is a small town, and folks started talking pretty quick. I'm lucky it didn't get back to Lissy. But I was unlucky in that it did get back to Granpa, who was a really old coot by this time and mean as a hornet when he had a mind to be.

Granpa came barreling into that roadhouse one afternoon just as me and my sweetheart had settled down in a nice comfy booth with a couple of cold ones. "Junior!" he roared. Since he was deaf, he thought he should yell so everybody could hear him. He could get pretty tiresome at times. "You get your butt outta that booth this minute and come here!"

I sighed. "He won't shut up till I do it," I explained to my girl. I took my arm from around her shoulders and slid out of the booth to face the ornery old man. "What, Granpa?"

"Get outside right now, and let's talk about something."

I shrugged and followed him out the door, squinting a little when the sun hit my eyes. It was so dark and cool inside the bar that I sometimes forgot it was still daylight. Granpa tottered over to his truck—it's a wonder they still let him out on the road—and told me to climb up in the cab.

"I've got a story I need to tell you," he said grimly.

Now I sighed openly. "Aw, c'mon, Granpa," I protested. "I've got a date."

"Precisely." He punctuated his statement by slamming the truck door shut. "Back when your daddy was a little bitty baby..."

I groaned, and it must've been pretty loud because he heard it and scowled at me. "You'd better listen close, boy," he growled, gripping the collar of my T-shirt in one gnarled old fist, surprisingly strong for his age. "You'll end up like your daddy in a cold empty grave before your time!"

Well, this surprised me because he didn't talk much about my daddy. So I shut up and listened.

"I was young and foolish, too, boy, just like you. Henrietta, your granma, was a beautiful woman when I married her: full of fire, hair like midnight, and the sweetest laugh you ever heard—it sounded like all the bells in heaven ringing all at once."

His eyes glazed, and my mind wandered back to the sweet young thing waiting for me inside. I started to press down lightly on the door handle, thinking I could slip out of the truck and back inside the roadhouse while Granpa was lost in a daydream. But the click of the door handle snapped him out of it.

"Shut that door!" His old rheumy eyes blazed, and I was almost scared not to do what I was told.

"But five or six years after we got married, life just sort of wore her down. The farm was awful hard work, you know, and then she had your daddy and a string of babies that never lived longer than a day or two at most. She can still tell you their names, and you'll find their stones in the graveyard next to your daddy."

I nodded absently. None of this was new to me.

"There was a widow woman who had the farm down the road—not too far from this place." He rolled down his window and spit out a thick blob of phlegm to express his disgust. Then he rolled up the window tight and turned back to me.

"She was beautiful. I mean, it stole your breath away to look at her: creamy white skin, chestnut hair that caught the sun and made it flash like sparks—she was everything a man might look for in a woman."

He leaned closer, and his breath washed over me, a stale, medicine-tainted stench with just a hint, I thought, of death in it. I pulled back, my nose wrinkling.

"I couldn't help myself, Junior." His voice had a pleading note that made me exceedingly uneasy. "It started with me walking down the road to borrow her team to finish up the plowing when our mules went lame. And then I kept finding more and more excuses to go back until I was spending almost as much time there as I was at home.

"One night I stayed later than I should have. It seemed uncommonly dark along River Road, but I'd had a sip or two, and that can make things seem different than they really are, you know."

I nodded. Boy, how I knew that.

"I was right along about here, I suppose, and of course, they hadn't built this place yet. The road was black as tar, so I could barely see my feet stepping one in front of the other. I was moving along at a pretty good clip, it being late and all, when I heard a rustle out of the woods to my left. I just glanced that way thinking that it was a deer or a coon or something and thinking, God help me, that if I'd brought my shotgun out it would've made a good excuse to be out till moonrise, at least.

"I didn't see anything. I kept moving, and I guess I was just a quarter mile from home when I heard a crashing sound between the trees to my left again. I thought it might be a bear from the sound of it, but there hadn't been any bears around here since I don't know when. I turned to face whatever was coming at me and saw the evilest, cruelest eyes that ever lived outside of hell. They were a burning, pulsing red—four little balls with flames licking out at me. I thought it was Satan himself, and I took to my heels and ran like a deer all the way home.

"When I got there, Henrietta was as calm as you please, smiling as she hung up my coat and told me supper was warming in the oven. I don't think she even heard my little lame attempt at an excuse. A saint, that's what she is to this day—just a saint. If she noticed I was out of breath, she didn't say a word.

"The next day, thinking about it, I got to thinking that maybe I'd had too much to drink and I'd imagined it all. I had a powerful urge to go visit that pretty widow woman again, so I took up my shotgun and told your granma I was going coon hunting.

"I had me a nice little visit and was heading home a few hours after dark, whistling and practically skipping I felt so good—but not for long. Again, I heard some rustling and carrying on in the trees, just out of sight, and so I stopped and loaded that shotgun just in case it was something that needed shooting. Whatever was making that noise wasn't in any hurry to come out of the underbrush, and I walked along, cautious-like, for about a half mile, keeping one eye out for that animal and the other on the road ahead. I was nearly to the turnoff for our house when something big and white and completely terrifying came bursting out of the trees, lunging straight for my throat.

"At first I couldn't even tell what it was, I was so scared, and it was coming at me so fast. I backed off, nearly stumbling over my feet in my haste, holding the shotgun out like a stick between me and the creature. Just before he lunged again, glaring steadily at me with those awful eyes of fire, I could see, clearly, that he was a two-headed dog—a hound from hell."

Granpa looked at me steadily, and I got a queasy feeling. I was starting to worry that this story didn't have a funny punch line.

"Somehow that shotgun got twisted down, and it went off right at my foot. Blew my little toe right off. Luckily, Henrietta heard the blast and came out to get me. Otherwise, I might've bled to death right there. But while I lay there bleeding, I knew that dog was a messenger. And I got that message loud and clear—I was never unfaithful to your granma again."

He clapped me on the shoulder, and I squirmed a little under his grasp. Granpa had never been much of a moralist before.

"Son, I'm telling you—you don't have any business messing around on Lissy. She's a good woman, and you don't want to feel that hellhound's hot breath on your neck."

"But what does all this have to do with my father?" I asked sullenly.

Granpa sighed. "Well, boy, it's the same song, different verse. Not too long after you were born, your daddy got itchy feet. Everybody all over the county knew he was stepping out on your mama. They were living with us at the time, and I did my best to hide it from her, and with a new baby and all, I guess she was pretty preoccupied. I don't think your granma ever knew about it either.

"One night when he came back late, I pulled him aside to tell him what happened to me. He just laughed, called me a silly old fart, and kept right on making mischief."

Granpa's expression got darker, and he seemed to shrink a little in his dirty coveralls, practically turning into a shriveled old man right in front of my eyes. "The very next night, he was walking back along River Road after spending half the evening and most of his paycheck on some other woman.

"We don't know exactly what happened, but we found your daddy on our porch steps next morning at sunup. There wasn't a mark on him, but his eyes were opened wide, staring, and his mouth was all twisted up like he'd been trying to call out for help.

"In the dirt below the stairs were the tracks of an enormous dog. Your daddy was just plain scared to death."

The truck seemed suddenly chilly, and I shivered a little before looking out to see if the sun still shone as brightly as before. Just then, my little sweetheart burst out of the door of the roadhouse, laughing and swinging lightly on the arm of my best friend.

Without a word, I jumped out of the truck to go make my claim. I didn't even hear Granpa pull out of the parking lot onto River Road, his tires spitting gravel as angrily as he could spit words.

I stayed out a little later than I should have that night. When I pulled up outside our trailer, just down the road from Granpa's house where I'd grown up, I looked around, a little nervous. I didn't place too much stock in Granpa's tall tales, but most all of his stories have a little piece of truth in them somewhere, if you just know where to look. For my dignity's sake, I tried not to hurry into the safety of the brightly lit trailer, but my steps were probably a little livelier than they'd been the night before.

Lissy greeted me with a smile and told me both babies were sound asleep in their cribs. My supper was still warm on the stove, she said, and it was one of my favorites—fried chicken, peas, and mashed potatoes. I narrowed my eyes and peered at her closely, but her open, happy face seemed to hold no trace of trickery.

Next day was Friday—payday. I had every good intention of going straight home after a beer or two, but one thing led to another, and while I was shooting a little pool, my girl came through the door looking like a little angel. Well, maybe not an angel exactly, but she looked mighty good. I dropped a little money in the jukebox and had a few more drinks, and before I knew it, it was a lot later than I could possibly dream up an excuse for. I untangled myself from my sweetheart—who was looking a little bleary-eyed herself—and walked very carefully to my truck.

It was just a half mile or so home, and I crawled along, hugging the yellow center line like a baby hugs its blanket. I had both windows down and the radio blasting, and my mind was a million miles away, trying to come up with a plausible excuse for coming home at such an hour, in such a state.

I guess that's why I never heard the beast until it was right up on me. Somehow it was running alongside the truck, snarling and snapping at my arm that hung halfway out the window.

I did a truly stupid thing. I slammed on my brakes, and the truck shuddered to a stop, the engine stalling out because in my fright, I didn't push in the clutch. The dog backed up to take a running leap at me, and I could see its two heads clearly, four beady red eyes glowing fiercely, two slick pink tongues covered in froth dangling between his long, wicked incisors, and two black noses wrinkled in anticipation of a fight.

It was such a terrifying sight that I just knew it had to be a nightmare, but when I felt his breath hot on my cheek, I knew it was not. Something about his breath made me think of my girlfriend whispering nonsense in my ear, and I gagged. His two heads couldn't fit completely inside the window, just the first third of each snout, and I fell over toward the middle of the cab.

I heard his jaws snap shut—first one, then the other—click, click. They closed on empty air, and I dared to reach for the knob to roll the window shut. His paws skittered and clawed on the glass, trying in vain to reach me. Both heads were thrown back, and both mouths were flung open wide as he bayed and howled his disappointment at lost prey. The radio was still blaring, spilling out an absurdly happy noise in stark contrast to the absolute terror I had just lived through.

He bounded off into the woods—back to hell, I imagine—and I somehow managed to drive my truck the few hundred yards home. I slept in the cab of my truck, too afraid to get out, and woke to the sound of tapping on my window. It was Lissy, holding a steaming mug of coffee in her hand and a baby on her hip.

"Have a good time last night?" she asked cheerfully, but I could only groan.

"Well, come in, then, and get some rest on a proper bed." She very kindly led me in and tucked me into bed as gently as she tucked in the babies. Then she very thoughtfully went and spent the morning with a friend, her and the babies, so my sleep was only disturbed by terrible nightmares of that two-headed dog.

My truck to this day carries long, livid scratches down the door. They're filled with rust now, and Lissy says I ought to get a new truck or at least get this one painted. But I'd rather spend the money on her and the boys. I'm a changed man now, really I am.

The other day I was warming up a little coffee. It was on a Saturday morning, and Lissy had a friend over. The girl sat on our sofa, sniveling and crying, a fistful of tissues in each hand. I could barely understand what she was saying, she was gurgling and hiccupping so much. But I heard Lissy loud and clear.

"You should move out to the country, honey," she said, stroking her friend's arm. "I don't know why, but the air out here is good for men like Tommy. Even the wildest ones settle down out here on River Road."

god rest your soul

Pain. It exploded through his consciousness with the fierceness of a sudden storm. Unanticipated. Inexplicable. Curses flew along with the blows, hatred soaking every syllable. He lay still, pressing his body as close to the ground as possible and not making any move that might stoke the wrath to further heights.

The man stopped at last, spitting out one more curse as he strode away. The dog heard a door slam shut across the yard and knew the pain was over for the time being. His thick black fur was sticky with blood and matted with dirt from the ground outside the shed where he lived. His thick ruff, which by rights should have framed his regal face, broad nose, and almond-shaped eyes, lay as if dispirited, bedraggled around the neck that boasted no collar and no mark of civilized ownership.

He moaned and rolled over. Every little movement caused another explosion of pain. Staggering to his feet, he moved through the underbrush and into the scraggly woods beyond. The gentle, soothing sound of moving water came clearly to his ears, and even through his scratched and bloodied nose, he could smell the fresh, welcome scent.

He drank deeply, gratefully. Then the dog worked his way farther into the woods, found a slight depression in the earth, and made his nest.

●●●●●●

"Here, girl!" The man clapped his hands sharply, the empty collar in his hand jangling. He whistled again and again, the sound losing itself quickly among the thickly wooded rolling hills.

"Lacey, here!" The command was as convincing as he could make it, but still the mixed-collie did not come crashing through the leaves with infectious joy. The man continued to tramp through the leaves, following no discernible path.

Just as he noticed the clouds leaching daylight from the sky, he heard a short, high yip of excitement. His heart speeding up, he began calling again. Ahead he could hear the sound of Lacey dancing, spinning through the undergrowth, but he stopped in surprise to hear a deeper, throatier bark answering Lacey's yelps. Another dog? Way out here? He slowed, cautious, until Lacey came bursting out of the woods to his left, trailing a mass of dried kudzu vine that looked like a rustic leash and collar.

"Girl, where have you been?" He laughed in relief and tousled her head roughly but affectionately. Her head was wet in places, and her tongue was out as she breathed hard. As his hands moved on down her coat, he noticed without curiosity at first that her fur had patches of dampness, like she'd been randomly sprinkled. Or, as his mind quickly put a picture together, like she'd been wrestling another dog, exchanging playful nips as they romped.

He stood up, ignoring the wet muzzle insistently nudging his hand. The woods were full of shadows now, and he strained his eyes to make out another canine shape between the trees. A fat raindrop landed on his bare arm, startling him. Another and another fell, and he stooped to slip the collar and leash on his dog before jogging through the woods back to his car.

"You have some company out there, Lacey? He laughed as they ran, dodging raindrops. She made no reply, but her tail waved gaily as she bounded over the rough ground.

"Is that why you ran off, girl? I thought you were gone for good!" Back at the roadside park, he opened the rear door of his station wagon, so Lacey could leap in, shaking off the rain.

The first low growls of thunder came rolling in just as the man flipped the switch to raise the car window. He stopped the mechanism midway and cocked his ear to listen attentively. From the woods, not too far from the road, he could just make out an unmistakable sound—the sound of a big dog baying in utter desolation.

Lacey sent up an answering cry, and the man shuddered, wondering at her ability to sense another's pain. Before she could cry again, he pulled out into the road, too fast, tires squealing from the abuse.

•••••

When the sun was almost directly overhead, it warmed the little hollow on the forest floor. The big black dog luxuriated in the warmth, stretching each leg as he awoke and wincing as fresh scabs broke open from the movement. He stood stiffly and stalked through the woods toward the little stream. He drank and then stood still, listening, his black tongue slightly extended.

He couldn't hear the low burble of noise from the house that always signified the man's alert presence. But then he hadn't heard the roar of the car engine that guaranteed the man's absence, either. As he stood weighing his need for food against his desire to avoid more pain, he heard the back door of the house squeak open.

The dog tensed, ready to flee. His ears pricked forward, and his jaws snapped shut. A soft voice and light footsteps were his signal to move, hesitantly at first, from the shadow of the trees.

"C'mere, Demon. C'mere, boy." She was barely calling, and the dog was glad, afraid that a loud shout might wake the storm of fury that erupted too often from within the house. The woman held a can of something and a fork, and she crept quietly toward the old shed that housed the dog when life was peaceful. As she reached the shelter of the shed, the dog could see the bruises mottling her neck and arms, a play of light and dark that mocked the shadows from the tree branches moving softly above her.

The dog now stood in the shadows, too, and watched silently as she scraped the dog food into a rusty old baking pan. When she finished, he growled softly before walking stiff-legged to the dish.

"I'm sorry, boy." She tossed the empty can inside the shed and bent to wipe the fork clean on the ground. "I don't feel too good neither."

Before the dog had finished eating, the woman was gone, sliding back into the house like pale smoke. He shook himself, all over, a satisfying movement in spite of the lingering aches. Trotting through the yard and down to the road, he began to make his daily rounds.

••••••

"C'mon, Marian. I know it's around here somewhere."

"It's dark, Thomas, and I promised Mama I'd be home half an hour ago."

"Aww, please? Just a little bit farther?"

The boy led her by the hand, crashing heedlessly through the underbrush, blind in the darkness before moonrise.

"You're lucky I really love you, Thomas Peter Gaines." She pouted, but the effect was lost in the pitch-black woods. An owl hooted just overhead, and she sprang closer to him, as close as she could while he thrashed his way ahead.

"I found it yesterday, no problem," he mumbled.

"What exactly is it?" A briar bush had caught her hand, and she thought maybe she was bleeding. This was no fun at all, she thought crossly. They could have walked to town and gotten a Coke or something, but instead they were wandering around lost in a wilderness.

"It's a neat, uh," he considered his words—"a neat shed" wouldn't quite have the drawing power he was looking for. "It's like an old barn that probably was built in pioneer days. And it's got..." he winced as a low-hanging branch slapped him in the face. "It's got all these neat things inside, like old chests and stuff."

"Well, I don't know..."

Just then the moon appeared over the crest of the ridge in front of them, bathing the woods and the hollow in a weird, otherworldly light.

"Ahhh," she gasped.

"There it is," he shouted. "I knew we were close!"

He half-ran, half-stumbled to a dilapidated structure built carelessly with planks of knotted wood that had long since weathered to a battered gray. The knotholes looked like scars or eyes peering angrily out at the twisted mass of vines and saplings that threatened to tumble the haphazard collection of boards to the ground.

Without warning, the boy sank halfway to his knees in mud. The girl stopped so suddenly that she lost her balance, teetering and finally stumbling with a little splash into a narrow, muddy creek.

"My dress!" the girl wailed. "Thomas, I swear, I will never, never..."

"I'm sorry, Marian. Look, I'll help you clean it up. C'mon—don't be mad!" He pulled out his shirttail and, pulling her to her feet, began to gently wipe her hands clean of the sticky mud.

"C'mon, let's go see what's inside. I bet there's buried treasure!" The boy quickly grasped her arms and swung her safely over the little creek and then pulled her along behind him. "Won't you kiss me?" he coaxed her, once they'd reached the shelter.

"I ought to slap you, Thomas." Her hand crept shyly up to his face, and she traced his jaw line with her finger. "You tricked me—there ain't no treasure here."

"But we're alone, and you know how much I love you." His arm slipped around her waist, and she did not resist.

Outside a few tendrils of clouds snaked across the face of the moon, transforming its bland, open stare into something vaguely threatening. A breeze kissed the treetops, making a shushing sound the couple didn't even hear.

"You make me do the craziest things, Thomas Gaines," she whispered. "What would Mama say if she could see me?" The boy just groaned and pulled her close again.

More clouds slipped through the sky, moving quickly enough now to roll and tumble over one another as they masked and unmasked the sober face of the full moon.

The wind rose to a whine. Abruptly, the girl pulled free from the embrace. "What was that?" she gasped.

"Oh, nothing, Marian. It's just the wind," he moaned. "Come back here!" He growled playfully and wrapped his arms around her. Another growl echoed from the darkest part of the shed, and the couple sprang apart, electrified.

"Did you hear that?"

The boy tried to stand his ground. "It was just the wind," he protested, but his words fell flat.

A deep, throaty growl rolled out from the shadows, and the wind wailed shrilly outside. Now the two stood, hands clasped tightly, straining to see through the shadows into the corner beyond.

When lightning struck, just on the next ridge, it provided the illumination that a benign old moon had supplied just ten minutes before. But this light revealed a menacing green reflection from the left corner of the shed. Almond-shaped eyes glared balefully, surrounded by black fur that blended seamlessly into the shadows.

Without another word, the two people turned and fled.

●●●●●●

The dirt road was packed hard enough to make his travels quite pleasant. Keeping to the side of the road, ready to duck into the woods if anyone passed by, the dog trotted purposefully. A thick gathering of trees and saplings crowded close to the road, making the way dim and shadowed except for an hour or two around noontime.

There were three or four farms within easy range, if the term "farm" was not taken too strictly. Farming in such hilly terrain was never easy, and the soil, although a rich, dark brown, did not yield much more than stones. Folks around these Missouri hills raised a few chickens, a little corn, and usually a fair enough kitchen garden. They also raised a fair crop of bitter, unhappy children who felt cheated from the moment they were born.

A little town offered possibilities for forage, too, if the dog was inclined toward trash-can food. Chicken was really his favorite meal, fresh and hot and just enough of a challenge to get his blood going. His tongue fell out of his mouth in anticipation, and his tail curled tighter over his hocks. Sometimes, too, folks would see him around and bring him food, although this was very unpredictable. He never really knew when he might be met with a shower of rocks and curses, so he tended to avoid people as much as he could.

He turned off the main road and started up a deeply rutted, narrow lane that led to his closest neighbor's place. Their dog, a hound of indeterminate lineage, was kept chained in back of the house, out of sight of the barnyard. If the wind cooperated and he didn't stir up the chickens until he made his strike, the dog would not alert any people to his presence.

He moved off the track, keeping close to the trees now, weaving cautiously in and out like a sly, wayward shadow. Just where the trees stopped, cleared years ago to make way for the farmyard, he paused and surveyed the scene. His ears, although nearly hidden by his thick ruff, were cocked forward to capture every sound. He could hear an ax ringing on wood out by the dog's run, which would help conceal the noise of his progress. Inside the house, he detected a low, continuous murmur of noise and voices.

Closest to him, he heard a sound that made him begin to salivate in hopes of a feast. At the cackling and clucking of a half dozen hens, he wrinkled up his nose, scenting the air for any silent barriers to his attack. He could see the low wire fence surrounding the birds, but that would provide very little hindrance. Just as he tensed his legs in preparation for a dash into the farmyard, he heard the squeal of hinges on the screen door of the house. The hens raised their cackling to a fever pitch as the woman approached their pen.

"Hungry, are you?" She threw several arcing handfuls of feed into the yard, and the birds scrambled to reach every morsel. She turned to the henhouse to collect the eggs, and the dog slunk away quietly, defeated. If he had been hungrier, he might have tried to snatch a hen from under her nose, but he hadn't reached that level of desperation yet.

At the next house, a mile down the road, the dog found his meal all laid out for him. A garbage can had been overturned, and the contents strewn out across the yard, by possums, he thought when he caught the scent. He was nosing through the remains of a fried chicken dinner when the yard exploded into a cacophony of noise.

"Here, you! Get out of there!" A tin can flew past his nose, and he backed off, startled. Scraps of paper, still stained with the blood of fresh-ground meat, fluttered from his mouth.

The woman was striding closer, still yelling and waving a long wooden spoon threateningly. As she stooped to pick up a rock, he turned to flee back into the woods. With a final curse, the woman hurled the stone with amazing accuracy. It thudded against his ribs with great force, and he yelped in surprised anguish.

"That'll teach you, you stupid dog! Stay away from my trash!" Her angry shout followed him as he staggered painfully into the shelter of the woods.

••••••

"Where'd those dogs go, Jim?" The man wrapped his big hands around the thermos cup filled with steaming coffee. Leaning against the truck, he surveyed the terrain in front of him. It wasn't the trees that made the ground so treacherous, although the undergrowth could catch onto you and make it seem as if invisible hands held you back. It was the unpredictable dips and hollows that could make you lose your footing, and the steep, rocky hills that made you gasp for breath.

"You ready to head out again?" The other hunter winked. "Thought you was all tuckered out."

"I said I'd bring back supper tonight, and that's exactly what I'll do. Unless your dogs have run off," his friend drawled in reply.

"They're out there," Jim snapped testily. "Best dogs in the whole county for squirrels. Probably just catching their breath."

Twisting the cap back on the thermos, the other man tossed it onto the seat of the truck. "Let's go, then," he said, and Jim followed.

Just a few hundred feet into the woods, they heard the unmistakable sound of dogs fighting. Deep growls, yips of pain, and the sharp sounds of teeth snapping shut were clearly audible.

"Blue, cut that out!" Jim called. Abruptly the fight stopped, and the two men charged ahead. The man gasped when he saw his dog ahead, lying in a little hollow.

"Blue!" he cried. The little beagle raised his head and thumped his tail feebly. The man hunkered down on his knees to inspect the dog.

"What'd you tangle with, feller?" he asked, gently running his hands over the dog's skull and then down his neck and across his ribs. "What's wrong?"

Without warning, the dog leaped to his feet and bounded across the little clearing. In the distance, the two hunters could hear another dog howling. "What was that?" Puzzled, Jim peered after his dog. "Not a scratch on him!"

"Those your dogs howling?"

Jim stopped to listen, squinting as if that would make him hear better. "That's not anybody's hunting dog," he concluded, shaking his head. "I've never heard a dog howl like that."

The mournful noise rose and fell, rose and fell again. It seemed to echo off the ridge ahead and multiply until it was the cry of two, twenty, a hundred dogs. Its agonizing call raised gooseflesh on Jim's arms, and he snuck a glance at his friend to see his response to the unseen dog. His friend stood mesmerized, staring off in the direction where Blue had disappeared. His face was contorted by sadness.

"Let's go," Jim whispered.

Shaking himself all over, his friend complied. As the heartbroken howls died away, the two men trudged slowly toward the road.

•••••

The rain had been pounding down so hard for a night and a day that the big black dog had crept to the shelter of the shed near its owner's house. The discomfort of the rain outweighed his sense of danger at home. Besides, sometimes his owner could be kind, although those occasions were no more than a hazy memory. This shed was the only home the dog had ever known.

He twisted around to lick his ribs where the rock had torn the flesh. His eyes slit nearly closed against the pain, he swabbed at the wound again and again with his broad, black tongue. Without warning, a shadow towered over him. A growl escaped his throat before he could contain it, and with that growl, he knew he had made a mistake of colossal proportions.

"Don't you growl at me," his owner grunted. He poked at him, sharply, with the pointed toe of his boot. The dog lay still as death, a survival tactic learned at no small expense.

"Where were you yesterday?" His tone was brutal. The boot drew back and aimed a kick at the ribs.

The dog lay still, without a whimper, as the man savaged it with feet and fists and curses. Only once, at the height of the rampage, did the dog raise his head and a vagrant gleam of light caught his pupils. They glowed an eerie, otherworldly green, and the man drew back for an instant. Then, seeing the dog offered no resistance, he continued his pitiless assault. When the dog lay limp and lifeless, the man turned and left the shadow-filled shelter.

Hours passed, and still the dog did not move. His rib cage rose and fell, but the movement was barely perceptible. At last, long past sunset, the almond-shaped eyes opened and blinked. His tongue, swollen and dry, worked its way between his teeth, seeking moisture from the ground beneath its body.

He tried to stand, but his back legs would not support his barrel-chested body. Pulling with his front legs, he slowly, painfully, crossed to the door of the shed. Water dripping from the eaves had collected in a puddle at the entrance, and he gratefully lapped at the water. He lay his head down again as new waves of pain broke over his body. His eyes never closed—the deep brown pupils just glazed over as his chest ceased to move. The rain beat steadily on his skull as the night wore on.

●●●●●●

The note was grubby around the edges and the penciled script was smudged, but the message was still legible.

Andy looked across the rows of bowed heads in his math class and nodded. Carl was watching him, and he made a circle with his thumb and forefinger.

"Okay," he mouthed. Both boys bent again to the paper in front of them just as the teacher looked up, frowning, her second sense activated by some small disturbance in the room's air currents, perhaps.

After school, Carl and Andy ditched their book bags at their respective homes and met at the foot of Carl's driveway. "So where'd you hear about this treasure?" Andy asked, standing with arms akimbo.

"My aunt was talking to somebody on the phone, and I heard her say she'd been out here looking for it. It was a long time ago, but she didn't find it."

"How do you know it's not some dumb trick?" Andy asked skeptically.

"She didn't know I was listening. And she said there were wild dogs guarding it—she got scared and ran off."

"Huh."

"You got anything better to do?"

Andy shrugged. "Guess not."

The two boys bounded through the woods, ducking under vines and squeezing between thick stands of saplings. It was an early spring afternoon, and the ground was thick and spongy underfoot. The branches were all bare, but swollen buds were in evidence everywhere. Beneath the heavy layer of last year's dead leaves, the ground lay full of promise.

"Here's the creek!" Carl was elated by his discovery. "She said she fell into the creek!"

Andy eyed the lazy, ambling course of water no more than eighteen inches across. "Pretty small creek," he muttered, but Carl didn't hear. He had crossed the stream and was thrashing around just out of sight.

It took no more than a giant step to cross it, and soon Andy stood next to his friend. "So?"

Carl took a few steps in one direction and then the other. "She said it was just over the creek," he said. "I found the creek. Just give me a minute, will you?"

"What exactly are we looking for?"

"It's a shed..." Carl started.

"There it is!" Andy pointed with a shout to a structure so overgrown with honeysuckle and kudzu that it looked like a stand of saplings. In a few weeks, when the leaves came out, it would be indistinguishable from the rest of the forest.

The two boys rushed over and tried to part the tough old vines to peer inside the shed. Just then, a blood-chilling howl cut through the trees.

"Holy cow!" shouted Andy. The boys looked at each other uneasily. "What'd your aunt say about wild dogs?"

Another howl tore through the forest, this time louder than before. To their left, back the way they had come, they heard the noise of a large creature crashing through the dead leaves.

Without further consultation, the boys fled. Andy headed off to the right, fleet as a rabbit, and Carl wasn't far behind. Three crashing leaps between the trees, and he could hear something gaining on him— something at least as big as he was. An unexpected dip in the forest floor, a root exposed by winter rains, and he fell headlong, colliding hard with the ground.

Carl lay with his eyes screwed shut in terror. Andy was gone. The beast was upon him, its approach quiet now. He felt it snuffle along the length of his body, and he braced himself for the inevitable snap of teeth against his flesh. Fear numbed him.

There was a little whine and then nothing—no more hot breath against his bare skin, no sound of paws crunching in the leaves, nothing at all. After a long moment, he opened his eyes. There, under his nose, was a long cylindrical shape unnaturally white for a forest floor.

He blinked and pulled back. He touched it with his fingers and then picked it up to examine it closer—a bone, a big bone. He held it up against his own arm to measure its size. It came from a creature almost as big as he was.

Carl stood up slowly, the bone still in his hand. He began to trace back his steps, his eye now catching glimpses of gleaming white to his left and to his right. At the entrance to the old shed, after kicking the vines aside and scratching a bit in the moist soil, he found a skull.

The light was nearly gone by the time he made his final discovery. He made his way home quietly and quickly, and he didn't have much to say at the supper table.

When he was clearing his plate, he asked his mother a shy question. "Why do we bury folks when they die, Mama?"

She looked startled. "Why, I don't know, Carl. I suppose it's so their souls will rest easy. Ask your daddy."

Sneaking out of the house was never difficult. Carl's mother always checked on him before she went to bed, but after that, he was on his own. Staying awake until she went to bed was sometimes hard, but tonight he had plenty of thoughts to occupy his mind.

Slipping out his window, Carl crept to the lean-to where the gardening tools were stored. Selecting a spade with a stout wooden handle, his slight form merged with shadows as he stole into the woods to his self-appointed task.

••••••

Lacey yipped in excitement as they pulled into the roadside park. "I'm not letting you off your leash this time, girl," the man warned as he clipped the lead to her collar. "I'm ready to get home, and that doesn't mean another tramp through the woods to track you down."

She lunged into the woods, straining hard enough to nearly pull the man off balance. Scenting eagerly this way and that, she dragged him between trees and through low-hanging shrouds of kudzu just beginning to show the barest hint of a bud here and there until she arrived at a little clearing. Here, she stopped. A questioning whine escaped her as she cocked her head, listening.

"What's wrong, Lacey?" The man looked all around the clearing, only now remembering the uneasy feeling that he'd had the last time they passed through these woods.

She whimpered in response and started toward an indistinct shape wreathed in thick, old vines and crowded close by young saplings now bare of leaves. After studying it for a minute or two, the man decided that it had once been an outbuilding of some sort, although it was hard to tell how long ago it had fallen into disrepair.

Lacey moved stiffly and cautiously, and the man wondered at her lack of enthusiasm. She was hardly more than a puppy at three years old, and he had never seen her act so strangely. He dropped her leash, certain that she would not bound off into the woods as she had the week before.

She sniffed delicately at the earth in front of the shed and whimpered again, this time louder. Then, in the age-old instinct shared by dogs of all breeds everywhere, she circled three times before settling down, her tail curled neatly around her hindquarters.

As Lacey settled into her chosen spot, the man noticed that the earth beneath her was freshly turned. In fact, it had been dug up and replaced in a careful, symmetrical rectangle just a little larger than Lacey's reclining shape. He shrugged, unconcerned with little mysteries. Turning toward the roadside park and his car, he whistled for Lacey to follow.

"Sure is peaceful, isn't it?" he said absently.

After a brief hesitation, Lacey rose and followed him. As they left the woods behind, they heard a low moaning sound high up in the trees.

It was clearly nothing but the wind.

lily's gift

The boy's lip quivered—it was clear he was about to break out in disgraceful, heaving sobs. "Give it back," he demanded, barely choking out the words. He was no more than nine, but his defiant posture, legs spread wide and hands on hips, was the mirror image of the older boys tormenting him.

"You can't make me," sing-songed the ringleader, holding the precious leather glove high above his head.

Willy stood still, feeling as if his feet were weighted by concrete. He was unwilling to jump up and try to snatch the glove away, certain the bully would only raise it higher.

"Give it to me," he repeated stubbornly. "Or else..."

"Or else what, baby?" Another boy taunted him. "You gonna cry to Mommy?"

Just then a golden fury came cannon-balling down the street. In an instant, she was leaping, growling, and generally terrorizing the three older boys, while Willy looked on in astonishment. An instant later, the tormentors were gone, and Lily sat in front of her master with his baseball glove lying neatly between her front paws. Her tongue was fully extended in a most unladylike manner, and she grinned up at the boy as if to say, "Did I do well, Master?"

He threw himself down and wrapped his arms around her neck. There wasn't far to go because he was not especially tall—but the dog was. "Lily, you saved me! Oh, Lily, you're the very best dog there ever was!"

She diligently swiped his face all over with her tongue, effectively cleaning the soot and grime that had collected there during his long and circuitous route home from school. Then she stood and frisked around him, her tail held high, dashing this way and that, sometimes leaning low on her front paws and swishing her tail in an invitation to mischief. Short, high barks communicated her message: "I've been home all alone, all day, and there are so many garbage cans to investigate and places to see and people to sniff! Get a move on, will you?"

"Willy! That you?" the boy's mother called as she leaned out the window and looked down the street. She recognized the substance of the dog's yelping if not the actual content. Willy scooped up his glove and trotted down the street, Lily close behind.

"Go 'round to the butcher's, will you, and get a pound of burger for dinner tonight. Tell him to charge it."

"Can I get Lily a bone, Mama?"

The woman shrugged and smiled. "Why not? Come directly home with it now, so I can start dinner!"

Willy opened the door to the stairs that led up to their first-floor apartment and tossed the baseball glove up the stairs, where it landed safely in the shadows on the first landing. Whistling—unnecessarily—for Lily to follow, he skipped down the street and around the corner, his encounter with the older boys totally forgotten.

• • • • • •

Janie tucked the blanket tightly up against the girls' chins and planted a kiss on each forehead. "Sleep, now," she said firmly. "Tomorrow we'll get you started at your new school." Two pairs of round, slightly frightened eyes stared back at her.

"Everything will be fine," she assured them before ducking under the sheet that was tacked up across the little alcove, which opened out directly into the spacious living room. The windows in the apartment were still uncurtained, and the Chicago night was anything but dark—a row of streetlights illuminated the windows as brightly as daylight. Silently demanding attention, stacks of boxes confronted Janie, but she successfully ignored them. Instead, she collapsed on the sofa in front of the television, keeping the volume low so it wouldn't wake any of the sleeping children.

With that uncanny sense of hearing mothers seem to develop, she sensed the girls whispering beyond the sheet. "Go to sleep, now, girls," she said sternly. "I mean it!"

The noise subsided, and Janie lost herself in another episode of *Marcus Welby, MD.* It was twenty minutes before another sound registered on her acute second sense. It was a whining, snuffling sound, so faint she almost missed it. One of her girls was crying, Janie thought as she jumped up and twisted the television knob, cutting off the singers extolling the virtues of Gulf Oil in mid-verse. Tiptoeing quietly to the alcove, she gently lifted a corner of the temporary curtain.

Just enough light spilled in to reveal the softly rounded faces of her two daughters, nine and ten years old, relaxed in sleep. A little spit bubble had formed at the corner of Angie's mouth, and Carol was snoring softly—but there was no sign of distress on either face.

Janie shrugged. It had been a long, hard day—well, really, a long, hard week getting herself and her five children moved to Chicago, finding this apartment, getting furniture set up, and utilities turned on. So maybe she was imagining things, but there was nothing wrong with her that a little sleep wouldn't cure. She turned off the living room lamps, reducing the unpacked boxes to mere shadows. Then she stood for a moment and admired the graceful symmetry of windows in the main room of this fine old apartment before heading back through the kitchen to her own room.

••••••

The room was dim. All four windows across the face of the long formal living room were draped in swathes of lace and thick fabric that collected dust. When Willy hid in the curtains or pushed them aside to look out at the street, a fine, nearly invisible cloud arose and made him sneeze violently.

Right now he wasn't looking out the window—he was trapped, sitting on a little chair while his mother and her friends chattered on and on. The light clattering of teacups on saucers provided a perfect counterpoint to the women's casual tones. But listening closer, Willy was appalled at the horrific subject matter.

"Had to have it all taken out, dear, scraped her out like a melon."

"After the baby was born, she never walked upright again. Stooped over and scurried, like a crab, she was..."

Willy's face must have revealed his distaste. His mother, glancing over at him, snickered and then quickly covered her mouth with her hand. "Willy, dear, would you like to go outside and play?"

With great relief, he nodded and sidled out of the room in no time flat. He poked his head into the curtained alcove that served as his room to pick up his glove and call softly for Lily, who was lying patiently on the little rag rug by the side of his bed. They scampered out the front door, Willy waving to acknowledge his mother's automatic "Be careful!"

Outside it was a perfect spring Saturday. The sky was as blue as blue can be, with just a few high, thin clouds hurrying by. The breeze was light and playful, and Willy could smell the heavy scent of fish and water from the lake a half mile to the east. In just two short hours, the sharp crack of the bat and the roar of the fans would resound from the confines of Wrigley Field, and Willy was determined to be there.

"C'mon, Lily," he urged as he broke out into a half trot. Wrigley Field was two blocks away, and if they got there soon enough, they could squeeze through a hole in the fence and hide out under the stands until the game began. The bigger boys had bragged about it. Willy had found the hole last week, and he and Lily had spent a glorious twenty minutes exploring the darkened, empty stands before a prowling watchman had sent them hurrying back to squeeze under the fence. Today, Willy was going to try sneaking in to catch the Cubs playing.

He stopped running when he got to the field, put his hands behind his back and strolled nonchalantly, lips puckered up to whistle.

The sight of a big, tall policeman made a shiver run deliciously down his spine. Lily, always game for an adventure, trotted obediently by his side. Once around the corner, he began to scan the fence, looking anxiously for the remembered opening.

There it was—half hidden by a tall weed growing out of crack in the pavement. Willy dropped to his knees and wiggled through in a flash. Still on his belly, he called softly to Lily.

"Come on, girl, you can do it!" he held out his hand to encourage her. She whimpered just a bit and scratched at the concrete with one front paw. When he called again, she cried a little louder and dropped to her stomach, trying to pull herself through the opening with a frantic scrabbling motion of her front and back paws.

She couldn't fit. She squeezed and wiggled, crying softly all the while, but her rear half would not make it under the fence without getting caught on the jagged edges of the loose fence wire.

"Don't think she's going to make it, boy," a booming voice said in a conversational, relaxed tone. Willy tensed, raising himself into a half-crouch and staring up. It was the burly policeman from around the corner.

"May I?" With a gesture that was almost courtly, the policeman offered his arm to Willy. Stunned, the boy reached up and was hauled to his feet.

"Pretty dog," the officer commented as the man and the boy walked briskly to the gate. Barking shrilly every few feet, Lily was tracking their progress on the outside of the fence. "She a golden retriever?"

Willy could only nod dumbly in reply. At the gate, the officer bent over to look Willy straight in the face. "Don't do this again, young man," he cautioned. "You're getting off light this time. But if you try it again, I'm warning you, it won't go so easy!"

Willy hung his head. "Yes, sir," he replied, in a voice scarcely loud enough to be heard. On the sidewalk outside, Lily hung her head, too.

The day was too delightful to spend long in regrets. Out of sight of the baseball field, Lily's tail rose high like a flag again, and Willy's spirits rose to match. Finding discarded treasures at every turn, they picked their way through the alleyways. Lily even scared up a few cats scavenging for their dinners and thoroughly enjoyed the subsequent chases.

On the last chase, Willy laughed so hard that his stomach ached. Lily managed to corner a scrawny, ferocious-looking cat, who stood with its back arched, spitting fiercely at the big, barking dog. Lily turned to look at Willy, as if to say, "What on earth do I do now?" He howled with laughter, and Lily, her pride hurt, stalked off in the opposite direction and lay with her head on her paws. The cat abruptly sat down and began to wash its face as if nothing at all unusual had happened.

After a couple hours of roaming, Willy noticed the wind picking up. Ugly gray clouds were scudding in fast from the lake. The shirt sleeves that were perfectly adequate at noon now felt skimpy, so he called to Lily and headed home.

His mother's friends were fortunately all gone, so he could sit in the warm kitchen and recount his adventures to his mother—an edited version, of course. He spoke between bites of the delicate finger sandwiches left over from the afternoon tea party. Lily lay at his feet and watched hopefully for any crumbs that might fall.

"She's getting fat, Mama," Willy complained. "I think we're feeding her too much."

Without a word, his mother dropped to her knees and gently patted Lily's abdomen. A shake of her head was the only reply. Then, puzzling Willy even further, she fetched the jug of milk from the icebox, filled a bowl, and set it down in front of Lily. As the dog drank, both the boy and his mother watched her with love in their eyes.

••••••

Janie had a bag of groceries on her hip and two in her hands while she pawed through her purse for the key. The door on the street level slammed, and she heard footsteps ascending the dark stairs. It was Mrs. May, the upstairs neighbor.

"Let me help you, dear," she cooed. "Got your hands full?" She relieved Janie of two bags of groceries, freeing Janie's hands to fit the key into the battered old lock.

"Would you like a cup of coffee, Mrs. May?" Janie asked politely but hoped the woman would refuse. She had a lot to do, and she needed to leave in an hour to pick up the children.

"Oh, no, I couldn't." The woman was peering around, looking in every corner and cocking her head as if to hear some faint sound.

"Is something wrong?"

"No, no." Now the woman was peeking into the grocery bags.

"What is it, Mrs. May?" Janie spoke more sharply than she had intended.

"I just don't want you to get in trouble," the woman blurted. "I know how the landlord feels about dogs!"

Now Janie was thoroughly confused. "What dogs?"

The look her neighbor gave her was full of pity. "You can't hide it, dear. You'll have to give them up, or else the landlord will have you evicted. It's happened before!"

"Give what up?"

Now the older lady leaned close, a fellow conspirator. "You can trust me, honey," she whispered. "I just love puppies. I'd have one myself if I could!"

"Look, Mrs. May. I don't have a dog, I don't have any puppies, and I don't want any trouble, okay?" Janie picked up the groceries and stalked back to the kitchen. She stopped dead in her tracks, Mrs. May nearly treading on her heels, as an explanation occurred to her.

"You've heard them, too!" she cried.

Mrs. May gleefully clapped her hands. "Now will you let me see them? How many are there? Where's their mother, poor darlings?"

Janie shook her head. "There are no puppies." Mrs. May's face fell. "But if you want to come down here at about ten o'clock tonight, I'd like you to hear something." Now it was Mrs. May's turn to look puzzled.

"Will you do that for me?" Janie asked, gently propelling the woman toward the door.

"Certainly, dear, I'd be glad to. But the puppies..."

Janie put on a big grin. "Ten o'clock," she repeated as she softly shut the door.

Mrs. May's reply was faint beyond the door. "Ten o'clock."

Janie hastily ran all five children through the bathtub, feeling like the foreman on an assembly line as she checked behind their ears and issued clean underwear. By ten o'clock, the older ones were at least quiet in their rooms, and her two youngest girls were snuggled up together fast asleep in the little alcove.

A tentative knock on the door came at five after the hour. "Oh, my dear, I don't mean to make a pest out of myself," Mrs. May began, but Janie shushed her.

"Let's just have a nice cup of tea and watch the evening news, shall we?"

They hadn't been sitting for more than five minutes before the whimpering began. It was soft, not at all panic-stricken, and it immediately brought a smile to both women's faces.

"Oh, can I go see them?" Mrs. May was halfway to her feet.

Janie, still smiling, just nodded. They crossed the living room and pulled the curtain to the alcove aside, letting light from the room spill into every corner. The smile of anticipation on Mrs. May's face faded away as her head swiveled this way and that.

"Where are they?" She forgot to whisper, and one of the girls stirred uneasily in her sleep.

Janie shrugged, holding up her empty hands. Mrs. May got down on her knees, every joint cracking, and lifted a corner of the bedspread to look under the bed. Slowly, awkwardly, she stood up. Janie had backed up into the living room, watching her neighbor carefully.

"That is the creepiest thing, I declare." The garrulous woman was almost speechless.

"I'm glad you heard them, too. Sometimes the girls hear the puppies before they go to sleep, but it doesn't scare them."

"Well," Mrs. May admitted, "it's not really a scary or creepy thing. They don't sound sad at all."

"Do you believe me now when I say we don't have any puppies?"

Mrs. May could only nod, a little shamefaced at her earlier insistence on the puppies' existence.

"I wonder where they came from." Janie mused aloud as she escorted Mrs. May out the door. "And why would we hear them cry now?"

●●●●●●

Lily was going crazy. She would run a few feet in one direction, her toenails skidding on the highly polished floor, and then turn around and run the other direction, whining and yipping with every step. Sometimes she would cower close to the floor, looking up with wild eyes at Willy, begging him to do something.

"What is it, girl?" He pleaded with her to tell him what was wrong, but she could not obey this time. Willy's mother was upstairs visiting the neighbor, and he was frantic.

When he found a drop of bloody water on the floor, his panic reached new heights. Now Lily was panting so hard she barely had time to whine, and she lay next to his bed on the little rug she'd claimed as her own three years ago as a puppy. Her abdomen heaved and rolled alarmingly, seeming to have a life of its own. Willy watched with terrified eyes.

Finally, Lily raised her head and let loose a howl that set his teeth on edge. Willy began to howl and cry, too, his tears flowing even faster when she growled at his outstretched hand.

A key in the lock sounded like salvation. It was his mother, and she bustled in the door calling out his name. She had heard Lily's howl upstairs in the neighbor's kitchen.

"Willy," she said, "go get me a couple of old sheets from the rag bag. Then fetch my sewing scissors from the basket in the kitchen." She was rolling up her sleeves as she talked. "And an apron from the drawer."

"What's wrong with Lily, Mama?" He was gasping between sobs. "She'll be fine," she replied briskly. "Do what I tell you—now!"

Willy collected everything, his ears tuned to the turmoil in the alcove. His mother was in there now speaking softly to Lily, who whimpered in reply but did not growl. He thrust the sheets, scissors, and apron through a gap in the curtain and slipped outside, too scared to watch whatever mysterious ritual was happening on the floor by his bed.

In an hour, it was all over. Lily's yelps of pain had reached a crescendo and then slowed, finally stopping altogether. Willy's mother came from behind the curtain, her hands held high and smeared with a thick, curious layer of reddish-black gore.

"Go on in, Willy," she said softly. "Lily's got a surprise for you."

The reflected light of the candles danced on the windowpanes, and Janie felt her heart swell with the warmth of family and friends surrounding her. "Happy birthday, to you..." The sweet strains were a little off-key, and the birthday cake was undeniably lopsided, but the candles burned with a bright optimism. Her children sang with enthusiasm and unbidden tears rose to her eyes.

"Now for the biggest surprise of all, Mama," Angie said, and, leading Janie into the living room, she flung aside the curtain to the alcove with a flourish.

"Oh, Eddie!" It was her baby brother, all the way from South Carolina to celebrate her birthday. Now the tears began in earnest, and her brother laughed as he held her.

"Such a bad surprise that I made you cry, eh?"

Janie wiped her face with her sleeve (a gesture her oldest son stored away in his mind for future use as a defense), and the seven of them sat down to birthday cake.

The children went to bed, protesting mildly, at eleven o'clock, and Janie had her brother all to herself for a precious few hours. They talked till two, when Janie brought out sheets and a pillow to make up a bed on the sofa.

"We'll try not to wake you up in the morning," she promised. "The kids all leave for school at 7:30, so it'll be quiet after that."

Eddie unwound himself from the sheet and blanket at ten the next morning, moaning loudly and mock-staggering into the kitchen to find his sister.

"Coffee, Janie, coffee!" he moaned. "This is the noisiest house I ever slept in!"

Janie grinned as she poured him a cup, black and strong from several hours of stewing. She spoke over her shoulder as she rinsed out the pot and refilled it to make a fresh pot.

"What do you mean? The kids bother you?"

"No, I'm talking about those confounded puppies. They sounded like they were under my pillow."

"They weren't far—they're in the alcove."

He looked startled and then grimaced as he tasted the coffee.

"Oohh, boy, this is bad!" He pushed the cup away. "When did you all get a dog?" Janie's grin grew wider. "We didn't."

"You'll have to explain yourself. I'm just a country bumpkin."

She shrugged. "I can't explain it. Just sometimes, at night, we hear puppies cry. They're right there, in that little alcove, but we can't see them."

Eddie shivered. "Doesn't it scare you?"

"Not really. You weren't scared, were you?"

He considered for a moment. "Nah. Are you sure it's not your neighbors though?"

She shook her head, definite. "No, the upstairs neighbor was ready to get me evicted over the noise because she heard it, too. And the closest building is way too far away to hear it that clearly. You said yourself, it's right there, right in the living room."

"Weird—very weird. But it suits you." Janie swiped at him with a dish towel, and he ducked, his grin matching hers. "Is that coffee ready yet?"

••••••

Willy tiptoed into the alcove, full of fear but also filled with faith in his mother's goodwill. Lily was curled up in a rough nest of torn strips of sheet, and her tail thumped lightly when she saw his face. She looked up at him, her eyes filled with unquestioning trust.

In the half circle formed by her furry, golden torso, five misshapen lumps were staggering about on uncertain little legs. They butted up against each other and against Lily's neck and legs, searching blindly for her belly and her swollen nipples.

Willy's mouth dropped open in awe. Lily, watching his reaction, seemed to smile fondly at him. At last each of the five pups found a place, and their thin, mewling cries were stilled. Crouching next to his dog, Willy breathed a promise: "Oh, Lily, what a wonderful dog you are. I will remember this forever."

••••••

Janie was curled up on the sofa with a book. The house was quiet, peaceful. It was the kind of moment filled with an ordered sense of contentment that sustained her through all the other hours of chaos and disorder. Beyond her in the alcove, she heard the small whimpering noises of puppies looking for—and finding—sustenance, and the sound made her smile. It sounded like hope fulfilled.

firehouse annie

The dog was stretched out full-length in the sun. An observer, looking close, could see little tendrils of steam rising from her well-muscled flanks. After a long, cold winter, Annie was making the most of the early spring sunshine pouring through the tall windows lining the south dormitory wall. She was alone upstairs—all six firefighters on duty were downstairs. There were a thousand small tasks to keep them occupied during daylight hours: the stable where Nell and Bramble lived was kept immaculate, the horses themselves needed grooming, and their halters and traces needed regular inspections for signs of wear, the firetruck always had a bolt to tighten or a wheel to adjust, and the hoses and pumps required checking.

Annie yawned and stretched. She reveled in the on-again, off-again urgency of her work. There was nothing like the excitement of a good run through the streets, some of them bricked—but most of them good old-fashioned dirt or mud, barking with all her might to accompany the wild clanging of the bell on the wagon. Nell and Bramble loved it, too. The three of them would race flat out to the scene of the fire, while passersby gaped and other traffic scurried out of the way. No one could deny the absolute necessity of their work; no one could resist admiring the spirit and grace with which they performed it.

The dog rose to her feet and padded across the room. Soon it would be time for supper, barring any calls, so now would be the best time to go pay a call on Nell and Bramble. The stable cat might be around, too, and that was always good for a little fun. Annie and the old tom had an agreement: He would allow himself to be chased about a third of the way down the block before he turned to make a stand. Annie would pretend to be vanquished, and both creatures would return to the firehouse. Annie enjoyed the excitement, and the tom appreciated the boost to his reputation as a tough old warrior.

Just as she began to descend the stairs, a wave of noise and activity broke over the station house. A clangorous bell ripped through the everyday hum of chores and conversation, and the firefighters began to run in every direction. To an untrained eye, it became bedlam. But Annie could see a precise, well-rehearsed pattern to the movement of the men. Tom and Harold literally jumped into their tall black boots and then snatched up their coats and shrugged them on as they ran across the yard to the stable. Red coiled the big canvas hose back into its place on the tank wagon, and Bobby tightened the bolts on the two front wheels. The Chief and Slim, the driver, conferred hastily over a map as they fastened their coats. Nell and Bramble were brought around and harnessed in a flash, and the wagon thundered out onto the street in less than three minutes after the alarm was rung, Annie running fleet by its side, and Red flailing the bell on the wagon with gusto.

They saw the smoke first, an angry black column rising rapidly up to the sky. It didn't waver on its course; that was good—there was no wind to aggravate the fire. When they reached the block of the fire, a crowd of onlookers scattered as Annie burst through ahead of the wagon, barking furiously.

It quickly became apparent that the fire was in an outbuilding behind the main building, but there was no easy access from the street. Annie tore around the corner, and Nell and Bramble followed close behind, the wagon careening after them. Nell and Bramble just barely caught sight of Annie's jaunty tail, a whip-like cord with a stylish black tip, as she darted into an alley. They followed and pulled up with a jerk right beside a little shed that was burning merrily. Nell, Bramble, and Annie had done their job—now the firefighters got to work.

This was the course of Annie's life—long, lazy stretches of inactivity broken by spurts of thrilling and dangerous activity, racing through the streets of her small city. People all over knew her by name.

"Here comes Annie," the owner of the diner might say, seeing a blur of sleek black and white sprinting by.

"Did you hear what happened last week? When the Morris's place caught on fire?" Someone was always on hand to tell a story about Annie. "I heard that the youngest, Mary, I think, had been carried out of the house lickety-split by her mama. But she was standing on the sidewalk crying like the world was ending."

The diner owner stopped polishing the counter and leaned over, his attention caught. "Annie was watching her—you know how she likes children—and darned if she didn't look like she was listening to that little girl. Then, before anyone could stop her, that crazy dog dashes up to the porch, flames shooting out of the windows and doors like that house was hell itself, snatches up something in her mouth, and comes bounding up to little Mary to lay it at her feet."

"What was it?"

"The little girl's doll—soaked and covered in soot, but safe. It was the most amazing thing. Mary's mama says she'll do anything for that dog. Says Annie's the closest thing to an angel that ever walked on four feet."

The owner of the diner shook his head, smiling, and the story was added to the growing collection of tales about amazing Annie.

One late fall day, a call came from the candy store downtown, on First Street near the river. When the firefighters arrived, the first floor of the brick building was already consumed by flames. The second and third floors were threatened, so the firefighters had their hands full. Unnoticed by them, Annie ran around to the back of the building where the owner had constructed a little lean-to for extra storage.

Bobby was directing a stream of water into the front window when Annie bounded up to him and began barking furiously. "What, Annie? I'm busy now!"

Annie wouldn't stop barking. "Red," the firefighter shouted, "come see what's wrong with Annie!"

The second firefighter shook his head when he saw the narrow corridor between buildings that Annie intended him to pass through. "It's too dangerous, Annie," he said. "Come on—let's get back to work."

Then the dog did something so out of character that the firefighter was shocked. She ran behind him and turned to plant her feet, blocking his access back to the street—and she growled at him.

"This is really stupid, Annie," the firefighter protested, but he let her lead him through the passageway anyway.

Smoke was pouring out of the little lean-to. Red was horrified to see Annie run inside and then, almost immediately, begin to back out, obviously tugging hard on something many times her own weight. In spite of the heat and the showers of burning embers floating down from the main building, Red ran up to the little structure.

Annie was pulling hard on the belt of Mr. Patillo, the candy store owner—he'd been overcome by the smoke. Red grabbed the man and carried him to safety, Annie barking loudly at his heels.

Annie served the central fire station for eleven years before she died quietly in her sleep. Almost everyone in town had a story about a miraculous Annie rescue or a remarkable Annie feat. Her courage was legendary. The firefighters led a funeral procession through the streets, and she was buried in a corner of the yard next to the stables.

It wasn't even two years later that old Mr. Patillo reported seeing her again. "I swear to you by all that's holy, I saw that dog racing down the street!"

Mr. Patillo's son-in-law now ran the candy store, but he allowed the old man to sit around and tell his tall tales to the children who came in after school. "Papa, she died last year," he argued patiently. "They don't even have dogs anymore because they can't keep up with the new fire engine. You're seeing things in the rain."

Just then lightning flashed outside, and the rain poured down with renewed intensity. "I tell you, I saw her," the old man insisted stubbornly. "I think she was warning me."

"Warning you about what, Papa?" His son-in-law spoke kindly, but his tone was laced with a pity the old man despised.

"I don't know—a fire, maybe, or something. This rain. How high is the river?"

"They say it's going to stop raining tonight, and the river won't crest above flood level. Don't worry about it, Papa." The old man crossed his arms and sat like a stone on his stool behind the counter.

"Okay, then, worry about it—I don't care. I'll let you lock up. I'm taking the books home to work on them tonight. I'll see you in the morning." Mr. Patillo's son-in-law pulled the door shut. The little bell meant to announce customers jangled angrily.

The old man toiled for hours, watching through the big display window as the rain came down steadily. Up and down the stairs he walked carrying box after box of merchandise to an unused room on the second floor. Once, long after dark, he took his umbrella and went to stand at the edge of First Street. The river was lapping hungrily at the land, already out of bounds.

When he was finished, he climbed the stairs one last time to his apartment, empty now of his wife and his five noisy children. The sound of a bell woke him—it was the telephone, a contraption his daughter had insisted he install.

"What do you want?" he growled into the receiver. He didn't like the intrusion the little black instrument created.

"Papa, we're ruined!" It was his son-in-law. Mr. Patillo felt a small warm sense of satisfaction begin glowing in his stomach, which rapidly spread throughout his body.

"Have you looked out your window, Papa?"

Without a word, Mr. Patillo set the telephone down and crossed to the window. The sun had come out as promised. It sparkled and gleamed on the silvery surface of the water directly below him. The river had flooded in the night, and the store below was filled with five feet of river water.

"I've taken care of it, boy," he said gruffly to his son-in-law. "I moved the inventory upstairs last night."

In 1922, when Mr. Patillo's son-in-law was a cranky old man, he still told that story to anybody who'd listen. But Angie Lorino had no time to stop for an old man's tales. Her new husband ran a dry goods store on Third Street, and she had her hands full keeping it swept and stocked and waiting on the customers who were always in a hurry.

One afternoon in late spring, Angie had a moment to pause on the doorstep of the store, broom in hand, and admire the delicate blue of the sky. The gauzy clouds racing by almost looked like lace, and she daydreamed just for a moment about an elegant dress, just that color, trimmed with fine handmade lace. When she looked back to the street, a movement caught her eye—a spotted dog, long and lean and powerfully muscled, was tearing down the street oblivious to the occasional car or truck, every stride stretching its legs to their fullest extent.

"What a pretty dog," she thought to herself. "I wonder where it's going." In the hours ahead, though, Angie would completely forget the momentary encounter with the white dog with black spots because the little Midwestern city was hit by the most powerful tornado ever recorded, and she had her hands full salvaging what she could from the wreckage of her husband's store.

Over the years, stories about Annie continued to build. Mrs. Butler saw a Dalmatian rushing down the street the day before the boiler in her building exploded. Otto Sternhouser saw a strange dog on the street one day and told his wife over supper—the next day his delivery truck went out of control and plunged through the guardrail on the Seventh Avenue bridge. Time and time again, the sight of the powerful, sleek dog coursing through the streets was the harbinger of disaster, whether for one family or many.

The city grew and changed. All the streets were paved now, and traffic was controlled by electronic boxes sending signals to drivers; the vehicles all moved swiftly, each one hermetically sealed with its occupants isolated behind glass, steel, and plastic. A chemical factory was built across the river. Big supermarkets sprang up on the outskirts, and the little stores of downtown were replaced by strips of shops bordered by parking lots.

Hardly anything remained of the little city that Annie had known so well. Only the more substantial buildings still stood downtown—the two-, three-, and four-story structures of brick or stone. But even these were changed with new facades or garish signs covering the careful craftsmanship of builders long dead.

Still Annie was seen, and her presence reported. A local columnist even spent her week's allotment of words on the ghost dog that predicted disaster. But Mary Bolen prided herself on being practical, and she secretly scoffed at these stories.

"People should find better things to do than repeat such old wives' tales," she thought as she washed the dishes after a neighbor's visit. She didn't know it, but in a box in her attic was an old rag doll that still smelled strongly of smoke and whose smiling hand-stitched face was streaked with soot. It had belonged to her great-great-great-grandmother.

Mary had three children. Scott, the oldest, would be five soon, and she needed to buy party favors for his party coming up two weeks from Saturday. On a sunny Thursday afternoon, when the baby woke from her nap, Mary shepherded Scott and Andy, who was three, down the stairs and out to the car.

"Mama heard about a wonderful store," she explained to them, the baby squirming in her arms. "They have all kinds of neat toys and candy and stuff for parties!"

"Goo," said the baby sleepily.

"I wanna sit in the front seat," whined Andy. "How come Scotty always gets to sit in the front seat?"

"I'm bigger," Scott announced breezily, easily pushing Andy aside. Andy began to howl, and the baby started tuning up in sympathy.

Mary chewed the inside of her cheek for just a moment. "Scotty, I need you to help me with the baby," she said brightly. "Will you climb back here and get her buckled up?"

He looked at her suspiciously. "I wanna sit in the front seat," he complained. "You'll sit in the front seat on the way home," Mary ordered. "We take turns, and Mama gets to decide."

Andy stuck out his tongue at Scott. Mary ignored it and got all three children situated in their proper safety seats with the proper seat belts before releasing a very large sigh. Getting anywhere with three kids took an enormous amount of energy.

It didn't take long to get to the downtown area. Near the river, where the oldest buildings still stood, Mary navigated her way to the address she'd scribbled on a scrap of paper. It was a wholesale candy and toy place, but they sold to individuals, too. All these old, somber brick buildings looked half empty now, some with windows boarded up and scrawny alley cats sunning themselves on the stoops. The area seemed to be mostly a warehouse district. Big trucks thundered past, and Mary could see where the traffic had torn up the asphalt to reveal the old brick road beneath. She found a parking place a few doors down, and pulled the car up to the curb.

"Here we are," she said cheerfully. Thankfully, the baby had gone back to sleep, and Scott and Andy had forgotten their spat and jumped out of the car, intrigued by the unfamiliar neighborhood. They were talking animatedly, but since they were safely on the sidewalk, Mary didn't pay much attention. She was occupied with getting the baby out of her car seat without waking her up.

Scott was pointing at something, and Andy was jumping up and down when Mary straightened up, with the baby cocooned safely against her shoulder. At the end of the block, a sleek, lean Dalmatian was headed toward them, loping at a comfortable speed. It was this graceful creature who had captured the boys' attention. As Mary watched, admiring the dog's fluid, easy motion down the dead center of the road, her mind registered the rumbling noise of a big truck rounding the corner. In the split second it took to realize the danger to the dog, she pulled the boys to her to cover their eyes.

"Mama, make it stop!" Andy had seen the danger, and his trust in her abilities knew no bounds.

Mary couldn't tear her eyes away from the impending disaster. Just as the truck bore down on the unsuspecting creature, Mary winced in anticipation of the grinding, heartrending noise of the collision, and she closed her eyes momentarily. When she opened them, the truck was gone, and the dog was streaking down the block unharmed. Mary released the boys but still clutched the baby tightly.

"Mama!" Andy threw his arms around her leg, giving her a grateful squeeze. It took a moment for her to realize that he thought she'd saved the dog.

Mary felt distinctly queasy. She urged the children into the store, a dim, cavernous room with wooden floors filled with metal shelving stacked up to the ceiling with box after box of candy and trinkets. It was a treasure trove, a child's conception of heaven, and Mary watched, smiling, as Scott and Andy debated the relative worth of candy snot compared to little buckets of candy dirt and gummy worms. They made it out of the store just at four o'clock, thirty dollars poorer but enriched with the currency of childhood: car-shaped erasers, bright beads, long spaghetti-like strands of fluorescent-colored bubble gum, and fifteen miniature pails of candy dirt and worms.

Dinner was chaotic. The baby, refreshed from her long nap and taking her cue from the boys, happily slung food in every direction when Mary turned her back. Scott and Andy were keyed up by the afternoon's expedition and vied for their father's attention in voices that quickly escalated into shouting. It was all the adults could manage to keep the two little boys seated. In their excitement, they kept springing up to demonstrate one point or another.

"The shelves were this high, Daddy!" Scott rolled out of his chair and jumped, his hand held up in the air to show how tall.

"And they went on and on and on until it was dark!" Andy, not to be outdone, flung his arms out wide, forgetting that his fork had just speared a couple of green beans. Seeing them fly across the room, the baby chuckled and picked up a carrot and flung it in the same direction.

"And there was this dog, and Mama saved it!" This melodramatic pronouncement caused a momentary lull in the conversation.

John looked at his wife and raised his eyebrows. She just shook her head and smiled faintly before getting up to retrieve the green beans and the carrot. Remembering the incident made her feel queasy all over again.

Working swiftly and efficiently, the adults got each child cleaned up, tucked into pajamas, and situated in a bed or a crib. John read a story to the boys, stretched out between them on Andy's narrow bed, while Mary headed to the kitchen to start on the dishes. When her husband joined her, she was unusually quiet.

"What's wrong, honey?" John's voice was muffled—he'd thrust his head inside the cabinet to try to make room for the plastic salad bowl.

"I don't believe in ghosts."

"Ow." John came up, rubbing his head, and hastily shut the cabinet door before all the bowls came rolling back out again. "I know you don't."

"But that dog was really strange."

"You think it was that dog the columnist wrote about—the disaster ghost dog?"

Mary forced herself to laugh. "Of course not!" She threw the sodden dish towel at her husband's head.

When the lights were out and John was just rolling over to get to sleep, she prodded him with her forefinger. "John," she whispered. "I just remembered. Beth called and wants to know if we can come up this weekend. Is that okay?"

"Sure, honey," he muttered sleepily.

"Right after work tomorrow, okay?"

"Okay, okay. Did you set the alarm clock?" His last sentence dissolved into a snore. It was hours later before Mary could compose her mind enough for sleep.

Mary packed the car and had the children waiting when her husband came home from work. As they passed the city limit sign, on their way north to see her sister, it was as if an invisible burden had lifted from her shoulders. She breathed easier.

The children played well with their cousins, John enjoyed the company of Beth's husband, and Mary and her sister reveled in the domestic peace—each feeling blessed by their healthy, happy family. That sense of satisfaction, bordering on smugness, made the shock even more appalling when Mary saw the familiar lines of her hometown on the Sunday morning TV news broadcast.

"Explosion at the chemical factory..." said the reporter, and Mary's legs gave out. She sank to the floor.

"Families evacuated..." the reporter droned on. Mary's mind was processing only bits and pieces of the horrible newscast.

"Spokesperson for the company declined to comment," the reporter concluded, speaking over pictures of panic-stricken families throwing their belongings feverishly into their cars. "And in other news..."

highway 79

The day was charged with an invisible power. It hummed through the air, fairly making sparks fly as it battered itself against any resistance in its path. Trees, shrubbery, people, dogs, cars, loose windows in their frames, and even flimsy house trailers—all shuddered and shook with the power sweeping through the day. Later, when the rain came, people would struggle even more. The wind would snatch umbrellas out of the strongest grasp, twisting and snapping the gleaming ribs with breathtaking ferocity.

For at least one person, the uncivilized weather was welcome. Lying down on the grass and looking up, it was possible to see beyond the grim, ponderous clouds bearing rain. As the threatening gray clouds scudded rapidly across the sky, there appeared between the billowing masses glimpses of the *real* sky. A serene, Blessed Virgin blue, it soared above the storm, above the earth, with solemn majesty.

The blue was so perfect that it made her heart ache. It was so rich a hue that she yearned to touch it, feel it with her fingertips like a length of silk priced out of reach.

"Are you out of your mind?"

The tone of voice was a perfect match for her mother's, but it was her roommate who spoke. Without sitting up, the young woman replied. "If I had a dog to walk, I'd do that. But I don't—so I thought I'd lie here and enjoy the weather."

"Don't you have midterms coming up?"

"Irrelevant."

"Suit yourself."

A few minutes later Susan heard the front door slam. The heavy gray clouds above skidded to a halt, the wind paused, and the tantalizing hints of clear sky above disappeared. The rain began with a startling fury, pelting down so hard that the woman feared it would pierce her unprotected skin. Defeated, she rose and approached the nondescript brick facade of the apartment house.

Just as she pulled open the screen door, an invisible force wrenched the wooden frame from her hands, causing her to draw a little gasp of alarm. The thin frame wobbled, slammed into the side of the apartment house, and returned, docile, to her hand.

It was only the wind, she told herself. As she watched, it picked up again, driving the rain in near horizontal sheets across the narrow strip of lawn and the gray stretch of asphalt where she and the other tenants parked.

Inside the apartment house, she paused a moment at the threshold, waiting for the familiar clicking rush of paws bearing an ungainly body across the scarred wooden floor. Her heart sank again, as it had countless times in the past two weeks, when she realized what she was waiting for and that it was a sound she would never hear again.

"Nevermore," she sighed aloud. The word triggered a tangential thought. "Cassie has a point about that American Lit midterm." She wandered over to the table where her books were spread and turned over the anthology without picking it up.

"But I just don't have the heart for Poe today." The windows rattled in their frames, sounding a bit like teeth chattering or, it struck her, paws clicking across the floor. Her eyes fell on an old sock ragged from years of wear and then shredded by endless bouts of tug-of-war with a rapidly growing, energetic Labrador Retriever.

Fetching the sock from under a chair, Susan abruptly sat down on the floor, her eyes filling with tears. She thought she'd already disposed of all of Prissy's toys, but here was one she'd overlooked.

"Really, Susan, you've got to stop mooning around about that dog."

Susan looked up, surprised. "I thought you'd gone to the library."

"I'm going now." Cassie stooped to pull the sock out of Susan's hands. "I'll take care of this. If you're not going to study, call your mom—she said she'd like you to come for dinner tonight if you don't have any other plans."

Susan shrugged indifferently, but Cassie had already swooped toward the door, juggling a stack of books, her keys, purse, and the dingy gray sock. "See you," she called, without looking back. The door slammed, and Susan was alone.

Every movement leaden, she pulled herself off the floor and slouched toward the kitchen. On the way, her hand grazed across the stack of textbooks waiting for attention on the table.

"Okay, okay," she muttered. "But not Poe—biology."

As she put the kettle on and pulled a box of tea bags from the cabinet, she resolved to try and stop talking out loud when the apartment was empty. Somehow it seemed a little more cracked to talk to yourself when there was no other living presence in the room. Talking to Prissy had been different—speech directed to Prissy had always elicited a response, even if it was only a lazy thump of the tail or one delicately arched eyebrow. Energetic words to the young dog had always brought wild gyrations and a wave of uncontrollable, messy kisses before she spun off toward the door and her leash hanging nearby.

The kettle whistled in the middle of these reminiscences, and Susan splashed a stream of boiling water over the tea bag in her cup. All afternoon the rain coursed around the building, occasionally whipped into a frenzy by gusts of wind. Susan struggled first with her biology notes and then with various analyses of nineteenth-century American literature. Slowly, the light bled from the sky.

Near dark the phone jangled, jarring Susan from her third perusal of an obfuscated sentence about Poe's intent. Speaking in monosyllables, she agreed to drive the thirty miles to the city for a home-cooked meal with her family that evening. Her mother nattered on about the weather, and Susan watched with dull eyes as the rain came down, seemingly intent on battering the earth into submission. The asphalt was winning, she noted, but the thin patchy grass was a goner.

At last, her mother hung up. Susan closed her books, scribbled a note to Cassie, and then gathered laundry for the foray home—one good thing, she supposed, about her mother's call.

Her mood did not lighten as she piled into the car trailing a straggly armload of jeans, socks, and T-shirts. But at least the rain had subsided, reduced to only a sullen, spitting shadow of its former fury. It was full dark when Susan pulled out of the parking lot, her headlights only an insubstantial yellow haze in the gloom.

Just outside the drowsy college town, Highway 79 narrowed into a winding ribbon of concrete snaking east to the city where she'd grown up. The wind had picked up again, and she felt it gently rocking the car at irregular intervals. She clenched the steering wheel tightly, leaning forward to peer fiercely through the windshield and pierce the blackness ahead.

Without warning a shape materialized by her left front tire— shaggy, about two feet tall, it swerved at the same time she did. She gasped and slammed on her brakes, realizing a split second later that the wind had picked up a plastic bag and sent it billowing across her path.

The car shrieked to a standstill, slewed across both lanes. She sat still for a moment, panting slightly, willing her hands to stop trembling and her heart to stop pounding ferociously in her chest. With a deep breath, she pulled the car into the right-hand lane and continued, slower and more cautiously than before.

Her headlights illuminated a green mile marker reading 53 km, and Susan snorted at this incongruous European note and then saw a black shape bound out of the woods and run directly in front of her car. There was no time to brake before she was upon the hapless animal, and she watched in horror-stretched time as the creature pinned her with a glowing gaze at once accusing and forgiving.

Fighting the car to a standstill a few hundred feet down the road,

Susan hurried back to the site of the accident. An indistinct pile of darkness lay motionless in the center of the lane. Just as she approached it, bright white lights swept over the rise behind her and the long, moaning horn of a tractor-trailer cut through the sound of the wind.

She jumped, now shuddering from head to toe. When the truck passed and she turned back to the poor creature in the road, it was gone. Rain gusted suddenly, and she ran back to her car, shaking with the force of suppressed sobs.

Dinner that night was not a success. Her father badgered her about her choice of a major, her mother was weepy, and her brother only appeared at the table after dessert was served. Susan was so unnerved by the family atmosphere and her experience on the dark road that she completely forgot to load her clean clothes into the car when she left to go back to her apartment.

The party the next night, Sunday, was as pointless as any other party Susan had been to since she started college, and she wondered why she'd let Cassie talk her into going. The dimly lit house was filled with smoke and loud noise. The people were divided into two distinct camps, and Susan fit into neither. Half the people there were either obliterated, their brains stewed by an excess of alcohol, or they were trying to reach that point. The other half was dedicated to finding someone of the opposite sex to add to their scorecard. After an hour of successfully avoiding both states, Susan wandered through the house in search of Cassie.

"I'm ready to go home!" Susan screeched to be heard over the crashing music.

"I haven't had a chance to dance yet," Cassie protested, leaning over to yell in Susan's ear. "Find somebody to dance with!"

She rolled her eyes, but it was so dark that Cassie didn't see. The smoke was making Susan's eyes burn, so she slipped out the back door. She could hear someone being sick in the bushes, but at least the smoke wasn't so thick out here, and the music was reduced to less than a deafening roar.

The back door creaked open behind her, and she sighed. Solitude was apparently too much to ask for.

It was not immediately obvious that the young man was drunk. He carefully hitched up his pants before seating himself next to Susan on the cold concrete stairs. But when he leaned close, extending his hand in greeting, it was all she could do not to wince visibly at the stench of alcohol. A miniature cloud of his own making enveloped him.

"I'm in pre-vet," he said, carefully enunciating his words. "You like animals?" All but the human kind, she thought, and then mentally chastised herself for being so unkind. But he didn't require an answer.

"I got shook up tonight," he continued. "I hit a dog, and I really love dogs—really I do."

The back door opened again, and Susan saw with relief that it was Cassie. Light streamed around her ample frame.

"I didn't mean to do it," he protested, his voice rising. "I wasn't drunk—he just came out of nowhere."

"Where were you?" Her sudden intensity cut through his stupor, and he turned to look at her.

"Coming into town on Highway 79 West. I never heard him hit—I just saw him in my rearview mirror laying in the road like a pile of rags."

Ignoring the almost overwhelming smell of alcohol, Susan leaned forward to clutch his arm. "Did you go back to see how badly he was hurt?"

Susan was shaking his arm with such force that he recoiled. "You're hurting me! Let go a' me!"

Cassie came down the stairs to pull Susan away. "Let's go home now, Susan. I think you've had too much to drink."

"No—I've got to know!" Susan twisted out of her friend's grasp and turned back to the drunken student on the steps. "Did you go back?"

"I'm sorry." Cassie said, trying a second time to put her arms around Susan's shoulders. "Her dog got hit, and the creep who did it never came back." Susan shook Cassie's arm off again. "Did you?" she hissed.

The student shrank back until his starched white shirt was pressing hard against the unyielding cement step. "He was gone! I would've ... I would've taken him to the vet's, but he was gone!"

He buried his face in his hands and sobbed, and Susan finally let

Cassie lead her around to the front of the house and bundle her into the car. No amount of talking would persuade Cassie that Susan had not been drinking, so Susan sat silent all the way home.

Her shriek of rage was loud enough to wake the dead on Monday morning. "What's wrong with you?" Cassie appeared at her door, a cup of yogurt in her hand.

"I can't believe it! I left all my clothes at home, and I don't even have a clean pair of jeans to wear to class!"

"Wear sweats." Cassie disappeared, and Susan had to grudgingly admit that her level-headedness was an asset at times. Still, she'd have to rush to her parents' house tonight after her American Lit class and get her clean laundry.

It was dark when Susan's car finally headed east toward her parents' house. Her American Lit professor had given the class an idea of what the midterm would cover, and Susan was busy mentally reviewing the high points as she drove with one hand. The other hand was twisting the little metal shaft on her car radio that tuned in the stations. The plastic knob had broken off last week and rolled under the seat—now she felt a little flicker of annoyance every time she tried to use the radio.

At last she managed to tune in to the campus station and cranked it up, letting the music engulf her in waves of angry rhetoric. "Be my angel. Be my angel. Do you wanna *die*?" the singer mocked. Susan sang along. The bass pounded. Her headlights cut a steady path through the shadows, and she kept time on the steering wheel, letting all thoughts of midterms, grades, and professors slip from her mind. The trees crowded close to the road, some even leaning over, their branches interlacing high above her, but she was oblivious to their hovering presence.

Abruptly, the radio stopped playing, and her unaccompanied voice, a little flat, filled the car. Irritated, she gave the radio a slap on its face, trying to prompt it to start again, but the radio maintained a stony silence. Then the car engine sputtered, coughed, and quit, and the car rolled silently on the empty road. Distracted, twisting the key and searching the dash for clues, she only half noticed the green mileage sign reflecting her headlights as she coasted to a stop: 53 km it read.

Now Susan's hands hit the steering wheel in frustration. She wrenched open her car door and tumbled out. She had a date at nine o'clock. If she'd gone straight home and then back, she would've had nearly an hour to spare. But now here she was, stuck on a deserted road in the dark with a car that wouldn't run.

She considered opening the hood to check for something, but she didn't have a clue as to what to look for. She had plenty of gas. She stalked around the car in a big circle, muttering dire threats under her breath. It was a five-year-old Escort, not too old, and had never given her a minute's trouble since her dad helped her buy it two years ago.

Finally, she stopped and considered her options. Sitting in the car was one, but she was brimming over with impotent fury and the thought of sitting still was repugnant. Walking for help—that was the right idea. It was just as far in either direction, so she turned off the car's headlights, shouldered her purse, and struck out to the east toward her parents' house, walking carefully along the very edge of the pavement.

It was very dark out. Without the glow of headlights and the protective shell of metal, glass, and plastic, Susan felt small and vulnerable. Now she became aware of the trees pressing close around her and the myriad sounds coming from the shadows. She shivered and pulled her jacket a little tighter around her shoulders.

Behind her, she heard a sound that might have been a whimper—or it might have been a night bird calling. Remembering the events of her drive home Saturday night, her footsteps became a little more hurried. She wouldn't want to face an injured animal here, in the dark, without the shelter of her car nearby. The narrow road was crumbling on the edges, and she stumbled every now and then without even a sliver of moon to light her way and the trees obscuring even the feeble light of the stars.

Without warning, her eyes filled up with tears. What a terrible fix to be in—walking alone on a dark, deserted road without a light. Too late, she remembered the flashlight in her glove box back in the car, but it wasn't worth the terrifying trek back to retrieve it. Again, she heard a suspicious rustling between the somber looming trees on her right, but she refused to turn her head and put a name to her ears. She strode doggedly on, clutching her purse strap so tight that her fingernails dug little crescents into her palm.

Blinded by hot, angry tears, she first mistook the approaching headlights for stars—they were so far distant and shimmered so tentatively. Then, as it dawned on her, she began to wave her arms and call out, even before the battered old truck was within hearing distance.

He was going in the wrong direction but agreed to turn around and take her to a gas station on the edge of town, just ten miles distant. As Susan climbed into the rusted-out, hard-used Chevy truck, every nerve screamed out in silent protest. She knew taking a ride with a stranger was stupid—she'd had it drilled into her head since she was three years old. But what, demanded another part of her, was her alternative? Walk another ten miles?

She slammed the truck's door closed and squinted through the dim light of the dashboard instruments to see her benefactor's face. He was old—in his forties—and when he grinned, she could see a gap where he was missing a tooth or maybe two. He didn't look like a psycho killer, she told herself, and she relaxed enough to take a deep breath.

"Just quit on ya, did it?"

"Just died, uh-huh. It's always been such a good car."

That seemed to exhaust the conversational possibilities until they were halfway to the gas station. The truck's vents were pouring out an uninterrupted stream of hot, dry air.

"I hit a dog or something out here Saturday night," Susan spilled out when she could no longer bear the silence. "But it was gone by the time I got back to it."

"Yeah." He nodded, and Susan thought they'd dispensed with that subject. But a long minute later, he continued. "That happened to my aunt, 'bout three years ago. Same stretch of road."

"Was it a black dog?"

"Dunno—she never told me. She's over to the state hospital now."

Susan didn't know what to say. "I'm sorry," she offered lamely. The dry heat in the cab made her choke just a little.

The man shrugged. "Completely off her rocker," he continued. "They say grief will do that to you."

They were pulling into the gas station, and Susan was fumbling in her purse. "Did she, ah, lose someone?"

"Her son died of leukemia a week before she hit that dog." He stopped outside the brightly lit gas station and sat with his hands slack on the wheel. "I always did wonder if there really was a dog."

Susan pulled a crumpled bill from her wallet and pressed it into his hand without even checking to see what denomination it was. "I know I hit a dog," she told him vehemently. "I'm sorry about your aunt."

She slid out of the truck, relieved to be out of the airless compartment. "Thank you very much!" She hollered over the roar of the engine, and he grinned his gap-toothed grin and pulled away, heading back the way he'd come.

The following Sunday it snowed. It was just a light dusting of powder spiraling slowly from the leaden sky, so Susan decided to head to her parents' house for dinner. She needed to wash clothes, anyway, and a trip home would save her ten dollars plus the aggravation of the laundromat.

The day was prematurely dark when Susan pulled out onto Highway 79 East. Although there was very little light from the sky, the thin covering of snow caught every glimmer and reflected it, sparkling magically. The snow transformed the narrow road, making the dark tree trunks and long empty stretches seem romantic. She could almost imagine a sleigh pulled by horses, bells jingling and trotting merrily through the woods that had seemed so threatening just a few nights ago. Being safely tucked away in a car makes a big difference, she noted dryly.

The woods were thicker here, and Susan switched on her headlights just in time for them to flash on the rectangular 53 km marker. Then, out of the corner of her left eye, she saw a dark bulk separate itself from the surrounding shadows. Instinctively, her foot slammed down on the brakes. Fishtailing slightly, the car shrieked to a stop. Susan jerked around just as a large, black dog, wearing no collar and apparently unaware of the danger, trotted purposefully across the road.

"It's that dog," she gasped, and shoved her door open, disentangling herself from the seat belt as she stood. The dog seemed to pause at the shallow bank that led back down into the woods.

536

"Hey, dog," she called. The dog did not turn—he did not so much as twitch an ear back toward her in acknowledgment of her words.

Susan crossed the road diagonally to get closer to him. He moved ahead, just into the tree line, walking slowly but steadily, without sniffing the ground or even the air ahead. They moved this way, she trailing him, for a good two hundred feet. The dog never looked back at her, but he always seemed to know when to pause to give her time to navigate a little dip in the ground or to work her way free from a bramble bush or thorny vine.

"Hey," she called to him again, an uneasy laugh sticking in her throat. "Where are you going?"

Above her, the rays of the setting sun broke through the clouds. Tiny flakes of snow still filtered down, catching the half light and spinning like glitter or fairy dust between the branches. The leaves not covered by snow wore a thick burr of frost—fantastic sparkling crystals. Behind her the leaves moved restlessly, and she spun around, breathless—no one there.

She watched as the leaves, heavy with frost, rustled and moved in a lazy circle, as if stirred by a gigantic unseen hand. Suppressing a shiver, she turned back to find the dog that had led her this far into the woods.

He was gone. She took a step forward, straining to pick out any sign of movement against the spindly black tree trunks ahead—nothing there. She held her breath for a moment, cocking her head, listening intently for the sound of paws, however faint, scuffling through the leaves—nothing. She scanned the woods to her left, to her right. The dog had disappeared without a trace, although she could still see the faint imprint of his pads in the dusting of snow in front of her.

Now she realized that she was cold. She'd left her heavy wool coat right where she'd flung it when she climbed into the car—on the passenger seat. A blast from a car horn, prolonged and loud, helped her orient herself. Turning, she trudged back to the road and her abandoned car.

The days oozed by, each one tinged by a gray, heavy mist of indifference. She listened in class but didn't hear. Her friends and her roommate tried to pierce the shroud without success. She rarely slept anymore. At odd times, she would hear the sound of a dog barking or catch sight of a fleeting black shape in the distance in the park. It would cause a flicker of pain, but it became increasingly difficult to reach through the growing cloud.

Susan examined the list posted on her American Lit professor's door. She had failed the midterm—just like she had failed the biology midterm and her French exam. It really made no difference to her, but she winced a little as the thought of her father's reaction flitted through her mind. Just then the office door swung open, and she found herself face-to-face with the professor.

"Ah, Susan," he said in mild surprise. "I'm glad to see you. I think we should chat. You know, I'm a little concerned about you."

She choked. "I, uh, I can't right now," she blurted. "I, ah, I've got to get to the library." She turned and fled to her car.

Without any conscious decision, she turned left out of campus and headed east. The road was lined with the old-fashioned storefronts that are so common in small towns: a movie theater that played nothing but old movies, a drugstore, a pawn shop, a rent-to-own place with cheap, shiny fake leather furniture gleaming in the window. Through the blinking yellow light, past KFC and McDonald's, and then abruptly, the woods closed in around the road. In the late afternoon sunlight, the stark shadows cast by the bare tree limbs lay across the road like bars on a jail cell.

It came as no surprise when her car sputtered and died just past the 53 km marker. Rather, she felt a tiny thrumming note of satisfaction dulled by distance. She abandoned her car, leaving the door open wide, and slid between the welcoming arms of the darkening forest. She was barely past the first line of trees before she saw the weird green glow of the black dog's eyes as they caught the last of the afternoon sunlight.

She never looked back—she followed him unhesitatingly, afraid even to blink her eyes lest she lose her guide again. He moved as before, certain of his direction yet never stopping to find a scent or look for a track. Susan thrust her way through wild tangles of undergrowth, eased through impenetrable thickets of brambles, never taking her eyes off the dog. Her hands were scratched and dripping blood, leaving a faint gory trail, but she never felt a thing. Small branches whipped back, impeding her progress, but she pressed on, doggedly determined to keep up.

She lost sight of him only for an instant as he crested a little rise. Hurrying two or three steps to the top, she let out a fierce cry of disappointment—the dog had disappeared!

She walked forward a few steps and saw a slight depression in the earth covered by a deadfall of small trees, twisted vines, and desiccated leaves. She tore at the branches, ripping savagely to uncover the way. The rough bark shredded her skin, and she threw back her head and howled with loss and pain.

At last, the branches were all piled to one side. Before her was a rough set of stone steps leading down into an unfathomable place. She could hear, faintly, the sound of the dog descending. Without wavering, Susan plunged down to whatever mysteries lay sheltered in the dark.

closed doors

"I've found the perfect house." That was my first thought when the real estate agent and I pulled up into the yard, but I tried hard not to let my excitement show.

It was a long house facing south, shaped like a backward "L" and butted up against an odd-looking little hillock. The entire front was shielded by a wide, inviting porch, and although the yard was mostly red Oklahoma clay, the porch was covered with a riot of honeysuckle. The house looked comfortable, sure of itself, and in spite of needing a coat of paint, it seemed to be in pretty good shape.

"It looks old," I said, attempting to inject a note of doubt into my voice. I must have succeeded, because the real estate agent was instantly defensive.

"It's been very well taken care of," she hastily assured me. "The plumbing and wiring were updated just a few years ago, and let me see..." She shuffled through some papers from her voluminous purse. "Ah, here we are—the furnace was installed just last winter."

"Well, let's go take a look." I tried to restrain myself, but I beat my escort to the door by a good three paces. The view from the porch, especially the west end, was breathtakingly empty: a long, high vista of endless Oklahoma sky, only tenuously bound to the earth by gentle folds of prairie punctuated here and there by the strong black trunks of sturdy old cottonwoods. The grassland undulated softly, rising here and there to ridges feathered with supple red cedars.

The view was deceptive. We were only about an hour from the boot-stomping, Cherokee-driving mayhem of Oklahoma City. With a fax line and a modem, I would be as connected as any writer needed to be. But the seeming isolation would, I hoped, be just the incentive I needed to finish the second novel languishing in my head.

"Beautiful view, isn't it?"

I'd been caught. I could only nod dumbly, while the agent grinned at me and wrestled with the keys. The arm of the L-shaped house enclosed the porch, and the windows facing it were irregularly sized.

The door swung inward to reveal a deep room, richly shadowed, with wide pine planking on the floor, scarred and worn from years of use. The only light was indirect, coming from the open door and a small window that faced the porch—the afternoon sunlight was prevented direct access by the overhang of the porch.

"Oh, it's kind of dim, isn't it?" The agent was unable to mask her dismay.

When my eyes adjusted to the shadows, a massive fieldstone fireplace at the west end of the room caught my eye. "This looks pretty old," I commented, crossing the room to touch the cold, gray stone. I could hear the agent fumbling with her papers again behind me.

"Oh, my," she exclaimed. "Now I understand why this room's so dark. It's the original cabin, built on the homestead site in, let's see, 1893. Settlers didn't put windows in because they just let the cold in."

There was a little door to the left of the massive hearth. I turned the handle and pulled, but it wouldn't budge. "Wonder what this is?"

"Oh, Alice, come see the rest of the house!" The agent had left the main room and moved into the kitchen.

This room was flooded with light, I saw as I joined her, and its generous proportions and simplicity won my heart. It was just a big, old-fashioned kitchen, rectangular, with a window above the sink, another above the stove, and a third window looking out onto the porch. The appliances were all old, but I could picture my big round worktable in the center of the room, a kettle burping steam on the stove, and myself busily tapping away at my computer in the corner.

I didn't say a word, but I suppose the real estate agent had a lot of experience. "Isn't it lovely," she purred, after examining my expression.

I nodded again, feeling transparent. A door on the south wall led into the bottom of the L-shape. The little bathroom was obviously an afterthought, squeezed in between the kitchen and the bedroom—I had to walk through the bathroom to reach the only bedroom of the house. It, too, was filled with an abundance of light, with windows on all three exterior walls.

The agent was wisely silent for a time as I wandered back through the three main rooms of the house and out onto the porch. I could see from here that the door by the fireplace was access to a small lean-to; I made a mental note to get the key to the door and take a look inside as soon as I could. I left the porch to walk around the house, while the agent went back to her car and made calls on her cellular phone.

The lean-to had a row of windows, rather high in the wall but facing the west and that spectacular view of the prairie. I tried to jump up and peek in the windows, but they were too high. Walking farther around the house, I saw that the original cabin had been built right up against the little hill, which was only about six feet tall and covered with tall grass. It was a strangely symmetrical hill, almost exactly the length of the first cabin.

I'd only gotten halfway around it when it occurred to me that this might have been a soddy, a shelter half-dug, half-built from turf. The first settlers needed shelter fast, and the sod was the only building material at hand. Digging a sort of burrow in the ground gave excellent insulation against the winter cold, although I'd always imagined that housekeeping in a muddy soddy must've been rather difficult.

This endeared the little house to me even more. Obviously, the settlers had prospered enough to build a real house on their site after the first winter or two. There was probably access to the soddy from the house somewhere; the space would be cool in summer and warm in winter, an ideal root cellar. I finished my circuit of the house, my head teeming with images of all the people who'd grown up, lived, laughed, cried, and worked around my house. It had already become "mine," and I quickly dispensed with the formalities within a few weeks and moved in my belongings.

I discovered that the lean-to behind the main hearth was small: nine feet wide and seven feet deep. But the row of windows beneath the eaves provided a spectacular view of the sky and land beyond, and I promptly installed a floor lamp, a table just large enough to hold my tea things and a jar of pens and pencils, and a rocking chair. I do my best thinking in a rocking chair. This room I dubbed my "think tank"—it was spare and uncluttered except for the landscape beyond the windows. Just enough distraction to keep me from feeling like a loony locked up in a white padded cell.

It was three days after moving in that I first had the opportunity to curl up in my rocker and contemplate the empty prairie outside the windows and the empty notepad in my lap. Just as I reached out to pluck a pen from the jar, something nudged my arm sharply.

I flew up out of the chair to survey the room, badly shaken. It was empty. I prowled through the house, going so far as to fling open closet doors and peer inside. Nothing—it was as isolated and as empty as always. After making a pot of tea, I returned to the lean-to. I had convinced myself that what had felt distinctly like a nudge was, in fact, some sort of a muscle spasm—there was simply no other explanation.

I worked for a couple of hours undisturbed by anything except the flight of a few birds dramatically swooping across the sky just before sunset. The sunset was extraordinary, a play of light and colors that held me spellbound for a good twenty minutes. Satisfied with my work, scribbled notes and outlines for the next two chapters, I rose and went to the kitchen to prepare a meal.

The next morning, I spent several hours procrastinating. I paid some bills, made a few phone calls, and even contemplated baking a batch of bread, all the while studiously avoiding the accusing glare of my computer's blank screen in the corner of the kitchen. When the kitchen was spotless, the bed made, the pillows on the sofa fluffed up and placed just so, I had no choice but to turn on the computer and set to work transcribing and embellishing my notes from the previous day. Once I started, I got lost in the work, pounding my way through page after page.

When I got tired and stood to stretch, I was pleased to see that I'd been working steadily for three hours. I'd worked right through lunch. This solitude was going to be just the right ingredient for completing the book. Taking some cheese and few slices of bread, I wandered toward the lean-to to relax for a minute before returning to the computer.

I sat down and rocked and nibbled for a few minutes, not thinking about anything in particular, when I felt an extremely peculiar kind of pressure on my knee. First there was a warm sensation, followed at once by a light pressure directly on the top of my thigh, near the kneecap. Then I very distinctly smelled a very unpleasant odor—a stench of rotten meat, was my first thought. But it was the warmth and the sense of something weighty pressing on my leg that really unnerved me.

I lost my appetite. Standing up, I absentmindedly laid the bread and cheese on my little table, next to the sugar bowl I kept there for my tea. I decided to go to town the next day to finish up a bit of costume research and call on a friend of mine who was, very conveniently, a neurologist. Maybe he could shed some light on the strange symptoms I had been experiencing lately.

We met at the little sandwich shop in the building where he worked. "So tell me, Alan, what have I got?" I spoke around an enormous mouthful of tuna salad. Solitude had done little to refine my table manners.

He chewed thoughtfully for a few minutes. "Well," he said finally, "I couldn't rule out a brain tumor unless you have a CAT scan."

I gulped. This was most definitely not what I wanted to hear.

"But," he continued, "it's not really at all the right pattern. If you had these illusions randomly, then I might think so. But you only have them in the little room, right?"

I nodded.

"Don't worry," he said, patting my knee. "It's probably nothing. If it's still bothering you in a couple weeks, make an appointment to see me, okay?"

I nodded, at once reassured and irritated that I felt so enormously relieved. I had such faith in medical mumbo jumbo.

"You've got lettuce stuck between your teeth." I couldn't resist pointing it out. I didn't want him to be fallible, but at the same time, I needed him to be just a little less godlike.

He sucked his teeth a minute and stood to leave.

"Alan," I blurted out, "am I a hypochondriac?"

He considered again. He never, even years before he became a doctor, said anything without deliberating first. Then he shrugged. "If you are, it's better than the news you thought you'd get, right?"

He disappeared before I had a chance to digest that comment. His ability to annoy me had not waned at all. But I felt a little better as I headed out to the library to look up some trivial little details about hats in the nineteenth century.

I found what I needed after nearly two hours of shuffling through reference books. Restless, I strolled down to the archives to see if they had any information about soddies. The history of my little house intrigued me. But I couldn't lay my hands on anything right away, and the archivist was busy, so I decided just to head on home and get back to work.

On my way back, I drove right through the county seat. Impulsively, I pulled into a parking place next to the courthouse and went into the deeds office. "How can I find out about who owned my house?"

The clerk was very helpful and showed me the title books and how to use them. I spread them out on the table and began to take notes, chastising myself mentally for not going straight home to work. This was, clearly, another delay tactic.

The chain of ownership was very straightforward: from me, it went back to a man named Hall, who, I remembered hearing from the real estate agent, had inherited the house from an aunt. Her name, I discovered, had been White, and she and her husband had inherited the house from his father, also named White. All told, the Whites of one generation or another had owned the house since 1917.

"Excuse me," I said, wandering back up to the front counter. "There's no record of my house before 1917."

She pursed her lips while she thought. Then she snapped her fingers. "I know," she said. "This was all Indian territory then—nobody owned it."

"But I know somebody lived there," I protested. "My house or part of it, anyway, dates back to 1895."

She shrugged. "Have you checked with the State Historical Society? They might know something. If it wasn't bought or sold, we don't have a record of it here."

I thanked her and left a little disappointed, although I wasn't sure why. I stopped at the grocery store and made it home just in time for sunset. I sat on the porch and reveled in the glorious explosion of colors, consciously avoiding the "think tank" and a repeat of my curious experiences there.

I spent a couple of hours after dinner assimilating my day's research findings into my novel and then combing through the last three chapters for inconsistencies or outright errors. Feeling virtuous, I retired to the bathtub with a glass of wine and a book. When the water was unbearably cold, I toweled myself dry and climbed into bed, making sure the blinds on the east window were tightly shut. Sunrise through the uncurtained window was bright enough to wake the dead, and I wanted to sleep at least until seven.

Something woke me up a few hours later. I think I had a touch of heartburn from the red wine. Whatever it was, I couldn't get back to sleep, so I pulled on my robe and ambled through the darkened house. I sat in the dark in the great room for a few moments, amusing myself by imagining a pioneer woman stoking up a fire in that great hearth and cooking a meal. The image was so vivid that I could practically see her, and I moved closer to examine the stone. There must have been some kind of hooks to hang kettles and pots from, and the stone would surely have a mark showing where they'd been.

I noticed the little door had swung open, and when I peered into the lean-to, I saw an irresistible view. The moon hung full and low over the prairie, illuminating the gentle folds of land with an eerie, bluish tint. I slipped into the rocker to sit and watch, sure that such a soothing landscape would soon put me to sleep. My eyelids did become heavy, and my feet stopped pushing off the floor so the rocker ceased its calming motion. I sat still, half asleep, until something warm and moist pushed its way firmly between the top of my leg and the palm of my hand.

My heart started thudding rapidly. With wide eyes, I stared down at my lap, raising my hand with a loud and unpleasant screech. The sensation abruptly ended, and I reached with trembling hands to switch on the floor lamp behind my rocker.

The light revealed a mess that the moonlight had masked. My jar of pencils and pens was on the floor, and the sugar bowl had fallen, too. Sugar was spilled out in a wide swath next to the rocker. The bread and cheese I'd abandoned earlier was five feet away from the table where I'd left it. But most uncanny of all, the spilled sugar bore the distinct impression of a large paw print, four smaller round pads surrounding a central, curved one—clearly a dog's paw print. I stared at it, my mouth comically agape. The house had been locked. I didn't have a dog—in fact, I was allergic to any kind of animal fur.

As if to punctuate that thought, I sneezed explosively. The action propelled me up and out of the little room, not even stopping to turn out the light or clean up the mess. Maybe, I thought wanly, this is just a dream and it will all be gone in the morning.

The next morning I just ignored it. I applied myself diligently to the computer and spent four uninterrupted hours pounding away at the keyboard. I ignored the incident, in fact, for two and a half weeks, during which time I managed to write prodigiously. I wrote, I ate, I spooned my sugar directly out of the bag, I took my tea on the porch to enjoy the sunsets, I wrote some more in the evenings, and I slept like a baby.

After such a prolonged outburst of creativity, I needed to go to the library again to check up on a few facts. I took my time, spending almost all day to verify little details about long-ago flora and fauna, as well as some facts about nineteenth-century eating habits. The research part of my work never gets boring.

When I was finished, I made my way to the archives again with only the vaguest idea of what to ask for. This time the librarian was free, and he was quite willing to chat about early Oklahoma history.

"The county clerk is right," he nodded. "All that was Indian land until World War I."

"But people, white people I mean, lived there?"

"I think so. Just a minute." He disappeared into the bowels of the library and returned a few minutes later with a scraggly old cloth-bound book.

"Yes, it was settled during the land run of '91," he replied. "People were given leases on the land, ninety-nine-year leases, as long as they farmed on it."

"So do you know who could tell me who had my house?"

He shook his head. "I'm sorry," he said. "I don't know who would have those records. Have you tried the Historical Society?"

"No," I said. "It's no big deal, really."

I must have looked really disappointed, because he repeated himself. "I'm sorry," he said helplessly.

I scribbled down my phone number on a scrap of paper and handed it to him. "If you run across anything at all about Washita County in the 1890s, would you give me a call?"

His face brightened. "Sure, I'd be glad to." He glanced at the paper. "Alice. I'm Bill."

"Thanks, Bill. I appreciate it."

I left the archives and drove home. Some of what I had discovered at the library meant I needed to rework part of a chapter, which was frustrating. On the other hand, sometimes these little alterations opened up interesting new twists. I had plenty to occupy my thoughts as I drove.

I avoided the lean-to successfully for four more days. Then the phone rang, startling me so badly I nearly fell out of my chair.

"Alice!" It was a loud and cheerful voice.

"Mary Ellen," I said cautiously. "How are you?" She was a former roommate from college. I had borne up under her boisterous presence for one whole quarter before squeezing enough money from my parents for a single dorm room. I've never tolerated sharing living space very well, and Mary Ellen had been a trial by fire.

"I'm in OK City!"

My heart sank. I knew what was coming.

"I want to see you and your new house!"

"Okay, where should I pick you up?" A docile reply. I knew she'd get her way eventually, so why waste time? She told me she had an unexpected twelve-hour layover at Will Rogers Airport, so I arranged to pick her up in two hours and bring her home for a cup of tea.

It really wasn't so bad. She was still funny—and smart. When we pulled up in front of the house (there was no driveway, just a dirt yard), she proclaimed that she simply adored my little house, and she'd have to see every inch of it before we sat down to tea.

"There's not much to see, really," I answered her mildly. I led her across the porch and into the living room. "Living room, kitchen," I paused to put the kettle on, "little ugly bathroom, and bedroom."

"Tell me all about the history of it, Alice. I know you know all about it."

"Not that much, really," I said. We were headed back to the kitchen where the kettle was shrieking. "Do you take sugar in your tea?"

She was amused by my lack of a sugar bowl. "Really, Alice," she said as she watched me spoon it out of the bag. "Thirty-five years old and you don't have a sugar bowl yet?"

"I had one," I blurted.

"Let's have our tea on the porch," she interrupted. "I'll bet you see great sunsets here."

I mumbled something in agreement and followed her out to the porch. We had only just sat down with our tea mugs when she jumped up again. "There's something you haven't shown me," she cried, sounding hurt. "I can see from out here that there's another room."

I mumbled some more as Mary Ellen swept back into the main room of the house and went directly to the little door. She flung it open, and a thick wave of heavy odor poured out. Mary Ellen sniffed and then turned to me looking puzzled.

"Why didn't you tell me you had a dog?"

"I don't," I stammered.

Mary Ellen poked her head through the door and looked around. "Where is he?" she demanded. "You sly thing, you always said you were allergic to dogs!"

"I am," I insisted. "There is no dog, Mary Ellen."

Her eyes took in the whole mess: the upturned sugar bowl, the paw print, the stale bread and dried-out cheese lying against the baseboard.

She turned back to me, her tone aggrieved. "Whatever you say, Alice." She was cross for the next hour, as we tried to maintain a conversation. Finally, I gave up and suggested that we head back to the airport.

I was home only five minutes, reveling again in the quiet, when the phone shrilled. I hadn't had more than six calls since I moved in, and here was the second call in the day. It had to be Mary Ellen.

I stared at the insistent, jangling thing, debating whether to answer or not. Training prevailed, and I snatched it up.

"Hello?" I said, ungraciously—training only worked so far.

"Hello, Alice?" It wasn't Mary Ellen—it wasn't even a voice I could place. "This is Bill."

"Yes," I said cautiously. I was casting around in my brain for the connection.

"From the archives? In Oklahoma City?"

"Oh, sure, Bill, how are you?" I was so relieved it wasn't Mary Ellen that I became positively effusive.

"I found a book I thought you might be interested in?" His rising inflections were starting to annoy me.

"Yes?"

"It's about the German community in Washita County. I haven't read it all, but it sounds like the right time period and the right area?"

"Oh, yes, that's great." I tried to force some enthusiasm back into my voice.

"Do you want me to hold it for you?"

"Yeah, sure. I mean, I don't know when I can get back into town, but could you do that for me?"

"Oh, of course. It's not like anybody could check it out or anything, you know, since it's here in the archives." He gave a nervous little chuckle, and then there was a long, awkward pause.

"Well, thanks again," I said brightly. "See you later!" I hung up with a little click and then felt a little remorseful. I could have been nicer. Should have been, really, since he was going above and beyond the call of duty in looking for research material. Oh, well—I resolved to be extra nice when I went to see the book.

I was all jazzed up by the events of the day and decided to use up some of the energy by working. I plugged away on what was going to be the next-to-the-last chapter, fingers tapping steadily on the keyboard until nearly midnight. After half a glass of wine, I was struck by a debilitating sense of exhaustion, tired to the very bone. I managed to drag myself ten feet to my bed and fall across it, sinking immediately into a stuporous sleep.

It was the heavy kind of sleep where your body doesn't even twitch. I woke up four hours later in the same position: lengthways across the middle of the bed on top of the quilt and my head cradled in my upraised arms. I was instantly, fully awake—I woke as suddenly as I had fallen asleep.

My mouth had a sour taste, so I rose and brushed my teeth, moving confidently through the dark. In the short weeks since I'd moved in, my body had become adjusted to the space so completely that I rarely turned on a light when I woke in the middle of the night.

I had a sense that more sleep was out of the question, so I took a cup of tea and wandered through the shadowed, silent rooms. Without conscious choice, I found myself in the little lean-to behind the hearth. Beyond the windows lay an invisible vista, shadow layered on shadow, sky and prairie indistinguishable in the night. I sat and rocked, hands wrapped around my tea mug to soak in the comforting warmth and imagining the activity of the land before me. I thought of prairie dogs, coyotes, owls, rabbits, hawks, foxes—all the little lives busy, busy far beyond my prying eyes.

The thought of so many unseen endeavors must have been soothing because I believe I dozed off. My first coherent thought on waking was that the prairie dogs had invaded my house. My mind quickly dismissed that thought because, of course, prairie dogs are nearly extinct.

But there was the undeniable sound of an animal moving behind me, and that awareness pierced my sleepy consciousness with a sudden, sharp sense of danger. I froze, my eyes straining to see through the shadows and to my left where the noise seemed to originate. The noise was a distinct, precise clicking sound, rhythmic and quick—the sound of paws pacing the length of the room behind my rocking chair.

I exhaled softly, only then realizing that I'd been holding my breath since I woke up. Slowly, moving with infinitesimal care, I turned my head and then my shoulders to look behind my chair.

There was nothing to see. The sound of ragged toenails clicking against the wooden floorboards ceased immediately. I sat curled up in the rocker for several long moments, my brain taking this information and twisting it this way and that, trying to force it into some pattern that made sense. There was no sense—there was no explanation.

I continued to sit, watching the shadows bleed slowly from the sky, leached away by the rising sun. The changes were at first imperceptible, a lightening so gradual that it was as if my eyes were playing tricks. Then, at once it seemed, the landscape crossed the line from night to dawn, and birds began to sing.

Sleep was out of the question. I prowled restlessly through the house, moving from room to room, picking up a vase here and setting it down again there, sliding a pillow a little to the left or again to the right, twitching the slats of the blinds so they fell into place, dusting them—pointlessly—with my fingertips. At six I took a bath, and at seven I choked down a banana. At eight I snatched up a notepad and my car keys and left, at first driving aimlessly up and down the long, rolling prairie roads. At ten my nose told me I was on the outskirts of Oklahoma City—the stockyard stench was unmistakable. A few more miles, a few turns, and I found myself parked outside the library and the archives.

At the desk was a librarian I'd never seen before, and I was vaguely relieved not to have to see Bill. The woman handed me a thin, paperbound book when I told her my name, and I sat down at a heavy, scarred wooden table to read it.

It was somebody's master's thesis, typed on thin, now yellow paper, and handbound with cardboard. In detached, dry prose it described the German settlement in Washita County. They'd come from Missouri and Illinois to farm the rich Oklahoma land, and they quickly formed a tight-knit community complete with churches and schools. They helped each other out with planting and harvesting, barn raising and burials, matchmaking and births.

But it didn't last long. Other settlers moved in, and once World War I started, bad feelings began to grow against the German families, many of them now second- and third-generation but distinctly German all the same. The German families dispersed, other families took up the leases on the land in Indian Territory, and when the land was appropriated by the government, it was turned over to these relatively new settlers, who became the owners of some of the finest farmland in the country.

I read all this quickly, not even bothering to take notes. It seemed pretty clear that it was one of these hapless German families who had first built my home, first the soddy and then the one-room cabin with a lean-to for the livestock or maybe, I thought, for the privacy it might give the adults in the family. My mind boggled at the thought of an entire family, six or eight or even ten children and their parents, living together in that single room.

It was interesting information and seemed for some strange reason to settle my mind. I climbed back into my car and drove home, a pleasant, light weariness falling over me like a cloud.

At home I brushed my teeth and put on my nightgown, not caring that it was only two o'clock in the afternoon—I wanted to sleep. I closed the blinds tightly and curled up beneath my soft old quilt.

It was dark when I awoke. I groped for the clock on my bedside table and held it up to my face, squinting to see through my sleep-fogged eyes. It was almost midnight. Like the night before, I was as wide-awake as I could be, and I hated more than anything to lie in bed and try to sleep. I got up and wrapped a robe around me. The house seemed a little chilly, even though the real cold wouldn't arrive until October, a month away.

Stopping in the dim kitchen, lit only by the glow of the clock on the stove, I turned the flame on low beneath the kettle—a cup of herb tea might help me get back to sleep. I wandered through the rooms, running my fingers gently over many small treasures, their shape and texture reassuring even in the dark.

Again, inevitably it seemed, my feet led me to the small room behind the hearth. I curled up in the rocker, tucking the robe around my bare feet, and propelled myself gently back and forth. I stared out the window at the sleeping prairie, but my mind's eye turned inward. The rhythm of the rocking chair made me doze.

I smelled smoke—not the benign smell of a campfire or even the autumn-fresh odor of leaves burning briskly in the cool air. It was the dangerous, terrifying smell of flames out of control, fiercely, dispassionately burning everything in its path. It was an evil smell.

"Quick! In the wagon!" I heard the shouted command and looked wildly around. The smoke roiled, twisting thick and acrid, masking my vision. All I could see were vague shapes running panic-stricken through the dense, soot-laden air.

"I've got the team hitched up—let's go!" Now the command held a note of hysteria, as did the answering voice.

"What happened?" I could see a figure that must have been feminine; a long full skirt swung in an unconscious echo of the swirling, deadly smoke.

"They set the west field on fire, and I believe they set the barn on fire, too."

"But why?" A sob.

"I don't know, *liebchen*, but get in the wagon!"

The man's voice counted, up to five, and I realized he must be counting heads. "Emma, are you all right? Arthur? Grover?"

Just then pandemonium broke out in the room beside me. A deep, full-throated bark, repeated over and over, sounding every bit as terrified as the voices of the unseen people in the yard.

"The dog! John, we cannot leave the dog!"

The horses stomped and whinnied, a long, high shriek of panic. The man did not answer; I heard the horses gallop away, and the dog in the lean-to began to bay and cry.

When I woke up, covered in sweat and shivering from the cold, the kettle was shrieking in the kitchen. Shakily I rose and went to make a cup of tea.

Three months later, when I finally finished the book and turned it in to the publisher, I had a party at my new house. About twenty people came, some of them bringing housewarming gifts. The only person I'd had over to the house before the party had been Mary Ellen.

"I love your house, Alice," someone threw over their shoulder as they floated from the kitchen to the living room.

I was picking up discarded glasses when I saw Alan tugging gently at the door to the left of the hearth. He must have felt my eyes on him because he looked up and caught my gaze.

"What's this?" He gestured to the door with his half-empty beer bottle when I reached his side.

"Oh," I said lamely. "It's nothing, really. Just a little storage closet. I, ah, keep it locked because the door swings open at odd moments."

He looked at me with his eyebrows raised in an unspoken question. I made an excuse and left his side, leaving his question unanswered. Some doors are meant to be closed forever.

the wolf

With a roar of anger, he launched himself at his attacker, using his powerful haunches to spring a full foot off the ground before burying his teeth in the woman's arm. A growl bubbled up from deep within his chest but did nothing to lessen his ferocious grip. His ears lay flat against the dome of his head, and he held on with a frightening intensity.

"Aus!" the trainer barked.

The dog only growled lower. The trainer, watching the German shepherd's expression, sighed inwardly but made no visible sign of his displeasure.

"Aus!" he repeated from his position behind the assailant's shoulder. When the dog still did not let go, he jerked the lead, pulling the dog's head forward so he would be choked by the thick padding covering the decoy's arm. Reluctantly, after the third sharp tug, the dog released his grip, and the decoy backed away, stripping off the protective sleeve.

"I've had it for today, Jimmy," she said, keeping an eye on the German Shepherd. The dog was still snarling and standing in a half-crouch, ready to leap again.

"Yeah, okay, I'm beat, too," the trainer conceded. "Let me put this boy up." He led the large black-and-brown dog to its kennel, detouring to grab a handful of tidbits on the way. He opened his palm, holding his fingers flat as he offered the treats to the dog.

The German Shepherd wolfed them down, his long, white tapered canines exposed in an expression that was mostly frustration. This, he seemed to be saying, is not the kind of meat I would have preferred.

"Good boy," said the trainer, although he didn't really mean it. With a cursory pat on the head, he guided the dog into the kennel, unsnapped the lead, and locked the gate, double-checking the bolt unconsciously.

When he got back to the training area, his decoy was lounging against the fence, watching another dog and trainer work through some basic steps. "I don't know what to do with that dog, Kathy," he admitted. "He's got a great attitude most of the time, but sometimes he just doesn't know when to quit."

"You can't train an unpredictable dog, Jimmy," the woman advised. "Even if you do, you couldn't, in good conscience, take him out on the streets. What happens if he tears out some guy's throat? That's the kind of thing any sleazy lawyer would love to get his hands on. Police brutality with a dog—I can see it now."

The trainer shrugged. "I'd feel safe out on the streets with him. He's got a great bite and nothing scares him. He'd make a better partner than a lot of cops I know."

"I know what's wrong with him."

"What?"

"Same thing you've got—testosterone poisoning." She cuffed the K-9 officer on the shoulder and turned to leave.

••••••

The children were screaming. Lydia sighed and rose, her needlework falling to the floor as she crossed to the window. Out in the yard, two girls and one small boy played some incomprehensible game involving running, stopping, and starting again, with the three children shifting allegiances as fluidly as only siblings can. The game was apparently enhanced by shrieking, and Lydia allowed herself a small smile at the sheer pleasure they could find in physical activity.

She stooped to retrieve her work as she returned to the rocking chair by the fire. Although it was April, she still felt a chill in the air in the late afternoons. The modest fire sent flames licking up and around the logs in a satisfying, contained way, like a cat thoughtfully grooming itself.

As soon as Lydia had the thought, a cat materialized and sprang gracefully into her lap. She had just enough warning to lift the needlework out of the way—a fancy collar for her oldest granddaughter's Sunday dress.

"Tabby," she protested mildly, but the cat could sense she meant no real reproof. The creature curled up in her lap, and she rocked, needlework forgotten. She fought briefly to keep her eyes open but soon gave it up. Both the woman and the cat slipped in and out of a trancelike doze.

The children's shrieks startled her awake, and the cat leapt down from her lap to slink around the corner and away. The old cat still wasn't used to the children, and neither, thought Lydia, am I. It had been too long since her own daughter had been a child—and too soon since her daughter had died—for Lydia to have the heart to raise these children.

"But here they are," she sighed, "and I guess they're here to stay." She picked up the abandoned needlework and began to work again, but she had hardly taken a stitch before the door slammed open.

"Ahh," she cried. The needle had neatly pierced her heart-finger, but she barely had time to perceive this before the children were upon her with cries of acute distress.

"It's a wolf, Grandmama, a wolf!" Edward, the baby, was panting and struggling wildly to crawl into her lap. Lydia, the middle child and her own namesake, was tugging relentlessly on one arm, and Elizabeth was dancing about in front of her, first on one foot and then the other, babbling incoherently. The elder Lydia felt as if she would fly apart in the face of so much undirected anxiety.

"Stop, stop!" she commanded, and for a moment all was still. "If there's a creature outside, don't you suppose you'd better shut the door?" Her tone was biting, and she immediately regretted it. Elizabeth scurried to shut the door, and Edward's whimpers increased.

"Now, tell me," she ordered, in a slightly more kindly manner. "What happened?"

"We were playing..."

"It came from the woods..."

"Its teeth, Grandmama..."

All three children began at once, and Lydia had to calm them again. "Elizabeth first," she demanded.

"We were playing," the girl began again, twisting her skirt nervously in her hands. Lydia thought about telling her to stop but decided to hear out the story first. "Edward saw something in the woods, but we thought he was just being a baby, you know?"

Lydia felt a response was called for, so she nodded.

Encouraged, her granddaughter continued. "Then, when Lydia ran close to the woods, it ran out and growled at her, Grandmama—a big wolf!"

"With enormous fangs!" chimed in Edward.

Young Lydia only shuddered, while her grandmother considered the story. "There haven't been any wolves around here since I was a girl," the woman finally said. "Are you sure it wasn't just a big dog?"

The children were adamant that the creature was a wolf. Since it was nearly dark, they were easily persuaded to sit quietly by the fire while Elizabeth read to them. The evening passed without incident, but as Lydia braided her hair in preparation for bed, the wind picked up and began to whip angrily around the corners of the house. When she blew out the candle and crawled between the chilly, stiff sheets, she imagined that the sound of the wind was in reality the cry of the wolves, plaintive and cold.

••••••

The dog was near his limit for this training session, Jimmy could tell. He'd lost none of his enthusiasm—he still bounded with incredible energy toward the decoy every time he was given the command—but he was taking a split second too long to disengage and back off.

One more exercise, the trainer thought. "Let's set up the blinds," he called to Kathy. The lightweight, portable shelters would let the dog practice searching for a suspect and holding him—or her—at bay until a police officer arrived to make the arrest. They quickly set up the exercise, and Kathy crouched inside one shelter, out of the dog's sight.

"Revier," he commanded, and the dog dashed away. When he took the corner to thrust his head inside the first blind, his pumping legs struck the shelter and nearly toppled it over. Angry, the dog turned and snapped at the nylon before tearing off to the other blind fifty feet away.

Something about the dog's demeanor triggered caution in the trainer, and he followed the dog at a half-trot. There had been no lapses in his behavior at training sessions for weeks, and Jimmy was almost at ease with the dog's performance. He was working off the lead now, and next week he'd start working out on the street.

The dog threw himself at the blind with all the mindless ferocity of a tornado. The shelter shook and toppled, becoming a shapeless mass of nylon with the indeterminate shape of Kathy, the decoy, writhing underneath it.

"Aus!" Jimmy roared, feeling the situation spin out of control. "Hold still, Kathy!"

The dog thrust aggressively at the nylon with his nose, looking for a purchase. He was snarling angrily, his lips pulled back to expose sharp white teeth.

"Pfui," Jimmy ordered, deepening his pitch, hoping that the dog was not completely out of control. Just then Kathy moved, rolling over, Jimmy found out later, to cover her unprotected face.

The dog lunged. Jimmy dove, twisting as he fell, to put his body between the dog and the decoy to avert the vicious attack.

The dog's teeth ripped a flap of skin from Jimmy's cheek that was almost five inches wide. The long, tearing bite missed his eye by a scant half inch—the trainer would have nightmares about the incident for weeks to come.

"I've never met a dog who'd bite his handler," he'd say to anyone who would listen. "Most dogs would rather die than hurt their trainer."

"The dog's obviously psychotic," Kathy said quietly a week after it happened. "You don't have any choice."

"I hate to put him down. He's so good at the work, and he enjoys it so much." Jimmy was stubborn.

"Well, sure, let's send him to the local kiddie park—he's such a good dog." Her voice oozed sarcasm.

Jimmy eyed his friend. "He really scared you, didn't he?"

She laughed, a short bark without much mirth. "If he didn't scare you, then you're a lot dumber than you look."

"I'm sorry, Kathy. I forget, sometimes, how close you came to this." He gestured to the Frankenstein-like row of black stitches marching crooked down his cheek. "I'll deal with the dog—and we'll find a nice, tractable rottweiler to start training next week."

••••••

Lydia got her hired hand to hitch the mare up to the buggy first thing the next morning. Although the children were a bit apprehensive about leaving the protection of the house, it was easy to see that their grandmother would not take kindly to an outright refusal. So they reluctantly scurried out to the yard and into the buggy. They felt a little better when Lydia explained the mare's ability to sense the presence of wolves.

"Horses and wolves are natural enemies," she stated, sounding a lot more confident of her facts than she really was. "If there was a wolf within five miles of here, old Nellie here wouldn't even poke her long nose out of the barn."

They rode about two miles down the road before arriving at a prosperous-looking farm. As the buggy creaked and jingled up to the barn, three dogs raced into the yard, all of them barking ferociously. Edward immediately shrank back into Elizabeth, sobbing hysterically. Little Lydia paled and began to gulp and gasp, trying unsuccessfully to hold back her tears. Even Elizabeth turned a chalky white as she wrapped a protective arm around her brother and sister.

The elder Lydia pulled herself up as straight as she could and whispered, "Don't be afraid, children." Then she called out loudly and imperiously, "Ames! You, Ames! Call off your dogs, I say!"

A tall, impossibly thin man, wearing a battered black hat and carrying a pitchfork, shuffled out of the barn. At the sight of him, the dogs immediately stilled, and when he waved his pitchfork, they slunk off in three directions. The smallest dog curled up on the kitchen doorstep, keeping a wary eye on the visitors; the other two large, shaggy creatures, of indeterminate breed, went around to either side of the barn and, presumably, off to the fields and their work beyond.

"Lydia." His greeting was accompanied by the barest of nods, and the woman stiffened, aware of the slight.

"I'll thank you to keep your dogs off my land," she said coldly. "They frightened the children very badly yesterday, and I'll not have it."

He regarded her for a long moment before turning and ambling back into the barn without a word.

"I'm warning you, Ames, I'll have them shot if I see them again," she called. She was proud that she spoke without revealing a trace of the tension that stirred within her. The children stared after the man, their fear of the dogs forgotten in their amazement at the man's audacity. Lydia cleared her throat and chirruped to the mare to get her moving.

"Well, children," she said crisply as they drove away. "I expect we should be seeing about your lessons some time this morning, eh?"

••••••

Jimmy put down his fork and wiped his mouth with a napkin, half concealing a satisfied burp. "That was good, Kathy," he said. "Thanks." Tomorrow he would go back to work, and Kathy had brought by some takeout to celebrate. The stitches were out of his cheek, but there remained a red, livid scar that made Jimmy uncomfortable to be around strangers.

"What'll you do with that dog tomorrow, Jimmy?" They were sitting in the living room, feet propped up and staring at the TV. It was a commercial break on one of those real-life cop shows. They both had a weakness for the gritty drama; the unwitting comedy was pretty good, too.

"What?" Gee, she's not going to let that go, he thought.

"You know, that dog," she said sarcastically. "That little angel that caused you to miss three weeks of work?"

"Well, I'm going to talk to the vet tomorrow," Jimmy said, hoping that would put her off.

"You think he'd respond well to Prozac or something?"

This woman's sarcasm would choke a horse, Jimmy thought. He chose not to respond, and she was wise enough to drop it—that was how their friendship had been preserved through six years of association. They watched TV in silence for twenty minutes more.

"Look," Kathy burst out just as she was getting her keys out to leave, "I know you really like that dog for some sick reason, and you don't want to put him down."

Jimmy opened his mouth to speak but Kathy held up her hand to stop him. "Here's something for you to think about. I've got a friend of a friend who's renovating an old house out in the country and wants a dog for protection. There are no kids, the people working there won't even live there, so the dog can rip off the legs of anybody who startles him without any repercussions."

Jimmy was touched, though he tried not to show it. "Thanks, Kathy" was all he could manage to say.

She shoved a scrap of paper with a number scribbled on it into his hand and patted his arm awkwardly as she left. As he cleaned up the plastic forks and paper trash from their dinner, Jimmy marveled at the wonderful complexity of human beings. "Just when you think you've got them figured out," he mused.

••••••

Lydia wrung out a rag in the china basin and spread it across young Lydia's forehead. It was so hot that she imagined the water would sizzle when it dripped onto the girl's skin, but it only made the child stir uneasily and mutter. Next to her, propped up on two pillows, was her sister Elizabeth, two hectic spots of color high on her cheeks.

"Grandmama," she said dully, "is Lydia going to die?"

The woman gasped, taken aback by her bluntness, but she quickly regained her composure. "Of course not, Elizabeth," she said matter-of-factly. "You will both be well in the morning. It's only old women like me who get sick and die."

As soon as she said it, she regretted it. She had no wish to frighten the girl with the specter of the death of her only adult family left. She also had momentarily forgotten the death of her daughter, the mother of these children—a very young, healthy woman before a fever much like this had snatched her away.

"And I'm too mean to die soon, child," she amended hastily, swooping down to plant a light kiss on the girl's cheek. "You feel better? You want some warm broth?" Elizabeth shook her head and lay down, rolling on her side and closing her eyes.

In the corner of the sickroom, Edward played listlessly with some smooth round pebbles, clicking them together occasionally. Another game I will never comprehend, Lydia thought, carrying the basin out of the room and down the stairs. Her housekeeper had stopped coming, she said because of the back wages Lydia owed her—Lydia suspected it was just as much for fear of the fever as anything else.

When Lydia climbed wearily back up the stairs, carrying the basin full of fresh, cool water, she heard an odd sound from the room. It was a jerking, slithering sound that made her take a few running steps in alarm. Elizabeth was sitting up again, drawing back from the convulsing figure of her sister. Edward watched from the corner, his eyes wide with shock. The sound was the child's thin, hot limbs flailing against the linen sheets.

Lydia gathered her namesake up into her arms and held her as she died. So much death, she thought numbly. My husband, my daughter, now this child. When will it be my turn? I want it to be my turn next.

The tears were hot as they coursed down her cheeks. The fever that had taken young Lydia's life now finally left her, and her grandmother rocked the slight young body until it was cold.

••••••

"What is that?" The young man stared into the car, thankful that a sheet of glass separated him from the dog whose lips were drawn back to expose his teeth and, the man thought, an oversupply of mindless rage.

"Protection," his dad answered shortly. "Help me unload these two-by-fours."

The young man stood his ground. "Not unless that dog's tied up first," he answered firmly. "I don't know what happened to him, but I don't like dogs that look at me like that."

The older man shrugged and opened the door to grab the dog's leather leash. The dog bounded out of the car, rushing to attack anything within range, but a complicated muzzle kept his teeth from tearing anyone's flesh.

The older man struggled momentarily with the leash and then dragged the dog inside the building. His son followed at a respectful distance.

"That dog trained?"

"They said he was—and a great protection dog, too. Just a little aggressive sometimes."

"Ha! I'd say so."

The dog lay down quietly after his leash was attached tightly to the newel post of the main stairs. The two men unloaded the lumber, discussing the project at hand. The whole family was involved in renovating the old house for use as a restaurant; it had been a restaurant in the late sixties but had fallen into disrepair since then. Built in 1740 with a major addition in 1861, it was ideal for their purposes. It would require months of hard labor, but they were skilled and eager to make it work.

"If I'm going to work here, I guess I'd better make friends with this old boy," the younger man commented. "What's his name?"

"They called him 'Wolf,' " his dad replied. "He apparently had that kind of a disposition."

The dog was acting strangely, crouched with his belly low to the ground, when the young man knelt and held out his hand.

"Hey, boy," he said gently. "How's it going?"

The dog whined again and crouched still lower.

"Do you think the muzzle's hurting him, Dad?" Without waiting for a reply, he began to unbuckle and unstrap the contraption.

The older man watched, puzzled. The dog's behavior earlier had been completely different. He'd been belligerent, ready to charge practically anything that moved. Now he cringed, tense on the floor, his tail curled tight around his hindquarters.

"He acts like somebody's been beating him," his son commented.

"I'm sure he's been well treated," his dad objected. "K-9 officers have to be able to count on their dogs. A dog that's scared would make a lousy partner." The young man shrugged. "I'm going to take him off the leash," he said.

"Does he know commands like heel, stay, and all that?"

His dad fumbled in his pocket. "No, he's been trained using German commands. Here's a list of the words."

The young man studied the paper. "My German's a little rusty, boy, but here goes: Heir!"

The German Shepherd jumped to his feet and trotted over to the young man. "Good boy," he said, approvingly. "Let's show you around, okay?"

At the door to the kitchen, on the ground floor, the dog stopped dead in his tracks. When the young man called him the second time, he entered the room, but not before releasing a little yip of protest. The dog stuck so close to the young man's side that he had to be careful not to stumble over the powerful, furry body.

After a tour of the first floor, they climbed the stairs to an area that would be converted into more dining rooms. The dog's tail remained firmly placed straight down, not quite tucked between his back legs but ready to protect his vulnerable rear end at a moment's notice. The dog followed the young man cautiously, creeping from room to room.

The dog balked at climbing the narrow stairs to the third floor. The young man called and cajoled, but the dog would not move from his position at the foot of the stairs. He barked, growled, and finally cried when the young man gave up trying to convince him to make the climb. The big dog hovered at the bottom step, looking up anxiously and whining every so often, waiting for human company to rejoin him on the second floor.

••••••

It was Elizabeth's turn next. When she died, Lydia had no more tears left. She drew the sheet up over the girl's face, exhaustion making the linen feel as heavy as lead. A small whimpering sound made her look into the corner. Edward sat there, clutching the cat who had apparently decided that even small human company was preferable to no company at all.

"Oh, Edward," Lydia cried softly. She crossed to the shadowy corner and knelt gracelessly on one creaky old knee. She'd forgotten about the poor boy during the last twelve hours of battling Elizabeth's fever.

The child was shuddering, great heaving motions that Lydia thought masked unvoiced sobs. But the instant her fingertips touched the boy, she knew with a shock what was wrong.

"Not you, too, Edward," she whispered. His skin was fiery to her touch. Lydia never knew, in all her long sixty years of life, the kind of weariness that settled into her heart now. It was a tiredness so heavy, so relentless that she felt as if she should just lie down and let the darkness overtake her.

Instead, she pulled the little boy to her chest and stood, an old woman holding an armful of burning sticks. Since when had the child been so insubstantial?

She couldn't bear to move Elizabeth, so she went to the stairs and climbed, flat-footedly and clumsily, to Edward's little room on the top floor. She laid her grandson gently in his bed and began to stand vigil against the fever, now and then taking a damp rag and wiping it ineffectually across his forehead. His skin was papery and almost scorching under her hands, and when she held him close, she could practically smell a burning odor as the fever consumed him from the inside out.

After hours of mindlessly trekking up and down the stairs for cool water and stooping over his frail, shuddering body, she noticed the moon setting between the trees, framed by the attic window. Just then, Edward woke up.

"Grandmama," he croaked, and she jerked upright. "I'm thirsty."

She hurried to prop his head up and fed him a few sips of water. Even this small effort seemed to cost him untold energy. He started to slide back down on the bed but suddenly, savagely pulled himself back up.

"Grandmama," he gasped, pointing into the darkened corner. "How did it get in here?"

She peered into the corner, her tired eyes stubbornly refusing to focus on anything but shifting, insubstantial shadows. "What, Edward? I can't see anything."

The boy's feet were sliding and scrabbling underneath the light sheet, trying to find a purchase as he struggled to raise himself. "It's the wolf, Grandmama! Can't you see it? It's come to get me!" His cry was a pitiful mewling, his voice thin and cracking.

"Shhh, boy, it's all right," Lydia tried to soothe the child, holding him close. His body was stiff with terror, and his eyes remained focused on the empty corner. "Don't, don't let it get me, Grandmama," he whimpered.

His delirium continued throughout the night and into the next morning. At some point, he even lost awareness that it was his grandmother nursing him. "Mama," he sobbed, "Mama, the wolf is here!"

In her desperation, Lydia took to crossing the room to the corner where Edward pointed. "There's nothing here, dear, see?" She would take the fireplace poker and sweep it through the corner or kick with her feet at the empty air. "There's nothing here, darling, now please rest!"

She went through these motions over and over, but nothing could soothe the poor child's hysteria. When he died in her arms, he was still sobbing raggedly about the wolf in the corner.

•••••

The dog had been living in the house for a week, and his behavior had gotten increasingly timid. He lay by the front door and bolted out when he could, bounding through the yard and into the woods with high spirits. Recaptured, he would walk reluctantly back into the house. When someone was working, he liked to keep them within sight, unless they went up to the third floor. He never, never ascended those stairs no matter how badly he seemed to need companionship.

"I think we ought to rename this dog," the young man said to his father one day, roughly patting the big creature on the head. "Instead of 'Wolf,' we should call him 'Lamb' or maybe 'Chicken.'"

"I don't know what happened," the older man answered. "He's worse today than I've ever seen him." The dog was whimpering, pressed so close against the younger man's leg that his weight nearly threw him off balance.

"I hope he'll let you get some work done," he continued. "If he gets any meeker, we'll have to hire a nursemaid just to look after him!" With that, he waved and left.

"I'm going upstairs, boy," the young man said gently to the dog. A shudder coursed across the dog's back, visible even through his thick fur.

"C'mon," he said, encouraging the dog to follow. "I've got to finish putting that molding up on the third floor."

He climbed the stairs to the second level, the dog hovering close by his feet. When he started the climb to the third floor, the dog, as he expected, stopped at the foot of the stairs, whining softly.

"Oh, stop that, you big baby," the man said, annoyed. "There's nothing up here that could hurt you." He ignored the animal and went up the stairs two at a time.

He could hear the dog, pacing and crying softly on the second floor. Then, with a great clattering of toenails and yelping cries, the dog rushed up the stairs and appeared by the young man's side.

"Well, aren't you a brave dog," he said, pleased. "Lie down over there and stay out of my way." The dog padded obediently over to the corner, still whining quietly, and crouched uncomfortably, his head swiveling to follow the young man's every move.

Kneeling to hammer in a loose board, the young man saw motion out of the corner of his eye. It was the dog, flinching as if something struck it. He moaned, just a light breath of anxiety. As the young man watched in amazement, the dog's tail shifted, pulled back as if in anticipation of a blow. The dog cried again, softly.

"That dog is seriously psychotic," the young man muttered to himself and continued at his work. From time to time he could see the dog flinch or hear a terror-stricken moan.

At last the dog leapt to his feet, growling furiously. Then, with a yelp of surprised pain, he flung himself across the room and lunged through the open window, his sleek, powerful body propelling itself into open space. He fell, plummeting like a stone and landing in the yard below. The dog's crumpled body twitched once and then was still—finally at peace.

••••••

Lydia didn't look back as she jolted away on the hired cart, bearing a haphazard collection of what few belongings she could take. The sheriff's sale, for back taxes on the property, had taken all the good furniture, the piano, even her daughter's old clothes and the clothes of the children. All had been sold to her neighbors and strangers who came from far and wide. None of them could look her in the eye as she wandered straight-backed and proud through the rooms.

She was so preoccupied that she didn't hear the sound of a horse approaching, heading for her home. Lydia looked up and saw that it was Ames, grinning nastily at her, barely holding his seat on a horse that was far too spirited for a poor rider. He had bought the house and land for a fraction of its value.

"Got me a pretty nice house now," he crowed. "Fill it up with dogs if I like."

She wanted to ignore him, but she could not. "You'll never be at peace in that house, Ames," she told him, just barely managing to croak out the words. "Not you, not your dogs—ever. Mark my words!"

Ames wheeled and rode off. The dust he raised made Lydia cough before she commanded the driver to go on.

"The Wolf" grew out of a story told about the Crier in the Country Restaurant in Glen Mills, Pennsylvania.

looking for
the light

I had some friends who lived in New Orleans once. They'd dropped out of college and remembered that apartments in the French Quarter were always available—and fairly cheap. The first time I went to visit them, I was on spring break and recovering from a grueling winter of Shakespearean tragedies, Calculus 103, and French Composition 378. I was ready to let my hair down in the worst way, and I'd heard New Orleans was the place to do it.

What a great place, I thought to myself when I found their apartment building. It was on Rue Dauphine, and the entrance was a three-foot cranny between two buildings. After Madeline and Mark had buzzed me in, I'd sidled down a dark, dank, brick-lined corridor, my green canvas rucksack awkwardly scraping against the walls. The corridor opened abruptly into a little piece of paradise.

The courtyard was lush and green, even in early March, when my native city was still brown and lifeless. In the center was a little pond, and through the dark, cloudy water, I could sometimes catch a glimpse of orange or silver as a venerable old goldfish made a lazy circuit of his tiny fiefdom. Plants were everywhere: exotic flowering plants nodded dreamily to me, ferns peeked out demurely from behind cracked cement urns, and climbing plants seemed to grow before my eyes, straining to reach out a tendril and clinging languorously to any available surface. The courtyard was paved by bricks that were mossy and as uneven as a drunkard's steps.

Looking up, I saw that the main house had broad, tall windows that winked in the afternoon sunlight. The windows were thickly curtained, and I could sense that even the linings of the draperies would've cost my friends a couple months' rent—they obviously did not live in an apartment facing the street.

Reaching out on either side of the house, like arms opened wide (to embrace or to strangle, I wondered), were shabby little extensions—former slave quarters, I learned later. Constructed of wood, not stucco-covered brick like the main house, they nevertheless had fine verandas and views of the exquisite jewel, the courtyard.

My friends came out of a door three stories up, hailing me from their little stretch of the veranda. I hauled my suitcase up the stairs, which creaked and moaned like a live thing. Still out of breath, I commended Madeline and Mark on their apartment before I even set foot inside.

"It's pretty small," laughed Madeline, "but we can afford it, and it's close to work."

She wasn't joking about it being pretty small. The living room was twelve by ten and had a little table squeezed into one corner for eating. The kitchen was really a kitchenette—diminutive appliances in a straight row, hidden by a gray plastic folding screen that never would quite close all the way. The bedroom held a bed and exactly enough space to turn around. The bathroom was just as cramped, with a moldy, doll-size shower enclosure whose floor popped up and down like some kind of percussion instrument depending on where you set your feet.

We made room for my stuff in the corner next to the couch where I'd be sleeping. Mark had to leave right away to go to his job waiting tables, but Madeline and I had time to sit and catch up.

"So what's Susan up to? And Jo? And Annie? Is she still with Ed, or did that go down the tubes?"

I filled Madeline in on all the gossip while we drank thick black coffee out of heavy, cheap white mugs. In the middle of some long, pointless story about a classmate and her doomed love life, I heard a strange noise outside on the veranda.

"What's that?" I half rose from my seat. "Don't tell me Mark let you get a dog?"

Madeline laughed. "Of course not—he sneezes if he even passes a dog on the street. That's our resident ghost."

"Ha! A ghost! That's a good one, Maddy."

She looked a little offended. "It's true."

"Well in an apartment this size, I guess a dog ghost is all that would fit." I laughed again. When I realized that Madeline wasn't laughing with me, I tried to back up. "I'm sorry. You're serious, aren't you?"

She got up to slosh a little more coffee in our mugs and shrugged when she sat down again. "It's really strange. We don't hear it every night, but Mark swears it gets closer to the door every time we do hear it. Nobody in the building has a dog, and nobody's ever seen it, even though we've been sitting on the veranda when we heard it walking toward us."

Now I was getting curious. I went to the window and lifted the curtain to look outside. The veranda was completely empty, although a dog could've just gone around the corner of the building or down the stairs and out of my line of sight.

"Just wait," Madeline said defensively. "You'll see—I mean, you'll find out for yourself that it's a ghost."

"Where can we go to scare up the ghost of Jelly Roll Morton?" I responded. "I'm in the mood for some jazz and some serious fun."

Madeline was a good friend. She'd taken the night off from her job as a bartender just so she could show me around. We had a blast, and it was early the next morning before we made our way back to their little place on Rue Dauphine.

"Look at that moon," I gestured, a little widely, to a sliver of innocent white that seemed to be pinned between the tall chimneys of the building beyond the courtyard. Madeline and I were sitting on the veranda appreciating the fresh cool air after the dense, smoky atmosphere of the clubs.

Just then I heard a distinctive click-clicking sound on the old floorboards, and my heart sank. I was not in a fit state to scientifically observe a supernatural phenomenon.

"Here it comes," whispered Madeline. "Shhh!"

It wasn't necessary to hush me. With my mouth open, I stared down the length of the narrow veranda as I heard the sound of a small dog approaching. It was so distinct that I strained my eyes to make the shape of the dog appear—I expected to see the floorboards give slightly under the creature's paws as it came toward us. Just when it seemed the invisible hound would end up in my lap, the sound of its steps swerved right and went through the door into Madeline and Mark's apartment.

"It's never gone inside before!" Madeline's eyes were wide as she looked at me. Just then we heard an explosive "bang" from the living room. Madeline shrieked and ran inside, with me close on her heels.

"Mark," she shouted wildly. The living room was pitch-black—the curtains on the inside and wooden shutters on the outside effectively blocked the wan moonlight.

Mark stood in the door to the bedroom, silhouetted against the light, sleepily rubbing his head. "What was that?"

"Are you okay?"

I pinched myself. Too much excitement or too much to drink—I couldn't decide which.

Madeline found the lamp switch, and we surveyed the living room—not a thing was out of place. The noise was a mystery. It was so puzzling, in fact, that we forgot to tell Mark about the little ghost dog coming into the apartment.

We all slept late, and by the time I'd had my full complement of "morning" coffee, the sun was practically going down. I was beginning to like this city. Mark and Madeline both had to work, but they left me with a few pointers on safety (stay in the populated areas, watch my back, don't flash money around, etc., etc.), a list of clubs, and my own set of keys. I was going to do blues clubs tonight.

We went our separate ways. I thought about telling them I'd take along the invisible pooch for security, but I didn't want to make Madeline mad. I had just about convinced myself that I'd had too much fun the night before and had fallen victim to Madeline's powers of suggestion.

Well, I had too much fun again. But this, I reminded myself on the way home a little bleary eyed, was what New Orleans is all about. I had to watch the sidewalk very carefully because it buckled in all the wrong places and several times nearly sent me sprawling gracelessly.

At the courtyard entrance, I fumbled with the keys as I let myself in, and then I climbed the stairs to the top floor. I assumed that Madeline and Mark were fast asleep, so I tried to be as quiet as I could. When the key would not fit the lock, I cursed under my breath and sat down under the window. I stared at the keys in my hand and struggled to remember what they'd said about the front door lock.

When I heard the dog's nails, clickety-click on the floorboards, I exhaled loudly. "You're not real," I said pointedly, forgetting that I'd been trying not to wake up my friends. "Just quit it, all right?"

The noise of the dog's passage swerved again, moving effortlessly through the door that had stymied me. Before I could get to my feet, the explosive "bang" resonated through the air. This time it was immediately followed by the shrill, anguished yelping of a mortally injured dog.

"What happened," gasped Madeline, who had inexplicably appeared at my shoulder. She began stabbing at the lock with her key. Footsteps pounded up the stairs, and Mark arrived and rattled the door as Madeline inserted the key.

"Where did..." I began when another shot rang through the air. We all three tumbled through the door, falling over each other in our haste to see what was going on.

Nothing—the living room was exactly as we'd left it. I was now stone-cold sober, shivering a little in the early morning breeze.

"I thought you guys were here," I blurted out. "Where did you come from?"

"Mark came over to the bar when he got off work," Madeline explained.

"On Sunday nights the bar closes a little early, so he came to walk me home."

"What was all that racket?"

Madeline looked at Mark, and they shrugged simultaneously. It made me think of Siamese twins for some reason.

"Well, something's going on," I said, a little irritated. "Aren't you curious?"

Madeline snapped her fingers. "I know how we can find out what's happening," she said. "Wait."

She disappeared into the bedroom, and I stared at Mark, my eyebrows crawling up into my hairline. He shrugged again and went to the kitchenette. "Join me in a glass of milk?" he asked over his shoulder.

"Here it is!" Madeline appeared waving a shabby, taped-together cardboard box triumphantly over her head. "I knew I still had it!"

I saw with some dismay that the box held, of all things, a Ouija board and a little plastic planchette.

"You're nuts, Madeline," I said, quite rudely. "You don't believe in that crap, do you?"

She looked hurt, and I kicked myself mentally for not being more diplomatic. I heard a snicker from the kitchenette. Madeline heard it, too, and that's when she got mad.

"Okay." She stormed to the table and yanked the chairs out from under it. "I guarantee that you won't be skeptics for much longer. Get your butts over here right now."

Madeline the drill sergeant is not one to be ignored, and Mark and I sat down in the straight-backed chairs around the table, meek as lambs. When we were sitting still, Madeline took two deep breaths and ordered us to place our fingers lightly on the edge of the planchette.

"Is there a ghost in this house?" Her voice was still fierce. The planchette quivered, but I think Mark's fingers were trembling.

Madeline took another deep breath and spoke again, this time in a calmer voice. "Is there a spirit here?"

The planchette twitched and began to glide smoothly across the board. I yelped and snatched my fingers away. Mark's face bore a horrified expression so extreme that it was almost comical. Madeline looked grim. The planchette landed on the "yes" and stopped.

Madeline glared at me. "Put your fingers back on the planchette," she said.

"I, ah, look, somebody pushed it," I said. My voice cracked, and I knew I wasn't a bit convincing.

Madeline's voice got even softer. "We'll let you do it all by yourself," she whispered. "Just put your fingers on it, now."

I didn't believe in this hocus-pocus. I didn't like this game, but for some reason, I did as Madeline instructed. My fingers were anything but steady as I rested them on the edges of the little plastic triangle.

"Are you the spirit of a person?"

The room seemed darker suddenly. I could hear my friends breathing, but I couldn't quite make out their faces. The cheap ivory plastic of the planchette seemed to glow, and my eyes were drawn to it. The fingers resting on its edges were mine, I knew that, but they seemed unattached to my body—they barely brushed the top of the plastic triangle, little feather strokes or light breaths against the smooth, cool surface. It began to move, hesitantly at first and then so briskly that it nearly left my fingers hovering over empty air.

The plastic thing had its own life. Inanimate had become animate—I was terrified.

The planchette stopped over the word "no," and my stomach heaved. I pushed up from the table and bolted to the bathroom—I made it, just barely. I huddled for a long time in the bright clinical light, my cheek resting against the cold, solid, assuring, inanimate ceramic of the toilet bowl.

Madeline and Mark were very solicitous. Mark made up my bed on the sofa, and Madeline made some peppermint tea to soothe my stomach. The Ouija board was put up out of sight, and we spent the rest of the night in relative peace.

The next night was Monday, and Mark's restaurant was closed. He took me to a party at a friend's house, and I managed quite admirably to put the whole dreadful incident out of my mind. We stopped off at Madeline's bar after the party and kept her company until the bar closed down, and then the three of us made our uneventful, if unsteady, way home in the chilly, misty predawn hours. Then it was Tuesday, and I was crowned with a headache like none I'd ever had before. All I could do all day was groan and nod when aspirin and sympathy were offered.

"Didn't you tell her to stay away from hurricanes?" Madeline scolded Mark, but softly in deference to my pounding head.

Mark shrugged. Mark's good at shrugging—he has broad, expressive shoulders.

"I never saw her drink a hurricane," he said. "It could have been that Mexican coffee you made last night."

"My drinks don't make people this sick."

Mark just shrugged again, and I pulled the blanket over my head and wished for a peaceful, sudden end.

Right at sunset I was vaguely aware of Madeline touching my big toe and saying something softly. The door latched shut with a click, and I fell into a sodden, uneasy slumber.

When I awoke, I felt refreshed—even invigorated. My head was clear, my stomach growled in a healthy but undemanding way for solid food, and when I stood, the room did not tilt at all, much less begin that awful spinning that had ruined the earlier part of my day.

In fact, I felt so much better that I considered going out for a drink or two. But when I checked the clock and saw that it was past one, I decided to stick around at the apartment. Madeline and Mark would be back from work soon.

I constructed myself a sandwich out of assorted leftovers from the munchkin-size refrigerator and wandered out to the veranda to admire the courtyard from above. I couldn't remember when I'd last felt so crystal clear, so mentally sharp. The moon hung suspended between the sharp angles of the skyline, and gauzy fragments of clouds slid silently, swiftly across the crescent shape.

Then I heard the clicking sound of tiny paws across the wooden floor, and I turned to stone. The sandwich fell from my lifeless fingers, and I had to coax my limbs into turning to face the source of the noise. There was, of course, nothing there to see. The little paws clicked purposefully, busily down the veranda and turned into the door of the apartment I'd just left. I took three large steps and was in the room right behind it when the first gunshot rang out so loud that my hands, unbidden, flew up to protect my ears. Again the shrieking, agonized howl of a wounded dog—again a second gunshot and silence.

My legs were trembling so violently that I couldn't stand. I fell into the kitchen chair, my heart thudding so fast that I was afraid I was having a heart attack. I wondered what kind of insanity had caught me. Then I caught myself—this was real. This was not—could not be—some chemically-induced hallucination. After a few minutes, I was able to stand again, and I made myself a pot of coffee. While it dripped, a homey comforting sound, I searched for the Ouija board—I knew it couldn't be too hard to find in such a small space. At last I found it tucked above the cabinets in the kitchenette.

I took a slug of coffee and then placed my fingers resolutely on the edge of the planchette. Every light in the place was glowing brightly—I'd turned them on in the course of my search.

"Who are you?"

The planchette stirred slightly under my fingers, and I had to resist the impulse to snatch my hands away. I remembered Madeline's calm tone of voice and tried to replicate it. "Who are you?" I repeated.

The plastic triangle quivered again and began to slide slowly across the board. It came to the "B" and stopped.

"B," I repeated.

It shuddered and began to move again. Painstakingly at first but with increasing certainty, it crept from letter to letter: "B-E-L-L-E."

"What are you?"

Again the planchette glided from letter to letter: "S-P-I-R-I-T." I repressed a sigh of annoyance. "What were you here on earth?" "C-H-I-E-N."

"Dog!" My dad would be proud that the expense of college was bearing such fruit—it was his idea that I learn some French.

"What happened?"

"M-O-R-T-E." I heard a gasp behind me just as the planchette slid to a stop on the "E."

"What are you doing?" It was Madeline.

I raised my hands off the planchette. "Figuring out what's going on here," I said. "Isn't that obvious?"

Madeline slipped into the chair opposite me. "Don't let me interrupt then," she breathed. "Don't stop."

She watched with wide eyes as I asked another question. "How did you die?" "F-U-S-I-L."

"What's that mean?" Madeline couldn't take her eyes off the planchette. Sweat was collecting at my hairline, and I flexed my fingers for a moment, easing the tension.

"Gun," I replied. "Poor booger got shot. I figured as much."

"Why?"

"Let's ask," I answered. "Belle, why'd you get shot?"

This time the planchette moved swiftly from one letter to the next. "T-R-I-S-T-E."

"Who was sad?"

The planchette crept over to "yes."

"Was your master sad?" Madeline interrupted, but I didn't mind. I was getting pretty worn out. Mark slipped in the door and stood over Madeline's shoulder, his mouth hanging open as he saw the planchette jerk and then move decisively to the "yes."

"Why aren't you at peace?" The lights seemed dimmer now than when I'd started, and in the shadows, it was hard to tell, but I think I saw a tear slip down my friend's cheek.

"P-E-R-D-U."

"Lost," I translated, and a shiver ran down my spine.

"P-O-R-T-E."

"Door," I translated again, and the meaning hit me. "You can't find the door?" The planchette spun wildly, moving so rapidly that my fingers could barely keep up. Finally, it settled on "yes."

"Look for the light," Mark whispered. The planchette shuddered and remained on the "yes."

"Can you see a light?" The lamp behind Madeline flickered and the bulb expired with a soft pop. I moved the planchette to its starting place.

"Can you see a light?"

The plastic triangle vibrated under my fingertips. The little light over the stove dimmed and went out. The planchette began to inch slowly to the left toward the word "no."

"Look," Mark said, urgently, "look all around. There must be a light!"

The planchette trembled again and stopped. The air was electric. My fingers felt cold, bloodless—I felt like I'd been hunched over the little triangle of plastic since the dawn of time.

Now it began to move to the right. Calmly, smoothly. When it touched the "y" of the "yes" it was instantly drained of its vitality. The light over the stove shone with a renewed intensity. Madeline's and Mark's faces were ashen. I suppose I must have looked pretty wiped out, too.

Without saying a word, we put the Ouija board away. We poured a round of fresh coffee and traipsed down to the courtyard, where sleepy birds were just beginning to try on their morning songs. The sky above us began to lose its coal-black luster. As a pearly new light flooded the garden, we became immersed in the raucous, joyous sound of birds greeting the day.

tracking

I did the very best I could. I'd been taught from the very earliest days of my life that fighting was not the kind of behavior expected of me, but what happened that night was surely justifiable by the circumstances. I've also known, you see, that my primary mission in life is to protect my loved ones, and it was this very strong instinct that won out and provoked me to my actions.

But I should start at the beginning, like all good storytellers. I was young and impulsive and very, very attached to my pet. He was young also, and we would swim together, hunt together (along with our respective fathers), play together, work together (I was a creature of many talents and as good with livestock as I was with wildfowl), eat together, and even, when we could get away with it, sleep together.

This steady rhythm of life continued until I was a young adult. Our farm was on the edge of a small village, and one momentous day, there was a great hullabaloo on the green. People were running this way and that, shouting and waving their arms in a most excited way. Now this is behavior my pet sometimes indulged in, but never in such an uncontrollable manner for very long.

Just as things began to settle down, I saw coming into the village a long, straight line of men stepping along smartly, all in a neat row and dressed alike in red.

I immediately wondered whose pets they were and where he or she might be hiding, for these were very well-trained pets indeed. The man at the front of the line stopped and proceeded to have a very long and sometimes heated conversation with the men of the village, including my pet's father. I sat in a corner, in the shadow of the church, keeping my pet well out of harm's way.

When the conversation was over, my pet's father came toward us, obviously in very dejected spirits. "What's wrong?" I asked him, but he was too distraught to reply. He ruffled the hair on my pet's head and told him things were about to change.

"We have no choice, Henry," he said. "It's do what they say or be thrown in jail. It sticks in my craw, it does, but you and your mother can't manage the farm without me."

He clearly had no high regard for these fellows in red. I must admit that I never could discover who they belonged to, but I noticed that one man in particular was always shouting at them. I don't find that to be the best method of control, although it does work wonders with certain stubborn sheep and cows.

At first the activity of the red-coated visitors did not affect me and my pet too much. A few of them moved into the house, but since spring was here, that just meant that Henry was allowed to sleep out in the barn with me. Henry's father was continually downcast, and his mother was kept busy feeding all of us, but it was no great hardship for me.

Henry and I were finished with our chores one day and romping through the woods stirring up whatever excitement could be found, when one of these men in red jumped out at us from behind a tree.

"Who goes there?"

I hate more than anything to be surprised, and I instantly braced myself for a fight and growled ferociously. My pet, too, immediately stiffened and crouched low.

The stranger looked very fierce at first, but when I noticed that he was not much older than my pet, I could sense that he was frightened beneath the bravado. I relaxed somewhat and asked him what he was doing on our farm.

Henry put a hand on my neck to silence me and told the stranger, rather belligerently I think, that we lived here and asked what he was doing.

"This land belongs to His Majesty, the King," he growled in response, still pointing his fire-stick, with a wicked-looking blade attached, directly at us. "You'll have to turn around and go home."

We huffed and puffed a bit but eventually had to turn around. After we'd gone a ways back between the trees, Henry turned and asked me, "What are those sneaky redcoats up to now, Riley?"

I suspected it was no good, so I just growled low in my throat. The incident had taken the edge off the day, and we just trailed back to the barnyard to wait for supper.

The next day we traveled to a neighboring village to visit some of my friends. Fortunately, Henry and his father had family there, so we all enjoyed our brief stay. Just before they came out to load the wagon, Henry had an odd conversation with someone I'd never seen before.

The man crouched down low so that his eyes were level with Henry's. I trusted him immediately. "Are you a patriot like your father, boy?" He was whispering low, although there was no sign of anyone else in the barn.

"Of course." Henry could puff up like a bantam rooster when he had a mind.

"Can you keep a secret?"

Henry nodded, his eyes wide.

"General Washington needs brave lads like you to help him," the stranger continued. "But it's very dangerous work."

"I'm willing," Henry said eagerly. "I'd do anything to get back at old King George for what he's done to us."

"I have a letter that needs to be taken to the tavern keeper at...," here he named a village just two miles west of our own. "Can you do that without being stopped by any redcoats?"

"Sure I can." If I had thought Henry couldn't puff up any bigger, I was wrong—his chest swelled another inch.

The man took out a folded sheet of paper and placed it in Henry's hand. "Do it as soon as you can," he said, "but be careful. Take your dog with you and pretend like you're just out making mischief, like all boys do."

"Yes, sir." I thought Henry would burst, he was so full of himself.

"I've trained my pet better than to make mischief, thank you," I told the impertinent man, but he just laughed and patted me roughly on the head.

We returned to our own village, and the next day, we completed the errand as the stranger had instructed. It was easy, and the tavern keeper paid me with a nice juicy bone. A week later, a different stranger came by the farm—a risky business, if you ask me, since the redcoats were right there living with us, but he spoke with some urgency.

"Boy, I need you to carry this to Thomas at his tavern right away," he said abruptly. "Lives are depending on you. When can you leave?"

Henry stammered a bit, and I threw in my opinion, but as usual no one paid me any attention—pets can be such a chore at times.

"Yes, sir, I can go as soon as I get the cows in and milked," Henry managed to say.

"You call this mongrel a hunting dog?" The stranger swore and aimed a kick at me. I backed off, wondering about this sudden change in conversation.

Two redcoats strolled into the barn, coming to fetch their mounts, no doubt. "Here, here, what's this ruckus?" The taller one spoke lazily.

"This boy told my cousin that he had a good dog to sell, but this cur isn't worth any price. I wasted a trip all the way out here for nothing."

The men in red just laughed and muttered about country bumpkins. I bristled, but the insult was a very clever way to disguise the stranger's true intentions. He left, and Henry and I went to go fetch the cows before we set out on our errand. We took care of our chores as quickly as we could, and then Henry made some excuse to his parents and we were off.

The fastest route to the tavern was through a wide band of woods that was intersected twice by roads well-traveled by the redcoats. It took an hour in the daylight because the woods were pretty thick, and it was now just at sunset. The light was failing as we crashed through the underbrush at the farthest corner of our farm, and I felt a prickling of my skin, a sure sign of something dire about to come.

It was even darker in the woods, and the night creatures were beginning to stir from their burrows and nests. My eyesight is not so good in the dark, but my sense of smell is just as keen, so I led the way. Poor Henry was jumpy—my nerves were a bit frazzled, too.

An owl swooped out low, nearly brushing the top of Henry's head with his wings, and we both about jumped out of our skins. Near the edge of the first road, I made my pet stand still in the shadows while I crept up to the embankment to listen for the jingle and stomp of men on horseback. All was quiet, so I returned to Henry, thrusting my nose against his hand for reassurance. The sudden contact startled him, and he let out a little shriek before we scurried like timid little squirrels across the road.

Something still didn't feel right, but we made it safely across the second road. Then, quick as a wink, we were at the back door of the tavern. We sent a serving girl to fetch Thomas, and he came out, drying his big red hands on his apron.

"Thank you, boy," he whispered. "General Washington would thank you, too, if he knew what a service you've done for your country tonight. But be gone! My tavern's full of redcoats, and I've got more work than I can manage. Be exceedingly careful—I believe we may have a traitor among us."

He swatted Henry on the behind but ignored me completely. I didn't appreciate such an oversight, but I kept silent to prove that I too was a true patriot.

Henry was so unnerved by this time that he scampered through the field and across the road without me. When I caught up to him, I nipped his hand, lightly, in reproach—I've trained you better, my eyes told him. I would not speak aloud until we were safe in our own barn—I knew that we were still in grave danger.

We made our way through the first patch of forest without any mishaps. My ears and nose warned me about the location of the little brook and also steered us clear of a bumbling old skunk out for a moonlight stroll. I cautioned Henry to wait while I reconnoitered the second road crossing, leaving him safely stationed in the shadow of a great old elm. I crept quietly up to the road, my belly almost on the ground because my sense of danger was so great. Although I scented the air and listened with sharp ears, I discerned no peril in crossing the road. I turned to find my pet—and heard the yell.

"Who are you?" called out a stranger's voice. I bounded through the scraggly trees to see a redcoat struggling to pin down the arms of my young pet, who was fighting like a panther, I'm proud to say.

"I'm Henry Smithfield, now let me go!" With a final grunt of effort he worked free but stood his ground defiantly.

"What are you doing out here in the woods, young Henry?" The soldier eyed him suspiciously.

"I was," he took a deep breath and started over. "I was out tracking deer with my dog, and he got lost. He's a big black dog, about this high?" He held up his hand about three feet off the ground—that was my cue.

I limped up to him, holding up my left front paw and whimpering piteously. "Riley!" he fairly screeched. "Where have you been?"

"Where do you live, Henry Smithfield?" The man still sounded stern, but I could tell his suspicions were unraveling.

"The last farm outside the village, just up ahead."

"Hasn't anyone told you that there's a nighttime curfew?"

"I'm sorry, sir." Henry hung his head, sounding genuinely contrite. "We left in the afternoon, and he got lost, and I couldn't just leave him!"

"Make sure I don't catch you again, boy. There are spies and traitors all around us, and you wouldn't want to be mistaken for one of them!" The redcoat cuffed my pet on the head, and I had to swallow a growl. The man watched us as we crossed the road and headed through the woods on the other side.

I had the presence of mind to fake my limp until we were out of sight, and then I leaped up, putting my front paws on Henry's shoulders and knocking him down. I licked him until he cried for mercy, and then we continued toward home and a good night's sleep.

We carried messages to the tavern all winter on an irregular basis. I believe my pet's father may have begun to suspect some purpose behind our long ambling walks through the countryside, but he never said a word. Henry turned fifteen that winter, nearly a man grown, and his father was no doubt proud of his son's efforts to help the struggling patriot cause. We were cautious and had no more close scrapes like the encounter in the woods that first evening.

With spring came a rapid increase in the number of our errands. The abrupt stranger returned, purchasing a pup from Henry's father and cornering my pet again in the barn.

"I can't be seen around here anymore," he hissed, leaning close to Henry's face. "There's an oak tree on the road to the village—it's the tallest tree around, and it has a hollow in it. Do you know it?"

Henry nodded.

"Check it on Saturdays. If there are three stones inside, that means you are to pick up a message from a hiding place. Someone will be along next week to show you where."

Henry nodded again, the urgency in the man's tone having struck him temporarily dumb.

The stranger left, and we never saw him again. Just two days later, Henry's Uncle Isaiah rode up to the house, a grim expression on his face. After a brief conversation with his sister, Henry's mother, he suggested we three go out and bring home a rabbit or two for supper. Once we were away from the house, he spoke.

"I don't like this business, Henry," he said gruffly.

"What business, Uncle?" My pet was all innocence.

"I've been sent to help a courier find a secure place to pick up letters en route to General Washington. I thought I was meeting your father, but I find it's you instead. How long have you been doing this?"

"Nearly a year now, Uncle. Riley and I are always careful, and who would suspect a boy like me?" He grinned, and I could have kissed him, he looked so frisky and full of life. I settled for a short exclamation, and my pet and his uncle looked at me thinking I'd spotted a rabbit.

"You're not a young boy any more, Henry," his uncle spoke soberly after a moment. "I can't tell you what to do, but I beg you to give this up. Spies are hung without mercy, and that would break your mother's heart."

"I won't get caught, Uncle," Henry said confidently. "Let's find a really good spot for those messages, so we'll all be safer, all right?"

We arranged for a spot that was well-concealed, and Henry's uncle hugged him fiercely before we turned back home. I flushed out a pair of rabbits, so we all enjoyed a taste of rabbit stew that night.

I didn't always travel with my pet to check the oak tree hollow, but we always made the trips to collect the letters and to the tavern together. Three or four times that spring we went, and what news of the patriots reached us was mostly cheering. Then one night, we heard hoof beats late, and I came out of the barn to see Uncle Isaiah jump down from his horse.

He made some pretense of his wife being ill and needing Henry's mother, but in the flurry of preparing to carry her back with him, he thrust a small packet of letters into Henry's hands.

"God help us all," he muttered in the shadows, "but these have to go on to the tavern keeper tonight. Can you slip away without your house guests noticing?"

Henry's eyes shone bright in the dark corner of the barn. "Of course I can, Uncle. I'll leave at once."

"Go with God, boy," the man choked, and I thought he might cry, he was that fearful. Some men have a keener sense of perception than others. "I shouldn't do this to you, I know."

"Don't be silly, Uncle. Riley and I will be fine—won't we, boy?" He tousled my head, and I whined. I knew something was wrong, but I couldn't put my paw on it.

We slipped out the back of the barn while Isaiah and Henry's mother made a big fuss of leaving from the front. Across the fields, over a small stream, through a stretch of woods, and we were at the first road crossing. As usual, Henry waited while I checked the road for any riders. It was deserted, and we hurried across and through the woods again.

All at once, three men materialized from behind the trees, all of them dressed in red and armed. They took my pet roughly and carried him to a clearing not too far away where a small campfire burned. Why hadn't I smelled that fire? I will never understand how I could have failed my pet so badly. They did not notice me in their excitement at having caught someone out where he should not have been.

There were eight of them altogether, and I watched warily from the woods as they carelessly searched Henry's pockets.

"Aha!" cried the leader, a man with a distinct odor of cruelty about him. He waved the packet of letters. "What have we here?"

"Just some letters for my master, the tavern keeper," Henry cried desperately. The big man casually backhanded him across the mouth, and a growl rose from my throat as I saw my pet's blood well up bright and red.

"D'you write to your master in code, then," sneered another soldier. "Mighty unusual, that."

Henry was silent. Despair rose from him in waves—I could smell it from my hiding place. But I did not know what to do against so many men.

They wrapped a rope around his neck while I watched, puzzled. Clearly their intentions were not good. They lifted Henry up to a horse and threw one end of the rope around a stout branch of a nearby tree. When the horse was slapped, he ran off, and Henry dangled from the end of the rope.

The redcoats ignored Henry for a while, and I lay in the shadows trying to formulate a plan to get Henry and myself away. When they cut the rope and Henry fell down to the ground with a thud, I circled around in the woods, so I could reach him and wake him up. Pets don't always show the best of judgment—this was not a good time for a nap.

When I reached him, a terrible fear began to grow inside my belly. I washed his face thoroughly, even tugged on his shirttail, a strategy that never failed to rouse him, but Henry did not stir. I growled in his ear, but still there was no response. Finally, giving in to this awful, consuming terror, I threw back my head and howled.

I was so wrapped up in my own pain that I didn't see the redcoat approach me. It was the big one—the leader.

"Shut up, you stupid mongrel," he snarled. He directed a savage kick at my side, and, unthinking, I sprang at him, my teeth bared for attack.

I had failed to notice that in his hand was his fire-stick, with the long, sharp blade attached. He raised it and, in an oddly stretched-out moment, used the blade to neatly sever my head from my neck.

With a curious sensation of floating, I hovered above the camp.

The soldiers sat back down around the fire, eating some sort of a meal and talking aimlessly among themselves. My pet's body lay beneath the tree where it had fallen, and my own body, headless, lay crumpled beside it. It is a very singular feeling to see one's body without a head. Finally, I stopped staring and lay myself down by the fire to think what I should do next.

I could hear a dog howling in the woods. It sounded vaguely familiar, but I pushed that thought aside. I had to think, to plan—it was hard to concentrate. "You hear that?" One of the redcoats looked up from his plate.

"It's nothing. Probably just some farm dog."

"Sounds like that dog." He pointed with a knife at my body and then shifted uneasily.

"You'd be afraid of your own shadow, you would, Smitherman," the big one jeered at him. The dog's crescendo of howling peaked, fell off, and then began climbing again.

"There's a difference between foolhardy and brave, man," said a third soldier, speaking quietly.

"Well, I've never been afraid of no mongrel dogs or mongrel patriots, and that's the God's truth." The big redcoat scraped his plate into the fire, making the flames leap and hiss. "I'll take the first watch."

"You'd best take care out there in the dark."

"I don't know what you mean," the big one said, standing to walk around the fire. I swear, he must have seen me lying there because he paled and swung his foot at my ribs angrily. Of course, his boot went right through me, and he stumbled a bit.

"Take care," his fellow soldier repeated. As the big redcoat strode out into the shadow-filled forest, I rose and followed him—I was just another shadow in the woods.

We were only just out of sight of the fire's glow when I sprang on him. I know I shouldn't have. I know it was not a prudent decision. But we struggled mightily, and I growled, barked, and snarled all the while.

I took hold of his arm and his fine red coat and shredded it between my sharp white teeth, and then I sank my fangs into his tall black boots, relishing the taste of leather and the bite of the boot blacking on my tongue. When he had weakened, I jumped up on his chest and pushed him over, so I could reduce his white shirt and fancy coat to tatters. Brass buttons tasted cold and metallic, but the pain of their contact on my torn and bloody mouth was a pain that lessened my anguish over losing my dear pet. Finally, I was done—the man could only lie there and moan.

His companions came to take him back to the fireside. "What if the beast is still here?" asked the fearful one, looking all around—looking right through me.

"Let's just get him to camp and bandage him up. Heave, ho!" They toiled to lift and move his bulk, at last reaching the campsite. Curious, I padded along behind them.

"I've never seen such a thing."

By the light of the fire, they examined their leader. Every last piece of clothing he wore was slashed to ribbons. My teeth had ripped and shredded the arrogant red and white clothing until it barely covered the big one's body—but there was not a mark on his flesh.

"He's breathing all right," one soldier said, straining to see beyond the circle of light cast by the campfire. "What could have done this to him?"

No one answered, but I threw back my head and howled. All night, I paced round and round that campsite searching and watching the soldiers huddle together and try to overcome their terror. In their midst lay their leader, his chest rising and falling, rising and falling. Still drawing breath while my pet lay dead.

The big redcoat lay in a delirium for three days. His fellow soldiers were afraid to move him, and I circled the camp searching and howling until he finally breathed his last.

Now my search is over. After covering the ground all through the woods, I've finally found my pet's trail. I will follow it until I've found him. After all, I am the best tracking dog in the colonies, if I do say so myself.

"Tracking" has been adapted with permission from a story collected by Ruth Ann Musick.

a light too late
in coming

The legend of the ghost ship *Isadore* has been told and retold for more than a century along the blustery coast of Maine, where the rocky, treacherous cliffs of island Cape Neddick Nubble have sealed the doom of many a sailor. Here, jagged outcroppings known as the Bald Head Cliffs stretch northward into the icy waters, creating perilous conditions.

In 1837, Captain Joseph Smith petitioned for lighthouses on York River and Cape Neddick Nubble. Money was allocated for a small lighthouse at York Ledge, but the cape remained dark, and schooners continued to be lost against the treacherous Bald Head Cliffs. When another petition was introduced in 1852, Congress allocated $5,000 for a beacon, but after an inspection of the area, the project floundered. Then, in 1874, Congress appropriated $15,000 for a lighthouse. On July 1, 1879, the Cape Neddick Nubble beacon was finally lit eighty-eight feet above the water.

Unfortunately, the light had come too late for many a fearless seafarer, particularly thirty-six-year-old Captain Leander Foss and his crew aboard the *Isadore*. The ship set sail November 30, 1842, from Kennebunkport harbor, despite the strong misgivings of its crew.

Two nights before the *Isadore's* departure, Thomas King, a young seaman who had received a month's wages in advance for his anticipated tenure, had a nightmare. He dreamt of turbulent waters, the ship wrecked amid a swirling storm, and all aboard doomed. Shaken, King relayed his premonition to Captain Foss, whose scorn turned to suspicion when King requested to be relieved of his duties. Unwilling to give up the young seaman or the wages already paid to him, the captain would not let King out of his contract. Dispirited, King weighed his options but couldn't reconcile himself to the journey. In the end, whatever the consequences, he refused the captain's order. Instead of boarding the ship with the other crewmembers, King hid in the nearby woods. An angry Captain Foss ordered the crew to search the port and surrounding areas for King. Despite a burgeoning snowstorm that threatened their departure, the men searched relentlessly until evening but found no trace of their missing crewman. Finally, on that fateful Thanksgiving night, the *Isadore* set sail without Thomas King.

Unbeknownst to King, another crewman had dreamt of the ship's demise as well. In his dream the crewman had seen seven coffins, including his own, washed up on Maine's shoreline. Like King, he had told others of his dream, but no one had taken his apprehension to heart. He set sail along with the others.

Nineteen-year-old William Thomson was also aboard the *Isadore* that day. It was to be his first journey at sea, and he was filled with nervous excitement. His mother, who adamantly opposed the life that her husband had urged their son into, was filled with a nameless dread. She had wanted William to be a farmer, safe and sound on dry land.

Aside even from the warnings and premonitions of Thomas King, there was something ominous about the ship's departure that November day. The snowstorm had ushered in violent winds, and visibility was poor. Crew members and their families, who had gathered along the wharf to see them off, were equally concerned that the day was unfit for sailing. It was later rumored that, even as the ship drifted out to sea, the men onboard could hear the wails of their wives and mothers out on the wharf.

Those watching and weeping on the wharf were eventually blinded by the snow, and the ship was lost from sight. Not long after, the dreaded news arrived from Ogunquit: the *Isadore* had wrecked in the Bald Head Cliffs north of Cape Neddick Nubble. Already, the lifeless bodies and splintery remains of the ship had begun to wash ashore. All were lost: Captain Leander Foss, the young crewman who had dreamt of the seven coffins, and William Thomson. The sole survivor was Thomas King, who narrowly escaped death in the snowy woods of Kennebunkport harbor.

Ever since the *Isadore* was lost in the jagged rocks of Bald Head Cliffs, locals, particularly fishermen and those standing watch at the Cape Neddick Nubble Light, have reported seeing the shadowy likeness of a ship sailing up and down the coast. One fisherman claimed to see men on board the ship. They stared straight ahead as they passed from view, diligently working their stations though their clothes dripped with water.

The *Isadore* and its crew are still believed to haunt the waters off the northern coast of Maine. Most often, sightings occur where the Cape Neddick Nubble Light now stands. If only it had been standing that November night so many years ago.

here walks the ghost of william teach

Ocracoke Island was discovered in 1585 when a group of English explorers wrecked its ship into the island's sandy shores. However, it remained undeveloped for roughly two centuries. Today, Ocracoke is one of the North Carolina coast's oldest communities; and with only about eight hundred year-round residents, it maintains a markedly slower pace than the mainland. Sometimes, when lightning knocks out power on the island, residents rely on the Ocracoke Light to get them through the night, just as they used to do in the old days. Such occasions afford the perfect opportunity to gather around a fire and tell blood-curdling tales of the island's past.

The first lighthouse in the Ocracoke inlet was built on Shell Castle Island in 1794, but due to a migration of the channel, it was useless by 1818—the year it was struck and destroyed by lightning. By 1822, the government had appropriated $20,000 for a new structure on Ocracoke Island. It was built by Noah Porter for $11,359.35. Today, at 179 years of age, it is the second-oldest working lighthouse in the country. It is also, at seventy-five feet, the shortest lighthouse on the North Carolina coast.

The waters off the North Carolina coast have sunk more than two thousand ships since authorities started keeping records in 1526. Here, in the outer banks, ships hug the coastline to avoid the havoc of the warm Gulf Stream and icy Labrador Current. Add to that the area's ever-changing sandbars and dangerous Diamond Shoals, and the coast is ripe for maritime disaster. Not surprisingly, it's come to be known as the "Graveyard of the Atlantic." With a name like that, it's bound to host a number of local legends—not the least of which concerns the country's most famous brigand, Edward Teach, otherwise known as Blackbeard, the pirate.

Over the years, many versions of Blackbeard's story have evolved. One version even goes so far as to suggest that he is responsible for Ocracoke's unusual name. According to legend, on the morning of his death, before dawn, the pirate tossed and turned, impatient for daylight. Finally, at his wit's end, he cried, "Oh, cock, crow!" thus giving the island its name. While the tale is likely a tall one, this is certain: Blackbeard called Ocracoke home and met with a grisly death on its shores.

During the 1700s, Ocracoke was one of the busiest inlets on the East Coast. At that time, it was the only accessible waterway to Carolina port cities like Edmonton and New Bern. Eventually, it got a reputation. With the large number of vessels carrying goods to be sold, crime was inevitable. Pirates attacked and robbed ships, and kidnapped and even murdered sailors. The most infamous marauder of them all was a wealthy Englishman, Edward Teach, whose name came to be known and feared in the outer banks.

A restless spirit drove Teach from a privileged life. Bored with tradition, he turned to a life at sea, pillaging unsuspecting ships for sport. Though he wanted for little as an aristocrat, he made an unprecedented fortune pirating, and he built grand homes with dirty money in Bath, North Carolina, and on Ocracoke Island. He is even said to have had thirteen wives.

Blackbeard delighted in his attacks. In fact, he made a production of them. Just before boarding a trade ship, he tied red ribbons to his long black beard and braided slow-burning fuses into the hair, lighting the fuses with matches. Fire and smoke curled around his face, giving him the appearance of a devil. He wore daggers at his side and kept a variety of pistols strapped to his chest, loaded, cocked, and ready. Word of his monstrosity spread, prompting many a targeted captain to surrender on sight, or jump overboard. At the height of his career, Blackbeard commanded four hundred pirates and four ships.

North Carolina residents were acutely aware of Blackbeard's debauchery, and they wanted it stopped. But Teach had powerful allies, such as Royal Governor Charles Eden, and his offenses went unpunished. Eventually, unable to bear the grisly tales of his conquest another day, angry locals turned to the governor of Virginia, a man by the name of Alexander Spotswood. Lacking the men to outfit such a campaign, he made a plea to the English government, which ultimately sent Lieutenant Maynard to search for and capture or kill Blackbeard.

Maynard sailed down the Atlantic Coast, searching for the pirate's ominous black flag. He looked for days. Then, early one November morning in 1718, the crew spotted Blackbeard's ship, *Queen Anne's Revenge*, anchored among the islets. They fired a cannonball, and Blackbeard's crew fired back, tearing a hole in Maynard's vessel. Maynard and his crew ran aground on a nearby sandbar. There, they awaited the inevitable. When a fire-lit Blackbeard and his crew boarded the vessel from Virginia, Maynard and his men were prepared for combat. Daggers drawn, pistols cocked, the two forces fought a savage, bloody battle.

At last, Maynard came face to face with the pirate. He advanced, but Blackbeard was quicker. Swinging his sword across Maynard's, Blackbeard broke the lieutenant's blade in half. Maynard was helpless and stunned. With a glimmer in his eye, Blackbeard bore down upon his enemy. Just then, one of Maynard's crewmen came from behind, and with one clean swipe, beheaded the fiend. Maynard watched in awe as Blackbeard's head dropped to the deck.

The crew rejoiced over their victory and dumped the pirate's body overboard, where, according to legend, it swam three times around the ship before sinking into the dark waters of the Atlantic. As a final gesture, the crew tied Blackbeard's head to the bowsprit. It dangled off the end as a trophy and symbol of their success. For days, the ship sailed brandishing the rotting head, its black hair blowing in the wind. It was a challenge to pirates everywhere that their reign over the region was waning.

Often this tale is told on stormy nights, when the island is dark, save for the intermittent flash of the lighthouse beacon, and residents gather by their fires. There, it is whispered that, beneath the steady beam of the Ocracoke Island Light, in among the shadows of the trees, walks the headless ghost of Blackbeard, and, out across the illumined depths, his flaming vessel haunts the coast in search of its missing captain.

what the reef takes, the reef gives back

A dory breezed through the Long Island Sound, rocking gently on the waves. The day was warm and quiet, except for the squall of the gulls gliding overhead and the soft sound of water lapping against the base of the boat. The vessel's occupants steered carefully toward the reef, cautiously maneuvering their boat around the rocks beneath the surface.

On the right, they passed the Penfield Reef Light. One of the last offshore masonry lights built, it was erected to warn sailors away from the dangerous shoals they now crossed. Knowing the area well, the two sailors picked an opportune spot for a day of fishing and anchored their vessel near the lighthouse.

The low afternoon sun cast gold-laced shadows across the water as they tossed their lines into the sea. Hoping to catch cod and flounder, maybe even a few tuna, for the evening's supper, they cast and reeled their lines back in again all afternoon. It was a perfect day for fishing, and the young fishermen were determined to fill their buckets.

As the day wore on, the two young enthusiasts lost track of time. They had caught nearly enough fish to fill the freezer, but they continued, knowing they could give the extras away to neighbors and friends.

Late in the afternoon, the weather began to turn. The gentle breeze rolled and shifted. Ominous storm clouds slid across the sky, dulling the shimmering water, and the boat began to rock among the waves.

The two young sailors were startled by the sudden change of weather. Without a second thought, they packed their belongings and pulled the anchor back onboard. They knew what they were up against.

Their fishing reef was actually a peninsula, worn down by rough and restless waters into a series of small islands. Eventually, over hundreds of years, even the islands themselves had eroded into the mile-long stretch of shoals beneath their boat—one of the most dangerous areas in the Long Island Sound.

The fishermen knew, if they didn't leave the reef immediately, they would never leave. As they pushed off, rain erupted out of the sky in sharp, stinging drops, and the small mast of the boat pitched wildly in the wind. A wave rose, casting its shadow over the side of the boat and drenching the hapless sailors. Water spilled across the floorboards and into the buckets of fish as the men struggled to steer their dory. In an instant, they lost control; the vessel spun recklessly into the rocks and capsized.

The men came up coughing, fighting to stay above the thrashing waves. Both were strong swimmers, but no match for a tempest. They were on the verge of drowning when, out of nowhere, a man appeared on the rocks near the lighthouse. Without hesitation, he swam out to the men, whose arms and legs flailed desperately in an attempt to stay afloat. The stranger grabbed one of the men and dragged him to the rocks beneath the lighthouse. Then, with equal resolve, he swam out to get the other man.

The two young fishermen lay on the rocks, weary and in shock. When they looked up to thank the man who had rescued them, he was nowhere to be seen. He had disappeared as quickly as he had appeared.

A number of local legends share themes common to this story: a shipwreck, drowning fishermen, and a small vessel too close to the rocks. In the end, the savior of all onboard appears and disappears, leaving no clues as to his identity. One similar tale involves two boys who were fishing just off the rocks in a small canoe. When their canoe flipped, and they were thrown into the choppy waters, a man appeared and dragged them to the shore of the lighthouse. The lighthouse figures prominently in each of the tales, leading many to seek answers there.

The Penfield Reef Light was built in 1874 atop a cylindrical granite pier. It was designed by renowned architect F. Hopkinson Smith, who also designed and built the lighthouse at Long Island Sound's Race Rock and laid the foundation for the Statue of Liberty. The lighthouse cost a steep sum—$55,000—and, like the Ledge Light in New London, Connecticut, it resembled a large, well-to-do home. The keeper's dwelling was attached to the thirty-five-foot tower, whose beacon flashed fifty-one feet above the sea.

A two-story, four-bedroom house with an oil room, kitchen, first-floor den, and second-floor bedrooms, the dwelling was more than sufficient for a keeper and his assistant. Penfield Reef had a series of keepers over the years, including two female assistants, before the much-remembered Fredrick A. Jordan served.

On a cold December day, Jordan left the lighthouse in his small boat, bound for a Christmas holiday on the mainland. He'd made all the necessary arrangements for his leave, including last-minute cleaning and maintenance on the tower. With a final wave, he wished his assistant keeper, Rudolph Iten, happy holidays and pushed off. But just as Jordan left the lighthouse, his small boat capsized. Iten did all he could to rescue the keeper, but in the end, his efforts were fruitless. He recorded the events of the day in the keeper's log:

> Keeper left station at 12:20 p.m. and when about 150 yards NW of the light, his boat capsized, but he managed to cling to the overturned boat. He motioned me to lower the sailboat, but on account of the heavy seas running from the NE, it was impossible to launch the boat alone. At 1:00 p.m. the wind died down a bit and shifted to the south. I then lowered the

boat safely and started off after the keeper who had by this time drifted about one and one-half miles to the SW. When about one-half mile from the light, the wind shifted to the SW, making a head wind and an outgoing tide which proved too much for me to pull with the heavy boat. I had to give up and returned to the station with the wind now blowing a gale from the WSW. Sent distress signals to several ships but none answered. Lost track of the keeper at 3:00 p.m. He is probably lost. [*sic*]

Indeed, he was. Soon after 3:00 p.m., Jordan's body was found adrift in the waters near the lighthouse. He had fallen victim to the very reef over which he kept his watch.

Jordan's death was the second tragedy in a month. Just weeks before his own ill-fated journey, nine barges belonging to New York's Blue Line had wrecked upon the reef, which is now known as the Blue Line Graveyard.

Since these tragedies, tales of a mysterious lifeguard who saves drowning fishermen have become almost commonplace on the Long Island Sound. A spectral figure also has been seen shifting about the lighthouse. Keepers have reported seeing a form, dressed in white, floating about the lighthouse tower. At times, the form floats down the staircase and out the door, where it promptly disappears. Locals have also seen the figure in the lantern room, particularly on stormy nights, swaying in the light. On other occasions, some have caught glimpses of the shadowy spirit on the rocks at the base of the lighthouse.

It is said that Iten himself, having become keeper after Jordan's death, saw the apparition slide out of an upstairs room. As he stood watching, it made its way down the stairs and vanished. When Iten reached the first floor, he found that his journal had been placed on the table and opened to the entry recorded December 22, 1916, the day Fred Jordan died.

When asked about the ghost of Fred Jordan, Iten is said to have responded matter-of-factly, "There is an old saying, 'What the reef takes, the reef gives back.'"

a keeper reclaims
his post

St. Simons Island Lighthouse towers over the entrance of St. Simons Sound just east of Brunswick, Georgia. The original lighthouse was constructed in 1808 on the very site where the colonial Fort St. Simons once stood. Built under General James Oglethorpe to protect the southern portion of the island, the fort was destroyed in 1742 by retreating soldiers during the Battle of Bloody Marsh.

At the start of the nineteenth century, a plantation owner named John Couper took possession of the land and named it Couper's Point. Because Couper supported the idea of a lighthouse, a few years later, in 1804, he sold it to the government for a dollar. It was to be the site of the island's first harbor light.

The original St. Simons Light was built of tabby—a building material composed of sand, lime, oyster shells, and water—which was taken from the remnants of nearby Fort Frederica. James Gould, the tower's chief architect, became its first keeper. President Madison appointed him to the post, at a salary of $400 a year. He served for twenty-seven years.

In 1857, the island's harbor light was raised to the rank of coastal light. But just five short years later, the seventy-five-foot tower was reduced to rubble. In 1862, in order to prevent Federal troops from utilizing it, Confederate forces used black powder to level the lighthouse and keeper's dwelling. It took ten years and many lives to rebuild.

Finding and obtaining appropriate equipment was often difficult in post-Civil War America. It took weeks or even months to replenish needed supplies. But for the building crew of St. Simons Lighthouse, this was not the only setback. Stagnant ponds around the building site bred malaria. Several members of the construction crew, as well as the first contractor and the investor who replaced him, contracted the illness and died. On September 1, 1872, the St. Simons Lighthouse was completed under the direction of another investor. It stood 104 feet above the water.

A target for intense rains and wind, the new keeper's dwelling had been fortified with walls a foot thick. However, while these walls successfully kept the fierce storms that slam against the Georgia coast out, they were unable to quell storms brewing within.

Originally, the St. Simons Lighthouse was built as a single-family residence, but it was later converted into two separate apartments. The lighthouse keeper and his family typically shared their home with an assistant and his family. It was an ideal solution to the problem of long hours and isolation. Yet, in the case of keeper Fred Osborne and his assistant, this arrangement failed miserably.

Osborne served as keeper toward the end of the nineteenth century and was notoriously meticulous in his care—so much so, in fact, that, when the position for assistant keeper became available, there were very few applications. One gentleman, John Stevens, felt he was up to the task. He was ultimately awarded the position and trained under Osborne's tutelage. Nevertheless, Osborne never trusted him with significant duties. In retrospect, it could be said that Fred Osborne was wise not to trust John Stevens.

Unable to foster a friendship with the keeper, Stevens eventually found comfort and companionship in the keeper's wife. When Osborne found out, he flew into a rage. He confronted Stevens, and the two had a bitter and bloody argument on the front lawn of the lighthouse. Osborne pulled a pistol, but Stevens, who was carrying a shotgun, fired first.

Not wanting to face murder charges, Stevens rushed the dying Osborne to Brunswick Hospital. He told the nurses that Osborne had been shot by accident. Then, dutifully, he returned home to tend the unmanned lighthouse. Upon Osborne's death, the sheriff brought Stevens in for further questioning, but with no one else trained to tend the lighthouse, it was decided that he should return to his duties until his trial or, if necessary, until an appropriate replacement could be found. Stevens ultimately claimed self-defense, and the charges were dropped.

Prior to the murder of Fred Osborne, there had never been any indication of a ghost at the St. Simons Island Light. Ever since, keepers, locals, and visitors have reported unusual and unexplainable activity. From 1907 until 1936, Carl Svendsen served as lighthouse keeper. When he and his family moved into the lighthouse, they had no prior knowledge of the lighthouse's haunted history. In the evenings, while preparing dinner, Mrs. Svendsen would hear sounds of footsteps walking on the staircase. Assuming it was her husband coming down for dinner, she was particularly alarmed when she realized no one was there. She shared this news with her husband, who at first thought the lonely isolation of their lighthouse life had taken its toll on his wife. But eventually, he too began to hear the footsteps.

On one occasion, Mrs. Svendsen began setting the table and heard what she thought was her husband coming down to eat. When the heavy sounds of the footsteps reached the bottom of the staircase, the kitchen door swung open and, instead of Carl, a cold wind slid through the room, frightening both Mrs. Svendsen and the family dog. The dog's fur stood on end, and he began barking hysterically, as he too sensed the presence of an invisible force. The ghost never harmed the couple, and eventually, they learned to live with its presence.

Those involved with the lighthouse are hard pressed to find a reasonable explanation. Current curator, Deborah Thomas, reports that people who visit the lighthouse alone at night sometimes hear things. Most feel that Osborne's spirit returned because of unfinished business. His subordinate, John Stevens, had taken his wife, his life, and in the end, his post. Revenge was in order. But why he continued to haunt the lighthouse even after Steven's death is anyone's guess. Perhaps, as in life, he's loath to trust anyone else with its significant duties.

a spirited place

In the 1800s, industrialization started to boom in the Midwest. Charles Mears built the first sawmill on White Lake in 1838. In 1849, the Reverend William Ferry and his son, Thomas, built a water-powered sawmill at the mouth of White River, where White Lake meets Lake Michigan. Their farmed lumber went partially toward new construction in nearby Whitehall, but for the most part, it was shipped to larger cities like Chicago and Milwaukee. With an increasing number of ships transporting lumber, White River became congested, especially after the Great Chicago Fire of 1871, when lumber was in absolute demand.

As ships began to wreck more frequently, it became clear to the Michigan Legislature that a new lighthouse was needed at the entrance to White Lake. At the same time, those making their profits in the lumber industry were seeking money for the expansion of the shipping channel. Business was booming, and the lumber barons hoped to build an additional channel between White Lake and Lake Michigan.

In 1866, Congress agreed to a sum of $67,000 for the shipping channel and $10,000 for a new lighthouse at the entrance of the harbor. However, there was immediate disagreement as to the most appropriate position for the lighthouse. Construction was indefinitely halted until the channel could be built and authorities could reassess the area. It was important to position the tower where it would be most beneficial.

Work on the channel progressed slowly. In the meantime, ship captains needed a navigational aide. One shipping captain from England, William Robinson, took it upon himself to ensure the safety of his fellow sailors. He often built fires along the beach of White River to guide ships along the river.

In 1869, another $45,000 was appropriated for completion of the channel. Two years later, in 1871, it was finished. By that time, the original budget for the lighthouse had been long spent. Little more than $1,000 remained to construct a small wooden light at the end of a pier. This pier-head light guarded the new channel rather than the harbor, contrary to what ship captains had once hoped.

The faithful Captain William Robinson became the first keeper of the pier light in 1872. When the Lighthouse Board requested $4,000 for a keeper's dwelling, they were rebuffed. The next year, the board proposed a larger shore light. This time, their request was heard. In 1874, they were granted $15,000 for a new lighthouse and keeper's dwelling.

Captain Robinson and five other men assisted in the construction of the new lighthouse. Built with yellow Michigan brick and limestone blocks, the tower included a long, cast-iron staircase that ran from the cellar to the top of the tower. Robinson saw the project from start to finish and again took over his duties as keeper upon its completion.

After years of waiting, when the devoted keeper finally moved into the lighthouse with his wife, Sarah, he vowed never to leave it. The happy couple built a home in the tower, as Robinson had always envisioned, and together they raised eleven children.

Day in and day out, the keeper tended his lighthouse with wisdom and enthusiasm. He and his wife saw to the maintenance of the tower and home, raised their children, and made it their personal mission in life to protect ships along the shores of White River. Life was good. They were very much in love with one another and perfectly fulfilled by their duties. They imagined a long, happy life together in the lighthouse, but it was not to be. Sarah died suddenly at the age of fifty-eight. Robinson was unprepared for such a loss and inconsolable. To keep his spirits up, he concentrated all of his energies on the care of the lighthouse.

As the keeper grew older and nearer the age of retirement, his grandson and assistant, Captain William Bush, took over as keeper. The captain, however, was reluctant to loose his grip on the White River Light. Even though government regulation allowed only one lighthouse keeper and his family to reside in the lighthouse at a time, Robinson refused to leave. Out of respect, Bush deferred to his grandfather's seniority and allowed the captain to remain in the house and tend to the beacon as he had always done. Though the tower technically belonged to his grandson, Robinson carried out most of the work until well into his eighties.

After many years of this arrangement, it was a well-known fact, even to the Lighthouse Board, that Robinson was still residing and working in the lighthouse. In 1915, the board insisted that the keeper retire from his duties and the house. At eighty-seven, Robinson was no longer deemed capable of tending the light. He walked with a cane and couldn't get around as well as he once did, which made him a liability. They wanted Bush, a much younger and more capable man, permanently on duty. Robinson was unmoved. To the dismay of the organization, he refused to abandon the light.

At this point, the Board realized that significant measures would have to be taken. They never got the chance. Determined to live out his last years in the home he'd shared with his beloved wife, Captain Robinson died less than two weeks after their decree—and still he didn't leave. The ghost of Captain William Robinson has been a constant presence at the White River Light since the hour of his death.

Today, Karen McDonnell serves as director and curator, tending to the lighthouse. A self-described skeptic, she lived in the lighthouse for two years before experiencing any of the phenomena described to her by her predecessors. "By that time, I had dismissed it," she says. "Then I began to hear the footsteps on the stairs." Always between the hours of 2:00 and 4:00 a.m., McDonnell heard the sound of footsteps, accompanied by the sound of a cane, steadily climbing the stairs. "There's really no explanation, not wind or anything, that would create that sound pattern of someone walking with a cane," she explains. "So, I had a hard time dismissing it."

Once the captain had introduced himself to the new keeper, his wife was soon to follow. However, before that could happen, McDonnell had to make a change. Feeling that the devoted wife of the lighthouse's longest keeper ought to be remembered as well, McDonnell tracked down a portrait of Sarah Robinson and hung it on the wall beside one of the captain. Since then, she's noticed unexplained behavior that previous curators never mentioned. Putting two and two together, she's come to attribute this behavior to none other than the captain's wife.

"For one thing," McDonnell says, "the pictures that hang in the hallway, the pictures of the captain and Sarah, always go askew in different directions. If it were the wind, or something like that moving them, it would be a uniform movement, not this way and that."

Another time, McDonnell encountered an even more significant clue as to the spirit's identity. She got some help with a household chore. "I was dusting a glass display case, when the phone rang," she explains. "I went to answer the phone and left everything as it was. I have a photographic memory, so, when I got back, I noticed that the rag had been moved and a whole section of the case, which had been dusty when I left, had been cleaned. I don't know why, but I felt that that was definitely Sarah's doing."

Over the years, McDonnell's affection for the couple has grown. "I've just always felt that theirs was a great love story," she says, "and I'm not the only one who feels that way either." One day, a young professor who visited the lighthouse with a group of students substantiated her opinion about the Robinsons. "He was taking a bunch of students up the peninsula in a boat," McDonnell says. "The lighthouse was not on their itinerary at all. But when he saw it, he was absolutely riveted. He decided he had to see it. So, on the spur of the moment, the group docked its boat at the yacht club—a good mile and a half away—and walked to the lighthouse! After they'd toured the place, the professor asked me if I'd ever sensed a presence there. I told him that, yes, I had. Then he told me that he'd seen an image, like a flash in his mind, of a couple, obviously very much in love, sitting in one of the [recessed] windows. Later, he and his fiancée came back and had their picture taken in front of that window."

There is little doubt that the devoted lighthouse keeper, Captain William Robinson, and his wife, Sarah, remain in the lighthouse, but you won't hear Karen McDonnell say that they "haunt" the premises. "I don't like to say that the place is haunted," she muses, "because the word 'haunted' brings to mind dark and frightening things. I like to say that it is 'spirited.' This is a spirited place."

the light, the keeper, his wife, and her lover

What could be more chilling than a haunted mansion floating above a reckless sea? Here, at the entrance to New London Harbor, sits a grand three-story lighthouse in the French Second-Empire style. With eleven rooms, the house exhibits the grace, sophistication, and opulence of homes along the Connecticut coast. This was by design. Wealthy homeowners on the coast demanded that the building blend in with its surroundings. Constructed at the start of the twentieth century of red brick and granite with a mansard roof, New London Ledge was a jewel among lighthouses—one of few not built of cast iron. Any keeper would have been proud to call it home.

Lit in 1909, the New London Ledge Light was one of the last lighthouses built in New England. Its sister light, the New London Harbor Light, had been one of the first. Lit in 1760, the New London Harbor Light had begun as one of only three lights illuminating the coastline in colonial America. Its ninety-foot tower was designed to warn sailors away from rocky shoals in the harbor. Yet, tragically, sailing vessels continued to wreck against jagged shoals at the mouth of the Thames River. The light simply didn't reach that far. For many years, sailors complained of this dark and treacherous stretch, but it wasn't until 1890, nearly a century and a half later, that statesmen began lobbying for an additional lighthouse. Then, it was another nineteen years before the New London Ledge Light was built—and for the astronomical sum of $93,968.

Built by New London's Hamilton R. Douglas Company, the Ledge Light was truly an island unto itself. A timber crib had been towed twelve miles upstream, sunk on top a two-hundred-foot-long shoal and filled with concrete. An eighteen-foot-tall pier had been constructed on top of this foundation, and the house, in turn, had been constructed on the pier. From a distance, the structure seemed to float among the waves.

For lighthouse keepers and their families, life was a lonely and isolated existence in the middle of the ocean. Thick fog slid through the harbor and eerily wrapped around the dwelling. Loud, swelling waves crashed against the base of the lighthouse. And the only way in or out of the lighthouse for keepers and their families was by boat. The conditions left little to be desired, especially during inclement weather. The threat of flooding winds and rain instilled fear in any keeper who ever lived through a massive storm.

Especially difficult were times when harsh winter storms would blow in for days. As long as the storm persisted, keepers and their families were forced to remain indoors, and the lighthouse became a place of insufferable confinement. One hurricane, which occurred in 1938, created waves so fierce they were as high as the second-story windows. Keepers and their families were forced to watch the rough waters slam against their home and could only hope the windows wouldn't break before the storm subsided.

Even when days were pleasant, those who tended the lighthouse were housebound unless they took leave and went inland. Getting outdoors for a walk was confined to small strolls around the deck. The isolation was enough to drive the average person out of his mind.

In 1936, a young man moved in to tend the lighthouse. Day in, day out, the new keeper worked hard to keep the lighthouse in perfect working order; he swabbed the decks, polished the brass, cleaned the stately building, and tended the light. However content the new keeper was, this was not the life his young bride had dreamed of. She lived alone in the town, kept away from her husband for days, sometimes weeks on end. Eventually, the monotony and seclusion began to torment the young bride. But the keeper was loyal to his job. He didn't want to resign.

Inevitably, the young wife began to resent her husband and her life of isolation. Seeking companionship, she ran off to seek a more adventurous life with the captain of the Block Island ferry. From then on, her husband felt firsthand the isolation of which she'd so often spoken.

Shortly after his wife's departure, the keeper was found dead of an apparent suicide. Some believed that he had jumped from the catwalk surrounding the lantern gallery. Others said that he had been so distraught by his misfortune that he lost his concentration and fell. All agreed that his pretty young wife had led to his ruin.

Today, his ghost, who's come to be known as Ernie, haunts the New London Ledge Light. One keeper claimed that Ernie called out his name as he descended a ladder. Others have spotted his likeness at the top of the stairs. In some ways, Ernie seems to be tending to the only thing in life that never disappointed him—his faithful mansion light. On good days, he has been known to polish brass and swab the decks. In other ways, he seems as distraught as he must have been on the night he died. Bad days find him leaving tools lying about, setting boats adrift, turning televisions and foghorns on and off, opening and closing doors, and rearranging books on shelves.

In 1939, the United States Coast Guard assumed control of the lighthouse. Its crews tended the light until 1987, when it became automated. The day before automation, a Coast Guardsman summed up his opinion of the Ledge Light in the keeper's log: "Rock of slow torture. Ernie's domain. Hell on earth? May New London Ledge's light shine on forever because I'm through. I will watch it from afar while drinking a brew." Clearly, not everyone can cope with the isolation of the New London Ledge Light. But even in death, Ernie remains loyal to the post he did not want to resign.

a light in the darkness

Otherwise known as The Rock, Alcatraz prison has housed some of the country's most dangerous convicts. Today, the spirits of these iniquitous criminals still haunt the island. Thieves, rapists, military deserters, serial murderers, gangsters, and outlaws have served time here, and some say their evil energy still exists.

In the early 1850s, when ships arrived daily for the California Gold Rush, government officials saw the need for a series of lighthouses. Because the bay was difficult to enter and ships often wrecked into the island, the Alcatraz Island Lighthouse, resembling a two-story California cottage with a tower in the middle, became the first active light on the Pacific Coast. A fog bell was added in 1856.

Named La Isla de los Alcatraces, or "The Island of the Pelicans," by Spanish explorer Juan Manuel de Ayala in 1775, Alcatraz was once barren, with little vegetation. Flocks of pelicans soared about the small island, peaceful in its isolation. In the early nineteenth century, the United States Army took notice of its isolation. In its estimation, the island was the ideal location for a military fortress. Rough currents and poor weather conditions hindered access to the island, which commanded a strategic view of San Francisco. About the time the lighthouse was erected, the military began building its fortress to prevent enemy ships from entering the bay. It added a wharf for supplies and built storehouses, roadways, barracks, and a number of offices.

In 1859, a group of men was locked in the basement room of the guardhouse for unexplained crimes. The men's crimes went unrecorded in army files; however, their incarceration became significant in the island's history. They were to be the first in a long line of prisoners. By the summer of 1861, Alcatraz became the official military prison for the Department of the Pacific, housing Civil War prisoners and Confederate sympathizers caught celebrating Abraham Lincoln's murder.

In the early years, prison conditions were deplorable. Men were packed into cold, filthy cells and forced to sleep almost on top of one another. There was no running water or heat, and inadequate plumbing. Over the next forty years, the prison grew and crowded out the lighthouse, which met its end in 1906. An earthquake leveled San Francisco that year and extensively damaged the lighthouse. Longtime keeper B.F. Leeds was present during the quake. Like many who experienced the disaster, he thought the end of the world had come—a reasonable conclusion considering his surroundings. Afterward, the damaged light was torn down, and a new lighthouse was commissioned. It took three years to complete the eighty-four-foot concrete tower. It was powered by electricity, but a keeper was still needed to man it and service fog signals on the north and south ends of the island.

The life of a keeper on Alcatraz Island was bleak. With the living quarters so close to the prison, keepers had to use extreme caution when going about their daily activities. Their children, who attended school in San Francisco, rode across the grounds in a guard bus. Then, a prison boat transported them across the bay. Keepers' wives followed the same precautions whenever they had to leave the island. What's more, all outgoing and incoming passengers were counted to ensure that there were no stowaways. The families of keepers had to endure this indignity as often as twice a day. For their own safety, every aspect of their lives was regimented in this way. Even their trash was confiscated. It had to be crushed and dumped into the waters off the island to prevent prisoners from acquiring materials for weapons.

A keeper's duties were equally regimented. For example, when the fog signals needed servicing and the keeper had to cross to the other side of the island, the prison went on lock-down. No prisoner was allowed in the compound as the keeper crossed. The entire operation was carried out with the utmost caution and secrecy. The guards gave secret hand signals as a way of communicating the keeper's progress from gate to gate.

During the Great Depression, a wave of crime swept across America, and the population at Alcatraz boomed. The prison housed several of the age's well-known criminals. Included among the residents were Al Capone, George "Machine Gun" Kelly, Alvin Karpis, and Arthur "Doc" Barker.

By 1933, the Federal Bureau of Prisons had taken over The Rock, and by 1934, it had established a maximum-security prison. It was indeed, as originally intended, a fortress. Guards lined the grounds with machine guns, and barbed-wire fences punctuated the perimeter. Even the lighthouse keeper, isolated within his concrete watchtower, must have felt imprisoned in these new surroundings. Like the inmates, who by this time had nicknamed the prison "Hellcatraz," he suffered greatly from the monotony and loneliness. From his tower, he could see the bustling port, party boats, trade ships, and glowing city lights. Ironically, the Alcatraz Island Light afforded an enviable view of life in San Francisco. But everything about the life of a keeper on Alcatraz Island was decidedly unenviable—especially his view of the depravity below.

On May 2, 1946, the keeper had a bird's eye view when inmate Bernard Coy escaped. He killed a guard and secured weapons before freeing his five accomplices. The Marines were called in to restore order, and in no time, the fugitives hit a massive roadblock. They couldn't open the gate that led into the recreation yard. For close to two days, the lighthouse keeper watched in horror as the trapped prisoners waged a bloody battle against guards and Marines. After an apocalyptic fight, three of the six escapees were dead, as well as a number of guards. The lighthouse keeper later described the standoff as "forty-four hours of hell."

After more than half a century of hell on the "Island of Devils," keepers, guards, and inmates alike were liberated from its shores. In 1963, the lighthouse was automated and the penitentiary closed. Six years later, the lighthouse mysteriously burned, leaving the keeper's dwelling in ruins.

With such a dark and haunted history, Alcatraz was destined to remain a topic of profound interest. Today, curious travelers flock to see it, hoping to experience some of its horror firsthand. The D cellblock, also known as "solitary," is a particularly popular tourist attraction. Said to be the most haunted area on the island, to this day, it remains colder than any of the other cellblocks. Psychics and ghost hunters have reported intense paranormal activity here, and visitors have reported feeling cold, tingling sensations in their arms and fingers. The sounds of screams, rattling metal, and marching footsteps have also been heard here, and many have sensed the presence of evil spirits.

In the 1940s, legend had it that "The Hole," a dark, cold, windowless room in cellblock D, was haunted by an evil spirit. Prisoners feared isolation in The Hole because a pair of glowing eyes reportedly glared at them in the darkness. Inmates and guards had often seen a man dressed in nineteenth-century clothing wandering the corridors of D-block late at night. They speculated that perhaps he was the evil presence whose eyes shone out in The Hole.

One night, as was often the case, an inmate who had been confined to the dark cell began screaming. The guards jeered and laughed, assuming that the ghost story had gotten the better of him. All night he screamed, and all night his screams went unheeded. By morning, his cries had subsided. When the guards opened the cell, the man lay strangled, finger marks around his neck. Autopsy reports showed that the inmate could not have strangled himself—another force had to have been present in the cell. The news spread like wildfire: the evil spirit with the glowing eyes had claimed its first victim.

The following day, guards lined up the prisoners in cellblock D for a head count and came up extra. To their dismay, the murdered inmate stood in the line as usual. The block went silent, and everyone stared at the man, aghast. Within moments, the ghost vanished without a trace.

A dark energy ricochets off the walls of Alcatraz still. Repugnant odors sift through the salty air, mixing with the sea spray and fog. Wailing sobs, low moans, and piercing screams can be heard on the breeze. Apparitions of ex-prisoners and guards have appeared to visitors and rangers alike, and all who visit are left with a sense of unrest. The only benevolent spirit on the island is that of the original lighthouse, which is said to appear in times of intense fog, accompanied by a loud whistle and a flashing green light. Perhaps, just as it used to warn sailors of the island's dark shore, the lighthouse now warns visitors of the island's dark past.

a tale of
two keepers

The sparkling, emerald waters off Florida's most southern tip hide
an ocean floor littered with the skeletal remains of ships. Here, a
number of factors work against safe passage. During hurricane season,
driving winds and rain pound across the open waters of Key Largo.
Sudden squalls have thrown many a sailor spinning into the wild,
storm-driven seas. Moreover, just off Key Largo lies a vast and
dangerous stretch of reef. In 1695, the TMS *Winchester*, a sixty-gun
ship, met its ruin on the reef. Seventy-five years later, on October 23,
1770, the HMS *Carysfort* wrecked on the same stretch. Afterward, the
reef became known as Carysfort Reef. In 1824, Congress allocated
$20,000 for the posting of a lightship in the area. At that time, no one
knew of a way to build a sound structure on the reef itself, one capable
of surviving the force of the turbulent sea. Even lightships in the area
proved to be no match for the rough, choppy waters around the
reef. Five short years later, the first lightship, *Caesar*, had already fallen

prey to the elements. Its replacement, the lightship *Florida*, eventually met with some trouble of its own.

The largest of the Florida Keys, Key Largo extends thirty miles from end to end and was originally called Cayo Lago, or "Long Island," by the Spanish. Pirates and smugglers once used the island as a base of operations. Many believe, however, that the Indians were its first inhabitants. As settlers moved into Florida, the Seminoles became especially protective of their land. In a well-documented strike, they attacked and extinguished the light of the Cape Florida Lighthouse.

For some time, the lightship in Carysfort Reef had a significant presence, as it was one of few navigational aids for miles. A blow to it was a blow to Florida's citizens. Thus, like the Cape Florida Lighthouse, it was a logical target. On June 26, 1837, the Seminoles launched an attack.

Friends were visiting Captain John Walton and his crew aboard the *Florida* that day. Wanting to prepare an adequate meal for his guests, Walton had decided to go inland and gather vegetables from a garden he kept onshore. As the vessel approached, the Seminoles watched from the shore of Key Largo, prepared to strike. Just as the vessel docked, they charged, shooting the captain and his crew. Walton and one other man died instantly. Three other men, two of whom were wounded, narrowly escaped.

As it turned out, the lightship was of as little help to other seamen on the reef as it had been to Captain Walton and his crew. As a strategic presence, it drew too much attention to itself; as a navigational aid, it didn't draw enough. From 1833 to 1841, despite the ship's constant vigilance, more than sixty vessels were lost on the reef. Finally, in 1848, Congress appropriated funds for a masonry tower. Notable lighthouse builder Winslow Lewis submitted the first plans; however, there were delays in the building, and his plans were never fulfilled. In 1852, America's new Lighthouse Board chose plans submitted by Lewis' nephew, Isaiah W.P. Lewis. These plans called for an iron-pile lighthouse.

Having invented a new method for securing reef lighthouses to the coral rock beneath, Captain Howard Stansbury started the project. When the foundation had been laid, construction halted. The project met with delays, and when it was time to start up again, Stansbury was indisposed. A new contractor had to be obtained. The project endured two such replacements before its completion on March 10, 1852. The beacon towered one hundred feet above the high-water mark.

Living in an offshore, iron-pile lighthouse was a unique experience to say the least. High winds cut against the iron poles. Rough waters rushed through the stilted base. Heavy rains washed over the glass enclosure at the top, eliminating visibility. In short, conditions were severe. Among other things, keeping adequate food supplies proved difficult. With no means of refrigeration, food was kept cool in the water below the lighthouse; but as Florida waters are relatively warm, it spoiled within a couple of days. Denied even the pleasure of a wholesome meal, keepers were forced to rely on canned food. In all respects, the situation was far from ideal. Yet, true to form, a series of loyal keepers tended the Carysfort Reef Lighthouse until the 1970s, when solar panels were installed. More amazing than their devotion in the face of such discomfiture was their devotion in the face of Captain Charles M. Johnson. Keepers also had to put up with the ghost of this former lightship captain who had died during his short service.

The cantankerous Captain Johnson died just after the lighthouse was lit, to the sorrow of no one. Generally regarded as a heathen, he was despised by his assistants. In truth, they were relieved to see him go. However, it seems they were destined not to be so easily rid of him. After his death, his disquieting presence continued to plague keepers and their assistants. Deep, guttural groans rolled through the rafters. These sounds began soft and low, growing louder as the hours passed and the night grew old. Eventually, they intensified to high-pitched, human-sounding screams. Needless to say, on top of everything else, it was hard to get a good night's sleep in the Carysfort Reef Lighthouse.

Some now attribute the scary noises to the joints in Isaiah Lewis' iron plating. Of course, those who knew Captain Johnson were certain that it was he who roamed the halls. He had never been the type to rest in peace—or, as his assistants well knew, to allow anyone else the pleasure.

the infant and
the lady of dusk

Hendricks Head Lighthouse sits on a rocky, windswept shore on the east side of the Sheepscot River, six miles from Boothbay Harbor. Biting winter gales and towering, storm-driven waves have sent many an unfortunate soul into the razor-like ledges of Hendricks Head. At the start of the nineteenth century, these perilous waters were nearly impassable. As a remedy to the situation, the first Hendricks Head Lighthouse was built in 1829; it was replaced in 1875 with the existing tower.

Like many coastal towns in Maine, Hendricks Head boasts a wealth of legends and lore. These legends have been passed down over the years, told and retold on winter nights to wide-eyed children. One such story involves a much-disputed shipwreck.

According to the tale, in March of 1870, lighthouse keeper Jaruel Marr and his wife, Catherine, stood huddled together, watching helplessly as the tumultuous Atlantic assaulted a wayward vessel. A whirling snowstorm blinded the captain of the ship and obstructed his view of the lighthouse. He was dangerously close to the rocks on Hendricks Head. Marr knew the vessel was in trouble as large waves drove it closer and closer to a dangerous stretch of shoals.

Debating whether his small dory would make it the half-mile out to the ship, the keeper crawled down to the rocky edge of the water to check conditions. He realized then that the waves were too intense, the winds too brutal, and the air too cold. From this vantage point, he could see that all those aboard the unfortunate ship were getting washed over by the pounding waves. The water froze on impact with the ship, and crewmembers were becoming encased in a layer of ice. Marr knew his small dory was no match for the waves. Much to his despair, he was resigned to wait, hoping for a lull in the storm.

Together, the Marrs stood watching the hapless ship well into the night. As the gray sky faded to black, they lit a large bonfire on the beach, hoping to encourage anyone still alive to hang on. Not long afterward, the couple noticed a large bundle bobbing over the waves. Marr crawled down to the edge of the water and reeled it in with a boat hook. To his dismay, he realized he had rescued two feather mattresses. He scrutinized the bundle to see if there was something he could have missed. Then, it dawned on him: something must have been sent between them. Quickly he cut the ropes and found a box. Sure enough, inside the box was a baby girl. Miraculously, she was still alive.

Marr gathered the baby up and held her close to his chest. He and Catherine ran with the crying infant up to the keeper's cottage. There, Catherine took the baby into the house, bundled her in warm blankets, and rocked her by the fire. Marr returned to the beach to send a signal to the ship. He was determined to let those still alive know that he had received their package. Later, when the storm let up, he could no longer see the ship; it had been ravaged by the sea. Soon after, wreckage began to wash ashore. The saddened keeper examined the remnants of the ship that he had been unable to save. Before long, he came upon the box that had borne the child. In it, he found blankets, a small locket, and a note from the baby's mother, commending her soul to God.

The Marrs already had five children of their own and couldn't afford another. Nevertheless, they took it upon themselves to find a home for the orphaned baby. They were delighted when a doctor and his wife, summer residents at Hendricks Head, came forth to claim the child.

Extensive arguments have been made to discredit this account, but word has it that Marr's great-great-granddaughter, Elisa Trepanier, validated the story, claiming she'd heard it spoken of all her life. She even knew the baby's name: Seaborne. Fact or fiction, the legend of the rescued baby remains a favorite among lighthouse enthusiasts.

Another favorite legend, passed down for more than seventy years, is that of the "Lady of Dusk." One cold December day in 1931, an unaccompanied woman took a bus into Boothbay Harbor. She wore a smart, black dress. As the bus, filled mostly with locals, rumbled into town, she sat poised and made no conversation. When the bus stopped in the harbor, she climbed off, carrying only a small suitcase.

The afternoon was warmer than usual for December in Maine, but still cold by most standards. Wind rolled lightly across the jagged, naked branches of the trees. The sun hung low in the sky and cast shadows across summer cottages that would remain locked until well into spring. Waves spilled across the deserted beach.

The woman walked through town with her head held high, before slipping inside the Fullerton Hotel and asking politely for a room. The clerk nodded, assuming the woman was in town on business or perhaps to purchase summer property. Giving the woman a key, he wished her a pleasant stay.

Once upstairs, the woman unlocked her suitcase. She freshened up from her trip but didn't rest. Apparently, she had somewhere to be. Moments later, she let herself out of her room and locked the door behind her. Back in the lobby, she slipped past the desk and out the front door. On the street, she came upon some passersby and asked them to point her in the direction of the open ocean. They suggested she visit the wharf, which offered the most charming view in Boothbay Harbor. Showing little interest in the view, she thanked them just the same and went on her way, continuing up the looping road that wound around the harbor to Southport and Hendricks Head.

By this time, the delicate wind had picked up. It rose and fell and was at times still, at times quite restless. Dark clouds pushed across the low afternoon sun, and a threat of snow loomed on the horizon. The dignified woman didn't seem to notice or care. She continued with long, determined strides up the road to Southport. Mrs. Pinkham, who ran the Southport Post Office, was outside locking up for the evening when the woman passed. Her husband, Charlie, was finalizing the day's sales in his general store and overheard their conversation.

The woman saw Mrs. Pinkham and stopped to ask for directions to the ocean. Naturally, Mrs. Pinkham pointed her to the stretch of shore directly across the highway. The woman nodded, obviously aware of the ocean's proximity. But instead of moving on, she inquired again about a particular sweep of ocean. Confused, Mrs. Pinkham suggested Hendricks Head. The woman nodded. She seemed familiar with the name and wished for directions there. Knowing the sun would soon sink below the horizon and concerned with the weather, Mrs. Pinkham warned her against taking the lonely road to Hendricks Head that night. But the woman couldn't be bothered. She thanked Mrs. Pinkham and went on her way. As the clouds slid over the sun, Mrs. Pinkham watched the woman fade into the distance. She could see her black dress flapping in the wind as her long hair tossed behind her.

When his wife came in from the cold, Mr. Pinkham questioned her about the mysterious woman. Who was she, and where was she going? Why was she so determined to reach Hendricks Head in the dark? Mrs. Pinkham told him of the woman's intentions, but he wasn't satisfied. He felt uneasy about the whole affair.

Alone, the woman continued up the sandy path until she heard someone approaching. Not wanting to be warned away again, she slipped into the trees and watched quietly as Charles Knight, the keeper of the Hendricks Head Lighthouse, passed on his way to the post office. When he was a good distance from her, the woman stepped out of her hiding place and continued her journey.

Back in town, the Pinkhams told Knight about the strange woman heading to his part of the island and asked whether he had passed her along the way. Knight was perplexed. He'd seen no one on his way into town. The whole story was extremely curious. What could warrant so dangerous an excursion? Vowing to look for her on his return, Knight wished the Pinkhams a good evening and set out. He wanted to overtake the woman before it got dark.

Knight grew more and more apprehensive as darkness began to cover the island. With the thick clouds hovering overhead, it was becoming almost too dark to see. Having walked the route time and again, Knight had no trouble finding his way home, but he was nervous for the woman. She didn't know the way.

As he approached the lighthouse, he saw a figure dart behind one of the summer cottages. Sure it was the woman the Pinkhams had told him about, he called out but received no answer. Again, he called. And again, no answer came. By the time he reached the summer cottage, whoever it had been was gone.

The woman never returned to the Fullerton Hotel that evening, and by morning, everyone in Southport was uneasy about her mysterious disappearance. Willis Brewer, a fisherman in the area, agreed to go look for her. He retraced her steps from the Southport Post Office to Hendricks Head. He discovered the place where she stepped off the road as Charles Knight passed and found her trail to the summer cottages. He followed her steps west, but upon reaching the water, found nothing. For days, the mystery remained unsolved.

Almost a week later, on Sunday, December 6, Charlie Pinkham, who volunteered at the firehouse, gathered a couple of men and headed down to the waters below the lighthouse. They scanned the open sweep of the ocean but saw nothing. Finally, one of the firemen caught a glimpse of something bobbing in the water. The undertow had pulled the body of the woman up to the surface. When they pulled her in, they discovered that a flatiron had been tied to her body in order to weigh her down. Rumors spread of the woman's suicide, but there were some who suspected foul play.

Southport authorities conducted an extensive background search, but unfortunately, the woman had left nothing to be overturned. Her suitcase in the hotel had not a trace of identification. Detectives arrived from New York City. Reporters from all over ran stories. The Missing Persons Bureau checked time and again for leads, but in the end, no one came forward to claim her. In January 1932, she was buried in the cemetery along the road to Hendricks Head. No headstone marked her grave.

For years after the incident, an unidentified black limousine was seen in the area on the anniversary of her death. To add further mystery to the story, locals began seeing the ghost of a woman in black wandering the area around Hendricks Head Lighthouse. Upon closer inspection, they found footprints in the sand but no other trace of her. Known as the Lady of Dusk, she is often seen roaming the beach near the lighthouse in the early evening. She's also been seen on the stretch of road between Boothbay Harbor and Hendricks Head. It's even been rumored that she walks dignified, steadfast, and determined toward the water, just as she did on the night she drowned.

The mystery is still a hotly debated topic of conversation in Hendricks Head, Maine. Locals and visitors alike enjoy speculating as to the cause of the woman's death. Some have suggested that she lost her family fortune during the stock market crash and was unable to face a life of poverty. Others assert that the woman was in mourning and sought solace in the deep, dark waters. One far-fetched argument goes so far as to claim that she was involved in liquor smuggling and had crossed the wrong people. But for all their speculations, no one knows for sure what befell the Lady of Dusk that night, or why she darts among the cottages, beneath the soft glow of the Hendricks Head Light. She remains as elusive and mysterious in death as she was in life.

heroism and hauntings

Just where Owl's Head got its name, no one is entirely sure. It's been suggested that the jagged promontory, named Medacut by the Indians, resembles an owl: two hollows in the rock form the shape of eyes, and a small ridge juts out like a beak. Despite this explanation, few here see anything but rugged terrain, pine trees, and a few spruce trees at the top near the lighthouse.

The great height of Owl's Head allows the thirty-foot lighthouse, built in 1825, to tower one hundred feet above the water. The rocks below are razor-like, the waters rough, and the storms fierce. Not surprisingly, before the lighthouse was built, as well as after, the area bore witness to innumerable shipwrecks.

During the bleak days of winter, when the sky fades to white and the clouds grow thick with snow, locals retell the tales of fearless sailors and the loyal lighthouse keepers and their assistants who served here. Then they speak in hushed tones of the phantom at Owl's Head Light.

The Tale of the Fearless Sailor

During a brutal December storm of 1850, five ships were trapped in the freezing waters off Maine's rocky coast. All five had been tossed off course and into the shoreline. As the temperatures plummeted well below zero, the salt spray of the waves froze as soon as it hit the vessels. Inches of ice encased each ship, making it impossible to escape.

That same night, a ship headed for Boston was docked at Jameson's Port, an area close to Owl's Head. With no explanation to his crew of three—seaman Roger Elliott, mate Richard Ingraham, and Lydia Dyer, Ingraham's fiancée—the captain climbed off the boat and never returned. To this day, no one knows why he left. He may have been troubled by the storm and sought news in town. There, he may have learned of the five lost ships and lost heart. Or, as many believe, he may have had a premonition about the fate of his own ship and simply fled.

The winds howled that night, and the snow blew with fury, but the loyal crew patiently awaited the return of their captain. To keep warm, they huddled together, listening to the assault of the waves. Their boat rocked recklessly in the raging surf, straining the cables that held the ship at port. Inevitably, these cables snapped, sending the boat and its crew careening across Penobscot Bay toward the rocky ledges of Owl's Head. The schooner hit sharp rocks and its base was shattered, but somehow, the decks remained above water. Freezing waves crashed upon the ship with savage force. There was no way off the boat. With each passing second, the crew grew more and more horrified. They huddled under a wool blanket beneath the weight of the ice that was mounting on top.

Eventually, the ice cut off the oxygen inside their tent, and Lydia and Ingraham fell unconscious. Roger Elliott spent the night picking away at the ice with a sheath knife, working to maintain a small air hole. By morning, the storm had calmed. Exhausted and desperate, Roger Elliott used his fists to break free from the block of ice that had formed around them during the night.

As water kicked the boat against the edge of the rocks, Elliot jumped. He managed to climb onto a landing and pull himself up a steep precipice. Steadily he climbed up the slippery, ice-covered rocks to shore and found the road to the lighthouse. He'd seen its light from the port and knew that someone would be tending it.

Remarkably, lighthouse keeper William Masters came upon the disheveled seaman in the road. He gathered the stranger up in his sleigh and took him back to the lighthouse. Inside, Masters got Elliott into some warm clothes and served him hot rum. Before passing out, Elliott managed to tell the keeper about the two crewmembers he'd left behind on the boat.

Masters sprung into action. He gathered twelve men, and together they headed for the wreck site. The search crew quickly located the schooner and climbed aboard. There they found the young couple lying frozen under a block of ice. Believing them dead, Masters lost heart. But he refused to leave them within their icy coffin. He insisted that the men thaw the ice and work to retrieve the bodies. For hours, the rescue crew chipped away at the ice. Finally, they pulled the blue and lifeless bodies of Lydia Dyer and Richard Ingraham from the ship.

Inspired by this small success, the group carried the couple to the house and attempted to revive them. They poured cold water across their bodies and started massaging their limbs. Little by little, color came back into their faces. After two hours, Lydia began to gain consciousness. An hour later, Ingraham opened his eyes, reportedly demanding, "What is all this? Where are we?" Unfortunately, the brave Roger Elliot wasn't so lucky. He never recovered, and the lovers, who have come to be known as the "Frozen Couple of Owl's Head," were never able to thank him.

The Tale of the Loyal Assistant

In 1930, keeper Augustus B. Hamor came to Owl's Head with his Springer Spaniel, Spot. The faithful dog served by Hamor's side, assisting with many of the keeper's duties. He learned to bite down on the rope of the fog bell as ships approached, giving them fair warning. Then, he would race along the edge of the rocks and bark a greeting to each vessel as it passed. Ships' captains often blew their whistle or rang their own bell to thank Spot for his care.

One night, during an intense snowstorm, the captain of the mail boat *Matinicus* had not reached home at his usual hour, and his wife had become concerned. She called Mr. Hamor at the lighthouse to see if his dog had heard the whistle of her husband's boat. Sensing her alarm, the keeper sent Spot out into the biting storm. After thirty minutes, Spot returned and settled himself by the fire. Hamor could tell by his demeanor that he'd heard nothing. Just then, the dog leapt up from the hearth and ran back to the door. He scratched madly to be let out. Hamor could only assume that Spot had heard the ship's whistle at last. Relieved, he opened the door and followed his faithful companion out into the snow.

Spot labored through snowdrifts in a mad dash for the fog bell, but he couldn't reach it. Then, as if sensing the boat's danger, he made his way down the rocky promontory and ran to the edge of the water, barking hysterically. The captain heard him barking just in time, and steered his carrier away from the treacherous rocks. The *Matinicus* then gave three long whistle blasts to signal its appreciation.

Years later, when Spot died, his beloved keeper buried him near the fog bell he'd so faithfully tended.

The Tale of the Owl's Head Phantom

Like many lighthouses along America's shores, the Owl's Head Light is thought to be haunted—whether by the ghost of Roger Elliot or someone else, no one seems to know for sure. But there have been a number of unexplainable occurrences over the years.

For example, after snowstorms, mysterious footprints have been found to line the walk that leads to the lighthouse. The prints clearly belong to a man, size ten and a half. Perhaps the ghost of Roger Elliott retraces his steps along the snow-covered road. Or maybe Augustus Hamor has been out to visit his long-dead assistant. On occasion, keepers have reported seeing the specter, which resembles a man, in the windows of the lighthouse.

Whoever he is, the spirit at Owl's Head likes to be of assistance. From time to time, he polishes brass or frugally turns down the heat—a practice that seems to rule out the ghost of frozen seaman Roger Elliott.

a lighthouse built
for one

Florida's hot summers send everyone searching for air conditioning. However, at Pensacola Lighthouse there is no need for it. Even when the heat is stifling, the air in the lighthouse is downright bone chilling. It's as if a cold, invisible force moves through the tower, inching its way through the cracks and sidling up to visitors as they make their way up the winding steps.

Haunted by the sounds of laughter that rattle the walls and windows, the lighthouse is shrouded in mystery. Doors slam on their own. The unmistakable smell of pipe tobacco floats gently upstairs when no one is smoking. Footsteps have been heard ascending and descending the staircase, and a glowing, ghost-like form has been spotted in the top window.

In the early nineteenth century, Pensacola Bay was a significant port. Its deep waters made navigation easy for trade ships, but with more and more traffic, a navigational light was needed to guide mariners safely to port. The lightship *Aurora Borealis* provided that much-needed beacon from June 23, 1823, until 1825. However, as was the norm then, the light was weak and didn't always provide adequate protection during storms. Moreover, it was often dry-docked for maintenance and out of commission. Clearly, a more permanent light station was in order.

The Pensacola Lighthouse took only two months to build; negotiations and clearance took almost three years. In 1826, it was completed on a forty-foot hill west of the Spanish Fort San Carlos de Barrancas. It was the fourth lighthouse in Florida, and no one yet knew that it would necessitate a fifth.

Unfortunately, the light's construction was shoddy and its placement ill-planned. The tower was too short, and the many trees around it often obstructed its beam. In 1847, changes were made to the reflector lenses, but in reality, they were temporary fixes that did little to aid in navigation. Sailors still had difficulty detecting the light. After repeated complaints, a 160-foot tower was erected 1,600 feet west of the original. This time, construction crews took their time. The tower was lit in 1859.

Shortly after its completion, the new lighthouse was taken over by Confederate soldiers. Officers broke in and stole oil and other supplies. Eventually, the lighthouse itself was used as a lookout tower during the siege of Fort Pickens, a Union stronghold across the bay. With Confederate cannons placed nearby, the lighthouse suffered its share of retaliatory fire by the Union army, but it ultimately survived. Over the years, it would survive its share of natural disasters as well. On several occasions, the Pensacola Light was struck by lightning and, in 1875, the tower fell victim to the Charleston Earthquake. Unfortunately, keeper Jeremiah Ingraham proved less resilient than the tower he tended.

In August 1826, Ingraham moved into the lighthouse with his young wife, Michaela Penalber. Michaela had all the characteristics of a proper lighthouse keeper's wife. She helped with the cleaning and maintenance. She stood by her husband while he tended the light and showed the lighthouse a great deal of deference, as any good wife would. However, it could be argued that, when all was said and done, she had cared for the lighthouse a little too much.

Though some believe Ingraham simply became ill and died, others believe that his wife murdered him when they were alone in the tower. It's a tantalizing theory, especially considering the fact that, after her husband's death, Michaela took over as keeper.

While not all believe that murder was to blame for the keeper's death, more than a few visitors have experienced unusual phenomena that suggest the presence of a decidedly perturbed spirit. The ghost in the Pensacola Lighthouse has been known to hurl objects at overnight guests in the keeper's quarters. One workman even described having a water hose yanked from his grip.

Moreover, when the lighthouse was refurbished in later years, blood—or something uncannily like it—was discovered in more than one room. Once hidden by layers of tile, the original wood floors revealed dark red stains that no amount of scrubbing has ever been able to remove. For those who had always suspected Michaela Ingraham a murderer, this was evidence enough.

Perhaps Jeremiah Ingraham is still trying to wrestle his lighthouse from the grasp of another. Or perhaps Michaela's jealous spirit is once again demanding exclusive ownership of her beloved dwelling. Whatever the case may be, the unsettling tale of Jeremiah and Michaela Ingraham is destined to leave its mark on the storied history of the Pensacola Light.

the light that doesn't look haunted

The Fairport Harbor Light isn't like most haunted places. Its furnishings are not covered in dust. The stairwells don't creak with age. Cold drafts don't shift through the room. The corridors don't howl when the wind slips through window cracks. No, the Fairport Harbor Light has been sufficiently restored. It was the lighthouse of the past, in its dilapidated state that looked haunted. At one time, razing it seemed the best thing to do. However, the people of Fairport realized how much they valued the old lighthouse. It had become a beacon of safety, a symbol of the past, and a historical marker. The citizens of Fairport Harbor banded together and asked that the government turn the lighthouse over to them for five years. The government agreed, on condition that the town raise funds for the building's restoration as well as find a use for it. Otherwise, they warned, the structure would be demolished.

The Fairport Harbor Historical Society succeeded in raising sufficient funds to refurbish the lighthouse, and in 1946, opened its doors to the public. The restored site became the first marine museum in Ohio and the first lighthouse museum on the Great Lakes. Today, about fifty volunteers maintain the lighthouse and run the museum.

In the early nineteenth century, before Fairport Harbor (then called Grandon) had developed as a port town, traffic began to increase in the harbor. Shortly, the need for a lighthouse arose. Several contractors bid on the project, but the contract was ultimately awarded to Jonathan Goldsmith and Hiram Wood and their bid of $2,900. They completed the tower and the keeper's house in 1825, but a dispute erupted over a cellar that was to be built beneath the keeper's dwelling. Goldsmith claimed that the cellar had never been a part of the bargain. He agreed to build the addition for an extra $174.30. The Collector of Customs in Cleveland, who was overseeing the project, had no choice but to accept this sum. Hiring a new contractor would prove even more costly.

The lighthouse was finally finished and activated by the fall of that same year. Ten years later, however, the foundation beneath Goldsmith's expensive lighthouse had settled so much that a hefty sum of money was needed to restore what had only recently been built. Again, the Collector of Customs was forced to come up with a sum of money that had not been accounted for in the original budget. Ironically, six years later, Jonathan Goldsmith applied for the position of lighthouse keeper. Not surprisingly, the Collector of Customs flatly refused him. He wanted nothing whatsoever to do with the man.

Problems with the Goldsmith-designed tower continued to trouble Fairport Harbor until the winter of 1869. By then, it had fallen into such ill repair that a temporary tower had to be erected so that the original could be torn down. The new contractors were given a budget of $30,000 to work with. However, after the foundation and twenty-nine courses had been laid, they experienced a setback. Funds were suspended, and work was delayed indefinitely, leaving the unfinished tower exposed to the elements. By the time construction resumed, another $10,000 was needed to repair damage done by the weather.

On August 11, 1871, the light was finally activated, and the harbor was officially rid of Jonathan Goldsmith's legacy. Captain Joseph Babcock was the next to the last of seventeen keepers in Fairport Harbor. He served the newer light from 1871 to 1919—a total of 48 years. He and his family worked together to man the lighthouse. In fact, one of his sons, Daniel, served as his assistant from 1901 to 1919 and eventually took over the duties of chief lighthouse keeper from 1919 to 1925. Sadly, another son, Robbie, never had the opportunity.

Young Robbie, who had been born in the lighthouse, died of smallpox at age five. Today, some believe that his ghost haunts the downstairs rooms. Staff members note cold air and a foul odor. They've also described feeling a pervasive sense of dread in this area of the lighthouse. They've experienced altogether different phenomena in other areas.

Evidence suggests that Robbie's is not the only spirit to haunt the Fairport Harbor Light. While in the lighthouse, Mrs. Babcock also became extremely ill and was ordered to remain in bed until she recovered. Confined to her bedroom, her only source of entertainment was a litter of several small kittens that played about her bedside and kept her company.

Mrs. Babcock favored one of the kittens in particular, the gray one. From her bed, she tossed a ball to it, and the kitten fetched it for her. The playful pet enlivened many a long afternoon for Mrs. Babcock in her upper-level room, and apparently, its game continues. Museum keepers and curators claim to see the ghost of the gray kitten scurrying about the floor, as if in pursuit of something.

Of course, as with any ghost story, there are skeptics. But recently, they were dealt a blow when workers installing air conditioning vents came upon the remains of a gray cat in the crawl space. Its mummified body is said to be kept in the lighthouse museum.

Much about the Fairport Harbor Lighthouse has changed over the years. Above all, it's gone from looking haunted to looking picturesque. But don't be fooled. There are some things that even renovations and a few coats of paint can't change.

a tale of
two lighthouses

The Dark Tower

Few visitors to the town of Newport, Oregon, miss the chance to visit the Yaquina Bay Lighthouse. Built in 1871, it is the oldest building in Newport and the second-oldest lighthouse in Oregon. It remained active only three short years before a more impressive tower was built three miles north. Charles H. Pierce, his wife Sarah, and seven of their nine children lived in the lighthouse during its activation. However, it wasn't until long after the tower's deactivation that anyone took up permanent residence.

The Yaquina Bay Lighthouse has been cloaked in mystery for more than a hundred years. Gloomy hallways and a creaking spiral staircase are all part of its lure. A strange light in the third-floor window, smears of blood at the bottom of the third-floor staircase, and the eerie sound of screams reverberating against the lighthouse walls keep locals and visitors curious about the tower's past, which, according to legend, is dark. There were several mysterious deaths in the lighthouse. However, one story in particular has survived since the turn of the nineteenth century, and it is still very much alive in the Newport community.

Muriel, the delicate, sweet-tempered daughter of a sea captain, came to the shores of Newport with her father in 1899. It was the captain's intention to go back to sea while she remained on the island with relatives. She spent her first days alone, walking along the beach and sketching in notebooks, but it was not long before the amicable girl made friends. Together, she and her new acquaintances delighted in exploring the island, searching for adventure, and hoping to stumble upon mystery.

One dark night, she and her friends set out to explore the abandoned Yaquina Bay Lighthouse. Once inside, they crept up the stairs to the top of the tower and looked out over the vast stretch of sea before them. They began opening closet doors and mysterious panels. One iron door opened to a cavernous hole that appeared bottomless. Peering into the dank, black pit, the teens began scaring one another, and their wild imaginations got the better of them. As the empty lighthouse howled with the sounds of wind and screeching seabirds, the startled teens decided it was time to go.

Once outside and a good distance from the tower, young Muriel realized that she had forgotten her handkerchief. She returned with an escort to retrieve it. Not wanting to go back in himself, the boy elected to wait outside and stand guard. Muriel steeled herself for the task of reentering the dark tower. She planned to dash in and dash out and then be on her way. However, it didn't prove so simple a task.

When Muriel was out of sight, the boy heard a shriek and a call for help. The others came running back to the lighthouse. They did found find Muriel, only a pool of blood and her small, white handkerchief crumpled on the floor and spotted with blood. They proceeded up the stairwell and noticed a trail of blood leading to the iron trapdoor. The door, which had opened freely only moments earlier, was now locked. As much as they tried, Muriel's friends were unable to open the door. Frantically, they left the lighthouse in search of help.

For hours, search crews poured over the grounds and investigated the site. They searched from top to bottom, but no one found another trace of Muriel. It was as though she had vanished into thin air.

Detractors say that this story was originally a fictitious account written by Lischen M. Miller for an 1899 issue of the *Pacific Monthly*. Others, however, have reported seeing the young girl in the lighthouse and believe she haunts the tower.

Reportedly, a homeless man went to the lighthouse one rainy winter night in hopes of finding shelter. He ducked out of the rain and knocked on the door. To his surprise, the door opened, and a young girl stood before him. The figure disappeared, but he remained in the lighthouse all night, sheltered from the rain.

Members of the Coast Guard have also reported strange occurrences. One night, a Coast Guardsman noticed what looked like a person carrying a lantern in one of the lighthouse windows, but before he could look again, the image had disappeared and the light dimmed. Other Coast Guardsmen claim to have seen a mysterious light emanating from the third-floor window. Though the beacon atop the tower is electrified, there is no reasonable explanation for this light.

Today the lighthouse serves as a museum. On some mornings, museum keepers have difficulty opening the door, only to find, when they succeed, that pieces of merchandise had been moved during the night. Muriel very well may be behind these unexplained happenings; then again, so may the phantom that spirited her away all those years ago. Whatever the case, teenagers in Newport are liable to think twice before setting out to explore the Yaquina Bay Light on dark, uneventful nights.

The Taller Tower

Yaquina Head Lighthouse replaced the light at Yaquina Bay in 1873, after the U.S. Lighthouse Board decided that Newport needed a taller tower. At 162 feet, Yaquina Head is the tallest tower on the Oregon coast. It still shines today after more than 130 years.

Like Yaquina Bay, Yaquina Head has experienced its share of mysterious deaths. During construction of the tower, two supply ships met their doom on its shores. Another story that circulates in Newport concerns a father and daughter who were staying in a hotel, named the Monterrey, between the Yaquina Bay and Yaquina Head towers. One evening, the father, Tom Briggs, was returning to his hotel when he was caught in a flooded creek and swept out to sea. When his daughter heard the news, she shot and killed herself. Ever since, locals have claimed to see her ghost wandering the beach between the two lighthouses. She appears most often during intense storms along the coastline, searching for her lost father.

Yet another story involves an assistant keeper named Herbert Higgins who served from 1918 to 1929. The main keeper, a man named Smith, had plans to go to the mainland for a brief stint. He wished to spend time with his family and get a small reprieve from his lighthouse duties. Higgins, his faithful assistant, had agreed to man the light and attend to maintenance while Smith was away. Smith had full confidence that Higgins could handle the job.

Several days after Smith went inland, Higgins became very ill. Weak and in need of bed rest, he was in no shape to tend the light. He asked another assistant keeper, Frank Story, to take on the responsibility. Hardly the ideal replacement, Story was careless and spent the evening drinking. When the time came to tend the light, he was in no condition, and Higgins realized it was up to him after all. With great effort, Higgins climbed the long, spiral staircase to the top of the tower. But the exertion proved too much. He collapsed in the tower of the lighthouse before he could light the lantern.

In the meantime, Smith had noticed from the mainland that the light was out. Sensing something awry, he returned immediately. Upstairs, he found Story drunk and Higgins, his assistant keeper, dead. Smith blamed himself. The lighthouse was his responsibility. He never should have left Higgins alone.

Soon after Higgins was laid to rest, Smith began to hear the sound of heavy footsteps climbing the vacant staircase. Guilty of conscience, he became unnerved and feared that Higgins' ghost had returned for retaliation. From then on, he was never alone in the lighthouse without his trusted bulldog, but that didn't stop the footsteps. They continued to haunt him for the rest of his tenure.

spook hill

The tired couple literally fell into their small rental car. Although both of them were in pretty good shape, the Maryland portion of the Appalachian Trail had really taken the wind out of their sails.

They sat for a moment without moving, heads against headrests, eyes closed. Then they slowly turned their heads toward each other, opened their eyes, and exchanged a small smile. The look in their eyes said it, "I'm tired, I'm hungry, but I'm happy."

"We did it," the young woman, Jane, said quietly.

"Yeah," Russell, her husband, said contentedly. Neither was feeling particularly eloquent at the moment, but those few words said all they wanted to say.

They had just recently gotten into hiking, so they still didn't have the endurance to take on the entire trail—far from it, in fact. They had lugged their packs through most of a portion of the Maryland section of the trail, which was only a small and relatively easy part of the daunting Appalachian Trail, but they were beginners who were pleased with this little victory. First a bit of Maryland, then all of it, then on down into West Virginia. Who knew, maybe one day they would start in Maine and go the whole nine yards, which was really more like 2,000 miles.

"So how about the whole thing? Think we'll be ready next year?" Jane asked her husband.

Russell chuckled and replied, "Maybe in our next life. Ready to head out?" Their packs stowed safely in the rear portion of their car, they pulled their tired legs into the car, buckled up, and headed out.

The country in the hills of Maryland was beautiful, so the couple decided to take a few more days to see some of it by car, giving their legs a much deserved rest.

What these ambitious hiking upstarts didn't know was that they had been hiking and driving on and around the ridge of South Mountain. The beautiful foliage and breathtaking views were a visual feast for the nature buffs, but history enthusiasts had an interest in the area that was quite different.

A Civil War battle occurred at South Mountain, a battle that immediately preceded Antietam. That was probably why the young couple had no idea that they were even on or around a historic site. Antietam, located in Sharpsburg, Maryland, overshadowed this smaller battle, although it was strategically important and the death toll significant.

Robert E. Lee, the legendary Confederate general, had decided to go on the offensive and invade the North. The battle started on September 14, although it would be more accurate to say "battles." They were fighting over three different mountain gaps: Crampton's Gap, Fox's Gap, and Turner's Gap. As a result, both armies were somewhat scattered and confused. Lee eventually retreated, and a few days later came Antietam.

This Maryland battle may be overshadowed by the larger, later battle of Antietam, but legends still survive.

One of these legends is that in order to gain the upper hand, the Confederates had decided to move their cannons to the top of a hill, separating them from the Yankees. They would do so quietly and in cover of night, and when morning came, the Confederates could slaughter the surprised and unprepared Union soldiers. They pushed and pulled the heavy armaments up the grade, trying to do so as quickly and quietly as possible. Little did they know, the jig was up.

Union scouts had seen what the Rebels were up to. The Yanks quickly but quietly made their way to the top of the hill, leaving heavy and cumbersome equipment behind. When they crested the hill, they beat the Rebels at their own game by firing on them. The Rebels were just as they had hoped the Yankees would be: surprised and unprepared. They were picked off like fish in a barrel and suffered many losses that night.

The young couple knew none of this however, and as they drove along the mountain road they were astounded by the incredible beauty of the Appalachians. They were glad they had decided to rough it a little on their anniversary instead of just lying around on a beach somewhere. They had never been to this part of the country before, and now that they were here, they realized they didn't know what they were missing.

After driving for some time, they checked the map and figured that they were approaching a town called Burkittsville. As they passed the sign that read, "Welcome to the historic village of Burkittsville, 1825," Jane thought it looked familiar.

"Say, isn't this where that Blair Witch documentary or movie or whatever took place? I could have sworn it was Burkittsville. I think it was the same sign," she said interestedly.

"Hmm. Good thing we already stopped for gas," Russell said with a wink.

"I think we should stop for the night," Jane suggested. "It's not like we're gonna find anything else interesting way out here in the middle of nowhere."

"All right, Burkittsville, it is. Only don't wake me up when you get all freaked out," Russell said teasingly.

They pulled into the sleepy little town and slowly cruised down the street. They didn't really see much in the way of lodging, but a local suggested they try Franklin. There were all kinds of affordable hotels over in Franklin. He also suggested they check out the Gathland State Park while they were so close, a park which was situated in Crampton's Gap.

They thanked the man and rolled up the window.

"Wanna check it out?" Russell asked his wife.

"I'm pretty tired, but we might as well. Either way I'm gonna sleep like a log tonight," Jane replied with a yawn.

Following the local's directions, they drove out of town on Gapland Road. They admired the pastoral vistas in the late afternoon sun.

They passed a barn and began to crest a hill. Admiring the view from the top, Jane asked, "What was the name of this road again?"

"I was just wondering the same thing myself. Gapland Road or something. Come to think of it, I'm not sure if this is exactly the way that guy told us to go."

"Oh, ha ha ha," Jane said sarcastically with a wry smile, "you're such a liar. You think I'm gonna get all freaked out because we're lost near the woods and the Blair Witch is gonna get me and leave weird stuff outside your tent and blah, blah, blah. C'mon, hon, you can do better than that, can't you?" she asked with a smirk.

"No, really," Russell said as they coasted over the hill. "I really think we're going the wrong way."

Jane just sighed and shook her head bemusedly as she realized that they were coasting to a stop at the bottom of the hill.

Russell shifted the car into neutral and pulled the map out from the glove compartment. He furrowed his brow and began to look for the name of the road they were on. It was always so hard to find these little country roads, not to mention the fact that he was lousy with a map.

"Exactly how long do you plan to keep this little charade up?" Jane asked, a little annoyed this time. "Honey, I'm tired and hungry and more than a little bit…why are you driving backwards?"

"What are you talking about?" Russell mumbled, still studying the map in his lap.

"You obviously have your foot on the gas and the car in reverse or something," Jane said quickly, looking over her shoulder and up the hill to make sure no other cars were coming.

Russell glanced up quickly, looked back at his map, and then looked up again. He cocked his head with a look of bewilderment as a speed limit sign passed behind his wife's head.

He looked quickly at his feet, which rested flat on the floor nowhere near the gas or brake. With his right hand he jiggled the gear shift, which swung idly back and forth in neutral.

All the while they moved not only backward, but uphill.

"Stop it, Russell," Jane said in a panicked voice. "Someone's gonna come flying over that hill and nail us!"

"I'm not doing it! I swear! Look," he said, and jammed his foot onto the brake pedal. The movement slowed slightly, but slowly continued its gravity-defying movement in reverse.

"What is going on?" he said in frustration and a little bit of panic.

"Here, I'll get in the driver's seat, you push the car down," Jane tried to say calmly, though she realized how crazy it sounded.

"Good idea," Russell said, and jumped out of the car. It wasn't moving terribly fast, but this defied all logic. As he trotted around to the rear of the car he shook his head and thought about how strange it was to be pushing a car down a hill instead of up.

"Hit the gas! I'm gonna push," Russell called, trying to disguise the bewilderment and growing panic in his voice.

Jane did just that, and he hefted all of his body weight against the bumper. He felt the car move slightly downhill, but as soon as he stopped pushing, it began creeping up again.

"Oh, come on," he said and slammed his body into the rental car. He gritted his teeth and strained, letting forth the pained sound of a man exerting all of his physical strength. Jane gunned the engine, and looked into the rearview mirror in a growing panic, praying she didn't see an eighteen-wheeler barreling over the hill and straight into the rear of their oncoming car.

Finally, as if exhausted from resisting, the car started to slowly accelerate downhill. It picked up speed not from restored gravity alone, but Jane's defiantly heavy foot on the gas as well.

"Thank God," Russell thought as he trotted down the hill alongside the road.

"I kept it in first and put on the emergency brake," Jane said when her husband returned to the car, shaky and out-of-breath from running on tired legs and pushing a stubborn car. "I say we go straight to a hotel."

"Fine by me," the winded young husband said as he flopped into the passenger seat. "You're driving."

They rode in silence for a few minutes, neither wanting to be the first to broach the subject of the strange phenomena they had just experienced. Russell turned up the radio which had been playing softly since they left the hike.

"So, um, that was pretty weird," he said finally.

"Yeah," Jane said quickly, as if she had been waiting for him to say something, anything. Neither really knew what to say, but those few words seemed to be enough.

They didn't bother to stop and relate what had happened to any local residents for fear of not being believed. Maybe they were just loopy from the hike, they thought.

Had they stopped and told their story, however, the young couple might have felt a little better. Well, at least they would have known they weren't both simultaneously going crazy or gravity didn't momentarily stop working. For what they didn't know was that that hill, known to some as "Spook Hill," was the very one over which the Confederate soldiers had attempted to muscle their cannons in silence, only to be swiftly cut down by the Union soldiers who had crept up the other side.

What local residents believed was that each and every day, if you paused at the bottom long enough to let the Rebel soldiers get a good hold on your car, they'd push that piece of equipment right up that hill, struggling valiantly against the gravity that wished to push it down. About halfway up the hill, however, about where they were when the Union troops had opened fire, they would release their burden and let it fall, just as they had released their souls and let them fly. On they pushed, day in, day out. Maybe one of these days they'll finally make it to the top.

there are no happy endings

The dark and choppy waters off Biddeford Pool, Maine, were once ideal for fishing. An abundance of lobster, mackerel, and herring brought an influx of fishermen to the area. But turbulent waters and vicious storms were ever present.

Even with the lighthouse, constructed in 1808, Biddeford Pool has remained an unpredictable and dangerous area. Voracious storms have slammed ships into the rocks and killed everyone onboard.

At times, the lighthouse keeper or the warning light could do nothing to save a ship blown off course by the area's notoriously tempestuous weather.

In the past, such weather has made trips inland impossible. If, for example, there was an emergency at the light, and someone needed to see a doctor, life and death depended entirely on the weather. This was the case in 1960, when Coast Guardsman Laurier Burnham was tending the light without an assistant. His two-year-old daughter, Tammy, became extremely ill. He knew he had to get her to the mainland, but with no one to take over the lighthouse, he was forced to call on the Coast Guardsmen at the Fletcher Neck Lifeboat Station. Shortly after his call, two Coast Guardsmen arrived and took the child into their boat.

The waters that day were turbulent, and before the men knew it, their small boat had capsized. One man was able to grab hold of the boat and stay afloat, but the other, Edward Syvinski, was swept out to sea with the baby in his arms.

The Coast Guard searched for an hour before giving up, agreeing both their friend and the keeper's daughter were lost at sea. Burnham wasn't prepared to give up that easily. Despite orders to remain in the lighthouse, he left the tower unmanned and climbed aboard his own boat to search for his missing daughter. Against all odds, he finally found the two castaways near one of the neighboring islands, wearied from exhaustion but still alive. Turning his daughter over to another Coast Guard vessel, Burnham returned to the light. Little did he know the ordeal wasn't over.

Unbelievably, the second boat had trouble as well, and the crew was forced to turn the sick child over to a local lobsterman named Preston Alley. It was he who finally delivered Tammy Burnham to the Biddeford Pool hospital. In 1993, Tammy's father, Edward Syvinski, and Preston Alley were recognized by the South Portland Coast Guard Station for their extraordinary heroism. Unfortunately, not all of the island's tales end so happily.

Locals believe the island is haunted by the ghost of a man who committed a brutal murder at the end of the nineteenth century. According to a local tale, a twenty-five-year-old drifter came to the island and built a small shack on its western side. Easily bored with the calm of island life, he frequently visited the mainland's local pubs, where he drank himself into a stupor. One afternoon, the deputy sheriff came upon the young man in the street. The youth had just returned from a trip inland, drunk and belligerent. He wandered aimlessly and carried a long rifle. The lawman asked him to release his grip on the gun, but the young man refused. Then, without provocation, he shot the deputy sheriff in the gut and fled.

In a daze, the young man stumbled into the lighthouse. There, the keeper, Thomas Orcutt, questioned him and discovered what he'd done.

Dutifully, the young drifter had reported his actions. He'd killed a man in cold blood. Orcutt knew the deputy that the boy had killed, but he managed to remain calm. He insisted that the boy return to the mainland immediately and turn himself in to the police. The drifter agreed to do just that, but in truth, he had other things in mind. He left Orcutt, returned to his shack, and shot himself in the head.

Since the murder-suicide, islanders have felt an eerie presence. Window shades are raised and lowered, locked doors unlock themselves and swing open, and open doors swing shut. And, locals have reported hearing a medley of unexplainable sounds.

The lighthouse keepers claim that the ghost lives with them. Perhaps the restless spirit of the troubled young drifter finds solace in the dwelling of his only confidant, keeper Thomas Orcutt.

the lady with
the lantern

"Welcome to the Matanzas Hotel, Mr. Elliot," said the hotel's proprietress, as she turned the registry book for him to sign. "Are you here for business or pleasure?"

"A little of both, ma'am. A little of both," he replied.

Elliot couldn't help noticing that the innkeeper, a widow he'd heard, was a beautiful woman. Unlike many of the women he'd met lately, she wore her thick, dark hair long and her face was almost devoid of makeup. He so disliked the short hair, dark eyes, and red lips of those "flappers." Women who cut their hair and wore all that paint were women of questionable morals, Elliot thought. They were women who smoked cigarettes, drank whiskey, and, now that whiskey was prohibited, frequented speakeasies. Obviously, the widow here was a much finer woman.

The woman in question smiled at her new customer and handed him a key to a room at the back of the inn on the end furthest from the bay. As he hefted his valise and strode out of the lobby, she turned the registry around and examined his signature, a knowing smile on her face.

"More business than pleasure, eh, Mr. N. Elliot?" she mumbled to herself. Stepping from around the desk, she wandered out the front door. On the veranda, she hugged herself and took a quick look around the grounds of the hotel, solely hers since the death of her husband a year ago.

She had to admit, she loved the place. She loved the shady, bougainvillaea-framed veranda and the stately, Mediterranean-style building with its elegant interior. She loved the tropical scent that wafted to her from the hotel gardens and the silky feel of the salt-laden air on her skin. And she loved the fact that it was hers and hers alone. Not that she hadn't cared for her husband; she had. But he'd been so much older. She married him mostly for what he could give her, thinking she could stifle her youthful spirit and be happy with being mistress of the grand hotel. But, oh, he had been such an old Mrs. Grundy, always going on about the evils of alcohol and the moral depravity of the women who cut their hair and wore paint on their faces.

Her husband's idea of fun had been sedate walks around the grounds, topped off by a rousing game of mahjong with some of his old cronies in the hotel lobby. A night out on the town, of course, never included dancing or even a show. They maybe went to dinner at a local restaurant, and then she was all tucked into beddie-bye— alone—before 10 p.m. Holy moley! Things had been pretty boring around here.

She gazed across Matanzas Bay and smiled. Not anymore, she thought. Never again would she feel the overwhelming ennui that had gripped her in those days. Not since she'd met Bill and his friends. Since meeting the dark-haired, blue-eyed Bill six months ago, she'd felt a constant tingle of excitement that she'd never experienced before, a surprising self-awareness that kept her senses humming at a sometimes alarming pace.

No doubt about it, she was carrying a hot torch for the man. He was a dashing sea captain with dreamboat eyes and a heart as big as Matanzas Bay. Always fair with anyone he worked with, he had gained a reputation as the real McCoy in his business dealings. And, she almost giggled out loud, his mustache tickled when he kissed her. Since he'd stepped into her life, her days had become positively thrilling—and, by golly, quite profitable! Darn it. Because of her new guest, she wouldn't get to see him for another two weeks!

Thanks to the arrival of Mr. N. Elliot, she fumed, Bill and his fellow rum runners would have to bypass their stop at Matanzas Hotel. And she'd lose out on seeing Bill and on a lot of moola. She had everything ready. The back room of the hotel was set up for guests, and all the locals who were savvy had been notified that the party would be on tomorrow night. There was to be music and dancing and fun. And hooch. Bill always had the best Canadian and Irish whiskey and premium rum from the islands. He had promised some real French Champagne in this shipment—just for her.

The Champagne, he said, was to toast her—to celebrate their love and their success. Her hotel had become the hub of liquor smuggling, and they were both making a pretty penny off of it. So what if it was against the law? It was a stupid law. Who were these people who thought they had the right to tell her or anyone else that they couldn't have a drink or two when they wanted it?

She didn't feel the least bit guilty. In fact, she knew deep in her soul that when she was old and gray, rocking her last days away here on the veranda, these were the days she'd most cherish, the ones she'd prattle on about to anyone who'd listen.

It didn't matter to her that she'd been called in for questioning about the smuggling activity in St. Augustine. They had questioned her endlessly, but she'd never given up anything to the Feds. And she never would. Why would she even consider letting her life slip back into a boring day-to-day existence with nothing to look forward to? She loved the excitement of it all—the tingling anticipation of another shipment arrival, the flash of heat brought on by the thought of Bill's arms around her.

They had nothing on her and they knew it. They just wanted to scare her. So she did her best to keep up appearances. It's why she hadn't cut her hair and why she never wore a lot of makeup. Her demure look and manner, accompanied by a flutter of her long, dark lashes, she knew, often convinced the G-men that she was just the

victim of vicious rumors. Huh, she thought, they don't scare me.
They're just a bunch of pussy cats if you play 'em right. And she was
going to play them just right.

Well, can't keep sitting here, she thought. Plenty to do before
tonight. She'd have to post the secret warning to her anticipated guests
that they shouldn't show up tomorrow night. And there was still the
marketing to do. Sighing, she rose from the veranda railing and started
walking toward town.

••••••

It was well past midnight, and Mr. N. Elliot was out and about,
walking lightly along the hotel path to the bay, trying to keep his
footsteps from crunching and giving him away. He knew the rumors—
that the Matanzas Hotel was the hub of smuggling here in St.
Augustine, and that the good widow ran a speakeasy in a back room.

Yeah, he'd heard the rumors, but after meeting the modest widow,
he found them hard to believe. He could no more see her touching
illegal rum to her lips than he could see himself breaking a law. And
that just wasn't going to happen. One thing he did know, however:
there was a shipment due in to Matanzas Bay tonight and he planned
to catch the brigands and bring them to justice.

Reaching the bay, his eyes scoured the water for anything
untoward. Nothing. Moonlight shimmered on the placid bay waters,
and for a moment he found himself enjoying the feel of the warm
night air on his skin. For the merest split second, a desire hit him, a
desire for dark eyes looking into his and the tickle of sweet breath
caressing his neck.

Shaking it off, he strained his eyes to make out the silhouette of
any boat that might be trying to sneak in under the meager light. But
even his eagle eyes could discern nothing out of the way.

He turned west and started walking, skirting the bay and keeping
his eyes and ears trained on the water. If they were here, he'd catch
them, he knew. The information the Bureau had on St. Augustine was
solid. Rum running was going on here and lots of it. Gallons of illegal
liquor were docking here and finding their way into the country's

interior. That's why he'd chosen the town for his trip. Nothing wrong, he smiled, with a little working vacation.

After he'd walked at least a mile, he turned and looked back toward the hotel. A light caught his eye. Someone was up high, waving a lantern of some sort. Waving it back and forth. Glancing back out to the waters, he knew its gleam would be visible way out at the mouth of the bay. He knew without a doubt that it was a signal for the smugglers to stay away. Chagrined, he realized they knew he was here. Jeepers. He'd traded in his department-issue suit for casual trousers and a pullover shirt, clothes he never wore unless working undercover. He looked like a typical tourist, didn't he? What could have gone wrong?

Well, he'd get nothing done here, he thought. Might as well move on—further south, perhaps. As he started walking dejectedly back to the hotel, he strained his eyes to see which roof the signal was coming from, but he was too far away. Could be any roof. Could be the roof of the Matanzas, but he couldn't prove it. And he couldn't believe it, either. The widow was too genteel. Her hotel too elegant. Why would she get herself involved in something illegal? Those dark, guileless eyes. That halo of ebony hair. A silky voice that made his stomach flutter. He just didn't believe it. Hmmm, maybe he should hang around awhile? No, he decided, duty calls.

Back at the Matanzas Hotel, the widow handed in her lantern and climbed back into the hotel from a window that looked out over the roof. She smiled at her assistant, Clara, and nodded. The deed was done. She'd watched Mr. N. Elliot, and had seen him walk around the bay. She had watched him as he paused momentarily, as if a bit wistful, then slowly moved on.

When he'd gotten far enough away, she'd climbed out onto the roof and with her lantern, she'd warned Bill and all the other smugglers out there that it wasn't safe to come in. She knew they'd simply leave the bay and move on up the coast, selling their wares further north, returning to St. Augustine in two weeks time. She'd sure have to figure out a way of getting rid of Mr. Elliot by then.

She needn't have worried. Early the next morning, Mr. N. Elliot presented to the front desk, valise in hand, and informed her that he was checking out.

"Oh," she said. "I hope there was nothing wrong with the accommodations," she said.

"Not at all," he replied with a smile. "It seems that my business here did not work out. I'm going to have to move on."

"Oh? And which way are you headed?"

"Further south, I guess. Maybe on down to the Keys. I've heard business is hopping down there."

The widow flashed him a big smile that made his heart lurch. "Oh, yes, Mr. Elliot. It really is hopping down there." She handed him his receipt. "You have a good trip, now."

Two weeks later, Mr. N. Elliot strode into the Chicago branch of the FBI. He was tanned, but the relaxation you'd expect from a man just returning from a Florida vacation wasn't there. He was strung tight. Not that it was a surprise to his coworkers. He was well-known for his devotion to duty and they knew that, although he had protested he was only going on vacation, he'd had business in mind. They knew, too, that he'd failed.

"So, Chief," braved a wet-behind-the-ears feebie. "Guess things didn't pan out in St. Augustine."

Mr. N. Elliot caught the guy in his blue-steel gaze and held him there long enough to make him squirm. "No, Johnson. They didn't. The smugglers got warned off at the last minute. But we'll get 'em next time. Now get off your butt and get busy. There're people breaking the law out there."

••••••

The tale of the Lady with the Lantern is a well-known story in St. Augustine, mainly because the widow is still making her presence known. Her beloved Matanzas Hotel, one of the first buildings constructed after a fire destroyed six city blocks in 1914, is now the Casablanca Inn. As she wanders the halls, she's no doubt proud of how things have turned out. Listed on the National Register of Historic Places, her graceful Mediterranean revival house is considered one of the ten best inns in the Southeast.

That's not what makes it so interesting, however. The interesting part is the fact that periodically, late at night, a lantern can be seen waving upon the roof of the inn. The phenomenon has been reported by the guests of surrounding hotels, who noticed a light coming through their windows. Thinking it was the lighthouse on Anastasia Island, they peeked out of the curtains to see a swinging light on the roof of the Casablanca Inn.

Sailors out in the bay also have reported seeing a light swinging from the inn's roof on many a dark night. Many of them also report seeing a dark figure holding the light and waving it back and forth.

In addition to these sightings, there have been reports that the widow has appeared inside her beloved inn. Guests report catching a fleeting glimpse of something or someone moving in hallways and stairways and incidences of items missing from their rooms, only to reappear in strange places later.

The present owners of the Casablanca Inn say they discovered the story of the widow when they were doing some remodeling. They've declined to name her in deference to her descendants who still live in St. Augustine. No doubt they're delighted that, thanks to the widow and her swinging light, the inn is now included in St. Augustine's walking ghost tour. And thanks to the fact that folks love a good ghost story, the tour has become an excellent marketing tool.

No one knows why the widow still climbs the roof to swing her warning lantern. One story says that her rum runner lover was lost at sea when, after she'd warned him with her lantern, he'd stayed on in the waves of a coming hurricane. She never got over losing him, and that's why she continues to make her journey to the roof.

But we romantics discount that story. We think that no matter what became of the widow or of her seaman, the reason she still climbs out there on the roof with her lantern is that she's remembering. Remembering and reliving the best times of her life.